CRESCENT CITY WOLF PACK

COLLECTION
✠ ONE ✠

USA Today Bestselling Author
CARRIE PULKINEN

WEREWOLVES ONLY

❖ ONE ❖

CHAPTER ONE

Detective Macey Carpenter ducked under the police tape blocking off an alley on St. Peter Street and smoothed her hair toward the tight bun she wore near the nape of her neck. Storm clouds gathered in the darkening sky, and the summer air hung thick and wet. It was a typical steamy August night in the French Quarter, but the heavy humidity did nothing to quell the chorus of offending odors dancing in the air. She wrinkled her nose.

Slipping her hands into a pair of blue latex gloves, she snapped them at the wrists. The slight sting helped to separate the gruesomeness she'd soon see from the ordinary life she'd return to later. Disconnecting the good from the bad in her mind kept the nightmares at bay.

She paced into the alley, and three men in blue nodded curtly as they passed. "Carpenter," the blond with a crew cut muttered.

She nodded back and inhaled a deep breath. Angling up her nose to catch the wind, she rifled through the array of scents it presented her. The overpowering aroma of the female victim's Chanel couldn't cover the metallic reek of blood. Lucky for the woman, most of the blood seemed to belong to the attacker.

Macey shook her head. Seven sexual assaults in three weeks' time.

In each case, the victims described a different man. Different, yet similar enough that they had to be connected. But how? The assailant had disappeared every time but this one. What the hell was going on in this town?

She stepped into the courtyard and took in the landscape of the crime scene. Six nineteenth-century buildings backed onto a shared park. Willows lined the square, their sorrowful branches looming over the grief-stricken scene. A weathered stone fountain bubbled at the center of the wooded garden, and a thirty-foot magnolia tree towered in the corner, the perfume of its citrusy, white flowers mingling with the stale stench of death, creating a sickly-sweet fragrance that made her stomach turn.

"It's about time you got here, boss." Bryce Samuels winked and sauntered toward her.

Macey stopped and put her hands on her hips before shaking her head at her partner. "Traffic. What have we got?" After dropping her bag near a wall, she knelt to examine the alleged rapist's body. A series of jagged, foot-long gashes stretched from chest to pelvic bone, almost as if it had taken three slashes with the blade to lay the guy open. The pupils were dilated—the blood-red eyes frozen in a look of surprised terror.

"Victim's over there." Bryce gestured with his head to a stone bench near the common's entrance. A green-eyed redhead sat, wrapped in a stiff blanket, giving a statement to a uniform. "Same story as the others. Difference is, this time…there's evidence."

Macey followed his gaze to the body that lay before her. "Unless it was a sloth, I don't see how a dog or a bear could've done this with only three nails. Look here." She traced her gloved hand along each rip in the flesh. "It doesn't make sense."

Bryce crossed his arms. "No, it doesn't. But this is the first time the attacker is actually still at the scene."

"I know." Macey pulled off her gloves and dropped them in a trash bag. "Let's talk to the victim."

"Shall we?" Bryce motioned with his hands, and Macey took the lead. The uniform had finished his questioning, and the woman sat alone, shivering in the sweltering August heat. Funny how shock could do that to a body.

Her dark green blanket slipped off one slumped shoulder, revealing a black T-shirt with a restaurant name embroidered on the breast. The woman inhaled a shaky breath as Macey approached, but she didn't lift her gaze from the cobblestone path.

Macey sat on the edge of the bench, the cool stone taming the Louisiana summer. Bryce leaned against the wall behind her.

"Hey there. I'm Detective Macey Carpenter, but you can call me Macey."

The redhead sniffled and wiped her eyes.

Macey folded her hands in her lap. "What's your name?"

"It's Amy. Couldn't you read that in your report?" Her sarcasm didn't mask the fear in her voice. She wiped her eyes again and stared straight ahead.

Macey's chest tightened. She'd dealt with her own personal grief, so she could imagine what this poor woman was going through. Although, Macey had spent more than her fair share of time in denial, and Amy seemed to have skipped that stage and plowed straight into anger. "I could have looked at the report, but I'd rather hear it from you. You know…since you were here and all. I want to help."

"Doesn't everyone?" Amy wrapped the blanket tighter around her shoulders, her bobbed hair swishing forward to cover her face as she stared at the ground. "Everyone says they want to help, but when you tell the truth, do they believe you?" She blinked at Macey. "Hell no, they don't. And why am I not in the hospital? I was raped, for Pete's sake. Just because some…*thing* saved me and killed the asshole, I have to be questioned first? What? You think I killed him? I didn't, but believe me, if I could've…I would've in a heartbeat. Men like that don't deserve to live."

Macey took a deep breath. She understood anger. Resentment. Desperation. Those feelings were nothing new to her, though she'd buried them long ago. And though they rarely reared their ugly heads anymore, she still hadn't mastered acceptance. "What *thing* saved you, Amy? Was it an animal?"

Amy scoffed. "Animal. Man. Alien. It doesn't matter. No one believes me anyway."

Macey placed her hand on Amy's. "I believe you. Trust me. I've been on the trail of this *thing* for weeks. You aren't the first victim to tell me this story, but you are the first to have evidence. Please…I need you to tell me everything."

Amy took a deep breath and looked her square in the eyes. Holding her gaze, Macey gave her all the trust and reassurance she could without words. Amy exhaled and slumped her shoulders. "Okay. I'll tell you."

As Luke Mason stepped through the door of O'Malley's Pub, a curtain of cool, crisp air blasted his sweat drenched skin. At ninety-eight degrees and one hundred percent humidity, the Vieux Carré felt more like a Dutch oven than a French Quarter. He closed his eyes and let the coolness soothe his aching limbs as he entered the building. The low ceiling and bare brick walls were typical of the nineteenth-century structures in the Quarter. Shaded lights hung from exposed beams, casting a smoky glow over the bar.

He sat on a stool and took a long, refreshing gulp of the Blue Moon beer that sat ready on the counter, waiting for him.

"Rough day at the office?" Chase, the bartender, cocked his head toward the scar across Luke's bicep. Luke looked at his arm and shrugged. The thin, raised scab had been a gash two hours ago.

"Piece of scaffolding jumped out and got me. No biggie." He downed the rest of his beer and asked for another.

"Well, if that's all." Chase set down the mug he was polishing and poured another Blue Moon. At six foot one, he stood several inches shorter than Luke, but his height didn't make him any less of a fighter. If Luke trusted anyone to have his back no matter what, it would be him. An intricate series of tattoos sleeved Chase's arms, and he sported piercings in his ears and eyebrow.

Luke's only tattoo occupied his right shoulder. A fleur-de-lis designed from a wolf head signified his allegiance to the pack. The star in the center symbolized his bloodline—a direct descendent of the first family. And he wasn't just a descendent; he was next in line for pack leader. He finished his beer and slid the empty glass to his friend.

"What are you gonna do about James?" Chase placed the glass in the sink.

Luke wiped his hand down his face. "Is he back there?"

Chase nodded. With his hands on the bar, Luke heaved himself from the stool and shuffled toward the back room. He chuckled at the sign on the door—*Employees and Werewolves Only*—written in marker on a piece of cardboard. It came about as a joke from the customers—that his father, with his long, salt-and-pepper beard and almost-furry arms, looked like a wolf-man. They didn't know how right they were.

The Crescent City Wolf Pack—at two hundred members strong and growing—was the sixth largest in the nation. Werewolves tended to congregate in towns with immense wooded areas. While New Orleans itself consisted of more city than forest, the vast swamp lands surrounding the area made for prime hunting grounds. And for tough wolves.

Hunting gators wasn't any easier than it looked on television. While a bite rarely killed a werewolf, it sure hurt like hell. But the thrill of the hunt was worth double the pain. What other choice did they have? Nutria? The beaver-sized swamp rats satisfied the hunger, but they did nothing for the rush. Deer were abundant—and fun to chase—but nothing beat the thrill of hunting gators. They made worthy opponents.

The door shut behind him with a *thud*. Bright fluorescent lights hummed from above, giving the stone corridor a greenish glow. He turned the corner and descended a short flight of brick steps to the office.

The blinds drawn over the window blocked his view of the scene inside. He tried the knob but found it locked. It must've been more serious than he'd thought. He fished in his pocket and pulled out a key to unlock the door. When Luke stepped inside, James sat slouched in a chair, shaking his head. Stephen, third in command and Luke's cousin, leaned against the oak desk, his arms crossed over his chest.

"What are you going to do about this?" Stephen spat, shifting his weight to his feet and gesturing to James. "The cops are going to be looking for him."

Luke raised an eyebrow and regarded his cousin. Everyone knew Stephen wanted to be pack leader—and he already had a mate—but his moral compass didn't quite point in the right direction.

"No one will know who—or what—to look for." Luke turned to James. "The woman never saw you in human form?"

"No." James shook his head and dragged his hands down his face. "I don't know what happened. He should've disintegrated like the others. There wasn't supposed to be blood. Demons don't bleed."

Stephen cut him off. "This obviously wasn't a demon."

James sighed as Luke took the chair next to him. "It was a demon, Luke. I smelled it. Its eyes were red, and…"

Luke put a palm on his shoulder, and James covered it with his own four-fingered hand. He'd lost his pinkie on a construction site when he worked for Luke. "It's okay, man. We'll figure it out."

"Figure it out?" Stephen paced the floor, his hands balled into fists. "What's there to figure out? He killed a human, and he needs to be dealt with. You should put him in the pit."

Luke narrowed his eyes. His cousin would happily throw people into the pack's specially designed prison for minor infractions without learning all the facts. "I'll take that into consideration. You can go now."

Stephen's jaw tightened with an audible *click*. "You'd better take care of this."

"I said you can go."

Stephen glared at James and stormed out the door, slamming it behind him.

Luke shook his head. "Ignore him. He's peeved because he has no power in enforcing."

"He will if he has his way."

"He won't." The good of the pack always came first. He'd learned that by watching his father lead.

James's face went serious. "I hope not. I'll go rogue before I'll serve a tyrant like that. I know he's your cousin and all…but, shit. He scares me. A lot of us."

"Nothing to worry about. He won't become alpha."

James furrowed his brow. "You've only got about a month before your old man retires. You can find a mate by then?"

"If I'm going to become alpha, I don't have a choice." He rose to his feet and stepped around his desk, settling into a large leather office chair that squeaked as it absorbed his weight. He'd have to get the WD-40 after it soon. Picking up a pen and a pad of paper, he squared his gaze on James. No more friendliness. It was time to play his role as enforcer.

"The monster attacking that woman smelled like a demon. He gave you every reason to believe he came straight from hell, but he wasn't a demon. At least, not full demon."

James twisted in his seat. Sweat beaded on his forehead. Luke's main job was to deal with rogues and other rule-breakers. Not a job he enjoyed, but he didn't have a choice. His father was pack leader, which made Luke second in command. He couldn't stand seeing his friend cower like this, but he had to keep his aura of power strong to keep the pack under control.

"Tell me what happened, James. From the beginning."

CHAPTER TWO

MACEY GAVE THE VICTIM A SAD SMILE AS THE EMT CLOSED THE ambulance door. *Poor woman. The nightmares she's going to have.* She shook her head and returned to the scene.

As she walked up the alley, a sultry breeze wafted the scent of burnt flesh to her nostrils. Surely Bryce hadn't dropped a cigarette on the body again. Though it had only happened once, five years prior, no one on the force would let him live it down.

"Bryce!" She quickened her step and found him talking with the coroner. "Why do I smell burning flesh?" She wiped a bead of sweat off her brow as she marched toward her partner.

"I know what you're getting at, but I haven't smoked in years, so don't you even start on me with that crap, blondie." He signed the coroner's tablet and turned to face her. "Anyway, I don't smell anything but death."

Macey bit her bottom lip and glanced around the alley. Two men with a stretcher loaded the body into a van as the rest of the uniforms packed up their stuff to head out. Nothing appeared to be burning, but she couldn't deny the distinct, sharp scent of cinder in the air.

She trailed her hand along a building as she paced toward the courtyard, allowing the stories of long ago to seep into her senses. That old carriage house had seen so much. If only it could talk to the rest of the world the way it spoke to her. If only it could tell her who the killer was…

"You coming? Donuts are on me tonight." Bryce jingled his car keys in his hand, pulling Macey out of her mini trance.

She looked at her partner. He wore his light brown hair cut short on the sides, shaggy on top, and his goofy smile made his eyes sparkle when he laughed. If she didn't think of him so fondly as an older brother, she might have been attracted to him. Good thing she wasn't. Being partners was close enough for her comfort. Macey preferred to keep everyone at arm's length, and Bryce had already worked his way up to her elbow.

"Nah. I think I'm going to hang around here a while. See if anything comes to me. You know?"

He knew more about Macey's "ability" than anyone else. She hated calling it an ability, but wasn't that what it was?

He wrapped his arm around her. "You do that, boss. But don't spend too much time alone out here."

"No worries."

Macey stepped out of the alley and into the courtyard. Undoing the second button on her once-crisp, cornflower shirt, she rolled her sleeves up to her elbows. A bead of sweat dripped between her breasts. *Damn this heat.*

She sat on the edge of the fountain and closed her eyes, letting the melody of cascading water clear her mind and open her soul. There had to be something there. Some clue she'd missed. The dead man's energy tumbled through the air, teasing her, twisting, swirling, dancing around the edges of her senses. So close, yet unattainable because she couldn't touch it.

Seven women. Four rapes, three attempted rapes. No words had been exchanged. A man with red eyes had grabbed them and assaulted them in an alley. For the first two, the story ended there. The perpetrators got away. But for the remaining five victims, the story took an unimaginable twist. A beast, they'd called it, or some kind of animal that moved so quickly they couldn't identify it, swooped in and allegedly killed the attackers.

So, why was this the first body they'd found? In the four previous cases, the investigators had discovered nothing more than a pile of ash left behind. If an animal killed the rapists, where had it taken the bodies?

And where had the ashes come from? The lab hadn't determined what they used to be, though they definitely weren't human remains.

But the dead guy this time looked like...a dead guy. Why was there a body and no ash? There had to be something else to all these incidents. The women must have been leaving some important detail out of their stories.

But what was it?

An icy breeze tickled the back of her neck, raising goose bumps on her skin. She shivered and reached behind her to peel the sweat-soaked shirt away from her back. *Probably a ghost. Maybe the attacker's ghost.* She'd heard of people who could talk to spirits. People who could manipulate energy and communicate with entities in other dimensions. She truly believed they could, though most called it bogus. People tended to only believe in things they could see.

Macey believed in spirits. When a person died, their energy had to go somewhere. Objects—buildings, furniture, trees, anything really—absorbed a lot of it. That kind of energy, she could see. Though, saying she "saw" it was a stretch. Images could appear in her mind, but not before her eyes.

She blew out a hard breath and rose from the fountain. Her ability had gotten her nowhere in this case. It took time for objects to absorb energy, and this string of crimes was happening far too rapidly.

Seven incidents within a three-week span. New Orleans was never considered the safest city in the world, but this...this was outrageous. She shook her head. She needed a vacation. A nice, long break somewhere cool. Maybe Alaska. Let Bryce handle this one. He excelled at old-fashioned police work, which this case obviously required.

Macey's ability seemed useless.

She trudged toward the alley, berating herself for even considering a vacation. She wouldn't abandon this case any more than she'd abandon—well, anything. If she'd learned one thing from her childhood, it was to stick by something or someone until the end. No matter what. She'd had first-hand experience with having her world ripped apart when the people she'd needed most left her alone, and she would never let it happen again.

A light breeze blew up the alley, making the sticky August heat minutely more bearable. Macey took a deep breath, welcoming the relief. The scent of cinder tickled her senses again. Thunder clapped in the distance, and an ominous black sky threatened to downpour at any second.

Her shoes squeaked on the cobblestone as she hightailed it back to where the body had lain. The cleanup crew hadn't arrived to wash the pavement, so she had a chance. She closed her eyes and inhaled. The scent grew stronger.

She knelt, studying the cobblestone. This didn't look like blood. Rain began to fall in thick droplets around her, splashing into the semi-dried coagulation.

Crap. Not yet! Where were her gloves? She glanced across the alley to find her bag resting twenty feet away, where she'd left it.

Thunder cracked as the droplets fell quicker. Macey reached out and swept her fingers through the muck that was once blood. Closing her hand, she darted under an awning to examine the substance. She rubbed her thumb across the tips of her fingers and brought them to her nose.

A quick sniff determined what she'd stuck her hand in wasn't blood.

It was ash.

Sticking to the shadows, out of the detective's line of sight, Luke ran a hand through his hair as rain pelted him in the corner of the courtyard. The towering magnolia tree provided a shield from the downpour, but thick drops bounced off the waxy leaves and splattered around him. "You're sure no one saw you?"

"Just the woman," James said.

Luke looked at his friend. James was the quickest shifter and most skilled attacker in the pack. That's why he was the lead wolf on the demon hunting team. He'd never considered James careless enough to mistake a human for a demon. Something didn't add up.

"I trust you. The guy was most likely half demon, and it's hard to tell on those. We'll have to figure out where he came from—and who made him—if we're going to stop this fiasco before the cops find out too much. If it's the same person who's summoning these new demons, we can stop it all with one punch."

James shoved his hands in his pockets. "Let's hope it is."

"You too rattled to patrol tonight?"

He chuckled. "Nah. I'm good."

Luke rested his forearm on the tree above his head and shielded his eyes from the rain as James trotted away. This was the same female that showed up at every one of these incidents. He'd been watching her for the past three weeks. Detective Macey Carpenter. Everyone in the Quarter knew who she was, whether personally or not. She'd busted more criminals since she'd joined the force than anyone he'd ever heard of.

Macey had a tough, no bullshit reputation, and he'd seen her around enough to know it was true. When she walked into a room, she did it like she owned it—with strength and confidence. Maybe a little too much confidence. She was only human, after all. She didn't realize how fragile she was, and he was done with women like that. That's what he told himself as the familiar fluttering in his stomach— that happened every time he saw her—had him leaning away from the tree, the desire to erase the distance between them pulling him from the shadows.

He shook himself to break the trance. The truth was, he found himself oddly attracted to the petite fireball. She may have been tough, but her feminine side always showed through, no matter how much she tried to hide it. She always wore her golden hair slicked back into that damn bun, but he could imagine what it looked like falling down around her bare shoulders—

Nope. He had to stop right there. When he did mate, it had to be with another werewolf. There was no way around the antiquated law. He'd be alpha in a month, and he *had* to have a mate for that to happen. He didn't need to waste his time with a human. Especially one who had gotten dangerously close to discovering a secret she shouldn't know. So why was he hiding in the courtyard, watching her like a stalker?

He told himself it was his job. The pack did its best to keep peace in the supernatural community and to keep their existence a secret from the humans. Psychics and witches may have found a way to coexist…exposing *some* of their powers to the mundane…but there was no way in hell people would be as accepting of a predatory species like his. He had to stop Macey from learning anything about the demons…and especially the werewolves. Keeping tabs on the sexy detective proved a nice bonus, and it helped to quell the odd feeling of possessiveness brewing in his chest. His wolf had decided she was his to protect.

Macey bent down to tie her shoe, and her shirt gaped at the second button, revealing the lacey edge of a light pink bra. He took a deep breath to slow the sprint of his heart. *Not wasting my time with humans.*

Still, he did admire the way her black pants hugged her curves as she strutted through the rain and into the alley before disappearing around the corner.

With Macey out of sight, Luke stepped out of the shadows and made his way toward the alley. As he passed by the fountain, he paused to take a deep breath. The scent of rain mixed with the magnolias' sweet perfume smelled like summer in New Orleans. Like home. He smiled, relishing the downpour, even if it did add steam to the sauna of the Quarter.

The detective had found ash; that had been obvious from the curious look on her face as she'd swiped her fingers through the substance on the ground. A cop wouldn't have put her hand in a puddle of blood. Luckily, though, she wasn't able to save any as evidence.

And lucky for James, this confirmed Luke's belief that he hadn't killed a human. A heaviness lifted from his chest, and he tilted his head back, letting the rain fall onto his face. He wouldn't have to punish his friend.

He strode to the spot where the half-human body had lain, but the demon ash had already washed away. He surveyed the area for any other signs of the supernatural but found none. The rain had taken care of everything for him; a steady stream flowed between the worn stones, twisting and jutting right, then left, before cascading down a storm drain.

Now, he had to get to the morgue and decapitate the body before the damn demon came back to life.

The chances of reanimation were slim—or so legend stated—but it was best not to take chances. Besides, he had no idea what one looked like on the inside. Maybe it didn't have all the same human organs.

He had to get that body out of the morgue before the autopsy. And since the alpha was vacationing in Europe, Luke was the man to do it. His father had offered to come home when the outbreak started three weeks prior, but Luke assured him he could handle it. His parents had scheduled their two-month-long trip for right before his old man's retirement so Luke could work out the kinks in his new leadership role before it became official.

Of course, his dad had planned the retirement three and half years ago—when Luke had a fiancée and actually met all the qualifications to become alpha—and by law, it couldn't be changed. But if he could wipe out the demon infestation on his own, that would surely make his old man proud. This would prove to the pack that—mate or no mate—he was ready to be alpha.

He exited the alley onto St. Peter Street and turned right. His truck sat parked at the bar, and he needed to get to the morgue on Earhart. He fished in his pocket for some change and handed it to a bum huddled under an awning.

The man responded with a gnarled smile. "Bless you, sir."

Luke nodded and stepped past him. As he rounded the corner, he glanced up to see a pair of gleaming crimson eyes watching him. He inhaled sharply, and a low growl escaped his throat. Though the figure looked like a man, the creature ahead was all demon.

CHAPTER THREE

MACEY TAPPED HER PEN ON THE DESK AND STARED RIGHT PAST the case file she should have completed half an hour ago. What piece of this puzzle was she missing? She glanced at her right hand and ran her thumb across the pads of her first three fingers where the ash had been. She'd stopped by her house on the way to the station to wash up and change into dry clothes. And though the black residue had completely washed off on her trek through the rain, she could still sense the gritty substance on her skin.

A rap on her door brought her back to the present.

"Need some help with that paperwork, boss? We need to get it filed." Bryce leaned a shoulder against the door frame and took a bite of a Snickers bar.

Macey shook her head. "Do you ever eat real food?"

Bryce examined the candy, turning it over in his hands. "Looks real to me. I can feel it. I can see it." He held it up to his nose. "I can smell it." He took a bite and mumbled with the chocolate in his mouth. "And I can definitely taste it. Wanna bite?" He offered her the half-eaten bar.

She wrinkled her nose. "No thanks. All you eat is junk food."

Bryce swallowed the candy and snorted. "You're one to talk. I've seen how many beignets you can put away in one sitting."

She signed the last page of the file and stacked the papers without making eye contact with her partner. "That's different."

"How so?"

She looked into his eyes. "I eat healthy food too. You should think about taking some cooking lessons or something."

"Nah." He plopped into the chair across from her desk. "I need to find me a wife. Have a little lady in the kitchen making gumbo every night. That'd be nice. 'Course, she'd have to quit her job so she'd have time to iron my clothes and take care of all the babies we'd be making."

Macey bit her bottom lip. *Ten…nine…eight…*She knew he was messing with her. *Seven…six…five…*He was trying to get her riled up. Trying to get her to react. *Four, three-two-one.* Damn it, she was taking the bait.

She slapped her palms on her desk and lifted out of her seat. "You just keep on with that little fantasy, mister. And if you find a woman like that, you'd better keep her away from me, or I'll knock some sense into her myself." She dropped into her chair and crossed her arms over her chest. "Quit her job to take care of a man. Men can take care of themselves."

"What?" Bryce raised his hands. "C'mon, Mace. You know I'd take care of her too. I'd make her real happy…if you know what I mean." He raised his eyebrows in emphasis.

His goofy grin melted the tension in Macey's chest. Why did she let him get to her like that? "Oh, please. You know you couldn't make a girl any happier than BOB could."

"Bob? You mean I've got to compete with another man for my imaginary wife?"

She laughed. "No, dummy. B-O-B. Battery Operated Boyfriend?"

"Bob." He pressed his lips together and gazed at the ceiling. "Battery Oper—oh! I get it. Clever. And I'm offended."

"No, you're not. All done." She pushed the file across the desk. "Any word on the autopsy report?"

And just like that, they were back to business. That was the good thing about working with a bunch of men. She could switch gears in the middle of a conversation, and they didn't mind at all. And they didn't gossip…as much. So she constantly had to prove her worth as a female detective. She'd done fine so far.

Bryce picked up the file and flipped through the pages. "You know they won't get to it 'til the morning."

She groaned. "I know, but it's killing me." She lowered her voice and leaned forward. "After y'all left, I went back to the scene…where the body was. The blood was gone."

"That's good. Don't want to leave the city dirty. The cleanup crew is working fast these days."

"No, Bryce, listen. It hadn't been cleaned up yet. I didn't find any blood, but I did find ash. Ash…like at the other scenes."

He gave her a puzzled look. "Ash, huh? Did you turn it in to evidence?"

She let out a long sigh. "No. The bottom dropped out as soon as I found it. Washed it all away."

"Damn."

She slumped in her seat. "Tell me about it."

"Where do you think it came from? I'm sure there's a logical explanation somewhere out there."

Was there? She was beginning to wonder.

"Maybe all the attackers were carrying something," he said.

She raised an eyebrow. "Like what?"

"I dunno. Something burnt." He flashed a grin and winked.

Macey rolled her eyes. "You think? But that still doesn't explain why the blood was gone. It's strange." She rubbed her temple with two fingers, trying to ward off the impending headache that threatened to make her night even worse. "I'm wondering if it could be something…paranormal."

Bryce heaved himself up from his seat. "What? Like ghosts? Did you see something out there tonight?"

She shook her head. "No. Nothing's soaked in yet. I can't see anything, and you know I don't talk to ghosts. I…" She traced her finger along the faux wood pattern of her desk. He was going to think she'd gone insane. "I don't think the rapists are human." She bit her bottom lip and implored him with her gaze. It was the only explanation.

He stared at her and blinked. "Not huma—c'mon Mace. You know I believe in your ability or intuition…or whatever you call it, but that's as far as I'm willing to go. If they weren't human, they'd have to have been animals. And all the victims identified them as men."

"With red eyes."

"Contacts. Drugs. Or glare from the streetlights. *Something.*"

"You saw the body; they weren't contacts." Macey exhaled sharply and narrowed her eyes. She yanked open the desk drawer, grabbed her purse, and flung it over her shoulder. "*Something's* not right about this, and I'm going to find out what." She rose to her feet and strutted toward the door.

Bryce touched her elbow. "Where are you going?"

"To the morgue. I need to see the body."

When Luke made eye contact, the fiend grinned and tilted its head before it shimmied up a drain pipe and crouched on a rooftop over-looking an alley. With the black sky as a backdrop, it appeared as nothing more than a fuzzy mass—nothing a human eye would detect. Luke held its gaze, watching its crimson eyes as it crawled across the roof and disappeared into the alley below.

Shit. The morgue's gonna have to wait.

His beast wanted to take over. If he shifted, and stalked the demon in his wolf form, he'd have a better chance of making the kill. But the rain had let up, and locals and tourists alike were out, braving the steamy streets to make it to their destinations. There were too many people around. He'd have to chase his prey into the woods, where he could shift without being seen. He trotted up the sidewalk, and with his back to the wall, he peered into the passageway. The demon stood frozen, its back to the exit, as a growling wolf stared it down.

Goddammit!

Thick chocolate fur stood on end over the wolf's solid body. It shifted its weight back onto muscular haunches, preparing to pounce.

With his lips peeled back over ferocious fangs, Chase, in wolf form, snarled at his prey. Luke stepped into the alley, blocking the exit. Chase would hear about this. How would they explain the appearance of a giant wolf in the French Quarter?

The demon lunged left, its talons hooking onto a second-story windowsill. Before it could drag itself up, Chase snapped onto its leg and yanked it off the wall. The fiend skidded across the cobblestone and landed at Luke's feet. Without his own claws or something sharp to behead it, Luke's chances of killing the demon were nil, so he grabbed it by the neck and hauled it off the ground. "My friend wants to play with you." He shoved the fiend toward Chase, but it ducked and rolled, avoiding the werewolf's advance.

"Playtime's over." Luke picked up a metal trash can lid and hurled it at the demon, striking it in the back of the head. Chase sprang forward, teeth bared and claws extended. He swiped a massive paw across the demon's chest as his jaws snapped down on the fiend's face. Before Chase's paws hit the pavement, the demon fell into a pile of ash. He'd hit the sweet spot in one swipe.

All a werewolf had to do was puncture the demon's heart with a claw, and it was vanquished. Unfortunately, demons didn't really die. They went to their own hellish dimension, where they waited for some other idiotic human to conjure them back.

The sound of laughter and footsteps echoed down the alley. Luke snapped his head to the left to find a group of people sipping hurricanes twenty feet away. In their drunkenness, he could probably explain away their visions of a wolf in the French Quarter, but why take the chance? He turned to his friend. "Go."

Chase jumped behind a wall and ran toward a park. Luke casually walked down the passageway, stopping to kick his boot through the ash to spread out the evidence, and followed the wolf's path. Chase's shift at the bar didn't end for another three hours. He better not have been skirting his duties to play with the demons.

Once they were safely out of sight, human Chase stepped out from behind a sycamore and smoothed his T-shirt down his stomach. "Third one tonight. Thanks for your help."

Luke marched toward his friend, ready to give him a reaming, but Chase's statement caught him off guard. "Third one?"

"Yeah. James found one off Rampart shortly after he left you at the other scene. Tracked him two miles out of the city before he got him."

He shook his head. "Damn. All right. But you need to be more careful where you shift, man. You were *in* the Quarter."

Chase shrugged. "I know. But I saw you, and when it jumped off the roof, I knew we had it."

He had a point. Hell, Luke probably would've done the same thing. They'd vanquished the fiend, and that was the important thing. His cousin would say he was being too lenient. Shifting in the city went against the rules—unless it was absolutely necessary to save a human. But they'd ridded New Orleans of one more demon, hadn't they? Who gave a shit what his cousin would've said?

"Who's covering the bar tonight?" He motioned with his head for Chase to follow.

"Amber. She had a vision it'd be a busy night, so she let me go early."

The hair on the back of his neck stood on end at the mention of his sister. Her gift of premonition proved useful in the battle against the demons, but it wasn't always accurate. "Any details?"

"Nah. Just said she had a feeling."

"We need to get back." Luke picked up the pace, stomping through the mud toward the city. Chase followed on his heels.

"Noah and Cade are there. She's safe."

She better be. Chase would have to be out of his mind to leave Luke's little sister alone at the bar. She couldn't protect herself if anything… He stopped the thought right there. Only the eldest offspring of werewolf couples could shift, and Amber was as defense-less as a human. So was Melissa, his former fiancée. She'd been a second-born were, and he'd let her get killed three years ago.

He couldn't bear it if he lost another vulnerable female he loved. "I'm not worried about her," he lied. "I need to get my truck."

"Where you headed?" Chase asked.

"We're going to the morgue."

CHAPTER FOUR

JIMMY HANCOCK SAT ALONE ON THE PORCH OF THE TWO-ROOM cabin in the swamp, watching the neon-blue glow of the bug zapper. Mosquitoes the size of horseflies encircled the glimmering death trap. One by one, the brave insects would venture into the light they were so enamored of. And one by one, they'd die in a sharp pulse and a *zap*. Occasionally, the light of death would draw in a gray moth. It took more than a quick singe to kill those. The rapid flicker and *buzz, buzz, buzz...zap,* made Jimmy's skin crawl.

What did it feel like for the moth? It must've been worse than for the mosquito.

He wrung his hands and stared at the puddle of sweat on the floor beneath them. It was nothing compared to the amount his once-white T-shirt had absorbed from his pits and back. The thick mass of trees around the cabin blocked any chance of a breeze, but even that wouldn't have helped. Jimmy's nerves were making him sweat.

His younger brother should have been home hours ago, and Jimmy didn't know what to do. He could go looking for him, but what if someone found the cabin? All the work they'd done would be exposed. Or worse...destroyed. What would Ross do to him then?

Another moth met its fate with a crackling *zap*. Jimmy cringed.

He'd prefer the bug zapper any day to what his brother could do to him. What Ross *would* do to him.

He looked at the scar on his left palm. A thick black scab covered the thin line he'd opened the night before. He was supposed to open it again tonight, but not without Ross.

Jimmy couldn't control the demons. His brother did that part, so what was he supposed to do? He couldn't very well conjure one on his own. But if he didn't, he'd be in deep shit. His heart raced at the thought of the shit he'd be in. He must've screwed up already. Why else wouldn't Ross be home? Jimmy had done something wrong. It was his fault; it always was. He was only human.

Ross was the blessed one. Being half demon made him special. Jimmy wasn't special. He was a stupid idiot. He was lucky to have Ross as a brother. Damn lucky. And that's all Jimmy was. He wasn't smart. Wasn't handsome. He didn't have any friends because nobody liked a stupid idiot. Jimmy was lucky. That was all. And he was okay with that.

He opened the screen door and stepped inside the main room of the cabin. An old, rusty stove, sink, and ice box lined one wall, creating the small kitchen. A dilapidated futon leaned against another. That was where Jimmy slept. He was lucky to have such a soft place to sleep. He'd been real good that week when Ross brought it home for him. How long had it been? Fifteen years? Jimmy hadn't been good since.

He ran his hand along the wooden altar in the middle of the room, and his scar tingled. He didn't know why it did that. He picked up the ceremonial knife in his right hand. It was really a kitchen knife Ross had scratched some symbols into. Jimmy knew that, but Ross said the symbols made it special, so it wasn't just a kitchen knife anymore.

He held it up to the light. "*Hmpf.* Still looks like a kitchen knife."

"*Put it down, you stupid idiot.*"

"Huh? What?" The knife clanked on the linoleum floor. "Ross? That you?" With a trembling hand, he picked up the blade and put it back on the altar. He searched the room, but he couldn't see his brother.

"Where are you? On the porch?" He threw open the screen door, and it slammed against the wall with a loud *crack*. Jimmy jumped. No Ross.

"Ross?" Oh, no. His brother had seen him with the knife. He probably thought Jimmy was about to do something stupid again. "I…I wasn't gonna do it yet. I was waiting for you. I…I…I didn't know when you were coming back."

He tried to swallow, but it felt like his heart was lodged in his throat. It couldn't have been in his throat, though. It was beating in his chest like a race horse's hooves pounding the ground. He tentatively took a step back, bracing himself for the blow his brother was sure to give him. Would it be the head or the gut this time?

When nothing happened, he took another step back…Then another. With a maniacal squeal, he leapt to the futon and curled into a ball. He squeezed his eyes shut and mumbled into the dust-filled cushion. "I'm sorry, Ross. I'm so sorry. I screwed up again. I'm sorry."

"Shut up, moron."

Cold shivers ran down his spine. Where was his brother?

"Get up and get a hold of yourself. You have to do something for me."

Jimmy turned his head slightly and opened one eye a slit. No one was there. He opened the other eye and raised his head. "Where? I can't see you."

"Of course you can't, dimwit. I'm dead."

CHAPTER FIVE

"What do you mean you can't find it?" Macey balled her hands into fists as the lab tech blinked at her. She wanted to slap the annoyed expression off the kid's face. Of course, she wouldn't *actually* slap him, but the thought entered her mind, and she considered it. He couldn't have been more than twenty—with his acne-covered face and scrawny arms—and was obviously new to the job. "You *lost* the body?"

The tech sighed and rolled his eyes. "*I* didn't lose it." He tapped on the clipboard. "Says right here it should be in locker fifty-seven."

"But it isn't."

"Nope." The tech pulled up his social media account on the computer.

Macey snapped her fingers. "Hello?"

He slowly turned his head toward her, keeping his gaze on the monitor until the last second. "Yeah?" He flicked his eyes toward her before focusing on the computer again.

"If the body isn't in locker fifty-seven, then where is it?"

The guy shrugged. "How should I know? My shift just started twenty minutes ago." He clicked the play button on a video post, and a kitten wearing a top hat danced across the screen.

Macey's nails cut into her palms as she tried to maintain her composure. He was a kid. She shouldn't take his lack of respect personally. "I need you to…"

Click. Click. Click. He ignored her. With every muscle in her body tensed, she reached across the counter and switched off the monitor. She put her hands on her hips and glared at him.

The tech crossed his arms over his chest and glared back. "Look, lady. I dunno what you want *me* to do. It's not my problem."

Lady? She took a deep breath and let it out ever so slowly. *Ten. Nine. Eight. Seven.* She had to keep her cool. *Six. Five. Four…Keep your voice low, Mace…Three. Two…One.* She put on her biggest fake smile and took one more breath before she spoke.

"I realize you're new here, but let's get a few things straight. First, my name's not Lady. I introduced myself as Carpenter. *Detective* Carpenter. You saw my credentials, so I expect to be addressed accordingly. Second, you are the tech on duty, so, yes, it is your problem." Her blood boiled at the blasé expression on the kid's face. Who did he think he was? "Third, when an officer requests to see a body, you have to produce it. If it isn't where the log states, you need to *find* it."

The sound of the door opening behind her stopped Macey's rant. Bryce sauntered to her side. "I figured you'd have been in and out of here already. How goes it?"

Macey let out a cynical chuckle. "I would have been if this young man would do his job and find the body."

"Find it?" Bryce cut his gaze toward the tech. "Where is it?"

He shrugged. "I dunno. Not where it's supposed to be."

Bryce furrowed his brow. "Then go look for it."

The tech let out a long sigh and nodded. "Yes, sir." He rose from his seat and shuffled out the back door.

"Sir? You've been here for thirty seconds, he calls you sir and does what you ask. I've been here for fifteen minutes arguing with the little bastard, and what do I get? 'Look, *lady.* I dunno what you want me to do.' Jeez!"

Bryce shook his head. "You're a girl. And a little thing at that."

"It doesn't matter."

"It *shouldn't* matter. But it does. No one said it would be easy, Mace. You know that."

She closed her eyes and rolled her head from side to side, stretching her sore neck. The pain in her temple that had been threatening her earlier had turned into a full blown headache. "I've worked hard to earn the respect of the boys at the station. Even the Chief respects me. Why's it so hard for people like this kid to?"

"Why do you let it bother you?"

That was a good question, with a long list of answers. After being abandoned by her family at such an early age, she rarely felt like she belonged anywhere. Her life was a never-ending balancing act, trying to prove her worth while keeping everyone at a safe distance to avoid getting hurt. But standing under the fluorescent lights of the stark white morgue, waiting for a disrespectful kid to find a missing body, wasn't the time or place for a pity party. She'd thrown enough of those in her lifetime.

"No reason, I guess."

Luke and Chase sat in the cab of the pick-up and stared at the back door of the morgue. A single security camera hung loose from its mount, the frayed wiring sticking out of the device rendering it inoperable. They'd have no problem picking the lock and getting in, but finding the body without being caught might prove difficult.

"What's the plan, man? Just run in and grab it?" Chase circled his shoulders as if loosening up for a fight.

"Right. And not get caught. You ready?" Luke didn't wait for an answer. He stepped out of the truck and closed the door, searching the area for witnesses. They were alone. With long strides, he made his way to the door, Chase close behind. He pulled his lock-picking tools out of his back pocket, and within seconds, the door opened. As he peered inside, a scrawny kid with messy orange hair slammed a drawer shut and sulked out of the room.

"Now," he whispered, and they slinked inside. Bright fluorescent lights illuminated the cold, dreary room. Rows of metal doors lined three of the walls, their two-inch thickness the only thing separating the living from the dead. A lone steel table stood in the center of the room—probably where they did the autopsies. The stale smell of death lingered in the air.

Luke shivered. He'd done more than his share of killing animals, but that was for food. Dead humans were another story. How anyone could work in such a dismal place, he'd never understand. Why would someone want to be surrounded by death all night? The sour look on Chase's face said he probably thought the same thing.

Luke pointed to his nose, an indication for them to use their senses to find the body, rather than opening every drawer. Chase nodded, and they stepped farther into the room.

"You're sure you checked every locker?" A female voice floated in from down the hallway, and Luke held his breath. He'd recognize Macey Carpenter's melodic cadence anywhere, and though his mind told him he needed to move, his body betrayed him, freezing him to the spot. What was it about this woman that had him aching to know her?

Chase knocked him on the shoulder, bringing him back to the present. They needed to get the hell out of there. Now. Macey's voice drifted closer; they'd never make it to the back door. There was no time to escape. Nowhere to hide, except...

Chase yanked open an empty drawer and crawled inside. Luke's heart threatened to beat a hole through his chest. He couldn't stand being inside an elevator, much less a body locker. But what other choice did he have? He spun around and found number fifty-nine ajar. He peeked inside. No body.

He could do it. But the space was so small...Would he be able to breathe?

"I opened them all twice." The door knob twisted.

Now or never. He slid inside and the door closed behind him, the *click* of the latch sounding so final, his breath caught. Total darkness engulfed him. Utterly still. Cold. One twitch would give away his location, not that he could've moved a muscle if he'd wanted to. The confined space had him paralyzed with dread.

He closed his eyes and took several long, deep breaths, trying to slow his pulse. Now was not the time to panic.

"Well, it didn't get up and walk away. Where's fifty-seven?"

Macey's boot heels thudded across the tile, the sound echoing in Luke's constricted chamber like a hammer driving nails into a coffin.

"It's over here," a male said. "But, I told you. I opened it twice already. It's not there."

The *clack* of the latch and the sound of metal sliding on metal sent his heart racing again. They were so close to finding him.

The *bang* of the drawer slamming shut shook the wall of lockers. Luke held his breath.

"Let me see the report." He heard Detective Carpenter flipping through the pages, sighing heavily as the clipboard clanked on metal. "Joseph filed it. He's been here longer than I've been on the force. He doesn't make mistakes like this."

"Don't look at me." The male again. "I just got here. He handed me the folder, asked me to enter it, and left."

"No one's blaming you," an older male with a deeper voice responded. "But we do need to get this figured out. Fast."

"You're sure it wasn't transferred?" Annoyance edged Macey's words.

"There are two ways in and out of the building, and no one has taken a body out the front door since I got here." The younger male sounded indignant as he stomped across the room. "The back door locks automatically, and Joseph and I are the only ones with the key." He banged on something metal. "It's closed tight."

Luke allowed himself a small sigh of relief. At least they'd closed the door behind themselves when they broke in.

"Is there a security camera?" Macey's voice sounded closer, and Luke's head spun. Either she'd find him soon or he'd have a heart attack in this confined space. He clenched every muscle in his body to stop himself from shaking. *Please get this over with.*

The younger man sighed. "It's been broken for a week."

"Dammit. You're sure no one stuck the body in an adjacent locker by accident?" Macey again. Another drawer slid open. "Not in fifty-six."

Shit. His pulse pounded in his ears. The combination of fears called on his flight instinct. His beast begged to take over, the primal urge to shift and get the hell out of there overwhelming him. *Not now…*

"What about fifty-eight?" The drawer next to him slid open.

It took every ounce of control to tame his beast. He could not shift. Not there. He clenched his trembling hands into fists and fought to breathe. The air in his chamber grew heavy. He couldn't get enough of it into his lungs. He would suffocate if he didn't get out of there fast.

The adjacent door slammed shut. Was his next? The sharp screech of fingernails sliding across metal. A slight jiggle of the latch. He could practically feel her hand resting on the handle of his drawer. He closed his eyes, willing her to let go.

"Did you check fifty-nine?"

This was it. He swallowed hard.

"You know, boss. I think we need to call Joseph," The older man said. "Maybe he can shed some light on it."

"You're right." The handle clicked as she released it. "Let's get him on the phone." Her footsteps thudded across the room. A door opened and closed again.

Silence.

He couldn't wait another second. Fumbling his arms over his head, he gave the door a solid push.

It didn't move. *Crap!*

He pushed it harder. Still nothing.

Cold sweat trickled down his forehead, stinging his eyes. He was trapped. He ran his hands across the metal, searching for a latch to release him from the frigid tomb. The damn things only opened from the outside. He pressed his boots against the end of the chamber for leverage and slammed both fists against the door.

It didn't budge. That was it. He was going to suffocate. There was no way out, and he would die an excruciatingly slow death trapped inside a meat locker in the morgue. No…It couldn't happen. He banged frantically on the door, using all his strength to will it open. With his feet against the wall, he gave it a thrust with all his might, and the door flung open. His momentum sent the drawer shooting out, his body flying off the platform and crashing to the floor.

With a smack, his breath *whooshed* from his lungs. Pain shot through his limbs, and he gasped for air. He was free. Momentarily blinded by the overhead lights, he rubbed his eyes and shot to his feet. His entire body trembled, no longer with the need to shift, but with sheer terror.

"Dude, you okay?" Chase must've opened the latch.

"The door wouldn't open," Luke muttered.

"You closed it all the way." Chase chuckled under his breath.

"Yeah." Luke ran a hand through his sweat-soaked hair. With the racket he'd made, he was surprised no one had come running back into the room. It was time to jet. "I'm good. The body's not here."

"So I heard." Chase motioned toward the exit.

Luke paused and inhaled deeply. "I don't smell it in here either." He followed Chase out the door and jogged to his truck. He couldn't get away from that place fast enough. What kind of alpha gave in to irrational fears like that? He needed to get his act together if he ever wanted to be pack leader. Taking one last look at the closed door, he peeled out of the parking lot.

With the morgue in the rearview mirror, Chase turned to him. "You think it already…woke up?"

Luke sighed. "God, I hope not."

CHAPTER SIX

Jimmy was a hero. His brother would be so proud of him. He just knew it. He'd gotten Ross's body out of that place, and no one even saw him do it. He beat those flea-bag werewolves and that pretty cop too.

He grinned as he thought about what their faces must've looked like when they noticed his brother was gone. They didn't have a clue. Even the werewolves didn't pick up his scent as he hid out in the dumpster behind the morgue until they'd left. They'd run out the back door so fast, you'd have thought they'd seen a zombie or something.

"Who's the idiot now?" Jimmy shoved his brother's body over the edge of the dumpster and cringed when it thudded on the ground. Ross was dead. He couldn't feel that, could he? Jimmy swallowed. He hoped he couldn't.

He didn't know where Ross's ghost was. He'd said something about checking on a host and a birth—whatever that meant. It was confusing. He was supposed to get the body and bring it to the shack in the swamp. If he thought about anything else for too long, he'd get distracted. And the last thing his brother had told him before he left was *don't get distracted.*

He heaved his large frame from the dumpster to the ground and picked up the sack that held his brother. Good thing Jimmy was strong, because his brother was heavy. And it was a good thing he'd found that big duffle bag last spring. He'd had to fold him up just right, but Ross's body fit perfectly in the sack. It zipped up and everything.

With a proud grin stretching across his face, Jimmy slung the bag over his shoulder and trudged across the street. As long as he could make it to the forest without being seen, he'd be fine. He might even make himself a bed of leaves to sleep on the rest of the night. It had taken him two hours to walk to the morgue. It would take even longer to get home.

He stepped behind a fat tree trunk and gently dropped the duffle bag. That's what he'd do. He'd get some rest and go home in the morning. Ross would be so proud of him that he wouldn't mind waiting.

CHAPTER SEVEN

O'MALLEY'S PUB DIDN'T LOOK LIKE MUCH. SMALL. QUIET. Exactly the kind of place Macey needed to clear her mind. She'd walked by the bar dozens of times, always ignoring the urge to step inside. Something about the run-down building called to her. Beckoned her to open up and let it tell its story. That was the reason she'd steered clear of the establishment. Any structure that called that strongly had to be bad news.

And she didn't need any more of that.

The only lead on the case had disappeared. Now, she had nothing. No one at the morgue knew anything. They remembered checking the body in, and it ended there. She reported the broken camera to the head of security, but it wouldn't help with this case. If someone had taken the corpse out the back door, they'd never know.

She put her hands on her hips and shifted her weight from side to side. A change of scenery would help clear her mind. O'Malley's couldn't be *that* bad. Biting her bottom lip, she took a deep breath and pushed open the door. She braced herself for the onslaught of memories into her psyche. A building this old had to have an interesting past, and even without opening herself up to them, she expected the stories to hit her like a wall.

Nothing happened.

Hmm...Kinda disappointing. A smile tugged at the corner of her mouth. Maybe she could actually relax tonight. It was her night off, after all. She deserved a break, even one she'd been forced to take.

She adjusted her bun and smiled at the bartender. With his tattoos and piercings, he had a rough appearance, but the way he grinned gave away his sweet personality. He raised his head to acknowledge her. "What can I get you?"

Macey made her way to a stool at the corner of the bar. "Abita?"

"Sure thing." He filled the glass and set it in front of her, then went back to washing dishes. A news program played on the sole television, but it sat too far away to read the closed captioning.

The phone rang, and the man crossed the bar to pick up the receiver as Macey took a long drink of her beer. The icy bubbles tickled her throat on the way down to her stomach. It'd been way too long since she'd savored the malty goodness. Too long since she'd savored—or even enjoyed—anything. She'd been so caught up in the case; it was all she thought about. If the Chief hadn't insisted she take the night off after the body disappeared, she'd have been thinking about it now.

Damn it. It was still on her mind. After the fitful sleep she'd endured that morning, she needed to loosen up. The bartender hung up, punched in some numbers, and spoke to someone else briefly. The sparkle in his eye disappeared after the phone call, and he shuffled toward her, tensing his jaw and grumbling something under his breath.

"Everything okay?" She absently rubbed the condensation off the glass with her finger.

The bartender wiped the counter with a rag. "Yeah. It's...a family thing." His head snapped up when a side door opened, and he hurried over to the hunk that entered the room.

Wow. Macey scooted closer to the corner of the bar so she could watch the exchange without being seen. The man who entered from the back of the pub stood at least three inches taller than the bartender. He ran a hand through long, wavy, caramel locks, and his black T-shirt stretched tight across muscular pecs when he moved. His sapphire eyes held brotherly concern as he looked at the other man. "What's up?"

"Bekah's damn sitter canceled on her again, and she's gotta go to work. Amber's not due in for another two hours, and—"

The taller man raised a hand to stop him. "It's okay, Chase. Go do what you gotta do. I'll cover."

They walked toward the bar, and Macey gulped her beer to cool the fire that stirred in her core. She gripped the nearly empty mug with both hands and swallowed down a giggle. Had the alcohol already gone to her head? She chewed her bottom lip and focused on the tiny bubbles in her beverage, trying to make her eavesdropping less obvious.

"You sure, man?" The bartender reached into his pocket and pulled out a set of keys. "You've been on site all day."

"Go take care of your niece." He lifted the hinged part of the bar and stepped inside. Macey chugged what was left of her drink.

"Thanks, and I think the lady needs another round." His glittering smile returned as he bounded out the front door.

Macey took a deep breath and forced herself to make eye contact with the gorgeous man.

"What are you drink...ing?" A look of recognition flashed in his eyes before he composed himself.

"I...uh..." A lump in her throat had formed in the half second she'd caught his gaze. She cleared her voice. "Abita, please."

The corners of his eyes crinkled as he smiled. "Have you ever tried Blue Moon? I know Abita's the local favorite, but it's got nothing on this one." He poured the drink without waiting for a response and set it down in front of her.

"Well, no...but I..." Macey stumbled over her words. What the hell was wrong with her? She was a confident, kick-ass detective, but in half a minute, this guy had turned her into a babbling idiot.

He squeezed an orange slice and dropped it into the glass. "On me. If you don't like it, I'll buy your next Abita."

Fair enough. She picked up the beer and took a swig. It was smooth, like liquid gold, and the burst of citrus made her taste buds dance. "Wow. That is good." Finally, she'd found her voice. "Looks like you're off the hook. I'll keep the Blue Moon." She took another drink and toyed with the glass as her heart pounded hard against her chest.

"This your first time in?" His deep-blue eyes drew her in, and she had to look away.

"Yeah. I've lived here most of my life, though. I guess I don't get out much." *Good job, Mace. Way to sound pathetic.*

He chuckled. "Well, welcome." His gaze locked with hers for what felt like an eternity, holding her still, making her forget how to breathe. How did he do that? "I'm Luke Mason, by the way." He held out his hand to shake. "My old man owns the bar."

She hesitated to take his hand. Something inside her screamed to stop. Instinct told her this was the beginning of something bigger than she could imagine, but she chided herself. It was only a handshake. She reached across the bar and shook.

As soon as her skin brushed his, a buzzing sensation shot up her arm, making her hairs stand on end. It paused at her elbow, stinging like she'd hit her funny bone, before it lurched up to her shoulder. It spread through her body in a jolt, and she jumped. *What the hell?*

He gave her a quizzical look. "Interesting."

"Sorry." She jerked her hand away and rubbed her palm on her jeans. "I'm Macey. I must've built up some static electricity or something. You kinda shocked me."

"You shocked me too." Luke ran his hands through his hair and tied it at the nape of his neck with a band. "Do you want a menu? I recommend the steak. Made the marinade myself."

"You cook?"

"Does that surprise you?" His grin sent her heart racing again. What was wrong with her?

"I guess not. I'll stick to the beer, though. Thanks." She tugged on her bottom lip as she watched him wash his hands, pull a lemon out of the small fridge under the bar, and begin cutting it.

The muscles in his forearms flexed and extended with each chop of the knife. Her gaze traveled up to his biceps, where a thin, pink line scarred his otherwise perfect skin. His black T-shirt blocked her view of his obviously muscular shoulder, and warmth pulsed from her core out to her fingertips and toes. Was it the beer or the amazingly hot man across the bar making her feel this way?

Whatever it was, she needed a distraction, so she turned her attention to the video trivia machine at the end of the bar and dropped in a quarter. She touched the screen for eighties pop culture and began answering questions about music and movies from the decade. Her second beer was half empty, and she hadn't been in the bar half an hour.

She sipped her drink, occasionally stealing glances of the sexy bartender, as more and more patrons filled the bar. By the time she drained the glass, people wearing small white stickers on their shirts had packed the establishment, and Luke had filled three rows of plastic cups with ice on the bar in front of her. "What's going on?" she asked.

"Haunted French Quarter tours. They happen every night at six and eight."

"Ghost tours?" She chuckled.

He shrugged and poured a drink that looked like red Kool-Aid into the cups—New Orleans' infamous hurricanes. "My dad thought it would help with business."

She traced her finger along the rim of her empty glass. "Does it?"

"At six and eight. Excuse me." Luke stepped toward a group of customers and handed a patron two of the drinks. He reached for another plastic cup and glanced at Macey. Then he stopped, picked up a beer mug, filled it, and slid it toward her.

She would have thanked him, but he turned away to help the onslaught of customers getting ready for the tour. The once dark, quiet bar now bustled with activity. People filled every chair, lined the walls, and chattered incessantly. She popped another quarter into the machine. Luckily, the tour started in fifteen minutes. She could hang on until then. In the meantime, at least she could enjoy the view.

Luke finished serving the customers, and as the last one left the bar, he turned to face her. He looked at her quizzically, slightly cocking his head to the side. He narrowed his eyes and focused on her so hard, the rest of the world slipped away. Was he judging her?

Checking her out? Whatever he was doing, it made her palms sweat and her heart race. He went utterly still.

Then, he inhaled deeply and shook his head like he didn't believe something. He dropped his arms, and his smile returned, as if that awkward moment never happened.

"So, Macey…You're a detective, right? I think I've seen you on TV a few times."

"Yeah." She grimaced. Never one for the spotlight, she'd managed to keep her face off the evening news for years, letting her charismatic partner handle all the on-screen interviews. With the nature of this case, though, NOPD decided to be politically correct and have a woman on screen for a change. Lucky Macey.

And now Luke knew who she was. When men found out her occupation, some of them bolted immediately. It took a strong man to handle an equally strong woman, and it would've been nice if he'd gotten to know her personality before her reputation.

Wait. What was she thinking? It didn't matter what this guy thought of her; she wasn't looking for a relationship. She had no intention of setting herself up to be hurt again. Still, something about Luke drew her in.

"You've got quite a rep," he said. "I mean…you bust a lot of bad guys."

"I know. But it's my night off…" She batted her lashes, hoping he'd get the message that she didn't want to talk about work. He didn't.

"Can you tell someone is a criminal by looking at him?"

"There are certain qualities I look for, but I've learned not to judge a personality by the package." She took another sip of beer and let her gaze travel from his face down his muscular chest to his pants. "No matter how tempting the package may be." *Crap.* She didn't mean to say that last part out loud. Heat crept up her cheeks as she cleared her throat. "Why? Do you have something you want to confess?"

He chuckled and leaned toward her. "If I did, you'd have to beat it out of me." He winked before standing up straight and crossing his arms. Was he flirting with her? One way to find out.

"You'd like that, wouldn't you?"

The corner of his mouth pulled into a crooked grin. "Maybe."

He *was* flirting. A fluttering sensation formed in her stomach, like butterfly wings beating against a net. She leaned her elbows on the bar, resting her chin on her fist. "Hmm…"

He scratched behind his ear. "Anyway…you're working on the rape cases right? How's that going? Any leads?"

"Ha. I *had* a lead…until the body walked out of the morgue." *Crap!* What was her problem tonight? Was it the man? Or the beer? Whatever it was, she needed keep herself in check before she jeopardized her job.

His eyes widened in surprise. "You lost a body?"

"*I* didn't lose it. But…just…forget I said anything. I'm not supposed to talk about it." She gazed into his eyes, willing him to understand. "Please?"

He raised his hands in a show of innocence. "Okay. I didn't hear a thing."

Nothing he didn't already know, anyway. He probably could've gotten her to say more, but he didn't want to take advantage of her. She wasn't drunk, but she was obviously buzzed. And, damn, she was cute.

"Good. Because this case is tough enough. I don't need to lose my job over it."

He couldn't help but grin at the beautiful woman before him as she reached behind her head and loosened the bun at the nape of her neck. Silky blonde hair flowed over her shoulders, accentuating the delicate dip at the base of her throat in the center of her collar bone.

His mouth watered as he imagined his lips pressed against the indention and the sweet taste of her skin as he trailed kisses across her chest. "Wow."

"What?" She shoved the hair band into her purse and pushed her beer away. "I think I've had enough."

"Your hair is pretty. You should wear it down more."

"Oh." Her gaze shifted to the bar, and she blushed. "Thanks. I would, but…it gets in the way at work. I've been thinking about cutting it—"

"Don't."

She looked into his eyes, and a sly grin curved her lips. "Is that an order? Because I don't like being told what to do."

He slid his gaze down to her tempting mouth and lingered there a moment too long. What would those lips feel like pressed against his? "Just a suggestion."

"Suggestions I can handle."

What the hell was he doing? He needed to stop flirting with her. No matter how hot an inferno she lit inside his core, she was human for Christ's sake.

Or was she?

When he'd touched her, some kind of magic had shot up his arm. Possibly a witch. For a split second, he'd felt the electricity of a were… but she couldn't be. There was no way a were could live in the Quarter for as long as she had without the pack knowing. Rogues were required to register.

If she wasn't a werewolf, he didn't need to waste his time. But the longer she sat there in front of him, the less he cared about pack laws. When he became alpha, he could make his own laws.

Damn it. No! She'd gotten too close already. To the crimes. To the demons. Her job was to figure out what was happening, and his was to keep her from discovering the truth.

Her jingling cell phone pulled him back to reality. She dug in her purse and held the device to her ear. "Hey, Bryce." She mouthed the words *It's my partner* to Luke.

Even if she hadn't told him, she had the volume on her phone up so loud, he could hear every word Bryce said.

"Listen, Mace. We've got an issue with the first victim."

Macey rolled her eyes. "Oh, c'mon, Bryce. It's my night off. Yours too. Can't someone else handle it?"

"They are, but…she's dead. Ripped open…and eaten. Her entire abdomen."

"Come again?"

"That's all I know. On my way to the scene now. 857 Masters Street. Meet you there?"

She ran her hand over her face from her forehead down to her chin. "Actually, could you come pick me up? I'm at O'Malley's on St. Philip."

"Are you drunk, Mace? Do you need to sit this one out?"

"Hell no. You know me better than that. I've had a few, and I don't want to drive, that's all."

"Be there in ten."

She shoved her phone into her purse. "Sorry about that. Guess it's not my night off after all." Sliding off her stool, she hesitated, tugging on her bottom lip. "I have to go. How much do I owe?"

"It's on me tonight. It was nice to meet you, Macey." He held out his hand.

"Thank you." When they shook, the same buzzing electricity shuddered up his arm. Definitely some kind of magic. He held on too long. After the conversation he'd overheard, his instinct told him not to let her go. To protect her above all else. But what could he do? She wasn't his to protect, no matter what his wolf wanted.

Her eyes widened as she pulled her hand away. "I'd like to see you again sometime."

The energy faded, and a new heat flushed his system at the thought. He'd like to see her again too. Naked. In his bedroom… But he couldn't. His duty to the pack came first. "I'm sure we'll run into each other again." Even if he couldn't be with her, he'd be damned if he'd let any harm come to her.

Her expression dropped, the light in her eyes fading, as she turned for the exit. "Um…yeah. See you."

As soon as the door closed behind her, Luke hopped over the bar and called for one of the guys in the back to cover for him. There was no way he'd make it to the scene before Macey. Even if he did, the place would be crawling with cops. Two hundred pack members, and they still didn't have a man on the inside. He shook his head and bounded for his truck.

From the sound of it, whatever ate that woman had come from inside her.

CHAPTER EIGHT

Jimmy's body felt like lead. His muscles ached, and he trudged along like he was moving in slow motion. He'd carried his brother's body across the swamp and all the way to their house. It took him all day. He didn't mean to sleep so long, but that bed he'd made in the leaves was so comfy.

Ross would be mad. But maybe, since Jimmy had the body, his brother would forgive him.

A thick layer of mud covered his sopping wet boots. Dead leaves crunched under his steps as he hoofed it through the last few yards to the front door. It wasn't dark out yet, but heavy clouds covered the sun, casting an eerie haze over the already spooky house. Jimmy shivered. He didn't like living in the swamp. A small apartment in the city, with people all around, would have been nice. He liked people. But Ross insisted on the swamp because it gave them privacy. Being half demon, he needed his space.

But Jimmy didn't. The only reason he didn't leave was because when Ross was born, he'd eaten Momma. He said if Jimmy ever tried to run away, he'd eat him too. Jimmy swallowed hard. He didn't want to get eaten.

Still, he didn't like being alone. He had a dog once, but a gator ate it. He didn't get any more pets. As long as he stayed by himself, nobody got eaten.

He dragged the sack up the front steps and flung open the screen door. "Ross? You here?"

He took a tentative step inside and dropped the body bag at his feet. "Ross?"

"I'm here."

"Oh, good. For a minute I thought somebody—" Before he could finish his sentence, something crashed into him, knocking him to the floor. Jimmy stared up into the bright-red eyes of what looked like a ten-year-old boy. But Jimmy knew better. This wasn't a boy. He smiled and tried to get up as the boy backed away.

"Hey there! I didn't know we had a visitor. What's your name?"

The boy snarled, baring sharp teeth, and leapt toward Jimmy. Jimmy was about to scream when the boy stopped in mid-air and catapulted to the floor like he'd been hit. Jimmy screamed anyway.

The boy got up, dusted off his too-big trousers and crossed his arms. "I'm sorry. I didn't know you were Master's brother."

Jimmy's mouth fell open, so he snapped it shut. His brother hated it when he gaped. "Master?"

"He means me, you idiot. I should've let him tear you up. What the hell took you so long?"

Jimmy didn't know what to say. So many questions ran through his mind, but he knew he'd get in trouble for asking something stupid. "You were heavy." That was the truth. He couldn't get in trouble for telling the truth.

The impact of a hand across his face made his head jerk to the side. Pressure built in his eye like it would explode, and his cheek stung. Was it wrong to say Ross was heavy?

"It doesn't matter now. I don't want it anymore."

Confusion made Jimmy's thoughts tumble. "You don't want your body? But how will you—" He received another blow, this time to his gut. He doubled over as the air *whooshed* out of his lungs.

"Does it feel like I need a body?"

He coughed. "No, sir. It doesn't."

"Good. I don't have enough energy to knock any more sense into you. Besides, I can use your body when I need it."

"How can you—" A piercing pain shot through Jimmy's body, like he'd been stabbed with a million straight pins all at once. For a moment, he couldn't breathe. He stood frozen in the sensation of his skin being turned inside out. Then the pain stopped just as suddenly as it had started. His arms moved up and down, and he jumped. His body crouched and leapt into the air, but he wasn't controlling it. He tried to speak, but his mouth wouldn't move. All he could do was think. *What's happening? Why am I doing this?*

"Because I'm controlling you." He felt his mouth form the words, but they didn't come from his brain. It was almost his own voice, but Ross was speaking. "It's a little trick I figured out while I was waiting for you to get back. Fun, huh?"

Not really.

"Sure it is. And get used to it, because I like it. You and I are gonna have some fun. Maybe we'll go into town tonight and find a woman."

Oh, no. He can hear everything I think.

"Damn right, I can. Good thing you don't think much."

The sharp, tearing sensation returned, but this time it felt like the pins were pushing from the inside out. As Ross ripped himself from his body, Jimmy collapsed to the floor, gasping for breath. He ran his hands over his arms, patting his body to make sure his skin was still there.

"I…I didn't like that, Ross."

"Neither did the boy here. He's only a day old, but he's a lot stronger than you. You're easier to control." Ross laughed. *"That's no surprise."*

"What are you going to do with him?" Jimmy gestured to the boy who stood silently against the wall. Though, calling him a boy was a stretch. He'd be full grown in a couple of days, just like Ross had been.

"He's gonna be my eyes in the city. I'm gonna turn him loose and let him wreak his havoc or do whatever the hell he wants to, as long as he keeps an eye on those damn werewolves."

At that, the boy bolted through the house and out the door.

Jimmy wanted to ask a question. He knew he shouldn't, but he really wanted to know. "Why are we doing this? Calling demons and stuff?"

"You're doing it because I told you to. I'm doing it because…I'm bored. I'm tired of living in the swamp. I'm going to run this city one day, and all its magic will be mine."

He was able to ask that question without getting punished. He started to smile, but stopped himself. Maybe he could ask some more.

"What do the demons do after we call them?"

"They rape and murder. What else, moron? Then we get more half breeds like the boy."

"Why?"

"Because they obey me. And the more evil there is in the world, the better. Once I get enough of them, I'll build an army. Then I'll get rid of those damn werewolves, and every magical being in the city will answer to me."

CHAPTER NINE

MACEY MUNCHED ON A BEAR CLAW DURING THE FIFTEEN-MINUTE drive from the French Quarter, down the dusty country road, to the victim's home. She hadn't been drunk when Bryce called her, but a little food in her belly would sober her up if any tipsiness remained in her system.

The comfort food also helped ease the sting of rejection. She must've read Luke wrong. His glittering smile and flirtatious conversation couldn't have been what she'd thought. He probably flirted with all the customers. A guy that good-looking…Women probably went to that bar for the view of Luke alone. It was just as well. Getting involved with a man like that was the last thing she needed. No matter how much she'd wanted it at the time.

She swallowed the last of the pastry and reached for the cup of joe Bryce had so thoughtfully picked up for her on the way. She took a sip and wistfully stared out the window.

Her partner broke the silence. "You know, I expected you to be stumbling over your feet when I picked you up. But you only had three? I've seen you drink way more than that and be fine."

Macey took another sip of her coffee and put it in the cup holder.

"I'm sure my BAL is over the legal limit. It was high enough to screw up my judgment of the bartender, anyway."

Bryce flicked his gaze over to Macey for a second. "Do I want to know?"

She sighed and ran her hands through her hair, pulling it into a low ponytail. Holding a rubber band in her mouth, she twisted her mane into a tight bun. "It's just…" She spoke with the band between her teeth. "I really thought he liked me." Yanking the elastic out of her mouth, she twisted it in her hair. "He smiled and flirted. I thought he was flirting."

Bryce glanced at her with raised eyebrows.

"He was definitely flirting, Bryce. Ugh! Why do I care? I shouldn't care. I don't *need* a man." Honestly, she didn't even *want* one. As long as she didn't open herself up to anyone, no one could get close enough to hurt her.

"How do you know he's not interested?"

"Because I told him I wanted to see him again, and he said, 'I'm sure I'll see you around,' or something like that. He blew me off."

Bryce drew in a long breath. "Well, then he's an idiot, Mace. Forget about him."

"You're right. It's not like I ever have to see him again. I just won't go to that bar anymore." She inhaled deeply and closed her eyes, pushing the thoughts of Luke and his amazing biceps out of her head.

The sedan chugged down the dirt road, jolting over bumps and through potholes. The seatbelt pressed into her lap, each bouncing bump making the need to pee overwhelm her.

"Are we there yet?"

Bryce chuckled. "Don't make me turn this car around, young lady. We'll be there when we get there."

Macey groaned. "Seriously. I need to pee. If you see a store, you have to stop."

Her partner grinned silently as he made a sharp left turn into a driveway. "We're here. If the bathroom's been cleared, you can go. Otherwise…you'll have hold it."

Her mouth fell open. "You want me to pee in the victim's house?

At the crime scene?" She got out of the car and slammed the door. "You're nuts. I can't do that."

"Suit yourself." He shrugged and shuffled toward the house.

Macey glared at his back, but she followed. It was only three beers. She could hold it.

Monstrous pine trees towered over the small yard, creating a canopy across the walkway. The usually-green needles appeared as black silhouettes against the darkening sky. Gravel crunched beneath her flip-flops—not the shoes she'd have chosen for police work, but she didn't have time to change. Her denim capris clung to her skin, and she fought the urge to pop the button to relieve some of the pressure on her bladder.

Four stone steps led up to the entrance of the white Creole-style cottage, and green shutters framed the windows. Two men in blue greeted Macey and Bryce at the front door. "Victim's in the back yard," one of them said. "There's blood in the kitchen. Trails out the back door."

"Thanks." She smiled at the man and brushed past him into the small living room. Beige Berber carpet lined the floor from white wall to white wall. A canary yellow sofa sat across from a small television. Various trinkets lined the built-in bookshelves, all evenly and meticulously spaced. Nothing appeared to be out of place. No sign of a struggle so far.

Bryce cleared his throat and pointed his thumb toward an open door. "Bathroom's clear."

"Bryce!"

"Just saying. I'd use it." He grinned and took the lead as they headed into the kitchen. The chrome sink and faucet shined in the brightness cast from the recessed lighting. The cabinets gleamed a pristine white, and a large bouquet of sunflowers overflowed a blue vase on the center of the island. Except for the bloody hand print lying bright red against the pale gray granite, it was the most cheerful kitchen Macey had ever seen.

Bryce laughed.

"What?" She shifted her weight and fought the urge to bolt to the bathroom.

"You're doing the pee pee dance, Mace. Go use the toilet."

She glanced down at the awkward position she was standing in. "Oh, fine. But you better not tell anyone."

He drew a cross over his heart and pretended to zip his lips.

Macey ducked in and out of the restroom as fast as she could, and no one noticed her using the crime scene facilities. Men were lucky. Any tree would do when they had the urge. She trekked through the house and onto the back porch where Bryce stood, talking with a uniform.

"Feel better?" the man asked. Her partner tried to muffle his laughter.

"Not funny, Bryce." Her face burned with embarrassment, and she punched him on the shoulder. She had to be as red as a beet. She'd get him back, though. One way or another.

Down the steps and to the right lay the body of the first victim in the string of crimes. Her limbs were contorted, like she'd fallen and writhed in pain as whatever attacked her turned her into a meal. Macey peered over the railing at the bloody sight. The woman's abdomen was nearly nonexistent. She'd almost been chewed in half, but her still intact spine glistened white in the harsh, artificial light that had been set up to illuminate the scene.

The blood-soaked ground looked black beneath the mauled body, and bits of flesh lay scattered around the yard. Macey covered her mouth and fought the urge to vomit. She had to get a closer look, but this image would surely invade her nightmares. She followed Bryce down the stairs and stopped a few feet away from the victim.

The coroner was crouched by the body, and he rose to his feet when the detectives approached. He peeled the soiled latex gloves from his fingers and tossed them into a bag before he spoke. "Stomach and uterus are completely gone. What's left of the other organs is shredded to bits."

Macey's gaze darted from the victim to the examiner. "Any idea what could have done this?"

The man shrugged. "Something hungry. Or someone completely twisted. She's been here nearly twenty-four hours. That's all I know."

"Thank you." She glanced at the body again. Could the same creature that attacked the rapists have been responsible for the carnage here? If so, why would it have come back for the woman? Nothing about this case made sense. Turning to Bryce, she took a deep breath and immediately wished she hadn't. The stale scent of death mixed with flesh on the verge of decay made her stomach turn. "Do you think a *person* did this?"

He looked at the body and grimaced. "I sure hope not, but who knows? Do your thing, and maybe you'll get something."

She pursed her lips. Her ability hadn't helped so far, but she'd give it a try. She trotted up the porch steps and put her hand against the wall. The old cottage's secrets danced through her mind as fleeting images and short movies. She saw a Creole woman giving birth, a couple cooing over a baby, a soldier heading off to war as his wife cried over a cradle. Other images flitted in and out of her consciousness too quickly for her to grab onto. What was the house trying to tell her? Where was the victim's energy?

Macey took a deep breath to clear her mind. Then she closed her eyes and focused on the victim, willing her energy to come forward. A single picture flashed through her senses: the victim standing sideways in front of a mirror with her hand on her pregnant belly. Macey tried to grab hold of the picture, to make it stay so she could explore it. But it flitted away as quickly as it had come.

She dropped her hand and exhaled a sigh. It didn't make sense. The victim wasn't pregnant. Macey had spoken to her a few weeks earlier. She didn't have any children, according to the police report, but the woman in the vision was at least eight months along. Maybe she'd had a miscarriage at one time?

"He's here."

Macey jerked her head around at the whisper. It sounded as if someone stood right beside her. "What?" She scanned the scene, but she stood alone on the porch. The rest of the people there were men, and the whisper had been female.

A prickling sensation made the hairs on the back of her neck rise. A static electrical charge had her body humming. Was it the woman's spirit? It had to be. Like in the courtyard a few days prior, the spirit's energy danced around her...so close, but she couldn't grab onto it.

"I heard you," Macey whispered, so no one would hear her talking to a ghost. "What happened to you?"

She strained to hear the spirit again, but nothing happened. The energy dissipated, leaving Macey alone. Had she imagined it? She turned to report what she'd seen to Bryce, but movement in the line of trees behind the house caught her eye. The shadow of a man darted from behind a trunk and disappeared into the thicket.

What if it was the killer? If anyone was sick enough to do something like this, he'd probably return to the scene. Or was it a ghost? In the darkness, it was hard to tell. Macey slipped off the porch and tiptoed through the grass toward the woods, careful not to draw attention to herself.

She crept past the tree line and swept the area with her vision. She didn't see anything unusual, but the crunch of a breaking branch drew her attention deeper into the forest. She reached for her gun, but she didn't have it. Her heart pounded, the sound thrumming in her ears, as icy adrenaline flushed through her system. Her muscles tensed, and she tried to slow her breathing. What was she thinking heading into the woods unarmed and unprepared? If she called for backup now, whoever—or whatever—she was tracking would surely bolt. She was already here. She could handle it.

The figure took off, sprinting through the trees. She caught a glimpse of it—tall, broad shoulders, definitely masculine—before he disappeared into the thickness. Macey gave chase, running in the general direction he'd gone. She dodged tree stumps and stumbled over roots, nearly losing a flip flop, before she stopped.

She'd lost him.

"Where the hell did you go?" Standing utterly still, she held her breath and hoped a sound of his movement would betray his location. A soft breeze tickled her skin, and she inhaled deeply. The only scent that danced on the wind was the putrid death of the scene behind her. She crept forward through the brush, taking care to place each step with precision. The last thing she needed was a broken branch piercing the thin, floppy sole of her shoe.

A noise to her right made her heart leap. She stumbled back and caught herself on a tree trunk as a flock of quails squawked and flew from their nests. She swallowed and wiped the sweat from her brow. *Get a grip, Mace.*

As she continued to inch ahead, a thick, frigid gust of air enveloped her. It pricked at her body like thousands of dry pine needles piercing her skin. Ice formed in her veins as the atmosphere around her closed in, choked and heavy, with an aura of something… familiar. It slithered up her arms and swirled around her head as it made its presence known—the spirit from the courtyard. Instinct told her to bolt, but she tried to stay calm as whatever—or whoever—continued to torment her. If it was the rapist whose body went missing, maybe she could communicate with him.

"Who are you?" She gritted her teeth as the pricking sensation grew stronger. "What do you want?"

She strained to hear the faint chuckle that danced through her head.

"I want you, Detective."

"What the hell?" The voice had come from inside her head. With one sharp rip, the spirit entered her body. She'd never been possessed, but she knew without a doubt the ghost had gotten inside her. She could feel it rolling through her limbs, trying to control her mind. She couldn't move herself, but her head jerked toward a sound to her right.

A sharp exhale. A rustling in the brush. Her pulse thrummed in her ears and her stomach dropped as a creature appeared from the shadows. Shiny caramel-colored fur rolled over its muscular haunches as the biggest wolf she'd ever seen stepped toward her. It crept slowly, lowering its head and peering at her with piercing blue eyes.

"Not another one," the voice echoed.

Though the intelligent look in the wolf's gaze intrigued her, Macey didn't hesitate when it bared its teeth and growled a warning. Spirit or no spirit, she needed to get the hell out of there.

She clenched her fists and opened her mind like she did when she read an object. The rapist's face, with a snarling grin, flashed before her. The same man whose body went missing from the morgue. Without thinking, she grabbed on to the image and forced the parasite from her consciousness. Sharp pain ripped through her pores like she was sweating nails as the spirit left her body and circled above her head.

"Another time then."

She didn't have time to consider what had happened, and instead backed up carefully, never taking her gaze off the sapphire canine eyes. Something about the wolf seemed familiar, but she'd never seen it before. Had she dreamed of it? Seen it in one of her visions?

She inhaled sharply as the creature took another step toward her. Was this animal responsible for the horrific scene she so desperately wished to return to? If so, would she be its next victim? One foot behind the other, grasping at branches and tree trunks for support, she edged her way toward the house. When she reached the clearing, the wolf bowed its head and bounded away, deeper into the forest.

Once it was out of sight, Macey turned on her heels and sprinted for the house. She ran past Bryce and the body, took the stairs two at a time, and stopped on the porch. Heaving giant breaths, she leaned her hands against the railing and fought the urge to vomit yet a second time. What the hell had happened?

"You okay, Mace? You're white as milk." Bryce trotted to her side and placed his palm on her back. The warmth of his touch slowed her breathing enough for her to speak. But should she tell him about the spirit? Not yet. Not until she had time to process it.

"The woods. Back there." She pointed to the thicket behind the house. "A wolf." She turned to face her partner, resting her backside against the wooden rail. "I saw something in the forest. When I went to check it out, a wolf was checking me out."

"Are you hurt?" Bryce looked her over, concern dancing in his gaze.

"No. It growled at me, and I backed away. Do you think it could've…"

"Without a doubt. Wolves don't normally attack people, but if they're hungry, sick, or frightened enough, they will. Is it still out there?"

"No. It ran off as soon as I got to the clearing." Finally catching her breath, she shuffled across the porch to look at the body. "I don't know, Bryce. Why would a wolf just eat her abdomen?" *And why would the ghost of a rapist be hanging out in the woods?* "Wouldn't it go for the throat first...you know...to kill its prey?"

He shoved his hands into his pockets. "I don't know. But right now, it's all we've got. I'll let the coroner know to be looking for teeth marks and animal hair. And next time...let me know before you take off like that. We're partners."

She stiffened. "I had it under control."

"You also could've been eaten. No need to take chances like that when you've got a partner you can depend on. Sometimes it's okay to ask for help."

She smiled and patted his shoulder. "Thanks. I'll remember that." *But I can take care of myself.*

Luke watched from the shadows as Macey climbed into the car with her partner. Had he imagined her eyes? When she'd frozen and started talking to the air in the forest, she seemed to...change. At first, she'd almost appeared to be in pain. Then her eyes had glowed red for a minute...

Nah. Couldn't have.

They hadn't been the same deep crimson of a demon. They had only seemed a little red, hadn't they? It was a glare; that was all.

Whatever it was, he hated scaring her like that. But being in the forest alone with who-knew-how-many demons on the loose was dangerous. Deadly. He hadn't thought about it at the time—his main goal had been Macey's safety—but showing her his wolf form might have helped with the case.

At least the cops would be looking for an animal now rather than a murderer. And it might have bought him enough time to find the halfling that ripped its way out of the poor woman's stomach before it caused any more trouble.

He jogged to his truck, which he'd parked at the last restaurant before the road turned to dirt, and ran a mental to-do list. He'd have to get James to check on the other females to be sure none of them were pregnant. The weres had stopped most of the demons before they could spill their seed, but he needed to be sure. The half demon body from the morgue was still missing, but there wasn't anything he could do about that. The fiend would either come back or he wouldn't.

Luke needed to get some rest. All the demon hunting had made him lose focus on his regular job, and the deadline for the current building renovation his crew was working on was only a week away.

And on top of all that, he had to figure out what to do about his growing feelings for the sexy detective. If he could act on instinct, he'd take her to his house and keep her there until he vanquished every last demon. The intense urge to protect her barely overshadowed the *other* urges he felt every time he looked at her.

But the pack came first. Always.

He growled as he started the truck. What was he going to do about that woman?

CHAPTER TEN

MACEY SAT ALONE IN A CORNER BOOTH AT THE GUMBO PLACE, perusing the menu as she sipped an iced sweet tea. After the gory scene she'd witnessed last night, and the nightmares that followed, the fact she even had an appetite this evening should have surprised her. But she'd tucked the ghastly incident into a compartment in the back of her mind, like she always did, and now her mouth watered at all the delicious temptations the menu offered.

Whatever had happened to her in the woods was a memory now. The spirit hadn't tried to contact her since. In fact, she hadn't sensed *any* spirits since the incident. The day had been so normal, she'd begun to doubt if her ghostly encounter had even happened.

Scooting to her right to avoid the tear in the faded, red vinyl seat, she scanned the restaurant, making note of her surroundings. Booths lined the walls of the large, open dining area, with tables scattered about the center. Zydeco music piped through the speakers, muffling the incessant hum of the overhead fluorescent lights, and patrons occupied four of the tables: a man at the table next to her, a couple in a booth by the window, and two families across the room.

The ambience wasn't much, but this place had the best fried crawfish tails and étouffée in town. She ordered a dish that contained both her favorites and glanced up when the front door swung open. Her breath caught as Luke stepped across the threshold. He'd tied his light-brown hair back in a band, and a tight, heather gray T-shirt stretched across his chest. An intricate tattoo on his bicep peeked from beneath his sleeve. Heat flushed her cheeks as the image of him shirtless skittered through her mind. Did he have any more tattoos?

He looked right at her. Macey averted her gaze, staring intently at her hands folded on the table. Maybe he didn't catch her looking. She ignored him as long as was politely possible, but when his approach was obviously directed to her, she lifted her eyes and smiled.

"Hi, Macey. Is this seat taken?" He gestured to the bench across from her.

She shook her head. A minute motion, but he must've picked up on it because he slid into the seat and folded his hands on the table to match her posture. The waitress approached and set a glass of tea in front of him.

"Good evening, Luke." She grinned at him and offered a menu, but he waved it away.

"I'll have the same as the beautiful lady here."

The waitress shrugged and shot a heated glance at Macey. "Suit yourself." She turned on her heel and strutted away.

What was that about? Wait…had Luke called her beautiful? She hardly knew the man, but the words he'd uttered shot thrilling tingles to her core. He shouldn't have affected her that way. Not that soon. And especially not after he'd blown her off the way he had. She smoothed her hair toward her bun, hoping to smooth the thoughts from her head. "You don't even know what I ordered."

He raised a shoulder in a dismissive shrug. "I trust your taste. Everything's good here anyway."

She raised an eyebrow. "Oh, you trust me, do you?"

He cleared his voice. "I said I trust your taste."

"Mmm-hmm."

Leaning back in the booth, he stretched his arm across the back of the seat. "If you don't mind my asking, why are you alone again? No friends to hang out with?" He winked as if to show he was joking, but the truth of his statement stung.

"Honestly? I've always been kind of a loner." Her ears burned with embarrassment, but she didn't know why. Her lack of a social life was no secret at the station. She kept everyone but her parents at arm's length. She'd turned down so many invitations, her coworkers rarely asked her to hang out anymore. This virtual stranger's opinion shouldn't have mattered so much to her.

But it did.

He put his hands on the table and leaned forward. "I'm sorry. I didn't mean any—"

"It's okay." Her hard shrug made her bounce in her seat. "I've never really felt like I fit in anywhere. I've gotten used to it."

She picked up her glass and gulped down the contents, hoping to end the conversation. Their food arriving saved her from the awkward moment, and from Luke's response.

The waitress set the plates down and touched Luke's elbow. "It's good to see you again."

He inclined his head toward her. "You as well, Jackie. This is all we need." He all but dismissed her. She pursed her lips, trained her gaze on the floor, and scurried away. The pair obviously had some sort of history, though Macey didn't dare ask. She didn't want to know if they'd dated. For some reason, the image of Luke in the arms of that woman—of any woman—made her shudder. Possessiveness clutched at her heart, but why? He didn't belong to her any more than the man at the table next to them.

And she didn't want him. Why did she have to keep reminding herself of that?

Luke looked at the plate in front of him. "Good choice. One of my favorites." The corner of his mouth pulled into a wicked grin. "Of course, I like *everything* here."

His gaze locked with hers, and her heart stuttered. Was he implying he liked her? Surely he wasn't. She scooped a forkful of étouffée into her mouth and savored the flavor explosion on her tongue. The zing of spicy crawfish danced on her taste buds, and she closed her eyes to relish the moment. Opening them again, she found him grinning at her.

"What?" She wiped her mouth with the napkin.

"Nothing." He picked up his fork and pushed the food around on his plate. "You really enjoy your food, don't you?"

"I savor the things that bring me pleasure."

"Words to live by."

Luke stabbed the crawfish tails and shoved them into his mouth. What the hell was he doing flirting with the detective again? He was either out of his mind or masochistic, but he couldn't help it. The more he got to know her, the more enamored of her he became. He adored everything about her, from the way she closed her eyes with each bite she took to the way her brow furrowed when she caught him staring at her.

When werewolves found their fate-bound mates, they felt an instant connection. Others had described it as an overpowering sense of possessiveness. Protectiveness. A basal instinct to grab hold of the other person and never let her go. A feeling of completeness that could only be achieved with the person as his mate.

In the past, werewolves couldn't mate with anyone but their fate-bound, and if they didn't find the one they connected with on that primal level, they spent their lives alone. The law was meant to ensure the strength of the species, but with so few weres finding that deep connection with another, the threat of extinction forced the congress to change the law.

Now they could mate with anyone they chose, but they had to mate for life. Unless they were part of the alpha bloodline. No dilution allowed.

Sitting there, looking at Macey, Luke felt that instant connection. Hell, he'd felt it the moment she touched him at the bar. The protectiveness. The completeness. She was meant to be his.

But she was a human, damn it. She couldn't be his fate-bound mate…or even his regular mate. When he saw her sitting in this booth, he should've turned around and walked out the door. He was wasting his time and leading her on, but he couldn't help himself. The woman was magnetic.

If he were honest with himself, he'd admit Macey was the reason he came to this damn restaurant in the first place. He'd been tailing her for weeks, hiding evidence and trying to throw her off the trail of the demons, and he knew her schedule like clockwork. Tonight was Gumbo Place night, and he'd wandered there on autopilot, subconsciously hoping to get a glimpse of her. He hadn't planned on joining her for dinner, but here he was, enjoying every second of it.

"You said your dad owns the bar? And you work there?" The melodic cadence of her voice roused him from his thoughts.

He blinked as the question registered. "Yeah. I mean...my dad owns it, but I don't technically work there. I'm a contractor."

"Oh, that's cool. So, you do remodeling and stuff."

"And stuff." He chuckled. "You have a way of simplifying things."

"You have to in my line of work. There are only three things that motivate people." She ticked them off on her fingers. "Money, power, and love."

"And, which one motivates you, Ms. Carpenter?"

She grinned slyly. "I guess that depends on the situation."

He finished the last bite of his food and rested his elbow on the table. The silence must have made her uncomfortable because she babbled through the rest of her answer.

"I mean...I'm okay money-wise. And power? I guess I have more than I need."

"So all that's missing is love." As soon as the words left his lips, he wished he could take them back. Love was one thing he couldn't offer her.

She shifted in her seat to sit on her hands. "I...yeah. But it's... Who am I kidding? It's missing." She let out a half-hearted laugh and cast her gaze to the table.

He'd done it again—hit a sore spot with her for the second time in one night. *Real smooth.* Maybe he could change the subject. He cleared his voice. "Do you have family close by? Brothers or sisters?"

She sat up straight and inhaled slowly before she spoke. "My adoptive parents live in Metairie. My biological parents died when I was young. I had..." She put her fingers to her lips. "I don't know why

I'm telling you this. It's not something I talk about." Folding her hands on the table, she gazed up at him with sad eyes.

Instinct told him to comfort her, but what could he do? It was an ancient pain she held deep in her heart. It would take more than a few kind words from him to help her heal. He placed his palm over her petite hands, almost covering them completely. Vibrating energy seeped from her skin, snaking up his arms, and she sucked in a sharp breath as the fine blonde hairs on her arms stood on end. He followed the trail of goose bumps over her shoulder and up the delicate curve of her neck. She licked her lips. That tiny flick of her tongue had him groaning inwardly, his mouth watering with the need to taste her. He released her hands and fisted his in his lap. The need to pull her into his arms and kiss away the pain overwhelmed him.

She possessed some sort of magic, but he couldn't figure out what kind. Did Macey even know? She didn't act like any sort of magical being. And if normal humans had adopted her, not knowing... Thoughts raced through his head, but he needed to focus on the present.

"I'm sorry," he said. "We don't have to talk about anything you don't want to."

"It's okay." She rubbed her hands together and gazed at them quizzically.

She must've felt his energy too. A pure human would never notice it.

A smile brightened her face as she dropped her hands into her lap. "You're easy to talk to. I don't mind, actually."

Leaning his elbow on the table, he rested his chin on his hand. "Do you still see your parents often?"

"Two or three times a month."

"Must be nice. I see my folks nearly every day. It gets old."

She inclined her head and looked at his arm. "Hey, what's your tattoo of?"

"It's kind of like a family crest." He lifted his sleeve and slid his arm toward her.

"It's beautiful." She traced her finger across the design and yanked her hand away as a jolt of energy shot straight to his heart. She looked at her fingers, furrowed her brow, and looked at him. "Why does that happen?"

"What?"

"Please tell me you feel it too. Every time I touch you, it's like...I get shocked."

He considered lying, saying he didn't feel a thing. But the way her gaze implored him, he had to admit it. "I do. I guess we have a spark between us." He chuckled, trying to play it off. He felt more than magic of the supernatural kind. The chemistry between the two of them was undeniable.

She smiled, the delicate curve of her lips sending his heart into overdrive. "It does feel that way, doesn't it?"

"Yes, it does."

They stared at each other for a moment, and he lost himself in the emerald sea of her eyes. She was a witch. Or maybe some type of fae. She had to be. Could an alpha werewolf mate with a witch? Would her magic be enough to produce werewolf offspring? He'd have to do some research. Maybe somewhere along the family lines...It would explain how the younger siblings got their powers—like his sister who could see the future in her visions. But how could he find out if Macey truly possessed magic? "Can I ask you something?"

"Why not? I've already told you my dirty little secret."

"I'd hardly call it dirty."

She shrugged and folded her arms on the table. "Shoot."

"Do you know anything about...er, do you believe in magic?"

She stopped breathing for a moment. Straightening her spine, she opened her mouth as if to speak, but shut it with a *click*. "Why? What have you heard?"

Not the response I was expecting. "Nothing. I just wondered if you do."

She pursed her lips into a thin line as her brows drew together. "I...don't know. Do you?"

"Sure. Why not? I'm curious about your response, though. Should I have heard something?"

She took a deep breath and blew it out hard. "I can't believe I'm telling you this." Leaning forward, she lowered her voice to just above a whisper. "There might be a rumor going around that I can talk to the dead. Some people say that's how I close so many cases—that I can communicate with the victims."

He tried to hide the surprise in his eyes by blinking.

Macey held up her hands. "It isn't true. I can't really talk to dead people."

"How do you solve so many cases, then?"

She bristled. "What? You don't think I'm capable of capturing criminals with my brains and wit? Because I'm a woman I have to have some kind of magical powers to do my job?" She flung her hands about as she spoke; he'd hit sore spot number three. Or was it number four? He'd lost count.

"Macey, I have no doubt that you are the best detective New Orleans has. You're one of the smartest people I've met. My question had nothing to do with you being a woman."

Her shoulders dropped as her anger tempered. "I'm sorry. I feel like I have to defend myself a lot...to get respect. It's hard being a woman in a man's field."

"I'm sure it is." And he would have loved to let her vent; he could've listened to her voice for hours. At the moment, though, he needed to figure out her magic. "But you can't communicate with the dead at all? It's just a rumor?"

She hugged herself with her left arm and tugged at her bottom lip with her right hand, an adorable nervous habit. "I can't. But I can sort of sense things, I guess."

"The dead?"

"Sort of."

"Amazing." She was a necromancer. Or a psychic medium. He couldn't fight the smile that tugged at his lips. There was hope for them yet.

Macey snorted. "Hardly. I can't control it, and it only helps sometimes. Mostly after the energy's had time to..."

He raised his eyebrows.

"When it's had time to soak into an object. If I can touch something—usually a building—that's when I can sense things."

"That makes sense."

She cocked an eyebrow. "Does it? I'm glad you understand because it baffles and annoys the hell out of me. But, listen. I have to get back to work." She reached for the check he hadn't noticed the waitress deliver. The plates had been cleared as well, but he'd been so focused on the sexy detective, the rest of the world had slipped away.

That was fine with him, anyway. The waitress was one of several pack members after his affections. His upcoming pack leader status appealed to the weaker wolves. As his father's retirement date inched closer, the number of ladies vying for his attention had gone from zero to about fifteen.

"Let me take care of that." He pulled the ticket from her hand.

"That won't be necessary." She slapped a twenty on the table. "That should cover my part."

He sighed and laid a few bills on the table to cover the rest of the check. How many times could he offend her in one night? She was a strong, independent woman, and that was only one of the many things that made her so attractive. As they stood, he reached for her hand, expecting her to jerk away when the electricity surged between them.

Instead, she inhaled a sharp breath, glancing at their entwined fingers, before smiling at him. Hand in hand, they shuffled out the door.

His heart thudded a beat of exhilaration. Had he found his mate? The likelihood of a simple psychic being powerful enough to bear a were-child was slim, but he felt so much more power coming from her. A sliver of hope was all he needed. He'd start researching the family lines as soon as he got home. There had to be a way to make this work.

Sticky summer heat caressed his skin as they strolled up the street. A bead of sweat rolled between Macey's breasts, and he had to tear his gaze away before she caught him looking. What he'd have given to be that drop of moisture...

"Thank you for the company. It was nice." She paused at the intersection and blinked up at him. "I have to go this way." She pointed to the left.

"It was my pleasure, Macey. I enjoyed it."

"I guess I'll see you around?"

His stomach tightened. Hopefully she didn't notice his sweat-slickened palms. "It would be easier for me to find you if you gave me your number."

Her smile widened. "Okay." She recited the digits as he clumsily punched them into his phone with his right hand. He favored his left, but he wasn't ready to let her go.

"Got it. I'll let you get to work now." He leaned down and pressed his lips to her cheek. Her skin was warm and slightly salty. A shiver ran down his spine as the urge to take her mouth with his rose through his core. Her breath caught, but she didn't move away. He lingered there, his lips barely brushing her skin as she tightened her grip on his hand and turned to meet his mouth.

He hesitated, gazing into her emerald irises and reveling in the warmth of her breath on his skin. She closed her eyes and touched her mouth to his. Liquid warmth flowed to his core as he wrapped his arms around her waist and pulled her body closer. She melted into his embrace, her body conforming to his in a way that felt so damn right. He shuddered, slipping his tongue between her lips, and she moaned softly, the vibration of her voice sending a wave of electricity through his body. He had to pull away, or he'd never let her go.

He stroked her cheek with the back of his hand and memorized the hungriness in her eyes. He could get used to her looking at him like that every day. "I'll see you soon, Macey."

Macey couldn't help but grin as she made her way up Conti Street toward the police station. *What a way to start the night.* Her logical mind told her not to get excited. Letting people in, getting close, led to heartache. But she couldn't deny the way her body reacted when she was near Luke. It was almost as if some other-worldly force drew her to him. He'd talked about believing in magic, and that's how this connection she had with him felt.

Maybe it wouldn't hurt to let Luke get a little closer. Let him satisfy her physical desires without getting her heart involved. She'd managed to keep the rest of her emotions compartmentalized since she was a kid; she could keep it casual with Luke, couldn't she? Lord knew it had been a while since she'd had any kind of satisfaction…

She strolled into her office and dropped her purse into her desk drawer before firing up her computer.

"What are you smiling at?" Bryce leaned in the doorway and crossed his arms.

"Nothing you'd be interested in, trust me." She logged into her e-mail and pretended to focus on the screen, but her grin widened.

"As long as it doesn't have anything to do with your date with BOB, I'm all ears." He pushed off the wall and sauntered into the room.

Macey leaned back and spun in her seat to face him. "I did have a date, but not with BOB."

He plopped into the chair across from her desk. "It's about damn time."

CHAPTER ELEVEN

Luke managed a grumbled, "Hello," as he shuffled past the morning bartender. Six a.m. was too damn early to start work. Too early for a bar to open, too, but his old man had the crazy idea they should serve breakfast. To Luke, a bar was a bar. Drinks, beer, maybe some hot wings or cheese fries...They didn't need to serve anything else.

But the bar didn't belong to him, and as soon as his dad retired for good, it would fall into his sister's hands. Luke's contracting business was lucrative enough, and he was about to become alpha. He didn't need the hassle of running the bar too.

If he became alpha. The archaic law that he had to have a mate would be the death of him if he couldn't figure out a way to get the pack to accept Macey. He barely knew the woman, but she already had his heart in her hands.

And he was running out of time.

He ground his teeth. His heart didn't matter to the pack, but he *would* become alpha. It was his duty. His birthright. He shouldn't have to give up his dream of waking up to a woman he loved every morning in order to fulfill his destiny. With the intense connection he felt with Macey, he couldn't imagine falling in love with anyone else.

A grin tugged at the corner of his mouth as he imagined waking up with her, seeing her silky blonde mane tousled from a night of lovemaking. Her sleepy smile greeting him as he rolled over to embrace her.

He rubbed his eyes to wipe away the image. *Focus, man.* His first order of business was to register the new rogue who'd just come into town. He powered up his MacBook and glanced at the clock. The rogue's appointment was at six-fifteen. Hopefully, she wouldn't be late. His men were already on site at the remodel, and they needed all the help they could get.

After his dinner with Macey last night, he'd joined Chase and James on a demon hunt, so he hadn't had time to research the family lines for magic, but that occupied the next spot on his list…after he handled the pack business, caught up on the remodel, and took a second to breathe.

At ten past six, someone knocked on the office door. Luke double-clicked the shortcut to open the pack database and picked up his coffee. "It's open."

He raised the cup to his lips and nearly spilled it in his lap when the tall blonde stepped through the threshold. She had wavy, shoulder-length hair, and long bangs framed her bright-green eyes. If he didn't know any better, he'd have said this felt like a set-up.

"Are you Luke?"

He stared at her. His predicament was no secret, and word could have spread to the neighboring packs that the soon-to-be-alpha was in the market for a mate. But to send someone disguised as a rogue could be grounds to start a war. He dismissed that idea as quickly as it formed. No pack would be that stupid.

"Is this a bad time? I can come back later."

He rubbed a hand over his face. "No, no. Sorry. I'm Luke. You must be Alexis Gentry." He stood and held out a hand to shake, and when she accepted, the familiar tingle of werewolf shimmied up his arm.

"Have a seat. Do you have a driver's license or ID, so I can enter your info into the database?" The chair creaked as he sank into it again. He really needed to get the WD-40 after it.

The woman reached into her pocket and pulled out a small piece of plastic. Sliding it across the desk, she avoided looking into Luke's eyes and rubbed the back of her neck. "You're staring at me."

He picked up the ID and turned toward the computer screen. Holding the card in one hand, he tried to focus on typing the information with the other. The rogue was beautiful, no doubt about that. And he couldn't ignore the coincidence that she showed up now, as his deadline to select a mate was fast approaching. While he doubted another pack sent her, he wouldn't put it past his old man to send in a new "rogue" every day until he'd chosen one.

But this woman didn't hold a candle to Macey. In fact, he couldn't get the sexy detective off his mind. He needed to see her again. Soon.

He huffed and handed the card back to her. "How long do you plan to stay in New Orleans?"

She raised one shoulder and stared at her ID card. "I don't know. It depends on how things work out. A few months, maybe?"

"Good enough for me. What brings you here?"

Alexis put her card in her pocket and fiddled with the buttons on her shirt. When she spoke, her voice sounded strained. "Oh, I just like to move around a lot. I get bored, I guess."

She wasn't telling him everything, but he didn't have time to pry the answers out of her. If his old man had sent her, the most harm done was the waste of her time. If she was hiding something else...one of his men could keep an eye on her; he needed to get to work. "How long have you been rogue, and why did you leave your pack?"

She straightened in her chair and folded her hands in her lap. "I've never belonged to a pack. My parents were rogues, and I've been on my own since the change came." Her gaze steadied, locking with his as if challenging him to judge her.

Luke held her gaze until she looked away. "All right. I've got all your info. Do you have a place to stay?"

"Yes. One of your pack members gave me the name of a boarding house. I'll stay there until I get my feet back under me."

"Good. I have to get to work now. If you need anything else..." He rose and motioned toward the door.

Alexis stood and stepped toward the exit. "Actually, I could really use a job."

He blinked at her. Most rogues wanted nothing to do with the pack. They especially didn't want help. Every now and then a needy one would pass through, but he never understood why someone so willing to accept pack support would want to be on her own. "What can you do?"

She shoved her hands in her pockets. "This and that. Mostly carpentry, plumbing, a little auto work. I can usually fix whatever I get my hands on."

He raised an eyebrow. If she was telling the truth, this rogue could come in handy. "I'm a contractor. My crew is working on a remodel on Decatur. If you're any good, we could use some help. I'm heading there now."

"Oh, I'm good." She grinned. "What's the address?"

He scribbled on a scrap of paper and handed it to her.

"I'll be there in half an hour. And…thank you." She nodded her head and stepped through the door.

Luke did a few more things at the office, and by the time he arrived at the work site, Alexis stood in the parking lot, waiting for him.

"What took you so long, boss?" She grinned and playfully punched him on the shoulder. "Your boys here didn't believe you'd offered me a job."

"We didn't believe a rogue would accept help her first day in town." James approached Luke and lowered his voice. "Is she legit?"

"Yeah. I hired her." Though her casual way of addressing him tempted him to regret his decision. She had a rogue attitude, and if she planned to stick around, she'd have to learn the pecking order. Still, something about her didn't sit quite right with him. "Show her the ropes," he said to James. "I've got to go over the plans with the client."

"Sure thing." James led Alexis into the building.

After his meeting with the client, Luke checked in on the rogue from time to time, but apparently he'd worried for nothing. She fit right in with his team, pulled her weight, and didn't get in anyone's way. Any doubts he'd had about hiring her had washed away by the day's end. And her lack of…interest in him quelled his worry about his old man's matchmaker games. Then again, his dad probably had another female waiting in the wing if Alexis didn't work out.

As the crew put their equipment away and headed to their vehicles, Alexis dusted her hands off on her pants and strode toward Luke. "Same time tomorrow?" She flashed an anticipatory grin.

"Yeah. Good work today."

"See you tomorrow, boss." She turned and strode toward her beat-up Honda Civic.

Luke checked his watch. Seven fifteen. Macey would either be at home or the coffee shop she frequented in the evenings before work. She'd been on his mind all day; it wouldn't hurt to swing by and see if she was out. Maybe he could get her to elaborate on her ability to read objects. Then he might be able to figure out exactly what kind of magic she possessed and whether or not it would be strong enough for her to be his mate.

Macey pulled into a parking space at her favorite coffee shop and slid out of the driver's seat. After her dinner with Luke, last night had been alarmingly quiet. Nothing even remotely related to the case had required her attention, and while she didn't wish for another incident, a break that led to solving the case would have been nice. She'd have to do some more digging. Maybe look into recent cult activity in the area.

She paced through the parking lot toward the entrance, acutely aware of a man following behind her. With everything that had happened the past few weeks…and being this close to an alley…her senses were on high alert. She turned to greet the man and assess if he presented a threat.

Her heart dipped into her stomach as she gazed into Luke's bright-blue eyes. "What are you doing here?"

He grinned. "I felt like having a cup of coffee after work. You?"

"Same…but before work. My shift starts in two hours."

His gaze traveled from her eyes to her mouth, and back up again.

She tugged on her bottom lip, trying to think of something to say to ease the tension. It had only been twenty-four hours since she'd seen him, but she'd thought about him so much it felt like days. "You keep showing up like this, and I might start thinking you're following me."

Luke inclined his head and opened the door. "How about that coffee?"

"Okay."

A single barista stood behind the counter of the dimly lit shop. Sleek blue hair hung over her face, and a dozen earrings glinted in her ears. She put down her book and stepped toward the cash register. Macey ordered a decaf latte. Luke took his coffee black. They sat at a table by the window, and he reached across to take her hand. Tingling electricity shot up her arm, and his eyes gleamed devilishly as he gave her a knowing smile. She was getting used to the spark, but she would never get used to the way the rest of her body reacted to his touch. What was it about this man that got her so worked up?

"That's a beautiful bracelet." He ran his finger across the hammered copper band adorning her wrist. "I like the stones. Are they turquoise?"

"Yeah. It belonged to my biological mother."

"Oh?"

Why did she tell him that? She seemed to dredge up her tragic past every time she talked to him. "I don't remember her. I was three when my parents died."

He laced his fingers through hers and stared deeply into her eyes. "What happened to them?"

"Car crash. That's what I was told, anyway."

"You don't believe it?"

"I do. It's on the official report, but..."

He raised an eyebrow, urging her to finish.

She let out a nervous laugh. "I don't know what it is about you, but I always seem to spill my guts anytime you're around. I'm sorry. I don't mean to burden you with my life story."

He leaned forward, resting his elbows on the table. "It's not a burden. I want to know everything about you. So it's on the report, but…"

"But I've always had this weird feeling there's more to the story. I don't know. I did some research, and everything checks out, so…" She shrugged. "At least I know why they're gone. My sister…" She clamped her lips together. When would she learn to keep her mouth shut?

He leaned toward her. "You have a sister?"

She sucked in a breath and blew it out hard. She'd already opened the can; she might as well deal with the worms. "She ran away when we were in our third or fourth foster home. One day, everything was fine. Then she was just…gone. She didn't even say goodbye." A tear slid down her cheek, and she brushed it away. "I'm sorry. I don't think I've ever told anyone this. I didn't realize it still hurt so much."

Tightening his grip on her hand, he placed his other one on top of hers. She needed to pull herself together before she turned into a blubbering mess. Straightening, she wiped beneath her eyes. "My new parents adopted me not long after that, and they brought me here. All's well that ends well, right?"

The concern in his gaze felt way too heavy. "Do you know where she is now?"

A familiar pang of sadness shot through her chest. "I've been angry with her for so long; I've never tried to find her. But let's not talk about that, okay?" There were a million better ways to spend time with a guy as hot as Luke, and none of them involved crying over her tragic past. She locked the unwanted emotions away in the vault in the back of her mind and forced a smile. "What about you? Tell me something I don't know about Luke."

He chuckled and stared at their entwined fingers. "Well, I—"

"Excuse me." The barista approached their table. "Aren't you that detective? The one they keep interviewing on TV?"

Macey pulled her hand from Luke's and sat up straight. This was why she preferred to avoid the cameras. "Yes, I am. But I'm not at liberty to discuss an open case."

"That's okay." The barista grabbed a chair and joined them at the table. "You don't have to talk about it. Just listen. I have a theory."

"A theory." Macey looked at Luke who shrugged and crossed his arms. Everyone had a theory about it, and she'd have to hear this girl out if her time with Luke was to continue in peace.

"Yeah." The barista's eyes sparkled with excitement. "Werewolves."

Luke coughed.

Macey turned to the girl. "Your theory is werewolves?" She was nuts. There was no other way to describe her.

"Yes. See, all the women say they were raped, right? And that an animal or something killed the attacker. But what if the animal and the attacker were the same person? What if the werewolf assaulted the girl while he was in human form, and then he turned into a wolf and ran off?"

Macey *had* seen a wolf in the woods near that woman's house. Could it be possible that…no. She'd have to be nuts herself to even entertain the preposterous idea.

"Would you look at the time?" Luke tapped an imaginary watch on his wrist. "I didn't realize how late it was. I've got an early morning tomorrow, so we better get going." He rose from his chair, stepped around the barista, and offered Macey his hand.

"Yeah. You're right." Macey stood and looked at the girl. "Thanks for the coffee."

Luke led her out the door and around the corner of the building. Macey's car sat alone in the lot. "Well, that was weird." He ran a hand through his hair.

"Actually, I get that a lot. People with theories, I mean. Not werewolves. That was a first." She leaned her back against the car door and gazed up at him.

A sly smile curved his lips as he took a step toward her. "Werewolves. That's ridiculous." He leaned in closer, resting a hand against the car near her shoulder.

Her pulse sprinted. "Crazy." She could feel the heat radiating from his body. Her fingers twitched with the urge to run her hands up his chest and wrap them around his shoulders, but she resisted. She didn't want to get involved with anyone, but she wanted Luke so badly she could taste it.

Oh, to taste *him*…

"I wonder where she'd get an idea like that." He stroked her cheek with his thumb, and her breath hitched, her skin tingling where he touched her.

"I have no idea." Her heart pounded harder as he lowered his face to hers, their lips mere centimeters apart. Should she do this? It had been ages since she'd been with a man, and the way Luke touched her had her aching for more.

"You're so beautiful, Macey." His warm breath tickled her skin, and his mouth took hers. His lips were soft, the kiss firm, determined. He started to move away, but she slid her hand behind his neck, urging him to stay. She *needed* to do this.

A low moan resonated from his chest as he wrapped his arms around her and pulled her body close to his. She ran her hands over his arms and down his back, exploring every bulge and cut of his muscular frame. He broke away from the kiss to gaze into her eyes, his sapphire irises pooling with desire.

His voice was husky as he spoke. "I should probably let you get to work." He brushed his lips to her cheek, her jaw, her neck. When he reached her collarbone, he inhaled deeply, as if he were drinking in her essence. She shivered as he kissed the dip at the base of her throat and glided his mouth up to her earlobe.

"I've got a little over an hour, so I was planning to head home first. My place is just a few blocks away, if you wanted to come over." What was she thinking? This was only their second date, and she was already inviting him over? She needed to start thinking with her head and not her hormones.

Luke grinned wickedly. "Oh, I would love to, but..." He pressed against her, his arousal rubbing her hip. His lips brushed hers as he traced his fingers down her arms to hold her hands. "Not until we've had a proper date. A planned one." He leaned in and touched his lips to her ear. "And I'll need more than an hour with you."

His words seemed to suck the breath right from her lungs. She swallowed the thickness from her throat. "You would actually have to call me then. To plan a proper date."

He grinned. "I will tomorrow. I promise."

"I'm going to hold you to that."

"I never break a promise." He tugged her into a tight embrace. "I'll see you soon, Macey." The syllables of her name rolled off his tongue like music, weakening her knees.

Her chest ached at the thought of him leaving so soon. "Do you need a ride?"

"Nah. It's a glorious night. I think I'll walk." He kissed her once more and strolled away.

Macey bit her bottom lip as he sauntered out of the parking lot. He turned to wave goodbye before disappearing around the corner, and she let out a breath. How had she won the affections of such a scrumptious man? Her whole body tingled with the thoughts of how their next date might end. In her bed. Or maybe in his.

She couldn't wipe the grin off her face as she drove home and opened the front door. Her cat, Thor, greeted her with a hiss and darted under the sofa.

"Well, hello to you too, mister." She bent down and tried to coax the brown tabby out, but he met her with a swipe of his paw. "Are you jealous, Thor?"

The cat mewed.

"Well, you're going to have to get used to it. You aren't the only man in my life anymore."

CHAPTER TWELVE

"Detective Carpenter, it's so good to see you." Macey's father grinned as she approached.

"Oh, hush, Dad. I made detective years ago. How long is it going to take for you to get over it?" She skipped up the concrete path and threw herself into her father's arms. He squeezed her in a bear hug and kissed the top of her head.

"I'm just so darn proud of you, daughter. I'll never get over it."

"And the neighbors never hear the end of it. Come here." Macey's mother, Jenny, gave her a hug, wrapped her arm around her daughter, and walked her inside the small brick house.

The scent of oregano and thyme mixed with beef and carrots made Macey's mouth water. Her mom had made a pot roast—Macey's favorite. She followed the enticing aroma into the kitchen and lifted the lid on the slow cooker. Steam wafted out, tickling her senses and making her stomach growl. "Mmm…How much longer until dinner?"

Her mom took the lid, closing the pot and shooing Macey away from the food. "Another fifteen minutes or so." She took a large bowl out of the cabinet and handed her several bags of chopped vegetables.

"Here, mix the salad for me and tell me what's new with you. Any more trouble with…you know?"

Macey cringed. Her mother knew all about her ability, but she wished she hadn't told her about the spirit trying to possess her—or whatever had happened. All it did was worry her. "No. I'm sure it was my imagination. Forget I said anything about it."

Jenny pursed her lips and pulled a loaf of fresh, baked bread out of the oven. "Anything else going on?"

A grin curved Macey's mouth as she poured the cucumbers into the bowl. "Well, I've had a couple of dates."

Her mother paused and turned to Macey. "And how did they go?"

She dumped the bell peppers and carrots on top of the lettuce and tossed it around in the bowl. Her heart raced, and fresh adrenaline pumped through her body as she relived the surreal experience. "It was…weird. He's so easy to talk to. I told him way more than I should have."

"It's about time you opened up to someone."

"It's scary, though. You know?"

Her mom smiled. "I know you have reservations when it comes to relationships, but you deserve to be happy. Go ahead and enjoy it."

Macey grinned. Maybe her mom was right. She did deserve to be happy. Maybe it was time she opened up the gates to her heavily guarded heart and let someone in. "He's such a gentleman. He's got caramel-colored hair and gorgeous blue eyes."

"What's his name?"

"Luke Mason. He's so—"

"How do you know Luke Mason?" A musical voice drifted into the room, followed by a rotund, elderly woman with curly gray hair and dark brown eyes. She glided across the kitchen as if her feet didn't touch the floor beneath her long, burnt-orange skirt.

"Roberta! I didn't hear you come in." Jenny wiped her hands on a dish cloth and hugged the woman.

"William let me in. Your husband is such a charmer." Her smile lit up her face, and her eyes twinkled as she turned her attention to Macey. "You must be Macey. Your mother has told me so much about you."

Macey held out her hand to shake, but Roberta pushed it away, pulling her into a big hug instead. Macey tentatively hugged her back, patting her on the shoulder until she released her hold. She glanced at her mother, who smiled and busied herself with preparing the meal.

"Come. Sit." Roberta motioned for Macey to follow her to the dining room table.

Macey hesitated, looking at her mother.

"Go ahead," Jenny said. "Dinner's almost ready. I'll bring it to the table."

She followed Roberta, settling into a chair opposite her at the table. The woman's smile was so dazzling, she couldn't help but smile in return.

Roberta folded her hands on the table. "How do you know Luke?"

Heat rose to Macey's cheeks. "We kinda had a date last night." She picked at imaginary lint on her shirt, afraid to look in Roberta's eyes. Would this woman tell him what she said?

"Hmm…" Roberta picked up the small, red glasses that hung from a beaded chain around her neck and settled them on her nose. She narrowed a long and intense gaze at Macey. Then, she closed her eyes and inhaled deeply, absently nodding her head. The uncomfortable moment lasted no more than half a minute, but Macey's palms starting sweating.

"Interesting," Roberta muttered as she opened her eyes.

What had that been about? The woman seemed to have almost slipped into a trance. Desperate to change the subject, Macey shifted in her seat and asked, "How do you know my mom?"

Roberta's demeanor shifted back to cheerfulness. "I teach a meditation class at the civic center. Jenny joined a few weeks ago."

"That's cool." She had no idea her mother was into meditation. Maybe she needed to visit more often.

"It's been such an eye opening experience." The sound of her mother's voice startled her, and she jumped.

"God, Mom. I need to put a bell on you. You scared me!"

"Sorry, sweetheart." Jenny set the table with plates, silverware, and full glasses of sweet tea. Then she scurried to the kitchen and brought out the food. "Soup's on," she called over her shoulder to William.

With dinner on the table, they loaded their plates and began eating. The potatoes melted in Macey's mouth, and she had to remind herself to slow down. She didn't get home-cooking like this very often, and it was so good, she wanted to shovel it all in.

"Macey." Roberta dabbed the napkin at the corners of her mouth. "Your mother asked me to come over to talk to you about the trouble you had with a spirit. It seems you have an undeveloped gift you may need help with."

"Mom!" Macey glared at her mother. Her ability had always been their secret—she didn't want anyone to think she was a freak.

Jenny shrugged. "I was worried about you. Roberta is a psychic medium, so I thought she could help."

That explained the strange behavior. Macey's ears burned with embarrassment or anger—she didn't know which. Her mother had no right to share her secret. If Macey wanted to tell people, that was her business. But to go around telling complete strangers? What would the guys at work think of her if they found out?

She turned to Roberta and spoke through clenched teeth. "I don't know what my mother told you about my *ability*, but I'm handling it fine. And I'd appreciate it if you didn't talk about it to anyone else. My job depends on my sanity...or people perceiving me as sane."

Dropping her napkin on her plate, Macey rose to her feet and stormed out of the dining room. She wanted to slam the door behind her as she left the house, but she refrained from the childish action. Instead, she carefully clicked it shut, dropped down on the front steps, and sat with her head in her hands.

She'd overreacted, but embarrassment stopped her from going back inside. Her mother should've warned her. If she would have let her know why she'd invited Roberta, Macey would've had time to process. To avoid acting like she did. What a fool she'd made of herself. She needed to apologize to Roberta, at least.

She was about to do just that when the door opened and Roberta stepped onto the porch. Macey stood and leaned against the hand rail. "I'm sorry, Roberta. It's not something I tell many people, and you caught me off guard."

Roberta held up a finger. "No need to apologize. It can be hard accepting a gift you don't understand." She folded Macey's hand into her arm. "Let's walk."

They strolled up the driveway, and Macey led her to a walking trail through a wooded area behind the neighborhood. Massive oak trees created a canopy over the gravel path, their leaves dappling the sunlight on the ground. A gentle breeze rustled the branches, stirring the scent of earth and arbor in the air. Roberta's jolly demeanor slipped away, turning serious as she began to speak.

"There are things in this world that aren't as they seem. Some of us are gifted enough to see things as they are. Most of us are not. How long have you had the ability to read objects, Macey?"

She shrugged. "I don't know. As long as I can remember."

They paused at a bridge that crossed a narrow stream. "And you haven't sought help in developing it. Why?"

"My dad doesn't believe in it, so he won't talk about it. And, Mom…she taught me to keep it to myself. That's why it threw me off when she told you."

Roberta's musical laugh danced on the breeze. "Jenny is opening her mind to many things. I'm sorry it came so late. It must have been very hard keeping it to yourself."

"Not really. I've told a few people…People I trust. Some believe me, some don't."

"Luke believes you."

She pulled her hand from Roberta's grip. She'd trusted Luke, and to think he'd discussed her ability behind her back caused a sharp pain in her chest. How stupid of her to talk about herself with a man she barely knew. "How do you… Did you talk to him? How do you know him?"

"We run in similar circles, so to speak." She smiled knowingly. "He didn't share your secret with me, but I know him and I know he believes you."

Macey let out her breath as relief loosened the tightness in her chest.

Roberta stepped onto the bridge and turned to her. "Running water increases a spirit's ability to manifest. Were you near a stream when it happened?"

"It's possible, but I didn't see one. I was out in the woods…kinda like this." She spun in a circle, her senses suddenly heightened at the similarity of the scene. A warm breeze caressed her skin, and birds chirped in the trees above. Nothing out of the ordinary. No ghosts dancing in the wind. She turned to find Roberta staring at her.

"That's good. You should always pay attention to your surroundings."

Macey laughed. "As a cop, I always do. But now I have to pay attention to things I can't see?" She sat on the edge of the bridge. "It really happened, didn't it? I think I convinced myself it didn't."

Roberta eased down next to her. "It did, indeed. I sensed the remnants of its essence in you when we hugged. And I sense it is near now, though I can't tell where. Somehow, it's blocking me."

Macey swallowed. "It's here?"

"It's following you. And it's powerful."

"Well, crap." Just what she needed. As if her ability wasn't freaky enough, now she had a real ghost haunting her.

"Do you know what it wants?" Roberta asked.

She sighed and rubbed her temples. "It could only be after one thing. It wants to stop me. Have you heard about the case I'm working in the Quarter?"

Roberta raised her eyebrows. "I have."

"It's the ghost of one of the perpetrators. The one whose body we found." She rubbed her arms, suddenly chilled by the reality. "I saw his face when he got…inside me."

Her eyes tightened briefly before she forced a half-smile. "Try not to worry. You're strong, Macey. If you fought it out once, you can do it again."

She threw up her arms. "Well, that's great. I have to spend the rest of my life on the lookout for an evil spirit who wants to possess me? Do you think it'll leave me alone once I solve the case? *If* I solve the case?"

"If?"

"Well, so far, nothing in this case makes sense."

"That's because you're looking at it from a strictly human perspective. You need to open your mind to other possibilities."

"What kind of possibilities?" Werewolves? No, thanks. She'd already heard that one.

Roberta sighed and brushed a stray strand of hair from Macey's face, a motherly gesture that put her fears at ease. She could trust this woman. She felt it in her bones.

"There's only so much I can tell you. But if you'll allow me to help you develop your gift, the secrets will reveal themselves to you."

"But if you know something that will help solve the case, you have to—"

"I know what I know. This case is bigger than you, child. Truly solving it will change your life forever. I can help you if you are open to it. Are you ready?"

Macey chewed the inside of her cheek. Did she want her life changed? Did she have choice? "I guess so. Can you help me get rid of this spirit that's stalking me too?"

"I'm afraid only you can get rid of it for good."

An icy entity snaked around Macy's legs, spiraling up to her ear. *"You'll never get rid of me."* She jumped to her feet, spinning around, trying to locate the spirit.

"Roberta?" Her voice came out as a breathy whisper.

"It's here, isn't it?" Roberta said. "It's still blocking me. Don't let it in." She rose to her feet and stepped to Macey's side.

"Now, where did we leave off? Oh, yeah. I was trying to get inside you."

Her body trembled as the familiar prickling sensation covered her skin. "How do I keep it out?" Panic tipped in her voice.

"Same way you did last time, child. Use your mind to put up a shield."

Macey imagined a bubble of white light surrounding her body. She tensed her muscles, pushing back as the spirit tried to enter her. The sensation of a million needles lodged in her skin, the spirit pressing them in, her will pushing them out.

"Don't listen to that damn witch. I'm going to get inside you, so you might as well stop fighting."

"I won't let you in." She pushed back with all her might, gritting her teeth as sweat beaded on her forehead. A metal curtain slammed down in her mind, shutting the spirit out. Her body trembled, fatigue setting in and threatening to crumble the wall she'd so forcefully built. Then, the pricking stopped. The darkness that had closed in around her dissipated, lifting a weight off her chest.

"I'll get you another way, then." The spirit swirled around her in frantic circles before shooting up into the air.

Dizzy and drained, she leaned her hand against a tree trunk, trying to catch her ragged breath. "Did you hear what he said?"

Roberta put a hand on her shoulder. "I couldn't hear a thing. He was only talking to you."

In his wolf form, Luke crouched in the brush a few yards away from Macey. Initially, he'd berated himself for following her, but now he was glad he did. Something was tormenting her, though he couldn't wrap his mind around what it was. A regular spirit didn't have that kind of power, and once a demon was vanquished, it went straight to hell. It couldn't hang around in spirit form. Unless…

It had to be the half-demon James had killed a few days ago. But why wouldn't it have reincarnated its own body? Was it more powerful this way? A low growl rumbled in his chest. That explained why her eyes had turned red. The bastard had already gotten inside her.

Lying on his stomach, he inched forward on his haunches to get a better view of the scene. Macey leaned against a thick oak, her head tipped back so it rested against the tree. Long, golden hair flowed over her bare shoulders, cascading down to the center of her lavender tank top. Luke's chest tightened. So beautiful. Delicate. The fragility of human life made his heart ache.

The witch stood next to her, stroking her arm in comfort.

"He said he'd get to me another way." Macey's voice trembled as she spoke.

"You'll have to keep your guard up, then," Roberta said.

Macey shivered and whipped her head around. "He's here. I can feel him."

Luke rose onto his paws. He sensed the demon too. Scanning the scene, his gaze fixed on a branch, as thick as his thigh, swaying above the women. The air was stagnant; no breeze could've caused the movement. The branch pressed down, then snapped up as if it were pushed. He growled a warning.

Still out of sight, he crept closer, his gaze shifting from Macey to the tree. What the hell was the demon doing? Spirits weren't strong enough to move—

Before he could finish the thought, instinct took over. He leapt from his hiding place and bounded toward the women. Macey let out a yelp as he plowed into them, knocking them out of the line of the falling branch.

The bough crashed to the ground, splitting in half with a thundering *crack*. With the women safe, Luke prowled the area, howling a warning to the fiend. No one messed with his woman.

He lifted his muzzle, inhaling the coppery tinge of fresh blood. Macey was hurt. His stomach dropped, and he turned slowly to the pair. Roberta sat where she'd landed, dusting dirt and leaves from her skirt. Macey sat frozen, her gaze locked on his wolf form. Had she even noticed the gash on her thigh? Blood ran in ribbons over her knee, turning black as the ground absorbed it.

Luke cautiously took another step forward to examine her. Other than the cut on her leg, she seemed to be okay. He lowered his head and whimpered, trying his best to show Macey he wouldn't hurt her. It didn't work.

She grasped Roberta's shirt, never taking her gaze off him. "Roberta…I think we're about to get eaten."

"Oh, nonsense. It's just a wolf, and it saved our lives. Sit still until it goes away." Roberta looked into his eyes and raised an eyebrow as she spoke to Macey. "Do you sense the spirit, dear?"

Macey shook her head. "N-n…no. I think it's gone."

"Okay, then. We're safe." She looked at the cut on Macey's leg. "You've got a little scratch from your fall." She turned to Luke. "Nothing a salve and a bandage won't fix. I'm sure the wolf will leave now." She emphasized the last two words as if making sure he got the point.

He couldn't do anything else, so he blew a hard breath through his nose, turned, and ran into the woods. He'd have to trust Macey's intuition that the fiend had left. He didn't sense it there, but that didn't mean anything. It was only half demon, and it didn't have a goddamn body.

What the hell were they doing out in the woods again? Roberta, of all people, should've realized the danger Macey was in. That's if she knew it was a demon spirit.

When he first saw Macey with the witch, he'd thought he had it all figured out. That Macey was a witch as well, and she'd been holding back when they talked at the restaurant. But given the nature of the women's conversation, he wasn't sure now.

Could she really possess so much power and not even realize it? Growing up in the magical community, Luke couldn't fathom having no one to talk to about his abilities. Of course, the breadth of his abilities consisted of turning into a wolf on command and changing back into a human. Macey could read energy. And apparently be possessed by it.

He broke into a sprint, bounding through the forest with long strides, leaves crunching and twigs snapping under his massive paws. He needed to watch her more closely. To protect her. The thought of that fiend hurting her was enough to drive him mad. He'd already failed one woman. It wouldn't happen again.

At least she'd have Roberta coaching her now. Roberta was the most powerful witch he knew. She was a member of the local coven, but she didn't get involved in their politics. If anyone could train Macey to use her gifts, she could. The idea relaxed him a little, but he had to be extra vigilant to make sure his woman stayed safe.

His woman. He already thought of her that way, but she wasn't his yet. He still didn't know if it was possible for an alpha to mate with a non-were. He'd have to find out soon.

CHAPTER THIRTEEN

Two days passed with no word from Luke. Macey's elation after their dates deflated into a feeling of emptiness. And, they *had* been dates. Though they didn't start out that way, by the end of each evening, they were definitely in date mode. He'd even kissed her, for goodness sake! Then she'd invited him back to her house...

But he'd turned her down.

She gripped the steering wheel so tightly her knuckles turned white as she drove up Chartres Avenue. In the passenger seat, Bryce sat oblivious to the inner torment storming inside her.

"You trying to choke it to death?" Her partner nodded toward Macey's hands. Maybe he wasn't completely oblivious. "What's up, boss?"

She relaxed her death grip and let out a long sigh. "When two people have a...date...and they have a really good time...and the guy says he'll call, how long should it take?"

Bryce shook his head and mumbled, "Sorry I asked." He took a deep breath and peered thoughtfully out the window. "You're asking *me* for dating advice? The perpetual bachelor?" His goofy grin helped lighten the mood.

The tension in Macey's chest eased its grip. "You're the only guy I trust. The only person I can talk to."

He sighed. "Okay. How long has it been?"

"Two days." When she said it out loud, it didn't sound nearly as long as it felt.

Bryce laughed. "That's nothing, Mace. Give the boy time. He's probably trying to figure out what to say when he calls. Patience, grasshopper."

"It's hard to be patient after..." Heat flushed her cheeks at the memory of the kiss. Did she want to share all the juicy details with her partner?

"After?"

She huffed and fiddled with the AC controls. She had goose bumps thinking about the way she fit so perfectly into Luke's arms. At the personal information she'd shared so willingly with him. "He was easy to talk to. I told him a lot of things I don't normally tell people. He probably thinks I'm a freak now. That's why he hasn't called."

Bryce shifted in his seat to face her. "He doesn't think you're a freak." He tapped his finger against his chin, his eyes growing wide. "You're falling for this guy, aren't you?"

"What? Don't be ridiculous." She tried to laugh off the accusation. "I just...like him a little."

"Your confidence is slipping. I've never heard you question what a man thinks about you."

That's because I've never cared. "Okay, I like him a lot. Happy? He's different..." Cool relief flooded her system as a call came over the radio. At least she didn't have to talk about Luke anymore. Unfortunately, the call confirmed another murder.

Macey floored it, and five minutes later they arrived at the scene. As they approached the historic mansion-turned-apartment-building, the sharp, coppery scent of blood crept to her senses. In her line of work, she should've been used to the aromas of death. But the smell singed her nostrils. She paused in front of the structure, leaning her hand against the beige wood. Flipping open her notebook, she pretended to read as the images and energy stored in the building flowed through her fingertips and into her mind. She shuffled through the pictures, but found nothing of use. Maybe she'd get something inside the victim's apartment.

A steady stream of light from a gas lantern illuminated the sidewalk in front of the building. A glass fixture enclosed the flame, so the wind couldn't blow out the fire. Yet, the lantern in front of Macey flickered as if a breeze blew by. The flame danced, rising and falling as it shimmied in the non-existent wind. Even if the fire were exposed, the night hung dead still. Not even the slightest breeze alleviated the heavy, southern heat that clung to her skin like a wet blanket.

The flame stilled as the breeze circled Macey, raising goose bumps on the back of her neck. Was it another spirit trying to contact her? If so, it needed to try harder. She wasn't a psychic.

"The victim's this way." A uniformed officer motioned for them to follow him into an alley. A crowd had gathered behind the police tape, and they had to weave their way through to get to the courtyard and the body.

Macey swallowed down the bile that formed in the back of her throat as the stench assaulted her. What she would have given to have a man's nose. The smell never bothered them. Bryce wandered off to talk to another officer while she approached the body. She stifled a gasp as her gaze landed on the lifeless eyes staring into the night sky.

Another rape victim. Just like the last one, her abdomen was obliterated. But nothing ate this woman. The shot gun that lay at her feet was responsible for tearing the enormous gash through her stomach and out her back. Bits of flesh and bone lay scattered about the woman's head, no doubt the remnants of what blew out her back when she was shot. But why would the murderer leave the weapon lying at her feet?

She turned to the officer next to her. "Witnesses?"

"No one saw the shooter. Her roommate's out of town, but neighbors heard the shot. Only one fired."

"One was all it took," she muttered under her breath. "Has her apartment been searched?"

"Yes, ma'am. No evidence of a struggle. Victim was a neat freak, for sure. Carpets looked freshly vacuumed. The only interesting thing we turned up so far was this." He handed her a plastic bag containing a single slip of paper.

Macey squinted to read the pristine handwriting in the dark. Two lines centered on the page read:

I have to get rid of the devil inside me.
This is the only way I know how.

Macey returned the evidence to the officer. This wasn't a murder. It was a suicide.

*The devil inside me...*Was the woman possessed? Could the spirit that had tried to contact her earlier be the victim or the "devil" inside her? Too many questions clouded her mind.

"I've seen enough. How 'bout you, boss?" Bryce said.

"Yeah, me too." She raised her voice so the others would hear. "Pack it up, boys." As the myriad of questions spun through her head, she followed her partner toward the alley where the crowd was finally dispersing.

"I think I'm gonna hang behind and...you know."

A slow smile raised the corners of his mouth. "I figured as much. You always get that puzzled look on your face. I'll catch a ride back to the station and take care of the paperwork. Our shift's almost over anyway."

As Bryce strode off toward the other officers, Macey turned back to the scene. The coroner's men were already packing up to take the body to the morgue, but it was just as well. Macey was looking for spirits. Or at least the energy they left behind.

Inside, the victim's apartment appeared as the officer had described. Pristine. The trails left by a vacuum cleaner lined up evenly across the light beige carpet. Framed photographs on the mantle suggested the woman had many friends and a boyfriend. Macey rested her hand against the brick fireplace and closed her eyes. Happy images of the victim's life played in her mind like old home movies. She was rarely alone. Always surrounded by friends and family. And love. Only the most recent memories contained any sort of dismay.

"What am I missing?" Macey investigated the rest of the apartment, but couldn't find any physical evidence. No spirits tried to contact her. She made her way down the stairs and exited the building. She should go home. Bryce was taking care of the paperwork; there was no need for her to return to the station. But could she sleep after witnessing a gruesome scene like that?

She sighed. Of course she could. She'd lock the images away in the vault in the back of her mind where she kept every horrendous act she'd encountered. Before she left, she'd give her ability one last try. She meandered to the front of the building near the gas lamp that had flickered. That had to have been a spirit trying to contact her earlier.

As she rested her hand against the wood, a familiar silhouette flashing in the corner of her eye caught her attention. It had the same broad shoulders as the one she thought she'd seen in the woods at the other scene. He stood in a doorway across the alley, the backlighting making it impossible for her to discern his features. She stepped toward the figure, and he bolted from his position.

Damn it! She'd seen him. Luke dashed up the alley, walking as fast as he could. To run would only bring more attention to himself. He'd just had to get a closer look, hadn't he? If he'd have stayed in the shadows like he normally did, she would've walked right past him. James had beaten the officers to the scene and had already removed the bits of shattered fetus from the body, incinerating the flesh to conceal the evidence. Luke had no business getting so close. Or hanging around as long as he had. His emotions were making him sloppy.

"Excuse me, sir. Sir, stop!"

Busted. He slowly turned around and raised his hands in mock surrender. "Hey, Macey. Don't shoot."

She dropped her hands to her sides, and her mouth hung open. "Luke?" With three purposeful strides, she closed the distance between them. "Why were you running away from me?"

"I…" He huffed a hard sigh. *Might as well tell her the truth. A little of it, anyway.* "I didn't want you to think I was following you. You've already accused me of it once."

Redness rose on her cheeks, and she gazed at the ground. "Were you? Or…what are you doing here?"

He shrugged and shoved his hands into his pockets. "I saw the crowd and was curious. I might have lingered a little longer because you were there." That wasn't exactly a lie.

"Oh." She tilted her head and narrowed her eyes. "Do you ever go north of the Quarter? Masters Street area?"

"Can't say that I do." He would have to be more careful.

"No. I guess not."

Awkward silence hung between them. Her mouth opened a few times as if she were going to speak, but the words didn't come. As he watched the movement of her lips, all he could think about was how they'd felt pressed to his: soft, warm, moist. He could almost taste them.

"I'm sorry I haven't called you," he finally said. "I've been tied up with work." *And killing demons.*

"It's okay." She waved away his apology.

He took her hand and laced his fingers through hers. "No, it's not. I shouldn't have left you waiting like that."

Sucking in a sharp breath, she swallowed hard as she inched closer to his body. She glanced around at the empty alley and angled her head up toward his. Her pink tongue glided over her lips before she spoke. "You're here now."

He groaned. Did she have any idea how sexy she was? Of course she did, and she used it to her full advantage. He shouldn't have been pursuing her yet. Not until he had all the facts and had presented them to his father. He'd spent the past two days researching the family lines to see if there was any chance Macey could be his mate. A handful of cases existed where wolves had mated with other magic beings and still had were offspring. Mostly witches, mages, and fae, though—never with a simple psychic.

But Macey was more than that. Her power coursed through him every time they touched, taunting him with its mystery. And there was more magic in her. It had been suppressed long ago, or never formed, but surely he could help her chip away at whatever held it back. Then he could fulfill his duty as alpha and follow his heart as a man.

And right at that moment, with Macey's luscious lips parted and ready, he was all man. He leaned in and took her mouth in a gentle kiss. Her warm velvet lips sent tingling energy shooting straight to his heart. He expected her to pull away, but she leaned into the kiss, pressing her soft curves against his body and wrapping her arms around his waist. He cradled the back of her neck with his hand and slipped his tongue into her honey-sweet mouth. If only her hair hung loose; he'd have loved to tangle his hands in her silky locks.

He tilted his head back to look into her eyes. What thoughts swam behind those emerald pools? Did she feel like she'd known him forever, the way he felt about her? They were meant to be together. Could she sense it too? He hadn't spoken to her in two days, but the time and distance melted away as he held her in his arms.

Sighing, she leaned her head against his chest. "I was beginning to think you weren't interested in me."

How could she think such a thing? He placed his hands on her shoulders and gently pushed her away, so he could look at her. "I am *very* interested in you, but my life is complicated, and—"

She touched her index finger against his lips. "It's okay."

He grabbed her hand and playfully bit her finger. "Would you stop saying that? There's no excuse for my behavior, and I need to make it up to you. How about we get out of this alley? Can I buy you a cup of coffee? Or do you need to go back to work?"

She grinned. "Actually, my shift just ended, and coffee sounds fantastic." She looked at her watch and furrowed her brow. "Don't you have to be at work in a few hours? It's late for someone with a day job."

"I'm a big boy. I'll be okay." Werewolves didn't need as much sleep as humans, anyway.

"Well, all right then. My car's across the street. Do you want to follow me?"

"Actually, my truck's at home. I was out for a walk when I…uh… saw the commotion." He shoved his hands in his pockets and prayed she'd buy his story. Who went for a walk at one in the morning?

"Hmm…" Her emerald eyes narrowed briefly before a sly smile curved her lips. "Night owl, huh? Me too. C'mon, I'll drive."

Macey climbed into the driver's seat, and Luke slid in next to her. As soon as he closed the door, a static charge seemed to build in the confined space, drawing her toward him, making her palms sweat. She cranked up the AC and held her hands in front of the vents to dry them.

Luke buckled his seatbelt and chuckled. "Nervous?" He nodded to her hands.

She yanked them away from the vents and wiped them on her pants. "Not nervous. I don't know how to describe it. You…make me feel things."

"You make me feel things too." He caught her gaze, and the overwhelming urge to reach across the console and pull his mouth to hers consumed her. Something about Luke awakened a long-forgotten primal instinct deep inside her. The question was, could she keep her heart guarded while satisfying those instincts?

He reached for her hand and held it between both of his. "I have a confession."

"Uh oh. That doesn't sound good."

He took a deep breath and blew it out hard. "I *was* following you tonight."

Her heart paused for a moment before giving one solid slam against her chest, and a red flag planted itself firmly in the center of her brain. But Luke wasn't a stalker. His actions may have been questionable, but for some unknown reason, she trusted him down to her core. *Hear the man out, Mace. Surely he has a good reason.* "Why were you following me?"

"We have a police scanner at the bar. It's a…hobby of my old man's. When I heard the report come through, I figured you'd be at the scene, so I came out to see you. After not calling you for two days, I thought my apology would be more believable in person."

"Oh, that's nice of you." A little weird, but nice. "But, if you wanted to see me, why did you run from me?"

He let out an embarrassed chuckle and gazed at their entwined hands. "Once I got here, I realized how creepy it was, so I tried to get away before you found out it was me."

She chewed her bottom lip. So he wasn't the most suave person on the planet; neither was she. Plucking the red flag from her mind, she tossed it aside. "I see."

"I needed to see you again. I thought it would be a romantic gesture, but it turned out to be stalkerish." He shrugged. "With all our chance encounters, and your detective mind, I thought you might be suspicious. Better to come clean now, right?" He chuckled. "I just made things weird, didn't I?"

"Yes." Though, honestly, every time Luke was near, her brain seemed to shut down and let her hormones take over. The coincidence hadn't seemed odd at the time, but she may have been suspicious later, when her brain started working again. She squeezed his hand. "It's okay. I like weird."

Coming to a crime scene to see her was a strange choice, but no one had ever shown so much interest in her. She could forgive his lack of judgment this time. Besides, with his warm, musky scent filling the car and that strange energy dancing between them, all she could think about was what he would look like with his clothes lying on the floor beside the bed.

His shoulders moved away from his ears as his tension released. "That's good to know." He leaned across the console, as far as the seatbelt would allow, and stroked the back of his fingers down her cheek. "I'd like to kiss you now, if that's okay."

She didn't bother with an answer. Unhooking her seatbelt, she leaned into him, crushing her mouth to his. She shouldn't have been doing this. She didn't want to get involved with a man.

Damn it, why did her brain have to turn on now? She needed to plant her butt back in her seat and end this before he got close enough to hurt her. It would be the logical thing to do.

But as he cupped his hand behind her neck and slipped his tongue between her lips, her logic flew out the window right along with her inhibitions. Red flag? What red flag? She wanted this man.

And she could have him in a physical sense without getting her heart involved, couldn't she? It was worth a try.

She held his face in her hands and touched her forehead to his. "How about that coffee?"

"I've got a Keurig at my place...three blocks away."

She closed her eyes as a shudder ran through her entire body. "Show me the way."

Shoving the voice of reason into the vault, she drove to Luke's house and followed him inside. As soon as he shut the front door, she grabbed him by the shoulders and took his mouth again. If she stopped to think about what she was doing, she'd talk herself out it.

A growl emanated from Luke's chest as he slid his arms around her waist and held her close. The evidence of his desire pressed into her stomach, and she glided her hand between their bodies to rub him through his jeans.

He sucked in a sharp breath. "Are you sure you want to do this? We haven't even had a proper date."

It was just sex. As long as she could convince herself it didn't mean anything more, she'd be fine. This basal, primal urge she felt to possess him, to make him hers, was physical...nothing more. Grabbing his shirt by the hem, she yanked it over his head. Her mouth watered as she ran her hands along his firm chest, down his defined abs, and popped the button on his jeans.

He gripped her hips. "Can I take that as a yes?"

"Yes." *God, yes.*

He tugged her to the bedroom, took a condom from a drawer, and then tossed it on the nightstand. The nagging voice of reason tried to escape from the vault, warning her she was getting in too deep, but she locked it away.

The hunger in his eyes was unlike anything she'd seen, and as she undressed before him, his pupils dilated with desire. "Christ, Macey, you're gorgeous."

She unhooked her bra and dropped it on the floor, and another growl rumbled from his chest, awakening every feminine urge inside her body.

"Take your hair down."

She yanked the band from her hair, letting it spiral out of its knot and tumble over her shoulders. Then she slid down his zipper and pushed his pants and underwear to the floor.

Holy moly, he was huge.

"I need you, Luke." God, did she need him. She grabbed the condom and pushed him onto the bed. Forget about foreplay. It had been three years since she'd been with a man, and with Luke's dick hard and ready, she couldn't wait any longer.

She rolled the condom down his length and straddled him. Using her hand to guide him to her center, she sheathed him, moaning as his girth filled her completely. Never in her life had she felt so much desire, so much sheer need, emanating from somewhere deep inside her being. In this moment, he belonged to her...and she belonged to him.

Sliding his hands up her thighs, he clutched her hips and guided her up and down his thick cock. The electricity she normally felt when she touched him increased one hundred fold, rocketing through her body and setting her soul ablaze. She wanted to go slow, to make the searing intensity last, but as she moved her hips, the delicious friction of him sliding in and out sent her too close to the edge. With her hands on his chest, her nails digging into his skin, she lost herself to the moment. To the man.

He locked eyes with her, and licking his thumb, he pressed it to her clit, rubbing her sensitive nub in circles, sending more fire coursing through her veins. She couldn't take any more. Her orgasm ripped through her body, sending a shock of pleasure from her womb to her toes. Her legs trembled, and she collapsed on top of him, gasping for breath, burying her face in his neck.

He held onto her, moving his hips, each thrust sending another electric jolt of ecstasy through her system. He groaned as his own orgasm overtook him, showering her neck and shoulder in kisses, nipping at her sensitive skin as he found his release.

As her breathing slowed, she raised her head to look at him. His satisfied smile tugged at her heart, but the bright-red scratches trailing down his chest made her stomach drop. "I'm so sorry." She slid onto her side and ran her finger over the marks. "I hurt you."

"Nah. I'm fine." He rubbed a hand over his pecs. "They're already fading; no harm done." Rising onto an elbow, he kissed her cheek before whispering into her ear, "I liked it."

His breath against her skin made her shiver, and her stomach flip-flopped at his playful words. The marks faded before her eyes, turning into light pink lines before disappearing completely. She must not have scratched him as hard as she'd thought. She looked into his eyes, and her heart raced into overdrive. "I...liked it too."

Rolling onto her back, she stared at the ceiling. What had she just done? She'd acted like an animal, letting her primal desires overtake her, acting on instinct rather than listening to reason. For the first time in her life, she felt a sense of completeness. Something about being here with Luke felt so good...so *right*.

Luke slid out of bed and tossed the condom in the trash, and a smile tugged at Macey's lips. He was all smooth skin and hard muscle, and his backside looked as good as his front. Maybe she should let her instincts take over more often.

He climbed back into bed and pulled her close, and she allowed herself to get lost in the comfort of his embrace. Though he was nearly a foot taller than her, their bodies fit together perfectly, as if they were made for each other.

He pressed his lips to the top of her head, and his chest vibrated as he spoke. "If this is what I get for stalking you, I'll have to do it more often."

She propped her head on her hand and grinned. "Next time, I want a proper date first."

"So there will be a next time?"

She bit her bottom lip. If she had her way, there would be lots of next times. "I hope so."

"Good."

She laid her head on his shoulder. What was she saying? If she started going on dates with him, she'd start feeling things she didn't want to feel. She'd already opened up to him way more than she should have, and those feelings she didn't want to feel were starting to creep into her heart.

So much for the need being purely physical. Coldness flashed through her core, and she sat up. This couldn't be happening, could it? She swallowed the lump from her throat. The feelings weren't creeping; they'd slammed into her chest like a sucker-punch before she even had time to react.

"Where are you going?" He took her hand.

Good question. She had to get away or she would drown if she didn't come up for air. "You have to get up in a few hours. I should let you sleep."

He rose onto his elbows. "I'd sleep better with you curled up next to me."

His grin melted her heart, soothing her frazzled nerves. Something about his presence calmed her, making her want to stay in bed with him all night and all day tomorrow. But she couldn't. He needed to sleep, and she needed some alone time so she could sort out her emotions, decide what these strange new feelings meant. "I'm not tired. I work nights, remember?"

"I'll stay up with you then."

She smiled and rested a hand on his chest. The familiar tingle shimmied up her arm, and she was tempted to slide her fingers beneath the sheets. His smooth skin and intoxicating scent beckoned her to stay, but she fought the urge. She needed to gather her scattered thoughts and figure out if she was capable of letting Luke in.

Sliding out of bed, she picked up her clothes and dressed. "I'd rather you get some sleep, so maybe you'll remember to call me and ask me out on that date you keep promising me."

He sighed as he rolled out of bed and pulled on his underwear. "Let me at least walk you to the door."

He kissed her as she left and stood in the doorway until she got in her car and backed out of the driveway. Her chest tightened as she shifted into drive and headed home. She was in way over her head with this man. He was sweet, sexy, amazing in bed…

She'd built a fortress around her heart, but she may have found a man worth lowering the drawbridge for.

Luke only got three hours of sleep, but he woke the next morning feeling more refreshed and lively than he had in ages. Making love to Macey had been better than he could've imagined…and he'd imagined it plenty of times. It was a shame she took off the way she did, but he didn't want to push her to stay. Neither of them had planned on the night ending with them in bed together, but he was so damn glad it had.

He could've lain there all morning imagining her beautiful face. The way her warm, supple body would feel against his as they cuddled the day away. But he had a job to do and a pack to run. *Damn responsibility.* After last night, there was no doubt in his mind Macey was the one for him. She was his fate-bound; it didn't matter that she wasn't a werewolf. He couldn't deny fate.

The first order of business would be to convince the current alpha that Macey was an acceptable mate. Once his old man was on board, everyone else would follow.

After getting ready for work, he skipped down the stairs. Bypassing his truck, he took advantage of the gorgeous morning and walked to the job site. It was only six blocks away, and his body buzzed with excited energy. The morning sun hadn't risen high enough to peek over the buildings in the Quarter, so he was spared from the sweltering heat that would soon fry the dew from the grass. Jackson Square bustled with activity as the local artists and entertainers hurried to set up their displays as the tourists ventured out of their hotel rooms. Fortune tellers set up folding tables on the sidewalk, and painters hung their creations on the wrought iron fence that enclosed the grassy park. Luke waved at a man encrusted in gold paint from head to toe. He smiled to reveal a set of matching gold teeth.

A line of people had already formed outside Café Du Monde as they waited for their taste of the venue's famous beignets and café au lait. The sweet scent of fried pastries beckoned to him, and he almost stopped in for his own French donut smothered in powdered sugar.

But the pair of glowing red eyes watching him in the distance drew his attention away from the café. Luke stopped cold and returned the stare. *Christ! These things aren't supposed to be out in the daytime.*

A low growl resonated in his chest as he crept toward the fiend. The demon's wicked grin revealed a set of perfectly white, human teeth. Luke paused and eyed the creature. It looked too human to be a creature from hell. He angled his nose upward and inhaled a deep breath. The distinct demon-like smell of rotting flesh floated on the breeze. It was the half-demon born of the first victim. It had to be. He appeared to be a teenager, which put him at the right developmental age for a halfling.

Luke took two more tentative steps forward. When the demon merely sneered, he sprinted, barreling through the crowd toward the fiend. The halfling spun around and dashed away, cutting in and out of groups of tourists before darting into the French Market.

Luke cursed and skidded to a stop at the entrance to the bazaar. Row after row of tables filled with every kind of merchandise imaginable lined the shopping pavilion. People meandered up and down the columns of parcels, and the demon blended right in. At Luke's height, he could see over most of the patrons' heads, but the fiend was nowhere to be found.

Luke clambered his way through the market, checking the eyes of every male he passed. None were red. The demon was probably halfway to his hideout before Luke made it to the end of the pavilion. Exhaling a deflated sigh, he made a left on St. Philip to head to the bar. His civilian work would have to wait.

CHAPTER FOURTEEN

"What the hell is that bag doing here? People can probably smell it a mile away. Are you trying to get us caught?"

Jimmy curled into a ball on the corner of his futon. He didn't know where in the room his brother was, but the gash on his forehead hadn't healed from the last time Ross had struck him. He didn't want to get hit again.

"You never told me what to do with it. I...thought you might still want it." He ducked his head between his forearms and held his breath, waiting for the blow that never came. Instead, a cool breeze rustled through his hair.

"Don't worry, brother. I'm not going to hit you again. We need your face to heal for what I have planned."

Jimmy peeked his head up and looked around the room. He would never get used to his brother not having a body. It just wasn't right. He wished Ross would get back into his old body and leave him alone. Jimmy didn't like the way it felt to have his brother inside him. He didn't know what Ross had planned, but he was sure he wouldn't like it either.

Jimmy cringed before asking his next question. He hated asking questions because they were always stupid, and stupid questions got stupid answers. Or punches to the gut. "What should I do with you… uh…the bag?"

"Burn it…No. That would draw too much attention. Go find a cinder block to tie it to, and sink it in the swamp. It's no use to me now."

"Yes, sir. I'll do it right now." Jimmy swung the pungent bag over his shoulder, relieved to be getting rid of the awful smell. It probably wouldn't have been a good idea for Ross to go back into his old body now that it was so stinky.

He turned to leave, and the door swung open, smacking him in the nose. An explosion of pain shot through his face, but Jimmy forced his watery eyes to focus on the boy who came in. Though he was only a few days old now, the boy looked more like a man to Jimmy. Ross wouldn't give him a name, though, so all he could call him was boy.

The boy strutted into the shack and gave Jimmy a mean look. He didn't even say he was sorry for smacking him in the face. "Master?" the boy called. "Master, I saw the wolf."

"What?" Ross growled. *"When?"*

The boy stood straight as a rod with his hands by his side. "A few moments ago, Master. I came here right away."

A pan flew across the room, missing the boy's head by two feet. Jimmy cringed. If Ross had been aiming for Jimmy, he wouldn't have missed. Ross liked the boy better than he liked him. It wasn't fair.

"What do you have to report?"

"The wolf was with the cop last night. I saw her leaving his house. I think they're working together."

"The cop, huh? I'm not worried about her; she'll be easy to handle. It's those damn wolves that keep killing my demons. Although…" An icy breeze whirled around Jimmy, making him sick to his stomach. He didn't want Ross inside him again. Maybe if he tensed all his muscles, he could squeeze him out.

A hollow laugh echoed through the small shack. *"If the wolf is spending so much time with her, they must have more going on."*

"What do you mean, Master?"

Jimmy stood there. He was glad the boy asked the question that almost slipped from his mouth.

"*They're lovers. You two are both too naïve for your own good. We can get to him through her. Jimmy! Why are you still here?*"

"I'm sorry." Jimmy shuffled out the door to bury his brother's body. Whatever Ross was planning, Jimmy wouldn't want to do it. Maybe he would stay away for a very long time. Maybe he just wouldn't go back.

But if he didn't, where would he go?

CHAPTER FIFTEEN

"Absolutely not, son. You're alpha."

Luke sighed and ran a hand through his hair. The video call with his parents wasn't going as well as he'd hoped. "Technically, Dad, you're alpha. I'm still second."

"You know what I mean. You'll be alpha as soon as you find a mate, and it's not going to be the cop. Psychic or not, she isn't a werewolf."

"But I've researched—" He glanced at the door and lowered his voice to avoid any unwelcome eavesdroppers. Trying to control his frustration, he fisted his hands on the desk. "I've researched the family history. Our line has mixed with fae and other magical creatures for centuries. Macey is powerful. I can feel it."

"You feel it with your cock."

"Marcus!" his mother interjected. "Mind your words." She looked at her son through the computer screen. "You love this girl, don't you?"

He sucked in a sharp breath. If being in love meant wanting nothing more than to make the other person happy—to spend every day of the rest of his life with her—then, yeah. Sure it was way too soon to call it love, but he couldn't deny his deep, primal desire to protect her, provide for her. Werewolf or not, she was his fate-bound. "She's the only one I can even consider taking as a mate."

"Well, you're gonna have to *consider* someone else," his father said. "What about that new rogue?"

Luke huffed. "Nice try, but no. And don't bother sending another one. It won't work."

"You think we sent her to you?" His mom looked appalled.

"Didn't you?"

"No, son. We didn't." His father crossed his arms. "But since she's there, you ought to consider—"

"No, Dad. She's not an option."

"Neither is the cop."

Luke ground his teeth. Why did his old man have to be such a hard ass? He drummed his fingers on the desk, trying to keep his heart from racing out of control. Mating with anyone but Macey was… unimaginable. Maybe he could appeal to his mother's sensitivity. "Mom, you understand, right?"

She smiled sadly and folded her hands in her lap. "I do, sweetheart. In any other case, I'd say your happiness comes first. But your father has a point. You're going to be alpha. You can't dilute the bloodline by mating with a non-were."

He fisted his hands to stop his fingers from trembling, but nothing could halt the frantic sprint of his heart. If his own mother wasn't on his side…

He stopped the thought before it could form. There had to be another way. A life without Macey wouldn't be worth living. "You know, it's still just a fifty-fifty chance my offspring will be able to succeed me. What if my first born is a girl? Alphas have to be male, so—"

His father sighed. "Werewolves only, son."

"But—"

Marcus raised his hand to stop him. "Werewolves only."

They said their goodbyes, and Luke slammed the MacBook shut. He wasn't ready to give up, but damn it, his mother was right. He couldn't take a chance in diluting the bloodline. Too many weres were mating with humans as it was. An alpha couldn't add to the weakening of the species.

He pressed his index finger and thumb to the bridge of his nose and closed his eyes to stave off the impending headache that threatened from behind his temples. Pushing his love life to the back burner for the time being, he rose from his chair and followed the murmur of voices down the hall to the meeting room.

He pushed open the door, and a hush fell across the crowd. Nearly thirty pack members lowered their heads to greet him, already giving Luke the respect of an alpha. Though the meeting was open to everyone, he didn't expect anyone but the ten people on the demon hunting team to show. The pack must've been more concerned about the demon issue than he'd thought.

As he strode to the front of the room, everyone settled into the metal folding chairs that circled the space. Everyone, except his cousin. Stephen stood next to Luke, his arms crossed over his chest, a scowl on his face. The sharp sting of tension mixed with jealousy radiated from Stephen's body. He wanted to be in control so badly, it showed in every move he made.

Luke scanned the crowd, acknowledging each person's attendance with a nod of his head. His heart stuttered when he met Alexis's familiar gaze. If his old man hadn't sent her as a potential mate, what the hell was she doing at a pack meeting?

"First of all, I want to thank you all for coming. And I want those of you who aren't on the demon team to know that we have the situation under control."

"Do you?" An older were stood. "I'm afraid to let my daughters out of the house at night."

Luke bristled at the man's tone. "No weres have been attacked."

"Not yet. My girls are second and third born. They can't shift, so they have no way to protect themselves."

"We're all scared to death," a woman said.

"No incidents have been reported in the last week. My men have stopped three demons before they had the chance to find victims."

The man laughed cynically. "But have you stopped the person who's summoning them? Do you even know who he is?" He sat down and crossed his arms, murmuring to the woman next to him. Stephen shifted his weight as if he wanted to speak.

Luke took a deep breath. He'd had no idea his pack was this worried, and he should have. His mind had been so wrapped up in thoughts of Macey, he'd been neglecting his people. What the hell was his problem? He needed to get his mind off the sexy detective and focus on his duties. Hell, he needed to get his mind off women all together. As if to drive his point home, he caught Alexis's gaze. She pursed her lips and gave him a sympathetic look.

He needed to get this meeting under control. Get rid of the demons. Make things normal again. Then he could focus on making Macey his mate. He still had close to two weeks before his old man's retirement. He could do it all by then.

"I don't know who's summoning the demons," he said, "but I know how we can find out."

The whispering quieted as everyone focused on Luke. Stephen's mouth dropped open, and he clicked it shut. "When were you going to share this information with me?" he asked so quietly only Luke could hear.

Luke chuckled. "Right about now." He faced the crowd and raised his voice so they all could hear. "I saw the half-demon child this morning. He reeks of hell and has the same red eyes; he won't be hard to find again. With the whole team on the lookout, we'll find him and track him to his hideout. He'll lead us straight to his master; I'd put money on it."

From the whispers he overheard in the crowd, they seemed satisfied...for now. Leave it to Stephen to raise another concern. "What about the cops? That female detective is getting too close."

"No one needs to worry about the cops. I'm taking care of the detective." *And setting myself up for a major heartbreak.*

Stephen turned to Luke. "And just what are you doing about her?"

Luke fisted his hands and gritted his teeth. If the pack knew his true feelings for Macey, he'd lose their respect. "I befriended her. I'm giving her misinformation and guiding her away from the truth."

"You *befriended* her? You mean you're screwing her." Venom oozed from Stephen's voice. "You reek of human."

"It's strictly business. My relationship with Macey Carpenter goes no further than ensuring our secrets stay safe." He cringed inwardly. He hated lying to the pack, but what else could he do? Tell them he was in love with a human?

He scanned the crowd for their reactions. Most nodded their approval or whispered amongst themselves, but Alexis furrowed her brow and squirmed in her seat. Was she glaring at him? Surely not. Even rogues knew to respect an alpha. She shifted her gaze to the floor and chewed her bottom lip.

Before dismissing the meeting, he described the halfling in more detail, making sure everyone knew to be on the lookout. When the room cleared, Luke made his way to the bar for a beer. Lord knew he needed one after the week he'd had.

Chase poured him a brew as he plopped down on a stool. Most of the pack had left the bar, but a few people occupied the tables around the room. Alexis leaned against the wall in the back, talking to another female. He caught her gaze and nodded a hello. She responded by pursing her lips and giving him a curt nod in return.

Chase mixed a drink for a customer and turned to Luke. "Look, man. I know it's none of my business, but…"

Luke raised an eyebrow at his friend. "Then why are you asking?"

"There's more to the story with you and the detective, isn't there?"

He closed his eyes for a long blink. When he opened them, Chase stared intently at him.

"I'm asking because you're my friend. And I've seen the way you look at her."

Luke leaned forward, lowering his voice. "This is between you and me."

Chase nodded.

"She's amazing, man. I don't know what I'm going to do about it, but, yeah. I'm falling for her hard. As far as the pack's concerned, though, it's business. That's probably all it'll turn out to be anyway." He swallowed down the sour taste that formed in the back of his throat.

"I never thought I'd see the day you fell for a human."

Luke downed his beer and slid the glass to Chase. "Me neither.

But duty comes first." Maybe if he said it out loud enough, he could convince himself it was true.

"Right." Chase clapped him on the shoulder. "Who needs happiness when you've got duty?"

The front door swung open, and both men snapped their heads toward the entrance. James barreled through and skidded to a stop in front of Luke. With one hand on the bar, he heaved in a few breaths before straightening his posture. "I got another one. He was already on top of her, but I got him."

"Damn it!" Luke slammed his fist on the bar and rose to his feet. "Did it rape her?"

James shook his head. "I don't know. Possibly. Your girl is probably on her way to the scene now."

"Shit! All right. Let's go."

"Hey, Luke." Alexis's voice came from just behind his shoulder. How long had she been standing there?

"Make it fast. I have to go." He stalked toward the door, and Alexis followed.

"Let me go with you. I…want to help."

He paused to give her a once over. If she had a motive, he couldn't sense it. And he didn't have time to argue with her. "Stay in the shadows, and keep up. Don't let the cops see you."

He glimpsed a grin curving her lips before he turned and bolted out the door.

CHAPTER SIXTEEN

"It's about time we had another one." Bryce floored it and sped toward the crime scene. "It's been so quiet these past few days, I thought our cult had skipped town."

Macey groaned and gripped the door handle as the car lurched over the bumps on the narrow French Quarter road. He weaved around parked cars, blasting the siren to alert pedestrians to get out of their way. These streets weren't made for Bryce's kind of driving. Next shift, she'd have to be sure she was behind the wheel. "Do you think it's one group doing all this? That they're organized?"

Her partner shrugged. "Beats me. But they always seem to happen the same way."

"What about the animal that saves them? How do you explain that? And the body? And the ash? It doesn't add up."

Bryce turned left on St. Louise and headed toward Dauphine. "You're not still hung up on all that paranormal crap are you? Monsters don't exist, Mace. Not the supernatural kind anyway."

Macey crossed her arms and let out a long sigh. A month ago, she would've agreed with him, but that was before a mysterious animal started attacking rapists and turning them into ash. Ghosts were real, weren't they? So, why couldn't there be some kind of monster or spirit out there wreaking havoc? Why not werewolves, like the barista suggested? That would explain the strange wolf she'd encountered twice now. And why Roberta didn't seem the least bit scared of it.

What am I thinking? Monsters? Werewolves? She needed to focus on the facts. The answers had to be there in the evidence. But the evidence kept disappearing: first the attackers themselves, then the body from the morgue, and now the ash from the lab. Looking at facts and thinking like a detective was getting them nowhere in this case. Maybe it was time she opened her mind to other possibilities.

Could she convince her partner? "How do you know monsters don't exist?"

He chuckled. "Because I've never seen one."

"You've never seen God, and you believe He exists."

"That's different."

"How?"

"Because He's God. If monsters and vampires and werewolves were real, we'd know about them, Mace. C'mon. You have to think logically." He parked against a curb and unlatched his seatbelt.

Macey put her hand on his shoulder. "Thinking logically isn't helping solve this case. All I'm saying is that maybe we need to be a little more open-minded."

"Right. You crack open your mind. I'm going to look at the evidence." He got out of the car and slammed the door.

Great. Now he thinks I'm crazy. If she couldn't get her own partner to consider the possibility, she certainly couldn't expect anyone else to believe her. Except, maybe Luke. The way he'd asked if she believed in magic made it sound like he believed. And he was so accepting of her ability when she'd told him about it. It didn't even faze him that she might be able to talk to spirits. Did he know something?

She laughed at herself and got out of the car. Maybe she really was going crazy. Even if Luke did believe in monsters and magic, she couldn't discuss the case with him...no matter how close the two of them were getting. No, she needed to get him out of her mind for the time being and focus on the evidence. Bryce was right.

They were the first to arrive on the scene, and Macey rushed to the woman who cowered in the corner of the alley. With her knees pulled up to her chest, her matted brown hair swinging forward to cover her face as she buried it in her arms, the woman looked more like a terrified child. Macey's chest tightened as she approached the victim.

"Ma'am, are you okay?" Of course she wasn't okay. What a stupid question. "An ambulance is on its way. I'm Detective Macey Carpenter."

The woman scuttled away as Macey stepped closer, curling into an even tighter ball.

Macey squatted to her level. "I'm not going to hurt you. Can you tell me your name?" She glanced at her partner, who pointed to a pile of ash a few feet away. Macey nodded and returned her attention to the victim.

"Jessica." The woman wiped her face with the back of her hand and loosened her posture tentatively.

"Okay, Jessica. Can you please tell me what happened? Were you raped?"

Jessica sucked in a shaky breath. "No, thank God. He just beat me up pretty bad." She burst into tears and hid her face in her hands.

Macey put her arm around the victim, who shivered in the August heat. Sirens in the distance blared, getting louder as the ambulance approached the scene. She didn't have much time to talk to the woman privately. "What happened after he beat you?"

"He was trying to get my panties off when…" Jessica rubbed her face and shook her head. "It's crazy, but a big dog or something attacked him."

"A dog? What did it look like?"

"I don't know. It happened so fast. It was like…I heard a growl. No, it was more like a snarl, you know?" She looked at Macey, who nodded her head. "And one minute the guy was on me, but the next he was rolling on the ground with the dog. Then the dog took off, and I guess it dragged the guy with it. I don't know."

She'd heard the story what, seven or eight times now? It was the same as the other victims, but they'd never described the animal as a dog. Could it have been the wolf she'd seen before? What on Earth would an animal like that be doing in the French Quarter? Absolutely nothing about this case made sense.

The woman sobbed uncontrollably, and Macey gently rubbed her back. The ambulance doors opened and closed. She had to hurry. "I know this is hard, Jessica. But can you tell me what the dog looked like? Could it have been a wolf?"

"I guess so. It was gray, I think. Or black, maybe. But it was big. Way bigger than any dog I've seen. If it was a wolf, it was a monster of one."

"And you didn't see what happened to the man who attacked you?"

"No. I think the animal carried him off."

Macey smiled sympathetically and stood as the EMTs scurried over to check Jessica's vitals. "Thank you. That's exactly what I needed to know."

Luke, James, and Alexis watched from the shadows as Macey scooped up the demon ash and sealed it in an evidence bag. She handed the bag to an officer, slipped off her blue latex gloves and placed her hand against the wall. She must've been trying to pick up the energy of the scene from the building. Hopefully she wouldn't get anything useful.

"Looks like I'll be breaking into the lab again," James said.

Luke tore his gaze away from the beautiful detective to look at his friend. "At least you know your way around now. I've got it from here; you can go patrol. Alexis, you can head back too."

James nodded and took off up the alley. Alexis hesitated, her gaze shifting from the scene to Luke. "I'd like to stick around, if that's okay. I really want to help."

Luke furrowed his brow and narrowed his eyes at her. What was she up to? He preferred to be alone so he wouldn't feel the need to hide his feelings for Macey. But getting to know Alexis better was probably a good idea. If his old man really didn't send her, she must've had some other motive for wanting to be involved in the demon issue.

"Why are you taking all this interest in the pack? You thinking of joining?"

As she watched the detectives gather evidence, a look of sadness fell across her face. "I don't know. I like it here. I just figured you could use all the help you could get with your demon problem."

"Have you fought demons before?"

"No. But I'd like to learn." She turned to him and smiled. "If you need another person on the team, I'll volunteer."

"Let me think about it." What would the rest of the team think about working with a rogue? They'd accepted her on the job site, but carpentry wasn't demon hunting. He doubted they'd approve. Rogues didn't care about anything but themselves, but Alexis wasn't like any rogue he'd ever met. As he watched her watching the scene, she seemed to take a genuine interest in what happened. If only he could get inside her head and figure out why she cared so much. "What's your story?"

She sucked in a sharp breath. "I don't have a story. Why?"

"You're holding something back."

Her gaze landed on the detective. "I've told you everything you need to know." She looked at Luke, glanced back at the scene, and stepped away. "Well, it looks like you've got this under control. I'm going to jet."

"Okay..." Before he could say goodbye, she trotted down the street.

"Hey, Mace." Bryce paused before opening the car door.

Macey dropped her bag in the trunk, slammed it shut, and stepped to the passenger side. "Yeah?"

"Listen, I'm sorry about the way I acted in the car earlier."

She gave him a tight grin and slid into her seat.

Bryce got in the car and started the engine. "I don't believe in that stuff, and to hear you talking about it like it's real... It scares me."

Macey scoffed. "Nothing scares you, Bryce. You're a big, bad detective, remember?" She grinned, hoping to ease the tension that filled the car like static electricity.

"Now, hear me out." He gripped the steering wheel so hard his knuckles turned white. "I was thinking about what you said, and… Well, what if you're right? What then?"

She tugged on her bottom lip as Bryce kneaded the steering wheel like dough. "I don't know," she said. "But I did get a little more info out of the victim this time. She described the animal as a wolf."

"A wolf? Like the one you saw in the woods?"

"The coloring was different, but yeah. I think there might be a pack of wolves attacking people."

Bryce raised an eyebrow at her. "But—"

"I haven't figured out what they have to do with the case, but it's a start. Maybe they can sense the victims' fear, and they're attracted to it. Or maybe all the women have something in common. I don't know, but it's something to look into."

He let out a long breath. "So it's not a monster. Just a wolf. I'll give animal control a call."

As if on cue, Macey's cell phone rang. Another detective on the scene of another assault outside the Quarter. "Looks like our night is just getting started. Head over to the Hilton on Canal."

"Another one?"

When they arrived at the hotel, they took the elevator up to the fifteenth floor. "This doesn't seem right," she said to Bryce. "All the others have been in the alley or on a small street. Our guys don't operate in hotel rooms."

The elevator door slid open, and they stepped into a deserted hallway. A pair of guards stood outside the victim's door. Macey nodded to the men and stepped through the threshold. The basic hotel room held a king-sized bed in the center, a flat screen TV on a table, and a small desk in the corner. The twisted bed sheets lay half-pulled to the floor. Pens, a notepad, and a lamp lay scattered about the room. Obvious signs of a struggle.

The victim sat on a chair near the window. A sketch artist's pencil flew fervently across the page as she described the attacker. Her face was a mask of blankness, her shuddering breaths the only clue to the earthquake that must have been crumbling inside her.

Macey spotted the detective who'd called and motioned for him to talk to her. "What happened here?" she asked.

The man shoved a small notepad into his jacket pocket. "Sexual assault. Victim said she met the guy in a bar. He followed her and forced his way into her room. Did his thing and left."

"Why did you call me? This doesn't sound anything like the other cases."

The detective cut his gaze toward the victim and lowered his voice. "She said the attacker had red eyes."

***

Jimmy peeled the blood-stained T-shirt over his head, used it to wipe the clammy sweat from his face, and hung it on the arm of the futon to dry. His whole body felt raw, like he'd been dragged naked across the asphalt while tied to the back of a truck. He hadn't, of course. But that's what he felt like. Was it from Ross's spirit ripping its way in and out of his body? Or was it because of what Ross had made him do?

The back of his mouth tasted sour like vomit, and his muscles ached from the explosion of excitement he'd just experienced. Did he enjoy it?

A little.

He didn't want to hurt that girl. But Ross was controlling his body, so he couldn't help it. He could feel it, though. And it felt good. Jimmy had never made love to a woman before. He'd wanted to make love to her. When Ross had used Jimmy's body to talk to the girl, it was exciting. He said some clever things and made her laugh. Jimmy could never say such clever things on his own because he was a stupid idiot. But Ross was smart, and he made smart words come out of Jimmy's stupid mouth.

The girl liked Jimmy. Well, she liked Ross inside Jimmy's body, but that was close enough. When it was time to leave, Jimmy was sure the girl was going to say yes to sex. But when Ross made him ask if he could walk her to her hotel room, she said no.

"That's okay," Ross had said in Jimmy's mind. "We're still gonna screw her."

But she had said no, so Jimmy didn't want to do it anymore. Ross made him follow her and push his way into her room. Jimmy was strong on his own, but Ross made him stronger. The girl tried to put up a fight, but Ross made Jimmy smack her in the face. She screamed and stumbled backwards into the room, falling on top of the bed… right where Ross wanted her. She kicked and bit, but Jimmy's body was too strong.

Jimmy squeezed his eyes shut and curled up in a ball on the futon. "Why did you make me do that, Ross? She said no."

A cool breeze snaked up his arm and whispered into his ear, *"Shut up, moron. You liked it. I can hear your thoughts, remember?"*

Tremors shook his body as a deep sob escaped his throat. "I liked the way it felt. I didn't like hurting that girl."

CHAPTER SEVENTEEN

LUKE WAS READY FOR HIS DATE WITH MACEY BY SIX O'CLOCK, but he wasn't picking her up until eight. She had him so wound up, he couldn't stop his leg from bouncing under the kitchen table. He got up and paced the room. He needed a distraction, something to occupy his mind for the next two hours until he saw her again.

Why the hell was he so nervous? He'd gone out with her before; he'd made love to her for Christ's sake. Maybe the nerves were a warning from his subconscious to guard his heart. Nah, it was too late for that. His heart belonged to Macey, even though his old man had made it clear she was off limits. But he couldn't help himself. He had to see her again. He was still holding on to that tiny sliver of hope that things could work out.

He switched on the TV and flipped through the channels to the local evening news. A little doom and gloom would keep his brain busy while he waited. He plopped down on the sofa and rested his feet on the coffee table, but the screen didn't distract him from his thoughts. This was their first real date. The times before had been spontaneous...well, he'd followed her on purpose, but what had happened afterward had been spontaneous. This date had been planned. He'd called her and asked her out, and she'd said yes. And that made it so much more real.

He focused on the television. A journalist stood outside a hotel on Canal Street, her grim expression revealing the seriousness of the story she reported. He turned up the volume.

"…though the circumstances are different in last night's attack, the perpetrator had one thing in common with the others. The victim claimed he had red eyes."

"Shit!" Luke jumped to his feet. Why didn't he know about this one yet? A police composite sketch filled the screen, and he snapped a picture of it with his phone. Either the demons were getting smarter, taking their victims indoors, or this was the human who'd been summoning them. He had to warn the pack.

As he entered the bar, Chase and Stephen stood near the TV, the volume blasting to drown out the music. Another reporter told the same story on a different channel.

"You see this, man?" Chase said. "It's all over the news. Can't believe we missed one."

Stephen crossed his arms, tightening his jaw. "We wouldn't have missed it if I were in charge. Maybe we need to call your daddy, so a *real* alpha can handle this."

Luke glared at his cousin, holding eye contact to exert his dominance. Stephen returned his gaze, challenging him with his stare. Tension thickened between them as Luke took a step forward. The last thing they needed was to fight amongst themselves when they shared a common goal, but an alpha had to take every challenge seriously.

"Don't you have some accounting to do in the back?" Luke said. "I'm sure if you walk away now, I can forget this ever happened."

Fear flashed in Stephen's eyes, his resolve seeming to waver, but he didn't tear his gaze away from Luke's. He fisted his hands at his sides and gritted his teeth.

Luke took another step forward. "Or are we going to have a problem?"

Stephen let out his breath in a slow hiss, his challenging posture deflating. "No. We're good." He dropped his gaze to the floor, ending the confrontation.

Luke turned to Chase. "I'm texting you the police sketch. Send it to everyone on the team. This guy's M.O. is different, and that makes me think it might be the leader."

Chase's phone chimed. "Got it. You headed out for your date?"

"Is it that obvious?"

"Shirt's ironed. No holes in your jeans." He shrugged. "Pretty damn obvious."

Stephen stepped from behind the bar. "You're going out with the cop?"

"Yeah. I am. Got a problem with that?"

"Alphas can't mate with humans."

"I'm well aware of that."

Stephen shook his head and stormed through the door to the office.

Chase grinned. "Seems like he'd be happy if you mated with a human. With you out of the way, he'd be free to run his reign of terror."

Luke sank onto a barstool, a heaviness sinking in his heart. "She's not going to be my mate." And that was the truth, wasn't it? No matter how strongly he cared for Macey, she wasn't a werewolf.

"Then why are you going out with her?"

He traced the wood grain on the bar. "You know...to lead her away from the truth. Keep her from finding out too much."

Chase raised an eyebrow. "Uh huh."

"What am I supposed to do, man? She's incredible. I can't let a girl like her get away." He drummed his fingers on the wood. There had to be something he could do...

Macey freshened up her makeup for the fourth time and sipped a glass of chardonnay. Liquid relaxation pooled in her core and flowed out to her limbs, a welcome relief from the tension she'd carried in her muscles all day. Luke said he'd pick her up at eight, and she'd been a nervous wreck since he'd called. Butterflies flitted in her stomach just thinking about him.

An actual planned date with the man of her dreams. Wait…was he the man of her dreams? He was all she thought about, so he must be.

Thor jumped onto the bathroom counter and mewed for her attention. She stroked his soft brown fur, and his body vibrated with a satisfied purr.

She finished her wine, letting the soothing liquid calm her nerves. Running her fingers through her hair, she tousled the roots to give it volume. Luke had mentioned he liked her hair down. Would he remember saying that? Would he think she was trying too hard? Maybe she should put it up. She'd be more comfortable in her usual bun anyway.

She reached for her brush, and the doorbell rang. *Crap! He's here.* Thor jumped from the counter and darted under her bed. Macey checked her reflection one last time and padded into the living room. "Coming."

She opened the door, and her breath caught at the sight of him. He wore dark jeans and a deep blue shirt that matched his eyes. A crooked grin lit up his face as he offered her a bouquet of lemon-yellow daisies.

"They match your dress."

"Hmm?" She took the flowers and inhaled their sweet fragrance. "Oh, yeah. I guess they do. Thank you. Do you want to come inside?"

He shoved his hands in his pockets and rocked back on his heels. "Actually, we have a dinner reservation at eight-fifteen, so we should get going."

"Okay. Let me put these in some water." She trotted to the kitchen, shoved the bouquet in an empty vase and grabbed her purse. She'd worry about the water later. Right now, the only thing on her mind was the gorgeous hunk on her doorstep.

"Where are we going?" she asked as he opened the truck door for her.

"Captain Boudreaux's, if that's okay with you." He closed the door behind her and got in the driver's seat.

"Sounds wonderful."

They rode in silence up St. Charles, Luke kneading the steering wheel while Macey's leg bounced up and down. She rested her hand on her knee to stop the movement and tried to think of something to say. He'd always been so easy to talk to before, but now he seemed different. Distracted. She tugged on her bottom lip and swallowed the dryness out of her mouth.

"Is everything okay? You're quiet tonight," she said.

He glanced at her and relaxed his grip on the steering wheel. "Yeah. I've got a lot on my mind."

"Do you want to talk about it?"

"Nah." He reached for her hand, and all the tension drained from her body. How could a simple touch have such an effect on her?

"You look beautiful. I love it when you wear your hair down." He slid his hand up the back of her neck, his fingers combing through her hair. Her heart stuttered at the intimacy of his touch, and heat pooled below her navel. He glanced at her with palpable hunger in his eyes before returning his hand to the steering wheel. It was a good thing he hadn't come inside when she'd asked. They probably wouldn't have made it out of the house.

When they arrived at the restaurant, a line of people stretched out the door and around the corner of the Victorian style structure. Lavender and white striped awnings hung above the windows, matching the purple siding and white trim of the building.

"Looks like we'll be waiting a while," Macey said.

Luke grinned. "No worries. They know me here." He led her past the line of hungry patrons and ushered her through the door.

"Local celebrity?"

"Nah. I did the remodel after the last hurricane. They got eight feet of water inside. Almost tore the place down, but my team was able to restore it. The manager's a friend of mine."

As they entered the dining room, Macey's breath caught. Vaulted ceilings revealed exposed wood beams stained dark chocolate brown. Crystal chandeliers hung from above, filling the room with pale, warm light. Framed black-and-white photos of famous New Orleans buildings adorned an exposed brick wall, obviously original to the nineteenth-century structure. How many stories could this old building tell? And they'd almost torn it down.

"You did all this? It's beautiful." She picked up a menu.

"Me and a crew of thirty men." He scanned the room, eyes gleaming. "I'm glad we were able to restore it. Our city's so rich in history. It breaks my heart when we have to bulldoze a building."

She grinned at him.

"What?"

"Nothing. It's…you have a soft side. Artistic. I wasn't expecting it." She folded her menu on the table and took a sip of water.

"Well, you're a lot different than I expected too."

She raised an eyebrow and rested her hands on the table. "And how did you expect me to be?" She braced herself for his answer, unsure if she really wanted to know.

"Cocky. All business. You know the type." He reached for her hands across the table. "But you're not like that at all."

Electricity tingled up her arms. Her heart fluttered, and she leaned in, the urge to close the distance between them overwhelming. "What am I like then?"

He leaned in to match her posture and held her with a piercing gaze. "Kind. Caring. Beautiful. Amazing…in the bedroom and out."

It took every ounce of control she could muster to keep herself from climbing over the table and throwing herself into his arms. Simply touching him sent her body into overdrive. She leaned back and fanned herself with the menu. "Is it hot in here?"

A sly smile curved his lips. "No, I think it's just you."

The rest of their dinner went by in a blur. She was so caught up in this incredible man, she'd forgotten what she ordered by the time the food arrived. The line still stretched out the door as they left the restaurant, and they strolled hand-in-hand down Frenchman Street.

They stopped in front of a squat brown building with a red door. A saxophone's sad wail drifted to the street from somewhere inside. Live music was abundant in this part of town, tucked away from the flashy neon lights and cover music of Bourbon Street. A simple wooden sign above the door advertised the name of the establishment: Louie's. This was the street locals went to for live music.

None of those annoying hawkers trying to lure people into bars with the promise of cheap, watered down drinks and scantily-clad women.

"Do you like Blues? Or Jazz?" Luke asked.

"Love it."

"Good." He opened the door and led her inside.

A dozen people filled the chairs of the small room. Strings of pale white lights hung from low ceilings, giving the establishment a cozy feel. A sax, a bass, and a baby grand piano sat upon a tiny stage, their players belting out a soulful rendition of "Do You Know What It Means To Miss New Orleans." Luke led her to an empty table near the stage and wrapped his arm around her shoulders. He absently traced his fingers along her skin as he hummed along to the tune.

The band finished the number and announced a short break as a rough-looking man approached Luke. His jeans were torn and paint-stained, his shirt yellowing with sweat. His unkempt hair was greasy, and anger filled his eyes. He didn't speak, but his hands clenched into fists at his sides as he stared at Luke.

Luke sighed. "Will you excuse me for a minute, Macey?"

"Sure." She watched the exchange, though she couldn't hear what they said. The man's sharp gestures and accusing posture would have intimidated most people. Luke kept his cool, though she could tell he was agitated. He said something that appeared to appease the man, gave him a tight smile, and returned to the table.

"Sorry about that. Work drama." He settled in next to her and took her hand.

"Everything okay?"

"It will be. So, do you—"

The piano player clapped Luke on the shoulder. "Luke, my man. Long time, no see."

"Hey, Benny." He stood and shook the man's hand. Benny was a rotund character with leathery skin and canyons etched into his forehead. His bright brown eyes crinkled when he smiled.

"My old bones need a longer rest, but these guys ain't gonna let me have it." He pointed a thumb at the other musicians on stage. "Think you could take over the keys for a song or two to give my joints a break?" He splayed his gnarled fingers, cracked his knuckles, and winked at Macey.

Luke grinned. "Anything for you, Uncle Ben."

Macey arched an eyebrow. "You play?"

"A little."

Was there anything this man couldn't do? Luke slid onto the bench behind the piano, and Benny took the microphone, crooning "Sitting on the Dock of the Bay" while Luke's fingers flew across the keys like a professional.

Macey had to remind herself to breathe. Musicians had always made her heart swoon. There was something undeniably sexy about a man who could express his emotions through song. If she wasn't careful, she'd end up falling in love with this one.

He finished the song and took his seat next to her, resting his hand on her knee. His palm warmed her skin, and she leaned into his side. "You're good."

He chuckled. "My mom wanted to make sure I was a well-rounded person."

"Good for her."

His thumb tapped a rhythm on her leg. "Hey, you want to get out of here? Go have a cup of coffee someplace quiet?"

"I've got coffee at my place, and it's quiet. Want to go there?"

He looked at her, his smoldering gaze traveling from her eyes to her lips, down her body, and up again. "Yeah. I do."

"Here we are." Her voice cracked as she spoke, and she bit her bottom lip. Her cheeks flushed pink as she blinked those emerald eyes and opened the front door. "Come on in. So, this is my living room, obviously." She was cute when she was nervous. She stared at him, apparently waiting for a response, so he had to tear his gaze away from her little yellow sundress to survey the room.

Wood floors. White sofa. Teal pillows. "It's nice." He stepped toward her, sliding his arm around her waist. "But I'd rather look at you."

He lowered his head to kiss her, but a brown cat jumped onto the sofa and hissed. With its back arched and ears flat, the feline screeched a challenging meow.

Luke straightened his spine and eyed the furry creature. "You have a cat."

"Sorry. I don't know what's gotten into him. He's been acting weird lately. Shoo, Thor. Get down." She waved her arms at the cat, and it darted under the sofa.

He chuckled. "God of thunder, huh?"

"He may be small, but he's mighty."

The cat glared at him from under the couch. Luke sighed. Werewolves had a distinct animal scent. Though it was imperceptible to humans, other animals recognized it immediately. The cat didn't approve. "I'm more of a dog person myself."

"So am I, but don't tell Thor that." She bent down to look at the feline. "Cats are easier to take care of. Since I work so much, I needed a pet that didn't mind being alone."

"It's okay. I don't mind cats." He knelt and rested his forearms on the floor, palms flat in a submissive gesture. If his pack could see him bowing down to a cat, they'd never let him live it down. But he needed to win over the pet if he wanted to keep the woman.

"Come on, Thor. I won't hurt you."

The cat inched forward.

"That's a good kitty."

Thor slinked from under the couch and eyed him warily.

Luke blew out a breath and rolled over on his back, allowing the cat to jump onto his chest. *This is so demeaning.* Thor stared at him triumphantly and licked his paws.

"See? We're buddies now, right, Thor?" He scooped the cat into his arms and stood, scratching its ears.

"Well, how about that?" Macey took Thor from his grasp and put him on the floor. "Do you want me to make some coffee?"

He stepped toward her and traced his fingers along her jawline, raising her chin. Leaning in, he hovered his lips over hers, letting the anticipation build, fueling the fire in his heart. Heat radiated from her skin, awakening a primal desire deep inside him. He crushed his mouth to hers.

She moaned, wrapping her arms around his waist, molding her body to his. He wanted her. He wanted her more than he'd wanted anything his entire life, and she was his for the taking. She tugged at his shirt, leaving trails of fire on his skin as she slid it over his head. Desire pooled in her eyes as she ran her hands over his body and licked her lips. Her dress strap slipped off her shoulder, and he groaned, trailing kisses up and down her neck. She reached behind her back and tugged down her zipper.

His phone rang, but he ignored it, focusing instead on her sensuous curves as her little yellow sundress dropped to the floor. He glided his hands along her body and gripped her hips, pulling her against him.

His phone rang again. He groaned and fished it from his pocket to find Chase's name lighting up the screen. Cupping Macey's cheek in his hand, he pressed a tender kiss to her lips. "Hold that thought. This will only take a minute."

He held the phone to his ear. "This had better be important."

"We've got a problem." Chase's voice sounded grim. "Danny called an emergency meeting. There's a crowd at the bar."

"What?" He stepped away from Macey. "He doesn't have the authority."

"He saw you with the detective tonight. Rumors are flying that you're choosing a human over the pack. People are scared."

Damn it. He thought he'd appeased his pack member at the jazz club when he'd assured him he was trying to lead Macey astray. Apparently things were worse than he'd thought. "I'll be there in ten. Can you hold down the fort 'til then?"

"I'll do my best."

Macey picked up her dress. "Where are you going?"

The disappointment in her eyes tugged at his heart, and he wanted nothing more than to finish what they'd started. To take her to bed and make love to her all night long.

But as much as he wanted to be with this woman right now… forever…he couldn't. His pack was scared. Of the demons and of the possibility that Stephen could become alpha if Luke didn't get his act together. James wasn't the only one who'd threatened to go rogue if Luke let Stephen lead, and now it seemed the sentiment was spreading.

He was letting his heart get in the way of his duty, and it was about to tear his pack apart.

"It's a work emergency." He pulled his shirt over his head.

"At eleven o'clock at night?"

"I'm sorry." He kissed her on the cheek and opened the front door. "There are some things I need to take care of. I might be busy for a few days, but I promise I'll call you as soon as I can."

She furrowed her brow. "I don't understand."

What the hell was he doing? He had to make a choice between the woman he loved and his pack, and there was no right answer. He wanted both. He *needed* both. "I'll call you in a few days. I'm sorry."

CHAPTER EIGHTEEN

Jimmy held the ceremonial kitchen knife in his sweaty right hand and tried to keep it from trembling. The cut always hurt more when his hands shook. He wasn't scared. Ross had already made him summon so many demons, he was used to the pain. Jimmy's hands were shaking because he was mad.

He glared at the boy lying on his futon. That was Jimmy's futon, and the boy had stolen it. His back ached from sleeping on the floor, and he had bruises on his hips from where the bones dug into the hard linoleum. His brother said the boy was more useful. Smarter. Jimmy was a stupid idiot, and stupid idiots slept on the floor.

"What are you waiting for, dimwit? Do I have to possess you and summon the demon myself?" Ross's voice came from everywhere and nowhere all at once.

"No, please. I'll do it." He pressed the blade against his palm, only wincing a little as a fresh ribbon of blood pooled in his hand. He held it over the altar, counting as three drops fell into the ceremonial bowl. It looked like a cereal bowl to Jimmy, but he'd learned not to argue with his brother.

He whispered the special chant Ross had made him memorize. It took him two weeks to learn the chant because he was stupid and didn't know how to read. He'd learned a little before Momma died, but once she was gone, he didn't go to school anymore. He knew the chant now though, and he whispered it fast so he could move away. This was the scary part.

He grabbed a towel to stop the bleeding and clambered into the corner as a big mass of billowing black smoke swirled out of the bowl. All the air seemed to be sucked out of the room, ripped from his lungs like he was sitting inside a vacuum. The smoke spread out, hovering below the ceiling like thick carpet before tumbling back toward the bowl. A demon with bright red eyes and shiny black skin crouched on the altar and stared at Jimmy like it wanted to eat him. Jimmy's whole body shook, and his heart pounded like it was going to explode out of his chest. He *really* didn't want to get eaten. Sometimes the demons looked like mean people, with human colored skin. This one was slick like a snake, and twice as scary.

Ross said his own chant in a language Jimmy didn't understand, and the demon shot out the door. Jimmy whimpered.

"Why are you scared, idiot? I told you I won't let them hurt you. Only a pure human can raise a demon. You're special, brother."

Special? Jimmy was special? He must be if Ross said he was. His mouth curled into a smile, so he covered it with his hand.

"It's okay to smile. You did good. Now, get over there and raise another one."

"Another one? But I'm tired, Ross. Calling demons makes my tummy hurt, and it gives me a headache. Can't that be enough for today?"

A blow to his head knocked him to the ground. Jimmy clutched his eye, trying to hold it in because it felt like it was going to pop right out of his head. He was stupid. He deserved to be hit.

"As long as those damn wolves keep killing my demons, you'll keep raising more. And that bitch detective. I saw your face all over the evening news yesterday, and I know she was behind that. We've gotta take her out."

"Isn't she dating that werewolf? Won't they all be protecting her?" Jimmy braced himself for another strike, but it didn't come.

"You're right. You may not be as stupid as I thought you were."

Jimmy's mouth tried to pull into another smile, but he fought it this time. He could tell by the tone of his brother's voice that he wasn't going to like what Ross said next.

"I think it's time for us to pay Detective Carpenter a visit. But, first, we're gonna need a lot more demons."

CHAPTER NINETEEN

MACEY AND ROBERTA SAT IN A SWING ON HER MOM'S FRONT porch, sipping tea and trying to build Macey's powers. She took a deep breath and focused on the energy trapped inside an antique clock.

"It was in a Creole plantation. A young slave girl used to dust it every day, but she knocked it off the shelf once." Macey read the energy, relaying the melancholy story of the artifact to her teacher.

Roberta nodded encouragingly. "That's good. Now, I want you to see if you can release the energy."

"What do you mean?"

"When you touch the clock, you see a story. You understand why the item makes you feel a certain way. For most people, all they get is the feeling. This clock brings sadness into the home, but most don't know why. If you can release the energy into the universe, you'll be cleansing the item so someone else can enjoy its beauty without feeling the sadness that comes along with it."

Macey looked at the clock, turning it over in her hands. "You can do that?"

"I can, yes. And I think you can too, if you try. Find the energy inside the clock, and coax it out. Set it free."

Macey turned her focus to the clock and the energy that swirled inside it. She imagined opening the clock and warm, white light flowing through it, whisking the negativity away. An electric pulse radiated through her hands as the slave girl, and the horrible beatings she'd endured, broke free from the artifact and floated away. Then, nothing. She rested her hand on the clock, searching for a trace of the energy, for the story, but it was gone. "That's it? It's that easy?"

Roberta smiled. "For you, it seems it is."

"Huh." If she'd known using her ability could be that simple, she'd have sought out help a long time ago. "Thanks." She tugged on her bottom lip and stared at the clock. If only everything were this easy. "Have you seen Luke around lately?"

"I can't say that I have. Is there a problem?"

"He had to leave abruptly on our last date, and I haven't heard from him in a few days. He said he had a work emergency, but…"

Roberta inhaled deeply, and an unreadable expression fell across her features. "I'm sure there's nothing to worry about, child. He's probably behind on a deadline; give him time."

"Yeah." That's probably all it was. How many times had she pulled twenty-hour shifts when she'd been working on an important case? He probably worked all day, and then crashed from exhaustion as soon as he got home. It made sense. Still…he could've at least sent her a text by now.

"You're right." She had another question that had been burning in her mind. "I've been meaning to ask…Why weren't you afraid of that wolf the other day? Do you have some sort of animal power too?" Or were werewolves really a possibility? At this point, the idea made as much sense as any other theory she'd heard about the case.

She laughed. "I suppose you could say that. The wolves are our friends." She clamped her mouth shut, pressing her lips into a tight smile.

"Okay." Roberta was a mysterious woman, for sure.

"Same time tomorrow, then?" The old woman heaved herself from the swing and straightened her skirt.

"Sounds good."

Macey handed Roberta the clock and said goodbye. Maybe her

power could be of some use after all. Maybe not on the case, but at least it was good for something. The attackers had been quiet for several days, but it was only a matter of time before he—they—it—whatever it was struck again. The spirit that had tormented her was quiet too, and she wondered again if the two were related.

She wondered a lot lately. Thought about the case incessantly. Anything to keep her mind occupied, her thoughts away from Luke and the strange way he'd left.

"Macey, dear." Jenny stepped onto the porch and sat next to her daughter. "It's not that I don't love you being here, hon. But…don't you think Thor is getting lonely? You've slept here after work three days in a row."

She waved her hand dismissively and picked up her tea. "He's a cat, Mom. I stop by the house every day to make sure he's okay." *Please don't ask me about Luke.* "I better get ready for work."

She hopped off the swing and shuffled inside.

Her mom followed. "It's about that boy, isn't it? Did he break up with you?"

She groaned. "He's not a boy; he's a grown man, and he didn't break up with me. He's been busy."

"Have you tried calling him?"

"No, and I'm not going to. If he wants to see me again, he'll call me." And if he didn't, that was fine too. That's what she'd keep telling herself, anyway. It was her own fault for letting him in. For getting close. She'd ignored all the warnings her logical mind had thrown at her, and look where it had landed her. Missing him. She could hold on to the hope that he'd call for a few more days, but then what? Admit that yet another person she cared about had abandoned her? That she wasn't worthy of love?

Her mom rubbed her hand on Macey's back. "Men are complicated creatures. I won't even pretend to understand them. But there are other fish in the sea, right? Someone better will come along."

"I don't want another fish. I want Luke."

Luke sulked into O'Malley's and slid onto a barstool. He needed to get his shit together. The demon activity had been quiet the past few days, so there wasn't much to distract him from his thoughts. Every time he closed his eyes, he saw Macey's face. He'd purposely spent the last three days away from her to appease his pack. They needed the reassurance that he wouldn't let them down...that he *would* be the next alpha...but, damn it, why did he have to hurt Macey in the process?

His fingers itched with the desire to dial her number every time he looked at his phone. But as soon as he heard her melodic voice, he'd have to see her again. He wouldn't be able to help himself. What the hell was he going to do?

Chase slid him a beer, and Luke gulped it down. His mom would lecture him about daytime drinking, but he'd say it was her fault for raising him in a bar. Besides, it was the only thing that dulled the pain in his heart. His folks would be home in a few days, and the pressure to find a mate would pick up again. His dad's retirement would happen on the next full moon, but did it have to be at the cost of Luke's happiness?

"Slow day at the office?" Chase asked.

"You could say that." He should've been on site, helping his team, but he couldn't focus on anything but figuring out a way to make Macey his mate.

"What did you decide to do about your detective?"

Luke laid his palms flat on the bar and stared at his fingers. Only days ago, those fingers had caressed her supple body, twisted in her silky hair. They tingled with the memories. "I'm thinking about petitioning the council." They probably had more knowledge on the issue of weres mating with other magical beings. But a no from the council would be a conclusive no, and he wasn't sure he could handle something so final. At the moment, he at least had a shred of hope that his dad would change his mind.

Chase arched an eyebrow. "You sure you want to go over your old man's head? The pack bond's already volatile."

He closed his eyes and let out a low growl. "You're right. Even if they approved her as my mate, I'd lose the pack's trust if I disobeyed the alpha. I'll either make him change his mind or I'll have to break it off with her." His chest ached at the thought.

"I'm sorry, man."

"My duty to the pack comes first."

Stephen stepped through the office door and strutted to the bar. "It's about time you acted like an alpha. I was starting to think you *wanted* to be second the rest of your life."

Luke squeezed his hands into fists. "Don't start with me."

"Seriously, though, cuz. I'm sorry you couldn't make it work with your human. It would've been nice to have a cop on our side."

"What cop?" Alexis asked as she entered the bar, followed by a couple of Luke's employees. "What are you talking about?"

Damn it. Who else was going to eavesdrop on this conversation? He should've kept his mouth shut. Now the whole pack was in his personal business. Alexis was out of line questioning her superior like that. Being a rogue was no excuse for not following pack rules. The two workers sat at a table in the back, but Alexis lingered by the bar, waiting for an answer. When he didn't give her one, she glared at him before shifting her gaze to his cousin. What the hell was her problem?

Stephen wiggled his eyebrows and grinned. "Our soon-to-be alpha is going to stop screwing the detective." He leaned on the bar, resting his chin on his hand to feign interest. "How are we ever going to keep her off our trail now?"

A low growl resonated from Luke's chest, warning his cousin to back off. He didn't need this kind of disrespect. Especially in front of a rogue.

"You've really been screwing Macey?" Alexis sounded incredulous.

Luke turned to face her. "How I run my pack is not your concern, rogue."

She bristled. "It is when you're hurting innocent people. You can't use a woman, lead her on like that, to serve your *pack's* purpose." She spat the word pack in disgust. "Macey has feelings. She's not some pawn in your demon hunting game."

Luke rose to his feet, straightening to his full height. "You're a rogue. Why do you care so much about what happens in *my pack?*"

"I don't care about your pack. I care about my *sister.*" Her eyes flashed like she'd said more than she intended, but she set her jaw and gave him a challenging look.

"You…" He stammered, squeezing his eyes shut, clutching the edge of the bar to steady himself. His chest tightened, and he had to remind himself to breathe. Did he hear her right? "Macey is your sister?" His voice came out as a raspy whisper.

Alexis raised her chin. "Yes, she is."

Luke turned to Chase, who raised his eyebrows. If Macey was Alexis's sister, that meant she was…

"She's your *biological* sister? You have the same parents? The same blood?"

She crossed her arms. "That's generally what 'sister' means."

"Looks like we finally got our man on the inside," Stephen grumbled under his breath.

"Goddammit!" Luke pointed a finger at Alexis. "Stay here until I get back. I'm not done with you."

He stormed out of the bar and stopped on the sidewalk, resting his hand against the wall, heaving heavy breaths as his eyes adjusted to the blinding sunlight.

Macey was a werewolf.

Why hadn't he made the connection before? She'd told him she had an older sister. Macey had powers like other second-born weres. Hell, he'd even detected a hint of werewolf in her energy the first time he'd touched her, but he'd dismissed it—his ego insisting no werewolf could live in the Quarter without his knowledge. How could he have been so stupid? It made so much sense when he pieced it all together. Alexis was the sister who'd abandoned her in foster care.

He had to talk to Macey. He could make things right.

He jogged up St. Philip Street and made a left on Burgundy. He'd knock on her door and tell her everything. They *could* be together. Elation filled his heart, inflating his chest with joy. It was two in the afternoon. Would Macey be up? He'd wake her if she wasn't. This was too important to wait.

He lifted his face to the cloudless sky, letting the sunlight warm his skin as he trotted along the sidewalk. The answer to all his problems had come to him in the form of a cumbersome rogue. Who would've thought?

He chuckled as he rounded the corner, but the bookcase he plowed into cut his laugh short. He grunted as his knee made contact with the edge of the shelf, shooting stinging pain down his shin, and he knelt to pick up the second-hand novels he'd scattered on the sidewalk. The store clerk stepped outside, and he smiled at her as he returned the last book to the case and continued on his way. Nothing would spoil his mood today.

He could finally fulfill his duty as alpha *and* spend the rest of his life with his fate-bound mate.

But would Macey still want him after he'd blown her off? His run slowed to a walk. Would she be willing to open her heart to him after the way he'd acted? He had to find out. He'd beg if he had to.

He bounded up her front steps and pounded on the door. "Macey? Macey, it's Luke. Open up please." The seconds ticked by into an eternity as he waited for her to answer. He knocked again. *Please be home.* He held his breath as the lock rattled and the door cracked open.

Macey's face appeared between the door and the jamb. "Luke?"

"I need to talk to you. Can I come in? Please?"

She studied him for a moment, as if trying to decide whether or not she wanted to talk. Finally, she sighed and opened the door. "Come on."

The cool air of her living room made him shiver. Or was it his excitement? He wasn't sure. He closed the door behind him, blocking out the summer heat, and stared at her, another kind of heat pooling in his core. She was barefoot, wearing a silky green robe, and she'd piled her hair on top of her head in a messy twist. A few silky strands hung down around her face, framing her sparkling eyes. He'd always fantasized about what she'd look like if he woke up next to her. She was more stunning than he'd imagined.

"Well?" She picked up a coffee mug and settled onto the sofa, curling one leg underneath her.

"I'm sorry." He sat on the edge of the couch and turned his body to face her. "The way I acted was inexcusable, and I hope you can find it in your heart to forgive me."

She gazed into her mug and inhaled deeply. "Thank you for the apology. Is that all you needed?" She set her cup down and started to get up.

He reached for her arm. "That's not all."

She sat down and pulled her arm from his grasp. Thor jumped into her lap, and she held him close, stroking his fur.

"See, the thing is…oh, Macey, there's so much I need to tell you. I don't know where to start." He raked his hand through his hair, desperately trying to gather his thoughts.

She stared at her cat. "You can start with explaining why you ran off. One minute things were going great, and then you bolted." She lifted her gaze to meet his, and the pain in her eyes pierced his heart. "What happened?"

"It really was an emergency, but it wasn't for work. It was…" He let out his breath in a huff. How could he make this right? "Let me start this way. Your power? Your ability to read objects and sense spirits is real."

She squinted her eyes. "I know. Roberta has been helping me develop it."

"Roberta. Yes. She has powers, too, but they're different. So magic is real."

"What are you getting at?" She put the cat on the floor and crossed her arms.

"So, if you have powers, and Roberta has different powers…then other people could have even more different powers. Like me."

She raised an eyebrow. "You have powers?"

"Kind of. Yes."

"And what does that have to do with you running out on me?"

"It's complicated."

"And why haven't you called? Or at least texted?" She flung her arms about, irritated. "I was starting to think I'd never hear from you again."

He folded his hands in his lap and swallowed. There was no easy way to say it. "You've seen a wolf in the woods twice now, haven't you?

A light-brown one? It knocked you out from under a falling tree branch."

She gaped at him. "How did you know that?"

He tapped his fist against his chest. "That wolf was me. I'm a werewolf."

She stared at him, blinking. He waited for her to respond, but she just narrowed her eyes and stared.

"I know it sounds crazy, but it's true, Macey. That's why I ran off that night. The emergency had to do with the pack, and I didn't think I could tell you about it, but I was wrong. I don't want to keep secrets from you. I want you to know everything." He took her hands in his, and she didn't pull away. "I want to be with you, Macey. If you'll have me."

She opened her mouth to speak but snapped it shut again. Her gaze fell to their entwined hands and rose to meet his. "You're a werewolf? That's a real thing?"

"Yeah."

She let out a cynical laugh and shook her head. "So, I'm not going crazy then?"

"No, you're not. I'll prove it to you. Wait here." Heart thudding in his chest, he paced to the next room and shifted. Seeing his wolf form would be shocking enough. He'd save letting her watch the transformation for another time. Slowly, he padded into the living room, lowered his head submissively, and approached her.

"Oh, my God!" She folded both legs onto the couch and balled herself up in the corner. He crept toward her and rested his chin on the cushion, trying his best to look harmless. He whimpered, begging her to relax. If she could accept this part of him—all of him—they could spend the rest of their lives together. His stomach fluttered at the thought of spending forever with Macey.

Slowly, her muscles began to unwind; her eyes held an incredulous expression. "Luke? Is that really you?" She uncurled herself and tentatively reached a hand toward his head. "Can you talk?"

He stared at her. He could understand everything she said, but a wolf's mouth couldn't form human words.

"I guess not." She rested her hand on top of his head and stroked his fur. "You're so soft." Tilting her head, she studied him. Slowly, all traces of fear drained from her eyes, and she smiled. "I'm not crazy. This is…amazing."

He hopped onto the couch and licked her face.

She laughed. "Okay, enough of that, mister." She stroked a hand down his shoulder and shook her head. "You're really a werewolf. No wonder Roberta wasn't afraid of you. She knew."

The knot in his chest released, and he jumped down and trotted out of the room to shift back to human form. She was already taking things much better than he'd expected.

She giggled as he stepped back into the room. "So when those women claimed a big animal saved them from the attackers…that was you?"

"Well, me and my team."

"There's more of you? More werewolves?" She giggled again, covering her mouth with her hand. "It feels so weird saying that."

He smiled. "There's a whole pack in New Orleans. About two hundred of us."

"Two *hundred*?" She tugged her bottom lip. "But, the rapist. Who?"

"Demons."

Her mouth fell open. "Demons?"

He sank onto the sofa next to her. Closer this time, but still not close enough. "Yeah. Someone has been summoning them. We're working on finding the bastard and putting a stop to all this."

He could practically see the gears turning in her head as she shook it, narrowing her eyes, trying to understand. "But how come no one knows about you? How do you keep two hundred people hidden?"

"We're not hidden. We're regular people, who happen to have some special abilities. We try to keep it a secret." Silence stretched between them like an infinite sea. What thoughts were tumbling through her mind? He could only imagine the emotions she must have been enduring, but relief seemed to be somewhere at the top of the list. He wanted to scoop her into his arms and tell her everything would be fine now. To wrap her in comfort and reassurance. But she needed time to process, and he could give her that too.

Finally, she spoke. "And that's why you freaked out on me? Because you're a werewolf, and you thought I couldn't handle it?"

He knelt on the floor in front of her and grasped her hands. "I'm so sorry, Macey. Can you find it in your heart to give me another chance?"

She searched his eyes, and his chest tightened as he prayed she'd find what she needed. Tugging him onto the sofa, she held his face in her hands. A smile spread across her own, reaching all the way to her eyes. "I think I can."

He kissed her. Deep and slow. Passionate heat built in his chest, its flames licking out to set his body on fire. She'd taken him back, and he would never lose her again.

"Just promise me one thing," she said as she snaked her arms around the back of his neck. "No more secrets, okay?"

He swallowed. "Well, there is one more thing you need to know."

She pulled back, eyeing him warily. "What's that?"

"It'll be easier to explain it at the bar. That's our base. Can you go there with me?"

She hesitated, folding her hands in her lap. "All right. Let me get dressed."

A thousand emotions danced through Macey's heart as they approached O'Malley's Pub, but relief topped them all. Relief that Luke still wanted her. That she wasn't going crazy. The case was solvable now that she had some answers. It was all starting to make sense. She had hundreds of questions to ask him, but for now, she relished the elation of holding his hand.

"There's a hierarchy in the pack, a lot like regular wolves. We have an alpha who's in charge, and everyone answers to him."

"So he's like a king?" They turned right on St. Philip and stepped around a young man playing his guitar on the sidewalk. She dropped some change into his instrument case and wrapped her arm around Luke's bicep.

"Not really a king. More like a boss. The president of the

company. But the alpha is determined by bloodline, so I guess king works too. All alphas have to be descendants of the first family."

"Okay." She shook her head. It was hard to believe this was all real, but she'd seen it with her own eyes. What would her partner think now?

"When the alpha dies or retires, if his son is a full werewolf, he takes over. Otherwise, the oldest first family male steps in."

"Full? You can be half a werewolf?"

He smiled and kissed the top of her head. "Only the firstborn child of a werewolf couple can actually shift. The younger siblings are born with special abilities—my sister has premonitions—but they can't turn into wolves."

"Interesting. And what would happen if a werewolf and a human had a baby together? Would the baby be a werewolf? Or half a were-wolf?" She bit her lip. What was she thinking asking a loaded question like that? They'd just solidified their relationship, and she was already asking about their babies?

"There's a fifty-fifty chance the children will be weres. Mating with humans dilutes the bloodlines." He looked at her with an expression she didn't understand. Regret, maybe? If he married her, would he be shunned for not producing werewolf offspring?

They stopped outside the pub door, and he turned to face her. "That's the reason I ran off that night. Some weres do mate with humans, but the son of the alpha can't." He pinned her with an intense gaze, searching her eyes for understanding.

A heaviness settled in her core as the realization dawned on her. "You're the son...of the alpha?"

"Yeah."

She froze, a wave of nausea rolling through her stomach. Was all this for nothing? The revelation of his secret, her acceptance of his supernatural existence...and she couldn't be with him because he was werewolf royalty? "But I'm human, Luke."

He tucked a strand of hair behind her ear and gently kissed her cheek. His mouth lingered by her ear, his warm breath tickling her skin. "You're a werewolf, Macey."

She shook her head. "No."

"Yes. Your abilities? The way you can read energy? It's because you're a were."

She crossed her arms over her tightening chest. "I think I would know if I turned into a wolf."

He raised his eyebrows. "Only the first-born child can shift."

She covered her mouth. "My sister." Her head spun. She leaned into Luke for support, trying to understand what he was telling her. "But she ran away. How could she—? How did you—?"

He wrapped his arm around her shoulders and led her into the pub. "She's here, Macey. Alexis is here."

As Macey's gaze landed on the woman at the bar, the entire room became a vacuum, sucking the air from her lungs. She fisted her hands at her sides, using the burn of her nails biting into her palms to keep herself steady. Thoughts raced through her mind, turning her into a whirlwind of emotions…none of them pleasant.

She wasn't the gangly teenager Macey remembered, but the woman at the bar was definitely her sister. She laughed at something the bartender had said, but as soon as their eyes met, Alexis's face went slack with shock. She stumbled to her feet and pressed her back against the bar, gripping with her hands as if she needed to steady herself. "Macey."

Macey hadn't seen her sister in twenty years. What was she supposed to say? She rubbed the back of her neck and focused on the sensation of Luke's hand resting on her back, grounding her.

Alexis looked from Macey to Luke and back again. "Macey, I was going to find you—"

"Don't, Alexis. Just…don't." All the resentment she'd felt toward her sister bubbled to the surface, tainting her words with venom. She counted backward from ten, but this was an ancient anger that couldn't be quelled with tricks. "After all these years…you show up in *my* city, and you don't even have the guts to talk to me? You must have known I was here."

Alexis took a step toward her. "I did. That's why I came."

"Shut up. You don't get to talk to me." She couldn't deal with this. Not now. "I'm going home."

"Wait, Macey." Luke grasped her arm, but she yanked it away.

"I want to go home."

He followed her out the door as she stomped into the street. She fumed with anger. Her hands balled into fists, nails cutting into her skin again. *Focus on the physical pain. It hurts less than the betrayal.* She struggled to breathe. What did all this mean? Her sister was here, in New Orleans, and she was a werewolf. She'd only just found out werewolves existed, and now she was related to one?

Luke approached her tentatively. "Can I walk with you?"

She sucked in a deep, shaky breath and blew it out hard. "Yeah." She shook her head. "I…why didn't you warn me? I wasn't prepared for a shock like that."

He laced his fingers through hers and gave her a sheepish look. "I'm sorry. I thought it would be a good surprise to see her. I screwed up again, didn't I?"

"Yeah, you did." His touch calmed her. His intentions had been in the right place; she couldn't be mad at him. "But…it's okay. I need some time to process all this. I've got so many thoughts and emotions swirling around inside me, and I don't know how to sort it all out."

"Do you want me to come over? We can talk about it. I'll answer as many questions for you as I can."

She chewed her bottom lip, contemplating his offer. "Okay."

They walked three blocks to her house, and Thor greeted them at the door. He purred and wound his way through their legs, stopping to rub his head against Luke's calf.

"Looks like you won him over," she said.

Luke scratched the cat behind the ears. "Yeah, don't tell anybody how I gained his trust. I'm about to be alpha. I can't go around submitting to cats."

"It's weird he was never afraid of me."

"Why is that weird?"

"I'm assuming he didn't like you at first because he could sense you're a werewolf, right?"

"Sure. He's got animal instincts. He could smell the wolf inside me."

"So, why couldn't he smell the one in me?"

An amused grin curved his lips. "There is no wolf inside you. You're all woman."

She let out her breath in a huff. "I don't understand."

"You have the werewolf gene, but since you're second born, it's dormant. You're a carrier, but you don't have any canine traits yourself."

"So I'll never turn into a wolf?"

He shook his head.

That's a relief, but… "Why do I have a bloodhound's sense of smell?"

He shrugged. "Lucky, I guess. Like any other were, your blood is sacred. It's where your magic lives, and it shouldn't be taken lightly."

"Sacred?" A sinking feeling formed in her stomach. "I've donated blood before. Did I spread my magic? Or could I have hurt someone?"

His eyebrows scrunched together as he considered her questions. "I don't think so. Like I said, your werewolf gene is dormant; it shouldn't be a problem. The receiver's own white blood cells would have been able to destroy the foreign substance, so I wouldn't worry about it. I hope you won't donate again, though. Our laws forbid it."

Jeez. Special werewolf laws? She shook her head and motioned for him to sit on the sofa. "You've got a lot of explaining to do. Want a beer?"

"Yeah."

She popped the tops on two Blue Moons and tossed the lids in the trash. They landed on the wilted, brown flowers he'd given her on their date, so she pushed them farther down in the bin and laid a napkin over them. This was a fresh start. She didn't need a reminder of the trouble they'd been through.

He grinned as she sat next to him and offered him the brew. "I thought Abita was your favorite."

"You changed my mind." She held up her bottle. "Here's to starting over. Truthfully this time." They clinked the glass necks together and took a long drink. The frosty bubbles soothed the tightness in her throat and warmed her from the inside out.

Luke took her hand. "I will tell you everything you want to know."

They talked for hours, Macey listening intently as he explained the origin of the New Orleans werewolves and the way the pack worked. The politics confused her, but she tried to grasp the concepts. She must have had a glazed look in her eyes because he stopped and smiled at her, cupping her cheek in his hand.

"This must sound so strange to you. You're taking it like a champ."

"Really? Maybe once the shock wears off, I'm going to have a heart attack." She put her hand on his, leaning her face into his palm. The tingling energy that used to frighten her now provided comfort. Warmth.

"So this electric feeling is because you're a werewolf? And it will always be there?"

"It's like a paranormal calling card of sorts. All magical beings have a certain energy they radiate. Generally, you get used to it, but it's stronger with you. Stronger than I've ever felt with anyone. And different."

"I like it."

He leaned forward and pressed his lips to hers. Her pulse quickened, a different kind of energy racing through her veins.

"That spark though," he whispered, his mouth hovering over hers, "is only ours." He winked and pulled away. "Do you have any more questions? Or is that enough weirdness for one day?"

She shook her head. That was definitely enough. "I guess I should talk to Alexis."

"I can give you the number she registered with, if you want to call her."

Macey nodded. "I can't believe she's a werewolf."

"Technically, you are too. And so is your boyfriend."

There was no explanation for the way she felt about this man, and she wasn't going to question it anymore. If magic and werewolves were real, maybe this seemingly otherworldly force that drew her to him was real too. She gazed at the hopeful longing in his eyes as her heart flip-flopped in her chest. She'd finally found a place she belonged. "You're my boyfriend?"

"I'd like to be. If that's okay with you."

"I think we can work something out." Desire pooled below her navel, and her fingers twitched with the need to feel the sinew beneath his shirt.

As if he read her mind, he traced his fingertips along her jawline, leaving a trail of heat on her skin that tingled with energy. He hooked his finger under her chin and leaned in so close she could feel the warmth of his breath on her lips. He stayed there, letting the anticipation build until she thought she'd have to throw herself at him. She closed her eyes and inched closer to him. Electricity danced between their lips as he slowly leaned in and took her mouth with his.

His tongue slipped out to taste her, licking her upper lip, then moving down to trace her lower one. Every muscle in her body relaxed as she melted into his embrace. "I think that's been enough talk."

The corner of his mouth tugged into a wicked grin. "I agree." He stood, pulling her body to his, pressing the evidence of his own desire against her stomach and taking her mouth once more. She snaked her hands over the ripples of his abs, memorizing every cut of muscle with her fingers. He was warm and hard. All over. Never in her life had she desired a man this much, and it was all she could do to keep her knees from buckling beneath her.

He kissed along her jaw, trailing his lips up to her earlobe, down her neck, and across her collar bone. She slipped her hands beneath his shirt, kneading the tight muscles as she worked her way up to his chest. When his lips caressed the top of her breast in the dip of her V-neck shirt, shivers ran down her spine. She dug her nails into his skin, and a soft moan escaped her lips.

He scooped her into his arms, frantically kissing her as if she might slip away if he stopped. "Bedroom?" he breathed into her mouth.

"Down the hall on the left."

He carried her into the bedroom and stopped in the doorway. Soft sunlight filtered through the sheer white drapes covering the bay window, casting a golden glow on the alabaster bedspread. She slid from his arms and beckoned him into the room. Climbing onto the mattress, she held out her arms, inviting him in, but he stood by the bed with an expression of awe in his eyes. "You're so beautiful, Macey. I could stare at you all day."

"I can think of a lot more fun things to do, but that would require you climbing into bed with me." She rose to her knees, hooked her finger in the waistband of his jeans and pulled him toward her. Her gaze fixed on the bulge beneath his zipper, and she stroked her palm across the mound. He sucked in a sharp breath, and she clutched the bottom of his shirt, yanking it up over his head.

He caught her wrists in his hands, and she dropped his shirt on the floor. "Are you sure you want to do this? You've been through a lot today." His gaze was so intense, she almost second guessed herself. But his grip on her, though gentle, aroused a primal need inside her. His broad shoulders and perfectly chiseled stomach had her entire body aching with the need to feel him on top of her, inside her, becoming part of her.

"I want you to take me."

He cocked an eyebrow and released her hands. "You don't have to ask me twice."

She unbuttoned her shirt and slid it over her shoulders. "I didn't plan to."

"And if I'd hesitated?" His grin widened as he climbed onto the bed and laid her on her back.

"You wouldn't have." Desire filled her to the core, tightening her womb and making her mouth go dry as she reached behind her back, unsnapped her bra, and tossed it on the floor.

In an instant, he was on her, pressing his body against hers, taking her mouth in a passionate kiss. He trailed his lips down her neck, his tongue flicking out to taste her skin as he explored her breasts with his hands.

He moved down, tasting and caressing every inch of her bare skin. Every nerve in her body sung with electricity as his lips inched closer to her navel. He looked at her with passion-drunk eyes as he undid the button on her pants and slowly slid down the zipper. He worked the clothing over her hips, tossed it on the floor, and sat up to look at her. "You are the most beautiful woman I have ever seen."

He said it with such conviction, she believed every word. She bit her lip, anticipation tightening in her core as he removed his jeans. He cupped her breasts, teasing the sensitive nipples with his thumbs, and her breath hitched as he slid his hand down her body to caress between her legs.

She took his length in her hand, and he moaned.

She stroked up and down, reveling in his masculine groans and the way his body reacted to her touch. Who knew she could derive so much pleasure from making him feel good? His eyes closed as he tipped his head back and let his breath out in a hiss. He put his hand on hers to still her stroking. "If you don't slow down, this is going to be over before it starts."

She released her grip. "Well, we wouldn't want that now, would we?"

"No, we wouldn't. Let's take it slow this time."

She craved making him orgasm as much as she craved feeling her own, but she relented, lying back and letting him take the lead.

He trailed his lips from her belly button, across her hip and down her inner thigh, his velvet touch raising goose bumps on her skin. She spread her legs, offering herself to him to do with as he pleased, allowing herself to be vulnerable if only for the moment. As he flicked out his tongue to stroke her folds, fire shot through her core.

Fisting the sheets in her hands, she let out a soft moan. She'd have to let him have his way more often.

"You taste even better than I imagined." His voice vibrated across her sensitive center, tightening her stomach, making her ache for more.

Gripping her hips, he circled his tongue around her clit, sending waves of ecstasy pulsing through her body. He slipped one finger inside her, then another, moving them in, out, and around until she lost control.

She cried out, tossing her head back and tangling her fingers in his hair as the orgasm ripped through her body. "Oh my God, Luke! I need you inside me." She heaved heavy breaths as he slowed his stroking and gazed up at her hungrily.

"Yes, ma'am."

She reached across to her nightstand drawer and grabbed a condom.

He slid the rubber down his shaft and pressed it against her opening. His smoldering gaze locked with hers, and he pushed inside slowly, deliberately, stretching her to the point of pleasurable pain. She gasped as he filled her, and he slid back out, until only the tip remained inside her. He held it there, staring at her with so much adoration in his eyes her breath stilled in her chest. A thousand thoughts rushed through her mind, but she couldn't form the words she wanted to say.

He crushed his mouth to hers as he plunged inside her, and she gave herself to him. Fully. Utterly. Completely. She was done holding back. She'd spent her entire life guarding her heart, but from this moment on it belonged to Luke. She had to relinquish it because she wanted every part of him—body, heart, and soul.

He moaned, hooking his hands behind her shoulders and thrusting his hips. Each plunge sent electric tingles pulsing through her middle. He roamed his tongue over her shoulders and up her neck until he found her mouth again. He groaned against her lips as his rhythm increased, pushing her closer and closer to orgasm.

"You're incredible." His breath tickled her ear.

She tried to utter a response, but hearing his raspy voice, thick with passion, sent her over the edge again. Her orgasm overtook her, sending wave after wave of pulsing pleasure rocketing through her body.

As he found his own release, he relaxed on top of her and nuzzled his face into her hair. With a deep inhale, he rolled to his side and pulled her into his arms, grazing his lips across her forehead, her nose, her mouth.

"You are amazing."

She nuzzled into his chest and sighed. "You were pretty awesome, yourself." Though awesome didn't begin to describe what she'd just experienced. Astounding. Incredible. Mind-blowing. The best sex of her life. But it had been so much more than sex. So much raw emotion. So much…dare she say it? Love.

After cleaning up and snuggling under the covers, Luke dozed off in the warmth of Macey's embrace. The way she fit in his arms. The way he fit inside her. Everything about her was so…right. He had no doubt in his mind that she truly was his fate-bound. His soul mate. They were destined to be together.

As he lay on his back, she traced the cut of his muscles with her soft fingertips, and he opened his eyes sleepily and smiled at the beautiful creature in his arms.

A werewolf after all.

I love you. The words trembled on the tip of his tongue, but he bit them back. She'd been through so much today, he didn't want to overwhelm her.

"I'm curious." She propped her head on her hand. "Since I'm not a full werewolf, would our…" Her cheeks flushed pink, and she pretended to inspect her fingernails. "Never mind."

Rolling onto his side, he rested his hand on her hip. "Would our children be full werewolves?" His heart pounded, a smile stretching across his face. She was already thinking about their future; he couldn't imagine a life without her.

She pulled her hair over her shoulder, nervously combing it with her fingers, avoiding his gaze. "Yeah. I mean, not that I'm thinking about stuff like that."

"It doesn't matter whether or not you can shift. You've got were blood, so our first child would be full. The second would be like you."

Drawing her eyebrows together, she looked at him. "The second?"

He shrugged. "And the third and fourth."

Her eyes widened. "Four?"

He chuckled. "How many kids do you want then? Five?"

She playfully hit him in the face with a pillow. "Stop it. I don't know." She snuggled down into his side. "What time is it?"

He kissed her head before glancing at the clock on her nightstand. "Seven."

"Ugh. I have to go to work soon."

He held her tighter, unwilling to let her go so soon after he'd finally made her his. Lying there naked with her warm body pressed against him…he couldn't think of anywhere he'd rather be. If only he could make the moment last forever.

She sat up to stretch, and the sheet fell away, revealing her creamy breasts and perfect pink nipples. His cock went instantly hard, and he pulled her on top of him for another kiss. He could get used to waking up to this every day.

CHAPTER TWENTY

"Well, our rapist has definitely gotten smarter," Bryce said to Macey as they left yet another hotel room. "He's getting them out of the alleys, anyway."

"Yeah." It didn't make sense. This victim had given the same description of the attacker—he appeared completely human aside from the red eyes. And these weren't random attacks like the others. This guy met his victims in bars, charmed them, seduced them into trusting him. Maybe the incidents were unrelated. Maybe this attacker wasn't a demon.

Bryce cracked his knuckles as they stepped onto Bourbon Street. Later in the day, rap and hip hop music from various bars would mix with classic rock to form a cacophony of drunken sound, and inebriated tourists would stumble through the street in search of their next drinks. But this early in the morning, the only people milling about were the locals on their way to their jobs and the workers washing the streets.

"You pick up anything with your spirit sensors?" he asked. "Any paranormal theories about this one?"

"I think it's just a man. Probably wearing contacts. You know how people like to let their freak flags fly here. Normally, no one would bat an eye at a pair of red eyes."

Bryce rolled his neck as if the stress of the case was getting to him. It was getting to all of them. "And the ones from the alleys?"

She shrugged. "Same. Probably a group of men…a cult or a fraternity." Now that she knew the truth, she understood why Luke had tried so hard to cover it up. She'd be on a fast track to the looney bin if she tried to convince the police they were searching for demons. Better to play it down and let the werewolves take care of the problem.

"So, no evil spirits or monsters then?"

She forced a smile. "Come on, Bryce. You have to think logically. Those things don't exist."

"I'm glad you've come to your senses. Hey, want to grab a bite to eat before you head home?"

An icy breeze snaked up her arm, wrapping tightly around her neck. She froze. For a moment, she couldn't breathe as frigid tendrils of dread encased her racing heart. Then the entity released its hold and whispered in her ear. *"Did you think I'd forgotten about you?"* The sinister voice was unmistakable—the same spirit that had tormented her before. It had to be connected somehow.

"I'm coming for you." The spirit's energy circled her one more time before flitting away on the breeze. She reached out with her mind to find it, but the entity's essence dissipated as quickly as it had formed.

"Macey?" Bryce waved a hand in front of her face. "Did you hear me?"

She blinked. "Yeah. Sorry. I was…lost in thought."

"Everything okay?"

She forced another smile and nodded. "I'm fine. I'm not very hungry. Thanks for the invite, though."

He arched an eyebrow and looked at her skeptically. "No problem, boss. Take care of yourself."

The sun barely peaked above the horizon as she made her way toward St. Philip and O'Malley's Pub. Why a bar needed to be open at six in the morning was beyond her, but Luke asked her to stop by when she got off work. She quickened her steps as the anticipation of seeing him again built.

The spirit had rattled her, but since Roberta had helped her develop her powers, she was confident she could keep it out of her head. Still, she needed to let Luke know what was going on. She should have mentioned the spirit before, but it took a while for her brain to catch up with everything he'd revealed to her. Maybe he could figure out what the dead guy had to do with the demons.

She entered O'Malley's and made her way to the bar. The place sat empty, except for the tattooed bartender slicing lemons on the countertop. Her mind flashed back to the night she met Luke, to the image of his biceps flexing and contracting as he did the very same thing. She remembered the first time she'd felt that magical jolt of energy from his touch—a feeling she'd grown to love so much. Her stomach flitted at the memories, and she shivered.

"Not much business in the early morning, I guess?"

The bartender grinned. "Not of the human variety. I don't think we've been properly introduced. I'm Chase."

"Hi. I'm Macey."

His grin widened. "I know. Luke's told me all about you."

Heat flushed her cheeks, and her heart did a giddy little flip-flop. Luke was talking about her? She regained her composure before she spoke. "All good things, I hope."

He winked. "Of course. Luke's in the back. I'll call him for you." Chase picked up the phone and made the call as a dark-haired man with deep brown eyes entered the room. He narrowed his gaze at her and strode toward the bar, stopping two feet in front of her.

"Well, well. If it isn't our fearless leader's new plaything." He raked his gaze over her body and cocked an eyebrow as he stared at her chest. "I can see why he likes you."

Refusing to take the bait, she fisted her hands at her sides and counted backward from ten. She would not let this asshole get to her.

Chase hung up the phone. "Dude, that's Luke's girlfriend. Show some respect."

"Oh, I could respect her all night long." He slinked past her, his serpent-like gaze boring into her as he stepped behind the bar.

She locked eyes with the snaky brunet, daring him to make another comment. She'd dealt with plenty of men like him before.

Misogynistic jerks who thought they needed to keep women in their place. If he was trying to intimidate her, it wasn't working.

Chase shifted uncomfortably, his gaze flicking between Macey and the man. "Luke's finishing up. He'll be out in a few minutes. Can I get you anything while you wait?"

She ignored the snake and beamed a smile at the bartender. "Thanks, Chase. I'm fine."

The jerk ran his tongue over his teeth. "Yes, you are."

"Stephen..." Chase's voice was heavy with warning.

Stephen straightened his spine and eyed the bartender. "You need to remember your place." He returned his sickly stare to Macey's chest. "If you ever want to know what a real man tastes like, you come give me a lick, darlin'."

Her stomach churned in disgust, but she maintained her poise. She smoothed her hair into her bun and leaned her forearm on the bar. "Stephen, I'd sooner lick the sludge off the Bourbon Street sidewalk than get my tongue anywhere near you."

Chase laughed and slapped Stephen on the shoulder. "Sounds like you need to remember *your* place, buddy...and your mate."

He balked, but she was just getting started. Her entire career, she'd had to deal with disrespect. Condescension. She was sick of trying to prove her worth to men. "Luke is more man than you'll ever be. He—"

The front door swung open and a pair of college-age guys staggered in. The blond seemed to be drunk already—or still drunk from the night before. His friend looked rough, with messy hair and a crumpled blue shirt, but at least he could walk straight.

"C'mon, man. Let's go," blue shirt said.

"Hold on. Hold on. I need another beer." Blondie swaggered up to the bar. "Gimme a Coors Light."

An amused smile lit on Chase's lips. "We don't serve Coors here."

"Why the hell not?" He cut his gaze over to Macey and straightened his posture as if he just noticed she was there. "Hey there, sweetheart." He moved behind her and rubbed her shoulders.

Not another one. She stiffened as his fingers kneaded her muscles, and when he started to glide his hands over her shoulders and onto her chest, she grabbed him by the wrist. In one swift movement, she pivoted around and wrenched his arm behind his back, pinning his head to the bar.

"Ow."

Without loosening her grip, she leaned down to speak to him face-to-face. Her years on the police force had taught her to keep her voice calm and steady—a whisper was much more intimidating than a shout. "I just got off work, and I really don't want to haul your drunk ass down to the station right now. So I'll make you a deal. I'm going to let you go, you're going to take your friend and walk out of this bar, and we'll pretend like this never happened. Go back to your hotel room and sleep it off. Okay?"

Fear widened his eyes as his gaze darted about the room. "Yes, ma'am. I'm sorry."

She released him, and he grabbed his friend and scurried to the door.

"Go to your hotel."

"Yes, ma'am."

"Hot damn." Chase gave her a slow round of applause. Stephen gritted his teeth and glared at her as she settled onto a barstool.

"Impressive." The bartender nodded his approval.

Macey shrugged. "Not really." She'd dealt with worse. "Why don't you serve Coors Light here? It's pretty popular, isn't it?"

Chase chuckled. "Because it's also called the Silver Bullet."

It took her a moment to catch on. "Oh…Wait. That's a real thing? Can a silver bullet really kill a werewolf?"

"A silver bullet can kill anything if it hits the right spot." Chase grabbed a rag and wiped the counter where the drunk guy had been pinned. "But no. That's a myth. Silver doesn't hurt werewolves." He held up his right hand to show her a silver ring on his finger. "Not serving the beer is part of the so-called joke." He nodded to the cardboard *Employees and Werewolves Only* sign on the door.

Her cheeks flushed with embarrassment. Of course it was a myth. She was almost afraid to ask her next question. "What about full moons?"

Chase smiled wistfully. "Our wolves are more powerful under a full moon, and the urge to shift is stronger. Lunar cycles affect us, but they don't control us like the movies would have you believe."

"I guess I've still got a lot to learn."

"Oh, yeah." Stephen grumbled as he lifted the hinged part of the bar and headed toward the back. Luke stepped through the swinging door as Stephen opened it. "I thought you said she'd be useful." He shoved past Luke to get through the door.

Luke's face lit up as soon as he looked at her, and he strutted forward to greet her. "Hello, beautiful." He swept her in his arms and spun her around. "How was work?"

"Fine. What did he mean by useful?"

He shook his head. "Ignore my cousin. He has an inferiority complex."

"He's your cousin?" The two men looked nothing alike. Their personalities were even more different. How could Luke be related to a guy like that?

"Unfortunately." He trailed the back of his fingers across her cheek and planted a firm yet inviting kiss on her lips. Her head swam with desire. She slid her hands behind his neck and pulled him closer, deepening the kiss. She couldn't get enough of this man. His tongue brushed hers, and a shudder ran through her body, weakening her knees.

Chase cleared his throat.

Luke smiled. "Sorry, man. I can't seem to keep my hands off her." He turned his smoldering gaze back on her. "Ready to go?"

Boy, was she. But once they made it to his house, she'd lose the ability to think straight. "Before we leave, there's something I need to tell you."

A crooked smile lifted one corner of his mouth. "Uh oh. That doesn't sound good. It's not going to be the 'it's not you, it's me' speech already, is it?" He said it jokingly, but she detected a hint of apprehension in his voice.

She laced her fingers through his to ease his concern. "It's nothing like that." She glanced at Chase, who stared at the ceiling, doing a terrible job of pretending not to listen. "There's a spirit that's been bothering me."

The bartender raised his eyebrows and looked at Luke.

"I thought you couldn't talk to spirits." Luke eased onto a barstool and tightened his grip on her hand.

"I can't, normally. But this one talks to me."

His jaw tightened, concern etching lines in his forehead. "Is it the same one from the woods? When that tree branch almost…"

"Yes. And I know who he is, but I can't figure out how he's connected to all this."

A vein in his neck throbbed, and anxiety tightened his eyes. "Who is he?"

"Do you remember that body that went missing from the morgue?"

The men exchanged a knowing glance, and Luke nodded.

"It's him. He's been following me to the crime scenes, but I can't figure out why. Or how he's communicating with me…trying to get inside me. I can't talk to spirits."

He took a deep breath. "He's not just a spirit. He's a halfling."

"What's that?"

"Half human, half demon. He should've reincarnated into that missing body, but he's chosen to stay in spirit form instead."

"Well, that explains a lot." The werewolves hadn't accidentally killed a human criminal. They'd killed a monster.

"Are you certain it's the same guy from the morgue?"

She nodded. "I saw his face when he got inside my head. Right before I forced him out."

Anger flashed in his eyes before he softened his gaze. "Don't worry, beautiful. I won't let him hurt you." He traced his fingers across her forehead and kissed her cheek. "I will keep you safe. Always."

While the gesture was sweet, she certainly didn't need coddling. "I'm not worried. He only got inside me once, and I know how to keep him out now."

"Still. Just know that I'm here…that we're all here…" He glanced at the bartender. "To protect you."

Chase chuckled under his breath. "Like she needs it."

Luke ignored his friend's comment and wrapped his arms around her. "You've had a long night working. Let's go back to my place, and I'll take you to bed."

Her heart pounded at the thought, and she slid her arms around his waist. "Okay, but I do need to sleep *sometime* today."

"Oh, I know." He nuzzled her neck, his teeth lightly grazing her skin and sending goose bumps running down her arm. "And I promise I'll let you." He moved to the other side of her neck and trailed his tongue up to her earlobe. His breath warmed her skin, raising goose bumps on the other arm. "After I have my way with you."

"Here we are." Luke led Macey through the door and into the living room. "It's not much when you see it in the daylight, is it?"

She smiled as her gaze danced about the room. "It's nice. Cozy."

An empty beer bottle sat next to a crumpled chip bag on the coffee table, and he whisked them away to the trash. "Sorry about the mess."

"It's not messy."

She was right. That was the only piece of trash lying out, but he straightened the pillows on the couch anyway. They'd already shared themselves intimately, but something about having her in his house made him feel more vulnerable. Her presence seemed to fill the room with warmth, turning his eating and sleeping quarters into a place he'd like her to call home.

Clasping her hands behind her back, she bit her bottom lip and gazed up at him. His cock swelled at the sight of those hooded emerald eyes, and when her tongue flicked out to moisten her lips, his heart nearly beat out of his chest.

"So, about that *way* you wanted to have with me." She untied the knot in her hair, and it spilled around her shoulders.

Dear lord, he could have taken her right there on the living room floor. Just watching the rise and fall of her breasts as she breathed was enough to make him lose control. But he intended to make this moment last. "I've been out hunting all night. I could use a shower."

She stepped toward him and ran a finger down his chest, stopping at the waistband of his jeans. He held his breath as she popped the button and slid the zipper down. Another wave of heat flashed through his groin as she slipped her hand into his pants to grip his shaft, his body shuddering at the feel of her soft fingers wrapped around him.

"I'm feeling a little dirty, myself. Mind if I join you?"

He cupped her face in his hands and slid his fingers into her hair. "Let's go clean you up then."

"Okay." She smiled, keeping a firm grip on his dick.

"You might want to let me go, so I can walk." He laughed and tugged her hand from his pants before leading her into the bathroom.

Leaving their clothes in a heap on the floor, they stepped into the shower. Rivulets of moisture rolled down Macey's skin, sliding over her sensuous curves before falling to the ground. She was a hot, wet goddess standing before him, and all he could do was stare. "You're so beautiful. I really could just look at you all day."

A sly grin curved her pink lips. "And I really *couldn't* let you do that. I need you to touch me."

A low growl resonated in his chest as he lathered his hands and slid them over her body. Her soft skin was a stark contrast to his calloused hands, but the look in her eyes said she enjoyed his touch. Her breath hitched when his thumb brushed her nipple, and he cupped her breasts in his hands. She closed her eyes and moaned softly as he pinched the pink pearls between his fingers, hardening them with his touch.

He continued washing her, sliding his hands over her stomach, down one leg and up the other, and when his fingers reached the sensitive nub between her legs, she gasped. He slipped a finger inside her tight, wet warmth, and she moaned. Good God, how he loved this woman. He reveled in the sensuous sounds that escaped her lips as he caressed her.

She trembled as he rubbed her clit, her breaths becoming rapid and shallow. "Luke, I can't…I can't stand up."

"Hold on to me, baby."

She clutched his shoulders and pressed her head to his chest as she came. The sounds she made. The way her entire body shuddered with her orgasm. It was the most beautiful thing he'd ever seen. A sight he needed to see every day for the rest of his life.

Her breathing slowed, and she looked at him with mischief in her eyes. "You're still dirty. We need to fix that." The water beat down on his back as she lathered her hands and slid them down his chest, his stomach, his legs. Her skin felt like velvet rubbing against his, her magic energy mixing with the sparks of passion igniting in his core.

She knelt to the ground and took his length in her hand, circling her tongue around the tip. Fire shot through his veins as she took him into her mouth and gazed up at him. Never looking away, she moved her mouth up and down his cock, taking more and more of him in with each stroke of her lips. His stomach clenched as his orgasm built, but he put his hands on her shoulders to stop her.

"I need to make love to you. Right now." His voice was raw with need.

She released her hold and ran her hot tongue from base to tip before rising to her feet and kissing him. Grabbing his neck, she hooked her legs around his waist and pressed her slick, wet body against him. He fumbled to turn off the water and carried her to the bedroom to toss her onto the bed. He needed to be inside her. To fill her. To feel her.

He grabbed a condom from the drawer, and she yanked it from his hands, ripping open the package. "Lie down." Her command thrilled him, and he did as he was told. She straddled him and gave his cock a final lick before sliding on the condom and guiding him to her folds. Sweet elation engulfed him as she sheathed him.

Beads of water dripped from the ends of her hair, falling onto his stomach and rolling toward the place where their bodies joined. His gaze followed the trail, and he memorized the look, the sensation, of becoming one with the woman he loved.

"You feel so good inside me, Luke." She rocked her hips, gliding up and down his shaft, slowly at first, but increasing steadily as she held his gaze. Her hooded eyes. Her soft moans. He could feel her need as if it were his own—passionate, lustful, full of emotion. She ran her hands over his chest, her gentle caress making his entire body ache for her. For them. He belonged to Macey...in this moment and forever. Though neither of them had said the words aloud, she loved him too. He could see it in her eyes. Feel it in the way she touched him.

Her movements quickened, her breathing growing shallow, and she tossed back her head and cried out as the climax overtook her. Seeing her writhing in pleasure as she rode him sent him over the edge. His own orgasm exploded, and he ground his hips against her, thrusting deeper and deeper inside her.

As their rhythm slowed, she leaned forward, laying her breasts to his chest, touching her lips to his. His heart swelled with so much love for the woman in his arms, and he knew, without a shadow of a doubt, she was meant to be his mate. His wife. A satisfied *mmm* escaped her lips as she rolled off him and snuggled into his side.

As she started to doze, he slid out of bed. She reached for him, and his chest tightened at the gesture.

"Where are you going?"

"I need to throw this away. I'll be right back." He tossed the condom in the trash and closed the drapes.

She rolled onto her back. "Don't do that. I can barely keep my eyes open as it is."

"Then close them." He slid back into bed and held her in his arms. "Sleep here today. With me."

She snuggled her back into his front and tugged his arm around her chest. "I have to see my sister this afternoon." The sleepiness in her voice had him hard all over again. He could imagine falling asleep with her in his arms every day. Waking up wrapped in her warmth.

"What time do you need to get up? I'll set an alarm."

"Noon?"

"Consider it done." He kissed her neck as she relaxed in his arms and slipped into blissful sleep.

CHAPTER TWENTY-ONE

MACEY SHUFFLED INTO JACKSON SQUARE AND FOUND HER SISTER sitting on a bench facing the St. Louis Cathedral. Alexis smiled tentatively and lifted a hand to wave. She wore beige cargo pants and a fitted green tank top that revealed her muscular arms. Her nails were short, but clean, her hands calloused like she worked a manual labor job. Macey returned her smile and sat next to her.

She'd only texted her sister, not having the courage to speak to her on the phone. Now that they were face to face, she still didn't know what to say. She stared up at the eighteenth-century church and collected her thoughts. The shock of seeing Alexis after all these years had subsided, and now she wanted answers. "Why did you come here?"

Alexis stared straight ahead. "To find you."

Macey examined the cathedral façade, with its triple steeples towering over the square. She stared at the clock below the middle steeple, ticking away the hours, and contemplated all the years they'd lost. So much time gone. Their relationship had crumbled into nothing. Could they rebuild it? "How long have you been in New Orleans?"

"A few weeks."

She inhaled a deep breath and held it. A few weeks…and her sister hadn't bothered to contact her. "How did you know I was here?"

"I saw you on the news." She finally looked at her. "Macey, I came as soon as I learned you were here. I was going to talk to you myself. I just needed time to figure out what to say."

It had been twenty years; a few weeks didn't make much of a difference. She had her sister back, and that was the important thing. So why did it still hurt so much?

A bead of sweat rolled down Macey's neck, and she wiped it away. "You abandoned me. Why come back now?"

"I changed, Macey. I turned into a werewolf, for Christ's sake. What was I supposed to do? I didn't know what was happening to me. Mom and Dad never prepared me."

Her jaw tightened. "They died."

"I…" Alexis sighed. "I know. I'm not blaming them, but put yourself in my place for a second. Imagine being thirteen years old, having no knowledge that any type of magic exists, much less flows through your own veins. I freaked. I'm sorry."

She had a point. At thirteen, Macey's biggest concern was getting rid of the zit on her nose before taking her yearbook picture. Her sister turned into a werewolf. Still… "You could've come back for me once you figured it out."

"I did." Alexis rested her elbow on the back of the bench. "By the time I found some help and came back, you'd already been adopted. I tried to find out where they'd taken you, but I couldn't get to your records. I was only thirteen. I was a child too."

Her chest tightened. "You came back for me?" All these years Macey thought her sister had abandoned her without a second thought. But she hadn't. Not on purpose, anyway.

Alexis smiled. "Of course, I did. You're my little sister. I love you."

"I love you too." A glimmer of the bond they'd shared as children sparked in her core. Perhaps they could rebuild their relationship.

"Yoo hoo. Macey." A melodic voice drifted on the air. Macey looked up to see Roberta, dressed in a long brown skirt and a colorful blouse, sitting at a small folding table and shuffling a stack of tarot cards.

She turned to her sister. "Come here. I want you to meet some-one." They stepped around a juggler performing for a small crowd and passed two women in similar gypsy clothes with signs claiming they could read the future. Jackson Square overflowed with faux fortune tellers, so seeing Roberta came as a surprise.

They sat in the chairs at Roberta's table. "I didn't know people with real powers set up booths here," Macey said.

"There are a few of us." She nodded to an older man holding a crystal ball.

"This is my sister, Alexis." Macey leaned in and lowered her voice. "She's a werewolf."

A knowing smile brightened the old woman's face. "So the truth has revealed itself to you."

Macey glanced sideways at Alexis. "It's about time."

"And Luke?" Roberta asked.

Warmth bloomed in Macey's heart at the mention of his name, and she couldn't fight the smile that curved her lips. "He's good. Luke is…amazing."

Roberta patted Macey's hand in a motherly gesture. "Have you heard from our spirit friend?"

Macey gazed at the stack of tarot cards lying on the table. The thick card stock had yellowed with age, and the edges were frayed. "Yeah, actually. Yesterday…he said he was coming for me." She explained the demon spirit to her sister.

"Sounds like a halfling if his spirit is able to torment you like that," Alexis said. "He'll be hard to kill."

"Especially since he's already dead." Macey traced her finger across the top card, and crackling magical energy seeped into her skin. How many magical things had she touched in her life and written the sensations off as her imagination?

"A werewolf can kill a demon easily," Alexis said. "But a half-demon spirit? It would take a medium to capture something like that."

Roberta smiled. "Macey can do it."

A heavy feeling sank in her stomach. "I cannot." She'd learned how to release energy from an object a few days ago. She didn't have the power to fight a demon.

"The method is the same." Roberta picked up the stack of cards and laid a few of them on the table. A slight smile tugged at her lips before she scooped them up and returned them to the deck. "If you can release energy, you can capture it too."

Macey shook her head. "How?"

"Do the process in reverse. And if you can find out the spirit's name, that will help. A named thing is a tamed thing." Roberta shuffled the cards again. "Luke has an exceptional demon hunting team, dear. You'll be a great asset."

"An asset." Could she help them fight the demons? She'd busted plenty of human monsters since she became a cop, but demons? She chewed her bottom lip. Well, why not? She was a werewolf, after all. "Roberta, why didn't you tell me Luke was a werewolf? If you knew all along…"

"It wasn't my secret to tell, child. Think about how you felt when your mother told me yours."

"Oh." When she put it that way, it made sense. She probably wouldn't have believed her anyway.

Roberta rummaged through her bag and pulled out a rough, oval-shaped crystal, about the size of a potato. A kaleidoscope of colors sparkled in the translucent white stone as she turned it over in her hands. "I use it for releasing energy, but you can also use it to trap your spirit." She offered it to Macey.

She held up her hands. "Oh, I can't."

"Please, take it."

Macey sighed and slipped the rock into her purse. Her mentor made it sound so easy. Hopefully it would be. Trapping a demon spirit wasn't something she could practice beforehand. "Thanks, but…I'm not sure I'll know what to do."

"You will when the time comes." Roberta's gaze was intense, almost as if she were willing the information into Macey's mind. "Now, if you ladies will excuse me, I need to see some paying customers."

Macey and her sister walked up St. Ann and crossed Decatur toward Café Du Monde. They climbed the steps near the iconic green and white coffee shop and peered out over the Mississippi river. Barges drifted by in the distance, and a steamboat churned up the mucky water with its paddle wheel near the shore.

"I'm sorry for blowing up at you in the bar." Macey reached out to touch her sister's arm, but let her hand fall to her side. The anger and resentment she'd felt toward her had quelled, but having Alexis back in her life would take some getting used to. "If I had known you were going to be there, maybe I would have behaved differently. Luke thought it would be a nice surprise."

Alexis ground her teeth. "I understand. It was a huge shock." She chewed her bottom lip and stared at the ground. "Listen. There's something you need to know about Luke."

"He's in line to be the next alpha." That infectious smile returned to her lips. "I know what I'm getting into."

"No. Not that. He…" She shoved her hands in her pockets and kicked at the dirt on the concrete. "I don't know a nice way to say this, so I'm not going to sugar-coat it. He's only been dating you to feed you lies and throw you off the case." She looked at Macey, sadness filling her eyes.

Heat spread from Macey's neck up to her cheeks like fingers of fire burning a building. Why would her sister say such a thing? "That's not true. He told me everything. I know all about the demons and the werewolves, and we're still together. We're seeing each other tonight."

Alexis raised her hands. "I know. But I went to a pack meeting, and that's what he told us. He was keeping you occupied until they could defeat all the demons. He's been using you."

Macey crossed her arms, dread clutching at her heart. She refused to believe it.

"And when they found out you were my sister…that you were a werewolf too, they decided to use you as their 'person on the inside.' You're the only werewolf cop in New Orleans, so you can cover up their tracks for them."

Macey's nails dug into her arms. Every muscle in her body tensed at the accusations her sister made. Could Luke be using her? Was all the tenderness, all the passion, just a ploy to get her to cover up the pack's tracks? She shook her head. "Luke would never…" Would he?

Spikes of doubt began to bore into her mind. Was that what Stephen meant when he mentioned her being useful?

"He did. I was there when he said it."

How could she have been so naïve? Looking back on the path of their relationship, Alexis's words made sense. Luke had deceived her, then left her. But when he found out she was a werewolf, and he could still use her, he'd come running back. And she'd accepted him with open arms like a fool.

Tears welled in her eyes. "I see."

Alexis wrapped her arms around her. "I'm sorry, Macey. I hate being the one to tell you this, but I don't want to see you get hurt."

"Too late." She pulled away from her sister's embrace.

"Stephen said Luke was screwing you to keep you occupied. Did you sleep with him?"

"Worse. I gave him my heart."

Pity softened her eyes. "Oh, Macey."

"I have to go." She hurried down the steps and crossed the street into Jackson Square. This was her own fault. She'd let her guard down. She'd been distracted by his piercing eyes and sexy body, and she'd opened up to him. Made herself vulnerable. A mistake she wouldn't make again. There was a reason she'd guarded her heart so heavily all these years, and she was stupid to think Luke would be any different. People left. She was never worth sticking around for, and she still wasn't.

How long was he planning to string her along? Just until they'd vanquished the demons? Or would he keep using her until he tired of her?

She wiped her tears and straightened her spine. Love wasn't in the cards for her, and that was fine. She was done playing the fool.

As she passed in front of a candy store, the shop owner yelled at what appeared to be a homeless man, then he hit him on the head with a thick stick of summer sausage. The poor guy cowered in the corner, trying to inch his way toward the door, but the shop owner's relentless berating continued.

Tucking her emotions into the vault, Macey welcomed the distraction and stepped inside to flash her badge. "Is there a problem here?"

The homeless man whimpered.

"Every week," the shop keeper shouted. "Every week he comes in here and eats my samples. Every time he buys nothing!"

The cowering man covered his face and peeked at her through his fingers. Tears filled his frightened, brown eyes, tugging at Macey's heartstrings.

"Okay. How about I take him outside and have a talk with him?" she said to the shopkeeper.

"Tell him not to come back! Idiot!"

"Okay." She cautiously approached the man and touched his elbow. He recoiled. "Sir? Do you want to come take a walk with me?"

He ran his hand under his nose and wiped it on his sweat-stained shirt. "Please don't hit me." His bottom lip trembled as he spoke.

"I'm not going to hurt you. Come on. Let's take a walk." She ushered the man outside and guided him away from the store. She sat him on a park bench and waited for his sniveling to subside before speaking. "What happened in there?"

He wiped his nose and dried his eyes on his shirt sleeve. "I was hungry. I thought it was free." He sighed. "I'm a stupid idiot."

"No. No, you're not. That wasn't nice of the shopkeeper to call you that." She sat down next to him. Aside from his dirty clothes and greasy hair, something about the man wasn't quite right. Like his elevator didn't go all the way to the top. He almost seemed drunk, but she couldn't smell any traces of alcohol.

"Oh, I am. My brother told me so." He appeared to be about thirty years old, but he had the speech pattern of a six-year-old. His stomach growled, and he hit it with his fist. "Sometimes, if I punch it, I can make the roaring stop."

"When was the last time you ate?"

"The candy in the shop." He pointed.

"I mean a meal. Something that filled you up?"

He shrugged. "My brother brings me food sometimes. Well, he used to."

"Sometimes? Wait here." She trotted to the food vendor a few feet away and bought two hot dogs, a bag of chips, and a bottle of water. The man's innocent gaze flitted about the park like a little boy's would.

He smiled when he saw a dog pretending to be passed out on the street, a hurricane glass lying on its stomach and a patty of fake vomit near its mouth.

"That's a smart dog," he said as Macey returned to the bench. "It's not really asleep. It's just playing like it is."

She offered him the food and sat beside him. Though she was certain she'd never seen him before, his oddly familiar face pricked at her mind, raising the hairs on the back of her neck. She stifled a gasp as she realized where she'd seen him. She pulled out her phone and found the image of the police sketch. His features were similar to the rapist. It wasn't an exact match, but this was only an artist's rendition based on someone else's description. It could be the same man.

He inhaled each hotdog in two bites, then started on the bag of chips. How long had it been since his last meal? He certainly didn't act like a rapist. The women had described him as charming. Smooth. This was a child in a man's body. And he had brown eyes, not red. The guy in the sketch was most likely half demon. This man definitely was not. "What's your name?"

He finished the chips and chugged the water. "My name is Jimmy."

"Well, it's nice to meet you, Jimmy. I'm Macey."

"Thank you for the food, Miss Macey. That will keep my tummy quiet for a long time."

"My pleasure. Jimmy, do you come here often? The shopkeeper said he sees you every week."

"Oh, yes, ma'am. Mondays are my free days. I get to come here every Monday."

She tilted her head. "But it's not Monday."

"Oh, my brother told me to meet him here today. He said we're going to do something fun. I hope we can go to the aquarium. I want to see the fishies." He clapped his hands.

"Do you have somewhere to stay? A bed to sleep in?"

He nodded. "Yes ma'am. I have a futon. My brother got it for me when I was really good."

"Does your brother live with you?"

"Yes, ma'am. Well, kinda."

"Kinda?" She pulled a pen and a slip of paper out of her purse. She'd have to do some research on this brother of his. "What's his name?"

Jimmy's eyes grew wide. "Oh, I...I'm really not supposed to talk about him. I...I'm not supposed to talk to people at all." He jumped off the bench and tripped over his feet, falling back down. "I have to go." He clambered to his feet again. "Thank you, Miss Macey, for the food. You're a real nice lady." He turned on his heel and disappeared into the crowd.

"Well, that was strange." Macey picked up the food wrappers and tossed them in a trash bin. There was no way that guy was the rapist. He probably couldn't even operate a toaster, much less a woman's body.

CHAPTER TWENTY-TWO

As Luke strolled up St. Philip, the evening sun dipped into the horizon, painting the sky in shades of pink and purple. The afternoon clouds had dissipated, and the French Quarter buildings cast long stripes of shade across the pavement. The steamy scent of fresh rain drifted up from the puddles in the street.

He'd had the urge to dial Macey's number all afternoon, but she was spending time with her sister. He'd see her soon enough. As he approached the bar, he hesitated to go in. His mind was so wrapped up in his sexy detective—and she was *his* now—he didn't want to think about werewolf business.

But he had to. With Macey's help, they wouldn't have to worry so much about the humans finding out about the demons, but they still needed to catch the bastard who was summoning the fiends. His parents would be home tomorrow. He'd be alpha in five days. He needed to wrap this up.

The chilled curtain of air separating the inside of O'Malley's from the outside blasted his skin. Chase had his arms full of half-drunk hurricanes, and he dumped the contents down the sink before tossing the plastic cups in the trash. Alexis sat at the bar, nursing a glass of whiskey, a grim expression occupying her face.

"How'd it go with Macey today?" Luke asked.

"Oh, fine." She glanced at him before turning her attention to her drink. "Trying to repair twenty years of damage won't be easy."

"At least you made a start."

She shrugged.

Chase poured Luke a beer and handed it to him. "You've got a spring in your step I haven't seen in a long time."

Luke grinned. His life was finally starting to fall into place. "I'm in love. What can I say?" And he planned to tell her tonight.

Alexis's head jerked up. "Love? But you said—"

"Hold on." Luke's phone vibrated in his pocket. His grin widened when Macey's name lit up the screen. "Hello, beautiful. How was your day?"

"You can stop now, Luke." Her voice was strained. Irritated.

"What can I stop?"

"Pretending you like me. I know, okay?"

He tightened his grip on the phone. "Preten—Macey, what are you talking about?"

"You've been using me to cover up the truth. That's why you're dating me. Well, you don't have to anymore. Okay? I'll be your 'man on the inside,' so you can stop the charade. I won't tell anyone about the werewolves or the demons. No one would believe me anyway."

"Where on Earth would you get an idea like that?" He eyed the woman sitting at the bar, staring into her drink. He knew exactly where.

"Alexis told me everything."

His heart pounded like a sledgehammer as he glared at Macey's sister. "And you believe her?"

"Of course I do. She's my sister."

"Macey, none of that is true. Macey? Hello?"

Silence hung heavy on the other end. Final.

Angry heat rolled through his body as he dropped his phone into his pocket. He turned to Alexis. "What did you do, rogue?"

She shrank in on herself, wrapping her arms across her middle. "I...I was looking out for my sister. After what you said at the meeting, I thought you—"

"Well, you thought wrong." He raked his hands through his hair. "I'm not using her. I'm in love with her."

Alexis's mouth hung open, her bottom lip quivering. "I…"

He dialed Macey's number. Straight to voicemail. "Macey, Alexis was wrong. None of that is true. I…just…please call me." He pocketed his phone. "I've got to find her."

He strode toward the door, and James came flying through. "Demons. Three. On Rampart," he said between breaths.

"Shit. They aren't wasting any moonlight." Luke tensed. He *had* to hunt the demons, but Macey…

"I'll talk to her." Alexis downed the rest of her whiskey. "I'll make things right."

"You better."

Chase leapt over the bar, and the men rushed out into the night.

The French Quarter swarmed with people. They'd have to herd the demons out of the city to have any chance of battling them unnoticed. James led them up St. Philip to Rampart and stopped. "They're on the move."

Luke inhaled deeply, sifting through the scents of the Quarter. It was faint, but underneath the sweet smells of magnolias and pralines and the sour tinge of alcohol, the putrid scent of death and decay lingered like a long-buried secret. "This way."

They darted down Dumaine and skidded to a stop on Royal. There, in the shadows, indistinguishable from the darkness, save for the gleaming red eyes, three demons lurked in an alley.

"One man on the roof," Chase said. "The other two at each end of the alley. We surround them and get them all at once. They won't know what hit them." He shifted his weight from foot to foot, his eyes gleaming in the gas light.

"You got lucky last time," Luke said. "We're not shifting in the city again. Too many witnesses."

James cracked his knuckles. "Witnesses that are about to become victims if we don't act fast."

"Right," Luke said. "Wait…what's this?"

A black-haired man approached the fiends and spoke to them.

Luke couldn't make out their words over the chatter of tourists, but this guy had to be involved.

"That the bastard who's summoning them?" Chase clenched his fists.

The man turned his head and scanned the street with his own set of red eyes. Luke recognized him immediately. Though full-grown now, his face was unmistakable. "That's the halfling I saw last week."

The man pointed into the alley, and the demons' eyes followed his gaze. They slinked deeper into the shadows as the halfling turned and ran up Royal Street.

"Can you guys handle three on your own?" Luke asked.

"Are you kidding?" James bounced on the balls of his feet. "I was born for this."

"Good. I'm going to tail the halfling. See if he can show me where his master's hiding out."

Keeping his distance, Luke followed the man out of the Quarter. He slinked through the outlying neighborhoods and through the wards that still hadn't completely recovered from the last hurricane. Where was the fiend headed? With the last house behind him, Luke shifted into wolf form and stalked the halfling into the swamp.

Though he looked like a man, the half-demon moved with the speed and agility of an otherworldly creature. He leapt over fallen logs and ducked under low-hanging branches as if he had the entire forest memorized.

As the halfling approached a run-down shack situated on a piece of semi-dry land, Luke slowed his pace and ducked behind a tree. Crouching low, he belly-crawled closer to the structure. His back leg kicked a fallen tree branch, disturbing a nest of wild boar piglets. They snorted and squealed for their mother, scattering through the trees. The halfling snapped his head around at the sound and peered into the darkness.

Luke held his breath, anticipating the attack from the sow. Wild boars could be as mean as gators, especially the ones in the swamp. But the mother never came. Maybe she'd already been turned into someone's dinner. A piglet scurried past the halfling, and he sneered, picking up the squealing baby and carrying it inside.

Luke released his breath. The last thing he needed was for a pig to give him away. He crept closer to the shack and peeked through the window. A makeshift altar stood in the center of the room. It was nothing more than a wooden table covered in cloth and animal bones, but this had to be the place where the demons were summoned. He could just make out the designs drawn on a cereal bowl in the middle of the table. Black magic markings.

The halfling picked up the knife that lay beside the bowl and stabbed the piglet. It let out a piercing squeal before flailing and going limp in his hand. Luke didn't stick around to watch the rest. He could've easily taken out the demon spawn on his own, but the signs of struggle would let his master know he'd been found. He'd wait until the bastard was home and end this thing once and for all.

Macey took her frozen dinner out of the microwave and settled on the couch with a glass of chardonnay. Thor sat on the other end of the sofa and flicked his tail triumphantly.

"Don't look so smug." She eyed her cat. "He fooled you too."

She flipped on the television and shoveled a spoonful of mac and cheese into her mouth. Luke planned to take her to a new Italian restaurant in the Garden District tonight. It would have been better than the cardboard pasta and runny, half-frozen cheese sauce she was currently eating. *Stop it, Mace. Don't think about him.*

That was easier said than done. The harder she tried to get the image of his deep blue eyes and caramel hair out of her mind, the more vivid the picture became. She sighed and put the bowl on the coffee table. She'd get over him. Her life was fine before she met him, and it would be fine with him gone too. He had too many responsibilities, anyway. His job, running his pack, hunting demons. She was busy too…

And Thor would have missed their Saturday night Netflix binges.

She could think of a thousand reasons why not being with Luke was the best decision she could've made. As long as she kept her distance, he'd never have the chance to abandon her. This time, she was the one who left. The relationship ended because *she* wanted it to, and she would keep reminding herself of that until it stopped hurting.

She finished her dinner and set the bowl in the sink. Thor curled up in her lap, and she sipped her wine as she started season two of her new favorite show.

A knock on the door made her heart jump. Could it be Luke? So what if it was? He'd only fill her head with more lies, and she wasn't sure she had the strength to resist him. She'd probably fall for whatever story he fed her, so she'd better not answer the door.

The knock sounded again. "Miss Macey? Are you home?"

That wasn't Luke. She set Thor on the floor and tiptoed to the door.

Another knock. "Miss Macey? It's Jimmy."

The guy from the candy store? How on Earth did he know where she lived? She looked through the peep hole, and sure enough, Jimmy stood on the porch. He wore clean clothes, and his hair had been combed, but it was definitely him. She unlatched the lock, but kept the chain in place, and opened the door a crack. "What are you doing here, Jimmy?"

"I'm sorry, Miss Macey. My brother made me do it." He squeezed his eyes shut, a tense, pained expression masking his face, as a garbled yelp came from somewhere deep inside. His body shuddered, and a sinister smile curved his lips. He sucked in a deep breath and slowly opened his eyes.

Blood red eyes.

Macey gasped and stumbled back, trying to close the door, but he stuck his foot in the jamb. He slammed his shoulder against the door with inhuman strength, snapping the security chain in half. Thor hissed and darted into the bedroom as Macey backed into a table, knocking over a lamp and shattering it on the floor.

Jimmy wrapped his long fingers around her neck and pinned her against the wall. "You were kind to my brother today."

Brother? His voice was the same, but different. It no longer held the childish intonation it had earlier in the day. And his eyes...

"He likes you now." He slammed her onto the floor, and the air *whooshed* out of her lungs.

She gasped for breath. "Jimmy? What are you doing?"

"I'm not Jimmy."

She tried to scoot away, but he was on her in an instant, straddling her, pinning her to the ground. Her shoulder blades dug into the wood, sending piercing pain shooting into her arms.

"I was going to have some fun with you before I killed you, but now that my idiot brother has taken a liking to you, I won't. I don't want to damage his mind too much. Such a shame. You are a pretty little thing." He thrust his hips against her as he spoke. "He begged me not to kill you. 'Miss Macey's a real nice lady,'" he said in a mocking tone. "A nice lady who's been getting in my way long enough."

He stood, lifting her off the ground by the shoulders, her feet dangling three inches above the wood. "You see…" With his hand around her neck, he slammed her into the wall. Her head knocked against drywall, and her vision swam with stars. Clawing at his hand, she tried to peel his fingers from her throat, but he held her with otherworldly strength. The strength of a demon. The brother who terrorized Jimmy was the half-demon spirt who'd been taunting her.

"You see, *Miss Macey*, I've got a plan. I'm going to run this city. And I am trying to build an army of halflings to help me do it. But you and your werewolf friends are making my life difficult. How can my demons impregnate enough women to build an army, when the werewolves keep killing them?"

She tried to speak, but his grip crushed her windpipe. She could barely breathe, but she refused to be his next victim. If only she could reach her pistol; she'd left it on the kitchen counter with her badge. She clutched his arm and managed a strangled, "Please."

The demon in Jimmy's body sighed and shook his head. "I have to use a body to kill you, since I don't have one of my own. Making that branch fall on you took all the energy I had. It took hours for me to recover after that. Spirit energy isn't infinite, I'm afraid." He squeezed her throat tighter. "This way is much more efficient."

She couldn't breathe. Her vision tunneled, blackness closing in around her, when he suddenly let her go. She clutched her neck as she gasped for breath. Blinking away the darkness, she found Thor climbing up the man's back, his teeth slicing into his neck.

She took the chance and stumbled into the kitchen, throwing herself at her firearm. Jimmy flung Thor across the foyer and roared as he came barreling into the room.

Macey raised her gun and fired. The bullet burrowed into his shoulder. Jimmy fell against the wall and slid down. He reached for the wound and pulled away a shaking hand covered in blood. His bottom lip quivered.

"You bitch." The voice bellowed from every corner of the room. *"I need that body."*

She swung the gun around, frantically searching for the source of the sound.

"Miss Macey?" The childish tone returned to Jimmy's voice. He stood up and swayed on his feet. "I don't feel so good."

"Run, you moron. If you pass out here, I swear I'll kill you myself."

"I'm sorry, Miss Macey. You really are a nice lady." He stumbled into the living room and out the door. Thor hissed and darted into the kitchen.

The last thing Macey saw was a cast iron pan flying across the room, striking her head with splitting pain.

CHAPTER TWENTY-THREE

LUKE SHIFTED TO HUMAN FORM BEFORE HE REACHED THE CITY. He stopped by the bar, but his hunters were still on patrol. Macey didn't pick up her phone, so he tried Alexis. No answer. Could they be at Macey's house? It wouldn't hurt to look.

He stepped out into the humid night and headed toward her home. At worst, he could at least let her know what was about to go down in the swamp, so they could concoct a cover story to satisfy the police. At best, Alexis would have convinced her she was wrong, and Macey would throw herself into his arms as soon as he knocked on the door. His chest tightened. He could only hope for the best.

As he turned the corner on Barracks, he caught a whiff of rotting flesh as a black mass dropped from a rooftop into an alley. *Damn demons.* His reunion with Macey would have to wait.

With his back pressed against the wall, Luke peered into the alley to see what the fiend was up to. This was a residential street; attracted to the masses, demons usually stuck to the crowded areas. More victims. Easier targets.

This demon crouched in a shadow, rubbing its knobby hands together, and staring up at a balcony. Tendrils of ivy crawled across the cast iron railing and climbed up the poles. Soft rock music played from a speaker on a table, where a glass of soda sat, untouched, the ice melting in the heat. A girl stretched out on a chaise lounge; she couldn't have been more than fourteen. She punched in something on her cell phone, and the blue light illuminated an amused grin, her innocent eyes sparkling as she laughed.

The demon's nostrils flared. That thing could scale the balcony railing in a single leap. He had to stop it, but it was against the rules to shift in the city. Aside from piercing the heart, the only other way to kill a demon was to cut its head off. He scanned the area for something sharp. Nothing.

He could fight it in human form. Wrestle with it. Try to make it run. It rocked to the balls of its feet like it was about to jump.

Screw the rules. These were desperate times.

Luke leapt toward the demon, shifting in midair, bringing his massive claws down on...nothing. The fiend had disappeared, leaving behind nothing but a dissipating cloud of black smoke. *What the hell?* Demons couldn't disappear.

A maniacal cackle emanated from the balcony. The girl screamed. The fiend clung to the railing like a monkey, taunting Luke and scaring the girl to death. She scrambled back, curling into a ball and pressing herself against the wall. She glanced at the open door and focused on the demon.

Luke rocked back on his haunches and launched himself up. He swiped at the fiend, slicing a massive claw through its thick, leathery skin. It let out an ear-piercing squeal and lost its balance on the railing. Hanging from one arm, it let out a snake-like hiss. Luke growled in return.

The girl's shrill scream echoed through night as she stumbled off her chair and darted inside, slamming the door. The fiend looked up at the balcony and glared down at Luke. Its lips peeled back over dagger-like fangs in a sick attempt at a smile. Then, it disappeared in another cloud of smoke.

Shit! Luke ducked into the alley and shifted into human form. Where had the bastard gone? The girl's entire body trembled as she peeked through the curtains and clutched her phone in her hand. It hadn't followed her inside.

A freakish cackle sounded from down the street as the fiend jumped onto another rooftop. Luke gave chase, following it as it leapt from building to building, leading Luke up Chartres, closer and closer to Basin Street.

The demon jumped to the street and plowed through a group of people on a vampire tour. They squealed in surprise, laughing at their own reactions, probably thinking the fiend was part of the show. Luke slowed his pace as he wove through the crowd, trying not to draw any more attention to the chase. As soon as he broke from the mass, he sprinted after the beast. He wouldn't let this one get away.

"Smells like death around here. Need some help?" Chase and James caught up, flanking Luke on either side.

Luke pointed to the rooftop where the demon returned. "Tried to get a teenage girl on Barracks."

"The bastard," James said.

The demon darted across Basin street, weaving through traffic like a crazed animal. Drivers slammed on their brakes and honked their horns at what probably looked like a shadow to them.

The men followed, using the confusion in the traffic jam to their advantage and racing across the street. The demon scaled the wall of St. Louis Cemetery Number One and disappeared into the graveyard.

"Damn, that sucker's fast." Chase tried the gate. "Locked."

"Step aside, boys, and give me some cover." James took a lock-picking kit out of his pocket and stepped toward the gate. Luke and Chase stood in front of him, blocking him from view.

He tried to act casual, but so much adrenaline coursed through Luke's veins, he doubted he was pulling it off. "Make it quick," he said through clenched teeth as he nodded at a couple passing by. They slowed as they approached the cemetery gate—probably tourists wanting to experience the graveyard and all its spooky mysteries at night. But the St. Louis cemetery closed at dusk, and even daytime entry required a licensed tour guide. Breaking in was completely illegal, and completely necessary.

He straightened his spine and looked the man in the eyes. His girlfriend grabbed at his arm like she was nervous. "Evening," Luke said.

The man's eyes widened, a hint of fear draining the color from his face as he quickened his pace and hurried past.

"Got it. We're in." James popped the lock, and the others followed him inside the walls.

Stepping into the cemetery was like entering another world. Towering tombs rose from the ground in classic Spanish style. Row after row of white stucco structures housed the remains of generations of New Orleans residents. Most were well-kept, with elaborate statues adorning the crypts and long lists of names etched into plaques dating to the seventeen hundreds. Others had crumbled with decay, decades of weather eating away at the stucco, exposing the brick and mortar underneath.

"Welcome to the city of the dead," Luke mumbled.

"The demon could be anywhere," Chase said.

"We'll find him." James crept up the walkway, peering between each row of tombs. "Heeere demon, demon, demon," he called. "Come to papa, you disgusting piece of hell trash."

A shadow darted by in Luke's peripheral vision, and he took off after it. He sprinted up a row of tombs and made a left.

Dead end. No demon.

He backed out and continued up the path.

"Over here," James yelled.

Luke followed his voice across the cemetery and found the fiend perched atop an enormous mausoleum, like a hideous, living gargoyle. It peeled back its lips in a putrid smile and cackled wildly before disappearing in a cloud of smoke.

"What the hell?" Chase rubbed his eyes. "I've never seen one do that."

"I forgot to mention that," Luke said. "This one's gonna be harder to kill."

James grinned. "You mean more fun. Let's get this bastard." He shifted into wolf form and loped down the path. Chase and Luke shifted and took off in opposite directions. There'd be no more talk, but in wolf form, they had an almost telepathic form of communication. They couldn't exactly read each other's minds, but they always knew what the other was thinking.

Chase growled, and Luke turned a corner to find his friend face to face with the demon. It sneered as Chase leapt for it, disappearing in a poof before the wolf could make contact. It reappeared on a tomb four feet away, only to vanish and show up behind him. The fiend was toying with them.

James swiped at the creature, but it disappeared. Its teeth sank into Luke's shoulder before he even realized it was on his back. He howled and rolled, knocking the demon to the ground. Luke latched onto its leg, and it let out a screeching wail. It clawed the ground, trying to free itself from Luke's jaws.

They had it.

Chase pounced. Luke's teeth snapped together. The creature was gone.

It reformed two feet away, dragging its mangled leg and leaving a trail of smoking, black blood. The wolves circled it, closing in, growling. The fiend tried to disappear again, but the injury had zapped its strength. Fear filled its wild, red eyes as Luke stepped forward and swiped a claw across its heart. This time, the cloud of smoke turned into a pile of ash. They sent the demon back to hell.

The men shifted to human form and slipped out of the cemetery, locking the gate behind them.

"What a night," James said as they made their way into the French Quarter. "That one made six, all in a span of a few hours."

"I wonder what else he's going to throw at us tonight." Chase said.

"It's our turn to throw something at him." Luke glanced at his friends. "I know where the bastard lives."

"Macey?"

Macey's eyes fluttered open at the sound of her sister's voice. The kitchen lights pierced her eyes like daggers, and her stomach roiled at the pounding pain in her head. The cold tile floor chilled through her shirt, but it didn't stop the sweat from beading on her forehead. She rolled onto her side and clutched a cabinet, pulling herself into a sitting position.

"In here." Her voice came out as a croak. Her throat felt like she'd swallowed a desert. Glass crunched under Alexis's shoes, her pounding footsteps quickening like a jackhammer in Macey's skull.

"Macey!" Alexis dropped to her knees and reached out like she wanted to comfort her sister, but she hesitated. "Are you okay?"

Macey's vision wavered, but she managed to find her voice. "I'll survive. Help me up."

Alexis lifted her by the arm and steadied her on her feet. But as soon as she let go, the world turned on its side. Macey caught herself on the edge of the table, and her sister helped her into a chair.

"An ambulance is on its way," Alexis said.

"No. No hospitals. I just hit my head. I'll be okay."

"You could have a concussion."

Macey blinked away the stars in her vision and focused on her sister. "I'm fine."

Alexis crossed her arms. "You're going. I made the call when I found your front door open."

A fresh wave of nausea rolled through Macey's stomach. Maybe it wouldn't hurt to get her head checked. "Okay. Did you see Thor? My cat?"

"He hissed at me and ran down the hall." Alexis pulled a chair next to her and sat down. Her jaw flexed, the sound of her teeth grinding like crunching gravel in Macey's skull. Concern filled her sister's gaze as she reached out and gingerly brushed her fingers across the knot on Macey's head. She closed her eyes. "Who did this to you?"

CHAPTER TWENTY-FOUR

"HOLD STILL, YOU INSOLENT FOOL." ROSS'S VOICE SOUNDED LIKE IT came from inside Jimmy's head, but his brother wasn't possessing him. He squirmed under the boy's weight and screamed when the boy stuck his fingers into his wound. Ross wouldn't squirm or scream. Only stupid idiots did that.

The bullet made a squishy sucking sound as the boy pulled it out, and fire shot down Jimmy's arm. It wasn't really fire, but that's what it felt like. The real fire burned in the stove, crackling like a monster trying to escape a prison.

The boy wasn't a boy anymore. He was a full-grown man the same size as Jimmy, and he had no trouble pinning Jimmy to the floor. He stuck a long metal rod into the fire and poured alcohol into the hole in Jimmy's arm. Fresh flames seemed to engulf him, stinging like a thousand wasps.

"What are you gonna do with that poker?" Jimmy's voice sounded tiny.

"He's going to cauterize the wound. We can't have you bleeding out; I still need you."

"What's a cot-trize?"

"Cauterize, you idiot. Make it stop bleeding."

"Oh." It would be nice if it stopped bleeding. Maybe it would stop hurting too. "Is Miss Macey okay? You didn't kill her, did you?"

"If you wouldn't have gone and got yourself shot, I would have. Without a body, I barely had enough strength to knock her out."

Good. Miss Macey didn't deserve to die.

"Next time I see that bitch, she's dead."

Next time he saw her, Jimmy would fight back against his brother. He couldn't let Miss Macey get hurt. She was a nice lady. The nicest lady he'd ever met, besides Momma.

The boy who wasn't a boy smiled and pulled the poker out of the flames. The tip of the stick glowed red hot, and Jimmy squeezed his eyes shut. His heart pounded in his chest, and his wound bled harder.

The poker plunged into his shoulder, and he screamed. Then everything went black.

CHAPTER TWENTY-FIVE

"So, anyway, I was wrong. I'm sorry I screwed things up with you and Luke." Alexis brushed the hair out of Macey's face and sat on the edge of the hospital bed. A clock on the wall ticked the seconds away as the IV drip tried to keep time. The computer monitoring Macey's vitals hummed, quietly beeping every few seconds.

"Thanks for clearing that up." She patted her sister's hand.

The blood pressure cuff inflated, squeezing her bicep tightly before slowly, rhythmically releasing its grip as the pain medication relaxed her, easing the throbbing in her head to a dull ache. But it did nothing for the ache in her heart. She didn't know what to believe anymore. Did Luke care for her? Or was he using her? Maybe it was a little of both. Either way, she'd broken her sacred rule: don't let anyone get close enough to hurt her. It was time to repair the fortress walls she'd allowed Luke to break down.

"Do you think you'll get back together?"

Macey sighed. "I don't know. I've always had a hard time opening up to people, ever since…you know."

Alexis stared at her hands and sucked in a shaky breath. "I'm sorry."

"I know. And I understand why you did it now. I'm not blaming you. But it's going to take some time for me to learn to trust someone again. And Luke..." She shook her head. "I don't know. I've let my guard down too many times with him. He makes me want to open up and share everything about myself."

"Isn't that a good thing?"

"Not for me. I was vulnerable. If it was so easy for me to be *that* hurt over a misunderstanding, then I was in way over my head. I've never gotten so close to someone so fast. And now I know why."

A knock sounded on the door, and Bryce sauntered into to the room. He set a bouquet of pink roses on the table beside the bed and smiled at Macey. "How you feeling, boss?"

"A little headache. Any sign of the perp?"

"Not yet. Got word in at all the hospitals and urgent care clinics to let us know of any patients with shoulder wounds. Nothing so far."

Macey let out a sigh of relief. She'd given the first responders a false description of Jimmy and denied any knowledge of the attacker's identity. She'd even told them he wore a mask. "That's too bad."

Bryce's smile widened, and he ran a hand through his hair as if he just noticed someone else was in the room. "Hi there. I'm Bryce, Macey's partner." He reached across the bed to shake her sister's hand.

Alexis grinned as her cheeks flushed pink. "I'm Alexis. I'm...uh..." She looked at Macey, uncertainty causing her brow to furrow.

"She's my sister," Macey said.

Bryce stopped shaking her hand, but he didn't let it go. "I didn't know you had a sister, Mace." His gaze lingered on Alexis.

"It's a long story."

"Well, I better get going." Alexis slid her hand out of Bryce's grasp. "I'll check on Thor. Make sure he's okay. That's one hell of a cat."

"He deserves a medal," Macey said.

Alexis touched her fingertips to Macey's shoulder. "You'll be okay?"

The concern in her sister's voice touched her heart. She wasn't sure what to do about Luke, but she was glad to have Alexis back. "Yeah. Surprisingly, it wasn't a concussion. I'm sure I'll be released soon."

"I'll call you later. It was nice meeting you, Bryce." She smiled at him and slipped out the door.

Bryce stood there with his hands in his pockets, a goofy grin on his face as he watched her leave. "She's pretty."

Macey glared at him. "Don't even think about it."

He raised his hands. "What? I wasn't thinking."

"You never are. That's the problem."

He pulled up a chair next to the bed. "Is she single?"

She rolled her eyes. "She's not the type that wants to be your 'little woman,' making gumbo in the kitchen and having your babies."

"C'mon. You know I was kidding about that."

"She's off limits."

"Okay, boss. Whatever you say." He leaned his elbows on his knees, clasping his hands. "Do you really think this was a random attack? Nothing to do with the case?"

She cringed. Lying to her partner made her sick to her stomach, but what choice did she have? She had no idea how to cover everything up and solve the case in a way that would satisfy both the police and the werewolves. She needed to talk to Luke, but her chest tightened just thinking about him. "I don't know about random. I've put away plenty of bad guys, so someone could've been out for revenge. He wore a mask, so it could've been anyone. But I don't think it was the rapist." She smoothed the sheets over her stomach, trying to keep the bile from creeping up her throat. "He didn't seem interested in getting my clothes off. He wanted me dead. End of story."

"Well, I'm sure he'll turn up. He couldn't get too far with a wound like that. You're one tough little lady." He winked, always trying to get a rise out of her.

She was about to respond with a sarcastic comeback when the door flew open, thudding against the wall. Luke rushed in, his eyes wild with concern, and he threw himself onto the bed. "Oh, thank God." He stroked her hair and held her face in his hands. "I'm so sorry, Macey. Are you okay? What happened?" He kissed her forehead and both her cheeks.

She gripped the blankets in her fists to stop her arms from wrapping around his shoulders. Every fiber of her being ached to hold him, but she fought it. She would not lose her heart again. "I'm fine."

Bryce cleared his throat, and Luke looked up at him. His gaze danced between the flowers and her partner before landing back on Macey.

"Have you met Bryce?" she asked.

"Not officially." Luke shook his hand and focused his attention on Macey. "I'm so sorry, Macey. This is all my fault. I should have been there to protect you from that..." He cut his gaze over to Bryce. "That asshole."

She stiffened. "I don't need protection." Was that why he was concerned? Not because she was hurt, but because he felt guilty?

Bryce stood and shoved his hands in his pockets. "Don't let her size fool you. She's pretty good at protecting herself."

"No." Luke shook his head. "I should have been there for you."

"Well." Bryce shuffled toward the door. "I'll let you two work this out on your own. I'll call you if I hear anything, boss."

Bryce closed the door, and Macey glared at Luke. "I did fine on my own."

Luke looked at her incredulously. "He knocked you out. You're in the hospital."

"I'm alive, aren't I? I shot him and came out with nothing more than a headache." Did he honestly think she was that helpless? That he needed to spend every waking moment by her side to protect her from the bad guys? She'd been fighting bad guys without him for years.

"I..." He let out a heavy sigh.

"Why are you even here, Luke? What do you want?" Anger seethed in her voice, and anger was good. Anger would keep her heart hardened.

He took her hand in his and stroked it. "Isn't it obvious? Those things Alexis told you weren't true."

She looked at her hand resting in his. The warmth of his touch. The familiar energy dancing on her skin. How could something so bad for her feel so right? *Anger. Focus on the anger.* "You said them, though."

"I know. I did it to appease the pack. To keep things under control. But I didn't mean a word of it. She told you that, right?"

Macey's throat thickened. Her eyes stung with tears. Why did her resolve dissolve into nothing around him? He knew her weaknesses.

How to press every button to keep her wrapped around his finger. Tears shimmered in his sapphire eyes, and she wanted nothing more than to throw her arms around his neck and let him back in.

But she couldn't. She had to be strong this time. Her heart might not survive another beating from a man like Luke. "She told me, but…"

"But?"

"But I don't know." She pulled her hand from his grasp and hugged herself. "I don't know what to believe anymore."

His hands clenched into fists on the blanket. "Damn it, Macey. I love you. Believe that."

She sucked in a shaky breath and hugged herself tighter. She did believe him. The emotion in his eyes spoke volumes above the words, but it didn't mean he'd stay. Her sister and her parents had loved her, but they'd abandoned her anyway. Love may have been a glue that held people together, but life could always tear them apart.

"Detective Carpenter?" A nurse poked her head through the doorway and knocked before entering the room. "You're being released. Just sign here, and you're free to leave." She looked at Luke. "Do you have a ride?"

"Yeah, I'll take her home," Luke said before she could answer.

The nurse removed the IV and disconnected her from the monitoring equipment before handing her a plastic bag. "Here are your clothes. Let me know if you need anything else."

As the nurse left the room, Macey swung her legs over the side of the bed. Her head still hurt, but at least she could get out of this suffocating hospital room. Luke watched her as she pulled her clothes from the bag and started to untie her gown. "Do you mind turning around?" she said.

"Yeah. Sure." His voice was barely a whisper, made thick by the tears he tried to hold back. He turned his back to her and fiddled with his hands as if he wasn't sure what to do with them.

He'd seen her naked before. He'd touched every inch of her body. But now she felt vulnerable, exposed in front of this man who knew way too much about her. She dressed quickly and cleared her throat to let him know she was done.

When he turned around, light glistened off the dampness of his cheeks. "I love you, Macey."

"I know. But the way I reacted when Alexis told me those things scared me to death. It's not you. *I* scared *myself.* I'm not used to being close to people."

He shoved his hands in his pockets and let out a dry chuckle. "Great. The 'it's not you, it's me' speech. Classic."

Why did her heart feel like it was being ripped from her chest? "I just need some time."

"Take all the time you need. I'm not going anywhere."

As long as she made up her mind within the next few days, he'd be fine. While his dad's retirement date wasn't technically set in stone, it would take an act of congress to change it. Literally. His father had filed for retirement with the werewolf national congress three and a half years ago. An alpha resigning voluntarily wasn't taken lightly, and he had to file for permission years in advance. He had to prove he had an acceptable successor, and a second in line in case the first one didn't work out.

Three and a half years ago, Luke had been engaged to Melissa. As the oldest male of the bloodline after Luke, Stephen had been the obvious second choice. No one ever expected him to actually be in the running for alpha, and now he was—if Luke couldn't get his act together. If he couldn't convince Macey they belonged together, he only had two options. Mate with someone he didn't love or let the pack fall into Stephen's hands. Neither option was acceptable. He couldn't let his twisted, power-hungry cousin tear apart the pack. And he could never love another woman. He'd thought he loved Melissa, but she hadn't been his fate-bound. Hell, he'd never fathomed the depths of love he was capable of until he met Macey.

She was his fate-bound. Now, if he could just convince her.

He pulled up to the curb in front of Macey's house and shut off the engine.

"Thanks for the ride." She reached for the door handle.

"Macey."

She froze, her hand trembling on the latch. "I should go."

"We don't have to talk about us…until you're ready. But we do need to talk about what happened. It was him, wasn't it? The guy from the sketch?"

She chewed her bottom lip and stared out the window. "I think you better come inside."

Glass crunched under his boots when he stepped through the door. A white ceramic lamp lay shattered on the floor, and a cracked dent marred the drywall at Macey's head level. If the guy had knocked her unconscious, he could've killed her easily. Snapped her neck. Crushed her windpipe.

His stomach twisted. He'd come so close to losing her. All the blood in his head plunged to his feet, making the room spin, before a flash of anger singed through his veins. Anger at the attacker, but more than anything, anger at himself for letting it happen. "Christ! What did that bastard do to you?"

"It's fine." She grabbed a broom from the closet and swept up the mess. "He didn't know what he was doing."

"He didn't know?" How hard had she hit her head to think the man didn't know he was trying to kill her?

She continued her frantic sweeping, keeping her gaze trained on the floor.

"Macey." He put his hand on the broom to stop her. "Come sit down. Talk to me."

She tugged on her bottom lip as her gaze darted about the room. "Luke, I…"

"Hey." He took the broom from her hand and leaned it against the wall. "It's business, okay? No matter your feelings for me, we're on the same team. We're going to have to work together, so put your detective cap on and talk to me like a cop. Right now, I'm just the alpha, and you're a police officer, and we're trying to solve a case."

Her posture relaxed, the tension draining from her muscles as she stepped toward the sofa. A slight smile curved one side of her mouth, and the sparkle almost returned to her eyes. "But you're not the alpha."

"Not yet." His arms ached to hold her as she sank onto the couch. Days ago, she'd been his. Now she was like a stunning statue in a museum. Cold and untouchable. But not completely. That small smile, that tiny glimmer, gave him hope. She could be his again.

He sat on the opposite end of the sofa, not nearly as close as he wanted to be. "What did you mean when you said he didn't know what he was doing?"

Her fingers brushed the knot on her head. "He was the rapist. But he wasn't. He did it, but he didn't mean to."

He looked at her, hoping his silence would encourage her to explain. She wasn't making any sense at all.

She let out an exasperated sigh. "The man in that picture—the man who beat me up last night—he was possessed by a demon."

"A demon?"

"Yeah."

"How do you know?"

"Because it was the same demon that tried to possess me. The halfling that went missing from the morgue."

He raised an eyebrow. "You're sure?"

"It's him. He's the hotel room rapist. He's using his brother, possessing him so he can assault women and do whatever else."

He nodded. "And summon more demons. He was a halfling. His brother must be human. He's using his brother's blood to summon the fiends." Luke's heart pounded. It was all starting to make sense. "We've got him, Macey. I know where the bastard lives. We can take out him and his brother." He wanted to hug her. To sweep her up in his arms and kiss her. He refrained.

She shook her head. "You can't."

"Oh, yes we can. Werewolves were born to hunt demons. We can take them both down."

"You can't hurt his brother. Jimmy is innocent."

Luke scoffed. "Innocent, my ass. He's been summoning demons. Only a pure human can do that."

"You don't understand. Jimmy is...special. He's like a little boy stuck in a man's body. His brother abuses him into submission." She looked at him with pleading eyes. "He needs help, Luke."

Crap. "Well, that complicates things, doesn't it?"

She yawned. "I guess it does."

"You've been up all night. You should get some rest. I'll stay with you…I mean, I'll stay in the living room…so you can sleep."

She cocked an eyebrow. "I'll sleep fine without you here. Don't you have some demons to chase?"

"Not in the middle of the day. It's okay. I can stay and keep you safe."

Her nostrils flared. "I don't need you to keep me safe. I'm going to take a nap, and then I'm going to go to work."

"You're recovering from an attack. You shouldn't be going to work."

She stood and marched toward the door. "You shouldn't be telling me what to do. I appreciate the ride home, but now it's time for you to leave."

He'd done it again. The mere suggestion that she might need help always seemed to set her off. He should've known better by now to tread carefully around that subject. Standing, he cautiously approached her. He needed to defuse the situation before he walked out the door. He couldn't leave her mad at him…didn't want to leave her at all.

"I'm sorry. You're right, I'm being overprotective. I just…I came so close to losing you. I'm afraid for it to happen again."

He took a step closer and cupped her face in his hand. For a moment, she nuzzled into his touch, closing her eyes like she was giving in. Then she stiffened.

"You don't h…have me anymore." Her voice trembled as she spoke.

He dropped his hand to his side. "I know. But that doesn't mean I won't fight for you."

She took a deep, shuddering breath. "When I allow myself to get close to anyone, something always happens. Life always finds a way to take away the ones I love."

He reached for her hand, lacing his fingers through hers, his heart hammering at her use of that word. She didn't pull away. "Life never gives guarantees, but I can. I promise you this, Macey. I will love you with every fiber of my being for as long as I'm alive, and I will do everything in my power to stand by your side forever, no matter what life has in mind."

"I'm scared."

"I know. But don't be so afraid of dying that you never learn to live." He squeezed her hand and kissed her softly on the cheek. Her breath hitched when his lips brushed her face. Was it the supernatural energy or merely from his touch? "Please lock the door. And don't answer it for anyone."

She nodded and closed the door. He caught it with his hand just before it shut. He couldn't mask the pain of his breaking heart. "Come back to me, Macey. Please."

"I need more time. I'm sorry."

CHAPTER TWENTY-SIX

MACEY GAZED AT THE OBLONG CRYSTAL ROBERTA HAD GIVEN her. It weighed heavy in her hands, its uneven edges rough against her skin. *You'll know what to do when the time comes.* Hopefully, Roberta was right. Releasing energy from objects had become so easy, once she learned what to do. Would trapping a ghost be as simple? *Just do the same thing, in reverse.* She could do that, couldn't she? She had to. This was the weapon for stopping the demon spirit, and Macey had to wield it.

She sighed and dropped the stone into her purse before shoving it in her desk drawer. If Luke would even let her get close to the fiend. He had this crazy idea that she was a helpless damsel in distress who wouldn't be safe without a big bad werewolf watching out for her. Never mind that she was a police detective who fought human monsters every day. What was his problem?

She slammed the drawer shut and toyed with her copper bracelet. Had her mother been a full werewolf who could shift? Or her father? Her life would certainly have been different if her parents had survived. Maybe she wouldn't be so terrified of loving Luke if they had. Then again, she probably wouldn't have even met him.

Her chest ached with the thoughts. *Focus on one thing at a time.*

Right now, the most important thing was stopping the demon spirit and getting Jimmy the help he needed. Fixing her heart would have to wait.

"You okay, boss?" Bryce leaned in the doorway and took a bite of his Snickers bar. "I didn't expect you back tonight."

"I'm fine. Needed to get out of the house. Keep my mind busy."

He pushed off the door and sauntered toward her desk, dropping a Hershey Special Dark bar in front of her as he sat in a chair. "I hear women like chocolate when they're having man trouble." He winked.

"I…" She started to push the candy away but hesitated. The sweet chocolaty scent filled her nose, making her mouth water. "What the hell." She opened the wrapper and placed a square of chocolate on her tongue. Her eyelids closed as the bittersweet goodness melted, relaxing the tension in her shoulders. When she opened her eyes, Bryce grinned at her.

"Wanna talk about it?" he asked.

"Not really."

"Whew." He pretended to wipe sweat from his forehead. "Good."

Macey rolled her eyes.

"Can we talk about your pretty sister?" He wiggled his eyebrows.

"No."

"Well, it was worth a shot. Listen, Mace, I'm pushing them real hard to find the guy that attacked you, but they're coming up with nothing. Have you remembered any more details? Anything at all that could help our boys out?"

Her face tightened. She tried to relax into a neutral expression, but her heart rate kicked up, and her palms went slick with sweat. She looked him in the eyes, forcing herself to hold his gaze as she spoke. "I've told you everything I remember."

He squinted at her, studying her. Bryce could spot a lie a mile away before it even rounded the corner. He wouldn't buy it, but he might let it slide. "And you're not holding anything back? Nothing else is going on? That Luke guy—"

"Luke did not hurt me, so don't even go there." *Not physically, anyway.*

"Okay. But if you ever need any help with him…"

"It's not like that. I promise."

"But if it ever is."

She reached across the desk and patted his hand. "Thanks, Bryce."

The tune of Taylor Swift's "Shake It Off" drifted up from Bryce's pants. He grinned as he fished his phone out of his pocket. "Like my ringtone? It's new."

Macey laughed and leaned back in her chair. If only she could shake it off like Taylor. She trusted her partner. She hadn't opened up to him about everything in her life, but he knew a lot. And he'd been around for five years. Maybe Luke... She didn't have time to finish her thought.

"Got another one. Over on Esplanade. Let's go."

Luke brushed off his shirt and tied back his hair. His parents had arrived at the Louis Armstrong International Airport that afternoon, and his dad waited for him in the office. Dread tightened his chest. He'd hoped to have the demon infestation taken care of before his old man got home. He could imagine the disappointment his father must have felt to learn Luke hadn't taken care of the problem.

He hadn't seen his folks in two months, and he'd hoped their reunion would consist of a nice dinner and maybe a few souvenirs. His dad wanted to get straight to business.

He opened the door to find Marcus sitting behind the desk, a casual smile lighting his face as he stroked his wife's hand. Luke's mom perched on the edge of the bureau, toying with a tiny Eiffel Tower figure. She set the trinket on the desk and rushed toward Luke, wrapping her arms around him.

"Welcome home, Mom. How was your trip?"

"It was wonderful. I can't wait to tell you all about it."

"Hey, Dad." Luke reached across the desk to shake his father's hand.

"Sit down, son." Marcus's face was serious. "I'm concerned."

Luke sank into the chair and gripped the smooth, wooden arm rests. The disappointment in the old man's eyes stung. He'd failed him.

"I expected a debriefing from you first, but I wasn't home ten minutes before your cousin knocked on my door." Marcus folded his hands on the table and leaned forward, resting his weight on his arms. The chair creaked with his movement. Luke's mother settled into the chair next to him and clasped her hands in her lap.

Luke cleared his throat. "I've got the demon situation under control. I have a plan. I—"

"That's not what I'm worried about. I have no doubt you'll clean up that mess before the week is through."

He exhaled. He hadn't failed his father. Not yet. "Then what did Stephen want, if not to tattle on my lack of progress?"

His father held his eyes with a steely gaze. "He wants to be alpha, son. Rumor has it you haven't selected a mate. You know you can't be alpha unless you're mated to another werewolf."

Luke rubbed the back of his neck. "I have chosen one."

His dad crossed his arms over his chest. "The cop? I heard she dumped you."

Good news sure did travel fast in the wolf pack. "She just needs time. She'll come around."

"We don't have time."

His mom patted his hand. "I was ecstatic when I heard Macey was a were. I really was. But if she doesn't want to be with you…"

He jerked his hand away. "She does. I love her, and I know she loves me. She's scared. That's all. Macey *will* come back to me."

His old man leaned back in his chair. "And if she doesn't? I won't have Stephen tearing this pack apart."

Luke shot out of the chair, knocking it over. "He won't." He clenched his fists by his sides and raked in a ragged breath. "I *will* be alpha."

"Then you'd better choose an alternative mate. You're running out of time. After Stephen left, three different women knocked on my door offering to be your mate. The pack doesn't want your cousin to lead it. You have plenty of choices, son."

He swallowed down the sour taste bubbling from his throat. Choosing anyone but Macey was unthinkable. "I'll tell you what. If I can't win Macey back before the deadline...you can choose one for me. Anybody you want. It doesn't matter."

"Oh, honey." His mom's eyes held sadness, her voice pity. "We can't choose a life partner for you."

"Sure you can. If it isn't Macey, it might as well be anyone. It won't matter to me, because I'll never love anyone else. I'll do my duty. I'll run this pack, and I'll have offspring. But my heart will always belong to Macey." He reached for the doorknob. "I'm going to get her back. She just has to learn to trust me."

His mom smiled. "Then you need to learn to trust her."

Jimmy woke up to a throbbing pain in his shoulder. His back ached from sleeping on the floor, and his hair was soaked through with sweat. "Hello?" he called out into the shack.

No one answered.

"Ross? Boy?"

Silence.

He peeled himself off the floor and gingerly touched his wound. A big white blister surrounded by an angry red welt covered the hole where Miss Macey's bullet had hit him. It wasn't bleeding anymore, but it sure did hurt.

Miss Macey had looked so frightened when he went to her house. Ross had used him to scare the nice lady, and he'd tried to kill her too. Jimmy didn't like scaring or killing. Or being used. Hopefully Miss Macey was okay, but Ross would keep going after her until she was dead. He was sure of that. He wouldn't use Jimmy to do it, though. Jimmy would fight back.

His stomach growled, and the memory of those hotdogs made his mouth water. Maybe he could help Miss Macey. No one had ever been so nice to him, except for Momma. He picked at the scar on his palm. Ross had killed Momma. Jimmy wouldn't let him kill Miss Macey too.

CHAPTER TWENTY-SEVEN

As Macey climbed the creaky wooden steps toward the victim's apartment, she ran her hand along the cracked brick wall. Images of the building's history shuffled through her mind like a slide show of secrets to which only she was privy. A few weeks ago, the barrage of images would've overwhelmed her. Now that Roberta had helped develop her gift, she could easily grab hold of any image she chose and soak in the energy, the story, the building held.

She grinned as she watched the image of two young boys in knickers and suspenders sliding down the stairs on an old board like they were riding a sled. They hooped and hollered and crashed at the bottom, then ran back up and slid down again.

Would her own children be as rambunctious as these boys one day? Would they look like her, with small statures and pale hair? Or would they favor Luke?

She shook herself. *Don't think like that.* She needed to focus on the case. One step at a time.

"You okay?" Bryce paused at the top of the stairs; Macey had stopped mid-flight.

"Yeah. Just…reading." She continued her ascent.

Bryce raised his eyebrows. "Anything helpful?"

She shook her head and brushed past him. The victim's apartment showed no sign of struggle. A rainbow of pillows lined the sofa, each one tilted at a perfect diagonal and carefully laid in place. The shelves held rows of neatly stacked books, and a stick of burning incense filled the room with patchouli. Strings of orange beads hung over the doorway to the balcony, and Macey stepped through to find the victim sipping juice on a lawn chair.

The woman had dark brown eyes that crinkled in the corners when she smiled. "You must be the great Detective Carpenter. I've heard about you." She offered her hand, and Macey shook it.

A soft tingle buzzed up her arm, and Macey narrowed her eyes. The woman wasn't a werewolf; the sensation felt different. But she possessed some sort of magic. A small cut marred her forehead, and a clay pot lay smashed on the floor. Here had been the struggle.

"You seem awfully calm for being the victim of an attempted sexual assault, Miss…" She flipped through her notes to find the woman's name.

"Natasha."

"Natasha, can you tell me what happened?"

The woman waved her hand dismissively. "It was nothing a little voodoo magic couldn't take care of."

"Voodoo?" Bryce tried to step onto the balcony, but he got tangled in the beads hanging in the doorway. He stumbled and spun around and finally made it out the door.

Natasha glanced at him and focused on Macey. "That demon messed with the wrong priestess is all I'm saying."

"Demon, huh?" Bryce chuckled. "Let me guess. Red eyes?"

"Yeah," Macey said. "We've been getting a lot of reports of a guy wearing red contacts harassing women. It was probably him."

Natasha glared at Macey, her gaze heavy, full of warning. "I know a demon when I see one. You should too."

Macey stepped toward her partner and lowered her voice. "Why don't you let me handle this. Maybe I can talk some sense into her. You know…woman to woman."

"Gotcha, boss. I'll be right inside." Bryce swatted at the hanging beads and stepped through the door.

Macey pulled a chair up next to Natasha. "The demon," she whispered. "What did it look like?"

"Oh, you believe me now, do you?" Natasha spoke loudly, leaning back and crossing her arms.

"Shh…I do, but they don't." She nodded toward the men in the apartment. "Did you kill it?"

Natasha laughed. "Kill it? Nah. I can send a spirit on to the next plane, but I ain't mastered demon slaying. I sure did scare it off, though."

"Which way did it go?"

"Took off up the street there." She pointed. "He's probably still hanging around. I pissed him off, so he'll be back. You can count on that."

"Maybe you should stay inside tonight." Macey leaned over the balcony, scanning the shadows below. If only her werewolf blood enhanced her vision like it did her sense of smell. All she could see was darkness.

"I ain't afraid of no demon. The neighbors heard the commotion and called you, but I done blessed this place and set up a charm. Ain't no evil getting back in here tonight."

"All right. Just—" Something stirred in the corner of her vision. Two blocks away, a shadow morphed into a human-like form and slinked down the street. "That's it, isn't it?"

Natasha leaned forward. "Mm-hmm. That's a demon if I ever seen one. Check out them eyes."

The fiend turned its head, and crimson eyes flashed like glowing embers. Where were the werewolves? They were supposed to be stopping these things. Macey darted into the apartment and shoved past the officers in the living room.

"Where you headed?" Bryce called as she dashed through the door.

"I'll be right back. Stay here." She bounded down the steps and sprinted as soon as her feet hit the pavement. "Hey! Stop!"

The demon turned around and peeled its lips back into a reptilian sneer. It hissed and darted down an alley into the shadows. Macey veered around the corner and skidded to a stop. Dead end. She had it trapped.

The creature crouched by the wall, rocking side to side on its claw-like feet. It made a screeching sound like metal scraping metal and arched its back like a cat. Macey raised her gun. Head or heart? Would a bullet even kill a demon? She hesitated, hovering her sights between its eyes. No. It had to be the heart.

The demon screeched again, and another assaulting wail answered it. Macey jerked her head around as a second demon dropped into the alley from the rooftop above. Her heart jack hammered in her chest. The *whooshing* of her pulse pounded in her ears. She pointed her gun at the first demon. Then the second. What could she do? They had her pinned in.

They crept toward her, inching closer, their crimson eyes bleeding hate. The second fiend sprang, leaping toward Macey and knocking the gun out of her hand. It skidded to the feet of the first demon, who picked it up and tossed it aside.

The demons slithered closer, the odor of death and garbage emanating from their pores and assaulting Macey's senses. She stumbled back and tripped over a broken piece of wrought iron railing. She fell to the ground and quickly sprang to her feet, gripping the metal stake in her hand.

She couldn't breathe. Fear gripped her heart like a steel fist as she waved the pole at the fiends. If she was going down, she'd go down fighting. "Back off."

A massive, sandy colored wolf dropped into the alley from above. Without warning, it leapt toward a demon and clamped its jaws on the fiend's neck. Macey didn't hesitate. She charged at the second demon and drove the metal spike straight through its heart. The devil exploded into a billowing cloud of ash as the stake clattered on the cobblestone.

Macey gasped and stumbled back against the wall. The werewolf grunted, standing over the ashes of the other fiend. It nudged Macey's pistol with its nose, sliding the gun across the stones. Macey crept forward and picked it up.

"Thanks for your help. I know you're not Luke. Who are you?"

The wolf glanced down the alley toward the street and blew out a hard breath. It shifted its gaze back to Macey as its body began to vibrate. A shimmery mist enveloped it, and it transformed into a woman.

Macey blinked. "Alexis?"

She rushed toward her sister and embraced her. "Macey! Are you okay?"

"Yeah. I'm fine. But…your clothes." She ran her hands over Alexis's shirt sleeves. The wolf wasn't wearing a teal T-shirt and jeans, but when it morphed into her sister, she was fully clothed. "How?"

She shrugged. "Magic, I suppose. Whatever I'm wearing…or carrying in my pockets…gets absorbed in the shift. When I shift back, everything's in its place."

"That's…weird."

"It's always been this way."

"Well, how about that?" She shook her head. "When did you start chasing demons?"

Alexis dropped her arms by her sides. "I don't…officially. Luke won't let me on the team since I'm not a pack member. But I figured y'all needed all the help you could get."

"Thanks. You saved my life."

"Hardly. You slayed that demon like a pro." She wrapped an arm around Macey's shoulders. "You can take care of yourself, little sis."

Macey sighed. "I'm glad someone thinks so. Walk with me. I need to get back to my partner."

"Luke being over-protective?" Alexis followed her sister out of the alley.

"He's treating me like I'm helpless. I have one little altercation, and suddenly he thinks I can't be alone anymore."

"You have to remember…he's an alpha male. About to be *the* alpha male. It's in his nature to be protective."

Macey slowed her pace as they approached Natasha's building. "I know. You're right, but…"

"But you're scared."

"Terrified."

"I get it." Alexis nodded toward Bryce coming down the stairs. "There's your partner. You'd better get back to work. I'll call you later."

Macey jogged to the building and arrived as Bryce reached the street. Natasha still sat on her balcony, sipping her glass of juice and smiling smugly.

"Thanks, Natasha," Macey called up to her. "It's taken care of. You have a good night."

Natasha waved. "Yes, ma'am. I knew you could do it."

"What was that about?" Bryce said as they walked to his car.

Macey grinned. "It's a girl thing. You wouldn't understand."

Chase leaned against the wall outside Jean Lafitte's Blacksmith Shop. With his hands shoved in his pockets and one leg crossed in front of the other, he appeared calm, casual. To a human, he looked like a normal guy hanging out in the French Quarter. But Luke knew better. Chase's attentive eyes scanned the scene, raking back and forth across the shadows in the distance. He was hunting demons.

The old Blacksmith Shop-turned-bar was a popular place for ghost tours to stop and give the tourists a break. Built in the 1700s, it was one of the oldest buildings in the Quarter. Two attic windows jutted up from the sagging, shingled roof, and a brick and mortar chimney rose between them. Three shuttered doors stood open on the building front, and patrons filed in and out as they got their drinks and returned to their tours. The structure's sordid history alone would be enough to attract creatures from hell. The crowd swarming inside and spilling out onto the sidewalk made it all the more appealing.

"Quiet night." Luke sauntered toward his friend.

"Yeah." Chase smiled, but it didn't reach his eyes. He inhaled and opened his mouth like he was going to say something, but he shook his head instead. Luke leaned against the wall and shoved his hands in his pockets to mirror Chase's posture.

Chase glanced at him with a strange expression and focused back on the shadows. "How'd the debriefing go with your old man?"

Luke exhaled sharply and ran his hand over his face. "Not good, man."

"Not happy about the demon situation?"

"No. I've got a plan for that. We're going to take these suckers out tomorrow afternoon." He told Chase about the new information Macey had given him. "Soon as I find someone who can trap the halfling spirit, we're good to go."

"What's the problem then?"

"It's Stephen. Knocked on the old man's door as soon as he found out they were home."

Chase shook his head. "He's chomping at the bit to be alpha. Dude wants it bad. I hope he doesn't do anything stupid."

"He won't."

Chase hesitated, kicking at the dust on the ground. "He's not going to get the chance to be alpha is he?" He raised his eyes to meet Luke's, and they were tight with worry. "You'll mate?"

"C'mon, man. You know me better than that." He let out a cynical laugh. "I told my folks if I couldn't get Macey back before the deadline, they could choose someone for me."

Chase raised an eyebrow. "You'd go through with that?"

"As long as the mate understands it's just business, yeah. I'll do what I have to do for the good of the pack. But honestly?" He let his gaze drift toward the shadows as his throat thickened. "It *has* to be Macey. It *will* be."

"Yeah. Speaking of Macey and our quiet night, I talked to Alexis a few minutes ago."

A feeling of dread sank in his gut as he gave him his full attention. "What happened? Is Macey okay?"

"She's fine. But...a pair of demons cornered your girl in an alley. Alexis fought them off, sent them back to hell."

His stomach turned. "Holy shit. It must've happened when I was meeting with my parents. Goddammit! I should've been there to protect her. I've got to go check on her."

Chase put a hand on Luke's arm. "Slow down, Lancelot. Your princess walked away without a scratch."

Luke balled his hands into fists. His muscles tightened with the urge to run to her. To comfort her. But what good would that do? She didn't want to see him. He inhaled deeply and tried to relax.

"Look," Chase said, "I know you worry about her after what happened to Melissa."

"I worry about any were who can't shift. They're defenseless."

"Some may be, but Macey isn't one of them. She's a badass detective who takes down monsters on a daily basis. So the monsters she's used to are human. So what? Sometimes those are the worst kind."

Luke huffed. His friend had a point.

"I don't know much about women, but I'm pretty sure you rushing in to scold her for doing her job isn't going to help your case. Think about the things that attracted you to her in the first place. Her independence? Spunk? Confidence? Those things aren't going to disappear because you're in her life. They make her who she is. Macey doesn't need a knight in shining armor. She needs a partner."

"Damn it, Chase. Why do you have to make so much sense?"

He grinned. "Someone's got to keep you in line."

Across the street, the shadows moved. A drunk woman leaned against the wall near an alley entrance, her friends ignoring her as she doubled over and dry heaved. A fiend had found its target. Luke nodded toward the demon. "Looks like we'll have an interesting night after all."

CHAPTER TWENTY-EIGHT

Luke got up at dawn and headed to Café Beignet to meet Roberta. He could take care of the living halfling and the human, but he needed a medium to trap the demon spirit. Roberta would know who could help.

He turned onto Bourbon Street and headed toward Musical Legends Park. The café was located in the rear of the square. Foamy liquid flowed down the sidewalks and cascaded into the storm drains, and he inhaled the clean scent of soap. This was the best Bourbon Street would smell all day. Every morning, before the sun came up, a crew washed the streets in the French Quarter. Especially this one. The bubbly mixture rinsed away most of the beer, urine, and vomit the tourists had deposited the night before, but it wouldn't be long before the foul scents returned. As soon as the revelers finished nursing their hangovers, they'd start the party over again.

Laissez les bon temps roulez. Let the good times roll. It was the theme of the Big Easy, and he understood the appeal. He'd done his share of partying, and he couldn't imagine a greater city than New Orleans.

As he entered the park, he spotted Roberta sitting on an upstairs patio, sipping from a paper cup. Alexis sat next to her at the small, wrought iron table. What the hell was she doing there? Roberta waved, smiling brightly. Alexis swallowed hard and averted her gaze. At least she realized she was overstepping her boundaries.

"Thanks for meeting me, Roberta." Luke settled into a chair across from the women. "Alexis." He nodded.

The corners of Roberta's eyes crinkled, deepening her crow's feet into canyons. "Anything I can do to help my friends." She passed a knowing glance to Alexis.

Luke stiffened. Pack members couldn't keep secrets from the alpha. Normally he could demand they tell him whatever secret they shared. But these women weren't pack...and he didn't technically hold the alpha title yet. He'd have to coax it out of them gently.

"What are you doing here, Alexis?" Okay, maybe not so gently, but the woman had been a thorn in his side from the beginning.

She sat up straight. "Roberta invited me."

"She's as much a part of this mess as you are," Roberta said.

His jaw tightened as he glared at Macey's sister. She did look out for her family; he'd give her that. "Fine." He shifted his gaze to Roberta. "I need a medium."

Roberta started to answer, but remained silent as a waiter delivered a cup of black coffee for Luke and three orders of beignets. He hadn't planned on eating, but he couldn't resist the sugary pastries. He tore one in half and shoved the French donut into his mouth. Powdered sugar floated down, dusting the table and his pants in white.

Amusement turned up the corners of Roberta's mouth. "You have a medium. A powerful one."

"Who?" Luke sipped his coffee to wash down the pastry.

"Macey," Alexis said.

He choked, spilling hot liquid down the front of his shirt. He slammed the Styrofoam cup on the table, sloshing the coffee everywhere. Roberta handed him a stack of napkins, and he dabbed at the stain on his shirt. "No way."

"Why not?" Alexis's challenging tone grated on his nerves.

"She's the best one for the job," Roberta said. "Her powers are effortless. She's a natural."

Luke shook his head. Macey wasn't getting anywhere near that demon again. "There has to be someone else. I won't put her in harm's way. She knows virtually nothing about the supernatural world. She can't shift. She's defenseless against these monsters."

Alexis crossed her arms. "Defenseless? She killed a demon last night. I think she can handle herself around monsters."

He froze. The napkin fell to the table. "She...killed one? Chase said that you…"

"I didn't tell him the whole story. She was fierce, Luke. She rammed a piece of wrought iron fence right through its heart. She probably could've taken on both of them if I hadn't shown up to help."

His mouth hung open in disbelief. Thoughts tumbled through his mind as he tried to comprehend. "She killed it?"

"I'm telling you," Alexis said, "she can take care of herself. And she can trap this spirit. You need to give her a chance."

Maybe she could handle it. She was strong. The strongest woman he knew. "I… She…"

"She's a detective, dear," Roberta said. "It's her job to be in harm's way. She needs to end this as much as you do. Let her."

He ground his teeth and swallowed hard. A weight the size of a bowling ball formed in his stomach as he took a deep breath and nodded. "Bring her to the bar at eleven, then we'll head to the swamp."

Alexis stood. "I'm coming too."

"Damn right you are." His team could handle the halfling and the human. Alexis would help him protect Macey.

Luke brought Chase and James up to speed on the situation while he waited for Macey and Alexis to arrive. Stephen insisted on tagging along, but he probably only wanted to impress the alpha. He'd shown no interest in the demon hunting team before the old man came back.

"Don't kill the human," Luke said. "He's innocent."

"Are you kidding me?" Stephen crossed his arms. "He's been summoning *demons*."

Luke sighed. This part would take some convincing…for all of them. He wasn't sure he believed in the guy's innocence himself, but Macey insisted. "He's a few cards short of a full deck, okay? Macey says he's like a kid in a man's body, and his brother's been forcing him to do it."

Stephen's lip curved in disgust. "Macey? Now we're taking orders from a human outside the pack?"

"You know she's not human." Luke stood and stepped around the desk, asserting his dominance.

Stephen widened his stance. "She's not pack."

"She will be."

"Some alpha you're gonna be. Taking orders from a woman."

Luke slammed his forearm against Stephen's chest, pinning him to the wall. Heat rolled through his body, his beast begging to take over and fight. It might take an ass-kicking to keep his cousin in line, but now wasn't the time. He took a deep breath, and spoke in a low growl. "I *will* be alpha. And *I'm* giving the orders. You better learn to accept that." He leaned in, pressing the air from his cousin's lungs. "Show some respect."

He released him, and Stephen slumped against the wall, rubbing his chest. He mumbled something under his breath, but Luke ignored him. It was eleven o'clock. The women had arrived.

Luke stepped through the swinging door into the bar to find Alexis and Macey chatting with his sister. Macey wore dark jeans and a fitted black T-shirt that hugged her curves in all the right places. Her face was clean of makeup, and she'd tied her hair back into a bun. Her gun sat holstered on her hip, while a black messenger bag hung across her body on the other side. His heart flittered at the sight of her, his fingers twitching to untie her hair.

Her eyes lit up for a moment when they met his, but they quickly dimmed as she looked away. His chest ached, but he pushed the emotions aside. "Seen anything helpful?" he asked Amber.

"It's fuzzy. You guys are clouding my visions with all that testosterone." She smiled and motioned for Luke to come closer. Leaning in, she whispered, "Watch your back today. I'm sensing friendly fire."

"Details?" He glanced at his cousin.

She shook her head. "Good luck."

He turned to his team. "I'll drive the women as close as we can get, and we'll walk the rest of the way. Meet us there."

"Got it," James said, and the three men darted out the door.

He motioned for Macey and Alexis to follow him to his truck, and they all climbed in. The air hung heavy, tension thickening the atmosphere as Luke scrambled for something to say. Conversations with Macey had always been so easy before, flowing effortlessly like they'd never run out of things to talk about. Now he was at a loss for words. He couldn't talk about them, so he settled for talking about her. "I hear you killed a demon on your own last night."

Macey glanced at him. "I did." Wariness in her voice drew out her words. She sat in the middle of the bench seat, close enough that he could feel the warmth radiating from her skin.

"That's...amazing." His hand slid off the steering wheel, and he instinctively reached for her knee. At the last second, he played off the movement by reaching for the AC controls to crank up the air. Luckily, she didn't notice his almost-mistake.

"You sound surprised," she said.

"I've never seen anybody who couldn't shift take one on before. You're tougher than I thought."

Her posture relaxed, and a smile played on her lips. He'd finally said something right. If only he could keep the conversation going, but it was time to get to work. He pulled his truck to the side of the road and rolled to a stop. "We'll have to walk from here."

"How will we know if the spirit is even there?" Alexis asked a few minutes later as they trudged through the brush toward the shack.

"I'll sense it." Macey shivered. "I can always tell when it's around."

"Here's the plan," Luke said. "The guys will take care of the halfling. Alexis, you and I will guard Macey. Make sure nothing happens to her while she's trapping the demon. Once the demon's gone and Macey's safe, then we'll deal with the human."

"I don't need a bodyguard," Macey said.

"What if it possesses your friend again?" Luke said. "He knocked you out before; he can do it again."

Macey stopped and balled her hands into fists. She pressed her lips into a hard line and glared at him. "This has got to stop. Why do you treat me like I'm helpless? You want me to be your 'man on the inside,' but you don't want me close to the action. I'm not going to sit at home looking pretty while the boys fight all the bad guys. I'm one of the boys, Luke. I'm better than most of them."

What could he say? She was right. They were all right. Macey wasn't Melissa. He was letting his past control his future with the woman he loved. When he didn't respond, she turned on her heel and marched away. Alexis hurried to catch up to her.

"I had a fiancée once." He had to force the words over the lump in his throat. "Did you know that?"

Macey stopped and turned around.

"Well, it wasn't official. I didn't give her a ring yet, but we'd talked about it." He stepped toward her and ran a hand through his hair.

Her angry expression softened. "I had no idea."

He shrugged as a familiar ache formed in his chest. "She got killed because of me. We were supposed to go out to dinner that night, but I was working late on a construction site. Then I had to go to the bar to deal with some pack business. I canceled on her. That was the last time I talked to her."

"I'm so sorry." She tentatively stepped toward him. Her hands twitched like she wanted to offer him comfort, but she held it back.

"If I'd have gone home after work. If I'd have been there for her, those damn rogues wouldn't have kidnapped her." He dropped his gaze to the ground. "They found her body in an apartment in Shreveport. The rogues were dead too. Police said it looked like a drug deal gone awry, but Melissa wasn't into drugs." He shoved his hands into his pockets. "I could have protected her, but I didn't. I don't want to make that mistake again."

Macey's body trembled. She crossed and uncrossed her arms and shifted her weight from side to side.

"Please say something, Macey."

"Wait," Alexis said. "Melissa who?"

He tore his gaze away from Macey's shimmering eyes. "Taylor. Melissa Taylor."

Alexis stiffened. "I knew her." Her voice was a whisper. She shook her head. "Luke, she wasn't kidnapped."

"What are you talking about?"

Alexis took a deep breath and let it out slowly. "Melissa went to that apartment on her own that night. She knew those rogues."

His heart dropped into his stomach. "How do you know that?"

"Because I was supposed to be there too."

A wave of nausea rolled through him, and he gritted his teeth. "Explain."

"The rogues were dealers. It's how a lot of them make a living." She looked at Macey. "Not me. I never sold drugs, but I was dating one of them. Melissa was with the other one. The police are right. It was a drug deal gone bad."

He shook his head in disbelief. Melissa wasn't cheating on him. No way…

"I knew she had another boyfriend in New Orleans," Alexis continued, "but I didn't know it was you. She talked about leaving the pack. She liked the freedom of being rogue. I'm sorry, Luke."

He blinked, his throat thickening as his mind scrambled to comprehend. Melissa hadn't been kidnapped. She'd been cheating on him. He swallowed, and the sensation of hot coal burned down his esophagus, settling in his stomach like a boulder. The woman he'd once thought he'd spend forever with had betrayed him…but he couldn't be angry with her. She'd paid the ultimate price for her infidelity, and he wouldn't wish that fate on anyone.

Macey ran to him, finally offering the comfort she'd been holding back. She wrapped her arms around his waist and pressed her head against his chest. He held her, letting her warmth loosen the knots in his core.

Though his mind didn't want to accept the betrayal, in his heart he knew it was true. The signs were there, if he were honest with himself. The new wardrobe, excessive trips to the salon, how careful she was to never leave her phone lying where he would see it. In the back of his mind, he'd suspected it. But her death had washed away his doubt, leaving a thick layer of guilt in its place.

Though he'd cared for Melissa deeply, he'd used his anger at himself to cope with her death, feeling the sadness, but never truly dealing with it. Now, he expected the emotion to slam into his chest, knocking the air from his lungs. Instead, he let out his breath slowly as a hundred-pound weight lifted off his shoulders. The guilt he'd carried for three years floated away, and he hugged Macey tighter.

"Looks like we've both been letting our pasts mess with our lives," she said.

He looked at Alexis. "Yeah, I guess we have."

Alexis raised her hands. "Hey, I'll take responsibility for Macey's issues, but I had nothing to do with Melissa's choices. You can't blame me for that."

Luke laughed. Guilt was a useless emotion that did nothing but weigh him down and hold him back. Now he was free. Free to mourn Melissa's death properly and free to finally move on. "I don't. I'm glad to know the truth. Now let's go kick some demon ass."

Macey pulled away and gazed up at him, a timid smile curving her pink lips. What he would have given to know what thoughts tumbled through her mind at that moment. But it wasn't the time for talk. They'd already wasted too much with his confession and Alexis's revelation. He laced his fingers through hers and led them to the shack.

"It's there, through the trees," he said. Dirty white paint peeled from the rotted wood structure, and a lopsided porch crumbled in front of the house. A screen door hung loose, unable to latch closed because the house sank at an odd angle.

Macey gasped. "That's where Jimmy lives? No wonder he's starving. They don't even have electricity."

"Yes, they do." Luke pointed to a red engine near the back door. "There's a generator there. And there's a solar panel on the roof. Somebody was smart enough to set that up."

"Well, it wasn't Jimmy." Defensiveness sharpened Macey's voice. How could she be so fond of the man who'd attacked her? "And he's not here anyway. Neither of them are."

"Took you long enough." Chase and the other men approached from the left. He looked at Luke's hand, holding Macey's, and grinned. "Looks like nobody's home."

"We can wait," Luke said.

Macey shook her head. "It's Monday."

"So?"

"Jimmy goes to the Quarter on Mondays. He'll be in Jackson Square."

Stephen stepped forward. "How do you know so much about the rapist? Seems suspicious to me." He looked at the other men. "How do we know this isn't a trap? She could be working with the fiends. Setting us up."

Luke opened his mouth to defend Macey, but she didn't need his help.

"He's not the rapist," she said. "If you'd take a minute to look through all that testosterone swirling behind your eyes, you'd see the facts. The spirit is the one we're after. I met Jimmy. He's as helpless as a child." She was feisty. And so goddamn sexy.

Stephen looked at Luke like he expected him to step in, but Luke just grinned. His woman could take care of herself. He accepted that now. The only thing left to do was make her his again.

"What's the plan then?" he said to Macey. "Do we wait it out? When will he be back?"

"I think I should go to Jackson Square and talk to him. He'll listen to me. Maybe he can help."

"All right. Chase, James, Stephen, stay here. Stake the place out and call me if you see any action. Alexis and I will go with Macey back to the Quarter."

Stephen puffed out his chest. "You're seriously taking orders from that *woman?*"

Macey put her hands on her hips. "I think *he* gave the order. I merely made a suggestion."

Stephen narrowed his eyes in an icy glare, but he didn't say anything else. James bit his lip, and Chase rubbed his face, both trying to hide their smiles. Hopefully this was the extent of the "friendly fire" his sister warned him about. A sinking feeling in his gut told him there'd be more.

CHAPTER TWENTY-NINE

THE AUGUST SUN HUNG HIGH IN THE SKY, ROASTING JACKSON Square. Sweat stung Macey's eyes, and she wiped it away as she scanned the crowd for Jimmy. She checked the candy store first, but the owner hadn't seen him. Just her luck, he'd learned his lesson and wouldn't go there again. Hopefully she'd find him somewhere in the Square.

Luke and Alexis sat on a bench under a tree in the park. His gaze followed her as she walked around the perimeter. Protecting her from a distance.

At least he was giving her room to breathe now. Showing some trust in her abilities. Possessiveness gripped at her heart to think he had been engaged before. That he had loved another woman. She shook her head. He'd had a life before her; she'd have been a fool to think he hadn't. Still, a ball of jealousy knotted in her stomach every time she pictured him in another woman's arms. What did that say about her?

Did she want him back? Of course she did. Every fiber of her being ached to be in his arms. But if she needed him that badly, could her heart survive losing him? She'd given herself to him so easily before, and fallen apart so desperately when she'd thought he was using her. She couldn't take that chance again.

Focus, Mace. Find Jimmy. She'd have time to think about her relationship with Luke when this was over. She meandered through the crowd, searching the faces until her gaze landed upon Jimmy's innocent, brown eyes. He sat on a bench, facing the St. Louis Cathedral, and beamed a smile at the juggler tossing flaming batons into the air.

She approached him cautiously, assuming a cheerful posture and smiling to disarm his fears. His eyes widened when he noticed her, his gaze darting about like he might be watched. Seemingly satisfied with his observation, he waved and trotted toward her.

"Hi, Miss Macey!" He stopped, and his face fell as his gaze locked on her gun. He placed his hand on his shoulder and winced.

"I'm not going to hurt you, Jimmy. Is your brother around?" She didn't sense the demon, but maybe Jimmy knew where it was.

"Oh, no. He's not here." When he pulled his hand away from his shoulder, his shirt stuck to the wound.

"How's your shoulder?"

His bottom lip trembled. "It hurts."

"I'm sorry I shot you. I was scared."

He nodded, fat tears pooling in his eyes. "It's okay, Miss Macey. Ross made me do mean things to you."

"Ross? Is that your brother's name?"

His eyes widened, and tears dripped onto his cheeks. He nodded.

"Did you go to the doctor to fix your shoulder?"

"Oh, no ma'am. I'm not allowed to see a doctor. The boy cat-rized it for me."

"Cat-rized?"

"He burned it. To make it stop bleeding. It hurts really bad, but it doesn't bleed anymore. Just some green stuff comes out."

Macey cringed. "You mean cauterized?"

"That's what I said."

"What boy?"

"Ross made him. He's special like my brother. Half demon." His face pinched. "He lives with us now. He sleeps on my futon. I have to sleep on the floor because I'm not special."

"I think you're special." Her heart ached for the poor man, but she tried to keep her expression cheerful.

His eyes brightened. "You do?"

"You're very special, Jimmy, and I'd like to help you. Would you like to get away from your brother? To have a real bed to sleep in and food every day?"

"Oh, I would like that very much. But he won't let me leave. He said if I ever tried to go away, he'd eat me like he ate Momma."

"You mean when he was born?" Visions of the first victim's mangled torso made her stomach turn. Had Jimmy watched his brother claw his way out of his mother's womb? No wonder his brain didn't work quite right.

"Yes, ma'am. And I don't want to get eaten."

"I won't let him eat you. I promise I can keep you safe. Will you let me help you, Jimmy?" She placed a gentle hand on his good shoulder.

He looked at her hand, and confusion clouded his eyes. Had he ever been touched in a loving way? Probably not since his brother was born. "Okay, Miss Macey. You're a real nice lady."

"I have some friends with me. Do you want to meet them?"

He grinned like a child. "Friends? I don't have any friends."

"I'm your friend. Do you want to meet some more?"

"Yes, please!"

She led Jimmy through the park gates and introduced him to Luke and Alexis. He smiled timidly at her sister and waved, but when his eyes met Luke's, he cowered. He shuffled backward, tensing like he was about to bolt.

"What's wrong?" Macey asked.

"He…he's a werewolf. Werewolves are bad."

"No, Jimmy." She put her hand on his elbow. That bewildered expression crossed his face, but he relaxed under her touch. "Luke is my friend. Werewolves are good. He's going to help you too."

"But Ross says werewolves are bad. They keep killing his demons."

Luke grumbled under his breath, but he didn't say anything out loud. He was letting Macey take the lead. Trusting her. He pressed his lips into a tight smile.

"Do you think what your brother is doing is good?" Macey asked.

Jimmy hung his head and rubbed the back of his neck. "No, ma'am."

"We're going to stop him and find you a place to stay. Would you like that?"

"Yes, ma'am."

"How many halflings are there?" Luke asked. "We need to know what we're up against."

Jimmy's gaze darted about the square like he wasn't sure if he should answer. Finally, his frightened eyes locked with Macey's.

"It's okay. You can answer him."

"Well, there's one. Maybe two."

"Maybe?" Luke stood. The calmness in his voice sounded forced. His fists clenched and unclenched at his sides.

Jimmy stepped back, crossing his arms over his chest in an X—a defensive posture. "He's mad at me." He angled his body sideways, as if bracing for a blow.

"No one's mad at you, Jimmy." Macey mouthed the words *sit down* to Luke. He grunted, but he did what she asked. Alexis sank onto the bench next to him.

"What do you mean *maybe* two?" Macey said.

Jimmy relaxed his posture and scratched his ear. "Oh. He said he had to go see about a birth today. Last time he said that, he brought the boy home. I don't want another boy in our house. I want my futon back."

"I'm going to get you a real bed."

His face lit with a smile. "Then I won't go back. I don't want to raise any more demons. It makes me feel sick, but Ross said we have to raise a whole mess of them tonight. But if I stay with you, Miss Macey, you'll keep me safe, right? You won't let Ross eat me. You promised."

Luke ran his hand over his face. He was obviously losing patience with Jimmy, but Macey almost had all the information she needed.

"I will help you," she said. "But first I need you to go back, okay? And pretend like you never talked to me."

Jimmy knit his brow. "Why?"

"It's the only way to stop your brother from hurting more people."

His gaze fell to the ground as he shoved his hands in his pockets. "I don't want to hurt more people."

"Will you help me then?" She reached for his injured hand and turned it palm up to see the scar. "Help me help you?"

He nodded.

"Good. Here's what I need you to do."

Luke crouched in the leaves behind a bush, eyeing the dilapidated shack. It had taken every ounce of self-control he could muster to stop himself from beating the crap out of that guy for what he did to Macey. Once he met him, though, he understood. There was no way Jimmy had done all this on his own.

He watched the man pacing back and forth across the window, muttering to himself incessantly, wringing his hands like his nerves were tearing him apart. "How do you know he's not going to spill the whole plan to his brother as soon as he sees him?"

"I don't," Macey said. "But he trusts me. And if we move in fast enough, he won't have a chance to tell him anything."

He peered into the trees behind the shack. His team had already shifted, preparing to take on the two halflings at his command. Alexis was somewhere nearby. She'd be watching Jimmy. Macey didn't want to hurt the guy, but he trusted Alexis to do what needed to be done if Macey's life was in danger.

Luke grudgingly remained in human form. If it were up to him, he'd shift like the others and tear into that cabin like a storm, but Macey wouldn't let him near Jimmy unless he stayed human. He sure as hell wasn't letting her go in alone.

"What will they do with the baby?" She stared straight ahead, not meeting his gaze.

"The halfling?"

"If it's an infant, I…" She shook her head.

"By the time they get it back here, it'll be a child. Halflings grow exponentially, reaching full size in a few days."

"A child." She still wouldn't look at him.

"It may look like a child, but he'll be pure evil. Trust me. The spirit you're going to capture started out the same way. And it's already killed the woman who gave birth to it."

She nodded.

He rubbed his hand in circles on her back, trying to reassure her, and she leaned into him, resting her head on his shoulder. Her hair smelled like strawberries. He wrapped his arms around her and kissed the top of her head, his pulse quickening, his chest aching at how perfect she felt in his arms.

"I've missed you," she said.

His breath hitched, his stomach fluttering like a thousand butterflies emerging from their cocoons. "I've been lost without you, Macey."

She pulled away and looked at him. A sadness filled her eyes that he didn't understand. He was hers if she wanted him. Why wouldn't she let him in?

He cupped her face in his hand, running his thumb across her soft skin. "After this is over, can we give it another try? Can we give *us* another try?"

She took a deep breath and let it out slowly. "Luke, I—" She stiffened, her eyes growing wide with fear. "He's here."

CHAPTER THIRTY

Jimmy just had to act natural. Pretend like everything was normal and go along with whatever Ross wanted. That's what Miss Macey had said to do. He stopped pacing to stare out the window. She said she'd be out there somewhere, and she'd come in to help him as soon as she could.

Footsteps sounded on the front porch, making Jimmy's heart beat like a racehorse. Was she here? Had she come to save him early? "Mi —" He slapped his hand over his mouth. The boy stepped inside, followed by another boy. This one looked like he was five years old, but Jimmy knew better. He still had blood on his face from eating his momma.

Jimmy shuddered. If the boys were here, his brother must've been close by. Sweat rolled down his back, making his shirt stick to his skin. He shivered. Where was Miss Macey?

"Are you ready, dimwit?"

The voice snaked around him, slithering into his head. Jimmy swallowed down the sour taste in his mouth and nodded. "I guess so."

Bam! The blow to his head caught Jimmy off guard, and he stumbled into the altar. His face stung where Ross's spirit hit him. What if Ross hit Miss Macey?

"You guess so? Don't make me use up all my strength keeping you in line, idiot. We've got a lot to do tonight."

"Okay."

The boy and the little boy sat on Jimmy's futon. Something burned inside him. He ground his teeth, and his body tensed as he glared at them. But he would have a bed to sleep in tonight. Miss Macey promised. How would she fight Ross when she couldn't touch him but he could touch her? It wasn't fair.

Jimmy had an idea. His tummy did a little flip inside him, and he smiled.

"What are you so happy about?"

"I don't want to raise any demons."

This time the blow came to his stomach. He doubled over, clutching his middle, but he still smiled. If he could get Ross to use up all his energy now, he wouldn't be able to hurt Miss Macey or her friends.

"You'll do what I tell you to, you moron. Now pick up the knife and get busy."

"No." He braced himself for another beating, but it didn't come. An icy snake slithered up his body and whispered in his ear.

"What are you doing brother? You're acting suspicious."

"N…nothing. I just don't want to raise no more demons." His knees trembled, so he put his hand on the altar to hold himself steady.

A loud *bang* sounded in the swamp, and he jerked his head toward the sound. That was the signal. The boys were supposed to run outside to see what it was, and then the werewolves would get them. But the boys didn't move from Jimmy's futon.

"What was that?" Jimmy said. "M…maybe the boy and the little boy should go check."

"You'd like that, wouldn't you? Does it hurt your little feelings to see them sitting there? Or is something else going on? What are you scheming?"

"I'm not scheming n…nothing."

"You know I can get inside your head and see for myself, so you might as well tell me."

Jimmy clamped his mouth shut. He was a stupid idiot. He should have gone along with Ross's plans like Miss Macey had told him to do.

Good ideas never popped into his head. Only bad ones. He was a moron. Now what was Miss Macey going to do? She couldn't fight Ross and the boys at the same time.

"Why can't you follow orders like the boy there? If you weren't so easy to possess, I'd have let him eat you a long time ago."

Jimmy's whole body trembled. He didn't want to get eaten. "I'm sorry, Ross. Please don't let him eat me."

A million tiny razor blades sliced through Jimmy's skin as Ross pushed his spirit inside him. He wanted to collapse to the floor and cry, but he couldn't control his own muscles anymore. He could feel his brother prodding through his brain, sifting through his memories like someone panning for gold. Jimmy tried not to think about anything, but he couldn't get the image of Miss Macey's face to go away. And thoughts of Miss Macey led to thoughts of her friends, and before he knew it, he'd spilled the whole plan.

"Werewolves?" Ross growled the words with Jimmy's mouth. "You're friends with werewolves now?"

Ross ripped himself from his brother's body, and Jimmy crumpled to the floor. He gasped for breath and rocked back and forth on the hard linoleum. What had he done? He was such a stupid idiot.

"Thanks for bringing them here, brother. We're on my turf now. Killing them all will be fun."

CHAPTER THIRTY-ONE

"GODDAMMIT. THEY AREN'T MOVING." *I KNEW THIS WOULDN'T work.* Luke refrained from saying the last part out loud for fear of alienating Macey more. But, damn it, they couldn't depend on that guy. "He must've told them the plan."

"It's not his fault," Macey said. "You saw how his eyes glowed for a few minutes. The spirit possessed him. Maybe he can read his mind while he's in there."

"Could he read your mind?" Alexis leaned against a tree a few yards away.

"I don't think so. I forced him out as soon as he got in."

"Whatever the method, he spilled the plan," Luke said.

She crossed her arms. "It wasn't his fault."

"Why do you keep defending him?"

"He needs help."

Luke took a deep breath and chose his words carefully. "If it comes down to your life or his…"

"I know. But it won't."

"So," Alexis said. "What do we do now?"

Luke signaled the rest of his team to join them, and the men approached in human form. They'd lost the element of surprise, but they outnumbered them. "Looks like we're going to have to bust in with our teeth bared. You guys take out the halflings; we'll get the spirit."

"What about the halflings' spirits?" Alexis asked. "Won't they be set free like Jimmy's brother?"

"I don't think so," Luke said. "They're too young. Not strong enough. As long as you decapitate the bodies, they shouldn't be a problem anymore." He turned to Macey. "You've got your gun. My teeth and claws are my weapons."

"I understand. If you think you need to shift..."

He took her hand and led her away from the pack. "Listen, Macey." He lowered his voice so only she could hear. "If anything happens in there...and we need to get away fast...I want you to climb on my back, and we'll run."

"I can run."

"Werewolves are faster. Please. Promise me?"

A sly grin curved her lips. "You want me to ride you?"

"Every day of my life." He took her face in his hands and kissed her. Firmly. With purpose. If she wouldn't let him tell her how he felt, he was going to show her. At first, she stiffened, but she didn't pull away. Her body relaxed, her lips softening to accept him. Hope bloomed in his core, and he held on to it. When this was over, she would be his.

Macey's head spun from the kiss as she tromped through the brush toward the shack. Her body had reacted against her will, reciprocating the passion. She hadn't had time to consider the consequences letting him back in might bring, and she didn't have time to think about it now. She pushed those emotions aside and followed the pack of wolves as they stalked the demons.

They were all huge, but Luke outweighed them by at least fifty pounds. He stayed close, on her left side, while Alexis flanked her on the right. Her sister may have been the smallest, but she'd seen her fight a demon. Alexis was just as strong as the others. Chase had brown fur, and James was a dappled gray. Stephen's fur was also gray, but so dark it seemed almost black.

An icy chill crept up Macey's spine, raising goose bumps on the back of her neck. A sharp prickling sensation pressed into her skin, and she froze. The demon was trying to enter her. She pushed back, slamming down the iron curtain of her will, forcing the demon away. "Nice try."

"It was worth a shot." The voice swirled around her head. *"It would've been fun to make you kill your friends. I'll still enjoy watching my boys do it."*

The halflings stepped out of the shack. The bigger one dragged Jimmy through the door and shoved him off the porch. The wolves fanned out to face them, but Luke stayed glued by her side.

Tears streamed down Jimmy's face. "I'm sorry, Miss Macey. Please don't let your friends eat me."

"No one's going to hurt you, Jimmy."

"Get them!"

On the spirit's command, the halflings hurled themselves at the wolves. The small one carried a knife, and he stabbed it into the brown wolf's shoulder. Chase yelped, and James's jaws clamped down on the halfling's neck. The knife fell to the ground as the boy went limp.

It was a demon. Not a boy. Macey had to remind herself she wasn't witnessing a child's death. The older halfling darted into the trees, and Chase and James tore off after it. Stephen lingered for a moment, his fiery gaze boring into Luke, before running after the others. Jimmy dropped to his knees, cowering in the dirt, and covered his face with his arms.

"Your wolves are making my life difficult. Time to get rid of your sister."

Before Macey could react, a log flew through the air, pummeling toward Alexis. It collided with her head, splitting in two with a horrendous crack. Her massive body crashed to the Earth, and dark red blood matted in her sandy fur.

"Alexis!" Macey rushed to her sister, dropping to her knees at her side. She laid her head against the wolf's chest. Relief washed through her at the gentle rise and fall of her ribcage.

"Now that she's out of the way, I can deal with you."

Macey shot to her feet and whirled around at the voice. Luke growled, his gaze darting about as he searched for the demon. Jimmy curled into a ball in the dirt and sobbed.

Anger lit a fire in the pit of her stomach, and she burned to destroy the demon. With one hand on the crystal in her messenger bag, she reached out with her mind. At first she felt only the emptiness of the crystal, a black hole devoid of energy. When she read objects, the energy came to her. Now she had to search for it in the atmosphere. *Do the process in reverse.*

She tore her focus away from the crystal and sifted through the air around her, like fanning the pages of a book. The demon was here somewhere. She could sense his presence, even in his silence. A fleeting tingle tickled her senses, and she reached for it with her mind. The spirit sifted through her fingers like sand through a sieve.

Alexis whimpered, her body shifting to human form. Luke prowled around her, his gaze darting from the trees to Jimmy and back again. Dried leaves crunched under his paws. A heron squawked from above.

She shook her head. *Focus, Macey. You can do this.* She reached out again and grabbed hold of the ghost, pulling with all her might. If she could hold on long enough, she could transfer its energy into the crystal and trap it inside. But her feeble attempt at catching the spirit failed. It slipped from her grasp and floated away laughing.

"You've learned a thing or two since we last met. So have I."

A gush of frigid air blasted past her, slamming into Jimmy. He rolled onto his back, a strained groan filtering through his clenched teeth. His body stiffened like a rod and went slack. His entire demeanor changed as Ross took over his form. He rose to his feet, standing tall with his shoulders back, chest proud. He strolled toward her, a confident gait replacing Jimmy's awkward walk. A ring of crimson glowed around his chocolate irises.

Luke lowered his head and bared his teeth, inching closer to Macey. She raised her gun.

"You won't shoot me." Jimmy's voice was confident. Not his own. "You promised to help my brother. To give him a real bed to sleep in."

Macey's eyes grew wide.

"Oh, yeah. I can hear his thoughts. He thinks you're going to be his new mommy." Ross laughed. "But that's not what you had in mind, was it, bitch?"

Luke growled, rocking back on his haunches, preparing to launch himself.

"Don't," Macey whispered. "Don't hurt Jimmy."

"Don't hurt Jimmy," Ross said in a mocking tone. "Go ahead and kill him. It won't hurt me."

He was right. If she shot him again, or if Luke attacked, they'd only be hurting Jimmy. Ross could leave his body as quickly as he'd entered it, and then what? Could Macey grab his spirit and force him into the crystal? She'd never been able to grasp free-floating energy. But she could pull it out of an object. Maybe even out of a human. She needed to keep Ross just where he was.

"Come on, wolf man. Let's see what you're made of." Ross taunted Luke, feigning attacks left and right and then slipping away before getting within arm's reach. "No? You don't want a piece of me? How about if I take a piece of your girl?"

He lunged at her, knocking the gun from her hand. Before she could react, he gripped her neck and slammed her into the ground. The air *whooshed* from her lungs. She gasped for breath and clawed at his hands pressing against her trachea. *Not this again.* Lacing her arms between his, she scratched at his neck, prying his hands apart with her forearms. She would not let him hurt her again.

Luke barreled into him, sending him flying off her and into a tree. The rotted trunk split with the impact, and Jimmy's body slid to the ground. Luke pinned him down with his paws and snarled in his face.

"Don't hurt him!" She forced the raspy words through her bruised throat.

Ross laughed hysterically. "Jimmy is so scared right now. If you could only hear the thoughts racing through his mind. Go ahead and bite him. Snap his head off. I can find another human to raise my demons."

"Jimmy." Macey rose to her feet, "I know you're in there. I'm going to help you."

"By giving him a heart attack," Ross said, still laughing. "His chest is about to explode."

"Luke, please. You're scaring him."

"Trust her." Alexis sat up, cradling her head in her hand. "She can do this."

Luke blew out a hard breath and reluctantly stepped away from the man. Ross pulled himself up by the tree trunk, struggling to straighten and carry his weight on his feet. He leaned against the tree, squeezing his eyes shut as if the world were spinning.

Macey leaned in close to Luke. "I can catch him, but you can't help me like this…as a wolf. Do you trust me?"

He held her gaze for a long moment. Then he looked at Ross, struggling to right himself. In answer to her question, he shifted to human form. "What do you need me to do?"

"Hold him still."

"Finally, a fair fight." Ross stumbled forward. "Man to man. Don't let the injury fool you. I make this body strong."

He hurled himself toward Luke with inhuman speed, planting his shoulder squarely in his stomach. Luke went down. Ross drew his arm back and punched him in the face.

"Jimmy!" Macey screamed. "Take control, Jimmy. You can do it."

Luke caught the next punch in his hand and twisted Ross's arm, throwing him to the ground. Ross jumped to his feet, but Luke tackled him, wrapping his arm around his neck. Alexis threw herself on top of Ross, pinning his legs to the ground.

"Do your thing, Macey, but make it fast. He's strong." Luke tightened his grip on his neck. Any more pressure, and it might snap.

Macey dropped to her knees and rested a hand on Jimmy's head, gripping the crystal in her other hand. She closed her eyes and let the images fill her mind. Ross was a foreign energy inside Jimmy's body, just like the energy she read in objects and buildings. Flashes of Ross's life, the atrocities he'd committed, played through her mind like a movie. She saw it all—the assaults, the murders, the beatings poor Jimmy had endured at the hands of his own brother. Her insides twisted with nausea as the bloody scenes flashed behind her eyes.

"You can't do this!" Ross started to tear away from Jimmy's body, but Macey caught him this time.

She opened herself, allowing his energy to flow through her. "Ross, I'm banishing you from this dimension. You won't hurt anyone ever again." Her head spun. Vertigo threatened to pull her under, but she held on. Jimmy's body fell slack as she took the sickening essence of the demon into herself and pushed it toward the crystal.

Roberta was right. She knew exactly what to do. With one final push, the demon's energy left her body and filled the stone. It fell from her hands as she collapsed into Luke's arms.

"Macey, are you okay?" Concern furrowed his brow as he stroked her face and held her.

Was she okay? Memories of the demon's energy raking through her body made her shudder. She opened her mind to the energy in the air, but she no longer sensed the demon. His essence now resided in Roberta's crystal.

"I'm fine." She smiled, letting the warmth of Luke's strong embrace slow her racing heart. "We did it."

He pulled her closer. "*You* did it. That was amazing."

Alexis picked up the stone and turned it over on her hands. She curled up her lip at the pale red glow. "What do we do with it now?"

"I know a certain Voodoo priestess who can take care of it," Macey said. "How's your head?"

Blood had left a sticky red trail down the side of her face, but it was already starting to dry. She shrugged. "Werewolves are fast healers. I'll go check on the guys." She slipped the stone into Macey's bag and trotted deeper into the woods, leaving her alone with Luke.

Being in his arms felt so right. Maybe it was shock, but as his sapphire eyes searched hers, she wanted to give him everything he needed. All he wanted was to love her, and for her to love him. If she thought about it too much, she'd pull away. Guard her heart.

For now, she rode the adrenaline, allowed herself to be caught in the moment, and she pressed her lips to his. His breath hitched as she kissed him, uncertainty making him hesitate. She slid her hands behind his neck and kissed him harder, letting him know that—at least for now—in his arms was exactly where she wanted to be.

A soft moan escaped his throat as his passion finally met hers. His tongue parted her lips, and she let him in. The salt of his skin mixed with the sweet taste of mint as their tongues tangled, their bodies molding together. Thoughts of caution tumbled through her mind, but she ignored them for now.

"Miss Macey?" Jimmy interrupted them.

Tearing her gaze away from Luke, she looked up at Jimmy, who stood over them, clutching his back. The skin around his eye swelled purple, and abrasions reddened his neck and arms.

"Is m…my brother gone?"

"Yes, he is. You're safe now."

The other werewolves in human form approached from the trees. The men froze. The situation must have looked dire, with Jimmy towering over them, Luke clutching Macey in his arms on the ground. Alexis stood between Chase and James, and she put her hands on their arms to stop them. Stephen didn't hesitate. He barreled toward them, catching Jimmy around the waist and plowing him down. Jimmy yelped as his body crashed to the ground.

"Stop it!" Macey yelled. "Get off him!" She scrambled to her feet and rushed toward them, but Luke stopped her. He calmly wrapped his arms around her, pulling her against his chest.

"Stand down, Stephen. It's over."

Stephen stopped wrestling, but kept Jimmy's shoulders pinned to the dirt. "He's one of them. We should rip his throat out and end this for good."

"He's innocent." Macey struggled to get to Jimmy, but Luke's hold was firm. "He was possessed."

"Get off him, Stephen." Authority flowed through Luke's voice, calm with a hint of warning around the edges.

Stephen narrowed his eyes, his gaze darting between Luke and Macey, as he rose to his feet and dusted off his shirt like he was dusting off Luke's threat. "No alpha should take orders from a woman."

Luke tensed, gripping Macey by the shoulders. "The order comes from me."

"You're not qualified to give the orders." Stephen shifted, his body morphing into the black wolf.

Luke shoved Macey to the ground and sprang away from her, shifting in midair. She grunted as she hit the dirt. Something hard jabbed into her shoulder, and she reached her hand into the dead leaves to find it. Her gun. She shot to her feet and leveled the barrel at the black wolf. Jimmy scrambled behind her.

"Macey, don't." Alexis raced toward her.

The wolves squared off, snarling as they stalked circles around each other. Chase and James stepped back, their expressions grim.

"It's a challenge for rank." Alexis put her hand on the gun, lowering Macey's arms. "You can't interfere."

"What do you mean?"

"Luke's supposed to be the next alpha. Stephen wants to take his place."

Macey shook off her sister and pointed the gun at Stephen. "He can't do that."

"He can if he kills him."

"No." She tightened her grip on the gun, her finger hovering over the trigger.

"If you interfere, you'll jeopardize Luke's position. The alpha has to be the strongest. Now he has to prove it. If he has help, it will open him up to more threats. More challenges. He has to defeat Stephen on his own."

Her hands shook as she lowered her gun. "I won't let Stephen kill him."

"As long as the fight is between the two of them and no one else, you have to step aside."

She nodded. She'd let them fight it out, but Luke's words echoed in her mind. *If it's between your life and his…* She gripped her gun at her side.

Stephen sprang, his massive paws connecting with Luke's chest. The wolves tumbled over each other, biting and clawing until Luke found his footing. He charged at Stephen, his jaws clamping down on his neck. The black wolf yelped, and Luke knocked him to the ground. Stephen flailed, prying his flesh from Luke's grip.

They squared off again. The black wolf's lips peeled back over his massive teeth in a ferocious snarl. Luke exhaled, shaking his head. He didn't want to fight. Macey didn't want him to fight. Maybe he'd never abandon her willingly, but he might not have a choice if Stephen won.

Stephen lunged again. Luke's teeth tore into his shoulder as he threw him to the ground. His black fur shone with blood, but he scrambled to his feet. He lunged, and again, Luke deflected him. The fight stretched on endlessly. They were evenly matched; comparable in strength, though Luke's size gave him an edge. Macey flinched each time teeth tore into flesh. She didn't want to watch, but she couldn't look away.

Jimmy stepped from behind her. "Stop it, you mean black wolf. Mr. Luke is my friend."

"Jimmy, no!" Macey tried to hold him back, but he waved his arms and limped toward the wolves.

"You leave Mr. Luke alone!"

For a moment, the fighting stopped. Both wolves stared at the crazy man flailing his arms and moving toward them. Macey held her breath. Stephen sprang, claws extended, knocking Jimmy to the ground. Luke barreled into the black wolf as his jaws were about to snap on Jimmy's face. Jimmy squealed and crab-walked backward, scrambling behind Macey again.

She tore her gaze away from the fight to be sure he was okay. "Did he hurt you?"

"A big scratch." His shirt was torn, and fresh blood oozed from his bullet wound.

"Put pressure on it. You'll be okay."

Stephen limped in circles around Luke. Blood gushed from his flank, soaking his leg and matting his fur. Aside from a small gash in his neck, Luke appeared uninjured. There was no way Stephen could win this fight. He must have realized it was over because his gaze suddenly locked on Macey.

He sprinted toward her, and she froze. Panic gripped her muscles, turning them to stone. Luke leapt and tried to tackle the black wolf, but he was too late. Stephen pummeled into Macey, knocking her to the ground. The impact of her head slamming into the dirt brought back her control. Stephen snarled, opening his jaws above her face. Hot saliva dripped onto her cheek. Her shoulders were pinned, but she managed to raise her gun just enough to press the barrel into his fur.

In the split second he reared back, preparing to snap her face off, she fired. His body stiffened, his eyes going wild, as he rolled off her. She scrambled back as Luke clamped down on his neck and dragged him farther away.

Alexis dropped to her knees and held her, frantically searching her for injury. "Are you okay?"

Macey trembled, clutching her sister's arm as she watched the fight. "Is he going to kill him?"

"Challenges are fights to the death."

Stephen lay on his right side. His left back leg hung limp, but the gushing blood from the bullet wound had already slowed to a trickle. Luke stood with both paws on the black wolf's chest, growling.

Macey cringed. She couldn't watch Luke kill him. Justified or not, Stephen was already down.

Luke lowered his head toward Stephen and blew out a hard breath. The black wolf turned, locking eyes with Luke. Luke's gaze narrowed, a silent warning that the fight was over. Stephen sucked in a ragged breath and exhaled a sigh. He laid down his head and closed his eyes.

Every muscle in Macey's body tensed as she waited for Luke to make a move. He could have easily ripped Stephen's throat out, and apparently would have been justified in doing it. Instead, he walked toward his friends, his tail held high, chest proud. Chase, James, and Alexis dropped to one knee, lowering their heads in acceptance of his dominance.

Luke shifted and wrapped Macey in his arms. She covered her mouth with her hand and leaned into him, a shudder rocking her body. He worried she'd be afraid of him after witnessing the challenge, but she buried her face in his chest and slid her arms around his waist.

"You didn't kill him." She pulled away to gaze into his eyes.

"Of course not." As much as he'd wanted to tear the bastard's throat out for attacking his fate-bound, he wouldn't have killed his cousin whether Macey was watching or not. Stephen had relented, and Luke wasn't capable of murder. Even if their laws allowed it.

Stephen groaned as he shifted into human form and clutched his leg. The bullet probably cracked his femur. It would be a while before he healed.

"Get him out of here," he said to Chase and James. The men lifted Stephen and carried him toward the city.

"Wait," Macey called. "They can't take him to the hospital. My bullet is in his leg."

"They won't," Luke said. "His body will eventually expel it. He won't need medical attention."

"He's a bad werewolf." Jimmy rubbed a hand up and down his arm like he was trying to comfort himself. Jumping into the middle of a werewolf fight proved his insanity. Hopefully he really was as harmless as Macey made him out to be.

She pulled from his embrace and turned to Jimmy. "Sometimes good people make bad choices. We all make mistakes." She looked at Luke, and his heart stuttered. Was she admitting leaving him was a mistake? He could only hope.

"Do I get to stay with you now?" Jimmy said. "You promised you'd give me a real bed."

"No, Jimmy. The police are looking for you. Ross made you do some really bad things." She reached for him, but he recoiled.

"Will they hurt me?"

"No. You need to tell them everything that happened. Then they'll take you to see a doctor, and you'll get to stay in a hospital. People will take care of you, and you'll have a bed to sleep in every night."

Luke started to protest, but she raised a hand to silence him. Was she crazy? She wanted him to tell the police everything?

"That's sounds real nice," Jimmy said. "And will you come to see me every day?"

She patted his back. "How about once a week?"

He blinked as if contemplating her offer. Then he smiled. "I guess that will be okay."

"Go with Alexis. She'll take you to the truck, and I'll be there soon. I need to talk to Luke for a minute."

"Okay, Miss Macey." He turned and followed Alexis out of the swamp.

As soon as he was out of earshot, Luke spoke, "He's going to expose us all."

She shook her head. "No one will believe him. As soon as he tells them his brother's spirit possessed him, and the werewolves saved him, they'll chalk him up as a lunatic and put him in an asylum."

He raised an eyebrow. "*That's* the bed you promised him?"

"It will feel like a luxury resort after the life he's been used to. I'm going to take care of him. I've got a doctor friend who will keep an eye on him and make sure he's treated right."

He stared at the amazing woman standing in front of him. They ended the reign of demons because of her. She even killed one without his help. She fought off a werewolf attack, and in the end, it was her plan that saved the day. He'd never doubt her abilities again. He could feel the goofy smile tugging at his lips, and he probably looked like an idiot staring at her. But he didn't care. She was incredible.

She rubbed the back of her neck, her cheeks flushing pink under his heated gaze. "We should go before Jimmy changes his mind."

He grabbed her hand. "Go out with me tonight. Let me take you to dinner."

"I'm going to have tons of paperwork to file. I'll probably be there all night dealing with Jimmy. I want to be sure he's handled gently."

"Tomorrow then. Give me one dinner. That's all I'm asking."

A symphony of crickets chirped in the night, filling the sultry air with music. Macey adjusted the shoulder strap of her bag, and dry leaves crunched under her feet as she moved. A frog croaked nearby. She stared at the ground as she considered his request and inhaled a deep breath. When she finally raised her gaze to his, she smiled.

"I guess one dinner won't hurt."

CHAPTER THIRTY-TWO

LUKE HELD MACEY'S HAND AS THEY STROLLED UP DAUPHINE toward her house. The sweetness of the strawberry cheesecake they'd shared still lingered on his lips, but the memory of Macey's taste was sweeter. A gentle breeze caressed his skin, easing the stifling summer heat, making the night air almost pleasant. A lone musician played a haunting tune on his saxophone, and Luke dropped a dollar into his instrument case. Even the sad music couldn't dull the spark of happiness in his heart.

They'd spent most of dinner talking about the case, and how Macey had spun it at the station to ensure their secret stayed safe. And even though the talk was work related, the familiar ease of their conversations had returned. She hadn't pulled away when he'd reached for her hand across the table at the restaurant, and walking with her now felt like the most natural thing in the world.

She leaned into his side and sighed contentedly. "Anyway, he's got a psych evaluation scheduled. As soon as he told them his dead brother made him do it all, they called a doctor."

"So the only mystery that remains is what happened to the body."

She laughed. "No. Jimmy took it."

"What?"

"Right out of the morgue."

"No way."

"If you could have seen the kid on duty when it happened, you wouldn't be so surprised. It's funny though. All this time, I assumed you'd taken it."

"I tried. It was already gone. You almost caught me too." He told her about sneaking in with Chase and climbing into a locker to hide. "You had your hand on the latch, but then you walked away."

She laughed as she climbed the steps to her door. "Well, that was a close call."

"Tell me about it." He shuddered. "I hate tight spaces."

She arched an eyebrow. "*All* tight spaces?"

"Pretty much."

A mischievous grin lit her face as she ran her hands up his chest and over his shoulders. "That's a shame."

His eyebrows raised as her words sank in, and blood rushed to his groin. "I suppose *some* tight spaces aren't so bad." The mere thought of being inside her again had him rock hard in seconds. And when she pressed her body against his, he couldn't help but groan as he kissed her.

She tasted sweet, a hint of strawberry lingering on her tongue, and he slid his hands down her back to cup her butt and pull her closer. The rest of the world slipped away as he held the woman he loved. Caught in the moment, he forgot they stood on her front porch until a passerby whistled and shouted, "Get a room." He chuckled and leaned his forehead to hers.

"Do you want to come inside?" she asked.

"I do."

She fumbled with the key, her trembling hands making it hard for her to find the lock. He rested his hand on her back to steady her, and she opened the door. The familiarity of the scene gave him pause. He wouldn't make the same mistake again. They'd talk first, before they got carried away. Macey pulled him inside, but he lingered near the door.

"What's wrong?" she asked.

"Before we do this, I need to know. Are we official? Are we a couple again?"

Her gaze fell to the floor. "Oh. I...don't know." She held her left arm with her right hand. A wall clock chimed. Thor rubbed against Luke's legs and purred. "He likes you."

A sour sensation twisted in his stomach as his heart rate kicked up. "Don't change the subject."

She let out a heavy sigh. "I don't think I'm ready for anything serious."

"Really? Then you're sending me some pretty mixed signals." He crossed his arms.

"I'm sorry. Sometimes I can't control myself with you." She bit her bottom lip and gazed up at him.

"I know the feeling."

"I like you, Luke. I do. But you know I'm scared. I was hoping we could take it slow. Just date for a while and see how it goes. No expectations." She picked up her cat and scratched it behind the ears.

"You call what happened on your porch slow?"

She shrugged. "I need some time."

A groan rumbled in his chest. He was going to have to tell her. "Time is the one thing I don't have." He'd hoped she'd fall in love without the pressure of a deadline, but he was out of options. "I'm set to become alpha in two days. If we're going to be together, I need a commitment from you before then."

She blinked. "Or what?"

"Or we can't be together. Ever."

She put the cat down and fisted her hands on her hips. "That's the most ridiculous thing I've ever heard."

"You're right. It is ridiculous, but it's the law." A stupid, archaic law that would be the death of him if he couldn't get through to her.

"So we can't be casually dating when you become alpha?"

He shook his head. "It has to be official."

She crossed and uncrossed her arms, shifting her weight from foot to foot. He could practically see the gears turning in her mind. "Can't you lie? Tell them we're committed, and give me time to think about it? You've lied to them about dating me before."

If only it were that easy. "That was different. You would have to commit before the pack. In a ceremony. It would be binding."

She rubbed the back of her neck. Her gaze darted about the room, looking at everything but him. "Binding."

"As it stands now, you're not officially part of the pack. Now that we know you're a were, you're considered rogue, like your sister. But if you want to be with me…and I *really* hope you do…you'll have to join the pack. And follow pack law."

"So this is an ultimatum? Your pack is going to force me to commit to you or we're through?"

"No one's forcing you. That's why I'm telling you this. I love you, and I want to spend the rest of my life with you…if you love me too. Do you love me, Macey?" His chest tightened. He held his breath and waited for the answer he didn't want to hear.

"I…" Her chin quivered. Confusion clouded her eyes as she finally looked at him. "I can't do this now. You need to leave."

"Macey…"

"I need time."

Letting out a heavy sigh, he rubbed his head. He wasn't above begging, but the stubborn set of her jaw told him now wasn't the time. Macey loved him, and if she thought she didn't, she was lying to herself. She was his fate-bound, damn it, but if he tried to tell her that now it would drive them even further apart. She'd realize it eventually on her own, but then it might be too late.

He fought off the sickening feeling churning in his stomach and opened the door, pausing in the threshold. "I hope two days is enough."

Macey locked the door behind him and sank onto her sofa. Thor jumped up next to her and mewed softly.

"I like him too, but what was I supposed to do?"

The cat sat down and blinked at her contemptuously.

"He can't force me to spend the rest of my life with him with only two days' notice. What if I'd said yes, and he changed his mind later and left me? Or what if something happened to him? Then I'd be stuck in the pack and forced to follow their rules for the rest of my life. I can't do it, Thor."

He licked his paw and wiped his face.

"And anyway, I'm sure he's exaggerating. How could they stop him from dating me again after he becomes alpha? He'll be the one in charge; I'm sure he can do anything he wants. So we break up now, and maybe later we can try it again. It's the logical thing to do."

An impatient mewl sounded in Thor's throat.

"Oh, what do you know? You're just a cat."

She leaned back and closed her eyes. Two days. How could she make a decision like that in two days? She couldn't. She wouldn't. And that's all there was to it. Life would go back to normal, the way it used to be before Luke showed up. Everything would be fine.

She opened her eyes, her gaze landing on the black messenger bag lying on the foyer table. The crystal with Ross's spirit still rested inside. She shivered to think the half-demon soul may have heard her exchange with Luke. Tomorrow, she'd meet with Natasha and send the fiend to hell where he belonged. Tonight, she would do her best to not think about Luke.

Macey slung the messenger bag over her shoulder and walked out the door. The afternoon sun shone high in the cloudless sky, baking the city in relentless heat. Sweat immediately beaded on her forehead. She hurried across to the shady side of the street, resting her hand on her fabric bag. The only demon lurking in the shadows today was stuck inside Roberta's crystal. Hopefully she'd never have to see another one again.

Natasha sat on her balcony in a folding chair. An orange scarf circled her hair, thick braids sprouting from the center like a potted plant. Her red lips curved into a smile when she spotted Macey, and she waved. "Door's open. Come on in."

Macey's phone buzzed in her pocket as she climbed the stairs to Natasha's apartment. Another message from Luke. She'd programmed her phone to send his calls straight to voicemail after his third attempt to reach her this afternoon. If he didn't give up soon, she'd have to block his number all together. Still, the temptation to check the message had her fingers hovering over the screen.

She sighed and shoved the phone into her pocket. *Don't let him get to you, Mace.*

Even though Natasha had told her to come in, she knocked before opening the door. She looked forward to the relief of conditioned air, but the sticky breeze of a box fan blowing in the corner greeted her instead. Incense smoke hung in the humid air like fog, and she fanned it out of her face.

"I'm on the porch," Natasha called. "Come on out. I made some tea."

Macey stepped through the beaded curtain. "Hi, Natasha. Thanks for helping me with this."

"Ain't nothing. Sit down, have a drink." She offered her a tall glass of sweet tea.

Macey took a big gulp. The icy liquid slid down her throat, cooling her from the inside out. "Thank you." She set the glass on the table and pulled out the crystal. "Here he is. His name's Ross if that helps."

Natasha's face contorted with disgust as she eyed the stone. "That's a demon all right." She snatched the crystal from Macey's hands and dropped it into an empty clay pot on the floor. "I'll take care of it."

"Is there anything I can do to help? I want to make sure he can't come back."

Natasha straightened. "Not unless you're practiced in Voodoo rituals and know how to open the veil between worlds?"

Macey shook her head. "I'm sorry. I didn't mean—"

"Don't you worry, Detective. I said I'll take care of it."

"Please, call me Macey. This is strictly off the record. If the department found out…"

Natasha smiled and shuffled a deck of tarot cards. "I know how you werewolves like your privacy. I won't tell your secret. Never have."

Macey blinked at her. "How did you know?"

"I have a few powers of my own. I've been a part of this community my whole life, and I know how things work. Probably a lot better than you do. You're just coming into your powers, ain't you?"

Macey sipped her tea. Everything about the supernatural community was new to her, but admitting her own naivety was still difficult. "I'm learning to understand them. I've had them all my life."

"Mm-hmm. It ain't nothing to be ashamed of." She set the cards down and folded her hands in her lap. "Luke's a good guy, you know. You could do worse."

Macey swallowed. "You know Luke?"

She waved her hand in dismissal. "Everybody in our community knows who Luke is. Why anybody would dump him is beyond me."

"Wow. You are really good at reading people." Not that it was any of her business.

Natasha laughed. "I haven't read you yet, girl. I'm a good listener. Hair stylist by trade. I do Roberta's hair. Girl loves to gossip."

"Great." Her relationship with Luke—or lack thereof—was the subject of the supernatural community's gossip pool. *Fantastic.* "I appreciate your help with the spirit. If there's ever anything I can do for you, let me know." She started to stand, but Natasha closed her eyes and raised a finger in the air. Macey sank back onto the chair.

Natasha swayed from side to side, nodding her head. "Now I'm reading you."

"I really don't need to be read. I'm going to go now."

She opened her eyes. "Just like I thought." Her lips pressed into a disappointed line as she shook her head.

"What?"

"You think too much."

Macey scoffed. Like that was even possible. "Okay. Thanks again for your help."

"Your brain'll fool you. You need to listen to your heart more. It won't steer you wrong."

She forced a smile and stepped toward the doorway. "I think I'm doing fine."

"Don't believe everything you think."

CHAPTER THIRTY-THREE

THE SOUND OF A KEY IN HIS FRONT DOOR LOCK ROUSED LUKE from sleep. He grumbled and rolled over, squinting at the clock on his nightstand. As he blinked, the red digital display came into focus. Ten a.m. He'd been in bed since midnight.

"Good morning, sunshine. It's time to wake up." His mother's melodic voice drifted on the air, but he didn't respond. Maybe if he stayed silent, she'd go away and today wouldn't have to happen.

Sunlight filtered in through the mini-blinds, illuminating the dust motes floating in the air. If he lay still long enough, maybe he'd turn to dust and could float away too. He sighed and draped an arm over his eyes. Why couldn't he go back to sleep and let this all be a dream?

The scent of brewing coffee tickled his senses, clearing the fog from his mind. This was it. The first day of the rest of his life. The last day he'd have a chance at love. He checked his phone for messages. Maybe Macey had returned one of his calls or texts.

Nothing.

Time had run out. What the hell was he supposed to do now? He sat up and chunked the phone across the room, slamming it into the back of a padded chair. It bounced off the seat and slipped onto the carpeted floor. The phone remained in one piece, which was more than he could say for his heart.

"Everything okay in here?" His mom paused in the doorway, a cup of coffee in one hand, a tuxedo draped over her other arm.

A goddamn tuxedo.

"You almost broke your phone." She laid the suit on a chair and offered him the coffee. He only grunted in reply, so she set the cup and the phone on his nightstand. "It's a big day today. My little boy, becoming alpha. I'm so proud of you." She sat on the edge of his bed and patted his leg.

He sucked in a deep breath and blew it out hard. He was acting like a child. His mom deserved better. "Thanks."

She gazed at him, her eyes full of sympathy, as she rubbed circles on his knee. "Your tuxedo is pressed and ready to go. Make sure you do something about that bedhead before you get to the ballroom." She mussed his hair with her hand. Thankfully, she didn't mention the other thing that was happening at the ceremony…before he could become alpha. He still didn't know who they'd chosen as his mate. He didn't care.

"What time is the ceremony again?" he asked.

"Seven. But the meeting starts at six. Then dinner at eight."

"Right."

She stood and traced a finger over the suit. "You've got plenty of time if there's anything you need to do this afternoon. Any last minute business you need to take care of."

"I just have to show up, right? Or was I supposed to take care of the catering too?" He forced a half-hearted grin and winked at his mom.

A sad smile curved her lips. "I'll see you tonight, sweetheart. Don't forget about Great-Grand Ma Ma's ring." She blew him a kiss and shuffled out the door.

He lay there until he heard the front door open and close, her key turning in the lock. Then he swung his legs over the side of the bed and opened the nightstand drawer. There, in a burgundy leather box, sat his great-grandmother's wedding ring. He opened the lid and gazed at the stone.

A one-and-a-half carat round diamond sat atop an intricate platinum art deco setting. Three smaller diamonds accented the large one
on each side, trailing down to a detailed, tiny rose molded into the
metal. His great-grandfather had given this ring to her in 1933, two
years before he became alpha.

A small slip of yellowing paper sat folded in the lid. Luke pulled it
out, carefully unfolding the brittle note. The letters wobbled from a
shaky hand. His great-grandmother must have been eighty when she'd
written it.

For Luke.
May his true love bring him as much happiness as Arthur brought me.

He folded the note and placed it back in the lid, and then took the
ring from the box. The diamond glinted in the sunlight, and he laid
the ring on the table next to the box. There was only one person who
could wear that ring.

But she wouldn't answer his calls.

If he couldn't reach her by phone, she'd have to talk to him in
person. He couldn't go through with the ceremony tonight unless he'd
done everything he could to win Macey back. He jumped out of bed
and got dressed. Leaving the coffee on the table, he grabbed his phone
and slipped the ring into his pocket before darting out the door.

He tried Macey's house first, banging on the door until Thor
jumped into the window sill and rubbed his side against the glass. She
wasn't home. Where else could she be? He sat on her steps and pulled
the ring out of his pocket. Great-Grand Ma Ma's words rang in his
ears. *May his true love bring him as much happiness as Arthur brought
me.* Macey would make him the happiest man alive if she'd give him a
chance. He fished his phone from his other pocket and dialed Alexis.
Surely her sister would know where to find her. The call connected.

"Where's Macey?"

"Well, hello to you, too, Luke."

"Cut the crap, Alexis. I've got six hours to find Macey and convince her to marry me. Do you know where she is?"

She hesitated, her voice lowering in concern. "I think she's at her parents' house in Metairie."

"I know where that is. Thanks." He pocketed his phone and raced to his truck. His palms were so slick with sweat he could barely grip the steering wheel on the twenty-minute drive. Last time he was there, he'd approached through the trees, watching Macey and Roberta deal with the damn demon spirit. He had no trouble finding the one-story home from the street, and he barreled into the driveway, stopping just short of a row of hedges.

He jumped out of the truck and jogged up the front steps. Tendrils of ivy climbed a lattice behind a white, wooden porch swing. The red inner door hung open, a glass storm door separating the summer from the chilled air inside. The sounds of a pre-season football game drifted out from the living room, and he could see the back of a man's head through the door. Luke rapped on the glass.

The man was tall, with receding brown hair and glasses, and he paused when he saw Luke through the door. This must have been Macey's father. He rested his hand on the handle, but didn't open the door. "Can I help you?"

"Mr. Carpenter?"

"Yes." He drew out the word skeptically.

"I'm Luke Mason. Is Macey here? I need to talk to her."

An amused grin lit his face, and he opened the door. "It's nice to meet you, Luke. Come on in."

He stepped through the doorway into the small foyer. A bright yellow kitchen sat off to the left, and a hallway ran down to the right.

Mr. Carpenter straightened to his full height. "You've caused my little girl all kinds of heartache."

"I don't mean to, sir. I'd like to make things right."

He chuckled. "Macey, you've got company."

She padded down the hallway in denim shorts and bare feet. A white tank top clung to her curves, and her hair spilled around her shoulders like spun gold. His chest tightened, his arms aching to hold her. He wanted to run to her. To take her in his arms and never let her go. It was all he could do to keep his feet planted on the floor.

She stopped midstride when she saw him, her face taking on a range of so many emotions, he couldn't count them all. Her disapproving gaze flicked to her father before settling on Luke. "What are you doing here?"

"I need to talk to you."

She rubbed one arm. "I have nothing to say."

"Then listen. Please."

Her dad took her by the arm and led her toward him. "Give the boy a chance. He drove all this way."

She let out her breath in a slow hiss. Her teeth clenched, the muscles in her jaw flexing taut. "Fine." She threw the storm door open and stomped onto the porch.

Luke followed. "You didn't return my calls."

She spun around to face him. His expression must have been pained because all the anger drained from her face as she sank onto the swing. "I didn't know what to say. I...still don't."

"All you have to do is listen. If you're not convinced when I'm done, I'll leave and never bother you again." He sat down, his leg brushing hers. She scooted away, and a stinging pain shot through his heart. Resting his hand on his leg, he could feel the ring burning a hole through his jeans. It belonged on Macey's finger, and he ached to put it there.

"I love you, Macey."

"Luke, please don't..."

"Just hear me out, okay?"

She nodded.

"I've loved you from the moment you walked into my dad's bar in that tank top and flip flops. Hell, maybe I even loved you before then, but that's the moment I knew. I'd been watching you since the whole demon ordeal started and you took on the case. It was my job to get rid of the evidence and keep you from finding out the truth. And I told myself that's all I was doing when I hung around watching you clear the scenes. But it was so much more than that. I was enamored."

He turned in his seat to face her. "Then you came into the bar and shook my hand, and I knew you had magic in you. I spent the next week trying to find out exactly what you were, to see if there was any chance we could be together. My folks were in Paris, and I called them and begged my old man to let your magic be enough."

She stared at the ground. "I guess he said 'no?'"

"'Werewolves only.' That's what he said. Then I found out you *are* a werewolf. And, yeah, I said those things Alexis told you. But I said them before I knew what you were. There was enough tension in the pack with the demons and Stephen trying to step in. I couldn't let them know I was in love with a human, but you know what I figured out?"

She glanced at him, her eyes tight with worry or confusion, before returning her gaze to the ground.

"It didn't matter what you were. I was in love with *who* you were. Who you are. You could be a human, a witch, or even a vampire. I would love you regardless. But it doesn't matter anymore because you are a werewolf. We *can* be…we were *meant* to be together. You are the only one I'll ever love. You're my fate-bound, Macey. My soul mate. So, please. I'm begging you." He sank to his knees in front of her and took her hands in his. "Take me back."

Her lips parted, and she sucked in a breath as her gaze lingered on their entwined hands. Tears shimmered in her eyes, dampening her lashes when she blinked. He held his breath, a glimmer of hope sparking in his chest as she raised her gaze to meet his. She licked her lips and leaned toward him.

"Luke…"

The whisper of his name on her lips nearly crumbled him. He reached for her, taking her cheek in his hand, sliding his fingers into her hair as she nuzzled into his touch. "Please, Macey."

She shot to her feet, yanking from his grasp. With her arms crossed, she held herself, shaking her head. "I can't."

She had to. He couldn't let it end this way. Not after everything they'd been through. She was his world. His destiny. Screw the laws. Screw the pack. He couldn't live without this woman. Pressure built in the back of his eyes as he rose from the ground. "Then I'll step down.

I'll let someone else take over, and you can have all the time you want. We can take it slow, whatever you need."

"Don't say that. You can't let Stephen take your place; you can't do that to your pack. You're supposed to be alpha."

"I'm supposed to be with you. It's fate, Macey, and I know you feel it too."

She dug her nails into her arms. "No. You were born to lead the pack. I'm just a distraction."

"Macey, please. What do you want me to do?" He'd do anything —*be* anything—for her. Life would be meaningless without her by his side. Why couldn't she see that?

She sucked in a deep breath and looked into his eyes. "I want you to leave. Go back to your pack and become the alpha. Forget about me."

Her words severed his heart from his chest. With his hands in his pockets, he toyed with the ring. No matter her answer, it belonged to Macey. So did his heart. "If you change your mind, the ceremony is at seven. Once I become alpha, it will be too late."

She opened the glass door and looked at him with sad eyes. "I'm sorry. Goodbye, Luke."

———

Macey closed the inner door and watched through the blinds as Luke drove away, the hole in her chest where her heart used to be growing wider as his truck disappeared into the horizon. She stepped away from the window and followed the smell of coffee into the kitchen.

Her mom poured two mugs and set them on the table. "Do you want to talk about it?"

Macey picked up the cup and inhaled the comforting aroma. "Not really."

"What did he say?"

She shrugged and traced the swirling pattern on the tablecloth. "He said he loves me."

Her mom reached across the table and stilled her hand. "Do you love him?"

"No...maybe...I...I don't know." She sighed. "Yes. Yes, I do." She loved him fiercely, and she couldn't imagine spending the rest of her life with anyone but him.

"Then what's the problem?"

"What if he leaves me?"

"What if he stays?"

Macey folded her hands in her lap. "You don't understand. Everyone I've ever depended on has abandoned me. I can't take that chance again."

Her mom raised an eyebrow and sat up straight. "Everyone?"

She rested her face in her hands and took a deep breath. "Okay, not *everyone*. You and Dad never left."

"So, three people then? Your biological parents and your sister. That's not even close to everyone."

Her mom had a point. Put that way, her abandonment issues sounded petty. Almost ridiculous. But they had been the three people she'd needed the most. That counted for something. "I'm scared. I've never been in love before. I need more time."

"Why?"

Because he's a werewolf who thinks he can't date me after he becomes the alpha. But she couldn't tell her mother that. "It's scary."

"You don't think he's scared too?"

"No." Luke wasn't scared of anything. He was confident. Charismatic. Everything he did, he did with gusto, as if failure never crossed his mind. He was kind and sexy, and those piercing eyes were...and his body...Oh! She had to stop thinking about him.

Her mom folded her hands on the table. "You've rejected him, hon. What are you going to do when he moves on?"

Moves on? Thoughts of him finding someone else had never crossed her mind. She sipped her coffee to warm the chill that crept through her veins. "I don't... It's complicated."

"It's not complicated at all. He loves you. You love him. You're happy when you're with him and miserable without him. Love won't always be easy, but it's worth the risk."

Was it though? She'd sabotaged every relationship she'd had before anyone could get close enough to hurt her. It was easier that way.

Safer. She could easily spend the rest of her life alone, guarding her heart. But what kind of life would that be?

CHAPTER THIRTY-FOUR

LUKE SLOUCHED IN A CHAIR IN THE MEETING ROOM AND watched his mom fiddle with her hair in the mirror for the fifteenth time since they'd arrived at the hotel. All two-hundred pack members would fill the ballroom soon, and his mom had spent the entire afternoon running around, making sure everything was perfect for the ceremony. Seven members of the werewolf congress would attend to ensure they performed the rituals to code, making Luke's succession official.

The meeting would come first—a sort of state-of-the-pack address from the current alpha. They'd discuss the business of the year, and people could express any concerns they might have. Then the ceremony would begin. A new family, who'd recently moved to New Orleans, had applied to join the pack. Their admission would come first, followed by the announcement of Luke's mate.

His stomach turned. Could he spend the rest of his life with someone he didn't love? He'd have to figure out a way. He looked at his old man. "Why Jackie?"

"We interviewed several candidates," his dad said. "When I researched their lineage, hers was the strongest. No dilution in the bloodline."

He ran his hand over his forehead, trying to rub away the pounding in his head. "Have you told her yet?"

His mom settled into a chair next to him. "No. We wanted to give you a chance to…to make sure we made the right choice for you."

"It doesn't matter."

Concern filled his mother's eyes. "Do you have the ring?"

His hand instinctively went to his pocket, his finger tracing the outline of the cold metal. "I'm not giving it to her. It was meant for someone else. Someone I love."

He gripped the arms of his chair. He'd been on a rollercoaster of emotions all afternoon, from the slow build of anger to the sharp drop of fear and finally settling into the steady ride of resignation. Now the anger was back in full force like a tornado ripping through his chest.

"It isn't fair." He slammed his fist down on the table. "I'm the only one this damn archaic law applies to. Why can't I have more time?"

His dad steepled his hands under his chin. "You know why, son. It's to guarantee the lineage—"

"Yeah, I know. But I can guarantee Macey would come around if I had more time."

"Well, you don't," Marcus said. "It's the law, so there's no sense in whining about it."

"Our laws have changed before. Werewolves are evolving, and I think it's time this law changed too. Half the congress is here. If I appeal to them—"

His dad leaned forward, lowering his voice into a commanding growl. "You've made your choices and missed your chance. The ceremony will go as planned."

Luke reined in his anger, calming the burning flames down to a slow simmer. His father was right. He'd tried to win Macey, but she'd made her decision. There was nothing he could do about it, except go on with his life and become the best damn alpha New Orleans ever had. Still, it wouldn't hurt to check his messages one more time. He pulled his phone from his pocket and tapped the screen.

Nothing.

He tossed it on the table.

His old man grabbed it and slipped it into his jacket pocket. "I'll hold on to this. You don't need any more distractions."

He started to protest, but what the hell? If she hadn't called by now, she wasn't going to. "Did the congress approve Chase as my second?"

"Paperwork came in this morning. It's a done deal."

Since Stephen had attacked Luke's intended mate, he'd be spending the next six months in the pit. The council stripped his cousin of his rank, and since he'd been incapacitated in the challenge, he didn't have the strength to contest it. Chase would step in as Luke's second in command until a child of the first family bloodline was old enough to take over. Hopefully Luke's first-born son.

The son he wouldn't be having with Macey. He closed his eyes and imagined her swollen belly. Her golden hair cascading around her shoulders. The warm smile dancing on her pink lips as he rested his hand on her stomach to feel the baby kick.

He shook his head to rid his mind of the heartbreaking image. "I need to get some air."

"The meeting starts in fifteen minutes," his mom said.

"I'll be there."

A crowd had gathered in the corridor, so Luke straightened his spine and held his head high. He had to appear confident and strong, even though he was falling apart inside. People gathered in small groups to chat before the meeting while others filed into the ballroom to take their seats.

"Congratulations, Luke." John, a man around his father's age, clapped him on the shoulder. "Who's the lucky lady?"

Luke forced a smile. "It's a surprise."

He needed some privacy. Five minutes to compose himself, so he could go into his new life with a clear head. He wouldn't get any peace out here.

"Hi, Luke." Jackie approached him, prancing across the hall, her lavender gown swishing around her ankles. "I'm curious. Does your mate already know if she's been chosen? I don't want to get my hopes up if…" She ran her hand over his arm and grinned shyly.

He instinctively jerked away, the thought of enduring someone other than Macey's touch making his stomach turn.

Jackie shrank in on herself, and Luke patted her shoulder. *What an ass.* He needed to start acting like an alpha rather than a scorned teenager. Forcing a reassuring smile, he muttered, "It'll be a surprise to everyone. Excuse me."

He walked with purpose now, eyes straight ahead, his mouth pressed into a line. His pulse thrummed in his ears. He couldn't breathe. He had to get out of this crowd before he exploded. Skirting the wall, he checked the door handles, finding each one locked. There had to be another meeting room, or even a supply closet open. Just five minutes. That's all he needed. Five minutes to breathe.

The corridor made a T at the end, and he jutted right around the corner. The next door opened, and he rushed inside, slamming it behind him. The hotel's second ballroom sat silent. Empty like his chest. A massive chandelier hung in the center of the rectangular room, its dripping crystals glinting in the sunlight that poured in through the window.

Three wooden steps led up to a set of French doors that opened onto a balcony. He threw open the doors and stepped onto the terrace overlooking Bourbon Street. The sounds of jazz mixed with hip hop and pop floated through the air as the sun sank closer to the horizon. The revelers below went about their partying, oblivious to the events about to unfold.

Life went on. His would too.

"Luke?"

He turned around to find Alexis standing on the steps. Her emerald dress matched her eyes. It would've matched Macey's eyes too. "I didn't hear you come in."

She lowered her head sheepishly. "Sorry. I...followed you."

He stepped back inside and closed the balcony doors, bringing peaceful silence back to the ballroom. "It's okay. I needed a few minutes to compose myself."

"So, I guess Macey..."

"No."

Alexis shook her head. "I really thought she'd change her mind."

"I hoped she would." He sat on the top step and ran a hand through his hair. "I hurt her too much."

Alexis sank down next to him, resting her forearms on her knees and wringing her hands. "I'm the one who hurt her. The whole reason she's acting this way is because I ran away. Now I've screwed up her life and yours."

"You were a kid. I won't hold it against you."

"She does. And worse than that…she's holding it against you. I can't believe she'd step aside and let you take another mate when she's obviously in love with you."

He cleared his throat.

Alexis narrowed her gaze. "She does know you're taking another mate."

"I didn't tell her that part."

"What?" She jumped to her feet. "She doesn't know?"

He stood and crossed his arms. He didn't owe her an explanation, but he gave her one anyway. "She already felt enough pressure knowing there was a deadline. I didn't want to add to it."

Alexis crossed her arms to mirror his posture. "So you didn't tell her. She probably thinks she still has a chance with you."

"No. I told her she had to commit before I became alpha."

"But you didn't tell her why."

"It doesn't matter. She made it very clear she didn't want anything to do with me."

She blinked at him, her expression incredulous, before turning on her heel and marching away.

"Where are you going?"

"You may make a great alpha, Luke, but you're a stupid man." She stormed out the door.

He tried for a witty reply, but words escaped him. Time had run out anyway. The meeting was about to start.

Thankfully the corridor was clear as he made his way to the ball-room. Everyone would be taking their seats by now. Two guards stood outside the entrance, ensuring the pack's privacy. His mom had reserved the room under the pretense of an engagement party, with strict orders for the hotel staff not to enter until the ceremony had ended.

He nodded to the guards, gripped the door handle that would lead him to his fate, and closed his eyes. With one last deep breath, he pushed through and entered the ballroom. Twenty-five circular banquet tables drenched in white linen sat atop lush green carpet that stretched from wall to wall. A similar chandelier hung in the center of the room, but this one was lit and sparkled like a million diamonds. He pressed his hand against the ring in his pocket.

The entire pack had gathered for this momentous event, dressed in their best formal clothes. So much pomp and circumstance for such a heart-wrenching day. He scanned the crowd for Alexis. She'd been dressed for the party, but he couldn't find her. Apparently his stupidity was too much for her. He did spot Stephen's mate sitting at a table in the back, a sullen expression occupying her face. Luke had spared her mate's life, but she refused to make eye contact with him.

Luke's parents sat at a long, rectangular table at the front of the room. Behind them, on a raised platform, sat the seven congressmen. Luke straightened his spine and nodded to the men before striding to the table to join his parents.

At precisely six o'clock, Marcus commenced the meeting. Luke sat rigid, his face turned toward his father. He nodded occasionally, hoping to give the illusion he was listening intently, while his mind drifted a thousand miles away. He didn't hear a word his old man said.

"Son?" Marcus put a hand on Luke's shoulder, snapping him back to coherence. "Your report?"

"Right." He cleared his throat and stepped to the microphone. As he brought the pack up to speed on how they resolved the demon infestation, his heart clenched each time he mentioned Macey's name. Surely this would get easier with time. He sat down and slipped his hand in his pocket to feel the ring. As soon as he got home, it would go back in the drawer and stay there.

"If no one has any more comments, this will conclude our annual meeting," his father said into the microphone. The crowd remained silent. Marcus nodded. "We'll begin the ceremony with the pack pledge, followed by our new member initiation."

Luke stood and recited the words he'd known by heart since he was a child. His pulse raced out of control as his father conducted the initiation. The new family knelt before him as he went through the formalities, officially approving their membership.

It was happening too fast. He wasn't ready.

"As you all know, I'll be retiring." His dad glanced at his watch and grinned. "By the end of the hour." Some of the audience chuckled. "I'll be passing the torch on to my son, who I know will do a better job running this pack than I ever did. But before he can become alpha, there's the matter of selecting a mate."

His stomach roiled. Sweat beaded on his forehead.

"Since he's not married, Luke has decided to trust his mother and I to select a mate for him. We've thoroughly reviewed each applicant and chosen the woman we think will compliment him best. Son, would you like to make the announcement?"

No. The room tilted on its side as he rose from his chair. He caught himself on the edge of the table and let out a half-hearted chuckle to put the pack at ease. No matter how torn up he was on the inside, he had to give the illusion of control. Of dominance.

He stepped to the microphone and scanned the crowd one last time. She wasn't there. The tiny sliver of hope—that maybe Macey would show up and say she'd changed her mind—died away. He pressed his hand against the ring in his pocket, took a deep breath, and prepared to utter the words he'd never be able to take back.

CHAPTER THIRTY-FIVE

MACEY IGNORED THE POUNDING ON THE DOOR AND BURIED HER head deeper into the pillow. She'd come to her parents' house because she didn't want to be alone. Now she wished she'd stayed home.

"Macey, you have another visitor," her dad called.

She groaned and rolled out of bed, glancing at the clock. Six-fifteen. Luke would be at his ceremony, so it couldn't be him. A small part of her wished it was. If he came back now, she might not be able to say no. Would that be such a bad thing?

She pushed the thought aside and padded down the hallway into the living room. Alexis stood near the door while her mom and dad sat on the couch looking at her expectantly.

"Is this *the* Alexis?" Her mom's eyes darted back and forth between them.

"Yeah, Mom. This is my sister."

"We need to talk. Now," Alexis said.

Macey turned to her mom. "It's a long story. I'll tell you later." She motioned for Alexis to follow her. "Come on. We can talk in my room."

"We don't have much time," Alexis said as Macey closed the bedroom door.

"Time for what?"

"To get you back to Luke and stop the ceremony."

Macey let out a huff and plopped onto the bed. She picked up a fluffy pink pillow and hugged it to her chest. "I'm not going to stop him from becoming alpha."

"No, but he needs you to be his mate."

Mate. There was that word again. Luke had called her his soul mate, and the idea sounded too good to be true. They were meant to be together, though; she could feel it in her bones. But for something so huge…so monumental…she needed time to wrap her mind around it. Her entire world had changed in a matter of weeks, and she was still trying to absorb it all. She waved her hand dismissively. "He just thinks he needs me right now. I'll call him next week after things settle down, and we'll talk again. I don't want to rush into anything."

Alexis put her hands on her hips. "You don't have a choice."

"There's always a choice."

"Not if you want Luke. Do you love him?"

"Yes." She narrowed her eyes at her sister. Why was Alexis so wound up about this? Why wouldn't she have a choice?

"You're losing him. Every second that you sit there holding that stupid pillow, he's slipping further away."

Macey tossed the pillow aside. "Come on. You're being dramatic. I'm being cautious. It's not my fault I have abandonment issues."

Anger flashed in her sister's eyes. "How long are you going to play the victim, Macey?"

"I'm not—"

"You've changed. You used to be a fighter. Tough. Resilient. Now look at you. So scared to get your poor little heart broken, you're walking away from the best thing that's ever happened to you."

Macey clenched her hands into fists. How dare her sister talk to her that way? "You want to talk about walking away? You've been gone for twenty years, and suddenly you come back thinking you know what's best for me? You don't. I am strong. I am a fighter."

Alexis took a deep breath and exhaled slowly. "This isn't about me, Macey." Her voice was quiet. Calm. "This is about you and Luke. He's not going to be available next week. Or ever again if you don't get your ass to that ceremony right now and stop it."

Her breath caught. "What are you talking about?"

"He has to have a mate to become alpha." She glanced at her watch. "He's about to select one now."

Her heart stuttered, her veins running cold with ice. Did she hear that right? "He's...getting married?"

Alexis shook her head. "He's taking a mate. It's more like a business deal to ensure the alpha has children. He won't marry her, but he also won't be able to marry anyone else. Werewolves mate for life."

Her head spun. Or was it the room? Either way, her stomach lurched, and she ground her teeth to stop her lunch from making a reappearance. No wonder he was relentless in trying to talk to her. "Why didn't he tell me?"

"Because he's a man. He thought he'd pressured you enough. Said he wanted you to love him on your own."

"I do love him." She couldn't let him take someone else as his mate. *She* was his soul mate, his...what did he call her? His fate-bound. Yes, they were bound by fate, but in her idiocy, she'd torn them apart. She had to repair their bond.

Alexis tugged her to her feet. "Then get dressed and let's go. The ceremony is formal, and it's a twenty-minute drive to New Orleans."

She couldn't make herself move. What if she was too late? Would he really go through with it? Her throat tightened, and she could barely force out the words, "I don't have any clothes here."

"Trade with me then." Alexis unzipped her dress and tossed it to her sister.

Macey stared at the emerald fabric in her hands, the shock of the ordeal making her limbs heavy like lead. "What about you?"

"This isn't about me. Hurry up."

Her movements finally caught up with the urgency, and she stripped, giving her clothes to Alexis. Her sister's dress was made for someone taller, and the straps slipped off her shoulders.

"Safety pins?" Alexis said.

"In the drawer."

Alexis folded the straps and pinned them to the inside of the dress.

The sparkling gown hugged Macey's torso, flaring slightly at the hips to cascade down to her knees in the front. The back brushed the floor. "There. Now it's perfect. Shoes?"

Macey stepped into the pair of black flats next to her bed. "These are all I have here."

"They'll do." Alexis grabbed her by the arm and dragged her into the living room.

"Where are you going?" her mother asked as they rushed out the front door.

"To get Luke back," Macey called over her shoulder.

"Have fun."

Macey climbed into the passenger seat, and Alexis peeled out of the driveway. She tore through the neighborhood and merged onto the highway like a professional Indy Car driver. Macey clutched the door and closed her eyes. "How much time do we have?"

"Thirty minutes. Plenty of time if there's no traffic."

"Who is he going to choose if we don't make it in time?" Pain pierced her heart at the thought of him in another woman's arms.

"I don't know. He let his parents pick for him, and they haven't told anyone." She squeezed Macey's hand. "Don't worry. We'll make it."

Alexis zipped in and out of traffic, bouncing between lanes and cursing at the slower cars. Macey dared to peek at the speedometer. They were pushing one hundred. She said a silent prayer that they'd make it there alive. She'd only *thought* her partner was a scary driver. Alexis was a maniac.

As they climbed an overpass, a sea of red brake lights stretched out before them, disappearing into the horizon. Traffic slowed to a crawl as they descended the bridge and inched their way forward at an excruciating speed.

"Oh, no. No, no, no." Alexis blasted the horn. "Can't you wave your badge around and get these people out of the way?"

"Where would they go? It looks like an accident up ahead." She pulled out her phone and unlocked the screen. Six unread voicemail messages from Luke waited to be heard. Her fingers trembled as she opened the map app and typed in the hotel address. The phone slipped from her sweaty palm and bounced under the seat. "Damn it."

She reached beneath the seat and found the phone. "If you can get off at the next exit, we can take back roads to the Quarter."

Alexis gripped the steering wheel and checked her review mirror. "Screw the exit. I can run faster than this." She slammed on the gas and cut across the grassy median onto the frontage road. "Which way?"

"Take the next right."

She fishtailed around the corner and floored it. "Seriously, though. If it were dark out, I'd shift and run you there. It'd be faster than this."

Macey crinkled her nose. "Then I'd smell like dog."

"We *all* smell like dog."

"Good point. Turn left."

Alexis turned and rolled to a slow crawl behind a city bus. The damn thing stopped every fifteen feet to pick up more passengers.

Macey's head pounded. At this speed they'd never make it in time…and not making it was *not* an option. "Can't you pass it?"

Alexis leaned her head out the window. "There's too much traffic." She eyed something to the right and raised her eyebrows at Macey. "You can get me out of a ticket, right?"

"Probably," she said warily.

"Hold on." She cut the wheel right and lurched onto the sidewalk. Pedestrians scattered as she barreled toward the bus stop and made a hard right turn to skirt behind it. They barely fit. Bushes scraped down the side of the car like claws on a windowpane. She jerked the wheel left, and they bumped over the curb, back onto the road.

If I survive this, I will never complain about Bryce's driving again. "It's a straight shot from here to the Quarter. What time is it?"

"We've got ten minutes."

Her heart jack hammered in her chest. She dialed his number. Straight to voicemail. "He's not answering his phone."

"Text him."

I'm on my way. Please don't choose a mate. She pressed send and counted to fifty. No response. Tears stung her eyes. "We're too late."

"No, we're not."

"What if they started early?"

"They didn't."

"How do you know?"

"We're going to make it."

Finally, they crossed Rampart and entered the French Quarter. They raced up Bienville as fast as the bumpy, narrow road would allow and stopped just before Bourbon.

"You've got to be kidding me," Alexis said. "A parade? On a Thursday?"

"New Orleanians will find any excuse they can to have a parade. Try to find a place to park."

She pulled the car into an alley, and they jumped out. A man on a balcony yelled down to them. "Hey! You can't park there. I'll call the cops."

"I am a cop." Macey kept running. She plowed through the mass of spectators on Bourbon, shoving her way down the street, Alexis on her heels.

"It's there." Her sister pointed to a hotel across the street.

Macey leaped over a metal barricade and darted across the parade line, weaving her way through a sea of women in elaborate headdresses and sparkling masks, and narrowly missing a mounted patrol. She stumbled, caught herself with her hands before she fell, and looked up at the officer.

"Detective Carpenter?" The look on the man's face was incredulous. "Do you need backup?"

"No. No worries." She turned on her heel and dashed across the street.

"I'm right behind you," Alexis called as Macey paused to look for her. "Go! Go!"

She pushed through the door and skidded to a stop in the lobby. "Where's the ballroom?" she called to the hotel clerk.

"What?"

"The ballroom."

"Down there." He pointed. "But you can't—"

Macey sprinted down the hall.

Two burly men stood guard outside a set of double doors. This had to be the place. As she approached, they crossed their arms, widening their stances and blocking the entrance. She adjusted the straps on her dress and smoothed the gown down her torso. "Sorry, I'm a little late for the ceremony. If you'll excuse me." She reached for the door handle, and a guard grabbed her wrist.

"This is a private event." His grip was firm, his voice gravelly with warning.

"But I really need to talk to Luke." She considered playing the cop card, but these guys didn't seem like the type to back down, regardless of the law.

He released her arm and straightened his spine, crossing his thick arms over his chest. "Not today."

"Macey!" Alexis sprinted toward her.

"They won't let me in."

"Out of the way, guys," Alexis said. "This is official pack business."

The other guard looked down his nose at her. "I don't take orders from rogues."

Alexis gave her sister a meaningful look, a tiny nod of her head letting Macey know they were about to do something they couldn't take back. Then she launched herself at a guard. The surprise of her impact made him stumble far enough away from the door for Macey to get close. She threw herself at the entrance and screamed, "Luke!" Her fist slammed into the metal door with a *thud*, shooting tingling shards of pain up her arm. The guard grabbed her around the waist and pulled her back.

"Luke!" She flailed in his arms. "Luke, stop! Don't do it!" This couldn't' be happening. She *had* to get through that door. She didn't finally come to her senses and race across town to get to him, only to be stopped at the entrance.

She wiggled, twisting and turning, but the guard tightened his grip. Alexis climbed on the other guard's back, doing everything she could to keep him away from the door. The entrance stood unguarded. If Macey could just wiggle free and get to the door before the guard, she'd be in. But he held her around the waist, her arms pinned at her sides. She wiggled some more and managed to shimmy down far enough for her mouth the reach his arm. Her teeth sank into his flesh. The guard yelped, loosening his grip enough for Macey to break free.

"Luke!" Macey screamed again. Flinging herself at the door, she pounded it with her fist. Her trembling hands reached for the handle, and she pressed it down. The door opened a crack before the guard snatched her up again, yanking her away. The handle slipped from her grasp. The door clicked shut.

"Luke, please!"

"Luke!" Alexis's voice was hoarse. Her guard pinned her to the ground and slapped a hand over her mouth.

"Give it up, rogues," Macey's guard said. "You're not getting in that room."

"But I was supposed to be his mate." Macey stopped struggling. By now, he'd probably already chosen another. And it was her fault. She'd been so afraid of letting him get close enough to hurt her, she'd driven him into someone else's arms. She was too late.

Her body went slack in the guard's arms, the will to fight—to do anything—draining away like flood water after a rain. He let her sink to the ground and released her as she crumpled to her knees and buried her face in her hands. A deep sob hitched in her throat. She'd been so stupid. Her sister was right; she'd been playing the victim for so long she didn't know how else to act. Yes, she'd been abandoned. And, yes, it had hurt. But the events from her past didn't have to control her future. She knew that now.

Now that it was too late.

"Macey?" Luke's voice danced in her ears. She looked up to find him standing in the doorway, confusion furrowing his brow. He looked at the other guard. "Let her go."

Alexis scrambled to her feet and pulled Macey up by the arm. "Go," she whispered in her ear.

She took two tentative steps toward him. "Luke, I…"

He tilted his head and blinked. His left hand went to his pocket. "Macey."

She ran. Throwing her arms around his neck, she buried her face in his chest. He stiffened. His heartbeat slammed against her cheek, but he hesitated to hold her.

"I'm so sorry, Luke. I was stupid, and immature, and…"

He patted her back awkwardly.

"Oh, no." She covered her mouth with her hand as she stepped back to see his face. "I'm too late, aren't I? Have you already chosen a mate?"

His gaze lingered on her eyes before traveling down her body and back up again, the intensity of his stare piercing her soul. Why wouldn't he speak? "Say something. Please."

He swallowed. "I have chosen."

"No." Her body trembled, her heart wrenching as if being ripped from her chest. Tears welled in her eyes, and she dropped her gaze to the floor to hide them.

She'd lost him.

"Macey, look at me." He hooked a finger under her chin, raising her gaze to meet his. "I chose you. It's always been you." He took her in his arms, hugging her tight.

"So you haven't…"

"I told them they'd have to take me single or not at all."

She melted into his warmth, sweet relief flooding her body as the tension drained away.

"Son?" An older man stepped through the doorway. "You can't drop a bomb like that and walk away from the pack. You need to fix this."

"Just a minute, Dad." He gripped Macey's shoulders and stared intently into her eyes. "You need to know what you're getting yourself into. When we step into that ballroom, we'll take an oath. A pledge to the pack to be mates. Once you're in, there's no way out. Werewolves mate for life."

Life was exactly what she wanted. She slid her hands up his chest to cup his face. "Do you promise?"

A sly grin pulled up one corner of his mouth. "Yes, ma'am."

"I'll hold you to it." She rose onto her toes to place a soft kiss on his lips. "I'm yours."

Luke's dad cleared his throat. "We need to finish the ceremony." He motioned for them to enter the ballroom, his voice rough with warning. "The pack's waiting."

Luke nodded to his father and stepped toward Alexis, holding out his hand to shake. "Thank you for bringing her back to me."

She hugged him. "Be good to my sister."

"Always."

His dad clutched the door handle. "If you don't get your ass back in there, there's going to be a riot."

Macey took her sister's hand. "Come on."

Alexis shook her head. "Go in there? Dressed like this?" She motioned to Macey's shorts and tank top she now wore. "No way. I've got some unfinished business to take care of outside of town, anyway."

"You're leaving? I just got you back." Macey smiled at her sister. She could tell from the look in her eyes this wasn't goodbye.

"Not permanently. I need to tie up some loose ends. I promise I'll be back in time for the wedding." She nodded toward Luke.

Macey turned to find him standing in front of her, toying with a ring in his hands.

"I'll see you later, sister." Alexis kissed her on the cheek and shoved Macey toward him.

"This ring has been burning a hole in my pocket all day," he said.

"It's beautiful."

"It belonged to my great-grandmother. She left it to me when she died, with a note that she hoped my true love would make me as happy as my great-granddad made her. I wanted to give it to you this morning, but…" He held up the ring and examined it. The diamond glinted in the light, and he let out a nervous chuckle. "I'm going to try this again." He knelt on one knee and took her hand in his. The familiar electric tingle shot up her arm, making her breath catch.

"Macey, no one can make me happier than you can. If I spend every day with you for the rest of my life, it still won't be enough. I need more from you than a mate. I need you to be my wife. Will you marry me?"

"Yes. Yes!" Her hand trembled as he slid the ring on her finger and pulled her into his arms. "I love you, Luke."

"You have no idea how badly I've wanted to hear those words from you. I love you too."

CHAPTER THIRTY-SIX

"If you two lovebirds are done making up, we've got a ceremony to finish, a riot to stop, and a panel of hungry congressmen to feed." Luke's dad held out his hand for Macey to shake. "By the way, I'm Marcus. It's nice to finally meet the woman my son's been so worked up about."

Macey shook his hand, and the tingle of werewolf magic shimmied up her arm. The sensation was different than when she touched Luke, though. Duller. She might have missed it if she didn't know what to look for. It appeared only Luke's energy could make her heart skip a beat, and that's the way she liked it.

She slipped into the ballroom, and Luke held her tight to his side. From the noise and commotion, what he'd said to the pack must have meant mutiny because every person in the room looked either livid or terrified. Some grumbled. Others yelled, their fists clenched tightly at their sides. All because of her.

She gripped his bicep, her throat tightening. He did this for her. Even when she'd rejected him, he hadn't given up on their love.

A group of seven men standing on a raised platform turned toward them. "This is unacceptable," one of them boomed.

"It's taken care of." Luke pressed his hand into the small of her back and led her onto the stage. A hushed murmur befell the crowd as he stepped to the microphone and raised a hand to silence them. "There's been a change of plans." He pulled her into his side and wrapped his arm around her. "I'd like to introduce my fiancée, Macey."

Silence ensued as the pack seemed to hold a collective breath. Then Chase stood, and the remaining pack members joined him in a standing ovation.

"We'll take that oath now, Dad," Luke said.

Marcus read from an antique, leather-bound book, and Macey repeated the words required of her. She made promises to uphold the pack values and follow their laws. The entire oath sounded more like a business deal than a union, until she got to the part where they had to promise to have children together. Luke smiled and squeezed her hand as she agreed to everything.

As Marcus read the final words, making the union official, Luke leaned in and whispered in her ear, "I promise the wedding will be much more romantic."

The rest of the evening went by in a blur. She joined Luke's mother at the table as he and his father went through the ceremony of changing leadership. Luke accepted the role of alpha, and the pack cheered. The weariness in Marcus's eyes lifted, and a smile played on his lips as he and his wife stepped off the platform and joined the pack.

The sun dipped behind the horizon as they finished dinner, and the pack members slowly filed out the door. Luke stayed by her side, his arm around her possessively as they said their goodbyes. She leaned into his warmth, allowing him to lead her, to take care of her. For the first time in years, she opened herself to need, admitting—at least to herself—that it was possible to depend on someone and still be independent at the same time. She needed him in so many ways, and the smoldering look in his eyes told her he felt the same.

As the last guest left the ballroom, he wrapped his arms around her and caught her mouth with his. "Your place or mine?"

"I think my house is closer." She couldn't wait to get him home.

"Let's go."

Macey's hands were steady as she slid the key into the lock and opened the door. Luke couldn't keep his hands off her. As soon as they stepped through the threshold, he pulled her close, cupping her butt in his hands. His cock swelled, pressing against his zipper, and it took every ounce of self-control he could muster to stop himself from taking her right there in the living room. He'd come so close to losing her, but now she was his. A vise of possessiveness gripped his heart, and he held her tighter.

"I love you, Luke." Her breath tickled his ear.

"I love you too. And I can't wait to call you Mrs. Mason."

She stepped away, a playful smile dancing across her lips. "Macey Mason? What have I gotten myself into?"

"I don't know." He ran his fingers along her skin, sliding her dress straps over her shoulders. "But I know what I'd like to get *myself* into."

She bit her bottom lip and laced her fingers through his. "Well then, Mr. Mason, you should come with me." She led him to her bedroom, and Thor jumped off the bed to wind between his ankles. He let out a soft mew and rubbed his head against Luke's shin.

Macey picked up the cat and set him outside the door. "Thor says, 'Welcome home.'"

"I like the sound of that." He chuckled. "I'm going to be the only alpha in history with a pet cat."

"He's a good cat."

"He is."

Tugging on her bottom lip, she furrowed her brow. "Did you know I was coming? Is that why you said that to the pack? You caused quite an uproar."

He traced his fingers along her shoulders, marveling in the softness of her skin. "I've never been one to let an archaic law hold me back. I told them to give me a year." He shrugged. "I figured I could win you back by then."

"What if they didn't agree to your demands?"

"Then they would have had to find a new alpha. Good thing you showed up when you did."

Snuggling into his chest, she slid her arms around his waist. "Thank you for not giving up on me."

"I knew you'd come around." He glided his hand up the back of her dress and pulled the zipper down. The emerald fabric cascaded to the floor, revealing her porcelain skin wrapped in lacey pink lingerie. Soft moonlight filtering through the curtains gave her an ethereal glow. He watched as she undid the buttons on his shirt, memorizing every detail of the way she moved. The way her hair spilled over her shoulders. The fire in her eyes as she popped the button on his pants and tugged the zipper down.

She grinned wickedly as she unhooked her bra and slipped her panties off. All he could do was stare at the image of perfection before him. His hungry gaze traveled up and down her body, his cock aching to fill her, his heart pounding with the need to possess her.

Her fingers danced across his chest, trailing down to his stomach. "Now that you have me, what are you going to do with me?"

He grinned, scooping her in his arms. "I'm going to love you for as long as you'll let me." He laid her on the bed and climbed on top of her, pressing himself between her legs. Her breath caught as he filled her, and she gazed at him with eyes full of love. "And I believe you promised me forever."

"I did." She smiled and wrapped her legs around his waist, holding him tight. "Werewolves mate for life."

BENEATH A BLUE MOON

⚜ Two ⚜

CHAPTER ONE

CHASE BEAUCHAMP ROLLED HIS HARLEY TO A STOP OUTSIDE THE morgue on Earhart. He let the engine idle, the low rumble filling the humid night air with its sultry song. The stale stench of death seemed to ooze from the pores in the brick building, undulating into the parking lot like a suffocating fog.

He killed the engine and stared at the heavy, metal door, a chill creeping up his spine as the memory of his last trip to the morgue played in his mind. He still had nightmares about the twenty minutes he'd spent in the cold locker, hiding from the same cop he was about to meet now. Exhaling a curse, he dismounted his bike.

Go in. Check out the body. Get the hell out. That's all he had to do. At least he wasn't trying to steal the damn thing this time.

He heaved open the door and blinked as his eyes adjusted to the stark white reception room. Though what kind of reception one could give to anyone who came to identify a body, he had no clue. The sharp tinge of bleach in the air did nothing to mask the sour, musty aroma of dead flesh. He tried to keep his facial expression neutral as he scanned the empty room, but the smell was more offensive than a Saturday night on Bourbon Street. Something about preserved dead people gave him the creeps.

And where the hell was Macey?

The door swung open, and a man with clean-cut, light-brown hair ambled in. If his shoulder holster didn't give him away, his cocky gait screamed cop. Chase had seen this guy before. Macey's partner, Bryce.

"You Chase Beauchamp?" He raked his gaze over Chase's tattooed arms before lingering a little too long on the piercing in his right eyebrow.

Chase nodded and returned his stare.

"Detective Bryce Samuels." He held out his hand. "I'm Detective Carpenter's partner."

Chase shook his hand, and not a hint of magic seeped from his skin. This guy was all human. "Where's Macey?"

"She's checking up on a lead. Asked me to show you the body. Apparently, you might be able to *pick up* on something she didn't." He made air quotes with his fingers and looked toward the front desk. "Where's the mummy?"

A scrawny kid with shaggy red hair typed something into his computer and shot to his feet. "Locker twenty-six. Did you prepare him?" He cut his gaze toward Chase and grimaced.

Bryce slapped Chase on the shoulder and walked toward a swinging door. "She's a mummy. Prepared?"

"As I'll ever be." He followed Bryce down a narrow hallway illuminated in sickly-green fluorescent lights. The putrid color did nothing for the ambience. Then again, a storage house for the freshly dead didn't need to be warm and cheerful.

They turned a corner, and Bryce lowered his voice. "Macey tells me you have a similar ability to her spirit sensors."

"Something like that. I'd say mine's a little more pronounced." How much did this guy know about his partner? Macey was the alpha's mate and the only werewolf on the New Orleans police force. Being second born, she lacked the ability to shift, but nearly all werewolf offspring possessed some sort of power.

Bryce stopped outside a door. "So you can see ghosts? Or spirit energy? I think that's what she calls it."

"Sort of." *Not at all.* Macey suspected the victim died of supernatural causes, but she didn't know enough about the paranormal world to make the call. She'd had no idea she was a werewolf herself until a few months ago. Whether or not the pack got involved in this case would be up to Chase. Then it would be Macey's job to make sure the police never discovered the truth.

Bryce pushed open the door and strode toward a locker. Chase followed, trying his best to *not* think about how it had felt to be inside one. Suffocating. Cold. Morbid. Another chill spiraled from his tail bone up to the base of his skull.

Sliding the drawer open, Bryce pulled back the sheet to reveal the corpse. Dry, brown skin stretched tight across the boney figure, as if someone had wrapped a science class skeleton in leather and slapped a bleached-blonde wig on it. Thin lips stretched back into a torturous howl, and the sunken cheeks looked like they'd crumble to bits if he touched them.

But the most haunting aspect of all was the gaping, hollow eye socket.

Though his skin crawled like a swarm of spiders skittered across the surface, Chase leaned in closer to the shriveled corpse. "Any idea what happened to her eye?"

Bryce pinched his brows as if looking at the body caused him pain. "No clue. Can't you ask her ghost?"

"Right. Let me see if I can pick up anything." He closed his eyes and took a deep breath, trying to mimic the way Macey acted when she read energy.

Big mistake.

The rancid death stench made his stomach turn. How could humans not be bothered by this smell? He swallowed the sour taste of bile from his throat and raked his gaze over the body. "Looks like something sucked the life right out of her."

"No kidding. Autopsy says her blood has turned to powder. Pretty much all her insides have."

"Hmm. A vampire wouldn't have left any blood behind at all, so it's safe to rule that out."

Bryce blinked.

Crap, he shouldn't have said that. Chase shoved his hands in his pockets and forced a smile. "I'm kidding."

He chuckled. "You never know in this town. A few months ago, we had so many people trying to convince us werewolves were involved in a case that Macey started to believe it was true."

Chase shook his head, laughing off the statement. "Women."

"Right. So, no lingering spirits then?"

"None that I can see." Not that he could have detected one if it were there. Like most first-born weres, Chase's only powers were massive strength and the ability to shift into wolf form. "Does she have any other markings? Punctures or cuts?"

"She has a tattoo beneath her collar bone. It's hard to tell, the way the skin shriveled up, but it looks Celtic." Bryce pulled the sheet down to reveal a warped, black design on the woman's chest.

He could see how a human would mistake the twisting, knot-like pattern for Celtic, especially in this distorted condition, but the tattoo had nothing to do with the Irish. This woman belonged to a witch's coven, though which one, he couldn't be sure.

The sour taste returned to the back of his mouth. *Damn witches.* They were a bunch of selfish pricks who didn't give a shit about the rest of the supernatural community. This woman had probably pissed someone off high up in the coven, and they'd discarded her like trash, leaving the mess for the werewolves to clean up. It looked like the pack would be getting involved after all.

Bryce covered the body with the sheet and shoved the drawer shut. "Recognize the design?"

"No. You're right. It's probably a Celtic knot. Sorry I couldn't be more help."

Bryce narrowed his eyes, studying him. "Don't you need to touch something? Or meditate?"

"Pardon?"

"Macey always puts her hands on the walls and closes her eyes and starts swaying like she's hypnotized."

Damn, this guy was perceptive. If Macey had given Chase a head's up, he might have been prepared to put on a show. As it stood now, he just wanted to get the hell out of that stinking cesspool of death. "My ability doesn't work that way."

Bryce lifted a shoulder and nodded toward the door. "Whatever you say, boss. I won't even pretend to understand what y'all can do. Frankly, it's a little weird."

If he only knew the half of it. "I can see how it would seem that way." He followed the officer to the reception area, the tightness in his chest loosening now that a solid wall stood between him and the bodies.

Bryce stopped at the desk and signed his name on a clipboard before turning to Chase. "We rely on Macey's ability a lot."

Chase nodded. "Reading spirit energy is a handy talent."

"She said you'd fill in for her while she's on her honeymoon in a few months. Help us out if we need it." He raised his eyebrows, silently asking for confirmation.

"Did she?" Strange the alpha himself hadn't told him about this new assignment. Chase would need some lessons on pretending to be psychic if he was going to keep this charade up.

Bryce popped a piece of gum into his mouth and clenched it between his teeth. "That okay?"

"You get any more weird cases, give me a call. I like weird."

Bryce nodded curtly. "Will do."

Chase shook his hand and shoved open the door. Thick, sultry air enveloped him as he treaded through the parking lot to his bike, breathing deeper now that he'd gotten away from the damn morgue and its foul stench. Thunder clapped in the distance, and his arm hairs stood on end as the storm clouds gathered above.

He glanced at his watch and cursed under his breath. Luke would expect a full report, but he didn't have time to swing by the bar. Bekah had a class tonight, and the one thing Chase liked better than hunting demons was babysitting for his sister.

A text would have to do. *Victim's a witch. Insides turned to powder. Never seen anything like it. Babysitting tonight.* He mashed the send button with his thumb, shoved the phone in his pocket and then headed home.

He'd be happy if he never stepped foot inside that morgue again, but something told him he'd be spending a lot more time there, thanks to the alpha's mate.

Rain Connolly sat at a table in the darkened bakery and stared out the window. Using the side of her hand, she wiped the condensation from the pane and leaned toward the glass. Fat water droplets danced across Royal Street, pooling near the sidewalk and cascading down the storm drain, washing the sludge from the road. She'd always loved a good thunderstorm, and not just because of her name.

The cleansing act of water from above rinsing away the impurities on the ground soothed her. If only her own sins were so easily washed away.

The sudden showers had sent tourists and locals alike scattering for cover. Now the rain and the streetlights had the stage to themselves, and they created a choreographed routine Rain could've watched for hours. The boom of thunder interrupted the musical cadence of the shower, but the droplets found their rhythm again, falling individually before becoming one with the steady stream running down the street.

She sighed as a woman rounded the corner, stomping her heavy, black boots through the puddles, disrupting the dance of the down-pour. Though the hood of her jacket hid her face in shadows, the woman's deep-magenta aura and purposeful strides couldn't be mistaken. Rain leaned away from the window and clutched the pendant hanging from her neck. Though the goddess seemed to have abandoned her, a quick prayer wouldn't hurt.

The woman banged on the door as a bright bolt of lightning flashed across the sky, followed by a massive clap of thunder so loud it rattled the windows of the nineteenth-century building. She squealed and knocked harder.

As tempting as it was to leave her landlord out in the storm, Rain rose from her chair and opened the door. "I'm closed, Ingrid."

"I'm not here for cake." Ingrid folded her umbrella and left it on the front steps before striding inside and slipping the hood off her head. She shook out her crimson curls and huffed as she examined the wet ends of her hair. "Your rent is late, and your fees need to be paid."

"Fees for a coven to which I don't belong." Rain walked deeper into the storefront, but Ingrid lingered in the doorway.

"Do we have to have this conversation every month? If you want to operate as a witch, you either join the coven or you pay the fees. It's not a difficult concept."

She put her hands on her hips in a challenging pose. The *concept* wasn't the difficult thing. "Then let me join the coven."

Ingrid rolled her eyes. "Only real witches can join."

The corner of Rain's mouth twitched as a spark of heat flashed through her body, and she inclined her chin. "I am a real witch."

"You're cursed."

"Then let *me* join." Snow padded in from the back room and set a stack of freshly-washed plates on the counter.

Ingrid let out an irritated sigh and wiped the dripping hair from her forehead. "We're not taking chances with your sister either. You two don't know when to quit, do you?"

"Connollys never quit." Snow stood next to Rain and crossed her arms, her platinum blonde hair swishing as she shook her head.

Rain would argue to her last breath with any witch who challenged her heritage. Yes, she was cursed, but magic did flow through her veins. Unfortunately, though, even joining the coven wouldn't help her current situation. She sat on a barstool. "I don't have the money."

"Why not?"

"Business has been slow, but I have a potential wedding client coming in tomorrow. If they book, I can pay the rent or the fees. Not both. Not now. Can I have an extension?"

Ingrid opened her mouth as if to speak, but she closed it again. "You know I can't show you any kindness. Renting the building to you is all the risk I'm willing to take. I wouldn't have even let you sign the lease if I'd known about your curse beforehand."

Rain cringed inwardly. She'd been required by law to inform the coven priestess of her curse when she moved here, but she'd purposely signed the lease on the shop before she did. It wasn't a selfless act, but what else could she have done? She needed the prime location if her business would ever take off. "It's not a kindness. Decent landlords give their tenants extensions all the time. One more month."

"I'm not even going to chance being decent. Late fees started accruing last week. If I don't receive your payment in two weeks, you'll be evicted." Her eyes softened. "I'm sorry. I don't like being this way. It's not you…"

She stiffened. "It's my curse. I understand."

Ingrid attempted a sympathetic smile, but her mouth merely twitched as she opened the door. "Don't take it personally."

Rain returned the gesture with a faux grin. "How could I not?"

Snow locked the door after the landlord left and turned to her sister. "She's right, you know? You shouldn't take it personally. I bet they'd all love you like I do if they got to know you."

"It's not about being loved. Or even liked." She sighed and shook her head. "The second people find out about my curse, they act like I've got a contagious disease." And she deserved the punishment. She was lucky she'd gotten settled in before word of her curse spread through the community.

"They're being cautious."

She folded her hands in her lap and picked at her pale-pink nail polish. "What am I going to do? If I lose the bakery, I'll be on the street."

Snow sat on the stool next to her and wrapped her arm around her shoulders. How long had it been since another witch had gotten close enough to touch her?

Leaning into her sister's side, Rain let the affection calm her. "Careful comforting me. Don't be too kind."

"Don't be silly; I'm comforting myself." She laid her head on Rain's shoulder. "We can stop selling the enchanted cookies. If we're a human bakery, you won't owe the fees."

Rain let out a dry laugh. "The spells are what pay the bills between weddings."

"True. Spellbound Sweets wouldn't be much without the spells." She sat up straight. "Let me pay the fees. I'm the one operating as a witch anyway. I should be the one paying for the license."

Rain rose to her feet and shuffled around the counter to put the plates away. She'd drained her savings account to get the place up and running, not allowing her sister to pay for something as small as a can of rainbow sprinkles. It was the only way to make certain her curse didn't affect Snow. "It's a witch's bakery. *My* bakery. If you paid, it would be a kindness. I won't let you take that risk."

"What's the worst that could happen? Pneumonia for a week? A sprained ankle?"

Rain closed the cabinet, her heart sinking at the thought of what her curse could do to her sister. "You could get run over by a streetcar. Or struck by lightning. Or worse."

"Yeah, okay. Good point. The appointment tomorrow sounds promising, though. Werewolves tend to stick together, so if you can land the alpha's wedding, we'll have our foot in the door with their pack. They could bring in a lot of business." She spun a circle on the barstool and grinned. "Werewolves like to eat."

A tiny flame of hope flickered in her core before dying out. Her shoulders drooped. "Until another werewolf opens a bakery. They prefer to do business with their own kind. Don't get your hopes up."

"Well, there aren't any werewolf bakeries now, and now is all that matters at the moment." Snow leaned her elbow on the counter, resting her chin on her fist. "Let's focus on landing this gig, and it will solve half your problems."

"And the other half?"

She shrugged. "We're Connolly witches. We'll figure something out."

Rain smiled at her sister. Snow risked so much by being here every day, and gratitude didn't begin to describe the emotions Rain felt for her. "*You're* a Connolly witch. I'm just a Connolly." Or so everyone seemed to believe.

"Your powers may be bound, but there's magic in your blood." Snow leaned her forearms on the counter. "How many ingredients are left to find?"

She'd received an unbinding spell from the national witches' council in the mail three months ago on enchanted paper. Each time she retrieved an ingredient, the next one revealed itself. "I've got two ingredients left. As soon as I get my hands on some Bauhinia harvested by a priestess beneath a full moon in Peru, the last one will be revealed, and we'll be good to go. Do you really think it will work?"

Snow lifted an eyebrow. "Are you doubting my powers, sister?"

She laughed. "Of course not. But the council said only an ultimate act of selflessness could break the spell and unbind my powers."

"Then they said seven years of repentance is enough."

"I know that's what the letter said. It seems strange that they'd change their minds though. I bet Mom had something to do with it."

"So what if she did?" Snow lifted her hands as she shrugged and dropped them to her sides. "Maybe they weren't specific enough in what an 'ultimate act of selflessness' is. Maybe they feel like you've learned your lesson."

She traced the marble pattern on the countertop with her finger. "I guess." If the lesson was to put others before her powers, she hadn't had a choice but to learn. She'd been powerless for seven years. "Whatever their reasoning…I want my magic back."

"I understand. This will work." Snow stepped around the counter and gave her sister a hug. "I'm going home. Can I have today's pay so I don't get run over by a streetcar on my way?"

Rain chuckled and took two twenties from the cash register. "Be safe."

"Always."

After her sister left, Rain locked the door and turned off the lights before padding to her storage closet-turned-bedroom in the back of the shop. If this unbinding spell worked, and her curse could be broken, she might be able to save the bakery.

Bauhinia itself was easy to come by, but the stipulation that it be harvested by a priestess beneath a full moon made it difficult to find. She'd located a shop in Peru who could fill the order, but the cost of the ingredient, plus international shipping, had set her back several hundred dollars. But if she could get rid of this curse and be accepted into the witches' community again, she'd have more than enough business to pay all her bills.

Though she'd never achieve a spot on the national council after what she'd done to earn the curse, she might be able to work her way up in the coven once they let her in. At least she could hold a position of power within the community. It was better than nothing.

CHAPTER TWO

CHASE SAT BEHIND A MASSIVE OAK DESK AND EYED THE whimpering rule-breaker. The lanky teen couldn't have been more than seventeen, and he shifted in the green vinyl chair like his ass was sore. His dad most likely had torn the kid a new one the moment his little sister blabbed about what he'd done. Now he had to face the punishment from the pack.

With one elbow resting on the desk, Chase leaned his mouth into his hand, trying to hide the involuntary curve of his lips. Truth was, he saw a lot of himself in the rebellious teen. Growing up, he'd never been one for rules. Now his job for the next twenty-plus years was enforcing them. Who would've thought?

"What the hell were you thinking, Landon?" His smile under control, Chase steepled his fingers beneath his chin—a move the old alpha had pulled when Chase got in trouble himself—and leaned back in the squeaky leather chair. "You don't show your wolf form to humans."

Landon lifted his hands and started to speak, but he dropped them in his lap and let out a dramatic sigh. "You wouldn't understand."

He arched a pierced eyebrow. "Try me."

"He was kissing my sister in the back of his truck. In the swamp. *The swamp*. Who does that?" He fisted his trembling hands on the arms of the chair. "I was trying to save her."

The corners of Chase's mouth tugged upward, so he shot to his feet and paced around the desk. "Save her from what?"

Landon cowered in his chair. "He's going to break her heart. Dude's got a new girlfriend every week."

He stood behind the chair and peered through the mini blinds at the empty stone corridor. The kid's mom and sister waited in the bar down the hall, probably cowering in their chairs like rebellious Landon here.

The kid peeked over his shoulder and caught Chase's gaze. As soon as he made eye contact, he jerked his head forward and stared at his hands in his lap. "What are you going to do to me? Are you going to kill me?"

Now he didn't fight the smile. "For a first-time infraction? We're more civilized than that." He ran a finger across the back of the chair, and the kid froze. The hum of fluorescent lights and Landon's rapid, shallow breaths filled the otherwise silent room. The red numbers on the digital clock display flipped from eleven forty-five to forty-six. Forty-seven.

A little flush of fear ought to keep the kid in line for a while. It always worked on Chase when he was young. A pair of work boots thudded on the concrete outside, and Landon dropped his head into his hands. Being drilled by the second in command was intimidating enough. Now he'd have to hear it from the alpha.

The door flung open, and Luke sauntered in. He wore paint-stained jeans and a gray T-shirt, and his light-brown hair was tied back at the nape of his neck. Chase liked to think his own tattoos and piercings made him intimidating, but Luke held an aura of authority only members of the first family had.

The alpha dropped into the leather chair and leveled his gaze on Chase. "What did I miss?" Landon let out a whimper, and the corner of Luke's mouth twitched.

Chase crossed his arms and stood next to the kid. "Showed his wolf form to a human to stop him from making out with his sister."

"Did he now?" Luke pinned Landon with a hard stare. Both men had their own little sisters, so they could sympathize with Landon's need to protect his sibling. But the kid didn't need to know that.

The alpha rested his hands on the desk. "And what's the verdict?"

Chase strolled forward to lean against the desk. "Thirty hours of pack service and an apology to his sister."

Luke nodded. "Sounds good to me."

Landon lifted his head. "Thirty hours? That'll take forever."

Chase put a heavy hand on his shoulder. "We could put you in the pit. Or kill you."

His eyes widened. "No, no. Thirty hours sounds fair."

"Great." Luke smirked and took an old toothbrush from a desk drawer. "You can start by cleaning the toilets."

"Yes, sir." Landon took the toothbrush and sulked out of the office.

As the door clicked shut, Chase laughed. "That the same one your old man made me use when I screwed up?"

Luke nodded. "That toothbrush has seen more toilets than a frat boy during rush week."

Chase flopped into the chair and ran a hand through his hair. As second in command, his main job was to deal with rogues and rule-breakers. Lucky for him, Luke kept the pack under tight control. Rules were rarely broken.

Luke opened the laptop on the desk. "How's it feel being on the other side of the interrogation?"

"If you'd have told me ten years ago I'd be your second, I'd have laughed in your face."

The alpha chuckled as he punched the keyboard with his index fingers. "You've grown up a lot since we were kids. So have I."

"Yeah, but you knew you'd be alpha from day one. Responsibility's in your blood."

"It's in yours too. Just took you longer to figure it out." He hit the enter key and closed the computer.

"I suppose." Responsibility occupied ninety-nine percent of his time lately, but surprisingly, he didn't mind.

Luke's phone chimed, and he pulled it from his pocket. "Oh,

shit." He scrubbed a hand down his face. "I forgot about that. Come on, I need a beer." He paced out of the office before Chase had a chance to ask what was up.

He followed him up the short flight of stone steps into the bar, where Luke's sister stood behind the counter, polishing a beer mug. Amber wore the standard O'Malley's uniform—jeans and a black button-up—and she'd swept her light-brown hair into a high ponytail.

"It's about time you got here." She set down the glass and picked up a stack of notebooks. "I have to get the stock orders done. Just because you have rank now, it doesn't mean you get to make your own schedule. I own this bar." She winked. "I run the show."

Chase glanced at the clock. "I'm ten minutes early."

She lifted a section of counter top and sashayed toward him, a playful grin lighting on her lips. "Good." She glanced at Luke. "Keep him in line. I'm sensing change in his future."

Chase narrowed his eyes. "What kind of change?"

She shrugged. "Don't know yet. The feeling's building." She dropped into a chair at a table and opened the books, ending the conversation.

Luke settled onto a stool, and Chase slipped behind the counter and poured a tall glass of Blue Moon beer, sliding it to his friend. "Your sister's gift isn't very useful."

"She has her moments. Empathic premonitions are never exact."

He shook his head. She had helped a bit with the recent demon infestation, but change in his future? No, thank you. He liked his life the way it was. "What's going on?"

Luke took a swig and gripped the glass on the counter. "Damn cake tasting."

He cocked an eyebrow. "Cake?"

"For the wedding. Macey's dragging me to the bakery to taste the damn cakes for the reception. Like I give a shit if she chooses almond or butter cream. Cake is cake."

He laughed. "Better you than me."

The alpha narrowed his eyes. "It'll happen to you one day, my friend, and I plan to enjoy watching you squirm when it does."

Chase huffed. "You had to mate. I don't." And until recently, he didn't plan to. Ever. He had enough responsibility in his life without having to answer to a mate too.

"When you meet the right woman, you'll want to."

He crossed his arms. "I've met plenty of women. I don't want to."

Luke chuckled and downed the rest of his beer as his mate walked through the door. His entire demeanor shifted, and he shot to his feet and then sauntered toward her. Macey's smile reached all the way to her emerald eyes as she gazed up at Luke and wrapped her arms around his waist.

"Hi, beautiful. How's your day been so far?" Luke ran a hand over her head and tugged at the tight bun she wore at the nape of her neck.

Chase looked away from their affectionate display. Since Luke and Macey had gotten together, Luke had been the happiest he'd ever seen him. Apparently, love did that to a guy; not that Chase would know. But he'd reached the age where his mating instincts were kicking in hard. He wouldn't mind waking up in a beautiful woman's arms every morning, but he damn well wouldn't admit it to the alpha. It was hard enough admitting it to himself.

"Good." Macey pulled from Luke's embrace. "Hi, Chase."

"Afternoon, ma'am."

"How did it go with Bryce?"

"Oh, fine. A heads-up would've been nice. I didn't know I'd have to put on a show."

She turned to her mate, her eyes widening. "You didn't tell him I wasn't going to be there?"

"It may have slipped my mind." Luke chuckled. "Sorry about that, man."

Slipped his mind, my ass. He probably forgot on purpose to keep him on his toes. It wouldn't be the first time. "No problem."

Macey kissed Luke on the cheek. "Bryce is in the car waiting for me. I got called to a scene."

"So, no cake tasting?" Luke's voice sounded way too hopeful.

"I need you to go without me."

The alpha's mouth hung open, and Chase stifled a laugh.

Luke shook his head. "Reschedule it. I'm not going to pick a cake without you."

"I've already rescheduled on her three times." Macey walked her fingers up his chest. "You can do it, baby. I trust your taste." She kissed him on the cheek and headed for the exit. "Roberta says Spellbound Sweets is amazing. Just make sure nothing tastes gross." She waved goodbye and disappeared through the doorway.

Luke spun around, a look of terror freezing his features.

Amber shook her head. "Don't look at me. I've got a shipment coming in half an hour, and I have to finish balancing the books." She glanced at Chase, a sly smile curving her lips. "But I can man the bar if you want to take your second."

"Oh, hell no." Chase crossed his arms. "I'm not going to a witch's bakery. I'd rather go back to the morgue."

Luke raised his chin. "If another mummified body shows up, you will. Right now, you're tasting cake. Let's go."

Rain took a deep breath to calm her racing pulse as she arranged the cake samples on the platter. After they'd rescheduled the tasting so many times, she'd begun to worry this appointment would never happen. Snow had fielded all the calls from the alpha's mate, and they both stared at the phone, expecting it to ring any second with another cancellation.

"I think they're going to show this time." Snow drummed her lilac nails on the counter.

"Goddess, I hope so. I either get this deposit or I'll be sleeping on the streets." She eyed her sister. "Please be on your best behavior."

Snow pressed a hand against her chest, feigning shock. "Me? You think I'm going to screw this up?"

"Don't even pretend like you've cast a spell. And watch your temper. This is an alpha we're dealing with."

Snow smirked. "The hot temper runs in the family, love. I could say the same to you."

Rain huffed. Her sister had a point. Her temper had been what got her into this mess to begin with. "We've been here six months and haven't had any trouble with the werewolves. I don't want to start now."

Snow furrowed her brow. "What makes you think we're going to have trouble?"

"The Miami alpha's daughter went to culinary school with me, and we talked. Alphas are rough, no bull-shit men." She set the tray of samples in the fridge. "I guess they have to be in order to run a whole pack of werewolves. I hear their mates aren't any nicer." While she'd never met the New Orleans alpha, she couldn't imagine him being much different.

Snow blew her bangs off her forehead with a huff. "Jeez. They sound like the clients from hell."

"Yeah. But if we get this job, we'll be in. You said yourself how loyal werewolves are. Once the alpha accepts us, the whole pack will. I might be able to keep this place afloat after all." She dusted the powdered sugar from her pants. "At least I'll have a place to sleep for another month or two."

Snow rolled her eyes. "You'll sleep at my place before you'll be on the streets. I'll take my chances with the curse."

Rain pressed her lips together and peered at her sister. Snow would knock her out with a sleeping spell and drag her to her house before she'd let her end up homeless. And she could imagine the wrath her curse would bring down on her sister if she did. "That will never happen." She couldn't let it.

The front door chimed before Snow could argue, and a humming-bird took flight inside Rain's ribcage. She could do this. Be nice. Don't piss off the werewolves. Hope they like the cake. She took a deep breath, plastered a smile on her face, and sashayed into the storefront.

The alpha stepped through the door first, his deep-orange aura screaming power like nothing she'd seen before. He stood nearly six-foot-four and had light-brown hair and bright blue eyes.

He stepped aside for the next werewolf to enter, and Rain's breath caught in her throat. Another male, a few inches shorter than the alpha, shuffled into the store and shoved his hands into his pockets. His shiny, dark-brown hair was cut short on the sides, long enough on top to cascade to one side and curl down to his eyebrow where it accented a circular, silver piercing in his skin. He had a full, dark beard, and a series of intricate tattoos covered both his muscular arms, disappearing into the sleeves of his black shirt.

His deep-orange aura wasn't as strong as the alpha's, but he radiated sex and power. The man was scrumptious. His hazel eyes brightened as he caught her gaze, and one corner of his mouth tugged into a cocky grin.

Crap. He'd caught her staring.

Straightening her spine, she stepped toward the men. "Hi, welcome to Spellbound Sweets." She glanced to the door, expecting a female to enter, but the men appeared to be alone. Pausing, she cocked her head. The taller man was obviously the alpha, so did that make the sexy one his mate? Was that even allowed?

She cut her gaze between the two men, stretching the silence into awkwardness. Snow had never mentioned the mate she'd spoken to on the phone was male. Everything Rain knew about werewolves she'd learned from her friend in culinary school. Alphas had to be blood relatives of the first family, and they were required to keep the bloodline flowing. How could he continue the family legacy if his mate was…? She held back a sigh. All the hot ones were either gay or married, and this one was about to be both. Not that a cursed witch could afford to take a chance on any man, but still…

The alpha cleared his throat. "I'm Luke. This is Chase. We're here for a cake tasting."

Luke, that's right. Snow had written down their names, but Chase didn't ring a bell. She shook Luke's hand, and a jolt of magical energy shimmied up her arm. "I'm Rain. This is my sister, Snow. Thanks for coming."

Snow shook both their hands, and as Rain reached for Chase, a similar electric sensation danced from his skin, but it sent an extra jolt straight to her chest. He tightened his grip and furrowed his brow. "I thought this was a witch's bakery."

She pulled from his grasp. "It is. My sister is the witch. I'm the owner."

He narrowed his eyes. "That doesn't make sense."

"Snow? Do you want to bring out the samples?" She motioned to the table she'd set up with forks and water glasses. "Please, have a seat."

If they found out about her curse, they'd tuck tail and haul ass out of there before the sugar ever touched their lips. She'd have to do everything she could to steer the conversation away from the reason they didn't feel any magical energy emanating from her skin.

They settled into the chairs, and an amused grin lit on Luke's face. He looked at Chase. "This isn't so bad, is it?"

Chase's gaze slid over her body, feeling way more intimate than it should have. He was gay for goodness sake, and about to marry the alpha. But when he looked into her eyes, she couldn't stop her tongue from slipping out to moisten her lips.

Where the hell was Snow?

She needed to say something. Anything to break the awkwardness of his enticing gaze. If the alpha thought she was coming on to his future husband, she'd be toast. The first thought that crossed her mind tumbled from her lips before she could stop it. "I thought alphas had to ensure the continuation of the bloodline. How will you do that taking another male as your mate?"

A look of bewilderment flashed in Chase's eyes. "Your job is to make the cake. Pack business isn't your concern."

Luke crossed his arms. "I didn't realize you were *that* kind of bakery."

"I'm not." Oh, goddess, what had she done? If she had a shovel she'd dig a hole and bury herself for the rest of eternity. She mumbled a little prayer to the Earth Mother, asking for the ground to swallow her whole, which of course went unanswered.

She stepped to a display cabinet and took two cake toppers from a shelf, holding them up so the men could see. "I've done same-sex weddings before. You can marry a goat for all I care, as long as the goat consents."

The corner of Chase's mouth twitched. "A goat?" He crossed his arms, and Rain couldn't stop her gaze from sweeping over his muscular biceps.

Sweat slickened her palms, and she returned the cake toppers to the display. Why was she letting herself get so flustered? Sure, they were both powerful werewolves, but she'd been a powerful witch before the curse. She needed to pull herself together. Hold her ground.

Crossing her arms to mirror their posture, she shifted her weight to one foot. "You're half-animal yourself." She shrugged and returned to the table. "Pack business isn't my concern."

"Oh, Rain." Snow stopped in her tracks, gripping the cake tray in her hands.

Luke pressed his lips into a hard line.

Dear goddess, please don't let them shift in my store.

Fantastic. She'd pissed off the werewolves—exactly what she'd warned her sister not to do. Why couldn't she learn to think before she spoke?

She looked at Luke. If she could make peace with the alpha, maybe she could salvage the situation. "I'm sorry. My comment was out of line. I really take no issue in who you choose as your mate."

The alpha's eyes sparkled as his mouth split into a grin and he laughed. "Chase isn't my mate; he's my second."

She ducked her head. "Your second...mate?"

"Second in command." Chase leaned his forearms on the table. "Do I look gay to you?"

"Yes." *Damn it!* "I mean...you're hot, so..." *Jeez!* She covered her mouth with her hands before she could say anything else stupid.

"You'll have to excuse my sister." Snow dropped the tray onto the table, clanking the forks and shaking the water glasses. "She has no filter between her brain and her mouth."

Rain sank into her chair, afraid to make eye contact with the werewolves. Afraid if she opened her mouth again something even stupider would slip from between her lips and ruin her chance of getting this wedding...if she hadn't ruined it already.

Luke laughed again, and the corners of his eyes crinkled as he smiled. "No harm done; I'm sure it was an honest mistake." He winked at Rain and the tension in her muscles loosened. "My mate is Macey. She had to work and didn't want to cancel on you again, so Chase is here to help me pick the cake. His palette is a little more refined than mine. Right, buddy?" Luke clapped him on the shoulder, and Chase let out his breath in what could've either been a chuckle or a huff. It was hard to tell.

She caught Chase's gaze, and his hazel eyes held hers. Light greenish-gold with little golden flecks dancing around the pupils, they drew her in, pulling the breath from her lungs. She tried to look away, but her eyes ignored the command from her brain.

As his lips curved into that cocky smile, Snow cleared her voice. "Tell them about the cakes, hon, before they dry up."

Rain blinked, coming back to herself. Maybe the werewolves' power wasn't what had her flustered. Maybe it was the man. "Right, the first one is a vanilla-almond cake with classic buttercream frosting. It's the most popular for weddings because of its light flavor and moist texture." She needed to pull herself together. An attractive man shouldn't have made her this flustered. She'd never gotten this goo-goo eyed over one before. Not without the help of a spell.

Snow placed a sample of the cake in front of each man. Luke popped the whole piece into his mouth and grinned. He sure smiled a lot for a hard-ass alpha. "Tastes great to me. Chase?"

Chase used a fork to slice off a small bite and mushed it around in his mouth. He looked thoughtful for a moment before training his gaze on Rain. His piercing glinted as his eyebrow arched. "Too much nutmeg. What else you got?"

She straightened. Too much nutmeg? Was he insane? The nutmeg was what *made* this cake. How dare he insult her most delectable dessert? "There's only a pinch of nutmeg to enhance the almond and offset the sweetness of the vanilla."

Chase shrugged. "Whoever pinched it has a heavy hand then."

Heat flashed through her veins, her family's signature hot temper flaring to life. She'd won more awards with that recipe than she could count. No one ever picked up on the nutmeg. She couldn't help but glare at the man. He may have been as sexy as sugar was sweet, but his taste buds worked about as well as a busted kitchen scale.

Snow rested a hand on her shoulder. "Let's try the next one."

Rain let out a slow breath as her sister served the men the next slice. "This one is Italian cream cake with a cream cheese frosting. It has a stronger flavor and a denser texture, but it's also popular for weddings."

"This one's great too," Luke said with the food in his mouth.

Chase shook his head. "Way too dense. Shouldn't have to chew it this much."

Rain bit her tongue to stop from spouting off. She served them two more rounds of cake—raspberry-almond and lemon cream—and both men had their usual reactions. The alpha loved them all, but Chase found something negative to say every time.

Rain curled her hands into fists under the table. He was messing with her, getting her back for the goat comment. He had to be. Her lemon cream was divine, and he did *not* nearly choke on too much zest…because she didn't put any zest into the damn cake. "Are you this critical of everything you eat?"

Chase cracked his knuckles. "I know good cake when I taste it, and this isn't it."

"If you're upset because I questioned your sexuality, that says more about you than it does me." Clamping her mouth shut, she tried to keep her expression neutral. She should have clamped it shut before the insult tumbled out, but like Snow said, she had no filter. Words seemed to shoot from her thoughts to her lips, completely bypassing the rational part of her brain.

Luke made a strange sound in his throat that could've been a laugh or a choke. Chase leaned back in his chair. "You don't know a thing about me."

She arched an eyebrow. "And I don't care to." Unless it involved examining all those tattoos more closely…with her tongue. *Stop it, Rain.* What was she thinking?

The alpha rose to his feet. "Thank you for letting us sample your cakes. I'll talk to Macey, and we'll be in touch." He slapped Chase on the shoulder and shuffled to the door.

"Rain…" Snow whispered in her ear. "Stop them."

What was the point? The alpha wouldn't hire her for his wedding after that debacle.

Rain narrowed her gaze as Chase stood and gave her a curt nod. "Have a nice day, Rain. It was nice to meet you, Snow." He turned, and she caught a nice view of his backside as he sauntered out the door.

What the hell was her problem? He'd insulted her baking…several times…but all she could think about was what he looked like under those clothes and how much of him was covered in tattoos.

CHAPTER THREE

CHASE KEPT HIS GAZE TRAINED ON THE SIDEWALK AS THEY exited the bakery, fighting the urge to turn and catch a glimpse of the insolent witch.

"You want to tell me what that was all about?" Luke stared straight ahead, giving him ample time to formulate an excuse for turning a simple cake tasting into a fiasco.

He nodded and paced through the intersection, out of earshot and any magical enchantments the witches may have put on the bakery. He wouldn't have put it past them to cast a hunger spell on the sidewalk outside the shop to entice people to go inside and buy one of those mouth-watering cakes. Every damn one of them had melted on his tongue like an orgasm for his taste buds.

Stopping on the sidewalk, he glanced at the shop. "She's hiding something."

"Who? The owner?"

"Rain." Her name tasted as good on his lips as that lemon cake. Sweet and creamy and slightly tart.

Luke followed his gaze toward the yellow building. "Everyone's hiding something. Either tell me why you acted like an asshole, or I'm going back in there and picking the damn cake myself."

"She's hiding her magic. Didn't you notice when you shook her hand? Her sister's magic felt like a deep vibration. Strong. When I touched Rain, I didn't feel anything." Correction: he didn't feel any magic. When her delicate fingers wrapped around his hand, he'd felt plenty of other things. And damn him for feeling them for a witch.

Luke shrugged. "So? Maybe one of their parents was a human, and her sister got all the magic. I didn't sense any need to be on alert, and that bakery comes highly recommended."

"Recommended by another witch."

"Macey trusts Roberta, and so do I." He inclined his chin. "The owner is pretty, isn't she?"

He clenched his jaw. "Gorgeous." Could his nerves be on edge because of the way his body had reacted to the woman? Maybe the years of self-imposed celibacy were catching up to him. He shook his head. "She's a witch. She can't be trusted."

"I understand your aversion to witches, but they're not all bad." Luke shifted his weight to one foot. "Neither was the cake, was it?"

"Best damn cake I've ever tasted." Possibly the most beautiful woman he'd ever seen. And the way her temper flared and she bit back when he'd baited her…he could almost see the storm brewing in her dark-gray eyes.

Luke crossed his arms. "So you acted like an asshole because you're attracted to a witch who doesn't have any magic?"

"I was protecting the pack." And maybe his heart, but Luke didn't need to know that.

The alpha chuckled. "I see. Well, since you're so concerned about my mate's choice in bakeries for our wedding, you've earned yourself a new job."

"What's that?" Wariness stretched out his words. Whenever Luke got that look in his eyes, it usually meant trouble.

"You're in charge of all things cake."

A brick settled in the pit of his stomach. He'd been trying to avoid ever having to see the beautiful woman again, not end up as the cake liaison for the alpha's wedding.

"You're going to haul your ass back to the bakery, apologize for being a dick, and sign the contract so I can make my mate happy, understood?"

He met Luke's eyes briefly before shifting his gaze downward. "Yeah." What the hell kind of mess had he gotten himself into?

"And, since you're so concerned about her lack of magic, you're going to do a thorough investigation into her and her background."

He ground his teeth. "Damn it, Luke."

His friend laughed. "You're on witch duty until the wedding is done. Hopefully, by then, you'll get over your prejudice."

Second in command of the sixth largest werewolf pack in the United States, and he'd landed himself on witch and wedding cake duty. *Fantastic.* He grumbled under his breath as they walked away from the bakery.

Luke nodded to the left and crossed the street. "C'mon. We've got another appointment before you head back to apologize."

They rounded a corner to find a couple in the alley in the middle of what appeared to be a heated argument. The woman clutched her purse to her stomach, gripping the strap so tightly her knuckles turned white. The misaligned buttons on her waitress shirt indicated she'd gotten dressed in a hurry, probably trying to get away from the asshole pursuing her.

The guy's blond hair was slicked back from his face, his suit an Armani knock-off, his Rolex fake. He had a cocky grin and predatory eyes, and as he grabbed the woman's elbow, she jerked away. "Come on, baby. How many times do I have to tell you I'm sorry? She didn't mean anything."

The smooth insincerity of his voice raised Chase's hackles. He'd known plenty of assholes like this. Hell, he'd almost turned into one himself.

"We're through, Alan. Leave me alone." The woman turned to walk away, but Alan grabbed her bicep, spinning her to face him.

Chase strode into the ally and stood next to the woman, careful not to touch her—she'd been manhandled enough today—but close enough that Alan could feel the power in his aura. "Is this guy bothering you, ma'am?"

She glanced at Chase, her posture straightening. "He's leaving, aren't you, Alan?"

Alan flicked his gaze from the woman to Chase, and back to the woman again. The muscles in his neck worked as he swallowed whatever snide remark he was about to make and released his grip on her arm. "Yeah. I'm going." Maybe he wasn't as stupid as Chase thought. "See you around, Jamie."

Jamie inhaled a shaky breath and smoothed her crumpled shirt down her stomach. Her fingers trembled over the misaligned buttons for a moment before she fisted her hands and turned to Chase. "Thank you."

"Any time. Need me to walk you to work?"

She tugged on her blonde ponytail. "I'm already there." Nodding to a doorway a few feet away, she adjusted her purse strap.

"If you don't feel safe heading home after your shift, ask someone to escort you."

"It's fine. He won't try anything." She shuffled toward the door. "Thanks again." She cast a pained glance at Alan's back before disappearing into the building.

"You done playing Captain America?" Luke jerked his head, motioning for Chase to follow.

"Not quite." He intended to make sure the asshole never bothered Jamie again. "Hey, Alan."

"What do you want now?" As the man turned, Chase caught a glimpse of the tattoo on the side of his neck—a fleur-de-lis designed from a trinity knot. A coven crest.

Goddamn witch. His hands balled into fists as he barreled toward Alan. Grabbing him by his fake-Armani lapels, Chase twisted the material in his hands and slammed him against the wall.

Alan's eyes widened as his head made contact with the brick. "What the hell, man?"

"Chase." Luke growled a warning.

"He's a witch," he said through clenched teeth, never taking his eyes off the asshole. "Leave the woman alone."

Alan glanced at Luke, and a look of recognition flashed in his eyes. He lifted his arms, trying to shake Chase off, but Chase pressed him harder into the wall. "All I did was sleep with her friend. Aren't werewolves supposed to fight real monsters?"

"What do you think I'm doing?" He tightened his grip.

Luke moved toward him, but Chase didn't let up.

"You'll use her until she stops giving you what you want, and then you'll leave her. Or worse. I know your kind." Heat rolled through his body, his beast feeding off the emotions as memories flooded his brain.

Alan scoffed. "Sounds like you're speaking from experience."

Chase sucked in a breath to respond, but Luke's hand landed squarely on his shoulder, a silent order to end it. He pried loose his fists and released his hold on the man, taking a step back to surrender control to the alpha.

Luke straightened to his full height and looked down at the witch. "Actions always have consequences. Tread carefully."

"Yeah." Alan dusted off his jacket and narrowed his eyes at Chase before strutting out of the alley.

"This is exactly what I'm talking about," Chase grumbled. "Witches can't be trusted. None of them."

Luke crossed his arms. "This ends now."

"I just wanted to scare him. I know how it's going to end. He'll move on to the next woman, and Jamie will be left with the consequences." He glanced at the door the woman had disappeared through.

"They're not your concern." Luke uncrossed his arms, his eyes softening. "She's not your sister."

He let out a slow breath, the anger cooling to a mild burn. "I know. I got carried away. Sorry."

Luke nodded for him to follow him out of the alley. "You need to get over your aversion to witches."

"That won't happen any time soon." After everything he'd been through, it was ingrained in his soul.

"Then you're going to have to fake it." Luke hung a left on Ursulines and headed toward Rampart. "We need to pay a visit to the coven priestess."

Chase stopped short. "More witches?"

"We have to find out if the mummy is a one-off thing or if we should be expecting more victims."

Chase grumbled under his breath, but he followed the alpha to the coven house on the outskirts of the Quarter. Built in the 1800s, the three-story brick building once housed one of the most influential families of the nineteenth century. The wrought-iron galleries adorning the second and third floors overflowed with ferns and ivies and every other kind of plant imaginable. What was it about witches and nature? They could grow sunflowers in a frozen tundra if they had the mind to. Chase could barely keep the aloe vera plant Bekah brought home alive.

Luke knocked three times on the door, and Chase flanked him, standing a step behind his right shoulder. The sound of boots thudding on the hardwood floor seeped from inside, and Chase tensed. Witches and werewolves weren't mortal enemies. They had quite a bit in common if he paused to consider it. Magic in their blood, a shared affinity for the moon. Hell, some witches could even shapeshift.

But they were too powerful. With their spells, controlling the elements, the ability to bend people's will to do their dirty work for them… A chill crept up his spine.

"Relax," Luke muttered over his shoulder as the lock disengaged and the door swung open.

Like hell he would. His disdain for witches was purely personal, and he'd be damned if he'd ever let his guard down around one again. He'd learned his lesson. Twice.

"Can I help you?" A look of recognition flashed in the man's blue eyes before he cut his gaze to the left.

Getting a visit from the alpha werewolf would be enough to make any supernatural being nervous. Chase crossed his arms and widened his stance, adding to the intimidation effect.

"Is Calista here?" Luke asked.

The man swallowed. "Do you have an appointment?" His voice was thin, like it was a standard question he had to ask, but he knew what the answer would be.

Luke inclined his head. "Do I *need* an appointment?"

"No." He opened the door wider, motioning for them to enter. "Come in."

Chase's boots thudded on the floor as he stepped into the foyer, quieting as he reached a plush, green runner. A crystal chandelier hung in the entryway, casting golden light on the cream-colored walls. To the right lay a great room with a raised ceiling and polished wood floor. In the old days, the space would have been used for entertaining and could double as both a dancefloor and a massive dining room, depending on the occasion. Now, it housed some kind of altar, and the overpowering scent of incense made his nose burn.

"Have a seat in here." The man waved a hand toward a sitting room to the left. "I'll let Calista know you're here."

Chase shuffled into the sitting room behind Luke and lowered himself into a straight-back chair. Oil paintings adorned the dark-wood walls, and a baby grand piano occupied the corner of the room. The extravagant coven headquarters was a far cry from the squat Irish bar the pack called home base. With its low ceilings and bare brick walls, O'Malley's Pub would have these witches curling their lips in disdain.

What would Rain think of the bar? Or his tiny shotgun-style house for that matter? With her polished look, shiny hair, and perfect complexion, she probably came from money. Hell, she owned her own business. She wouldn't give a second glance to a rough-around-the-edges werewolf bartender.

He scrunched his brow. Why the hell was his imagination treading down *that* path? He shouldn't have given a second thought to a witch who was hiding her magic, but damn it, if he wasn't on the fourth or fifth.

Luke leaned forward, resting his elbows on his knees. "You okay?"

Chase blinked, banishing the image of the feisty witch from his mind. "Yeah. This place gives me the willies."

"Maybe someone's trying to cast a spell on you. Make you fall in love with a witch."

The sensation of a thousand ants skittering across his back made him shiver. "Don't even joke like that."

"Spells affecting free will are forbidden." A tall woman with long, dark hair and four-inch heels clicked into the sitting room. "Surely, you're aware of that, Mr. Mason."

Luke rose to his feet. "So is murder, but there's a dead witch at the morgue. Not everyone follows the rules."

Her eyes widened in shock for a split second before she composed herself. She opened her mouth to speak, but she hesitated as a pair of witches in Harrah's uniforms sashayed to the door. "Bye, Calista," the blonde called from the foyer. "See you tomorrow."

Calista waved over her shoulder and turned to the werewolves. "Let's have this meeting in my office." She motioned for them to follow her down a hallway and through a set of oak double doors.

A heavy wooden desk sat in front of a large window overlooking the courtyard, and the witch slinked behind it to lower herself into a tan leather chair. "How do you know it's a witch in the morgue?"

Luke sat in a chair across from the desk. "Tell her what you saw."

Chase settled into the one next to him. "She had a tattoo under her collarbone. Trinity knot with a coven crest."

Calista folded her hands on the desk. "Which coven?"

He huffed. "How the hell should I know?"

"No one in my coven has been reported missing." She took a sheet of paper from a drawer and offered it to him. "Do you remember what it looked like? Can you draw it for me?"

"Sure." He snatched a pen from the holder on the corner of her desk and leaned forward to sketch the design. The pen made a scratching sound on the paper as the crest came into shape. A trinity knot situated in a crescent moon with a string of six stars connecting the ends to form a circle.

As he finished the drawing, an honest-to-God black cat jumped on the desk and hissed before slinking across the surface. *Typical.* He pushed the paper toward Calista and glanced around the room, almost certain he'd find a pointy hat and a broomstick hanging on the wall.

He didn't.

Calista shooed the cat off the desk with her hand and pressed her lips together as she gazed at the sketch. "This witch belonged to the Miami coven. Her death doesn't concern us. Or you."

Luke straightened his spine. "It does when the cause of death was supernatural."

The cat jumped into the witch's lap, and she stroked its back. "How did she die?"

Chase cringed as the image of the mummified corpse flashed in his mind. "Something sucked the life right out of her. Took her eye as souvenir. Any of your minions have that ability?"

Calista bristled. "That's a weighty accusation to make." She shifted her gaze to Luke. "You need to keep this one on a tighter leash."

"No one's making accusations." Luke flashed him a warning glare. "But if you have any information, we'd appreciate your cooperation. It's our job to protect the secrecy of supernatural beings."

She inhaled deeply, cutting her gaze from Luke to Chase and back again. "You're looking for an energy vampire, and no, I don't know anyone with that power."

Chase shook his head. "The veins contained powdered blood. If it were a vampire—"

"Not the blood-sucking kind." She set the cat on the floor. "An *energy* vampire. Someone who can drain the magic and the life force from another being. Witches can develop the power by practicing the black arts, but I can assure you none of my witches would dare. We are a peaceful, goddess-worshipping coven."

"Thank you for your time." Luke stood, and Chase followed his lead.

Calista walked ahead of them toward the exit, her heels clicking on the wood in a melodic rhythm. She opened the door. "If I can be of any more service…"

Luke stepped through the door, but Chase paused in the threshold. "Actually, you can."

"Oh?"

"What can you tell me about the witch who runs the bakery?"

A strange look flashed in her eyes. "I'm afraid I can't tell you anything. She doesn't belong to the coven."

He rubbed the back of his neck. "Why doesn't she belong?"

"I'm afraid I can't answer that either. Have a nice day, gentlemen." She all but slammed the door in Chase's face.

Rain was hiding her powers *and* she didn't belong to the coven. She didn't look like the type of woman who'd drain the life from someone, but he'd learned his lesson giving witches the benefit of the doubt. Something wasn't right in that bakery, and he planned to figure out exactly what it was.

Rain leaned her elbows on the table and held her face in her hands. "What am I going to do now? I'll never be able to pay the rent without the werewolf wedding."

Snow rubbed a hand across her back. "I'm sure it'll work itself out. You put so much kindness out into the world; it's going to come back around to you soon."

"Sure." Like that could happen. She hadn't acted the slightest bit kind toward Chase. "Something tells me I'm not through making up for the bad things I've done."

"Bad *thing*. Singular. We all make mistakes."

"I'll be paying for mine for the rest of my life." Pinching the bridge of her nose, she squeezed her eyes shut. Why couldn't she have kept her temper in check? The alpha seemed to love every bite of cake he tried. But Chase...

Snow folded her hands on the table. "You have to admit, those werewolves were kinda hot."

"They were not..." Her stomach fluttered. "Yeah, they kinda were."

"Especially the tattooed one. What was his name?"

"Chase." Why did her voice sound so breathy, the S stretching out into a hiss? And why did his name taste so good to say?

"That's right." Her sister gave her a strange look. "Dark hair, ink, smoldering eyes."

"Mm-hmm." His eyes did smolder, didn't they?

"Exactly your type of guy."

Rain sat up straight. "He is *not* my type. I don't have a type. Anyway...he insulted my baking skills."

"I don't think he meant it." Snow smirked.

"He meant it. He was out to get me from the moment he stepped into the bakery."

Snow rolled her eyes. "Think about it. He knows enough about baking to taste the nutmeg in your classic vanilla-almond. You have to admit that turns you on. At least a little bit."

She wanted to argue. To insist his sensitive palate didn't interest her in the slightest. But she couldn't. "Yeah, okay. You made your point, but it doesn't matter. There's no way I'll be doing the werewolf wedding after that fiasco."

"You never know." Snow shrugged. "Maybe the alpha will bring his mate back and let her choose. We're the only supernatural bakery in the Quarter, and they seem like busy people."

"Maybe." Probably not.

The door chimed as a DHL delivery man carried a small cardboard box into the shop. Rain's heart sprinted as he shuffled toward her. "Rain Connolly?"

"That's me." She plastered on a fake smile to hide her nerves.

"Sign here please." He handed her a tablet. "My stylus broke, so you'll have to use your finger."

She scribbled her name on the device and wiped her sweaty hands on her jeans. "Thank you." Now if he would leave the store so she could open the box.

He shuffled toward a display case and gazed at the bite-sized delicacies beneath the glass. Snow padded behind the counter and jerked her head at Rain, a silent order to snap out of it and try to sell the guy something.

"Are you hungry?" Rain stood and joined her sister behind the display. "We've got a variety of mini cakes and cookies you can snack on while you're making deliveries."

"Not really." He shoved his hands in his pockets.

Damn. It seemed she couldn't even make a dollar today.

"These are interesting, though. What do the symbols mean?" He nodded at Snow's contribution to the bakery—cookies with a magic spell for clarity baked into them.

Rain gazed at the treats. They all contained the same spell, but the intent of the person eating it always focused the outcome.

"Oh, you have a discerning eye." Snow laid on the charm thick. "We're a witch's bakery, you know? And you were drawn to our spellbinders. They're magical cookies that help you realize your dreams."

He chuckled. "Is that so?"

Snow waved her hand over the glass in a flourish. "Need help finding your dream job? This is the cookie for you." She pointed to a green-iced cookie with a dollar sign frosted on the top. "Not doing so hot in the love department? We've got what you need." She indicated the cookie with a red heart. "If you're having trouble making a decision, this one can help." She used a piece of tissue paper to take a cookie with a blue question mark from the tray and offered it to him. "Clarity in a cookie for the bargain price of two ninety-nine."

He laughed unconvincingly. "If I give that heart one to the girl I like, she'll fall in love with me?"

"Oh, no." Rain pressed a hand to her chest and feigned offense. "Spells that hinder free will are forbidden. But if *you* eat it, it will help you realize if she's really the one for you."

"Hmm…" He narrowed his eyes. "I'll take the question mark one."

Snow slipped the cookie into a white paper bag and took his money. "Have a nice day."

"You too." He looked at the bag and shook his head before shuffling outside.

As soon as the door fell shut, Snow raced across the room and locked it. "Open it!" She scrambled back to the counter and gripped Rain's arm. "It's the Bauhinia, isn't it?"

"I think so." Her heart pounded. With a trembling hand, she grabbed a knife from a cutting board. The cool, steel handle slipped from her grasp. Like an idiot, she tried to catch the utensil midair, and the sharp end bit into her finger before it clattered on the floor.

"Crap!" A bead of warm, red blood pooled on her fingertip, and she gazed at it, mesmerized by the dim, magenta glow. She couldn't really call it a glow. It was more like a shimmer, proving her magic resided there and she'd moved one step closer to unlocking it.

"Are you okay?" Snow wiped her finger with a paper towel and wrapped a bandage around it, bringing Rain back to the present.

"I will be soon."

Snow handed her the knife. "Don't drop it."

Rain smirked. "Thanks." Pressing the sharp tip against the tape, she sliced down the center of the package where the two halves of the lid met in the middle. The flaps sprang open, and she yanked out the wad of paper sitting on top. There, nestled in a bed of packing peanuts, lay the Bauhinia.

She gingerly lifted it from the box and examined the container. A glass jar held a single pink flower attached to a stem with six green leaves shaped like a cow's hooves. Medically, the herb could lower blood sugar and treat diabetes. Magically, it could be used to resist the effects of controlling magic, like love spells and, more importantly… binding spells.

Excitement made her stomach turn. Two weeks and three hundred dollars later, and she finally held in her hands the second to last ingredient to unbind her powers and break the curse. "Get the bowl."

"One step ahead of you." Snow set the copper container on the counter and gently pried off the lid. A gelatinous mixture of mango, long pepper, agarwood, and a slew of strange liquids coagulated in the bottom of the bowl. She held out her hand. "Pay me first."

"Right." She yanked a twenty out of the cash register and pressed it into her sister's hand.

Snow shoved the bill into her pocket. "You're lucky this spell was written specifically for you. I hear I could get ten grand for one of these on the black market."

"Sure. Get caught and you'll end up with your powers bound like mine. Trust me. It's not worth it. Nothing is." Rain peered at the concoction, careful not to touch it for fear of contamination, and handed her sister the Bauhinia. Snow dropped the new ingredient into the bowl and crushed it into the mixture with a cast-iron pestle.

Holding her breath, Rain waited, anticipating some spark of magic or glowing aura to form from the potion. Nothing happened.

Snow set the pestle on a towel. "Huh."

Rain's shoulders drooped as she leaned her hip against the counter and shook her head. Could this entire spell be someone's idea of a sick joke? It hadn't been *that* long since she'd had the ability to make potions, and every time a new ingredient joined the mix, its magical properties changed the components of the spell, altering the appearance. She might as well have been staring at cake batter for all it mattered because this potion was as mundane as vanilla frosting.

Snow returned the lid to the bowl. "I'm sure the last ingredient will activate it. Unbinding potions are super powerful, and since this one takes so long to make, it probably requires the final step for the magic to galvanize."

The heaviness in her shoulders lifted, and she straightened her spine. Her sister's hypothesis made sense. "Let's find out what the final ingredient is." She padded through the kitchen to her bedroom in the back of the store and pulled a wooden box from beneath her bed. Retrieving the key from the closet, she opened the lid and took out the spell. The thick parchment felt like hope in her hands, and she ran a finger over the list. It had taken her three months to gather all these ingredients. Hopefully the last one would prove less difficult.

Returning to the storefront, she laid the enchanted paper on the bowl and chewed her bottom lip as she waited for her final task to appear.

"I can't look." Snow turned her back to the counter and pressed her fingers to her temples. "Tell me what it says."

Rain peered at the paper. The magic shimmered, a silvery mist swirling on the parchment as the words appeared on the page. Her heart sank. "Oh, no."

"That's a good 'oh, no,' right? Like, 'Oh, no. That's so easy to find.' Right?" Snow turned around.

A sour, burning sensation crept up Rain's throat. "Easy to find. Impossible to obtain."

"Oh, goddess, what is it?"

Rain sucked in a sharp breath and blew it out hard. "Two drops of blood from a first-born werewolf, given willingly, beneath a blue moon."

"You're joking. You have to be." Snow snatched the paper from her hands, her mouth hanging open as she read it. "How the hell are we supposed to manage that? No supernatural being is going to willingly give her blood away. Especially a werewolf. That's where our magic resides."

"No kidding." Rain looked at the bandage on her finger. Blood magic was a risky practice. Too little and the spell might only partially work...if at all. Use too much, and the consequences could be dire. "It must be the transformation and healing abilities that are needed to complete the spell."

"Maybe we can make a substitution. Maybe if we mixed this with a healing potion..." Snow drummed her nails on the granite.

"That won't work. This spell was written by a witch on the council, and it's a one-time deal. If we screw it up, that's it. Even if we did it exactly right the second time, it wouldn't work. They made that very clear in the letter that came with it." She carried the paper to her bedroom.

"So that's it then?" Snow followed on her heels. "You're giving up?"

Rain locked the spell in the box and slid it under her bed. "What else can I do? I've already pissed off the alpha, so the Crescent City Pack is out of the question. I won't go back to Miami. It's useless." She plopped onto her bed and rubbed her forehead. "Why did they have to throw the *given willingly* clause in there?"

Snow crossed her arms. "They're not going to make it easy for you, but you can't give up."

It was hopeless. Werewolves considered their blood sacred, and it was highly illegal for them to get it anywhere near another person. First-born werewolves weren't even allowed to go to the hospital. "Tell me what to do then, oh wise sister, who's only a year and a half older than I am."

"I'll tell you what you're going to do." She leaned a shoulder against the doorway and crossed her legs at the ankles. "You're going to the alpha and apologizing. You didn't piss *him* off. It was his sexy second who had the problem with you, and he's not the one getting married. Take a box of samples. Ask him to give them to his mate and let her decide."

"What good will that do? Maybe I'll get to do the wedding, but it won't help me with the spell." She sat up straight. "But maybe I'll get the wedding. Then I can pay my bills." Maybe she'd never be rid of her curse, but at least she wouldn't be on the street. "That's a great idea, wise one. I'll stop by their headquarters tomorrow morning."

Snow arched an eyebrow, and the corner of her mouth tugged upward, almost as if it were connected by a string.

A knot of wariness formed in Rain's stomach. That look only meant one thing. "There's something more sinister lurking inside this plan, isn't there?"

"Not sinister." Snow pushed from the doorway and settled on the edge of the bed. "I saw the way Chase looked at you. He wants you."

A fluttering sensation formed in her stomach before it sank to her knees. "I don't like where this is headed."

"You're attracted to him, right?"

"Who wouldn't be? The guy is like sex on a stick. But…even if I did apologize to him, you know what happened last time I fell in love. That's not something I care to go through again. Ever."

"First of all, you and I both know something *else* was going on last time…whether you can prove it or not." Snow grinned wickedly. "And anyway, who said anything about falling in love? Flirt with him. Earn his trust. I hear werewolves will do anything for their mates."

"I am *not* going to be his mate."

"Then be his friend. I may not be able to see magic like you, but I did see a spark between you two."

Rain chewed her bottom lip. She had to admit there'd been *something* between them. Was it a spark? It was hard to say. She had felt a bit of heat, which was more than she'd felt for any man in years. Then he went and insulted her cake. "I don't know…"

Her sister put a hand on her knee. "Everything happens for a reason. Chase coming into your life might be the end of your bad karma. Think of him as a gift from the universe. From fate."

"He does come in a nice package, doesn't he?" It wouldn't hurt to be nice to the man. Maybe they could be friends, but that was as far as she'd take it. She could enjoy his sex appeal from a safe distance, earn his trust, and when the time was right, she'd ask him for a small favor.

Yeah, right. Like that would work. No telling what kind of punishment he'd endure from his pack if he granted her request.

"It doesn't hurt to try." Snow stood and glided to the door. "I'm going to unlock the shop in case we get any customers."

Rain returned the key to the closet and straightened her sheets. It was the craziest, stupidest plan her sister had ever come up with, but it was the only one she had.

CHAPTER FOUR

CHASE SHUFFLED UP ROYAL STREET TOWARD SPELLBOUND Sweets and glanced at the time on his phone. Five-fifty-nine p.m. He'd caught a glimpse of the store hours posted on the door when he'd been there that afternoon, and the shop was scheduled to close at six. With any luck, the place would be empty when he got there.

He hadn't been avoiding talking to the witch. Not really. After their meeting with the coven, he'd spent the afternoon planning the bar menu for tomorrow and making sure they had enough ingredients in stock for the barbeque nachos he had planned. It wasn't his fault he didn't finish until five-forty-five. Sure, he could've taken care of the cake issue beforehand, but he'd dealt with enough witches for one day. Hell, he'd dealt with enough for the rest of his life.

Mumbling a prayer to whatever gods might be listening, he scrambled to find a way to approach the situation. He had to apologize for being a dick, number one. Even if the cake had tasted as bad as he'd pretended it did, he'd been out of line.

But there was something about the way her temper had flared that caused something to burn inside of him. And when the clouds gathered in her eyes, he couldn't help but want to experience the storm.

She was sexy as hell, and that was the problem. There were too many mysteries surrounding her. Too many red flags in his mind. But it was his job to get to know her—thanks to Luke—and he always followed through on his orders, no matter how ridiculous and scheming they may have been.

At five after six, he tried the door. Warm metal greeted his palm as he gave the knob a twist. *Damn.* Unlocked. Rain's dark curls bobbed as she snapped her head up and pinned him with a heated gaze. The gray in her irises seemed to swirl, undulating like a whirlpool, making the rest of the world disappear. She wiped her hands on a towel and glided around the counter with the grace of a swan.

"Can I help you?" She caught her bottom lip between her teeth, and the strength in his knees wavered.

He gripped the door knob tighter, his own body heat—combined with the sun-warmed metal—making his palm sweat. "I see you're about to close. I'll come back tomorrow."

"Please don't go." She reached toward him then dropped her arms to her sides. "I want to apologize for the way I acted. It was unprofessional."

"No. I want to apologize." He let the door fall shut behind him. "That's why I'm here."

The corner of her mouth twitched. "You *want* to apologize? Or were you *told* to?"

"Both. I was out of line. I'm sorry."

Her pink lips curved into a smile, revealing a set of perfectly straight, white teeth. He could imagine the way they'd feel nipping at his neck, gliding down his stomach to... *Whoa. Stop right there.* He cleared his throat and shoved his hands in his pockets.

"Apology accepted. I'd offer you a snack, but since my baking skills are apparently lacking..." She crossed her arms.

"Yeah, about that..." He stepped toward her. "Your cakes were amazing. Luke and Macey would like you for their wedding."

Her eyes widened briefly before she blinked away the surprise. "Why did you say they were terrible?"

"As second in command, it's my job to protect the pack. You being a witch made me wary. Then there was this." He took her hand and held it between both of his. Her lips parted as she sucked in a small breath, and then her eyes locked with his. What was it about her eyes?

He released her hand. "Why don't I feel your magic?"

She lifted her chin. "I don't have any magic."

"You have to. If your sister is a witch, that means at least one of your parents is. Magic is in your blood, but I don't feel it. Why is that?"

She lifted one shoulder as if to dismiss him and glided behind the safety of the counter. "I'm a dud, okay? Let it rest." She glared at him, daring him to press the issue.

He'd hit a sore spot. Maybe she was telling the truth. Some second-born weres didn't have special abilities, though he'd hardly call them duds. They had the magic in their veins, and they could continue the supernatural bloodline. He stepped toward the counter. "Is that why you aren't part of the coven? Because you don't have powers?"

"I'm not part of the coven, either." Snow's heels clicked on the tile floor as she approached her sister and wrapped her arm around her shoulders. "There's no requirement to join." Rain gave her a harsh look, and she dropped her arm to her side. "Sorry. Not helping?"

"Not really."

"Here." Snow handed Rain a stack of papers. "The wedding contract. I'll be in the back if you need me." She cut her gaze between Rain and him. "It's good to see you again, Chase." She strutted to the back before he had time to respond.

Rain slammed the papers onto the counter and paced to a glass display case. Now he'd hit a nerve. Hard. Would the coven deny someone entry because she didn't have powers? Leave it to witches to turn against their own.

"I'm sorry if I upset you."

"I'm not upset. Anyway, my sister and I belong to our old coven." She yanked a tray of cookies from the case, and it fell from her hands, scattering the confections across the floor. "Crap." She dropped to her knees, disappearing behind the display.

"Let me help you with that." He rushed around the counter and joined her on the floor.

She snatched the cookie he reached for. "I don't need help. Thank you." Scrambling for the rest of the cookies, she tossed them on the tray.

He reached for one that had landed halfway beneath the cabinet, but she grabbed his wrist. Her fingers were soft and warm wrapped around his arm, and while he didn't detect a magical signature from her skin, another kind of electricity shot straight to his heart. Why was he drawn to this woman? Was it her secrets? The mystery and danger brewing in her eyes? Or was it something else entirely?

Keeping a firm grasp on his wrist, she used her left hand to snatch the cookie and toss it on the tray. "Please don't show me any kindness." She released her grip and rose to her feet before carrying the tray to a waste bin and dumping the crumbling cookies into the trash.

What an odd thing for her to say. He spotted a cookie she'd missed and picked it up, examining the blue-frosting question mark drawn on the top. "Does the five-second rule apply?" He flashed a grin, hoping to get a smile out of her, and held up the cookie.

"I wouldn't."

Damn. No smile.

She set the tray on the counter. "You're already wary of witches. Those were clarity cookies. Snow makes them with magic."

He tossed it in the trash and wiped his hands on his pants, hopefully wiping away the damn spell before his skin absorbed it. "You sell spells to humans? That's allowed?"

She rolled her eyes. "It's a simple clarity spell, and they know it when they buy it. All it does is help them see their goals more clearly. Yes, it's allowed."

"Does it work?" He sauntered toward her and leaned a hip against the counter.

"Depending on the person's intent, yes." She moved toward him. Her eyes held a curious look as she dropped her gaze to his mouth briefly before flicking it back to his eyes.

A strange magnetism danced between them. Was she as drawn to him as he was to her? She seemed to be. But she was a witch, and his sudden urge to take her in his arms and kiss those soft, pink lips blasted a warning alarm in his brain. He had a job to do, and getting involved with the person he was supposed to protect the pack from wasn't part of it.

Then again, with the dead witch in the morgue and Rain without powers, maybe she was the one who needed protecting. Possessiveness coiled in his core as if his body had already decided she was his to take care of without consulting his mind first. Where the hell had this unwelcome emotion come from, and how could he get rid of it?

She cleared her voice and stepped back. Damn it, he'd been staring at her. And she'd been staring right back at him.

"Are you a chef?" She blinked twice, and her composure returned, the moment they'd shared dissolving as if it had never happened.

"No. Why do you ask?"

"No one has ever noticed the nutmeg in my classic vanilla-almond. And your comment about the zest in my lemon cream... There was no zest in it, but you must be familiar with cooking to make such an accusation."

"I'm self-taught. I do the menus for the bar and cook for my sister and niece." A pang of guilt spread through his stomach, and he rubbed the back of his neck. "I am sorry I said those things. All of the samples were delicious. Luke liked the vanilla best, so they're going with that one."

Her lips curved into a smile, and his heart slammed against his ribs. Damn, she was beautiful.

She scribbled something on the stack of papers and handed them to him. "If you can ask your alpha to sign this and bring the deposit by tomorrow, I'll add them to my calendar."

Chase grabbed a pen from the counter and signed his own name, adding the number for the bar and his personal cell to the form. "I'm on cake duty, so my signature will work. I can bring the money tomorrow."

She took the papers. "I'll look forward to seeing you."

"Me too." He shoved his hands in his pockets. That was his cue to leave, but he couldn't make his legs carry him to the door. He wanted to know this woman, but damn it, he didn't trust her. In the forty-five minutes he'd spent with her, his mind and his dick had waged a war inside his body. "Do you want to go to dinner?" *Crap.* It looked like his dick won that battle.

She opened her mouth to respond, but her brow furrowed, the storm in her eyes brewing as if she fought her own battle. "I…" She clamped her mouth shut and chewed her bottom lip. "Thank you, but no."

Snow emerged from the back of the store and flashed her a strange look, but Rain shook her head.

This cue to leave he didn't miss. "Right. Well, be careful heading home. I love this city, but it's not the safest place in the world."

"Don't worry. I live right here." Rain opened her arms, indicating the bakery.

"I'll bring the deposit by tomorrow. Good evening, ladies." He shuffled out the door and rubbed his chest, trying to rub away the sting of rejection. What the hell was he thinking asking her to dinner?

He wasn't thinking, and that was the problem. Not with the head on his shoulders anyway. The clicking of heels on concrete grabbed his attention, and he turned around to find Snow prancing after him.

"Chase, wait." She stopped a few feet in front of him and glanced at the bakery. "Rain's in the back. She doesn't know I'm talking to you."

"Okay." Why did that matter?

"My sister is a really great girl."

"I don't doubt that."

"She's kind of a tough nut to crack, though. I know she turned down your offer for dinner, but if you keep trying, she'll come around."

He held her gaze, trying to figure out her motivation. Was she attempting to play match-maker for her sister, or did she have an ulterior motive? He never knew with witches. "Thanks for the advice."

"She eats lunch in Louis Armstrong Park near the statue when the weather is nice. Tomorrow's forecast is sunny and warm." She smiled and spun toward the bakery.

"Hey, Snow?"

She stopped and faced him.

"Rain said she still belongs to her old coven. Which one is that?"

"We're from Miami. We've only been here six months, so we need to make sure things are going to work out before we change. See you tomorrow." She wiggled her fingers and strutted away.

His mind reeled. Miami? Did they know what happened to the witch in the morgue? Could they have been involved?

The battle to think with the right head raged inside him. He wanted to know every inch of Rain's body and every thought in her mind. The primal instinct to protect her, to make her his, roared inside him. If he listened to his beast, he'd know she couldn't be involved.

Then again, his wolf thrived on emotion. His feelings about the sexy witch could be clouding his judgment. Lord knew he'd been wrong about witches before. He wouldn't make the mistake of trusting one again, no matter how deep these strange, new emotions ran.

First order of business: report the new info to the alpha. Contract or no, Luke might change his mind after he heard the news.

CHAPTER FIVE

Isaac Mercado huddled under a scratchy, green blanket in the back seat of a Greyhound bus headed for Louisiana. Everything felt scratchy against his paper-thin skin, but the thought of his torment ending soon was reason enough to endure it.

Every time the bus hit a bump in the road, jostling him in the seat, sharp pain shot through his joints, threatening to shatter his bones. He shifted to his left hip and leaned his forehead against the window. The coolness of the glass did nothing to tame the fever trying to consume his entire body, and a bruise formed within seconds of the hard surface pressing against his skin. He attempted a sigh as he leaned on the cushioned headrest, but it turned into a hacking, wet cough, his chest threatening to explode with each forced breath.

A woman in the seat across the aisle covered her nose with the neck of her shirt and turned her back to him.

He splayed his fingers against his legs and winced as the knuckles cracked into place. The blue color that previously occupied his finger-tips had spread all the way to his wrists. His blood had turned against him, refusing to circulate properly through his veins.

His own magic used as a weapon to defeat him.

He rotated his wrists and wiggled his fingers, encouraging his cursed blood to flow again. A trip like this would require at least two weeks in the swamp to recover. Floating semi-submerged in the murky water eased the pain enough for him to focus his mind. The combination of mud and algae soothed his dry, cracked skin, and the remote location provided the privacy he needed to meditate for hours at a time.

The world thought him dead, and now that his true powers had been revealed, it needed to stay that way.

He closed his eyes and tried to ignore the prickling sensation in his legs. His feet had probably turned purple in the three hours since he'd boarded the bus in Florida. The pounding in his head was only matched by the pain of his predicament.

A witch of his magnitude reduced to meditating in a swamp, surviving on frogs and nutria for nourishment? Well, it was his own fault for tangling with a witch whose power matched—possibly exceeded—his own.

He'd be head of the council by now if his plan had worked, sitting comfortably in a mansion in the mountains. His tulpas—shadow-like entities he created with his mind—serving him, the entire witch community worshipping him.

But *she* had to screw it all up.

His revenge would be well worth the wait. If seven years of living alone in the swamp had taught him anything, it was patience. Two weeks of recovery would be plenty of time to get his body into shape enough to find and drain another witch. He could spend the days focusing on his tulpa, recharging the entity, increasing its power so it could walk the streets of New Orleans and execute his plan.

The witch he'd drained last week had been magnificent. Her life force had been strong like her magic, her gift of sight giving him the temporary ability to finally locate the one responsible for his demise. Too bad he'd burned through all her energy finding the bitch and sending his tulpa to New Orleans to dump the body. Hopefully, by now, his enemy was scared shitless, watching her back and jumping at every shadow. If she wasn't yet, she would be soon.

And then he'd make her suffer.

Slipping his hand into his pocket, he pulled out a small glass jar.

The witch's eye sloshed in the liquid as he turned the container and peered at the bright-blue iris. The orb contained enough magic for him to find his target once he arrived in the city.

A small child squealed from the seat in front of him, the shrill pitch of his young voice cutting through Isaac's ears like shards of glass. The boy reached his tiny hand around the seat, grasping the back as he squished his tear-streaked face between the seatback and the window. His eyes widened as he looked at Isaac, his mouth falling open, his body freezing in shock.

Isaac reached for the boy's hand, gripping the soft, life-filled skin in his frigid grasp. Warm energy flowed into Isaac's hand, restoring the tawny color to his skin as it cascaded up his arm to fill his chest. He inhaled the first deep breath he'd been able to take since he drained the witch and closed his eyes for a long blink to revel in the healing sensation.

The boy fell slack, leaning against the window before collapsing into his mother's lap. Isaac released his hand and stretched his arms over his head. What was it about young life that felt so damn good? He attempted a smile, but the shriveled skin of his upper lip split, and the coppery taste of his traitor blood oozed into his mouth. He hadn't drained nearly enough energy from the kid to make smiling worth it. Any more, though, and he'd have killed him. Now the boy would sleep for the rest of the trip and wake up with a vague memory of the monster in the seat behind him. He'd done the kid's mother a favor.

CHAPTER SIX

RAIN GLIDED UNDER THE ARCHWAY AT THE ENTRANCE TO LOUIS Armstrong park and passed the life-size bronze marching band statues on her way to her favorite bench. Settling onto the seat, she gazed out over the man-made lake, admiring the fountain flowing in the center of the water. The sound of the spray and the splash of the drops as they hit the surface caused a familiar ache inside her chest. As much as the sound brought comfort to her ears, it also reminded her of how much she'd lost.

A couple strolled along the brick path, pausing on the footbridge to steal a kiss before continuing on their way, and a woman spread a blanket beneath a massive oak while three small children played tag on the lawn behind her.

The early autumn sun warmed Rain's skin, and she closed her eyes for a moment, basking in the peaceful serenity of the scene. She smiled as she unwrapped her sandwich and took a bite. Not only had she won the werewolf wedding, but the pack's sexy second-in-command had been tasked to handle the cake.

Her knee bounced in anticipation at the thought of seeing Chase again. Him asking her to dinner had come as such a shock that she hadn't been able to form a proper sentence. Her first instinct had been to say yes. To go to dinner with him and hope he intended to have *her* for dessert. Thankfully, her brain had taken over before her mouth could react, and she'd said no. With her luck, he'd only asked her because he was suspicious about her lack of magic.

In fact, the more she thought about it, the more that seemed to be the case. He'd probably been assigned to watch her. To make sure she didn't pose a threat to the pack. The flitting elation at seeing him again that she'd felt a moment ago fizzled out like a can of soda left open overnight. Either she'd imagined the smoldering way he'd looked at her yesterday or he'd been faking the attraction.

Either way, it didn't matter. Her curse made getting close to people impossible. She wouldn't risk hurting anyone else. And with what happened the last time she fell for a man—whether she'd fallen on her own or had been pushed—getting anywhere near love was out of the question.

She'd go along with whatever charade he had planned. Build a friendship like Snow suggested. With the blue moon a few weeks away, she didn't have much time to earn his trust.

She sighed and took another bite of her sandwich. The cool cucumbers crunched between her teeth as she watched the colorful auras of the people in the park. Even humans had life energy that created a muted tone surrounding their bodies. Usually pale blue or green, it didn't sparkle with magic like that of a witch or werewolf.

Across the pond, stretched out on a blanket, a woman with a deep-orange werewolf aura lay next to a human. The man glided his fingers up her bare arm before leaning in and kissing her. Did the man know he was dating a supernatural creature? Most humans didn't know they existed.

Another orange aura caught Rain's eye, and she nearly choked on a cucumber as Chase came into view. A small girl, around six or seven years old, squealed in delight as she clutched his arm with both hands and he lifted her from the ground, setting her on her feet in front of him.

"Do it again," the little girl cried, and Chase beamed a smile, lifting her into the air once more.

Rain's mouth hung open, so she forced it shut. If Chase hadn't been scrumptious enough before, seeing him playing with a child—and enjoying it—made him mouth-watering. There was no pretense to his smile, no ulterior motive behind the sparkle in his eyes. He was simply happy, and the beauty of it whisked the air from Rain's lungs.

He caught her gaze and waved, and she swallowed the bite of sandwich she'd been grinding between her teeth since he came into view. She lifted her hand to return the wave, hoping to act aloof. He was just a client, after all. But her lips betrayed her, curving into a smile she couldn't have fought if she'd tried. If he had been sent to keep tabs on her, at least she could enjoy the view.

The girl had dark hair like Chase, and as he tugged her closer, Rain could see she also had his hazel eyes. He handed the child a pink plastic bottle and pointed to a group of children playing beneath an oak tree. She ran toward the kids, and Chase sat next to Rain.

"Coincidence seeing you here." He grinned and ran a hand through his hair. Did she detect a bit of nervousness in his movements? Surely not.

"Is it a coincidence? Or did my sister send you?"

He cleared his throat and glanced at the girl. "She might have mentioned you'd be here."

She'd have to have words with Snow later. Although…she did have a smokin' hot werewolf grinning at her, so maybe she should thank her sister. *No. He's here because his alpha ordered him to keep tabs on me.* She needed to remember that. "Is that your daughter?"

The same genuine smile she'd seen earlier returned to his lips as he glanced at the little girl again. "She's my niece, Emma."

"She's adorable." A flush of what she wanted to call relief washed through her body. Was she relieved? If the girl had been his daughter, then he might have been… "Are you married?" *Damn it!* Why did she ask that out loud?

He cast a sideways glance. "No, I'm not."

Oh, goddess, is that a good thing or a bad thing?

"Have you ever been?" She squeezed her lips together. The next question dancing through her brain involved whether or not he liked chocolate and from which part of her body he'd like to lick it, and she would not allow herself to speak that one aloud…no matter how curious she was for the answer.

He gave her his full attention, pinning her with his heated gaze. "I have never been married." He chuckled. "And I thought I'd be the one doing the interrogation."

"I'm not sure I like the sound of that." Unless it involved hand-cuffs and his detailed exploration of her body. *Stop it, Rain…*

Stretching his arm across the back of the bench, he shifted toward her. His position gave him view of both Rain and Emma playing in the grass behind her, and that was obviously why he moved, but when his knee brushed her thigh, her stomach clenched as if the touch had been intimate. She tried to hide her reaction, but his sly glance down at her leg and the crooked grin curving his lips said he knew exactly the kind of effect he had on her.

"Snow said you're from Miami."

"We moved here six months ago." She shoved her half-eaten sand-wich into its wrapper and tossed it into her bag. "What about you? Have you always lived in New Orleans?"

"Since I was a teenager. Are there any other Miami witches here?"

That didn't sound like a getting-to-know-you question. She narrowed her eyes in suspicion. "None that I'm aware of, but I don't pretend to know every witch in this city. Do you know every werewolf?"

He straightened. "Of course I do. It's my job."

"Uncle Chase!" Emma pranced toward them, swirling a plastic wand in her pink bottle. "Watch this." Pulling the wand from the soapy solution, she blew on it softly, creating a bubble nearly as big as her face. "Toby taught me if you're gentle, you can make it grow big without breaking it."

Emma waved the wand, and the bubble detached to float in front of them. Rain reached out a hand, and the bubble landed on her fingertips. "And if you're really gentle, you can catch them."

"Wow! How'd you do that?" Emma reached for the bubble, cupping her hands around the soapy sphere.

"Careful." Rain smiled as the girl tried to grasp the bubble, giggling as it popped in her hands. "My sister can make them freeze. She turns them into ice bubbles."

Emma's eyes widened. "Really?"

"Mm-hmm." She leaned closer and whispered, "She's a witch."

"Cool! I'm going to be a werewolf when I grow up, like Uncle Chase. My mom says I might not, but I know I am. Werewolves are the best."

"Witches are cool too." Chase said it to his niece, but his gaze locked with Rain's before lowering to her lips. She was definitely not imagining the attraction now.

She forced herself to look at Emma. "Maybe your uncle will bring you by my bakery sometime, and she can show you."

"Can we, Uncle Chase? Please?" She blinked at him expectantly.

Chase rubbed his beard as his gaze danced between Rain and Emma. "Sure, squirt. Anything for you."

"Cool!" She trotted off to play with the other kids.

Chase cast her an unbelieving look. "Snow can freeze things? Did she change her name after she came into her powers or is it a coincidence?"

"Nothing is coincidence. Our mother knew what her powers would be when she was pregnant. It's one of her gifts." A gift that had landed her mom a seat on the national council as foreign ambassador. She could read anyone's magic, tell exactly what they were capable of and whether or not they posed a threat.

Rain had been her protégé, and she'd learned the importance of power from her mother. Her chest tightened at the disappointment and embarrassment she'd caused her family. If she'd introduced her mom to her last boyfriend sooner, all the trouble might never have happened. She looked at Chase, and her heart raced. Could he be the answer to her prayers?

He arched an eyebrow, and the piercing glinted in the sunlight. "And what are your gifts, Rain? Controlling the weather?"

"I told you; I'm a dud." She should get up and walk away. If he continued to pry, she might slip up and tell him too much. Then she'd lose her one chance at paying the bills and lifting the curse. No matter how slim that chance might have been, she couldn't let it slip away. "Why does Emma's mom say she might not be a werewolf?"

His gaze hardened. "Because her dad's not. If both parents aren't weres, there's a fifty-fifty chance their kids won't be either."

"She idolizes you."

He gazed at the little girl. "I'm the only father-figure she has in her life. She and my sister live with me."

"It's nice that you're there for them." Her stomach fluttered. Oh, goddess, what was she getting herself into? The more she learned about this man, the more delectable he became. Helping raise his sister's child. Giving them a place to live. Second in command of an entire pack. He was powerful and kind. A provider. A protector.

"We take care of our own." Though he stated it as a fact, Rain couldn't ignore the jab to her heart, reminding her she wasn't one of them. She didn't belong.

She couldn't quell her curiosity. "It's acceptable for werewolves to date people outside their species?"

He glanced at his niece, keeping a close watch on her, before focusing on Rain again. "We can date anyone we want."

"What about marriage...or I think you call it mating, right? Can you mate with someone who isn't a werewolf?"

"We can mate and marry whomever we choose." The heat returned to his gaze, and his lips tugged into his signature cocky grin. "Are you in the market for a mate?"

She blinked, heat flushing her cheeks, as she realized how her question must have sounded. "No, absolutely not." Why couldn't she think before she spoke? She focused on the couple across the lake. "Take those two for example. Does that guy know he's dating a were-wolf? You seem so secretive; I would assume he doesn't."

Chase followed her gaze to the couple on the blanket. "If the rela-tionship becomes serious...if she decides to take him as her mate, she'll have to bring him into the pack. He'll be sworn to secrecy. We have rules in place."

"Interesting." The fluttering sensation returned to her stomach, as if the idea that she could potentially become his mate appealed to her. Did it appeal to her?

His gaze lingered on the couple across the pond for a moment before he shifted in his seat, his knee brushing hers again. "What's interesting to me is how you knew she was a werewolf from all the way across the lake."

What was it about this man that had her body reacting this way? One little brush of the knee shouldn't have sent her heart sprinting, but she couldn't deny the incessant palpitations she endured whenever he was near. "I can see her aura. It's part of my curse."

He leaned in closer. "Your curse?"

Her heart made a quick dip into her stomach before lodging itself in her throat. Oh, goddess, what had she done?

He took her hand, holding it between both of his. "Is that why I can't feel your magic? You're cursed?"

"What? No!" She pulled from his grasp and clutched her hands in her lap. She couldn't let the werewolves find out about her curse. It would ruin her.

And Chase...any chance she had at getting to know him better would crumble like a day-old, dried-out muffin. "I mean...I call it a curse...not having any powers. I guess my gift is that I can see other people's powers. I can see magic, but I don't have any of my own."

He leaned back on the bench and eyed her skeptically. "You can tell by looking at me that I'm a werewolf?"

She nodded.

"How?"

"Your aura is deep-orange, and it glows with magic. The stronger the magic, the more saturated the color." She was about to explain how deeply his aura glowed, but Chase scooted closer, the length of his muscular thigh resting against hers, making it hard for her to breathe.

It had been too long since she'd been this close to a man, and his warm, musky scent made her want to lean into his side. She felt herself drifting toward him, so she straightened.

"What about Emma?" He nodded toward his niece. "What do you see when you look at her?"

"I see a child who hasn't come into her powers yet. Her aura is pale blue like a human's. It could change as she matures." Or it could stay the same if her father was human, but the disappointment in his eyes stopped her from saying the last part out loud.

"Damn."

"I'm sorry."

Chase looked at her, his gaze dancing around her face, curiosity in his eyes. "You are a fascinating woman, Rain Connolly."

If he didn't quit looking at her mouth, she might not be able to stop herself from leaning over and kissing him. "You're pretty interesting, yourself."

A slow smile curved his full lips, and he gazed into her eyes for a moment before looking at her mouth again. Damn it, she liked him way more than she'd planned to. If he hadn't shown up in the park with his niece and acted all kind and fatherly, she could have continued admiring the package, assuming the inside was all testosterone and sarcasm.

Now she wanted to know him, and she wanted to start by finding out what those luscious lips tasted like. "If you want to kiss me, you—"

"Uncle Chase!" Emma climbed into his lap, breaking the trance he'd put on her and saving her from finishing the sentence that never should have left her lips. "Can we see the frozen bubbles now?"

He wrapped his arms around the little girl and kissed the top of her head. "We sure can, squirt. I need to talk to Miss Rain some more, anyway."

Emma took both their hands and tugged them from the bench. "Let's go."

Rain hesitated, her heart and her stomach tangling in a dizzying dance. Had they almost kissed? If he had tried to take her mouth with his, she'd have given it to him willingly. What happened to befriending him so he could help her break the curse? She needed to keep her priorities straight. Getting her magic back was her number one goal, but she couldn't deny the strange feelings stirring in her core.

"Do you mind if we walk you back to the bakery?" Chase asked.

She smiled at him before looking at Emma. "I'm sure my sister will be thrilled to meet you."

They strolled four blocks to the bakery in a line, Emma between them holding their hands. The adults remained quiet as the little girl babbled on about Toby from the park, occasionally hanging back and running forward for them to lift her in the air by the hands.

The whole scene felt surreal, walking hand-in-hand with this child, Chase by her side, glancing at her from time to time, a strange smile lighting on his lips. They must have looked like a family to passersby.

She'd better enjoy it now because this was the closest she'd ever get to having her own family, unless she could lift this curse.

As they crossed Bourbon Street, two boys with flattened soda cans attached to their sneakers performed a tap dance on the corner. The rhythmic beat of metal striking pavement created a percussive melody that drew a crowd of onlookers. The smaller boy rose onto the tips of his toes and spun, waving his arms in a windmill motion and ending the routine in a flourish.

"Cool!" Emma shouted, and she tugged Rain toward Chase, placing her hand in his and leaving them to run toward the boys.

Chase didn't jerk away. Instead, he tightened his grip, yanking her to his body and wrapping his arms around her, saving her from being flattened by a taxi. The driver blared the horn and shook his fist out the window, shouting a string of profanities at the people on the street.

"Best to keep to the sidewalks during the day, even on Bourbon Street." Chase's chest rumbled as he spoke, and with her face pressed against him, she couldn't help but notice the firm muscles beneath his shirt.

"You okay?" His chin brushed the top of her head, and…was that his nose? Did he smell her hair? The tingling, bubbly sensation shooting through her insides could have been an adrenaline rush from being nearly run over by a car, but the man holding her in a tight embrace was more likely the reason.

She peered up at him, and he didn't let her go. "I'm fine." This close to his lips, she could almost taste them on her tongue. Cinnamon, probably. Warm and slightly sweet. "Thank you for not letting me get run over. That was kind of you."

He smiled. "My pleasure."

Oh, goddess no. He'd shown her kindness. In keeping her from being struck by the taxi, he'd unwittingly set himself up for his own tragedy. How could she have let this happen? She'd rather be lying bruised and bloody on the blacktop than for Chase to endure some disaster for helping her. *Crap!*

Jerking from his embrace, she smoothed her shirt down her stomach and scurried away. "I need to get back to the bakery. Stop by when Emma's done playing and give me the deposit." She rushed across the street.

"Rain, stop."

She glanced behind her as Chase snatched Emma around the waist and threw her onto his shoulder before following her through the intersection.

His niece giggled as he caught up and set her on her feet. "That was fun! Do it again!"

He mussed her hair. "In a minute, squirt. Wait up, Rain. What's wrong?"

"Nothing." She continued her trek to the bakery, yanked open the door, and glared at her sister as she marched behind the counter. She needed to get herself under control. Change the subject before he pressed her for answers she couldn't give.

Chase caught the door and ushered his niece through. The girl ran to the nearest display case and stared, wide-eyed, at the treats inside. "Can I have a cookie?" She glanced at Chase before focusing on the desserts.

"Sure." He sauntered toward the counter, casting Rain a quizzical look, and opened his mouth to speak.

She cut him off. "Emma, this is my sister, Snow. Why don't you show her your bubbles?"

Emma's face brightened. "Give me my bubbles, Uncle Chase."

"I don't have them." His gaze lingered on Rain before he looked at his niece. "You must've left them in the park."

"Aw." Her entire body deflated.

Snow cut her gaze between Rain and Chase and grinned. "That's okay. We can make some in the kitchen with dish soap and a cookie cutter."

The little girl bounced on her toes. "And Rain said you can make them freeze."

Snow laughed. "I sure can. Come back to the kitchen with me."

Chase stiffened. "That's not a good idea, Emma. You need to stay out here where I can see you."

Rain crossed her arms, torn between swooning at his protective instincts and being offended that he didn't trust her sister.

"The sink is right here by the doorway," Snow said. "You'll be able to see her the whole time."

"Please, Uncle Chase?" Emma batted her lashes, her hazel eyes imploring him until he crumbled.

"Okay. But stay where you can see me. If you can't see me, that means I can't see you either, and then I'll have to hunt for you."

Emma curled her fingers into claws and growled at Chase before scurrying around the counter to the kitchen.

He kept his gaze trained on his niece until he appeared satisfied Snow wasn't going to kidnap her. Then he turned his green-gold eyes to Rain and took her hand.

She slipped from his grasp. "Witches don't eat children outside of fairy tales, you know. Emma is safe here."

He blinked. "I know. I'm not worried."

She scoffed. "You could've fooled me."

"Did I do something to offend you? I thought saving you from a head-on collision with a taxi was rather chivalrous of me, but it seems to have upset you."

She let out an exasperated sigh. "I said thank you. What more do you want from me?"

Leaning an elbow on the counter, he slipped his tongue out to moisten his lips before speaking. "I want you to finish what you were saying at the park. You said if I wanted to kiss you, I should..."

Emma giggled as a frozen bubble shattered on the floor. Chase glanced in her direction before focusing on Rain again. He really wasn't going to let this go.

Did she want to kiss him? Goddess yes, she did. She wanted to do a whole lot more than kiss the sexy werewolf, who had managed to inch his way around the counter to stand next to her, but she couldn't.

She'd already put him and his adorable little niece at risk by spending the past hour with them. This had to end. Right here, right now.

"I was going to say that if you want to kiss me, you should reconsider. I'm not interested." Lifting a shoulder, she turned her back to him and rummaged through a drawer to make herself look busy. Even if she wasn't cursed, he either had a grudge against her or witches in general, so things would never work out between them. Relationships had to be built on trust, and he hadn't shown her an ounce of it.

His sigh was audible, though she couldn't tell if it was from disappointment or frustration. "How much is the deposit?"

She straightened and slammed the drawer shut. "Three hundred dollars will reserve the date. I'll need half of the remainder one month in advance of the wedding. The second half will be billed after delivery."

He handed her a credit card. "It's got Luke's name on it, but I'm authorized to sign for it."

If this had been a human wedding, she'd have refused the card. With so much credit fraud going on these days, she didn't like to take chances. She had no doubts about Chase, though. If he'd stolen the alpha's credit card, he'd have to buy a lot more than wedding cake to make the punishment he'd likely endure worthwhile.

She swiped the card and handed him the ticket to sign. "That's all I need from you then, unless you're picking out the design as well."

He cringed. "God, I hope I'm not."

"Please let Luke and Macey know I'll need their design decisions in three weeks. It's been nice doing business with you." She inclined her chin hoping to end the conversation.

He didn't take the hint. "Listen, Rain…" He let out a heavy sigh and shook his head. "Are you sure you don't know of any other Miami witches in the area? No friends or family came to visit you or your sister this week?"

No one she knew wanted to be within one hundred miles of her and her curse. "No one; I'm sure of it. Why do you ask?"

"There's a body in the morgue."

That's what this was about? He'd stalked her in the park because someone was dead and he thought she was involved? She stacked the papers and jammed them into the stapler. "I'm sure there are lots of bodies in the morgue."

He laid his hands flat on the counter. "She's a witch...from Miami."

Her heart thrummed. "How do you know that?"

"She has a coven tattoo on her chest. The high priestess identified it as Miami."

Her throat thickened. If he'd talked to Calista, she might have told him about her curse. But surely, if he knew, the alpha wouldn't want her at his wedding. He wouldn't have paid the deposit... "I didn't know werewolves and witches worked so closely."

"We don't, unless our secrecy is threatened. She appears to have died from supernatural causes. Do you think you could identify her?"

Goddess, she hoped not. "Miami is a big city, and there are far more witches than werewolves. The chances of me knowing her are slim."

"Maybe you can identify the type of magic that killed her. You can see magic, right?"

She shook her head. "I can, but only in a living person. I don't think I can do much for you in this case."

He laced his fingers together. "Please? I could really use your help. I promise I'll leave you alone after this."

Her breath hitched. Leave her alone? That was the last thing she wanted, though it would be best for him...and for her since he'd apparently been acting interested so she would help him identify a body. Of course, her initial reason for befriending him wasn't exactly virtuous either. Maybe they were both feeling things they hadn't planned to feel.

Her curse specifically stated *witches* would be punished for showing her kindness, but she didn't want to take any chances with Chase. He was a supernatural being, so the curse might affect him.

Then again, she was supposed to be leading a selfless life, and he needed her help. She owed it to him for saving her life. "Okay. I don't know how much help I'll be, but I'll give it a shot."

He smiled. "Great. I'll talk to Macey and see when she can get us into the morgue."

"The alpha's mate?"

"She's a detective." He picked up a business card from the counter. "Is this the best number to reach you at?"

"Let me give you my cell. I don't answer that number after hours." She took the card and scribbled her personal number on the back before handing it to him.

"Thank you. I'll be in touch." He ambled behind the counter to the kitchen, taking his time as if he didn't want to leave yet. "Time to go, squirt."

"Can I take them home?" Emma scooped up an armful of frozen bubbles. "They're so pretty."

He laughed. "They'll melt by the time we get them to the house."

"I gave them an extra-hard freeze," Snow said. "They should be good for at least an hour."

"I guess so, then." With his hand on Emma's shoulder, he guided her to the storefront.

Rain handed him two chocolate chip cookies in a white paper bag. "Here's that cookie you promised her. There's one for you too."

He eyed the bag skeptically. "These didn't come from that shelf, did they?" He nodded toward the clarity cookies.

Irritation grated in her chest like sandpaper against her sternum. What would it take for him to trust her? "They're completely mundane. I'll take a bite myself to prove it to you if you want."

The look in his eyes said he was considering her offer. Luckily, he shook his head instead. "I'll take your word for it. Thanks."

He opened the door and nodded for Emma to pass.

"Call me," Rain said as he stepped through the threshold. She grimaced. *Why the hell did I say that?*

He paused and grinned. "I will."

As the door clicked shut behind him, Snow giggled. "Call me," she sang in a mocking tone.

Rain closed her eyes for a long blink, trying not to direct her irritation at her sister. "I did not mean to say that out loud."

"What did you mean to say?"

"Go away. I never want to see you again." Those cookies would be tossed into the first trashcan he saw, and the fact that he distrusted her that much when she'd done nothing wrong gnawed in her gut.

Snow laughed. "That's the fattest lie I've ever heard come out of your mouth. You want him."

"So?" She rolled her eyes. How could she be attracted to a man who emanated so much distrust?

"So...the bad boy werewolf turned out to be a family man. How hot is that?"

Then again, he was protecting his niece. She sank onto a stool and slouched her shoulders. "Extremely."

Snow climbed onto the stool next to her, excitement dancing in her eyes. "What are you going to do about it?"

She took a deep breath and drummed her nails on the counter. "I'm going to look at a dead body."

CHAPTER SEVEN

CHASE GRABBED HIS SECOND BLUE MOON BEER FROM THE fridge and settled into a chair at the kitchen table.

"You're taking her to the morgue on your first date?" Luke took a swig from his bottle. "Wouldn't be my first choice."

Drumming his fingers on the wood, Chase took a long drink, savoring the way the citrusy effervescence danced on his tongue, tickling his throat as it made its way down to his stomach. He could imagine what Rain's plump, pink lips would taste like...sweet like the beautiful cakes she created, maybe with a hint of strawberry to match their color.

He'd had the chance to taste them at the park that afternoon. Then he'd hesitated, and he'd dodged a bullet. His lips didn't need to get anywhere near the witch.

He set the bottle on the table with a *thud* and wiped his mouth with the back of his hand. "It's not a date; it's business. Anyway, she's a suspect. I'm not getting involved with a possible enemy."

Luke chuckled. "Is she really a suspect? Do we need to find another bakery?"

Chase grumbled. "No. She *should* be a suspect, but..."

"You trust her."

"I'm more afraid she'll be a target." The mere idea of finding Rain in the morgue with the life drained out of her had his beast begging to come out. He'd stalk the perimeter of the bakery, making sure nothing could harm her. Hell, if he had his way, he'd bring her to his house and keep her there until they figured out whether the murder was a one-off thing or they caught the bastard who killed the witch.

Luke nodded. "You feel a deep, primal need to protect her, don't you?"

"Yeah." It didn't mean anything. Ever since Emma was born he'd felt the need to protect his own. His family. His pack. Rain may not have been a werewolf, but the alpha had put Chase in charge of the witch, and he took his job seriously.

Luke clapped him on the shoulder and strolled to the fridge for another beer. "I know that feeling, my friend. Sounds like you found your fate-bound."

Chase stopped mid-swallow, choking and spewing beer across the table. "Bullshit." Fate-bound, his ass. She was beautiful, with a feisty personality. Independent. Strong. There was something inherently sexy about a woman who ran her own business. Who wouldn't be attracted to Rain? She was a witch, though, and that fact would never change.

And Chase would never trust a witch again.

A knock sounded on the door before James, his hunting buddy, let himself in. "What did I miss?" He strode straight to the fridge.

Luke grinned. "Chase was telling me about how he's met his fate-bound."

James grabbed a beer and paused, shaking his head before shutting the fridge door. "Not you too." He plopped into a chair at the table. "I'm going to have to find new hunting partners. Hanging out with a bunch of mated men cramps my style. You'll be slow."

Luke straightened his spine. "Mating does not make you slow. If anything, it makes you stronger."

"I'll take your word for it." James raised his beer in a salute and drained half the bottle.

Chase had just met the woman, and his friends already considered him mated. This nonsense had to stop. "I will not bind my fate with a witch."

Luke laughed. "You don't get a choice. Believe me."

"You're mating with a witch?" James's eyes widened in surprise. "You hate witches."

Chase chewed on the inside of his cheek. Luke was wrong. This was not happening. "I don't hate them; I just don't trust them."

"Except for this one." Luke tossed his empty bottle into the recycle bin. "Which proves my point."

Chase groaned.

The front door opened, and Emma darted to the table. "It's hunting night! Can I go this time? Please?" She hopped from man to man, batting her lashes and tugging on their arms.

Chase's heart swelled with love for the feisty little squirt. She'd be devastated if her witch genes turned out stronger and she didn't inherit the ability to shift. Of course, that was mostly his fault. He'd built up being a werewolf in her little mind and not done a thing to let her know it would be okay if she couldn't shift. That needed to change.

He pulled her into his lap. "You can't hunt gators unless you're a wolf."

"I am a wolf." She squirmed out of his arms and dropped to the floor.

"You might not be, squirt, and that's okay too. You've got magic in your blood, and that's all that matters."

Bekah dropped her purse on the counter and mouthed the words *thank you*. "Go get ready for your bath, Emma. I'll be there in a minute."

Emma let out a dramatic sigh, slumping her shoulders as if the request pained her. "Yes, ma'am." She trotted through the doorway into her bedroom.

Bekah crossed her arms, giving him a questioning look. "Where did that comment come from?"

"His fate-bound is a witch," Luke said.

"Wipe that shit-eating grin off your face, man. It's not happening." He rose and tossed his bottle into the bin. "Let's get this hunt started." At least in their wolf forms, he wouldn't have to listen to them run their mouths. Letting his beast take over for a while would help him clear his mind.

"Hold on." Bekah stepped toward him and grabbed his hand.

He tried to yank from her grasp, but she held a firm grip. Grinding his teeth, he muttered, "I don't need you to read me." His sister's empathic abilities came in handy occasionally, but not now.

She pressed her lips together, fighting a smile as she released his hand. "How about that. My brother has bonded with a witch." She shook her head. "What an unlikely turn of events. Finally letting go of your grudge?"

"I…" He rubbed his forehead. Damn it, why was this happening? "After what happened to me, and what Tommy did to you, I can't…" He couldn't what? Follow his fate? Trust his instincts and make the woman his? None of this made any sense.

Bekah rolled her eyes. "Tommy did what he did because he's an asshole, not because he's a witch. Same thing for your little school friends. They were jerks; you took the fall."

"If they weren't witches, they wouldn't have wanted my blood."

"I don't know what your friends were up to, but I believe that Tommy wanted it for your healing abilities. Healing is his gift."

He scoffed. "And then when I refused, he left you." He'd trusted the guy. Hell, he'd even liked him. But for a supernatural being to ask another for blood…especially to ask a werewolf…was unforgivable. His sister's ex-boyfriend had expected him to break an ancient, sacred law. Shit, it was one of the first and most important laws were-children learned. Rule number one: never fight a human while in wolf form, unless it's a fight to the death. Rule number two: blood is sacred and can never be shared.

Chase ground his teeth. "Witches are assholes."

Willingly giving his blood away would've landed him in the pit for the next twenty years. He'd have been middle-aged by the time he'd served his term in the werewolf prison. And that was if he received the lightest sentence. The national congress condoned death as a suitable punishment for giving blood to a witch.

No way. Not for anyone.

Bekah sighed. "I think his leaving had more to do with Emma than with you. Get over it. You can't fight fate."

Luke stood and cracked his knuckles. "Welcome to the club, man.

You're in for a wild ride." He jerked his head toward the door. "Let's hunt."

"Have fun, boys." Bekah grinned as Chase followed Luke and James out the door.

They loaded into Luke's truck and then headed down Interstate 10 toward their favorite hunting grounds. The massive swamp area was ripe with gators, wild boar, and plenty of other animals to satisfy the cravings of a wolf. Unfortunately, the beast inside Chase craved a lot more than the thrill of a hunt and the satisfaction of a meal. He craved a mate, and it seemed only one person would do.

He cranked up the AC, but it did nothing the cool the fire building in his core. "What if I date someone else? Find another mate? Surely this feeling will go away."

"I'm happy to play wingman if you want to hit the bars tonight." James raised his eyebrows, looking way too hopeful. "It's been a while."

Luke laughed. "Good luck with that."

"What's that supposed to mean?" Chase cut him a sideways glance, but he had a feeling he knew exactly what Luke meant.

"If Rain is your fate-bound, being with anyone but her will be unthinkable." He shrugged and pulled off the highway. "Might be a good test though. If you can pick up another female, then it's your hormones making you hot for the witch and not fate."

They bounced down a dirt path, heading deeper into the woods before rolling to a stop next to a massive cypress tree. Chase hopped out of the truck after his friends and gazed up at the half-moon brightening the night sky. Two more weeks, and it would be a blue moon, the second full moon of the month. He could almost feel the extra boost of magic pooling in his blood. Every first-born in the pack would be hunting beneath the blue moon. Their magic would be undeniable that night; the beast would take over whether they wanted it to or not.

Maybe that was what all this was about. His wolf's extra strength and his intense desire to mate had caused him to obsess over the first female he'd found attractive.

A test. That was exactly what he needed. Then he could prove to his friends, and to himself, that his fate was not bound to a witch…or to anyone for that matter.

"What do you say?" James cracked his neck and rolled his shoulders, his anticipation for the hunt evident in his posture. "Want to hit the bars after this? See if we can get you laid?"

"Hell ye—" A lump the size of a baseball formed in Chase's throat, and the *yes* he'd tried to answer got lodged beneath it. *Shit.* Hell yeah, he wanted to sleep with a woman. But the thought of climbing into bed with anyone but Rain Connolly made his skin crawl. He narrowed his eyes and glared at the moon.

"Can't do it, can you?" At least Luke wasn't laughing anymore, but his tone turned too serious. The last thing Chase needed was a therapy session.

"No." He called on his beast, letting the vibrating energy consume him, transforming his body into his wolf. He took off into the trees, putting space between his friends and him. His beast had the instinct to hunt with the pack, but the man needed to clear his head.

Why did he have to find his fate-bound? And why did it have to happen now? He liked his life the way it was. He was busy. Between his position as Luke's second, his job at the bar, and taking care of his niece, he barely had time for a social life, much less a girlfriend. And now he'd met the woman he was supposed to spend forever with, *and* she was a witch?

Fate had a sick sense of humor.

A rustle in the brush to his left yanked him from his thoughts. A shadow darted from behind a tree and disappeared as quickly as it had formed. *What the hell was that?* It had the silhouette of a man…sort of…but it's movements were more fluid, its shape seeming to roll and reform with each step.

He searched his mind for Luke and James. Though they couldn't speak in wolf form, they had a sort of telepathic connection. His friends hunted half a mile away, giving him the space he'd craved. He'd have to handle this one on his own.

Crouching low, he belly-crawled to the clearing where he'd spotted the shadow. It could have been a hunter, which would mean trouble for them all. Though werewolves were exceptionally fast healers, even he wouldn't recover from a bullet to the brain.

Dry leaves crunched beneath his paws as he dragged his body across the ground. Crickets chirped, and a sultry breeze rustled his chocolate fur, but the shadow…and whatever creature it belonged to…had vanished.

He stood and shook the dirt from his coat. Maybe he'd imagined it. He'd been caught up in his thoughts, not paying attention to where he was running. It was probably a trick of the moonlight. He needed to get out of his head and into this hunt before he drove himself crazy.

A high-pitched wail grated in his ears, making them twitch as something splashed into the water a few yards away. Instinct took over, and he dashed toward the sound, skidding to a stop at the water's edge. An air pocket covered in thick, green sludge bubbled to the surface, releasing a putrid steam as it popped.

The ground beneath his back paw crumbled, and he slipped, his right leg sinking in the sludge. He scrambled to grip the deteriorating soil with his left paw, digging his nails into the dirt for traction.

Something grabbed hold of his leg above the paw, and piercing pain shot straight to his bones. Chase yelped and clawed at the ground, but he couldn't get his footing. His other leg slipped into the muddy water, and jerking his head around, he clamped his jaws down on whatever animal had bitten him. Another sludgy air pocket bubbled from the surface, and the creature released its grip.

Using his front paws, Chase dragged himself from the water, letting out a howl he hoped his pack mates would hear. He collapsed on the bank as a throbbing pain spread from his leg, up to his haunches, all the way to his chest.

What the hell had bitten him? A venomous snake? Whatever it was, the poison spread quickly, making his entire body ache like he'd been hit by a truck. As the alpha howled his response, the world went black.

The trill of transformative magic surged through Isaac's veins, half-healing the puncture wounds from the animal's fangs before his own cursed blood vanquished the magic. Had he known it was a werewolf, he'd have put more energy into his tulpa and lured the beast farther into the water where it couldn't have gotten away so easily. The energy he could have gained from draining the creature dry would have more than made up for the amount he would have had to expend.

Even at optimum health, he'd be no match for a werewolf, though. Without his magic as a weapon, the beast could have ripped him to shreds before he had the chance to drain him.

Prying his lids open, he lifted his head above the murky water to peer at his victim. Matted, dark-brown fur covered the wolf's limp body, and it shimmered as he lost control of his magic and transformed into a man.

In the werewolf's current state, Isaac might've been able to take him, but the pain he'd endure dragging himself from the water wouldn't be worth it. He'd focus on his tulpa instead. Stick to the plan. Another week of recovery and he'd exact his revenge. He'd bide his time until then.

Two more wolves appeared in the brush. A light-brown one, the biggest of the three, nosed the body, rolling the man onto his back, while the gray one sniffed around the area. Its enhanced sense of smell led it to the water, and Isaac held his breath, sinking beneath the muck to hide his scent.

His lungs burned for oxygen. His blood barely carried enough to his cells as it was, and his entire body screamed with the need to breathe. Unable to stand another second without breath, he slowly rose from the muck until his nose broke the surface. He stifled a gasp and sucked in a breath as two men carried his victim away.

CHAPTER EIGHT

Rain closed her computer and dialed her landlord's number. After paying the utilities and buying supplies to run her store, she had enough money to pay the rent and the late fees, but the coven fees would have to wait until she got another big order or the werewolves paid the first half of their remainder.

"Hey, Ingrid, it's Rain. I have the rent check whenever you want to come pick it up."

Laughter echoed in the background. "I'm in Mexico until next week. I'll come by for it then."

It figured. Ingrid had rushed her to pay, and now that she had the money, she couldn't give it to her. "That's fine, but I expect the late fees to stop accruing as of today."

Ingrid paused, her voice sounding regretful. "I can't show you any kindness."

"It's not kindness; it's principle. I have the money, and I'm trying to make a payment. It's not my fault you aren't available to collect. I'll take it to your house and put under the doormat if I have to, but I'm not paying late fees anymore."

Ingrid sighed. "I guess you're right. But if you don't have the money when I come by, the fees will be doubled."

While that stipulation was nowhere in her contract, Rain understood Ingrid's position. Showing her kindness would result in a nasty accident or tragedy for her landlord. Rain wouldn't want to risk it either. "That's fair. I'll see you next week."

She hung up the phone and drummed her fingers on the counter. It had been two days since she'd heard from Chase. After the way she'd blown him off, she didn't expect him to show up for lunch again. But he did say he needed her to identify a body in the morgue, and she expected him to follow through on that.

Worry knotted in her stomach, and she chewed her bottom lip as she contemplated what to do. He'd saved her from getting hit by a taxi, and if that wasn't kindness, what was? If his punishment for saving her life were to lose his own, she'd never forgive herself.

Snow carried a tray of fresh clarity cookies to the display case and positioned them on a shelf. "Something's weighing heavy on your mind. Want to talk about it?" She wiped her hands on her apron and slid the case shut.

"Remember how I told you Chase asked me to look at a body in the morgue?"

Snow shivered. "You think it might be someone we know?"

"It's possible, but that's not what's bothering me. He asked me that two days ago, and I haven't heard from him since. If he was really concerned about a witch being murdered, don't you think he would have made an appointment to go to the morgue? Or at least called me?"

A mischievous grin curved Snow's lips. "You really like this guy, don't you?"

Who wouldn't? Simply looking at his sculpted body had her mouth watering and her fingers itching to peel away his clothes. He smelled like a forest after a cleansing rain, and he seemed to genuinely enjoy his niece. He was sexy and kind…

But his kindness could get him killed around her.

"I'm afraid that when he pulled me out of the taxi's path, he may have triggered the curse. What if he's sick…or dead?" Her stomach tumbled to her feet at the thought.

Snow wrinkled her nose. "He's not a witch. The curse doesn't count."

"It might."

She shook her head. "I remember it specifically said any *witch* who shows you kindness will be punished. There's no mention of werewolves."

Rain bit her lip. The curse did specify witches, and the words of a spell were taken literally. She'd found that out the hard way. But still... "He could have some witch blood in his veins. His niece is only half-werewolf. Who's to say his great-great-grandfather wasn't a witch? It's possible."

"Did you see it in his aura?" Snow leaned a hip against the counter.

"No, but he's a strong werewolf. If the witch blood is from a distant ancestor, I might not be able to see it." Her stomach twisted, the guilt churning in her gut.

Snow crossed her arms and drummed her fingers against her biceps. "Did you call him?"

"I don't have his number." She bit the end of her fingernail between her front teeth.

Snow pursed her lips for a moment before raising her eyebrows. "He put it on the contract."

She sucked in a sharp breath. "That's right; he did." Yanking open the filing cabinet, she grabbed the wedding contract and scanned the page. He'd checked the cellphone box next to the primary contact number and scribbled the digits on the line.

This was the right thing to do. Even if he told her he'd changed his mind and didn't need her help, at least she'd know he was alive. She took her phone from her pocket and dialed his number. Straight to voicemail. She hung up before the greeting ended. "His phone must be off. It didn't even ring."

Shaking her head and suppressing a smile, Snow uncrossed her arms. "If you're that worried about him, hon, go check on him. I'm sure someone at the bar knows where he is."

Rain gripped the contract in her left hand, wrinkling the pages, as she gnawed on her right pinkie nail. "Do you think I should?"

"You're not going to have any fingernails left if you don't."

Yanking her finger from her mouth, she examined her hand. She'd already chewed the first three nails down to nubs, and it was only ten o'clock. "You're right. I should. It will give me peace of mind."

Snow stopped fighting her smile. "And it will show him how much you care."

She did care, more than she wanted to. But her emotions didn't matter when he'd have to risk his life to be with her. She'd go to the bar, make sure he was okay, and then she'd shove her feelings for the sexy werewolf into the back of her mind and keep them there until the wedding was over. Then she'd forget about him.

Forget about breaking her curse. Willingly giving her his blood would be the kindest thing he could do, and he'd be met with the worst punishment possible...if he hadn't already. It was time to stop pretending she could have any kind of relationship with Chase... romantic or friendly. "I'll be back soon."

"Take your time," Snow sang.

The sun warmed her skin, chasing away the chill in the air, as she strode up Royal and made a left on St. Philip. She walked with purpose, ignoring her surroundings, anxiety tightening her muscles as her long strides carried her toward the bar. Something was wrong; she could feel it in her core.

A stream of cold water pelted her from above, jerking her from her thoughts, and she squealed. Jumping out of the way, she peered up to find a man watering a row of ferns hanging from a second-story gallery. The pots swung in the breeze from their wrought-iron hooks, and the man waved and shouted, "Sorry."

Rain forced a smile and returned his wave before continuing her trek to the bar. She'd passed by O'Malley's Pub plenty of times since she moved to New Orleans, but she'd never ventured inside. With her hand on the doorknob, she inhaled a deep breath and braced herself. With any luck, Chase would be behind the bar, a smile lighting up his handsome face as she entered the room.

But luck never was on her side.

As she stepped through the threshold, a crisp curtain of air blasted her skin. She made her way toward the bar, and a woman with light-brown hair and bright blue eyes greeted her.

"Welcome to O'Malley's. What can I get you?"

Rain gripped the edge of the bar. "Is Chase here?"

The woman tilted her head, studying her. "Are you Rain, the baker?"

"Yes." Her heart thrummed. Had Chase talked about her? Was that why the woman assumed she was Rain?

The woman smiled. "It's nice to meet you. I'm Amber. Luke is my brother."

Why was she giving her such a curious look? "It's nice to meet you too."

Amber wiped her hands on a dish rag. "Chase is at home. He got a nasty snake bite while he was hunting. Knocked him on his ass."

Icy tendrils of dread spiraled up her spine to squeeze her heart. Her curse had gotten him too. "Is he…will he recover?"

She shrugged. "Werewolves are fast healers. Must have been one hell of a snake, though. I've never seen him take this long to recover from an injury."

She lowered herself onto a barstool. He was hurt because of her. She had to see him…to do something to make this right. "I don't suppose you could tell me where he lives, so I could drop by and check on him?"

Amber grinned as she scribbled his address on a green Post-It Note. "I think he would love that. Here." She handed her the paper. "And tell him I said 'change is good.'"

"Okay." Rain gave her a quizzical look. Was that some kind of werewolf code?

"He'll know what I'm talking about."

Chase lay on the couch, flipping channels on the TV and cursing himself for falling into the water. The pounding in his head had subsided to a dull ache, and his vision had finally cleared, but at the rate he was healing, he'd be useless for another twelve hours minimum.

His mom had stayed with him yesterday while Emma went to school and Bekah worked, but he'd finally convinced the women he'd survive if they left him alone. That didn't stop his sister from taking an early lunch break to come home and check on him.

"You're sure you're going to be okay if I go back to work?" She refilled the water glass on the end table and rested her hand against his head. "You still feel like crap."

"Thanks, I hadn't noticed." He didn't need his sister to tell him what a wuss he was.

She sank onto the edge of the couch. "You can't fake feeling better around me. I'm an empath, remember?"

"You never let me forget."

She clutched his ankle, and shoving his sweats up to his knee, she turned his leg from side to side. "You don't find it strange that the puncture wounds healed when the rest of you is this sick?"

"Maybe they healed before the venom took effect." He turned off the TV and dropped the remote next to the water. "Can you get me a beer?"

Giving his leg a pat, she stood. "You can have a beer when you feel well enough to get off the couch and get it yourself."

"Gee, thanks."

Bekah picked up her purse. "Call Mom if you need anything. She'll be over in a heartbeat."

A knock sounded on the door.

Chase sighed. "Sounds like she couldn't stay away."

Bekah swung open the front door. "Hi. Can I help you?"

With the door half-open, he couldn't see the person on the porch, but Rain's melodic voice melted in his ears like ice cream—sweet and smooth. "Hi. I'm Rain. Is Chase home?"

"He sure is." His sister's evident smile gave her voice a musical quality. "You've got a visitor, Chase. Make yourself presentable."

As if he could haul his ass off the couch if he wanted to. He wore the same shirt and sweatpants Bekah had changed him into two days ago, and he hadn't brushed his teeth since before the hunt. Taking a big gulp of water, he swished it around in his mouth, hoping to wash away the grimy feel, and ran a hand through his disheveled hair.

Hell, maybe his gross appearance would be a good thing. Maybe she'd take one look at him and turn tail and run away. That might be best for both of them.

Rain tiptoed into the room, chewing on her bottom lip and looking at everything in the area but him.

"I'll see you later," Bekah called as she closed the front door on her way to work.

When Rain finally looked at him, it felt like the air had been sucked from his lungs. A possessive growl resonated deep inside his soul, and a single word echoed through his head: *Mine.*

Holy hell. His wolf had claimed her.

He expected his mind to reel with dismay or at least a little shock. Instead, the feeling settled in his core like it had been there his entire life, giving him a sense of completeness he'd never felt before.

She wore skinny jeans and a pink T-shirt with matching Converse, and her hair hung loose, her dark curls tumbling over her shoulders, accentuating her slender neck. As he held her gaze, her stormy eyes shimmered and liquid pooled on her lower lids.

Damn, how bad did he look? He swallowed the lump from his throat and shoved his wolf's desires to the back of his mind. "Hey. Thanks for stopping by."

She covered her mouth with her hand and shook her head. "I'm so sorry."

"It's not your fault." He scooted back on the couch, moving his legs to give her room, trying to keep his face neutral so she wouldn't notice the pain shooting through his limbs as he moved. "Want to sit?"

"Um...sure." Clutching her purse to her chest, she sank onto the edge of the sofa. "I looked for you at the bar. Amber gave me your address."

"Did she?" He wouldn't expect anything less of his boss. Between Amber and Luke, they were probably already planning his wedding date.

"I hope that's okay."

Okay? He felt better being near the woman. He'd had two days to mull over the fact that Rain could be his fate-bound, and no matter how hard he tried to deny it, he couldn't fight fate. She'd been on his mind every goddamn waking moment since he'd met her. "I'm glad you came. I wanted to call you, but today is the first time it hasn't felt like swallowing glass to talk."

"I'm so sorry. I have something that might help, but…" She clutched her purse tighter.

"But?"

She stared at the wall above his head. "It's a spell. A potion Snow made for you when I told her what happened."

"Ah…" A week ago, he wouldn't have entertained the thought of taking a witch's potion. Hell, he wouldn't have entertained a witch in his living room. But now, since Rain was the one offering it…

She looked at him, the tears sitting on her lower lids beginning to dry without falling. "Why don't you trust me?"

"I trust you." He blinked, his answer surprising both of them as the words tumbled so easily from his lips. It had been hard to admit the truth to Luke, and especially to himself, but the way his wolf reacted to seeing her again confirmed it. She was his fate-bound. It went against his better judgement and everything he'd believed since he was a kid, but he trusted this woman to his core.

The muscles in her throat flexed as she swallowed. "Then you've got something against witches."

Rubbing his forehead, he closed his eyes for a long blink. If he planned to follow his fate and let a witch into his life, he might as well tell her the truth. "It's a long story."

"I've got time." She offered him a smile and let her purse drop to the floor.

Oh, hell. He was doing this. He leaned his head back and stared at the ceiling. There was no sense in sugar-coating the story. If she knew the whole, messy truth, maybe she could forgive him for his initial mistrust. "I wasn't born into the pack."

Her brow scrunched as she tilted her head. His explanation would be harder than he thought if she didn't understand how strong the pack bond was.

He blew out a hard breath. "Do you know what a rogue werewolf is?"

"I'm guessing it's someone who doesn't belong to a pack. Like a lone wolf?"

"Exactly. We're pack creatures by nature. We crave the company of others like us, and we stick together. But sometimes we go rogue for various reasons. My parents were rogues."

"Why?" She scooted closer to him, her hip brushing against his leg.

That innocent touch sent a jolt of electricity shooting straight to his heart, easing the incessant ache in his muscles. "My dad had a wild side. Didn't care much for rules."

Her lips parted, but she paused before she spoke. "Had?"

"He died when I was five. My mom joined the pack because of me. To save me." A heaviness settled on his shoulders at the memory. When was the last time he'd talked about this?

"What happened?" Concern emanated from her eyes, and when she rested her hand on his knee, he fought the urge to lace his fingers through hers and bring them to his lips.

"We lived about a hundred miles northwest of New Orleans in Livonia. There was no pack, very few werewolves around, but even rogues are territorial. We got too close to another rogue's territory, and he and my dad had it out. Argued for years. When I was five, they got into a bar fight. Before they could take it outside and fight as wolves, one of the rogue's human friends shot my dad in the head."

She squeezed his leg. "Oh, Chase, I'm so sorry."

He shook his head. "I don't really remember him. Mostly things my mom has told me." He'd always have an ache in his heart that his father had been murdered. That he grew up without the man's influence. But he didn't lose sleep over it anymore, and it wasn't the point of the story.

He forced a half-smile. "I inherited my old man's rebellious nature, if you couldn't tell."

"No." She feigned shock. "The tattoos and piercing don't give that away at all."

He chuckled, and for the first time in two days, it didn't hurt to laugh. "My mom tried her best, but I was fourteen years old when I got in over my head. A small coven ran most of the town."

She moved her hand to her lap, taking the soothing warmth of her touch with her.

He inhaled deeply, silently wishing she'd touch him again to give him the strength to continue. This was the messy part. "I hung out with a group of kids from the coven, and we got into all kinds of trouble. Kids' stuff like graffiti, skipping school, you know… Anyway, one night we were hanging out, and they decided to do some kind of ritual that involved fire in the back of a store. We broke in, rearranged the furniture, and I watched them do their thing. They gave me a potion. Said it was the only way for me to participate since I wasn't a witch."

"Did you drink it?"

He clenched his jaw. "Remember when I said werewolves are pack animals by nature? I'd have done anything to belong. To fit in somewhere."

She sucked in a sharp breath. "I don't like where this is heading. Did they hurt you?"

"They tried to. Turns out, I was their sacrifice, and the potion was meant to knock me out. They tried to tie me up. They wanted my blood, and when I refused, they tried take it by force and throw me into the fire." A shudder ran through his body at the memory of the betrayal. "I'd come into my own magic by then, so I shifted and tore into them like I was fighting for my life."

She grimaced. "It sounds like you were."

"The fire got out of hand during the fight, and the building burned to the ground. Everyone got out alive, but they were in bad shape."

"And you?"

"Werewolves are fast healers. I didn't have a scratch by the time I got home, but I got blamed for everything. They claimed I ambushed their sacred ritual and started the fire myself."

"Oh, Chase, that's awful." She returned her hand to his leg, this time on his thigh.

"I was arrested for arson and assault. Spent some time in juvenile detention. Parole for a couple of years after that."

"And the other kids?"

"Nothing happened to them. I was blamed for everything." He laughed again, but he couldn't force any humor into it. "They covered their tracks with magic. Whether or not their parents bought their story, I don't know. As soon as I got out of juvenile detention, my mom packed us up and we moved here. She couldn't handle me on her own, so she sought out the help of the alpha…Luke's old man at the time. He straightened me out. If not for the pack, I'd either be dead or in jail by now."

"Wow." She stared straight ahead and chewed her lip. "Those kids were practicing black magic, which is forbidden. I hope you don't hold that against all witches. Most of us are peaceful, goddess-worshipping people."

How could he not? "That was my first run-in with witches. I've had bad luck with them ever since."

"Well…" She shrugged. "Maybe your luck is changing. Oh, that reminds me…Amber said to tell you change is good. She said you'd know what she was talking about."

He knew exactly what she was talking about. The beautiful woman sitting on the couch next to him, absently tracing circles on his thigh with her fingers. Did she even realize how intimately she was touching him? It felt so natural having her there, her gentle caress giving him the strength to tell his story.

She glanced at her hand on his leg and jerked it away. "Where does that leave us then?"

"I told you I trust you." He reached for her hand, and she let him take it. Her skin was soft, her unpainted fingernails stained blue around the edges from frosting. The temptation to bring them to his lips to taste them made his mouth water.

Luke was right; he couldn't fight fate. Didn't want to anymore. He could set his disdain for witches aside for Rain. His wolf wouldn't have it any other way, and if he had to swallow a spell to prove he trusted this woman, that's what he would do. "Tell me about this potion you brought."

She held his gaze for a moment before she took a vial of orange liquid from her purse. "It's a healing spell. It has mango leaves and rue and some other things, and Snow enchanted it with her power. It won't make you one hundred percent better, but it will speed up the healing."

"Give it to me." He held out his hand.

She eyed him skeptically. "Seriously?"

"I already feel better from you being here. If you're telling me this little bit of liquid will make me heal even faster, I believe you." Rain would never do anything to hurt him. He felt it in his core.

The corners of her mouth tugged into a hesitant smile, and she handed him the vial.

Holding her gaze, he popped out the cork and tossed the liquid back like a shot of tequila, swallowing it all in one gulp. It tasted like honey, and as the potion cascaded down his throat, a cooling sensation spread from his stomach to his limbs.

Rain's smile reached her eyes as she took the empty vial and returned it to her purse. "How do you feel?"

The ache in his legs subsided, and the pressure in his head lightened. "Like it's cooling me from the inside out."

She nodded "Because you're hot."

"Why, thank you." The widening of her eyes told him she didn't mean it that way, but he couldn't stop himself from messing with her. "That's the second time you've told me that."

She arched an eyebrow. "Bless your heart. You haven't seen a mirror lately, have you?" She chuckled and patted his knee. "I should let you get some rest."

What was it about a quick-witted woman that was so damn sexy? He grabbed her hand, not ready for her to leave. The temptation to pull her to his chest and plant his lips on hers built in his core, but he probably did look like hell, considering how he'd felt the past two days. His breath wouldn't be any better. "Can I ask you a witch-related question?"

The humor in her eyes faded to wariness. "Sure."

He turned her hand over and traced his finger on her soft palm. Her breath hitched as she gazed at their entwined fingers, and a battle of emotions seemed to play across her features.

"After I got out of juvenile detention, we moved, and I haven't seen those kids since. Do you know why they wanted my blood?"

"Blood magic." She slipped her hand from his grasp and wrapped her arms around herself. "Werewolf blood has healing and transformative powers. They were probably working on a spell that would elicit change or something that would be painful and would require healing. I can't say for sure." She grabbed her purse and stood. "I really should go. The potion should have its full effect in an hour or two. I hope you feel better soon."

"I already feel better." He sat up and put his feet on the floor for the first time in two days. Expecting the room to spin, he paused, giving his body time to adjust to the upright position, and then he pushed to his feet.

Big mistake. A wave of nausea washed over him, and he managed to catch the arm of the sofa to steady himself before he crumpled to the floor. Rain wrapped her arms around his shoulders and guided him to the cushions, getting him situated in his previous prone position before settling on the edge of the couch.

She brushed the hair off his forehead and glided her fingers down the side of his face. Though no magic seeped from her skin, her affectionate touch lit a fire inside his core. She smiled, her gaze drifting from his eyes to his lips and back again. "Not that much better, I guess?"

"Apparently not." What was it about her touch that derailed his thoughts? "I told you about my sordid past; it's your turn to tell me something."

She folded her hands in her lap. "What do you want to know?"

"Why do you know so much about black magic if you don't practice it?"

"Not all blood magic is black magic. Anytime blood is used in a spell, the practitioner has to be extremely careful to avoid contamination and to use the exact amount. I'm glad those kids didn't succeed, because if they'd screwed up their spell, the results could have been even more devastating than they were."

He sat up again, scooting to rest his back against the arm of the couch. For a powerless witch, she knew way too much about all this. "Have you ever practiced blood magic?"

She opened her mouth to respond but paused mid-breath. Pressing her lips together, she shook her head. "If you're trying to catch me in a lie, it won't work. I don't have powers. I can't cast spells."

Damn. Had his motive been that transparent? If she wasn't lying about her powers, what was she holding back? And *why* was she keeping it from him?

"I'm sorry." He rested a hand on her knee. "Here's the thing, Rain. I find you fascinating and alluring. I want to know you, but I can't shake the feeling that you aren't telling me everything. I already feel like a sentient being again from drinking your potion, which I think proves that I trust you. So, I've opened up. Now it's your turn."

She held his gaze, studying him, as she covered his hand with hers and gave it a squeeze. "You know everything you need to know." Moving his hand to his own lap, she patted it twice before standing. "I need to get back to work." She shuffled to the front door.

"Are you free tonight?"

Shaking her head, she turned to face him. "Chase…"

He wasn't about to let her shoot him down again. "I need you to take a look at the body in the morgue. If I can get Macey to meet us there, are you free around eight?"

Her chest rose and fell as she sighed. "Sure. I'll see you at eight." She opened the door and paused in the threshold, running her finger over the chipping paint on the jamb. "I did lie to you about something."

Swinging his feet to the floor, he rested his elbows on his knees. He'd have preferred to stand and face her for the admission, but he didn't dare risk nearly passing out in front of her again. He held her gaze, his silence encouraging her to continue.

"At the bakery, when I told you that I was going to say I wasn't interested and you shouldn't kiss me…That's not what I was going to say."

His heart slammed against his ribs. "What were you going to say?"

The corners of her mouth twitched into an almost-smile. "I was going to say that if you wanted to kiss me, you should do it, because I wanted to kiss you too. I'll see you tonight." She stepped through the door and closed it.

CHAPTER NINE

RAIN LEANED TOWARD THE MIRROR and applied a final swipe of mascara. As the brush reached the tip of her lashes, it slipped from her fingers and painted a thick black stripe down her cheek before clinking into the sink.

"Damn it." She glanced at the clock. Seven-fifty. No time to start over. Grabbing a washcloth, she wrapped it around her finger and held it under the faucet before swiping the smudge from her face. Ever since she'd left Chase's house that afternoon, her nerves had been on edge. What did one wear on a trip to the morgue with the man of her dreams?

She applied a fresh coat of powder where the smudge had been and jabbed the mascara wand into the bottle. This wasn't a date; she was doing him a favor, so she'd opted not to change clothes. It didn't hurt to freshen up her makeup and run a brush through her hair, though.

She tossed her makeup into its storage box and shoved it under the sink. Her tiny living quarters didn't leave room for clutter, so everything she owned sat either under the bed or in a cabinet or closet.

Chase's house was small, but what she'd seen of it had been clean. Cozy. Definitely not the bachelor pad she'd imagined him in before she found out his sister and niece lived with him. She smiled and flipped off the light switch before shuffling to the storefront to wait for him.

Hopefully, if her curse had caused his accident, she'd more than countered the effects. She hadn't expected him to actually drink the potion. And the way he'd tossed it back without hesitation did prove he was starting to trust her. But at what cost?

He could tell she kept secrets, but there was no way she could reveal her curse. She absolutely could not admit to needing his blood to break it. Not after everything he'd told her. The trust he'd shown today would dissolve into oblivion if he knew she needed him for the same reason his so-called friends had attacked him when he was a kid. She'd either have to find herself another werewolf or forget about breaking her curse.

The thought of living the rest of her life without her magic sat sour in her stomach like expired milk. What else could she do?

She caught a glimpse of Chase sauntering by the window, but he didn't stop at the bakery door. She hurried to the front and watched as he pressed the buzzer for the apartment upstairs. Her heart fluttered as she fumbled with the lock. *This isn't a date. Why do I have to keep reminding myself of that?*

She leaned out the door and admired his broad shoulders. When no one answered the buzzer, he stepped back and peered at the apartment above. The streetlights illuminated his strong jaw and high cheekbones. The color had returned to his skin, and his hair appeared washed and combed into that messy-chic style that was meant to look natural but he probably spent an hour perfecting. He looked scrumptious.

Not that he'd looked *that* bad at his house earlier. She'd only said he did to turn the tables on his cocky flirtation. He may have been a badass werewolf, but he wouldn't get the upper hand with her. Not if she could help it.

"Looking for someone?" She pulled the door shut and locked it. "No one lives up there at the moment."

He smiled and strode toward her, stopping short of wrapping his arms around her. Instead, he shoved his hands into his pockets and glanced up at the balcony. "I thought you lived there."

"I live in the back of the bakery. I can't afford the storefront and the apartment."

"Oh." He stared at her, and his magnetism made her lean toward him.

She slipped her hands into her own pockets to stop from reaching for him. "You look like you feel better."

He blinked, seeming to come out of whatever trance had been drawing them together. "I do. That potion you gave me was incredible. Tell Snow, 'Thank you,' for me."

"I will. It only worked that quickly because you're a werewolf, though."

"I guess I'm lucky to be a werewolf."

She smiled. "I guess you are."

"We better not keep Macey waiting. You ready?" He motioned toward the black motorcycle parked on the curb.

Sleek yet masculine, the bike sported black leather and shiny chrome. The closest Rain had ever come to a motorcycle was the one she made out of fondant and gum paste for a ten-year-old's birthday cake last year. It was so much sexier in person. Almost as sexy as the man who owned it.

She suppressed the giggle trying to escape her throat. "Seriously? That's your ride?"

"You didn't think I'd drive a Subaru, did you?" He unhooked a helmet from the back of the seat and tossed it to her before pulling a matching one onto his head. Maybe his hair did look that good naturally.

"A fast healer like yourself needs a helmet?" She shook her hair behind her shoulders and stuffed her head into the helmet, buckling the strap beneath her chin.

"I don't know anyone who can recover from having his brains splattered on the pavement." He swung a leg over the seat and straddled the massive machine.

Heat pooled below her navel as she ticked off the items on her mental hot-guy checklist. Tattoos? *Check.* Amazing body? From what she could tell with his clothes on, *check*. Kind, funny, caring, compassionate. *Check, check, check, check.* He got her motor running every time he looked at her, and now she was about to be painfully close to him. She'd have to press her body against his to hold on. His tight backside would fit snugly against her front. Goddess, help her.

"You coming?"

"I've never ridden a motorcycle before." She gripped his shoulders and swung her leg across the seat.

"Hold on tight, lean into the turns, and trust me to keep you safe. If you fight it, we could crash." He revved the engine and looked straight ahead, so she couldn't see his eyes, but the intensity in his words felt like he was talking about more than the motorcycle ride.

She wrapped her arms around his waist and rested her chin on his shoulder. "Contrary to what you think, I do trust you."

His chuckle vibrated into her chest. "You'll have to prove it."

They took off down the street, and Rain tightened her arms around Chase's firm body. At the slow speed they traveled through the French Quarter, she didn't have to hold him too tightly, but she'd have been an idiot not to take advantage of their close proximity.

His muscles were solid, and his woodsy, natural scent danced in her senses, making her head spin. She rested her nose against the back of his shoulder and took a few deep breaths. Sitting there, holding him, breathing in his intoxicating scent, her insides melted into goo.

Pheromones. His had to be so strong because he was a werewolf. No human—or witch for that matter—had ever affected her this way. Chase was, at heart, a pack animal. And pack animals drew others to them and were drawn to others in return. Instinct explained why the rest of the world slipped away when she was near him...and she couldn't fight instinct.

"Watch where you put your hands, *cher*. I might think you're trying to come on to me."

His deep, velvety voice roused her from her thoughts. They'd stopped at a light, and as her grip loosened, she'd unwittingly allowed her hands to rest on his crotch. Her heart rate kicked up, and she fought the urge to rub her palm across the mound in his jeans.

"Maybe I am." She slid her hands to his thighs and squeezed them before returning her grip to his stomach. With this giant machine rumbling beneath her and her body pressed up against him, how could she not be turned on?

He missed a beat in his reply, as if her response had derailed his thoughts. Good. Remind him he wasn't the only one with sex appeal.

"Hang on. We're heading onto the highway now." He took a left and zipped onto the road.

The speed and the wind rushing against her skin made her pulse quicken in exhilaration. They whizzed past cars and street lamps until they turned into a dizzying blur of light and shadow. Too bad the helmet kept the wind from whipping through her hair. That was the only thing that could have made this moment better.

He eased into the turns, and she tightened her grip as the bike leaned with the momentum. Chase commanded the machine like a man in control, as if it were an extension of his own self. The slight hint of fear she'd felt at the beginning of the ride drained away, leaving behind nothing but the thrill of excitement and the lust for the man. She could've done this all night long.

Chase pulled into the morgue parking lot and killed the engine. That ride had ended way too soon. Rain pried her arms from around his waist and yanked the helmet off her head, but she couldn't make her body move away from his. Being close to him felt way too good. Everything about this man had her mouth watering to taste him.

"You're hot, you're sweet, you ride a badass motorcycle... You must have a new girlfriend every week." She clamped her lips shut. She really needed to work on that filter.

He slid off the bike and set his helmet on the seat. Narrowing his eyes, he put his hands on his hips. "Is that what you think of me? Because I was a screw-up as a kid, I can't be faithful to a woman? Having tattoos and riding a bike automatically makes me an asshole?"

Uh oh. Way to piss off a werewolf again. She set her helmet on the seat in front of her and took a deep breath as she composed her answer. "I don't think you're an asshole. I assumed, based on how you make *me* feel, that a lot of women are attracted to you."

Something sparked in his eyes, and his entire demeanor softened.

The edges of his lips curved into a tiny smile as he crossed his arms over his chest. "How do I make you feel?"

Oh, goddess, she did not need to get into her complicated emotions with this man. He made her feel more alive than she'd felt in years. Like maybe there was more to life than power and position. For the first time since she'd been cursed, she had more on her mind than getting her magic back. "We don't want to keep Macey waiting. Let's get this over with."

She swung her leg over the seat and stumbled as she rose to her feet. Her legs felt numb, her knees weak, and Chase caught her by the hips to steady her.

"Careful. Your legs might be wobbly." And there he was, close to her again, his face a few inches from hers.

How easy it would have been to lean in and taste his lips. To feel his beard against her face. Would it be scratchy or soft? She straightened, grabbing control of her thoughts before they spiraled into all the other places she'd like to feel his beard against.

With her equilibrium returning, she stepped back before her desires overshadowed her rational thoughts. "How do you walk so easily after riding this thing?"

"You get used to it." He smiled, and taking her hand, he led her toward the brown brick building.

"Thanks for the ride. Having a man and a machine between my legs at the same time was exhilarating." She sucked in a sharp breath as heat crept up her cheeks. "That did not come out right."

He cast her a sideways glance, one corner of his mouth pulling into his signature cocky grin. "Sounded good to me. I'd like to take you for a longer ride when we're done here."

"I'd like that too." Way, *way* too much.

They stopped outside the door, and he turned to face her. "This body we're about to see is in bad shape."

She put a lid on the pot of emotions boiling over for Chase. As much as she'd enjoyed the ride over, this wasn't a date. It was time to be serious. "How bad?"

"She looks like a mummy. Dark, leathery skin. Missing an eye. If it's too much, let me know and we'll leave."

"I'll be fine." She wasn't about to show weakness in front of him. After everything he'd been through as a kid, for him to show her even the slightest bit of trust proved his emotional strength. But he hadn't gotten over it, and he'd need a strong witch to help him come to terms with his past and let go of his prejudice. She would be strong for him.

"All right then. Don't say you weren't warned." He opened the door and motioned for her to enter.

Bright fluorescent lights hummed from above, giving the plain reception area a clinical feel. Four empty chairs sat against one wall, and a petite, blonde woman leaned against the counter, chatting with a tall man with light brown hair. They both wore business casual clothes, but the guns holstered on the woman's hip and the man's shoulder gave away their occupations.

Chase placed his hand on the small of Rain's back and guided her toward the detectives, his touch sending a flood of warmth through her veins. "This is Macey and her partner, Bryce."

Rain shook Macey's hand. "It's nice to finally meet you. I'm Rain."

Macey smiled. "I hope Chase has been treating you right. I've heard good things about your cakes."

Chase crossed his arms and shifted his weight to one foot, casting Macey an unreadable look. The alpha's mate winked at him, letting him know whatever message he'd tried to send had been received.

Rain looked back to Chase. "We're getting along." That was an understatement. She turned to Bryce. "Hi."

"Nice to meet you." He shook her hand. "I seem to be the only person in New Orleans who doesn't have some sort of psychic ability."

"I'm not a psychic. I'm a witch."

Bryce scowled and looked at Macey, who shifted uncomfortably and glanced to the man behind the counter. "Is the body ready for us?"

"Yes, ma'am. Y'all can head back."

"This way." Macey whispered something to Chase as she strode for the door.

Werewolves may have kept their true identities secret from humans, but witches were well known, especially in New Orleans. They kept their more powerful abilities hidden, like Snow's ability to freeze things, but the practice of spells and rituals were common knowledge.

Bryce followed after Macey, and Chase put his hand on Rain's arm, holding her back a few steps. "Macey's partner doesn't know about us. He thinks I talk to ghosts."

"You could have warned me about that before we got here." She couldn't be expected to keep the right secrets if she wasn't made aware of which secrets she had to keep.

"Sorry." He gave her a sheepish look. "Having your arms wrapped around me for so long distracted me."

Her heart did this weird *thud...thud-thud-thud* thing, and she plastered on a smile. "I won't give your secret away." She moved toward the door, trying to put some distance between them before she wrapped her arms around him again.

"I trust you."

His words stopped her in her tracks, and she lowered her gaze, unable to meet his eyes. He had no reason to trust her. She'd been hiding things from him since the moment she met him, and it killed her to know their entire relationship was built on a lie. She wasn't worthy of his trust, but damn it, she wanted to be. Coming clean about her curse would be the first step. He deserved the truth. At least a little of it.

When she didn't respond, Chase brushed passed her and pushed open the door, leaving her alone in the reception area with the heaviness of her lies weighing her down, making it hard to move. She had to tell him. If she lost the wedding because of her admission, so be it. She couldn't lie to him anymore.

Rain followed the sound of their voices down the hallway and into the heart of the morgue. Her shoes squeaked on the white tile floor as she stepped in the room, and the sickly-sweet smell of decaying flesh made her wrinkle her nose as she took in her surroundings. Row after row of square metal doors lined three of the walls, all of them sealed shut, except one. Chase, Macey, and Bryce stood by the open door, waiting for her.

"Did you prepare her?" Bryce asked Chase.

He gave a quick nod. "She knows what to expect."

Macey reached for the drawer, but Bryce put a hand up to stop her. "Hold on. Before we do this, I've got to know. What's the difference between a witch and someone with psychic powers like Macey or Chase? You do Voodoo magic or something?"

Rain closed the distance between them and looked at both Macey and Chase, doing her best to assure them with her gaze that she wouldn't say too much. "Most witches are Wiccan. It's a religion; so is Voodoo. We worship a goddess and try our best to be one with nature."

Bryce arched an eyebrow. "Do the spells you cast work?"

A skeptic. Most humans were, but they rarely argued with her logic. "Casting spells is a lot like prayer. Do you believe prayer works?"

He shrugged. "Sure I do."

"Then why not spells?"

Bryce furrowed his brow as he contemplated her words. "I'm not even going to pretend to understand what y'all do or how you do it. The less I know, the better."

Rain gave him a reassuring smile. "I'm not going to cast any spells. I'm here to identify the body. She belonged to my old coven."

Bryce blinked.

"A coven is like a church."

"Hmm…" He rubbed his chin. "Witch church. If you say so." He pulled out the drawer to reveal the body.

Macey moved back the sheet, and Rain's breath caught in her throat at the sight of the remains. Based on the hair and nail polish alone—the only things left intact—she didn't recognize the woman. Her skin had shriveled on her bones, masking any features she might have had while alive. Rain's stomach twisted, and she swallowed the sour taste creeping up her throat. This woman wasn't mummified. She'd had the life sucked out of her, and Rain had only met one person with that ability.

"Here's the mark I told you about." Chase pointed to the coven crest on the woman's chest below her collarbone. "Calista said it was Miami. Do you recognize it?"

Rain nodded. "It's Miami. This is what it used to look like." She slid her shirt off her shoulder and turned her back so they could see the crest on her shoulder blade.

As she turned around and looked at Chase, his eyes held so much compassion, her heart thudded against her ribs.

"Do you know who she is?" His hands twitched as if he fought the urge to reach for her.

"Based on what I can tell from what's left of her, she's no one I was close to. I may have known her in passing, but it's difficult to say." She wrapped her arms around herself to chase away the chill penetrating her bones. Visions of the corpse would be invading her nightmares for weeks. "I've seen enough."

This time, Chase didn't hesitate. He wrapped his arms around her and tugged her to his chest, and the firmness and strength of his embrace warmed her from the inside out. She didn't know the dead woman on the table, but that didn't make it any less disturbing. He guided her out of the building and stopped on the sidewalk out front. The detectives followed on their heels.

"Thanks for your help, ma'am," Bryce said. "We better get back to the station, Mace."

Macey tugged her bottom lip and cut her gaze between Rain and Bryce. "Give me a minute. I need to talk to Rain about my wedding cake."

Bryce chuckled. "I'll be in the car."

As soon as her partner walked out of earshot, Macey turned to Rain. "Is there anything else you can tell us about the woman? I heard something about an energy vampire mentioned. Could you pick up on anything at all?"

Rain inhaled a shaky breath and leaned into Chase's side for support. Could her ex be alive? Surely not after what she'd done. "It does appear to be the work of an energy vampire, though I've never seen one drain a victim so thoroughly. In my experience, they usually take a little at a time…whatever they need to accomplish their task or recover from overusing their magic."

Chase stiffened. "In your experience?"

"I knew an energy vampire once, a long time ago. I was unwittingly his victim for more than a year before I caught on to what was happening." She shivered.

He tightened his arm around her protectively. "Do you know where this guy is now? Could he have done this?"

"I don't think so." Should she tell him the truth? What would he think of her if he knew what she'd done? "The last time I saw him, he was...ill. He was in no condition to perform any kind of magic, and I doubt he survived."

Bryce tapped on the horn and made a winding motion with his hand, telling Macey to hurry up.

She held up a finger. "Should I notify Miami we have one of their witches?"

Rain chewed the inside of her cheek. Surely it was coincidence the dead witch came from her hometown. If the Miami coven got involved in the investigation, they'd drag Rain into it—probably blame her or Snow. She'd lose the wedding *and* the werewolf she was falling for. "Can you wait? Let me see if my sister can scry for the attacker. She's good at locating people." She looked at Chase. "Having another coven in your territory could get sticky." How thick could she make this layer of lies?

Bryce honked again.

"Let me know what you find out. I'll have to contact them eventually." Macey turned to leave but paused. "And, Chase, I know this goes without saying, but..."

"I'll keep her safe."

Macey smiled. "I know you will." She climbed into the car with Bryce, and they pulled out of the parking lot.

"Are you okay?" Chase loosened his grip on her shoulder and moved to look into her eyes.

"I'm fine. A little creeped out, but I'll get over it." She had to. While the woman's death was tragic, it had nothing to do with her. The little wriggling sensation in the back of her mind was nothing. Isaac was dead. Her ex couldn't have been responsible for this.

"Will you tell me more about this energy vampire you encountered? How did he victimize you for so long without you knowing?"

Her stomach sank. She needed to tell him the truth. He deserved to know at least some of it, but first she needed to gather her thoughts. To figure out how much she was willing to risk. How much she should share. "Can we get out of this parking lot? How about that ride you promised me?" She flashed a weak smile.

"Rain…"

"I know. I will tell you, but it's not an easy story to share." Especially since what she'd done to Isaac had been a hundred times worse than what he'd done to her. "Take me for a ride, and I promise I'll tell you."

He arched an eyebrow. "I'll hold you to that promise."

"I hope you do."

CHAPTER TEN

THE BARK OF A CYPRESS TREE DUG INTO ISAAC'S BACK AS HE closed his eyes and leaned his head against the trunk. The hard ground beneath his legs did nothing to ease his aching muscles, but this would all be over soon. Once the witch was dead, the spell would lift and his body could repair itself...and stay that way.

The temptation to send his tulpa to kill her now was palpable. He could end his own anguish, but death was too easy for the one who did this to him. She deserved to suffer one thousand times worse for what she'd done.

He took the jar from his pocket and gazed at the orb rolling around in the liquid. This little act of magic would require another week of recovery, but he'd endure the agony in order to watch her suffer.

His knuckles cracked as he gripped the lid and twisted it from the jar. Sharp pain shot up to his elbow, the rotating movement threatening to rip it from its socket. Dropping the lid, he poured the contents into his palm, allowing the liquid to flow through his fingers. He closed his hand around the eye and concentrated on the magic within it.

"May the magic inside be my guide." His voice came out in a

croak. "I call on her sight to lead me through the night. Show me Rain, who has caused me insufferable pain."

The eye warmed in his hand, sending tingling energy up his arm and into his core. He closed his own eyes, allowing the visions to swim through his mind. Blurry at first, as his concentration focused, they came into crisp view.

"There you are, my little Rain. My, how you've grown." She hadn't been much more than a girl when he'd met her all those years ago. Powerful, but immature. She'd been an easy target, and once he'd cast his spell of obsession, she'd been his to manipulate. She was still beautiful, though her features had matured and her hair had grown. A familiar ache seized in his chest. He had cared for her once, but she'd hardly acknowledged his existence. Always focused on her magic and starting her business, power and position in the coven had been her main concerns.

His spell had taught her to love. To care for *him* above all else. He'd made her a better person, and she'd repaid him in the most inhumane way. The ache in his heart turned to a stab of anger, and he pushed the thoughts out of his mind and focused on her image.

But seeing her face didn't help him with her location. He concentrated on widening the vision. She was with a man. Tall with dark hair, he looked at her as if he wanted to consume her. The smile on her lips said she'd enjoy being eaten.

Isaac paused, his ragged breath catching in his throat as he looked closer in his vision. Though the man's face no longer contorted in pain, his features couldn't be mistaken. The werewolf from the swamp had caught Rain's eye.

Pain shot through his temple as he ground his teeth, and he lifted his injured arm. Cursed blood oozed through the moss bandage, and the burning from the beast's teeth had never ceased. Of all the men his Rain could have latched onto, why did it have to be the werewolf?

He closed his eyes and looked at her in his vision. The moment her wicked spell had taken effect on Isaac, his control over her had broken. He'd get her back, though. The little witch belonged to him, and she'd learn her lesson soon enough. He'd make the man suffer first. Then her sister and anyone else she cared about.

She would fear him, and in her fear, she would respect him. He had once made her eyes sparkle like they did for this man. Perhaps he could make them shine again. If he could drain a witch powerful enough to unbind Rain's magic, he could break her curse. With her magic restored, she could lift the spell she'd put on him and be his forever.

He gazed at her deep-gray eyes in his vision. She would pay one way or another—either sacrificing her life or devoting it to him.

He inhaled deeply, the humid air slicing like razor blades down his trachea, and reined in his emotions. "Show me where she's been."

His vision of Rain swam, drifting through time and space to a house—brown with white trim and green shutters. In his mind, he stepped inside and found her sitting on the couch next to the same man.

With a growl of frustration, he searched the vision again. Another building—bright yellow with a light-green door. A bakery. He peered through the window. Rain wore a blue apron and stood behind the counter, decorating a cake. His lips cracked as they curved into a smile. His pastry chef had made her dream of running a bakery come true.

Forcing his vision to the present, he watched Rain climb on the back of the man's motorcycle. Jealousy rolled through his shriveled veins like fire. The vision wavered as the magic subsided, flickering and losing focus. It was just as well; he'd seen enough. Fisting his hand around the eye, he squeezed until the gelatinous mess oozed through his fingers, ending the horrid vision.

Piercing pain ripped through his body as the magic dissipated, but he found the strength to call upon his tulpa. The shadow figure appeared before him, ready to do his bidding. He didn't need to speak to tell it his intent—*follow the man*. Make them both terrified for their lives.

CHAPTER ELEVEN

CHASE'S HEART POUNDED AS HE SPED DOWN THE HIGHWAY, BUT the rush he normally felt from riding on the open road paled in comparison to the way Rain's arms wrapped around him made his body hum. He could've ridden like this for hours, with her soft curves pressed into his back, her hands gripping his stomach.

He drove for half an hour, giving her time to gather her thoughts. Her secrets were about to be revealed, and he wanted to know everything. He took her over the bridge into Algiers and followed the back roads to a quiet spot on the riverbank. When he cut the engine, she tightened her arms around him as if she wasn't ready to let him go. He knew the feeling.

She loosened her grip, and he took off his helmet, hanging it on a handlebar. Climbing off the bike, he held out his hand to help her off. Her chest rose and fell as she took a deep breath and pulled the helmet from her head. Her soft, dark curls bounced as she shook her head and ran her fingers through her hair. She looked sexy as hell perched on the back of his bike...a sight he would love to get used to.

Setting the helmet on the seat, she held his gaze, and the confliction in her eyes tore at his heart. Whatever she was about to tell him wouldn't be easy.

Sharing his secret with her hadn't been a piece of cake either, but they'd get through it, whatever *it* was. It couldn't be any worse than the things he'd done.

She took his hand and swung her leg over the bike, stepping straight into his arms. Holding him tight, she pressed her face against his chest and inhaled deeply. If she was stalling, he wasn't complaining. Damn, she felt good in his arms.

He rubbed his hand across her back and pressed his lips to the top of her head. Her hair brushed his nose, the sweet scent of vanilla tickling his senses, and he tightened his arms around her. There was no denying the primal possessiveness he felt for this woman. His wolf had already claimed her, and now the man had finally accepted it.

Pulling from his embrace, she gave him a half-smile and slipped her hand into his. "I owe you an explanation."

"Then let's talk." He led her closer to the river, and they settled on a patch of grass. Light from the half-moon danced across the surface of the Mississippi, making the muddy water sparkle. The cosmos flowers growing on the bank filled the air with the sweet scent of chocolate, and he inhaled deeply, enjoying the unusual floral perfume.

Rain angled herself to face him, and her knee brushed his thigh. The heat radiating from her body called to him, urging him to take her in his arms again and find out if her lips tasted as sweet as they looked.

She rested her hand on his leg, the simple touch sending his heart racing. As she chewed her bottom lip, she looked into his eyes, her face taking on a mask of resolve. "I haven't always been a dud. I used to have powers."

He suppressed a smile. "I had a feeling you did." Finally, the truth came out. She was way too confident to be a magical being without magic. He'd peeled away one layer of the mystery surrounding Rain Connolly, but it wasn't enough. He ached to know her to the center of her very being. "Why did you lie?"

She let out a heavy sigh. "Let me tell you the story from the beginning. Hopefully you'll understand." She pulled her hand into her lap and clasped her fingers together. "You're not the only one who's had bad luck with witches. That energy vampire I knew…I used to date him."

He clenched his jaw as the feeling of protectiveness gripped his heart. "He took your powers?" If the guy was alive, and if Chase ever found him…

"Not exactly." She dropped her head and stared at her hands in her lap. "I was in love with him. I thought I was, anyway. Obsessed would be a better way to describe it, so I'm not sure if…" She exhaled sharply. "It doesn't matter. We lived together for almost a year."

She looked into his eyes. "I was like you. Second in command of the coven. I was training for a place on the national witches' council."

The fact didn't surprise him. "You must have been very powerful."

"I was. And Isaac…the energy vampire…was using my power without my knowledge. He'd take it, little by little, at night while I was sleeping. It was such a small amount, I didn't notice. I'd feel sick the next day sometimes, but normally I'd recover by the time I woke in the morning."

His jaw clenched. "Bastard." The mere thought of anyone hurting Rain was enough to drive him mad.

"It gets worse. I caught him cheating on me. A friend saw him out with another woman, so I followed him one night, and sure enough, he was seeing someone on the side. When he got home that night, I pretended I was asleep. He stood over the bed and touched my face. It felt like he was draining the life from my body, but I couldn't move. I couldn't stop him. I passed out, and when I woke the next morning, I confronted him."

Chase pried Rain's hands apart and slipped his fingers through hers. The lines in her forehead smoothed as she seemed to relax.

She straightened her spine and took a deep breath. "Long story short, we aren't together anymore. I ended up cursed and my powers are bound. Like I said before, the last time I saw him he was on his death bed. If he were alive, he'd be capable of doing what happened to the woman at the morgue, but I don't see how he could have recovered from his illness." She bit her bottom lip.

Chase ground his teeth as he tried to calm his pounding heart. "He cursed you."

She lowered her gaze to their entwined hands. "I lost more than my powers. And this is why I've been hesitant to get close to you...to anyone. If another witch shows me kindness, something bad will happen. Not to me, but to the person who was nice to me."

Chase closed his eyes and rubbed his forehead. What kind of sick bastard would do this to her? "If he can't have you, no one can?"

She glanced at him before returning her gaze to their hands. The muscles in her throat worked as she swallowed, and she placed her other hand on top of his. "I think that part of the curse was meant to teach me a lesson. I wasn't exactly kind when I confronted him. Now, no one can be kind to me without me unwittingly being *un*kind to them."

That explained her strange behavior. "What kind of bad things happen? And is it if they do *anything* kind? Or does it have to be something big?"

She let out a dry chuckle. "My parents took me out to dinner for my birthday a year after it happened. They both ended up in the hospital with pneumonia for two weeks."

"Ouch."

Nodding, she pressed her lips together, and her eyes shimmered. "The other day, you saved me from being hit by a taxi. Then you got sick when a snake bit you."

"You think the snake bite was because of your curse?"

She drew her shoulders toward her ears, and her bottom lip trembled. "What else could it be?"

Oh, hell no. He had to end this nonsense right now. No way was a stupid curse going to keep him away from his fate-bound. "Rain, listen to me. I was hunting in the swamp; I've been bitten before. That wasn't because of you."

"Have you ever gotten that sick?" A tear spilled from the inner corner of her eye, and he wiped it away with his thumb.

"No, but..." He had to fix this. No wonder she'd been holding back. She thought he'd get hurt if she let him in. "What *exactly* is the curse?"

"Any witch who shows me kindness will be punished."

"Any *witch*. Did it specify that it had to be a witch?"

"Well, yes."

He smiled. "Rain, I'm a werewolf, not a witch. Your curse won't affect me."

She traced her fingertips along the back of his hand. "What if one of your ancestors was a witch? If you have the slightest amount of witch blood in your veins, it could…"

"I don't. I swear, I am one hundred percent werewolf. Look at me." He cupped her cheek in his hand, drawing her face toward his. The sadness in her eyes stabbed at his heart. She'd opened up to him, finally letting him into her world, and now he understood her hesitation. "I'll take my chances."

She shook her head. "If anything happens to you…"

"Then it will be on me. You've warned me. I'm aware of the risks." He leaned closer, the tip of his nose brushing hers.

"Chase."

"I know you won't hurt me. Please let me in." He paused, his mouth lingering centimeters from hers, giving her plenty of time to move away. When she didn't, he brushed his lips over hers.

She responded, leaning into him, running her hand up his thigh to grip his hip. As her lips parted and her velvet tongue slipped into his mouth, fire shot through his veins. She tasted like peppermint, as sweet as the cakes she baked, and he couldn't get enough of her.

He slid his hand into her hair and moved the other to her back, holding her even closer. His entire body hummed, electricity igniting nerves he never knew existed, as if fate were smiling down on him as he held her. She was meant to be his.

Gliding her hand behind his neck, she tugged him toward her as she lay in the grass. He sidled next to her, afraid if he climbed on top of her they might not be able hold back. He wanted her. Needed her…to fill her, to feel her body wrapped around his, to become one with her.

She settled on her side, the length of her body pressed into his, and he closed his eyes to memorize the way she felt. Soft, supple, as if she were made to fit into arms. Tracing the contour of his lips with her tongue, she caught his bottom lip between her teeth.

He couldn't stop the moan vibrating from his throat. His fate-bound mate lay in his arms, and he wanted to taste every inch of her. He trailed his lips along her jawline and nipped at her delicate earlobe. Her breath hitched, and she tilted her head, giving him access to the sweet curve of her neck. He kissed his way down her throat, pausing to feel her pulse race beneath his lips, the intoxicating scent of her skin making his head spin.

He needed this woman, but not here. Not now. He pulled away to look at her, and she met his gaze with so much passion in her stormy eyes he almost gave in to desire. Instead, he took her hand and sat up, tugging her into his side. "A kiss like that is worth twenty snake bites."

She bit her lip and rested her hand on his chest. "Are you sure you don't have any witch in you?"

The warmth of her touch through his shirt made him shiver, and he longed to feel her bare skin against his. "Positive."

A genuine smile lit up her face as she leaned closer and whispered into his ear, "I think I'd like to have a little werewolf in me." She nipped his earlobe, and a flush of fiery heat spread through his chest.

"There's nothing little about this werewolf, *cher.*"

She ran her hand down his stomach, moving it over to his hip before she reached the good part. "I'd like to see for myself."

A shudder ran through his entire body. If he got any harder, he'd pass out from the lack of blood flow to his brain. "You're killing me, woman. Let me at least take you out to dinner first."

She sat up straight and studied him, her brow furrowing as if she wasn't sure. Her tongue slipped out to moisten her lips, and he couldn't help himself. He had to taste her again.

Cupping his hand behind her neck, he held her close and kissed her. She opened for him willingly, returning the kiss with as much passion as he felt. Closing his eyes, he drank her in, enjoying the sweetness of her tongue, the softness of her lips against his. He could've kissed her all night long, but she pressed her palms to his chest and pushed him away, laughing.

"Okay, you convinced me. I'll have dinner with you, but not tonight. It's late, and I have to get up early to deliver muffins to a daycare for a teacher appreciation breakfast."

"I love muffins. What flavor?"

"Banana nut and chocolate chip." She rose to her feet and dusted the grass from her pants.

"My favorite." Chase stood.

"Which one?"

"Both." He grinned at the beautiful woman before him. Anything she made would be his favorite. As he reached for her hand, a shadow passed in the corner of his vision. He jerked his head to follow the image, but it vanished into the trees. "Did you see that?"

Rain followed his gaze. "See what?"

"A shadow. It went that way." He pointed to the tree line, and the entity dashed behind a trunk. "Stay here." He took a few steps forward, keeping Rain within arms' reach. He wasn't about to leave her alone in the dark with no magic to protect herself, but he couldn't leave without investigating the shadow.

It could've been his mind playing tricks, but the sinking feeling in his stomach told him this was the same entity he'd seen in the swamp before he'd been bitten.

Rain stepped next to him and clutched his bicep. "What do you think it is?"

"It might be a demon."

She tightened her grip. "A demon?"

"I thought we got rid of the bastards a few months ago, but someone new might be summoning them." He peered into the trees, but in the darkness, and in his human form, he couldn't make out much. Though his vision was sharper than a human's, in his wolf form he could see fifty times better. If the fiend was alone, Chase could take him and keep Rain safe at the same time. More than one, though, and they'd have problems.

"What should we do?" She loosened her grip and stayed by his side, brave in the face of evil.

He glanced at her before a rustling sound drew his attention back to the trees. "Have you ever seen a werewolf shift?"

She blinked, a touch of uncertainty flashing in her eyes as she stepped away from him. "No."

"I promise I won't hurt you."

Her doubtful expression faded, and she lifted her chin. "I know you won't." She took a few more steps back, clasping her hands at her chest and watching him with wide, curious eyes.

His body tingled as he called on his wolf, electricity humming through his veins as the magic morphed his form. Dark chocolate fur rolled over his skin as he shifted, and his front paws landed on the ground with a thud.

Rain gasped as the transformation completed, but she didn't back away. Werewolves were massive—at least twice the size of a normal wolf—and his knife-like teeth could easily rip a person to shreds. She had every right to be terrified, but she wasn't. She moved toward him slowly and reached out a hand to stroke his fur. "Should I stay here?"

He jerked his head toward the trees to indicate she should follow him. For now, they were observers. He'd form his plan of attack—if he attacked—once he knew what they were dealing with.

They crept forward, Rain glued to his side, her hand resting on his back. He'd have time to consider how much he respected her bravery later. Right now, he had a demon to vanquish.

As he reached the first tree, the shadow darted from its hiding place and took off in the opposite direction. Torn between his duty to rid the city of demons and his instinct to protect the woman who would be his mate, he chose instinct and stayed by Rain's side. He swept his enhanced vision through the thicket, listening intently for any rustling or out-of-place sounds. Nothing.

He stood utterly motionless, breathing deeply for the scent of death, looking for movement. Still nothing. The fiend had been alone, and now it was gone.

He blew out a hard breath and swung his head around to see Rain. If she was scared, it didn't show on her face. Her eyes were tight, but with determination rather than worry. And he couldn't help but pause to admire her bravery. She'd planned to battle the demon by his side. He nudged her with his head and stepped away from the trees.

"I guess it's gone?"

He nodded. It was possible the demon had planned to attack but changed its mind when it discovered Chase was its natural-born enemy. He'd have to alert the pack, so they'd know to be on the lookout for a shadow.

Rain let out a breath as they walked up the riverbank and away from the trees, her posture relaxing, a sly smile curving her lips. "Are you going to be naked when you shift back to human?"

Thankfully not, or she'd see the raging hard-on she'd given him that was sure to return when he shifted. Then again, with the way she'd kissed him earlier, she might enjoy it. A chill ran through his body at the thought of her enjoying his dick, but that was a thought for another time. He called on his magic and transformed into his human self. Yep, the hard-on came back, tucked away inside his jeans.

Her shoulders slumped. "Damn. How come in the movies were-wolves are always naked when they turn back into humans?"

"Because the people making the movies have probably never met a real werewolf. I'm sorry to disappoint."

Her smile widened. "I don't think you could ever disappoint me."

He took her hand and led her to his bike. "Our clothes get absorbed by the magic when we shift. When we change back, everything is in its proper place."

"Fascinating."

He pulled on his helmet. "I need to report this to the alpha. Let's get you home, so you'll be safe."

Rain climbed onto the bike and wrapped her arms around Chase. Thank the goddess she had a helmet on, or she wouldn't have been able to stop herself from exploring the back of his neck with her tongue. The man was delectable.

And he'd been so confident when he saw the demon. Like he knew he could vanquish it and keep her safe at the same time. Brave, but not cocky about his abilities. A swarm of butterflies took flight in her stomach, and she closed her eyes, letting the rumble of the engine and the smell of his skin seep into her senses, relaxing her. She'd never been in the presence of a demon before, but she hadn't feared for her safety at all. She never would with Chase in her life.

As he stopped in front of the bakery, she tightened her arms around him. She'd been punishing herself long enough. Maybe fate had sent her a werewolf to show her life could still be fulfilling. Maybe the act of selflessness that would break her curse would be *not* asking him for the final ingredient—falling for a man who could end her punishment but caring so much about him that she never asked. But was it worth the risk after what happened before?

She'd been a strong, capable witch at one time before she'd let her emotions overwhelm her, and she'd done the unthinkable to the man she'd thought she loved. Her obsession with Isaac had driven her to use forbidden magic, and she'd been paying dearly for it ever since. What would happen if she allowed herself to fall for Chase? If Isaac didn't have her under a spell years ago, and those insane emotions had been her own, would she turn into a raving maniac this time too?

No, it couldn't happen. She cared deeply for Chase, but the feeling was completely different than before. She loved being near him, but when he wasn't around, she was fine. Sure, she missed him, but she didn't pine away, her thoughts becoming an obsessive whirlwind of anxiety like they had with Isaac.

She'd been young and dumb then. Even if she hadn't been under a spell, the last seven years had changed her, mellowed her. She was capable of having a mature, loving relationship now, wasn't she? There was one way to find out.

They climbed off the bike, and he guided her to the door with his hand firmly planted on her back. She doubted the demon had followed them home, but with Chase's stiff posture, he was obviously on high alert. He had a protective nature, and being near him gave her a sense of security she never realized she'd been lacking. She unlocked the door, and he ushered her inside.

"I'm sure the demon was targeting me, but I don't like the idea of you being here alone."

Was this his way of offering to stay the night with her? The thought of having his warm, hard body next to her in bed all night made her shiver. "What are you suggesting?"

He rubbed his beard and glanced at his bike on the curb outside. "Can your sister stay with you?"

Damn. "That's not the answer I was hoping for." She bit her lip. "I didn't mean to say that out loud."

He chuckled and wrapped his arms around her waist. "You didn't have to. I could see the disappointment in your eyes." He leaned in as if to kiss her, but he pressed his lips to her ear and whispered, "I would love to spend the night with you."

The warmth of his breath on her skin sent shivers running down to her toes. He caught her earlobe between his teeth before moving back to look at her. "But I texted Luke, and he'll have my ass if I don't get out there and stop the damn demon. Can you call your sister?"

"If I asked her, she'd be doing me a kindness. My curse may not affect you, but she would pay dearly for it."

He huffed. "What if I call her? Then she'll be doing *me* a kindness."

She rose onto her toes to kiss him. Her dream of feeling his soft, warm lips all over her body would have to wait, but that was okay. Letting their emotions simmer for a while would sweeten the reward. "There's no need. Snow cast a spell of protection on the bakery. There are totems placed around the perimeter, and as long as the doors are locked, nothing can get in."

He arched an eyebrow, giving her a wary look.

"I'll prove it to you. Go outside, and I'll lock the door. I'll bet you anything you can't get in."

He pinned her with a heated gaze that seemed to suck the breath from her lungs. "Anything?"

She swallowed. "Yep."

Running his fingers through her hair, he grazed her neck with his lips. "If I get in, you'll give me anything I want? Whenever I want it?"

"I will." Her knees weakened. *Goddess, please let it be the same thing I want.*

"And if I can't get in? Not that I won't be able to, but we need to make it fair." The corner of his mouth curved into a cocky grin.

She reached a hand to his face and ran her fingers down the soft hair in his beard. "Then you have to give me whatever *I* want."

"Sounds like a win-win to me."

She ran her thumb across his lips, and tingling magic seeped into her skin, sending a jolt through her heart. "You're assuming we both want the same thing."

He pulled her close, taking her mouth with his. The evidence of his desire rubbed against her stomach, and she fought the urge to slide her hand between their bodies to feel it. He had to be the sexiest man alive—his body, his scent, his soul—everything about him ignited a fire inside her like an oven on full blast. There was enough heat between them to fuel her entire bakery.

As the kiss slowed, he released his hold and stepped back. "I think we do." He winked and strutted out the door.

She turned the lock and watched as Chase rummaged through the compartment on the side of his motorcycle. Small black bag in hand, he returned to the door, his smile prematurely triumphant.

He held up the kit. "I know how to unlock a door."

How many times had he broken into a building to hide supernatural evidence? He seemed confident he could break in here, so he must have had a lot of practice. He jimmied his tools into the lock, his brow puckering in concentration.

Rain laughed as his smile slipped into a frown. With a huff, he shoved his tools into his back pocket and crossed his arms. He jiggled the doorknob, but it didn't budge.

"Try to break a window," she called through the glass, not even attempting to hide her smile.

He narrowed his eyes. "I don't want to damage your business."

"What's wrong? Scared the big bad wolf won't be able to blow the house down? I've got insurance."

"Oh, now you're asking for it. Stand back." He grabbed a helmet and hurled it into the small, vertical window next to the door, but the glass didn't shatter. Instead, the helmet bounced off the magic force field Snow had created and slammed into Chase's stomach.

He groaned and stumbled to his bike to drop the helmet. "All right. You win."

Rain pressed her lips together and opened the door. "Satisfied of my safety now?"

"I suppose." He rubbed his abdomen as he entered the bakery, absently lifting his shirt to reveal a few ridges of muscle along his stomach. A bird tattoo occupied three inches of space above his left hip, and she was overcome with the urge to explore it with her tongue. To lick every inch of him.

She sucked in a deep, shuddering breath. "Since you have to go, I'll collect my prize later, when you have more time." She'd need at least a few hours to explore his body properly.

He grinned. "I'm looking forward to it. I work at the bar every night until Tuesday. Want to have that dinner date then?"

Running her hands up his chest, she rested them on his shoulders. "I'm not sure if I can wait that long to collect."

"I'm afraid you'll have to, *cher*, if the prize you're looking for is what I hope it is. I'll see you Tuesday." He gave her one last kiss on the lips and slipped out the door.

Rain stood at the window as Chase got on his bike and rode away. As soon as he was out of sight, she plopped into a chair and sighed. She was falling hard and fast for the sexy werewolf, and there wasn't a thing she could do to stop it.

CHAPTER TWELVE

RAIN FINISHED COUNTING THE MONEY IN THE CASH REGISTER, and her heart did a little sprint as she prepared the deposit. Once word spread that the alpha werewolf and his mate had chosen her bakery for their wedding cake, business had picked up within the magical community. Pack members had come trickling in over the week, buying desserts and placing orders.

Snow padded into the storefront from the kitchen. "Smiling while you're counting money. That's a good sign."

Rain zipped the money bag shut and leaned against the counter. "It is. I took an order for a five-year-old werewolf's birthday party this afternoon. When they come in tomorrow to pay, I'll have enough for the coven fees."

"Those werewolves are turning out to be a blessing." Snow grinned. "Especially one werewolf in particular."

Warmth spread through Rain's body. Chase had met her in the park for her lunch break every day since that amazing kiss, and tonight would be his first night off. Their first official date.

Snow rearranged the cupcakes in the display case, filling in the empty spaces with items from the back. "Where's he taking you?"

"To dinner." She clutched the bag to her chest.

Her sister straightened. "And then?"

The heat in her body crept up to her cheeks. "He said, 'We'll see where the night takes us.'"

Snow wiggled her eyebrows. "That sounds promising. Are you nervous?"

Rain forced a laugh. "Me? Nervous? He's a smokin' hot werewolf whose kisses make me feel like a fireworks display with a very short fuse. I have nothing to be nervous about."

Snow wiped the counter with a rag. "You're scared."

"Terrified." She toyed with the zipper on the bag. "I haven't been with a man since Isaac." Her heart sank, a feeling of apprehension settling in her stomach like day-old meatloaf. "It's been seven years."

"I'm sure he'll go easy on you."

"I don't think I want him to." She fanned herself with the bag. Her date with Chase couldn't come soon enough.

"I'm supposed to pick Rain up in an hour. Can't someone else cover the shift?" Chase lowered his voice, using his hand to cover the phone, so his niece wouldn't overhear his conversation with Bekah. He loved spending time with the little girl, but tonight was his date with Rain, and his sister was screwing up his plans.

"No one else can do it. I should be home in an hour and a half." Dishes clanked in the background. "You'll be thirty minutes late. She'll understand."

He ran a hand down his face, muffling his frustrated sigh. "Okay. Get your ass home as soon as possible."

"I love you, big brother." Her voice took on that sing-song tone it always did when she knew she owed him big-time. As a restaurant manager, her schedule tended to be erratic, but it was flexible enough to enable her to go to college at the same time. She'd be graduating at the end of the semester, so her dependence on Chase as a free babysitter should lighten up soon.

"I love you too." He hung up the phone and glanced at Emma sitting on the floor in the living room. She smiled and clapped as the

Beast in her favorite Disney movie transformed into a prince, and his heart swelled with love. There were worse reasons for being late.

He dialed Rain's number. "Hey, *cher*, I'm going to be a little late for our date tonight. Someone called in sick on Bekah, and she has to cover until they can find a replacement for the shift. I'm watching Emma until she gets home."

"How late do you think you'll be?" The disappointment was evident in her voice.

"Could be half an hour." He sighed. Might as well let her know what to expect from his sister. "Knowing Bekah, it could be more."

"I see." She paused. "I've already closed the shop. I could come over and keep you company…"

A pleasant ache spread through his chest, and he couldn't fight his smile. "That's a thoughtful offer, but I had better plans than babysitting for our first official date."

"I don't mind. Emma is fun, and I'd…like to spend as much time with you as possible tonight."

The ache extended through his core. "Come on over then. Emma will be happy to see you."

Emma's movie ended, and he made a game of cleaning up her toys, attempting to make the place somewhat presentable for Rain. His niece squealed when the doorbell rang, and he had to jump over the coffee table to get to the door before she opened it. A week had passed with no sign of the shadow demon, but he wasn't taking any chances when it came to Emma.

He put his hand on the knob. "What have we told you about opening the door for strangers?"

"It's not a stranger." She glared at him accusingly. "It's Rain."

"But we don't know that unless we look out the window, do we?" He lifted her so she could see through the glass at the top of the door.

"It's Rain. Let her in!" She kicked her legs until he set her on the floor, and she twisted the knob and swung open the door.

His fate-bound stood on the porch in jeans and a purple shirt. Her dark curls spiraled over her shoulders, and her lips curved into the most breathtaking smile he'd ever seen. She knelt to eye-level with his niece and hugged her before standing and kissing him on the cheek.

She stepped back and held his gaze as his heart galloped in his chest. "Are you going to stand there staring at me all evening, or are you going to invite me in?"

"Come in!" Emma tugged her through the doorway, and he followed them into the living room, where Rain settled onto the couch next to his niece.

"You be Belle, and I'll be the Beast." Emma handed Rain a doll and began setting up a scene of other toys on the coffee table.

Chase sank onto the sofa next to Rain. "You don't have to do that if you don't want to."

She scooted closer to him, so the length of her thigh rested against his, and held the doll up to her face. "I don't mind. She kinda looks like me, don't you think?"

He couldn't help himself. Emma had her back turned, so he leaned in and gave Rain a quick kiss. Everything this woman did wrapped him tighter around her finger. She was smart, independent, brave, and beautiful, and she was amazing with his niece. Even if his wolf hadn't claimed her the moment he met her, he wouldn't have been able to stop himself from falling for Rain. She was everything he never knew he wanted.

They played with Emma for the next half-hour, stealing glances at each other as Belle and Beast went on their adventure. Every time Rain's stormy eyes met his, his pulse quickened. His phone buzzed, and he dug it out of his pocket to find a text from Bekah. He bit back the curse that tried to slip from his lips and tossed the phone on the table.

"What's wrong?" Rain had moved to the floor during their play session, so she settled onto the sofa next to him.

"Bekah isn't going to be home until nine. I'm sorry. If you want to leave and reschedule, I understand." Damn his sister. She knew how important this date was to him.

Emma froze. "Don't leave."

Rain smiled at her. "I'm not going to." She laced her arm around Chase's bicep and kissed him on the cheek. "I'm having too much fun."

"Yay!" Emma leaped from the floor and scurried out of the room.

He arched an eyebrow skeptically. "Seriously?"

"I like spending time with you, and the anticipation of getting you alone will make it that much better when it happens." She ran a hand along his inner thigh, stopping halfway up.

His stomach tightened, and he took a deep breath, trying to control the urge to lay her back on the sofa and have his way with her right then and there. He leaned close and touched his lips to her ear. "The anticipation might be the death of me."

He nipped her lobe, and a visible shiver ran through her entire body as her grip tightened on his thigh.

"A little delayed gratification will be good for you." She rose as Emma shuffled into the room, her arms full of coloring books.

"I'm hungry, Uncle Chase."

"I guess I could feed you ladies dinner since we're stuck here all evening." He'd planned to take Rain to his favorite Italian restaurant in the Garden District. Then they'd go for a ride on his bike so he could feel her supple body against his, her arms wrapped around his waist. Something about having her on the back of his bike—and the fact she enjoyed riding it—turned him on to no end.

But it would have to wait. Delayed gratification, she'd called it. He planned to gratify her until she screamed his name.

He shook his head to chase away the thoughts. "How about a pizza?"

"I want mac and cheese." Emma dropped the coloring books on the kitchen table and dragged Rain to a chair.

He followed them into the kitchen. "Don't you think we should offer our guest something a little more...substantial than mac and cheese?"

His niece poked out her bottom lip. "But you make the best mac and cheese in the world. Don't you want to impress your girlfriend?"

He sucked in a breath to respond, but he couldn't get the words past the lump in his throat. He did consider Rain his girlfriend. Hell, he was on a mission to make her his mate, but they hadn't discussed the terms of their relationship yet. He caught Rain's gaze, preparing to apologize, but the look in her eyes stopped him cold.

So much heat emanated from her gaze that it felt like she'd

stripped him bare and made love to him with her eyes. Her full lips tugged into a sly smile, and when she slipped her tongue out to moisten them, his knees nearly buckled. "Yeah, Chase." She leaned back in the chair and crossed her arms. "Don't you want to impress your girlfriend?"

His heart slammed against his ribs. Was that a confirmation? "I…" *Get it together, man.* "Let me see if I have the ingredients." He turned around and opened the fridge, hoping the chilled air would cool the heat from his cheeks. It didn't.

He rummaged through the drawers and found the cheddar, gouda, and Colby jack, but the only meat they had in the house was hot dogs. He couldn't feed his *girlfriend* hot dogs.

With his arms full of ingredients, he shut the fridge door with his knee. "You ladies are in luck. I've got all the supplies for my world famous three-cheese mac and cheese, complete with hotdogs for the little one."

Emma stopped coloring and glared at him. "I'll share my hotdogs with Rain."

"That's okay." Rain patted her shoulder. "I'm a vegetarian. I don't eat meat."

Emma scratched her head as if the idea confounded her. "I eat meat. So does Uncle Chase. He catches deer and alligators and sometimes wild hogs…"

"Okay." He dropped a pot onto the stove, hoping the loud *clank* of metal on metal would stop his niece from going into the details of a werewolf diet. "Yes, I eat meat." He looked at Rain. "Is that going to be a problem?"

"I wouldn't expect a werewolf to be a vegetarian. In fact, I would find it rather strange if you were."

"Good." He held her gaze a little longer, building the anticipation, sweetening the gratification his sister had delayed. The things he planned to do to his girlfriend…

He busied himself with his culinary masterpiece, which wasn't much more than some melted cheese and heavy whipping cream mixed with elbow pasta, while Rain entertained his niece with the coloring books. Half an hour later, he carried three heaping bowls of mac and cheese to the table. "Take your stuff to the bedroom, squirt. It's time to eat."

Emma dutifully scooped up all the coloring books and crayons and scurried out of the kitchen as Chase sat in the seat next to Rain.

She picked up her fork and swirled it around in the bowl. "Smells delicious."

"I'm sorry it's not the romantic dinner I promised you."

She reached under the table to rest her hand on his knee. "You cooked for me. I call that romantic." She parted her lips and slipped the fork into her mouth, closing her eyes before sliding it out.

His mouth watered as her jaw flexed, the muscles in her throat moving up and down as she swallowed the food. The woman made eating mac and cheese look sexy. If his sister didn't come home soon so he could get Rain alone, he might spontaneously combust.

"I could be a jerk like you were and find something wrong with it…but I won't."

He chuckled. "I'd call suggesting I mate with a goat a jerk thing to say, but who am I to split hairs?"

She glared at him, but the corner of her mouth tugged into a grin. "It's the best mac and cheese I've ever eaten."

"I told you it was good." Emma climbed into her chair and tore into her dinner as if she hadn't eaten all day.

By the time they finished eating and washed the dishes, the front door swung open and Bekah strutted in. "I'm so sorry I'm late."

"Mommy!" Emma ran to her mom and hugged her.

"Let's go pack a bag," Bekah said. "We're having a sleepover at Grandma's."

Chase arched an eyebrow at his sister. "A sleepover?"

"I owed you one. Now we're even." She followed Emma into the bedroom.

He pulled Rain into his arms. "Finally, some alone time."

She laughed and gave him a quick kiss before pushing him away. "We aren't alone yet. Wait until Emma's gone."

"What?" He took both her hands in his and looked into her eyes. "It's good for her to see a man treating his girlfriend right."

"Hmm…" She stepped closer. "You think you're treating me right?"

He rested his forehead against hers. "Am I?"

She smiled. "So right."

"Okay, we are getting out of your hair." Bekah slung a bag over her shoulder and tugged Emma toward the front door.

"Here, Rain, this is for you." Emma handed her a picture from her coloring book.

"Thank you, Emma. That's so sweet of you." Rain took the page and showed it to Chase.

"It's Belle and the Beast," Emma said. "Like you and Uncle Chase."

"See you tomorrow, squirt." He mussed her hair as she passed.

Bekah and Emma left, and Rain leaned against the counter and set the picture on the surface. "Does your mom live close by?"

"She's got a place in Algiers. Not too far away."

She chewed her bottom lip and fidgeted with her hands as if being alone with him suddenly made her nervous. "Does she live by herself?"

"Yes." What happened to the flirtation and that promise of gratification?

"She never remarried? Or…" She furrowed her brow. "Was she not allowed to remarry? I'm not sure how it works with werewolves."

Ah, it was the girlfriend comment. Werewolf relationships could seem complicated to someone on the outside; he could understand her confusion. He leaned on the counter next to her. "When a werewolf takes a mate, it's for life. Since my dad died, she is allowed to find a new mate, but…" He took her hand, lacing his fingers through hers.

"But?"

"He was her fate-bound. If a werewolf gets the opportunity to mate with their fate-bound, no one else will ever do. That's a bond that can never be broken or replaced."

Something sparked in her eyes. They widened briefly, a look of… recognition…flashing in her gaze before she furrowed her brow. His pulse thrummed. Could she possibly feel the same bond that tied him to her more strongly every day?

Bringing his hand up to her lips, she kissed it. "What is a fate-bound?"

"A fate-bound is your soulmate. The one you're meant to be with forever. It's a feeling we get, deep within our souls, that we can't deny. Our wolves usually recognize it first." He chuckled. "Sometimes it takes our human minds a while to catch up."

"I see." She wrapped her arms around him, resting her head against his chest.

He held his breath, waiting for her to ask the question that had to be burning in her mind. Could he bring himself to tell her she was his if she asked? Would the truth scare her away?

She didn't speak. Instead, she hugged him tighter. Maybe she was afraid of what his answer would be.

He kissed the top of her head, and his tension eased. Maybe after a few more dates. He'd have to tell her eventually, and all he could do was hope she could love him in return. "It's early enough to go out if you want to catch a movie or something."

She inhaled deeply, running her hands up and down his back before leaning away to look at him. "Your sister went out of her way to give us privacy. It would be a shame to waste the opportunity…and I believe you owe me my prize for not being able to break Snow's protection spell."

"I like the way you think." Cupping her cheek in his hand, he ran his thumb over her velvet-soft skin. She nuzzled into his touch, closing her eyes, letting him pull her close.

She parted her lips slightly and angled her face toward his. That was all the invitation he needed. Tangling his fingers in her hair, he crushed his mouth to hers. She responded, opening her mouth to let him in, brushing her tongue against his. Heat flashed through his body as she melted into his embrace, wrapping her arms around him, holding him tight.

She felt so damn good in his arms, her silky hair tangled between his fingers. Ever since his niece had been born, dating— and women in general—had taken a backseat to responsibility. He'd quit sleeping around the moment he saw what the consequences could be. Making love to Rain wouldn't be sleeping around, though.

She was the only woman he wanted to be with for the rest of his life.

Standing in the kitchen, with her curvy body rubbing against his, her lips searing him with kisses, he couldn't deny himself anymore. He wanted this woman. He needed her.

Taking her face in his hands, he kissed her forehead, her cheek, her mouth. He parted his lips to ask if she wanted to join him the bedroom, but the words didn't get a chance to leave his throat before she tugged his shirt over his head and ran her palms down his chest.

"Nipple rings." She licked her lips. "Can I play with them?"

Good God. Who knew something as simple as the aroused look on her face could nearly bring him to his knees. "They're all yours."

She danced her fingers across his skin, taking each ring between her thumb and forefinger and tugging gently. Electricity shot from his nipples to his dick, hardening him even more.

"Does it hurt when I pull on them?" She tugged again, watching his face intently.

"No." Damn. Breathless already? "It feels good."

She grinned. "Really?" A wickedly mischievous look flashed in her dark-gray eyes, and she lowered her head to his chest and flicked out her tongue. Warm moisture bathed his right nipple, and he couldn't help but groan.

Biting her bottom lip in that oh so sexy way of hers, she glanced up at him before moving to his left nipple. She lifted the ring with her tongue, then sucked it into her mouth.

His breath caught in his throat, his entire body humming with desire. If she could get him this turned on by taking his shirt off, he was in for a wild ride.

She released his nipple and glided her tongue up his chest before straightening. "You're so sexy, Chase. Your tattoos and piercings… Your body alone is a ten, but then add in your personality, and…" She grinned. "You're a nice guy wrapped in a bad boy package. The best of both worlds."

His chest tightened. She knew everything about his past, yet she still found him attractive. How did he get so lucky? "I wasn't always a nice guy."

"But you are now." She focused on his tattoos, running her hands up and down his arms, tracing the lines on the drawings. "Our pasts don't define us. Who we are now is all that matters." She looked into his eyes, holding his gaze, waiting for confirmation.

"I agree."

She traced a finger up his arm, indicating his tattoos. "Do they all have meaning?"

"Some do; some don't." He held his arms in front of him and looked at the ink. Full-color drawings ranging from traditional flash art to custom-made designs joined together to create intricate sleeves on both arms. "A buddy of mine is a tattoo artist. When he was starting up, I let him practice on me."

Her gaze traveled up and down his arms as she traced her fingers along the art. "That's nice of you."

He shrugged. "He needed a canvas; I like ink. We take care of our own." Running his hands over her hips, he toyed with the hem of her shirt. "My turn." He tugged her shirt over her head and tossed it on the table before stepping back to admire her.

A lacey, emerald-green bra wrapped around her full breasts, accentuating her slender waist. His fingers twitched with the urge to touch her, so he lifted his hands slowly and reached for her. She inhaled deeply as he ran a finger over the top of her breast, tracing the contour of her bra. Goose bumps rose on her skin.

"You, Rain, are the epitome of sexy. A beautiful soul wrapped in an equally beautiful package."

The muscles in her throat worked as she swallowed. Then, she straightened her spine and unhooked her bra, letting it fall to the floor.

Her perfect breasts beckoned him to taste them, so he cupped them both in his hands, leaned down, and took her nipple into his mouth. She gasped and clutched the edge of the countertop, and he moved to the other breast, circling his tongue around her nipple, hardening it into a perfect, pink pearl before sucking it between his teeth.

A high-pitched mewling sound escape her throat, and he paused.

Straightening, he moved his hands to her shoulders and looked into her eyes. "Do you want to stop?"

"No. Goddess, no. It's..." She lowered her gaze before blinking up at him. "It's been a long time since anyone has touched me like this."

He pulled her close, and the feel of her soft, bare skin pressed to his nearly crumbled him. If the intensity of his emotions was any indication of what was to come, he might not survive making love to Rain. He hadn't known it was possible to *feel* this much. "It's been a long time since I've touched anyone like this. We'll take it slow."

She nodded and nuzzled into his chest.

He stood in the kitchen, holding her, letting the idea of what they were about to do sink in. This would be so much more than sex for him, but he only wanted it if she did too. "Do you want to move to the bedroom?"

She paused, going utterly still for a heartbeat or two before looking up at him. "I do."

He held her gaze, giving her ample opportunity to change her mind. "Are you sure?"

"I've wanted you since the moment I met you. Take me to bed."

"Yes, ma'am." He scooped her into his arms and carried her out of the kitchen. "This is what's called a shotgun house." He stepped into his sister's bedroom. "If you open all the doors, you could shoot a shotgun from the front door, and it would go all the way out the back door."

"Interesting."

"Problem is, we have to go through Bekah and Emma's room to get to mine. Not much privacy." He opened the door to his bedroom and carried her inside.

She grinned. "I guess you don't get a lot of action then."

He chuckled. "Not since Emma was born."

"Your sister taking her to your mom's was quite a gesture then."

He lowered her feet to the floor and kissed her before stepping toward his dresser. "She knows how I feel about you." He took a condom from the drawer and tossed it on the nightstand.

Rain sat on the bed and ran her hands over the comforter. "How do you feel about me?"

He looked at the beautiful woman on his bed, her breasts rising and falling with each breath she took, and he ached with emotion. The words nearly spilled from his lips, but he bit them back. It was too soon to tell her how strongly he felt. He stood in front of her and rested his hands on her shoulders. "You are the most amazing woman I've ever met."

"You're pretty amazing, yourself." She kissed his stomach, trailing her tongue down, past his navel, to his jeans. His stomach tensed, a fresh flood of desire rushing to his groin, and he tightened his grip on her shoulders.

Moving her hands to his hips, she traced a finger along the waistband of his pants. "I believe I'm supposed to decide if there's anything little about the werewolf I'm about to make love to."

"Be my guest."

She popped the button on his jeans and slid the zipper down. Pushing his pants to the floor, she stared at the bulge in his underwear, her pupils dilating with desire. "So far so good."

He couldn't take it anymore. Kicking his jeans aside, he tugged her to her feet. His dick ached to fill her. His wolf begged to claim her. Why the hell had he told her they'd take it slow?

She ran her hands over his body, and every muscle he had tightened with need. As she glided her palm over his underwear and gripped his dick through the fabric, he closed his eyes and let out his breath in a slow hiss.

"Take these off." She released her hold and stepped back, her gaze locking on his crotch.

He obeyed, dropping his underwear to the floor. Her eyes widened, and she wrapped her silky fingers around his cock and touched her lips to his ear. "Definitely nothing little about this werewolf." She gave him a stroke, and his entire body shuddered.

Holy hell, he had to have this woman. He took her in his arms and kissed her as if she were the water to his insatiable thirst. The air to his lungs.

She released her hold on his dick to grip his shoulders, tugging him on top of her as she fell to the bed. He moved against her, but the coarse fabric of her jeans wasn't the sensation he needed to feel.

Rolling to his side, he continued exploring her mouth with his tongue as he unbuttoned her jeans. Rising onto his knees, he tore his lips from hers to work her clothing over her hips and toss the remaining garments onto the floor.

The woman of his dreams lay in his bed, gloriously naked and reaching for him. "Make love to me, Chase. I need you."

He lay beside her and kissed her, trailing his lips down her neck, nipping at her collarbone, reveling in her intoxicatingly feminine scent. She smelled like a meadow, with a warm, cinnamony undercurrent that was all Rain.

Her breath hitched as he glided his hand down her stomach, and when he stroked her soft folds, she let out a satisfied "*Mmm.*" He slipped a finger inside her, and she moaned. She was tight and wet, and he couldn't hold back any longer.

Grabbing the condom from the nightstand, he tossed the wrapper aside and rolled the rubber down his shaft. She watched him as he moved on top of her and propped himself on his hands, her gaze never straying from his as he settled his hips between her legs and pressed himself against her opening.

Her eyes bore into his soul as he filled her, became one with her, and a deep shudder ran through his entire body. He lowered his chest to hers and held still, memorizing the way she felt wrapped around him, squeezing him. She held his body, heart, and soul in her arms.

He pulled out until only his tip remained inside her, and he roamed his lips over her shoulder, up her neck to find her mouth. Sliding back in slowly, he reveled in the way she gripped his back, the soft moans vibrating from her throat. He took his time making love to her, cherishing her.

He had to move slowly or the overwhelming emotions of joining with his fate-bound, giving himself to his soulmate, would've ended this way too soon. If he could have paused time and made this moment last forever, he would have. The tremor in his soul told him his wolf agreed.

"Oh, Chase. This feels so good." The breathless sound of his name on her lips thrilled him, and he couldn't help but increase his rhythm.

She arched her back to take him deeper as he thrusted harder, his need growing stronger.

She hooked her legs behind his thighs and gripped his ass, guiding him faster and harder until she tossed her head back and let out the most beautiful moan he'd ever heard. She quivered around him, invoking her goddess and his name in the same breath.

He let go, giving himself to her. His orgasm exploded through his entire body as he pumped his hips, wave after wave of searing ecstasy burning through his veins. No woman had ever felt so good, so perfect in his arms.

As his climax subsided, he rose onto his elbows to look at his fate-bound. She *would* be his mate. She had to be. His wolf had claimed her, and now it felt as if an unbreakable cord ran from his heart to hers.

Her brow furrowed. Did she feel the strange connection too? Taking his face in her hands, she looked at him with a fierceness in her eyes. "You are mine."

She had no idea…

CHAPTER THIRTEEN

A JEALOUS RAGE BOILED INSIDE ISAAC AS HE TRUDGED AWAY from the werewolf's house. He ground his teeth as thoughts of *his* Rain spending the night with that creature plowed through his mind, digging up long-buried emotions he'd rather not remember.

He'd needed to get a glimpse of her, to see her with his own eyes. Could he possibly care for the woman after what she'd done to him?

Apparently, he could because the need to possess her gripped his chest, tightening his lungs until he couldn't breathe. Ducking into the shadows, he leaned against a wall and pressed a hand to his heart. The sluggish muscle beat lightly against his breast, when it should have been pounding.

Why hadn't he stuck to the plan? A week in the swamp would have been enough time to recover and implement his scheme. But he'd had to see her. *Idiot.*

After the energy he'd expended to satisfy his whim, he'd be forced to drain someone. He couldn't stand to spend another week in the putrid swamp when he was this close to getting his revenge.

His spine cracked as he straightened and pushed from the wall. Closing his eyes, he shut out the world, ignoring his senses and focusing on his tulpa. A mass of static energy buzzed before him, pricking at his skin as the entity took shape.

Peeling his heavy lids open, he gazed at his greatest creation. *Find me a witch. A beautiful one.* If Rain could give herself to another man, Isaac would take another woman.

The tulpa darted ahead of him, slinking through the shadows as it made its way toward Frenchman Street and its eclectic live music venues. He knew of one club in particular that drew a large supernatural crowd—a prime hunting ground for his next taste of life.

Isaac followed his creation, his dirty clothes and the smell of swamp that lingered on his skin causing people to keep a wide berth around him. A woman looked at him with sympathy and muttered something about too many homeless people, and a sinking sensation formed in his stomach. Rain would be repulsed to see him in this condition.

A groan rumbled in his throat. Why did he care?

Dragging his mind back to the mission, he focused on the entity, sending it his thoughts and connecting on a telepathic level. Though the vision was hazy, as if looking through smoke, Isaac could see with the tulpa's eyes. The shadow figure would need a face—a handsome man, tall and strong. Isaac's lip split as he smiled, and coppery blood trickled between his teeth. He found one who would do.

The man leaned against a wall and fiddled with a matchbook, attempting to light a cigarette, while his friend tossed a beer can into the trash. The tulpa moved like lightening, zipping through the darkness to rest a shadowy hand against its prey's cheek. The man's face fell slack. His shoulders drooped, and his friend barely caught him by the arm before he crumpled to the ground.

"What the hell? Did you see that?"

The man moaned in response.

The tulpa continued toward the club, its form wavering, rolling in on itself until it replicated the man's appearance. Isaac followed, curling his cracked lip at the man as his friend tried to drag him to his feet. The temptation to stop and finish him off gave Isaac pause. If he could take on the bastard's good looks by draining him like his tulpa could, he might have done it.

Instead, he ducked into the alley behind the club and cleared his mind. Through the smoky haze of the tulpa's vision, he searched the room for a beautiful witch to replace his Rain. Though muffled through the entity's senses, the music pulsed and vibrated as bodies writhed on the dancefloor. The tulpa slinked into the crowd, running its hand along the arms of its potential conquests, searching their skin for the magical electricity of a witch.

Through the tulpa's gaze, Isaac spotted dark curls bobbing across the dancefloor, and his throat tightened. He stumbled up the alley toward the door, the excitement that his Rain had left the werewolf driving him forward.

The woman turned, and he halted, the exertion sucking the air from his lungs. Even through the haze, her dark-brown eyes were unremarkable. While the woman held a certain attractiveness, she wasn't Rain.

How dare she have the audacity to resemble his woman? He urged the tulpa forward, and as it stroked her arm, her magical signature danced across the entity's borrowed skin.

The tulpa put a hand on her hip, moving its own in time with the music, and desire sparked in the woman's eyes as she ran a hand up the entity's shoulder. Isaac's jaw clenched. Rain had once looked at him that way.

Bring her to me. Isaac groaned and dissolved the connection, allowing the tulpa to do what was necessary to lead the woman to her doom. There would be no enjoyment in this victim. She deserved her fate for stirring these unwelcome emotions in his soul.

A giggle echoed from the alley entrance, and the woman appeared, her arms draped around the tulpa's shoulders. "Where are we going?" She buried her face in the entity's neck, and from this view, she looked so much like Rain, Isaac's heart missed a beat.

He closed his eyes and focused on the feel of her body pressed against the tulpa. The sensation felt distant, more like a memory, and when her nose glided along the entity's neck as she lifted her head, visions of Rain swam behind Isaac's eyes.

His knuckles cracked as he clenched his fists, and pain shot through his temple. Between his fatigue and the anger rolling through his system, his knees buckled beneath his weight. He leaned against the wall and scowled as the tulpa coaxed the woman deeper into the alley.

"Let's go back to the club." The first hint of fear raised her voice an octave as she tried to wiggle from the entity's embrace.

The tulpa tightened its grip and lifted her from the ground.

"What are you doing?" Panic laced her words as the tulpa carried her toward him. "Put me down!"

As she sucked in a breath to scream, Isaac took her face in his hands and gazed into her dark-brown eyes. Her life energy flowed through his fingers, spiraling up his arms to fill his body.

The woman froze, the frantic rhythm of her heart pumping her lifeforce into his veins. She clawed at his hands, but her strength faded quickly, her breathing growing shallow until a whisper left her lips. "Why?"

"Why, indeed?" Isaac's spine straightened as her energy spiraled through his body, mending his splitting bones, repairing his deteriorating muscles. Her lifeforce was strong, but unlike his Rain, her magic was weak.

The witch's skin shriveled on her bones, her eyes growing distant before the light in them extinguished. Shoving the empty body into his tulpa's arms, Isaac rolled his shoulders and cracked his neck.

"What a waste." Once again, he'd let his emotions rule, and he'd ruined his shot at draining a powerful witch. This one could barely cast a clarity spell, much less harness the amount of magic he'd need to defeat a werewolf.

He hadn't planned on leaving a trail of bodies in his wake, but he'd have to find someone stronger. Someone whose magic was worthy.

Making use of his temporary strength, he lifted the body from the tulpa's arms and tossed it into the dumpster. With any luck, he'd have Rain in his grasp before the rest of the witches caught on to his plan.

Dead or alive, she would be his again. Soon.

CHAPTER FOURTEEN

Rain woke with a strange sense of calm. Of security. She lay on her side, her back cradled into Chase's front, his arms wrapped tightly around her. A ceiling fan whirred from above, sending a cooling breeze onto the sheets, but the warmth of her werewolf kept the chill away.

Her werewolf.

What had come over her last night to claim him like she did? To tell him he was hers, as if he had no choice in the matter? Her pulse quickened, the flutter of a thousand butterflies taking flight like they had when he hadn't denied she was his girlfriend.

Everything about this moment felt right. Her lips curved into a smile. She could see herself spending forever with this man. This felt…real. So different from the way she'd felt with Isaac.

She'd been so desperate for Isaac's attention. Always worrying if he wanted her. Never feeling like she was enough.

With Chase, she didn't worry. He wore his emotions openly. In the way he looked at her. How he touched her. She'd grown up since her battle with her ex, and she'd never stoop to using a spell to harm someone again.

But she *had* harmed Isaac. She'd killed him.

Her stomach sank. Would Chase feel the same about her if he knew what she'd done? She had two choices: either tell him the truth now before she got in too deep or keep her mouth shut and pray that he never found out.

Rolling onto her other side, she lay face to face with him.

Her movement roused him from sleep, and he opened his eyes and smiled. "Good morning, beautiful. How did you sleep?"

"Good." The best sleep of her life. "I need to tell you something."

"Hmm…" He rolled on top of her and nuzzled into her neck, trailing his lips up to her earlobe and raising goose bumps on her arms. "Is it that you think your mind is playing tricks on you? That there's no way the sex last night was that amazing and you need to do it again, just to be sure?"

He kissed his way down her throat and circled his tongue around the dip in the center of her collar bone. "If that's what you need, I'm happy to oblige."

She could have lain there all day letting Chase cover her body in kisses. The softness of his lips followed by the tickle of his beard on her skin. The warmth of his tongue on her breast as he sucked her nipple into his mouth. Her will almost crumbled. "You might not want to after what I need to tell you."

He paused and looked at her. "That sounds serious."

As she opened her mouth to spill her awful truth, his phone rang from somewhere on the floor. He ignored it, focusing instead on her. "Is something wrong?"

She couldn't force the confession over the lump in her throat. "Aren't you going to answer your phone?"

"I suppose I should." He sighed and rolled off her, reaching for his jeans and digging through the pockets until he retrieved the phone. It had stopped ringing, but his sister's name lit up the screen as a missed call. "Why the hell is Bekah calling this early in the morning?" He sat up, furrowing his brow at the phone. "I better call her back." He ran his fingers down Rain's cheek and smiled his heart-melting smile. "Give me a sec."

She nodded as he pressed the button to return his sister's call.

"You rang?" He paused and listened, his grin falling into a scowl as his sister spoke. "They don't know what's wrong?"

Another pause, and he clutched Rain's hand in his. "Do you know where Tommy is? Surely he'd be willing to see you again to heal his daughter."

His shoulders drooped. "No. I suppose you're right. Bastard." He looked at Rain, and the brightness returned to his eyes. "I think I know another witch who can help. Hang tight. I'll be there as soon as I can."

Chase stood and gathered their clothes. "I'm sorry, *cher*, we're going to have to finish our conversation later. Emma's in the hospital."

Rain's heart thrummed in her chest as the pieces of the conversation began clicking into place. "What's wrong with her?"

He laid her clothes on the bed and put on his jeans. "They don't know. High fever. Vomiting. She's dehydrated and barely conscious."

Her throat tightened. "You mentioned Tommy…her father?"

"Yeah. Let me get your shirt." He paced into the kitchen and returned with the rest of her clothes.

Rain put on her pants and turned her shirt right side out. "How could her father heal her? Is he…" A sickening feeling swirled in her stomach, creeping its way up to her throat. "Is he a witch?"

Chase pulled his shirt over his head. "Yeah, but Bekah hasn't heard from him since he left her. He has decent healing abilities, but maybe Snow can make one of her potions, like the one you gave me?"

She sank onto the edge of the bed. *No, no, no.* This couldn't be happening. "Emma's half-witch?"

"Yeah, but…" His eyes widened. "Your…No, it wasn't your curse."

"It was, Chase. It is." She yanked her shirt down over her head and shoved her feet into her shoes. "She colored that picture for me. *Beauty and the Beast*, remember? She gave it to me…in kindness. She was kind to me, and now she's suffering for it."

He dropped his arms to his sides. "But she's a kid."

"So? She's a witch. That's what matters." She stood and paced to the living room. This was her fault. She'd let her guard down. Gotten close. And now a sweet little girl was suffering because she'd been careless with her curse.

"Rain, wait." Chase followed her. "This is not your fault."

She whirled around to face him. "No? Then whose fault is it? It's *my* curse. My burden."

"It's my fault." He caught her hand. "I'm to blame. I never told you her dad was a witch."

"Why didn't you?"

He squeezed her hand and let it go, a pained expression puckering his brow. "I don't know. It never crossed my mind. When I told you she was half-werewolf, I guess I assumed…I don't know." He let out a hard breath. "I'm sorry. I…this is one hundred percent my fault."

"No. It's mine. I've lived with this curse for seven years; I should know better. I assumed she was half-human when I should have asked." She was stupid and irresponsible, and now poor Emma had to pay the price.

"Look, we can argue over whose fault it is later. Do you think Snow will make a healing potion?"

She swallowed the sour taste from her mouth. "You'll have to ask her yourself. She can't do it for me."

Confusion clouded his eyes. "She did it for you when I was sick."

"She did that on her own. We've found loopholes…ways to get around the curse. I told her you were sick, but I didn't ask for her help. She made the potion on her own and made it very clear when she gave it to me that she did it for you, not for me."

He grabbed his keys from the counter and opened the door. "I'll ask her then. We'll take care of Emma. Come on."

She followed him outside to his bike. "My car is parked down the road." She texted him Snow's number. "You'll have to call Snow and ask her to meet us at the bakery."

"Okay." He fished his phone from his pocket, and Rain hurried to her car.

She started the engine and headed to the bakery before Chase finished his phone call and mounted his bike. What had she been thinking getting that close to him and his family? She'd been concerned about *him* having witch blood somewhere along the lines, but the thought that his niece might had never even crossed her mind.

Selfish. That was what she'd been. Only thinking of herself and her desires for Chase. So much for learning to lead a selfless life. This was why she didn't get close to people.

Parking in the alley behind the building, she shook her head as she climbed out of the car and slammed the door. Seven years. After the initial shock and the realization of how swiftly her curse worked, she'd spent the past seven years avoiding friendships like they were…well, a curse.

And then Chase came along with his hot body and tender touch, and her brain checked out, letting her hormones take over.

No more.

Her hands trembled as she fumbled with the lock and let herself in. The shop didn't open for another four hours, but she heated the ovens and took the dough and batter from the fridge to prepare the day's offerings.

Snow and Chase would handle the potion, and as much as Rain wanted to go to the hospital to comfort Emma, she couldn't. She could never see the little girl again. It wasn't worth the risk. How could she explain to a six-year-old that she was suffering because she'd done something nice for a cursed witch?

She couldn't, and the only way to make certain she wasn't a threat to Emma was to stop seeing Chase. Her heart wrenched at the thought of never feeling his strong arms wrapped around her again. But this was the way it had to be. She never should have tried to be with him in the first place.

A knock sounded on the front door, and she shuffled into the storefront to let Chase in. Snow wouldn't be far behind. She opened the door and stepped aside for him to enter, shutting it when he crossed the threshold.

He faced her, concern furrowing his dark brow. "We're going to fix this."

She wrung her hands and nodded, biting her bottom lip to hold back the tears. Thankfully, Snow stepped through door, saving her from having to answer.

She strutted past them toward the kitchen, waving a hand for them to follow her. "Give me ten minutes and I'll whip something up. What are her symptoms again?"

"Fever, vomiting, dehydration, but they've got her hooked up to an IV."

Snow grimaced. "Sounds like what happened to me that time I made a cake for your birthday."

The first tear rolled down her cheek. "I know."

Chase cupped her face in his hand, wiping the tear away with his thumb. "Hey, look at me." He stooped to catch her gaze. "I am taking full responsibility for this. You didn't know, so it's not your fault."

"It doesn't matter. I should have asked. I should have made sure."

Snow cleared her throat and busied herself with the potion, mixing eucalyptus with mango leaves and other healing herbs before reciting the spell and bottling the mixture. "Here you go." She handed it to Chase. "Don't expect it to work as fast as it did on you, though. If she hasn't come into her werewolf self-healing abilities yet, it's going to take at least a day for the full effect."

Chase pocketed the potion and took Rain's hand. "We better get this to Emma." He stepped toward the storefront, but Rain didn't budge. "Emma will want to see you."

"She can't. I'm too dangerous. It's best if she never sees me again."

He pressed his lips into a line and let out a sigh. "We'll figure something out. We can coach her on how to act around you so it doesn't happen again. We'll make a game out of it. She likes games."

Her throat tightened. "No. *We* won't do anything. It's best if you never see me again either."

The pain in his eyes tore at her heart. "Don't say that. I belong to you, remember? You told me so last night." He smiled weakly.

"I know what I said, but that was before..." She sighed. "I was careless, and a little girl is hurt because of it. She lives with you. She's family. I'm just a dud witch with a curse to keep me alone for the rest of my life."

"Rain." He reached for her, but she backed away.

"I'm sorry, Chase. Go to Emma. She needs you."

Snow glared at her with a look that said she'd be hearing from her later. "I'll go with you, Chase." She brushed past Rain and stomped out of the kitchen.

He pulled his keys from his pocket. "I'm going to find a way to break your curse. This isn't over."

She sucked in a shaky breath. "I'm afraid it is."

He shook his head and followed Snow out of the bakery.

Chase mounted his bike and slammed his helmet onto his head. He'd had a taste of his fate-bound mate, and he'd be damned if he would let some curse stand between them.

Snow opened her car door. "What hospital? I'll meet you there."

"Tulane."

She nodded and climbed into her Mazda. Chase revved his engine and peeled away from the store, leaving a black mark on the ground where his tire had spun. Childish? Yeah. But he was losing his fate-bound. He wasn't thinking straight.

His pulse thrummed in his ears as he wove through traffic on Basin Street and turned into the hospital parking lot. He'd help his niece. As soon as her condition stabilized, he'd go back to Rain and convince her they were meant to be together.

Why hadn't he thought to mention the fact that his niece was half-witch? He didn't care if he got hurt or sick. Nothing short of death could keep him away from the woman he loved, but he'd only been thinking about himself. He hadn't considered the effects his fate-bound could have on others. *Who's the asshole now?* He paced across the parking garage and jabbed the button for the elevator.

"Chase, wait up." Snow trotted across the pavement and stood next to him. "What did your niece do for Rain?"

"She gave her a picture she colored of *Beauty and the Beast*. Said it was Rain and me."

Snow smiled. "Aw, that's so sweet."

And she'd made their relationship official when he hadn't had the balls to bring it up. He'd always be grateful to his niece for that. "Sweet enough to land her in the hospital, apparently."

Her smile faded. "It wasn't *that* big of a kindness. I'm sure she'd recover fine on her own, but the potion will speed it up."

He slipped his hand into his pocket and toyed with the vial. "Thanks for this."

"My pleasure."

The elevator dinged, and the doors *whooshed* open, sending a gust of chilled air into his face. They rode the contraption to the third floor and paced down the hall to room 3C.

Emma lay in the bed, looking tiny and helpless, her dark hair matted to her forehead, her skin taking on an ashen pallor. Bekah sat in a chair next to her, holding her hand and softly singing "Belle" from *Beauty and the Beast*, Emma's favorite song. Chase had watched the movie with his niece so many times, he was tempted to sing along. Anything to make Emma feel better.

When his sister reached the end of the verse, she looked up at him.

"This is Snow, Rain's sister."

Bekah smiled weakly. "Frozen bubbles?"

"That's me," Snow said.

He took the spell from his pocket. "She made a healing potion. Like the one Rain brought over to me when I was down. It should speed up her recovery." He handed it to Bekah.

She took the vial and gently shook Emma awake. "Here, sweetie, you need to drink this. It will help you feel better."

Emma's eyes fluttered halfway open. Her dry lips stuck together at first, but she peeled them apart and let her mom pour the potion into her mouth.

"I can cool her fever." Snow held up her hands. "I did it for Rain when she was little. It won't hurt her."

Bekah gave her a confused look. "Like you froze the bubbles?"

"I won't freeze her. Just cool her down a little."

Chase stepped toward the bed. "You can trust her." He never imagined that phrase would pass from his lips when speaking about a witch, but he meant every damn word of it.

Bekah nodded, and Snow pressed her hands against Emma's forehead. She whispered something that rhymed—a spell, he assumed—and slid her palms down his niece's arms before resting them on her chest, her stomach, her legs. She repeated the movements three times and touched Emma's forehead with the back of her hand. "Should be 98.6 now. You can call in a nurse to take her temperature if you want."

Bekah placed her palms against Emma's cheeks. "Incredible. You've been so kind. Thank you."

"I'm glad I could help."

Chase shoved his hands into his pockets. "Speaking of kindness…" He nodded to Emma. "She's sick because of me."

Bekah furrowed her brow. "Full werewolves don't get viruses. She didn't catch this from you."

"She's sick because she was kind to Rain." He explained the curse, making sure to put all the blame on himself for not telling Rain that Emma was half-witch. "She never would have come over to babysit if she'd known."

"She feels terrible," Snow added. "My sister is very conscious about her curse. She won't let it happen again."

"I see." Bekah lowered her gaze and stared at her daughter. "It doesn't make sense." She motioned for Chase to move closer and whispered in his ear, "Fate wouldn't make you choose between your family and your soulmate would it?"

He tried to respond, but he couldn't get enough air into his lungs. Choose between his fate-bound and his family? It was an impossible decision, but it seemed he'd be forced to make it.

When he didn't answer, Bekah straightened her spine. "I'm sorry to say this, but as long as she's cursed, she can't be around Emma."

"I know."

"Emma is family, and she's pack. She's not going to stay home all the time because Rain is around."

He held her gaze. He knew exactly what his sister was saying. Family and the pack came first. Rain would have to be the one staying home, missing out on pack gatherings. Who knew how many other weres had witch blood flowing through their veins? He'd be putting his pack in danger by taking Rain as his mate.

Sharp pain flashed through his heart, and he placed a hand against his chest to rub it away. He looked at Snow. "Isn't there a way to break the curse?"

Snow's eyes tightened. "She hasn't talked to you about that?"

"No." If she had, he'd be doing everything in his power to break the damn thing.

"She needs…" Snow inhaled deeply, pressing her lips into a hard line. "She needs to commit an ultimate act of selflessness."

His head spun. Could she be any vaguer? "What does that mean? She needs to give her life to save someone?"

"No. If she gave up her life, that would defeat the purpose of breaking the curse, don't you think?" She laced her fingers together and gave him a strange look. Was it pity? Hope? She looked like she wanted to say something, and if she didn't spit it out, his head might explode.

"What then?" he said through clenched teeth. "What does she have to do?"

Snow deflated. "I don't know. She's become the most selfless person I know. She's reined in her temper. She gives, volunteers. Nothing has worked so far, but…" Her expression turned pained.

"But what?"

"You need to talk to her about it. Maybe the two of you can figure it out together."

"Uncle Chase?" Emma's voice sounded tiny. "Where's Rain?"

With two purposeful strides, he moved to the bedside and brushed the hair from his niece's face. The color was already returning to her cheeks, and she managed a weak smile. "She couldn't make it, squirt, but Snow is here."

"Hi, Emma." Snow waved from the foot of the bed.

Emma's smile widened. "When Rain becomes my aunt, will you be my aunt too?"

"Emma…" her mother chided. "Grown-up relationships are complicated."

She huffed. "Rain is going to be Uncle Chase's mate, Momma, and then she'll be my aunt."

A lump the size of a cantaloupe wedged into his throat. He could only hope. But as long as she was cursed, he didn't see how…

Snow suppressed a smile. "What makes you say that?"

"They love each other."

Warmth spread through his body. He obviously loved Rain. His wolf had made up his mind the moment he met her. The thought that she might already love him too sent his heart racing. Sometimes kids were more perceptive than adults.

Snow laughed. "What makes you say *that?*"

Emma sighed and rolled her eyes. "A girl just knows these things."

Snow arched an eyebrow at Chase. "A girl does, doesn't she?"

He raked a hand through his hair. A guy knew too. Fate would not send him a mate he couldn't be with. He had to figure out a way to break the curse. He pinched Emma's cheek. "How you feeling, squirt?"

"Better. The medicine tasted like bubblegum."

He looked at Snow. "Did you make the same potion you gave me? Mine tasted like honey."

"It tastes like whatever you need it to taste like. Does whatever it needs to do. That's how magic works."

That was how he worked too. He would do whatever he needed to do to keep his family and his pack safe *and* save the woman he loved from a curse. "What will you tell the doctors when she mysteriously recovers?"

Bekah shrugged. "They have no idea what's wrong with her. I doubt it's the first mystery illness they've encountered."

"I'm going to head to the bakery and see if I can talk some sense into my sister." Snow patted Emma's leg. "Take care of yourself, little one."

"I'll be there shortly." Chase nodded at Snow. "Thanks for your help."

He stayed at the hospital for a few more hours to make sure Emma's condition improved before heading to the parking garage. Hopefully Snow would have calmed Rain down by the time he got to the bakery. Seeing so much pain in her eyes had torn him to pieces.

CHAPTER FIFTEEN

RAIN SLIPPED HER HANDS INTO A PAIR OF OVEN MITTS AND pulled a tray of fresh-baked clarity cookies from the oven. Setting it on the counter, she dropped the mitts in a drawer and stared at the plain, beige treats. If she were to eat one now, before they were frosted, she could focus the effects on anything she wanted.

She chewed on her lip. Sliding a spatula beneath a warm cookie, she lifted it from the platter. Her breathing grew shallow as she gazed at the spellbound treat, and she let it fall back to the tray. *Don't be an idiot, Rain.*

She'd made the right decision about Chase; she didn't need a cookie to confirm it. Putting his family and his pack in danger wasn't a risk she wanted to take. No matter how much her heart ached to be with him, she couldn't. Even if he figured out a way to balance his time between her and his pack, she couldn't ask him to make that sacrifice.

Of course, if he gave her two drops of his blood, her curse would be broken and he wouldn't have to divide his time. But after everything he'd been through…asking him to give her a sacred part of himself, to break his pack laws and risk who-knew-what kind of punishment…she couldn't do that to him. What good would it be to have her curse broken but lose the trust of the man who'd broken it?

The door chimed, signaling a customer, and Snow's heels clicked across the tiles as she entered the kitchen. "Ingrid is here. She wants the rent."

"She told me she was coming for it tomorrow." Rain rolled her eyes. Leave it to Ingrid to insist on getting paid early. Though, the check was already late, so she couldn't blame her. "I'll bring it out to her. Can you take care of these cookies?"

"Sure thing."

Rain snatched the rent check from a drawer and padded into the storefront, but she stopped short at the sight of the person standing by the window. To the naked eye, the woman appeared to be Ingrid. She had the same red hair and slim build, but her aura was off.

Really off.

All witches' auras glowed a shade of magenta. Some leaned more toward deep purple, while others could be light pink depending on the level of their power, and Ingrid's aura usually had a dark, rosy radiance. This woman's aura didn't glow at all. Instead, a dull gray, almost mist-like form hovered around her body.

"Ingrid?"

Her landlord turned around. "I'm here for the rent check." She looked like Ingrid, but her voice…her expression…wasn't quite right.

Rain forced a smile. "How was your trip? Did you get home today?"

"I'm here for the rent check." She blinked rapidly, plastering a fake smile on her face. She never smiled at her.

Rain's pulse thrummed. This wasn't the Ingrid she knew. "You told me where you went, but I can't remember. Was it Cancun?"

"I'm here for the rent check." *Blink. Blink. Blink.*

A chill crept up her spine to pool at the top of her head. What if this wasn't Ingrid at all? Could demons shapeshift? Chase had mentioned they hadn't found the shadow he'd seen by the river. Maybe it had been hiding, gathering its energy so it could catch Rain alone and…what? Collect a rent check? It didn't make sense. If whatever had taken on Ingrid's form wanted Rain dead, it would have killed her by now.

Unless this really was Ingrid, and the demon possessed her, using her until her magic and energy were drained before moving on to the next host. And since Rain's magic was bound, the demon didn't deem her a potential target.

But Snow would be...

She shoved the check into her pocket. Whether or not this was really Ingrid's body, the entity in control was not her landlord. "I'll bring the money by tomorrow. It's locked in the timed safe, and I can't open it again until morning."

Ingrid stared at her blankly as if she only knew how to speak the single sentence.

Dread trickled from the base of Rain's skull down the length of her spine. "Will that be okay, Ingrid?"

She opened her mouth, and her lips trembled as she fought to form an *O* shape. "Okay." Her scratchy voice sounded forced. Not at all like Ingrid. She nodded and shuffled out the door.

Ingrid didn't shuffle; she always walked with purpose. Rain watched as she made her way down the sidewalk and disappeared from view.

What the hell was going on?

An image of the dead witch flashed in her mind. Could Isaac have summoned a demon and sent it after Rain? Not unless he'd summoned it from the grave. *Stop being ridiculous.* Seeing that body in the morgue was affecting her more than she'd thought. Isaac wasn't the only energy vampire to ever exist, and if he were alive, he wouldn't send a demon after Rain.

He'd want to kill her himself.

Rain yanked her phone from her pocket and dialed Ingrid's number. It rang five times before going to voicemail. She hung up without leaving a message.

What if this was an effect from her curse? Could Ingrid be deliriously ill because of her? No, she hadn't shown her kindness. She hadn't spoken to her in a week.

Rain dialed her number again. No answer.

Snow carried the tray of cookies from the kitchen and put them in the display case. "Rent's all paid?"

"Did Ingrid seem…off to you?"

"She wasn't her usual cheerful self." Snow winked. "She told me she was here for the rent check, so I came to find you. That's all she said to me. Is something wrong?"

What if she were dead? Rain couldn't live with herself knowing she'd been the last person to see Ingrid. Knowing she could have—should have—done something to help her.

"Her aura was off. I'm going to go check on her." She grabbed her keys and headed out the back door. A chill ran through her body as she climbed into her car and drove to Ingrid's house, a sure sign something was awry. A cyclist darted out on Esplanade, and Rain slammed her brakes to avoid a crash. She needed to calm down, but the closer she got to Ingrid's house the more thoughts swirled through her mind.

Focusing on the scenery, she took in the nineteenth-century mansions painted in shades of peach, lavender, and blue. White columns led up to second-story galleries, where colorful flags and plants adorned the buildings. Giant oaks towered from the neutral ground, the grassy median separating the opposing flow of traffic, and created a canopy over the street.

She accelerated, and the mansions gave way to smaller, more modest houses. Hanging a left on North Miro, she navigated through the neighborhood and found her landlord's home. Ingrid's car sat in the short driveway, and all the shutters were drawn.

Parking on the curb, she darted up the front steps and knocked on the door. "Ingrid?" Her hands trembled, so she clenched them into fists as the lock disengaged and Ingrid opened the door.

Ingrid squinted as she peered between the door and the jamb. "Rain? What are you doing here?"

"Are you okay?" Did she not remember coming to the bakery at all?

She opened the door wider. Her disheveled hair hung tangled over her shoulder, and indentions from a pillow marred one side of her face. Though her purple button-up had appeared freshly-ironed when she'd arrived at the shop, creases now zigzagged across it as if she'd lain in the same position for hours. "I've felt better. I must be coming down with the flu."

Rain's throat thickened. "Does your entire body ache? Like you've had the life drained out of you?"

Ingrid rolled her head from side to side, stretching her neck. "Yeah. Is something going around?"

That was the same way Rain had felt after Isaac stole her energy, but she'd always awoken coherent. The way Ingrid had acted that afternoon had seemed like it wasn't her. "Any other symptoms?"

She narrowed her eyes. "Not that it's any of your business, but I might be having hallucinations too. I thought I saw a shadow."

Rain clutched the doorframe. "A shadow?"

"Yeah. I was lying on the couch, and I heard a shuffling sound. Then this shadow appeared in front of me, and it touched my face. I must have been dreaming. I woke up when you knocked on the door, and now I feel like shit."

Rain tugged the crumpled check from her pocket and tried to keep a neutral expression. "Here's the rent. I'm sorry I woke you. I hope you feel better soon."

"Thanks." Ingrid took the money and shut the door as Rain darted to her car.

Collapsing into the driver's seat, she leaned her head against the headrest to stop the spinning sensation. Someone drained Ingrid's energy and then took on her form. It was the only explanation. She let out a slow breath and started the engine.

Rain drove to the bakery and double-checked the locks on all the doors and windows. As long as they remained engaged, Snow's charm would keep evil out of her space. If the demon decided to come back for her, it wouldn't be able to get inside unless she let it in.

She hung a sign in the door that read *please ring bell for entry* and shuffled behind the counter. Keeping the door locked wasn't the best for business, but at least she could check out the customers' auras before she invited them in.

Snow glanced at the sign and gave her a quizzical look. "We're screening customers now?"

"Ingrid wasn't okay. Something drained her energy."

Snow's mouth dropped open. "Isaac?"

Rain shook her head. "Isaac didn't do it, nor any other witch. Ingrid said she saw a shadow right before she passed out. Whatever came to the bakery wasn't our landlord; it was a shapeshifter."

Snow's shoulders relaxed as she let out her breath. "Didn't you and Chase see a shadow by the river last week?"

"He assumed it was a demon targeting him, but it sounds like it's targeting witches."

"Why would a demon be hunting witches?"

"I don't know, but it seems more probable than possible at this point, don't you think? *Something* is draining witches' energy."

Snow nodded. "I hate to say it, but I'd rather it be a demon on the loose than to think Isaac has returned from the grave."

She let out a slow breath. "*I* hate to say it, but I agree."

Snow's brow knit. "Why did it come here? Are we its next targets?"

"That's what I thought at first, but if it drained Ingrid's life force, it probably got a glimpse into her mind. And knowing Ingrid, she was thinking about getting the money, convincing herself she wasn't showing kindness by not evicting me immediately."

"So it took some of Ingrid's energy, took on her form, and showed up here because that was what she'd been thinking about?"

Rain bit her lip. "It makes sense, doesn't it?"

"I guess so." She nodded, the wariness in her eyes making way for resolve.

"And it didn't bother attacking us because it had plenty of Ingrid's energy running through its veins."

"Do demons have veins?"

Rain straightened her spine. "It doesn't matter. Demons are nasty creatures, hell-bent on causing death and destruction. We aren't targets any more than any other witches. And we're Connollys."

Snow put her hands on her hips. "That's right. We can take care of ourselves. No demon is getting past my charm." She leaned against the counter. "But you should probably tell Chase. Fighting demons is what werewolves do."

Her sister had a point, but to talk to him after everything that had happened? "I can't. You call him."

Snow crossed her arms. "You're the one who talked to Ingrid. It's your theory. Besides, I *know* he'd want to hear it from you."

Pressing her lips together, Rain closed her eyes for a long blink. As much as she ached to hear his deep velvet voice, she couldn't do it. Instead, she dialed the number for O'Malley's Pub and asked for Luke. Cool relief flooded her veins when he picked up the phone. She explained what happened with her landlord and her theory that the shadow demon had taken on her form.

"You're sure it came to the bakery because of Ingrid's thoughts? Someone didn't send it after you?" Concern emanated from Luke's voice.

Thoughts of Isaac raced through her mind, but she pushed them aside. "I don't have any living enemies. I don't believe it was targeting me."

"Okay. Let me talk to Chase."

Rain swallowed. "He's not here. We're...not talking at the moment."

Silence hung on the other end, stretching out until she thought the call had dropped. Finally, Luke responded. "I see. I can send someone else over to stand guard."

"That's not necessary. My sister is here, and the doors are locked. Please don't send anyone over."

Luke paused again. "If you insist. Chase will be informed, though."

"I understand." Hearing the news from his alpha rather than her would feel like betrayal. What had she been thinking calling Luke instead of Chase? Her mixed-up emotions had gotten the better of her. Maybe she should have eaten that clarity cookie after all.

"Thank you for the information."

She pressed *end* and looked at her sister. "I'm sure we're fine."

Snow furrowed her brow. "You don't think Isaac could have summoned the demon? I mean...you never actually saw him die."

She wrapped her arms around her middle, holding herself together. "There's no way he survived." He couldn't have. Even if he had, seven years had passed and he hadn't come for her yet. Why would he start now?

Snow nodded. "I believe you. Between your aura-reading ability and my magic, we'll be fine." She drummed her nails on the counter-top. "So…can we talk about Chase now?"

Chase strode into the hospital parking garage, heading for his bike, when a dark, human-like figure sprang from behind a pickup truck and darted around the corner.

"Shit." He picked up the pace, following the shadow, and stopped to peer around the corner. The figure stood at the garage exit, and it whirled to face him, cocking its featureless head before inching away from the building.

The semi-translucent figure was nearly solid black, but as it regarded Chase, its face seemed to morph, taking on liquid-looking features that smoothed into nothingness as quickly as they formed.

At midday, the sun had risen plenty high enough to chase away the darkness, and demons only came out at night. There was no mistaking this was the same shadow Chase had seen twice before, but if it wasn't a demon…what the hell was it?

It took two cautious steps backward before turning and running down the street.

"Goddammit." Chase took off after the creature. Mending his relationship with Rain would have to wait.

The figure jetted around a corner, sticking to the fence line as it ran, stopping every now and then to look back at Chase…almost as if to make sure he followed. Chase texted Luke and James, sharing his location and asking for backup. They'd call it his imagination if he claimed to see a demon out in the daytime.

He tracked the creature out of the Central Business District and into a dense patch of trees in City Park. Leaves crunched as boots pounded the ground behind him, and he looked over his shoulder to find Luke and James making their way toward him.

"What's going on?" Luke caught up first, followed by James.

"The shadow. It's out in the daytime."

"What the hell?" Luke scanned the trees. "Rain said it was a demon."

Chase froze. "When did you talk to Rain?"

Luke jerked his head, indicating they needed to walk and talk. "She called me half an hour ago. Said the demon attacked her friend and took on her form. I've heard of demons who can shape-shift, so I assumed she meant it happened last night."

"Goddammit, Rain. She was with me last night." He clenched his jaw to stop himself from asking permission to leave the hunt. His duty came first, but if his woman was in trouble…

"She's fine," Luke said, as if reading his mind. "You can go back to her as soon as we're done here." Thankfully, he didn't ask what happened between them. The fact that Luke believed in her safety eased his fears. His best friend wouldn't leave his fate-bound unprotected if she were in danger.

James squinted at the sky. "Can demons handle sunlight?"

"Not that I'm aware of." Hell, the first time Chase had seen a demon was a few months ago when a crazy halfling tried to build an army to take over the city. The werewolves had crushed his plans within a few weeks' time. They could take out one daylight-proof shadow demon. *If* that was all they were dealing with.

Luke turned in a circle, scanning the perimeter. "Weekday afternoon. Park's deserted. Humans rarely come this far out anyway. Duck into the trees before you shift. Vanquish it and get out."

Chase nodded, and they moved deeper into the thicket before shifting into their wolf forms. As Chase's beast took control, his first instinct was to run to Rain and make things right with her. He fought it, using his human thoughts to remain in control. One demon wouldn't be hard to kill. Then he could win back his woman.

The shadow moved from behind a tree. It barreled toward James, plowing into him and knocking him from his feet. James grunted as he hit the ground, but he sprang up, ready to attack. The creature tried to get Chase from behind, but he spun around, swiping his massive claws across the shadow's chest. His paw passed straight through the entity as if it didn't exist.

What the hell?

The thing stood there, tilting its head, its features wavering as if trying to take on a face-like form.

Luke and James fanned out around the entity until they all encircled it. Chase rocked back on his haunches, energy coiling in his legs, and sprang for the fiend.

No impact. His body propelled through the shadow; the surprise of not making contact threw him off-balance, and he tumbled into a tree, hitting the trunk with a *thud*. He scrambled to his feet and inhaled deeply. If this creature were a demon, the distinct scent of rotting garbage would have assaulted his senses. Instead, he smelled grass, earth, and trees. Nothing to indicate this creature had ascended from hell.

He growled low in his throat, and the wolves converged, stalking the...whatever it was...as it stepped backward in retreat. How the hell could they kill something they couldn't touch?

The entity took a few more slow steps backward before it stopped and dissolved into nothing. Chase scanned the area, but not a trace of the shadow remained. His friends split up, searching through the trees.

Nothing.

Luke shifted to human form, and Chase and James followed their alpha's lead. "Christ! What the hell was that?"

Chase shook his head. "I have no idea, but I'll see if I can get more information from Rain." His chest tightened. If she would even talk to him.

Isaac opened his eyes as his tulpa reformed before him. Perhaps draining a werewolf would be a better option for his next move. The healing abilities he'd gain might give him enough strength to create the spell he needed with his own magic. His body had burned through most of his last victim's lifeforce in less than twenty-four hours.

Using a tree for support, he pushed to his feet. The rough bark cut into his hand, tearing the paper-thin skin as he clutched the trunk. His back was stuck in a hunched position, and his spine snapped and cracked with splitting pain as he forced himself upright.

Werewolves were too strong, and they were on high alert since he'd allowed his tulpa to play with them. He'd drain a witch. Use her power to cast his spell, and then it would be his turn to play with the werewolves. First, he'd finish what he started with the one trying to claim his Rain. With his rival dead and his magic restored, he might stick around to punish the rest of the pack.

CHAPTER SIXTEEN

"You need him, Rain. Even if you don't have feelings for the guy, he's the key to breaking your curse."

Rain eyed her sister. The more she thought about it, the more she agreed with Snow; she did need Chase. Not to break her curse, though that would be a nice bonus. She needed him because life without him would be unbearable. If he thought they could make it work, who was she to tell him no?

"I suppose even seeing him once a week would be better than not at all." She wouldn't be able to go anywhere near his niece, and that thought made her heart ache. She loved the little girl, but seeing her wouldn't be worth the risk. And the other werewolves… Chase would have to talk to them. Explain her curse. Her throat thickened. How could he possibly think *she* was worth the risk?

"The blue moon is getting close." Snow wiped her hands on a towel and dropped it in the laundry bin. "But seriously, sis. You dig the guy. You get heart eyes every time you mention his name." Her heels clicked on the tile as she strode to the cash register. "I'm taking my pay for the day and heading home. He's coming over to talk to you. Please don't be an idiot."

"Thanks."

Snow left through the back door, and Rain shuffled across the store to check the lock on the front door. Glancing through the window, she scanned the street. No sign of Chase. Would he even show up? Snow had said Emma already felt better by the time she'd left the hospital. Maybe Chase had stayed there all day. Or maybe he'd had to work. Dozens of reasons could have kept him away. This didn't mean he'd given up on her.

It wouldn't hurt to send him a text to see how Emma was doing. Glancing through the window one more time, she sighed and padded to the counter. Climbing onto a stool, she tugged her phone from her pocket and typed a message to Chase. *How is Emma?*

Seconds stretched into painful minutes without a reply. Maybe he'd decided she was right. That her curse was too dangerous.

The phone buzzed, and his response lit up the screen. *Fine.*

Her stomach sank. Fine. A four-letter word loaded with so many meanings. The user rarely meant its literal definition. In this case, fine most likely meant final. It meant, "Emma is good, but I don't care enough about you to elaborate. You're only worth one word, so leave me alone."

The phone buzzed again. *Look up.*

She lifted her gaze to the window. Chase stood on the sidewalk outside, his phone in his hand. Her mouth fell open as she sucked in a breath. Maybe he did mean fine literally.

When she didn't move from her stool, he scrunched his brow and typed something into his phone.

Her screen lit up. *Can I come in? I'd like to talk to you.*

She smiled and slipped off her stool, forcing herself to stroll to the entry when she really wanted to run. Unlocking the door, she opened it and stepped aside so he could enter. His warm, musky scent filled her senses, lightening her head. She locked the door and turned to face him, and the sadness in his eyes crumbled her.

She wrapped her arms around him, burying her face in his neck. "I'm sorry."

The scent of soap lingered on his skin, and his hair was damp as if he'd showered shortly before arriving. "Rain." He held her tight. "We can work this out. I'm not letting you go so easily."

She leaned back and placed her hands on either side of his face. As she looked into his hazel eyes, she saw the rest of her life reflected in his tender gaze. "You don't have to let me go."

The worry lines in his forehead smoothed as the tension drained from his body. His lips curved into a tiny smile, and she couldn't resist. She took his mouth with hers, brushing her tongue to his. He tasted like peppermint toothpaste, and a deep rumble vibrated from his chest to his throat.

With his hands in her hair, he cradled her head and kissed her as if he were drinking in her essence. Held her as if she were the most precious thing in the world. He pulled back, searching her eyes as he grazed his fingers across her cheeks, running his thumb over her lips. "Luke told me you saw the demon. Are you sure you're okay?"

"I'm fine. We kept the doors locked all day. As long as Snow's charm is intact, nothing can get in."

He nodded, looking her hard in the eyes. "Next time, call me. I have a vested interested in your safety, and it goes far beyond wedding cake."

She took his hands, lacing her fingers through his. "I will. Emma's doing better?"

"She's almost fully recovered. They're keeping her overnight for observation, but she's going to be fine."

She swallowed the guilt that tightened her throat. "That's good. Did you tell her it was my fault?"

"Bekah knows what happened. Emma doesn't, but..." His eyes tightened in a pained expression. "My sister doesn't want you around her until we can figure out a way to break the curse."

"That's understandable." She chewed the inside of her cheek and dropped her gaze to the floor. It was a fitting reaction for Bekah to have, but the appropriateness didn't lesson the blow. "Being with me will make your life complicated. Your pack might not even accept me."

"They'll accept you." He hooked his finger under her chin, raising her gaze to meet his. "And I'll deal with the complications as they come."

"Are you sure it's worth it?"

"I've never been more sure of anything in my life. I love you."

His words hit her like a can of biscuits popping open in her chest. She couldn't get her breath to flow in nor out as the sensation expanded, spreading through her body.

Chase loved her.

A mix of warm elation and frigid fear swirled through her core, making her pulse race. How could something make her feel so incredibly happy and freeze her in terror at the same time?

She loved him too. There was no other way to describe her feelings for this man, but love could make people do terrible things. If she had truly been in love with Isaac and not under a spell…

But it wasn't like that with Chase. She felt real, raw, reciprocated emotions, and he deserved to know the entire truth about her past. The whole, horrible story. She shook her head. "Chase…"

"It's okay." He ran his fingers through her hair, tucking a curl behind her ear. "I know it's too soon, and you don't have to say it back. But you need to know…I'm not going anywhere."

The emotion…the passion in his eyes made tears well in her own, but she blinked them back. She had to be strong; she couldn't lie to him anymore. "It's not that." She doubled-checked the lock on the front door. "Come to my room. You might want to take those words back after you hear what I have to tell you."

He gave her a quizzical look and followed her through the kitchen into her make-shift bedroom. She grabbed her robe from the chair and motioned to the seat. "You might want to sit down for this."

He flashed his signature cocky grin, trying to lighten the mood. "Come on…it can't be that bad."

She raised her eyebrows, giving him her best *you'd be surprised* look without saying the words. No amount of banter could lighten the weight she was about to throw at him. Turning her back to him, she hung the robe on the tri-fold partition that separated the closet area from the rest of her bedroom. When she turned around, he sat in the chair and fisted his hands on his legs.

Rain lowered herself onto the edge of the bed, and her knee bumped his. "Sorry it's so cramped in here."

He lifted a leg, positioning it between her knees and resting his hands on her thighs. "Nothing to apologize for."

Her heart thrummed, her throat tightening and threatening to choke the words she needed to say, but she had to say them. She took a deep breath and blew it out hard. There was no easy way to put this. No way to lessen the blow. "I lied to you about my curse."

He straightened his spine, returning his hands to his own lap.

Crap. That wasn't how she wanted to start. "I didn't actually lie. I…let you believe a lie."

He arched an eyebrow. "And that's better?"

"No. It's…okay. Here's the truth. Isaac didn't put the curse on me. The national witches' council did."

Confusion clouded his eyes. "Why would they do that?"

She lowered her gaze to her lap. "Because of what I did to him. To Isaac." Tears collected on her lower lids. She tried to blink them back, but a single traitor escaped, dripping onto her jeans, darkening the fabric.

"Hey." Chase gripped her hands. "I'm not proud of everything I've done in the past. Whatever it is, we'll get through it."

His touch gave her the strength to continue. "When I confronted him about the cheating and the energy stealing, I cast a spell on him. A terrible spell that wasn't supposed to kill him…but I'm afraid it did. I broke the most sacred of all rules: harm no one."

He squeezed her hand, urging her to go on.

"I don't know if I was in love with Isaac or not. I know I was obsessed. Desperate for his approval. For his attention. My entire life revolved around him, and I thought that was what love felt like. But since I met you, I'm not sure, because I'm not obsessed with you."

She looked into his eyes, waiting for a reaction, but he kept his expression neutral. Neither of them moved, and for a moment nothing but the sound of her trembling breath filled her ears. "The way I feel about you is completely different. With you, I feel safe. I never worry if I have your approval because you show me every day that I do. Maybe it's because I'm older now and mature enough to not be so desperately dependent on a man. I don't know. I'm getting off track."

"I've got all night. Take your time."

She nodded. "When I found out he was cheating and stealing my energy, I went into a fit of rage. I cast a spell, thinking I'd stop him from being with the other woman by making her reject him. It was a spell meant to hinder free will, and that in itself is worthy of my punishment. But what happened was way worse than making his girl-friend hate him."

Chase moved to sit on the bed beside her and wrapped his arm around her shoulders. Supporting her. Giving her strength as she confessed the worst sin she'd ever committed.

"I wrote the spell so that the thing he loved the most would reject him forever, but the thing he loved the most wasn't a person. It was his magic. His power. Since magic resides in the blood, his own blood turned against him. Rather than delivering oxygen and nutrients to his cells to keep him alive and healthy, it stopped flowing like normal. He deteriorated rapidly. The last time I saw him, he looked like he'd aged fifty years. His girlfriend found him and reported me to the council. By the time they arrived to give me my punishment, Isaac had disap-peared. His girlfriend too. I assume she took him away, so he could die with some dignity."

Chase kissed the side of her head, leaving his lips pressed against her hair, his body going still. She held her breath, waiting for him to respond. To move. To do something to break the endless silence that felt too much like rejection. Had he changed his mind? Could he take away his love so quickly after giving it to her?

"It was a terrible thing for me to do, and I'm not defending myself. But I honestly think he had me under a spell first. That he had hindered *my* free will. The way I felt about him wasn't natural. I see that now. Now that I know what real love feels like."

Aside from the subtle rise and fall of his chest, he sat motionless. What was he thinking?

"If you want to leave, I understand. You can walk out, and I'll never bother you again. I'll be devastated, but I won't try to hurt you. Not that I could, since my powers are bound, but you know what I mean." She was babbling. She needed to shut up before she dug this pit any deeper. "Please say something."

He inhaled deeply, finishing the kiss as if he'd simply pressed pause while she explained. Then he slid off the bed and knelt in front of her, taking both her hands in his. "I love you. I will never walk out on you."

"I killed a man, Chase. I killed a man because he was cheating on me."

"He was also draining your energy. You saw the woman in the morgue; he could have done that to you. I don't buy for a minute that you are capable of hurting someone on your own. I think you were under a spell too. It makes sense. He wanted to steal your magic, so he had to keep you close."

Another tear rolled down her cheek. "What if I wasn't? What if I *am* capable of hurting people?"

He wiped the moisture from her cheek with his thumb. "You're the kindest, sweetest woman I know. Your past doesn't define you. I am in love with the woman you are today. And the Rain that's sitting here in front of me would never hurt anyone."

She looked at the man kneeling before her, and her chest ached with the amount of love he'd filled her with. He accepted her—sordid past, curse and all—and he loved her.

He sidled closer, spreading her knees apart so his body fit between them. "Who knows? Maybe falling in love will be the selfless act that breaks your curse."

She laughed. "As much as this feels like a fairy tale, I don't think true love's kiss is going to fix my problems."

A sly grin curved his lips. "It won't hurt to try."

"No, I suppose it won't." She took his face in her hands, running her fingers through his beard, and pressed her lips to his. The warmth and gentleness of the kiss loosened the tension in her muscles. He ran his hands up her legs, gripping her hips as his tongue brushed hers. His beard tickled her chin, and the softness of his lips sent buzzing energy zipping through her veins.

He moved his hands to the small of her back, holding her close as he deepened the kiss, and she got lost in the moment. In the man. They could make this relationship work. He believed they could, and now, so did she.

Pulling away, she rested her hands on his shoulders. "Still cursed."

He shrugged. "It was worth a shot." He rose from the ground and settled onto the bed next to her. "Seriously, though. I will do whatever it takes to help you break this curse. Just name it."

Her brow furrowed. Not if he knew what he'd actually have to do. And she certainly couldn't ask him now—when she'd confessed to murder.

The heat from his body so close to hers warmed her from the outside, but the fact that he forgave her for her past chased away the chilling guilt she'd been carrying in her chest since she first told him about her curse.

She couldn't ask him for his blood. What if he gave it to her and then he ended up in werewolf prison for the rest of his life? Or worse? She'd lived with the curse for seven years, and she could continue to bear it. She had to. "I know something you can do for me. It won't break the curse, but I think you might enjoy it." Leaning toward him, she glided her hand up his thigh, stopping half an inch shy from reaching his hip.

He closed the distance between them, lightly grazing his lips over hers. "Are we good now? Can I still call you mine?"

His breath against her skin raised goose bumps on her arms. "Yes, Chase. I'm yours."

He kissed her, tangling his fingers in her hair as he traced his lips down her neck, across her collar bone, and up the other side, leaving a trail of tingling magic on her skin, lighting her soul on fire.

She wanted to give him everything. To show him the love she felt for him before she said the words. Tugging his shirt over his head, she ran her hands over his firm chest and pushed him onto his back.

He grinned, pulling her down with him as he moved to the center of the bed. She showered his face and neck in kisses, allowing his masculine scent to intoxicate her, reveling in the hungry sounds he made in the back of his throat.

With one more deep inhale, she sat up, straddling his hips and running her palms up his stomach. On his left arm, the tattoo sleeve ended at his shoulder, but on the right side, it spilled over onto his chest. A series of roses surrounding an intricate compass occupied most of his right pec.

She traced the design with her fingers. "Does this one have a meaning?"

He placed his hand on hers, holding her palm against his chest. "I was lost for most of my childhood. Being in the pack helped me find my way."

She moved her hand to admire the drawing, following a trail of interwoven vines over his shoulder where they created a frame around another tattoo—a wolf head designed from a fleur-de-lis. "Is that why it's connected to your pack crest?"

"It is." He watched her with a heavy gaze as she ran her fingers over his tattoos. They were all beautiful. Intricate. Even without the ink, Chase had a body sculpted like a god. The gorgeous tattoos tipped his sexiness meter over the edge.

"Your friend is a talented artist." She used her thumbs to toy with his nipple rings.

He sucked in a breath. "He is."

She lowered her mouth to his chest, circling his nipple with her tongue before sucking the ring into her mouth. The sharp, metallic taste of the jewelry mixed with the slight saltiness of his skin, and his chest vibrated as he let out an aroused, *"Mmm."*

He caressed her shoulders. "You found my weakness on the first try."

She moved to his other nipple, sucking it harder as she tugged the other ring with her fingers. Another moan vibrated in his chest, sending her heart into a sprint. She loved that she could do this to him. Make him feel this way so easily. The pleasure it brought her to arouse him was palpable. This man was made for her.

She sat up and pulled her shirt over her head before unhooking her bra and tossing them to the floor. Lying on top of him, skin to skin, the tingle of his magic and the warmth of his body was almost too much to bear. "I'm sure there are other places you'd like to feel my mouth, aren't there?" As she glided her tongue down his chest, she slipped her hand between their bodies to rub him through his jeans.

His response came out more growl than words.

"I'll take that as a yes." She moved down his body, kissing, licking, and nipping her way to his navel. His stomach contracted as she reached the waist band of his jeans and undid the button.

He rose onto his elbows and watched as she slowly pulled the zipper down, the teeth coming apart one by one to reveal his dark-gray boxer-briefs. "You do that any more slowly, and I might explode."

She yanked the zipper the rest of the way down and slipped her hand beneath his underwear to grip his dick. "There will plenty of explosions tonight, wolf man. Be patient."

He grunted, his head falling back onto the pillow as she tugged off his clothes and dropped them on the floor. He had a sleek, powerful build, defined muscles rolling through his entire body, radiating a raw, primal strength. She sat back to appreciate his gorgeous perfection, her gaze traveling from his hooded, hazel eyes, down the length of him. He was thick and hard, and as a bead of moisture gathered on his tip, her mouth watered to taste him.

Taking his dick in her hand, she dipped her head and circled her tongue around the tip. He sucked in a sharp breath through his teeth and fisted the sheets in his hands. Her own stomach tight-ened, a giddy sensation bubbling up to her throat, escaping as a giggle.

"Something funny?" He rose onto his elbows again, arching a brow over his passion-drunk eyes.

"I like the way you react when I touch you." She held his gaze as she ran her tongue from base to tip."

His eyelids fluttered. "I like the way you touching me feels."

"Good." She took him into her mouth, and he let out his breath in a hiss. The weight of his gaze settled on her as she sucked him, and she took him in as deep as she could before sliding up until only the tip remained in her mouth. The taste of him made her heart sprint, and she wanted…needed…to take him all the way. She moved her mouth down and back up again, caressing his shaft with her tongue, and he moved his hips in unison with her strokes.

His hand on her shoulder slowed her rhythm, and when he stilled her head with his other hand, she released her hold. He sat up, pulling her into his lap, taking her mouth in a kiss. Gliding a hand up her back, he flipped her around, tossing her onto the bed, covering her body with his.

His strength amazed her. That he could pick her up as if she weighed nothing and put her right where he wanted made her stomach flutter. This was a man who was used to getting what he wanted. Good thing they both wanted the same thing.

He sat back on his heels and removed the rest of her clothes, his pupils dilating with desire as he caressed her with his gaze. He kissed her stomach, massaging her inner thighs as his lips neared her sensitive center. Her core tightened, anticipation building, coiling in her stomach. She arched her back, silently begging him to taste her.

His chuckle sent a puff of warm air across her clit, just enough sensation to force a whimper from her throat. He rested his cheek against her inner thigh, his beard tickling the delicate skin. "You are so sexy, Rain."

Her name on his lips. His breath teasing across her folds. It was enough to drive her insane. "Please, Chase."

"Tell me what you need."

"I…" Her voice came out in a breathy whisper. "I need you to touch me."

He slipped a finger inside her, and she gasped. "Like this?"

"*Mmm*…taste me. Please. I want to feel your tongue."

He moved his lips closer, a scant centimeter away from their destination. She could almost feel the smile playing on his lips as he made her wait, sweetening the reward. She'd take back everything she'd said about delayed gratification if he would just lick her.

The warmth of his tongue moved across her center, and she held her breath. When he reached her sensitive nub, the air left her lungs in a gush as tingling electricity shot through her core. His satisfaction vibrated across his lips, shooting another electric burst through her body, lighting every nerve on fire.

He knew where to touch, exactly how to move his tongue to drive her wild. He seemed to know his way around her body as if they'd made love a thousand times. When he slipped a second finger inside her, she couldn't hold back anymore.

Cresting like a wave, her climax crashed into her, tumbling

through her core, surging through her limbs. She cried out, arching her back as he continued to caress her, enchanting her senses until they were the only two people left in the world. Softly, slowly, he eased her down, gliding his tongue across her one more time before moving to lie beside her.

She rolled to her side, draping her top leg over his and taking his length in her hand. "You are the most amazing man I've ever met." She nuzzled closer, kissing him gently before catching his lower lip between her teeth.

He rolled to his back, pulling her on top of him, his lip slipping from her grip. "You're pretty amazing yourself."

She straddled him, sitting on his thighs and stroking him. "You didn't happen to bring a condom, did you?"

He closed his eyes. "No."

She spread the moisture beading on his tip over his shaft, allowing her hand to glide up and down with ease. She needed him inside her. Making love. Becoming one. He knew her so well, but she wanted him to know all of her. Body, mind, and soul. "I'm on birth control."

He opened his eyes and pinned her with a heated gaze. "Werewolves are immune to disease."

Her stomach fluttered, her pulse quickening with longing. "Sounds like we're good to go then."

His mouth tugged into a sexy grin. "I suppose we are."

Rising onto her knees, she guided him to her entrance, gasping as he filled her, his girth stretching her to a pleasurable ache. With her hands on his chest, she moved her hips, sliding up and down his length, each stroke shooting tingling energy to her womb.

He held her gaze, the look in his eyes so full of passion and love that she thought her heart might burst. Leaning forward, she rested her chest against his and kissed him, putting all of her emotions into the kiss, willing him to understand how much he meant to her.

He moaned into her mouth, and gripping her hips, he drove himself deeper inside her. She held still, allowing him to take her, giving herself to him as the overwhelming sensations of ecstasy drove her over the edge.

Her orgasm ripped through her body, shattering her soul into a thousand pieces that only Chase could put back together. He moved faster, his breath coming in short pants until he found his own release, and he held her tight, a low moan shuddering in his chest as he spasmed inside her.

Relaxing his grip, he glided his hands up and down her sweat-slickened back. She nuzzled into his neck, letting his intoxicatingly masculine scent fill her senses, relaxing her into a state of semi-slumber.

He was *her* wolf.

She blinked, lifting her head to look at him. Where had that thought come from? Though she'd always been aware of the duality of his being—even seeing him shift into his wolf form—she'd never thought of him as anything more than a man. But something about the intimacy they shared...the fact that she had finally given her whole self to him...created a strange bond she hadn't felt before. Deep. Primal. It was nothing scary or obsessive. It was rather... comforting. Something about being here with Chase lying in her bed...it finally felt like home.

He tucked a strand of hair behind her ear. "You look confused. What's on your mind, *cher*?"

Resting her weight on her right elbow, she placed her left hand over his heart. "I'm in love with you."

He smiled and took her hand, bringing her fingers to his lips. "You just made me the happiest man alive."

"And your wolf?"

He gave her a curious look. "That part of me has wanted you since the moment I saw you. The rest of me had to get over some misplaced anger issues first, but I'm all yours now. One hundred percent. I love you."

"I love you too." Her smile widened, and she moved to lie on her side, snuggling next to him and resting her head on his chest. "I like the way that sounds."

"So do I. You're way better than a goat."

She laughed. "You're not going to let me forget I said that, are you?"

"Not a chance."

She traced her fingers along the cuts of his muscles, and he let out a contented sigh. She loved Chase, and he loved her. Did that mean she was his fate-bound? When he'd talked about them, he'd made it sound like a werewolf could fall in love with someone who wasn't his fate-bound. If that were the case, what would happen if he met his fate-bound later? Would he stop loving her to be with the other woman? If Rain married him…if she was his mate…would he even be allowed to leave her?

A sickening feeling formed in her stomach as her mind spun with questions. If she was his fate-bound, none of them mattered, but… wouldn't he have told her if she was? She could ask him, but what would she do if the answer was no? She'd rather not know in that case. He loved her, and that was the important thing. She'd deal with the fate-bound issue when and if it ever came up.

His stomach vibrated as a deep growl rumbled from inside him.

She lifted her head. "I guess we missed dinner."

He chuckled. "And breakfast and lunch. I've been a little distracted today." He kissed the top of her head. "You wouldn't happen to have food other than cake in the kitchen, would you?"

She rose onto her elbow. "I do live here, you know. Of course I have food. No meat, but I can make a killer cucumber and avocado sandwich."

He wrinkled his nose.

She rolled her eyes. "Try it. I'll add extra cheese so it won't taste too healthy." Before he had a chance to protest, she rolled out of bed and put on her robe, cinching it at the waist. "You stay where you are. I'll be right back." She let her gaze wander over his magnificent body before turning and scurrying out the door. With Chase in her bed, she'd be back again and again. *What a man.* She grinned. Not gay, nor about to be married like she'd first thought. Lucky her.

Rain wasn't the type of woman who normally pranced, but she felt so damn giddy, she couldn't help herself. Happiness bubbled in her chest, its effervescence lightening her steps.

As she pranced into the kitchen and flipped on the light, her happy little heart got stuck in her throat. A man—or what was left of one—stood in the center of the room, toying with something in his hands.

Rain froze. Instinct told her to run or to call for Chase, but an icy flush of dread glued her to the spot, cutting off her ability to speak.

Ashen skin hung loose on the man's bones, giving him the appearance of having recently crawled out of the grave. His aura, once dark-purple and sparkling with magic, had turned a murky shade of brownish-black, illness dampening even the bluish glow of life. Though his dark eyes had dulled to a death-like state, they were unmistakable.

She clutched her robe together at her neck and forced out a whisper. "Isaac."

"Good evening, Rain." His voice came out as a croak, and his lips cracked as they peeled into a smile, revealing his rotted teeth.

Her stomach tumbled to her feet. Her heart pounded against her ribs. This couldn't be real. Isaac was dead.

"I think you've met my tulpa." He gestured to a darkened corner, and a figure emerged from the shadows. Though human-like in form, its featureless face made it look more like a nightmare than a person.

Her mind reeled, thoughts spinning through her head like a tornado. She blinked, cutting her gaze from the shadow to her ex-boyfriend. "You…made a tulpa?"

"I couldn't have done it without your help."

"That's not possible." Finally able to move her feet, she took a step back.

He sneered, the skin around his mouth cracking farther until a blackish goo oozed from the wounds. "It wasn't possible for *you*. The spell I had on you made sure you thought of little other than me. I, on the other hand, have had seven years of using nothing but my mind."

She shook her head, trying to bring herself up to speed with the situation. She'd been right about his spell, but she hadn't killed him. Now he stood in her kitchen, with a monster he'd created from his imagination, while Chase lay in her bedroom.

The blood drained from her head, making the room spin. *Chase.* Oh, goddess, she couldn't let Isaac get to Chase. If she stayed quiet, maybe Isaac wouldn't realize he was here. She could deal with her ex if he thought she was alone. She took another step back, and her body betrayed her, involuntarily glancing down the hall toward her bedroom. Faster than humanly possible, the tulpa swiped a knife from the block and pressed it to her windpipe.

"No yelling for your boyfriend." Isaac shuffled toward her. "I've got plans for him too."

She swallowed, and the edge of the blade scraped against her throat. The entity's hand held the back of her head, and she leaned into it, willing herself to pass through it. The tulpa only existed in Isaac's imagination. She closed her eyes and breathed as deeply as the cold steel against her trachea allowed. *It's not real. I can pass through it because it doesn't exist.* But the sharp metal pressing into her throat insisted on its reality. She opened her eyes. "How did you get in here? Snow set up a ring of protection."

Isaac held her broken totem between his thumb and forefinger and nodded toward his creation. Rain shifted her gaze to the shadow, and its faced morphed into a wavering, watery resemblance of her landlord.

She focused on the tulpa's aura—the same dull-gray she'd seen surrounding the thing posing as Ingrid. "You're the demon."

Isaac scoffed. "You've called me worse, love."

"You set this up. You sent your tulpa here to break the circle of protection so you could get inside my home." As her voice grew louder, the tulpa pressed the knife harder against her skin to silence her.

She clawed at the arm holding the knife, and her hands passed through it as if it were made of nothing. It moved its free hand to the side of her face. Though its touch felt cold, it was too solid to be a figment of Isaac's imagination. She couldn't convince her mind otherwise.

"Smart girl. But be quiet. I don't want to alert your werewolf boyfriend to my presence. I'm not strong enough to fight him yet."

Her stomach turned at the thought of him going after the man she loved. She had to protect Chase. "How did you find me?"

He clutched the edge of a countertop, and something thick and black oozed from a moss-covered wound on his wrist. "Surely, you've heard about the Miami witch that turned up dead in New Orleans? The one that was missing an eye?"

She cringed. "She had the gift of sight?"

"Eye, she did." He attempted a laugh that turned into a muffled cough. "Get it? Aye like yes, but also eye?"

Rain hardened her gaze. How had she found his sense of humor delightful at one time? Oh, right, because he'd had her under a spell. "Who was she?"

His eyes brightened. "You'll be happy to hear that was Giselle."

"Your girlfriend?"

He let out a wistful sigh. "I never had to put her under a spell. She liked me as I was…until you did *this* to me. She stuck around for a little while, until she figured out I wasn't going to recover."

"So you killed her?"

"I needed to drain someone to gain enough energy to make the journey to find you, my love." He shrugged. "She didn't have the sense to run away from Miami like you did. I took her life for her betrayal."

Rain narrowed her eyes. "And now it's my turn?"

A look of regret flashed in his eyes before he scowled. "You owe me more than your life. I'm going to make you suffer. Good night, sweet Rain."

The tulpa dropped the knife onto the counter and gripped the sides of her head. She struggled to free herself from its clutches as a dull ache spread across her scalp and her vision tunneled until two pinpricks of light remained.

Then darkness.

CHAPTER SEVENTEEN

CHASE PUT ON HIS UNDERWEAR AND SAT ON THE EDGE OF THE bed. How long did it take to make a cucumber and avocado sandwich? Maybe she had a garden out back, and she had to pick the vegetables first.

No, he'd been around back, and this building didn't have a courtyard like so many other French Quarter structures did. The only thing behind Rain's bakery was a dumpster that desperately needed emptying, based on the faint rotting smell creeping into his senses. Something wasn't right.

As he reached for his pants, she stepped through the doorway, grinning and holding a cookie in her hand.

"I was starting to worry about you, *cher*. Did you bake that from scratch?"

Her grin widened, and she shuffled toward him, offering him the treat.

He took it and held it up to his nose for a sniff. Chocolate chip. "What happened to the sandwich? I don't think a cookie is going to hold me 'til morning."

She sighed and tilted her head.

He started to ask if she'd put a spell on it but thought better of it.

That would've been a dick move, especially since they'd just declared their love for each other.

Lifting the cookie to his lips, he took a bite, and she watched him intently as he chewed and swallowed. He looked at her, and she nodded, encouraging him to finish. She was normally more talkative, but if she wanted him to eat the whole damn cookie, he'd eat it for her.

Finishing the last bite, he licked his fingers for emphasis. "Delicious as expected, though I was planning on having you for dessert."

She giggled.

"How about that sandwich? I need some sustenance for all the things I have planned for you tonight."

She turned on her heel and darted out the door.

What kind of game was the woman playing? He stood and peeked out the door, but she'd disappeared around a corner. As he stepped into the hall, a wave of fatigue crashed into him, spreading from his core to his limbs. His mouth went dry, and his head spun as his muscles contracted with searing pain. "What the hell?"

He stumbled down the hall into the kitchen, and his heart plummeted to his feet when he found Rain lying on the floor.

"Rain!" He rushed to her side, and dropping to his knees, he put a hand on her chest. It rose and fell steadily with her breaths, but his own breathing became labored and raspy. Rolling her onto her back, he patted her cheek gently. "Rain? *Cher*, are you okay?" *She's lying on the cold kitchen floor. Of course she's not okay, asshole.*

Her skin was clammy to the touch, and her eyelids fluttered as if she were trying to open them.

"Rain?"

She sucked in a sharp breath and opened her eyes. Blinking wildly, she darted her gaze about the room and locked eyes with him. "Chase? Is it really you?" She lifted her hand, slapping him across the face before letting her arm flop to the floor.

A stinging sensation spread from his cheek to his jaw, and he rubbed his face. "It's me. Ow."

"Sorry. I thought you weren't real." She tried to sit up, but her elbows buckled beneath her.

He caught her and scooped her into his arms. Had she always been this heavy? "What's going on? What happened?" He tried to stand, but his knees gave out before he could right himself. Setting Rain on the floor, he sat back on his heels. "What was in that cookie?"

She rubbed her temples. "What cookie?"

"The one you gave me. Wait…why did you think I wasn't real?" His head pounded, and he squeezed his eyes shut, trying to stave off the nausea that threatened to give that cookie a reappearance.

"I didn't give you a cookie." She moved to all fours, rocking slightly before steadying herself.

He scrunched his brow, shaking his head to clear the confusion clouding his mind. Shifting his weight to his feet, he tried to rise, but his knees wobbled. He put a hand on the floor. Why did he feel so weak? "Did you put a spell on me?" The moment the words left his lips, he regretted them.

Rain narrowed her eyes and peered at him through a curtain of her hair. "Seriously? You're really asking me that?"

Clutching a counter for support, he rose to his feet. "I'm sorry. I know you can't cast spells."

"It's not that you know I can't, Chase. It's that you thought I *would*." She stood and stumbled before catching herself on the wall.

"I don't think that, and I'm sorry I said it. Please explain what's going on. You came into the room and gave me a cookie. Then you ran out, and I found you unconscious on the floor. And I feel…" Ice flushed his veins. "I can't feel my wolf." He grabbed at his chest as if he could physically grab hold of the missing piece of his being. What the hell was happening to him?

Rain squinted, studying him. "Oh, goddess, no. Not you too."

"Me too what?"

With her back against the wall, she covered her face with her hands and slid to the floor. "I need to lie down."

Panic raced through his veins like a freight train. Reaching beneath her arms, he lifted her to his chest and carried her to the bedroom. His dizziness had subsided, leaving behind nothing but weakness in his muscles to indicate anything had happened to him. Weakness…and the absence of his wolf.

He laid her on the bed and sat beside her. "I know you don't feel well, *cher*, but I need you to tell me what happened. To you and to me."

She inhaled deeply, fluttering her eyes open to meet his gaze. "It was Isaac."

"Isaac? I thought he was dead."

"So did I, but he was standing in the kitchen with his tulpa when I got there."

"What the hell is a tulpa?"

"The shadow you've been seeing. It's not a demon. Isaac created it with his mind."

He squeezed his eyes shut and rubbed his forehead, trying to make sense of her words. He knew it wasn't a demon because he'd seen it in the daylight. Aside from the first time he'd encountered it in the swamp, it had only appeared when Rain was near. The damn thing hadn't been targeting him, it had been after his woman.

His spine went rigid, his muscles contracting as he fisted the sheet. How could he have been so stupid? "This tulpa...how did Isaac create it with his mind? Is it some kind of spell? A hologram? What is it?" He shook his head. "That's not important. What happened to you? Are you sick? What can I do?"

"The tulpa used my energy to shape-shift, like it did to my landlord, but I'll regain my strength." She inhaled a shaky breath. "My guess is that it made you think you saw me, so you would think that I..." She lowered her gaze to her stomach.

He clutched her hand. "That you what, Rain? Please tell me what's going on."

"Did you eat the cookie?"

"Yeah."

Tears gathered on her lower lids. "Isaac sent the tulpa, disguised as me, to give you a binding spell."

"A binding spell?"

She blinked up at him, and tears spilled down her cheeks. "He bound your power. Your wolf. You're like me now."

"No." He wouldn't believe it. Shaking his head, he stood and paced the small bedroom. His wolf was half of his soul. Without it, he wasn't himself. He was…nothing.

"Yes, Chase. I can see it in your aura. Or rather…I *can't* see it. Your aura looks mundane, so your power must be bound."

He jabbed his fingers into his hair, pulling it at the roots. "I can't shift? I've lost my strength?"

She nodded.

"I'm useless." He threw his hands into the air. This couldn't be happening.

"No. You're still you, like I'm still me. Your power is there, in your blood."

He stopped and leaned his head against the wall. Leave it to a witch to use someone he loved against him. "How did he find us? How did he know?"

"The witch from the morgue had the gift of sight. He…" She blew out a hard breath. "He killed her and used her gift to find me. To find us."

"Her missing eye." His muscles tensed, a sharp pain shooting through his jaw as he ground his teeth. The bastard would not get away with this. "How can I break the spell? What if I finished the job and killed him myself?"

She pushed into a sitting position and leaned her back against the wall. "Binding spells aren't tied to the caster. They get inside you, stay with you until they're broken."

"What about the coven? Or Snow? Can't someone write an *un*binding spell?"

A pained expression flashed across her features before morphing into sadness. "Unbinding spells are a bitch." She let out a dry laugh. "High-level witches have to write them, and they require months of preparation and ingredients that aren't easy to come by."

He sank onto the bed.

Rain scooted toward him and wrapped her arms around him from behind. "Snow doesn't have that kind of power. Anyway, if they were easy, don't you think I'd have found a way to break my curse by now?"

So…what? He was stuck this way? Was the universe playing some kind of cruel joke on him? Leading him to his fate-bound. Making her a witch of all creatures, and then waiting until he let his guard down to send in another witch to steal his wolf? "How'd he get in? You said no one could break the circle of protection."

"Remember what I told you about my landlord being drained by the shadow? I think it did that to gain the ability to take on her form. When it came into the bakery disguised as Ingrid, it took one of the enchanted totems. Breaking it broke the circle. The magic was tied to the lock, so we didn't notice the spell had stopped working."

"How did it know what to take?"

"I think Isaac can see through the tulpa's eyes. It's a projection of his mind, so wherever the tulpa goes, his vision goes. Isaac would have recognized the spell; it's basic witchcraft. He planned this. Knew you were here."

"And he's coming after me in order to hurt you."

She nodded and pressed her lips to his shoulder. "I'm so sorry. He's here for revenge. He'll go after you and Snow first—the people I love —to make me suffer. Then he'll kill me. The spell I cast on him is tied to me. With me dead, it will be lifted, and his power will return."

"We can't let that happen." No way in hell would he let anything happen to his fate-bound. "But I can't fight him like this. I'm weak."

"So is he. Chase, he's in bad shape. His arm is injured, and he looked like death. He must have drained another witch to get the power to create the binding spell he gave you. With his blood working against him, he doesn't retain power long. He'll need to recover before he strikes again. If we could figure out where he's hiding, we could catch him off-guard. Capture him and force him to remove the spell."

"He's in the swamp." He moved to face her and took her hands in his. "You said his arm was injured?"

"Yes, his wrist was wrapped in blood-soaked moss."

His heart raced. "A snake didn't bite me when I was hunting. I was following the shadow when I slipped into the water. I turned around and bit whatever had hold of my leg. It had to be Isaac. He was draining me."

Her eyes widened. "That's why he bound your power. He knew you were too strong for a fair fight."

"And if he knows anything about werewolf politics, he also knows

I'll lose my rank in the pack if anyone finds out I've lost my wolf." Not that rank mattered to him; his position was temporary anyway. But if the guy was out to hurt Rain by hurting the ones she loved…

"But you haven't lost your wolf. He's in you…bound in your blood."

He shook his head. "Doesn't matter. Only shifting wolves can hold rank." How long would Isaac try to stretch this out? Would he try to tear Chase's life apart before moving on to Snow's, saving Rain for last so he could watch her suffer?

"Then we'll fix this without telling the pack. Isaac isn't a threat to them. He's after me and the people I love, and he's probably at his weakest right now. Let me get dressed, and I'll call Snow." She slid off the bed, but as soon as she stood, her knees buckled.

Chase caught her by the waist and guided her to the bed. "You're not going anywhere in your condition. I'll get James and Luke to go with me. Snow and another wolf will stay here with you in case he comes back."

"But if you can't shift…"

He grabbed his shirt and pulled it over his head. "I wouldn't be where I am today if it weren't for the pack. I'm not going to turn my back on them now, but I have to figure out how we can get past the tulpa." He turned his jeans right side out and shoved in his legs. "We've tried to fight it before. It can touch us, but when we try to attack, it's as if the damn thing doesn't exist."

"That's because it doesn't. If you can convince your mind that it's not real, its blows will pass through you too. As long as it doesn't get ahold of a weapon." She rubbed her throat. "That knife was real enough."

He paused, and another flash of anger surged through him. "It had a knife against your throat?" And he'd been lounging in her bed, oblivious to the danger lurking a few feet away. *Asshole.* Fumbling with the button, he cursed at his jeans and yanked up the zipper.

"Don't you think I would have called for help if I'd been able?"

"This guy is dead. I'm going to take care of you, *cher.*"

Rain lay on the pillow, her lids fluttering shut as he spoke, and his heart ached for her. Even with his wolf bound, the overwhelming urge to protect his mate-to-be tore through him. He would do *anything* to keep her safe. "Before you fall asleep, is there a way to kill the tulpa?"

She shook her head. "Isaac would have to imagine it dead."

"If Isaac is dead himself?"

A tiny smile curved her lips. "Bye bye, tulpa."

CHAPTER EIGHTEEN

Rain woke with a start, sitting up in bed, her head spinning as she tried to regain focus. Memories began clicking together like pieces of a puzzle, expanding in her mind like a pressure cooker. "Chase."

"He's out looking for Isaac." Snow sat in the chair next to the bed and leaned her elbows on her knees. "How are you feeling?"

Rain blinked at her sister. The pounding in her head had subsided, and her muscles felt mildly achy. "Better. He told you what happened?" Her robe had come open while she slept, so she tied it shut.

Snow's lips quirked, suppressing a grin. "Not the whole story." She motioned with her head toward Rain's clothes discarded on the floor. "I take it you made up before all this went down?"

Warmth spread through her chest, elation tingling through her limbs. "You could say that. How long have I been out?"

"Chase left as soon as we got here…about twenty minutes ago, so maybe an hour."

She let out a slow breath. "I'm scared."

"For yourself or for Chase?"

"Both." She scooted to the edge of the bed and picked up her clothes. "Isaac is weak, but…"

Snow stood. "I made a new circle of protection, and I hid the totems this time." She nodded to a lumpy dishtowel lying on the table by the window. "And your boyfriend is a big, bad werewolf. He can take out your miserable ex with one swipe of a paw. I'm sure this will all be over soon." She smiled. "And the blue moon is right around the corner…"

Rain cringed inwardly but kept her expression neutral. How could she tell her sister—who had worked so hard on the unbinding spell, who had risked so much by simply moving to New Orleans and working with her—that she didn't plan on asking Chase for his blood?

She pulled her shirt over her head and shoved her legs into her jeans. "Chase said he was going to send a werewolf over to keep watch."

"He sent two. Why don't you come meet them?" Snow gestured toward the store front and stepped into the doorway.

Rain glanced in the mirror and tousled her tangled hair. "I suppose I've looked worse."

Snow rolled her eyes. "You're glowing like a woman in love. Now, come say hello to our guests before they start thinking we're rude."

After slipping on her shoes, Rain followed her sister into the storefront. Macey sat at the small cake tasting table in the corner with a tall, blonde woman. Though their statures were different, they both had bright-green eyes and similar facial features. The taller one's aura glowed the deep orange of a werewolf, while Macey's was a more muted tone.

Rain approached the table. "Hi. I'm sorry for dragging you out here in the middle of the night."

Macey stood and shook her hand. "It's no problem. I work nights, so I'm used to it."

The other woman rose to her feet and offered her hand. "Alexis Gentry. Nice to meet you."

Rain cut her gaze between the two women. Wasn't Macey's last name Carpenter? "You're obviously sisters, so I take it Gentry is your married name?"

She paused, her lip curling as if the idea disgusted her. "No, it's not."

Rain gave her a questioning look. Sisters with different last names? Did that mean they had different fathers? Weren't werewolves supposed to mate for life?

Alexis shrugged. "Long story."

She made a mental note to ask Chase about it later and turned her gaze to Macey. "Since you're here, do you want to talk about your wedding cake? I can show you my portfolio." She shuffled to the cabinet that held her books.

"Are you up for that?" Macey followed. "With everything that's happened…"

"There's a murderous madman on the loose, and people are dying because of me." A sob threatened to bubble from her chest, but she swallowed it down. She would not lose control in front of these women. Taking a heavy album from the shelf, she clutched it in her arms. "It will help keep my mind occupied until Chase comes back."

Macey nodded. "We'll be feeding several hundred people, but I'd like to keep it as simple as possible."

Rain set the portfolio on the table and sank into a chair. "Simple. Elegant. Big doesn't have to mean elaborate."

"Gentry…" Snow sat on a barstool and tapped a finger against her lips. "Where are you from?"

Alexis cut her gaze to Macey. "All over. Our parents were rogues, and they traveled a lot."

Snow smiled. "We might be related."

Rain's stomach turned. "What?"

"Way, way back…I'd have to look at my notes…one of the Connolly witches married a Gentry werewolf." She hopped off the stool and sashayed around the counter. "I researched our family tree as a gift for our grandmother's eightieth birthday. Coffee?"

Macey looked up from the portfolio. "That would be great."

Rain's throat went dry. "Why didn't you tell me that?"

Snow shrugged and filled the pot with water. "It was a long time ago; you wouldn't have been interested back then. Anyway, I think it was our great-great-grandmother's sister who married the Gentry. We don't have any werewolf in us." She smirked. "Well, *I* don't have any werewolf in me. You, on the other hand, occasionally do."

Heat crept up Rain's cheeks, but she wouldn't let her sister distract her. She looked at the women. "I'm sorry. You have to go. You can't be here. You can't show me kindness."

"Why not?" Alexis took a cookie from the plate Snow set on the table.

"You don't know about my curse?"

The werewolves shook their heads.

Rain's heart warmed. Chase hadn't told her secret. "Any witch who shows me kindness will suffer. Even if you have a little bit of witch blood, you're at risk. Being here, doing me a favor like this, you could end up getting run over by a bus."

Snow nodded. "It's happened to me. Well, it was more of a bump than a complete run-over, but it hurt like hell."

Rain gave her sister an apologetic look, but she waved it off. She'd lost count of how many times Snow had fallen victim to her curse, but every incident added another ounce of guilt to the weight she carried on her shoulders.

"Good thing we're not doing this for you, then," Alexis said around the cookie in her mouth. "We're under orders from the alpha."

That could've been a loop-hole, saving them from the curse, but it was best not to take chances. "You should leave."

"Are you kidding?" Alexis took another cookie. "I'm a rogue, and even I know better than to disobey an alpha. I leave, and I'll never be allowed back in New Orleans again. Especially since you're—"

"We'll be fine." Macey gave her a reassuring smile. "We're doing this for Luke...and for Chase." A funny look flashed in her eyes before she focused on the album. "I like this one, but it will have to be bigger, I'm afraid. Can you make this to feed four hundred?"

Rain let out a breath. Hopefully her curse would spare these women. They couldn't go against their alpha's orders. "Believe it or not, that one fed two-fifty. I can make it a little bigger. Is that the one you want?"

Alexis laughed. "She *wants* to elope and get married on a beach somewhere private."

Macey glared at her sister. "I'm adjusting to all the...people in my life. Before I joined the pack, it was just me and my parents. Now my family has grown by two hundred members."

Rain looked at Alexis. "You said you're rogue? Why aren't you in the pack?"

Her smiled faded. "Long story."

"And how is it that you and Luke are already mates but you aren't married?"

Snow set a tray of coffee on the table and cleared her voice. "Stop drilling them with questions. Some things are private."

Macey smiled and gave Rain that strange look again. "It's okay. I had a lot of questions in the beginning too." She pointed at a cake picture in the album. "Definitely this one."

"I'll write it down." Snow took the portfolio to the counter.

Macey folded her hands on the table. "Our parents died when we were very young, and we spent our childhoods in foster care. We didn't know we weren't human. Alexis ran away when she started shifting, and I got adopted shortly after. I had no clue I was a werewolf until I met Luke." Her eyes sparkled at the mention of her mate's name. "Being mates is different than being married. A couple can be mates without getting married because it's an oath you take before the pack."

Alexis took a sip of coffee. "It's binding. Marriage can end in divorce, but once a werewolf takes a mate, it's for life."

Macey nodded. "Normally, werewolves will become mates and get married at the same time. Luke was on a deadline. He had to be mated in order to become alpha, so we took the oath and then planned the wedding."

The look on Rain's face must have given away her confusion because Macey laughed. "Don't worry. The longer you're around Chase, the more things will start to make sense. Being loved by a werewolf is a gift to be treasured." The sparkle returned to her eyes, and Rain's chest tightened.

Did Chase's eyes ever sparkle when he talked about her? Rain's entire body tingled from thinking about him.

"Anyway…" Alexis said. "Tell us about the creature they're out hunting. Chase called it a tulpa. Where did it come from?"

Rain shifted her gaze to the last cookie on the plate. These women were risking their lives to protect her. They deserved the truth. "When I lived in Miami, I was in training for a spot on the national council. I had to complete a research project to qualify, so I was looking into an ancient form of magic that's no longer practiced. A tulpa is an entity created in the mind. It requires complete focus. The conjurer has to go into a meditative state for hours at a time, days and weeks on end. I thought it was impossible. A myth."

She looked at the women, who stared back at her intently. Snow pulled a chair beside her and rested her hand on her back.

"I was dating Isaac at the time…before I found out he was cheating on me and stealing my energy." A spark of anger ignited inside her, but she squelched it. Getting mad wouldn't do her any good. "I shared my research with him, and he apparently figured out how to make it work. I guess since he has the power to drain energy, his tulpa does too. It can shapeshift, and he can see through its eyes."

She shook her head. "But it doesn't really exist, so it can't be killed. Isaac is the only one who can destroy it."

Alexis lifted an eyebrow. "What if we destroy Isaac?"

"That would work too, but he's smart. He won't be easy to find."

"Have a little faith." Alexis crossed her arms. "Werewolves are excellent hunters."

She didn't lack faith. If anyone could find Isaac, it would be Chase and the other werewolves. But the fact that Chase couldn't shift had her trembling on the inside. That tulpa was fast, and Chase moved like a human. If he got hurt… His healing ability was bound with the rest of his magic. Did he realize that?

Macey put her hand on Rain's. "He'll be okay. They all will."

"Careful showing me kindness."

Macey gave her a sympathetic look and dropped her arm to her side.

"She's saying that to reassure herself." Snow looked at Macey, who nodded. "Her mate is out there too."

Rain's bottom lip trembled, so she bit it. She had to hold herself together. Becoming a blubbering mess would do nothing but make her look weak. Chase would be fine. They hunted in a pack, so the other werewolves would have his back. She took a deep breath and gave Macey an appreciative smile. "Can I ask you a personal question?"

Macey swallowed. "Sure."

"Are you and Luke...is he your fate-bound?"

Macey glanced at Alexis before focusing on Rain. "Yes. I didn't understand it at first...how someone could feel *that* deeply in a short amount of time."

Rain licked her lips and swallowed the dryness from her mouth. "Do werewolves ever mate with someone who isn't their fate-bound?"

"All the time," Alexis said.

"Why don't they wait? If their fate-bound is out there somewhere, why would they take someone else as their mate?"

Macey tilted her head. "There's no guarantee a werewolf will meet their fate-bound. It's not a rare occurrence, but many don't. Love is love, whether fate brought you together or if you met by chance."

"That makes sense." Even if she wasn't Chase's fate-bound, he could still love her deeply. And if they became mates, he'd remain faithful for the rest of his life. "But what if a werewolf takes someone as his mate, and then he later meets his fate-bound? What happens then?"

Macey grinned. "I don't think fate would introduce them if he'd taken another mate. I'd have to ask Luke, but I've never heard of that happening." She looked at Alexis.

"I've never heard of it either. If fate has plans, you can't stop them from happening, can you, Macey?" She smirked at her sister.

Macey returned the look, something passing between them that even Rain knew better than to ask about. Her filter did occasionally work, though Snow would say otherwise.

Macey smiled at Rain. "You don't have to worry about that."

"I—" A *bang-bang-bang* sounded on the door, rattling it in its frame.

"Who the hell?" Snow paced to the front window and peered through the glass. "Oh, shit."

Rain's heart raced. "Who is it?"

The werewolves rose to their feet, Macey's hand hovering over the gun holstered at her hip.

"It's Calista and her band of merry meddlers. Six of them."

"Six?" Why was the high priestess of a coven she wasn't allowed to join knocking on her door at three in the morning? "You're sure it's her?"

"Come check their auras. Unless the tulpa multiplied, I'm pretty sure it's the coven."

Rain shuffled to the front and looked out the window. Calista banged on the door again, her deep-magenta aura sparkling with power. This couldn't be good. "It's her. I guess we better let them in."

Snow opened the door, and Calista pushed past her, marching toward Rain. She spun in a circle, taking in the room, her gaze pausing on the werewolves, her lip curling in disgust. "Rain Connolly, you're charged with the murder of three witches."

Ice flushed her veins. "What? No!"

"Subdue her." Calista jerked her head at Rain, and two of her subjects marched toward her.

Her mind reeled. Three witches? *Oh, no.* Isaac did drain another one to gain the strength to come here tonight. One strong enough to cast the binding spell he'd put on Chase. "It wasn't me."

Macey and Alexis moved in front of her before the witches could reach her. "She's not going anywhere with you." Macey kept her hand resting on her gun. "She's under protection of the pack."

Calista crossed her arms. "The pack would protect a murderer?"

"I didn't kill them. I've been here all night. I swear." She clutched Snow's hand. How could they accuse her of such an atrocity?

"A body was found in a dumpster behind Frenchman Street."

Rain cringed.

"We found the other one on your back doorstep."

The room seemed to turn into a vacuum, sucking the air from her lungs. It wasn't enough for her cheating ex to kill innocent people and hurt the man she loved. He'd set her up to be charged with the crime too. "Isaac was here. The one who did it. Please, if you'll listen to me, I can explain everything."

Calista put her hands on her hips. "You can explain from your holding cell when a council member arrives. You are the only witch in New Orleans with no powers of your own, so you're stealing them from others. Take her sister too. She probably lured Jason here."

"Jason Clements?" Snow squeezed her hand tighter.

Sadness filled Calista eyes before she hardened her gaze. "Yes."

The other two witches advanced toward them. Macey drew her gun. "The order of the alpha is that she remains in this building, unharmed, until he returns."

The high priestess inclined her head, looking down her nose at Macey. "You're his mate, right? I've heard your story. You almost tore the pack apart once; are you sure you want to be the reason we start a war?"

Rain clenched her jaw. Three people were dead, a little girl was sick, and Chase's magic was bound...all because of her. She couldn't let anything else happen. "Stop." She wedged her way through her werewolf guardians. "I'll go peacefully."

"Rain, don't." Alexis took her arm, but she pulled away.

"You don't need to start a war over me."

Snow's eyes widened, but she stepped around the werewolves to stand by Rain's side. "I'll go too."

Macey holstered her gun and nodded. "Luke's not going to be happy about this." She narrowed her eyes at Calista. "Expect to hear from him soon."

The coven allowed Rain to lock up before leading Snow and her to the back seat of a black Mercedes. "Anything I do for the rest of the night that seems like kindness," Snow said, "is actually emotional support for myself." She flashed a small smile. "Just so you know."

They remained silent on the drive to the coven house, Snow gripping her hand the only thing keeping her grounded.

If the national council believed Calista's accusations, Rain was as good as dead. She'd been warned when they cursed her that the next step would be execution. Was that Isaac's plan all along? Not to be the one to murder her, but to let the council do it?

Flanked by four witches, Rain and Snow followed Calista into the house and down a flight of steps to the coven's makeshift prison. A single cot sat against one brick wall, and two lawn chairs occupied the center of the small room. Someone shoved her from behind, and Rain stumbled inside.

Snow rushed in with her and caught her by the arm. "Was that necessary?"

Calista straightened her spine. "The spell on this room neutralizes magic, and guards will be posted outside. Don't make this difficult by trying to escape."

Rain crossed her arms to hide her trembling. "There's nothing behind my building but a trash can. How did you know the body was there?"

"His girlfriend tracked his phone when he didn't come home." Calista mirrored her posture.

"Jason was my friend," Snow said. "We didn't do it."

"Save it for the council." Calista closed the door, and the sound of the magic lock clicking into place pierced the silence like a nail in a coffin.

Rain looked at her sister. "You knew Jason?"

Tears pooled in Snow's eyes, and her bottom lip trembled as she nodded. "Yeah." She wiped her cheeks. "He was powerful too. Whatever spells Isaac cast with Jason's magic will be hard to undo."

Rain sank onto the cot, dropping her head in her hands. "He bound Chase's power."

"Oh, no." Snow sat next to her.

"No kidding."

"I'm so sorry."

Rain let out a dry chuckle. "Looks like neither one of us will be getting our magic back anytime soon. If ever." She dragged her hands down her face. "He'll lose his rank in the pack. The council will have my head on a plate. The only good thing about this situation is that Isaac can't get to us in here."

Snow rubbed her hand across Rain's back. "There you go. Way to look on the bright side."

CHAPTER NINETEEN

CHASE STOPPED AT A RED LIGHT AND GROUND HIS TEETH. They'd searched every damn inch of a five-mile radius around the spot where Isaac had latched on to him the first time, and they'd found nothing. Not a trace of the tulpa or the bastard who created it. Chase would still have been out there searching if Luke hadn't called them back in.

They'd split up, each of them taking a third of the area, so he'd managed to keep the fact that he couldn't shift to himself so far. Sooner or later, though, he'd have to fess up and admit his problem. Sure, he might lose his rank in the pack, but he didn't give a damn about rank. Unlike witches, a werewolf would never turn his back on one of his own. He could go it alone or he could have the support of the pack at his back. His choice.

He'd keep it to himself for the time being though, to protect Rain.

How long was this damn light going to stay red? He needed to get back to his woman. With thoughts of running it skittering through his brain, he lifted his foot from the ground as his phone buzzed in his pocket. He checked the screen and found a message from Luke: *Get to the bar. Now.*

Cursing, he hung a right on St. Philip and headed to O'Malley's.

At six in the morning, the place sat empty, save for a few men on Luke's crew having breakfast. He nodded to the morning bartender and shuffled through the side door toward Luke's office.

As he entered the room, he found the alpha sitting in a chair behind the massive oak desk, his mate perched on the edge of the surface, holding his hand in both of hers. Alexis occupied a green vinyl chair facing the desk, and they all looked at him with grim expressions as he closed the door behind him.

A feeling of unease expanded in his chest like rising dough. If they were here… "Where's Rain? Is she okay? If that bastard got to her—"

"She's not hurt. She's…" Alexis looked at Luke.

"The coven has her. Two more witches were drained, and they're blaming Rain and her sister."

"What? That's insane." His nostrils flared, and he clenched his hands into fists as he focused on Alexis and then Macey. "How could you let them take her?"

"Watch your tone." Luke growled in warning.

Chase lowered his gaze, swallowing down his frustration. "Sorry."

"We weren't going to let them." Macey's voice held sympathy. "She chose to go with them to avoid a confrontation."

That sounded like Rain. The pack would go to war to protect one of their own, and since he'd let them know she was his fate-bound, she was included. Rain would never let a war happen over her.

But she didn't have a choice.

He turned and grabbed the doorknob.

"Where are you going?" Luke's voice held an edge of warning, reminding Chase he hadn't been dismissed.

His muscles tensed, and he squeezed the door knob tighter. "To get Rain."

"You can't bust into the coven house and take her by force. She's one of them. They have jurisdiction in this."

"She's not one of them." Frustration raised his voice, so he took a deep breath to calm himself. Luke might have been his best friend, but he could tear Chase's ass apart if he didn't show the alpha respect. "She's not allowed in the coven because she's cursed. If a witch shows her any kindness, they'll suffer for it. They're terrified of her, so there's no telling how they're treating her."

Luke glanced at his mate. "I'm aware of her problem, and the fact that I had to hear the information second-hand is another issue." He stood and walked around the desk to lean on the edge. "They found a body behind her building. It does look suspicious."

"I was with her all night, man. Don't tell me you believe them." He balled his hands into fists. If his own alpha wasn't on his side...

"I don't, but you need to go in there with a clear head and defend her logically."

Chase straightened his spine. "Yeah. Of course. I will." His head was as clear as spring water. His fate-bound needed his help, and he'd do anything to save her.

Luke cupped Macey's cheek in his hand and gave her a quick kiss. "Get some sleep today. I love you."

"I love you too." She cast a worried glance toward Chase. "Be safe."

"Always." Luke nodded to the door. "Let's go."

───────

Chase eyed the coven house as he marched up the sidewalk. No one would guess one of the best-kept houses in the Quarter housed a prison for witches in the back. Of course, no one would guess the quiet Irish pub on St. Philip held a prison strong enough to contain a werewolf either. New Orleans was full of dirty little secrets.

He stayed two steps behind Luke, silently thankful for his best friend's grounding presence. If Chase had come on his own, he'd have done exactly what Luke told him not to—busted in and taken his woman by force.

Alan, the witch he'd threatened in the alley, greeted them, crossing his arms and widening his stance in an attempt to look intimidating as he blocked their entrance. "Come to beg for your woman's release? Not so tough now, are you?"

Luke straightened to his full height, and Chase crossed his arms, mimicking Alan's posture. He'd show this asshole tough. A hint of fear flashed in the witch's eyes before he huffed and stepped aside, allowing them entrance.

Calista clicked into the foyer, wearing a pressed suit, her hair twisted into a neat knot on the back of her head. She appeared polished, but the dark circles beneath her eyes betrayed her. She'd lost sleep, whether from dealing with Rain or the loss of some of her own, Chase couldn't be sure.

Frankly, he didn't care. She had his love, and he wanted her back.

"Where's Rain?" His voice came out more hostile than he'd planned, but he couldn't hold back his anger. "If she's hurt…"

Luke put a heavy hand on his shoulder. "We'd like to negotiate her release."

Calista inclined her head. "I'm not releasing her. As soon as the hour is decent, I'll be placing a call to the national council and recommending immediate execution. We've put up with the murderous bitch and her curse long enough."

A deep growl rumbled in Chase's chest, and Luke tightened his grip on his shoulder. "She didn't kill those witches."

"Can you prove it?"

He attempted a step toward her, but Luke held him back. "I was with her all evening."

"You don't need to get your council involved in this." Luke dropped his arm to his side. "We know who's behind the murders, and we can stop him."

Chase moved closer to the witch. "We're not leaving without Rain and Snow. Let them go and no one has to get hurt."

Calista stiffened. "Call off your dog, alpha."

"Chase." Luke's voice was low with warning.

He needed to step lightly. Pissing off the high priestess wouldn't help his cause. He moved back, lowering his voice and speaking through clenched teeth. "Please let me see her."

The priestess regarded him, an amused smirk lighting on her lips. "She's special to you, isn't she?" She chuckled. "All this time I thought you had a grudge against witches, when it seems it's only me you can't stand."

Alan suppressed a chuckle. Calista cast him a sideways glance, and he stared at the floor.

Chase held her gaze, silently challenging her to continue mocking his emotions. He didn't have to explain himself to her, and he was done being civil. If she didn't take him to his woman within the next thirty seconds, he'd force his way in.

Luke must have felt Chase's intent because he stepped beside him, close enough to stop him from attempting anything stupid. "Listen to their story."

She shook her head. "How will I know they're telling the truth? Perhaps your second is in on it. Maybe he's an accomplice to her crimes."

"I'll vouch for him." Luke crossed his arms and gave her a challenging stare.

Her gaze danced between them before focusing on the alpha. "Luke, as much as I respect you, I can't…" She tapped a finger to her lips. "Although…I do know a way I could discover the truth on my own." She steepled her fingers beneath her chin and looked at Chase. "I offer you a trade."

"Name it." He'd do anything. Whatever she wanted was hers if she'd give him Rain.

"A pint of your blood. I can use it in a tracking spell to find the killer—whomever she may be—and I'll have enough left over for… future uses."

Her offer hit him like a meat cleaver to his heart. Of all the things for a witch to ask from him… No telling what she could do with that much blood. That much power. He swallowed the thickness from his throat and opened his mouth to respond.

Luke cut him off. "Not a chance. Werewolf blood is sacred for a reason. No witch is getting a single drop from my pack."

Chase pressed his lips together to suppress a sigh of relief. If he'd have answered the way he'd intended, he'd be facing twenty years in the pit…if Luke went light on his punishment.

Calista shrugged and cast Chase a knowing look. "That's a shame. Worth a try though." Alan whispered something in her ear. She paused, looking thoughtful for a moment before squaring her gaze on

Chase. "I like the idea, Alan. Unfortunately, spells that hinder free will are forbidden, even for the high priestess."

Damn, this witch seemed to know all his weaknesses. He couldn't give her his blood, but if he could get Rain back another way... "What kind of spell?"

"Alan suggested a truth spell. I have one; it's very easy to make, but the serum lasts twenty-four hours. You'd be forced to speak the truth for a full day."

"Give it to me. I've got nothing to hide."

She grinned and glanced at Luke. "What if I were tempted to make him spill your pack secrets?"

Chase answered, "If the pack has any secrets, I don't know them. I'm not first-family."

"Interesting..."

If she didn't wipe that shit-eating grin off her face, he'd be tempted to do it for her. He shoved his hands in his pockets to hold them still. His fate-bound was somewhere inside this house, and being this close without being able to see her grated on his nerves, making him want to snap.

She shook her head. "It's not worth the risk. Not when I'm about to get the council involved."

"Are there any side effects?" He couldn't let her dismiss it that easily. If he could get Rain back, he'd endure whatever the priestess threw at him. "Besides having to speak the truth for twenty-four hours, will anything else happen to me if I take the serum?"

She scoffed. "I'm a high priestess; no low-level witch could achieve a position like this. My spells do exactly as intended. Nothing more."

That was all he needed to hear. "You're not hindering my free will if I'm agreeing to it. I'll tell the truth for a day; no problem. Give it to me. I'll sign a release. Whatever you need."

"I'll sign it too," Luke added. "It appears to be the only peaceful way to solve this dilemma."

Calista narrowed her eyes. "I don't take kindly to threats."

Luke leaned toward her. "And I don't take kindly to you kidnapping someone who's under the pack's protection."

"She's not a werewolf."

"She's not a member of your coven."

She exhaled slowly and nodded to Alan. "Draw up the contract. I'll mix the potion."

Chase unclenched his fists as the tension drained from his muscles. Good thing this hadn't turned into a fight. A werewolf who couldn't shift wouldn't stand much of a chance against their magic.

"Lydia," Calista called to a woman down the hall. "Remove the dark-haired witch from the cell and take her and the werewolves to my office."

The mere thought of Rain being locked in a cell made his skin crawl. He followed the woman into the hall and down a short flight of steps. She opened a door and peered inside. "You come. You...stay put."

Rain shuffled into the hallway, and Chase swept her into his arms. "Thank God, you're okay." He held her tight to his chest, relief flooding his veins as he breathed in her familiar scent. She was warm and safe, and there was no way in hell he'd leave this place without her.

"Chase?" Her words vibrated against his chest. "What's happening? Am I free? What about Snow?"

"Not yet." He loosened his grip so he could look at her, but he refused to let her go. "We have to negotiate your release with Calista."

"This way." Lydia motioned them toward the office.

"I'm glad you're okay." Luke patted Rain on the shoulder before following Lydia.

Chase wrapped an arm around his fate-bound's shoulders and held her tight to his side as they entered the high priestess's office. The same black cat from his last visit sat in the center of the desk, and it hissed at Luke, making a wide berth around the alpha before brushing against Chase's leg on its way out the door.

Luke flashed him a questioning look, and he held his breath. He needed to come clean about his powers, but now wasn't the time nor place. He was about to let a witch cast a spell on him for the fourth time in his life, and the thought soured in his stomach like two-week-old buttermilk.

"Calista will be right with you." Lydia closed the door, the unmistakable sound of the lock sliding into place penetrating the silence.

"Did you explain what happened? Has she called the council?" Rain clutched his shirt. "She wouldn't listen to me."

He rubbed her back, trying to calm her. "She hasn't called them yet. We're going to explain everything as soon as she gets here."

"I doubt she'll believe us. She's had it out for me since she found out about my—" She looked at Luke.

Chase hugged her. "He knows about your curse." He leaned down to whisper in her ear, "But not about mine yet."

She nodded. "I'm sorry to be so much trouble."

Luke leaned against the wall. "We take care of our own. It's no trouble."

"I know, but I'm not—"

"You're with Chase; you're one of us. Simple as that."

Chase's heart swelled with gratitude. One—that he didn't mention the fate-bound bit. He was waiting for the right moment to tell Rain. And two—that the alpha, and therefore the pack, had accepted her without confrontation.

Luke sauntered to the window and stared at the garden behind the house. "They're awfully trusting leaving us alone in this room. We could easily bust out and be done with this nonsense."

"I wouldn't leave Snow," Rain said. "And I doubt you could break out."

Luke looked at her over his shoulder, arching an eyebrow in disbelief.

Chase laughed. "She's right. They probably have a spell on the whole building. Nothing gets in or out unless they want it to. Rain had one on her shop."

"Snow made a new one, and she hid the totems this time," Rain said. "It's secure."

Luke gazed out the window. "What happened to the old one?"

"Damn tulpa tricked her." He took a deep breath and let it out in a huff. Since Calista was taking her sweet time, he might as well come clean. "It tricked me too."

Luke turned around to face them. "How so?"

He opened his mouth to spill the truth, but the lock disengaged and Calista sashayed into the room. The liquid inside the shot glass she carried glowed bright blue, and Rain tightened her grip on his waist.

The priestess offered him the glass, and though his throat thickened to the point he could barely breathe, he took it.

"What is that?" Wariness edged Rain's voice as she cut her gaze between Calista and the glass.

"A truth spell." Calista smiled triumphantly. "Your wolf-boy has agreed to take it in hopes of saving you from execution."

Rain's eyes widened, and she fisted his shirt in her hand. "Chase, no. You don't have to do that."

"Yes, I do." He lifted the glass, but Calista rested her hand on top of it.

"Not until you both sign the waver." She set a sheet of paper on her desk and plucked a pen from a wooden container.

Luke stepped toward the desk and took the pen. "You're sure you want to do this?"

Chase couldn't force the *yes* through his throat, so he nodded. Luke signed the paper and handed him the pen. He scanned the words on the page. He'd be promising not to hold Calista or the coven accountable for anything that happened because of the spell. *Anything.* "This doesn't say what the spell does."

The priestess narrowed her gaze. "It says it's a truth potion. Self-explanatory."

He shook his head. "I want it in writing. This contract absolves you of *any* harm done for any reason. I'm agreeing to a truth serum that you swore would only force me to tell the truth for twenty-four hours. If you're so sure of your magic, guarantee that's all that will happen to me in writing."

She glared at him before snatching the pen from his hand. "Fine." She scribbled the guarantee onto the page and initialed the change.

Chase took the pen, fisting it in his hand to stop his trembling. Taking a potion from Rain had been one thing. He trusted the woman with every fiber of his being. He couldn't muster a single iota of trust for the priestess, but he pressed the pen to the page and scribbled his name anyway. As he formed the final *P* in his last name, he hesitated, crushing the ball-point into the paper until black ink puddled around it. Calista pried the contract and the pen from his grip and shoved them into a drawer.

He looked at the potion in his hand. His stomach roiled, his breathing growing shallow as he lifted it to his nose to sniff. It smelled sweet, like cotton candy, and tiny bits of silver sparkled in the liquid.

His mind flashed back to his childhood. The witches, his so-called friends. The ritual. The pain he'd endured from whatever potion they'd convinced him to take. They'd almost killed him. His body swayed, the sensation that he stood in the center of a merry-go-round spinning out of control, making it hard to breathe.

Rain put her hand on his back, steadying him. "If there is anything other than a truth spell in that glass, Calista, I swear on my life—"

"If he doesn't drink the potion, you won't have a life much longer. I suggest you keep your mouth shut."

Was he being naïve again? Maybe. But Luke and Rain would have his back if this went south.

He closed his eyes and tossed back the potion. The sticky, sweet liquid burned down his throat as if it took a layer of flesh with it to his stomach. He braced himself for the sensation to spread through his core, but the burning ceased.

Rain put a hand on his chest. "How do you feel?"

"I expected worse." Aside from a slight tingling in his head, he didn't feel any effects from the spell. "Are you sure you did it right, Calista?"

She sank into the chair behind her desk. "We'll find out, won't we? Have a seat."

He crossed his arms. "I'd rather stand." Sitting would make him vulnerable, and he couldn't give the priestess any more of an edge.

Luke looked him in the eyes, silently asking if he was all right. Chase nodded.

"Suit yourself." Calista leaned back in her chair. "I'll ask you a few test questions first to make sure it's taken effect."

Chase exhaled slowly. The smirk on the witch's face told him he wouldn't like what she planned to ask.

"You said you aren't first family. Luke has a cousin who is; why isn't he second in command?"

He ground his teeth and looked at Luke. Pack business wasn't *her* business, but what Stephen did was no secret. "He tried to kill Luke's mate."

She nodded. "Where is he now? Dead?"

He chewed the inside of his cheek, fighting the compulsion to spit out the answer. "Why do you want to know?"

"Answer the question, please."

The tingling in his head increased, willing him to tell her the truth. "He's in the pit. Our pack prison. Luke spared his life."

"Interesting." She folded her arms on the desk and leaned forward. "You said you and Rain were together all evening. Tell me what you were doing."

He clenched his jaw, hoping the sharp pain shooting through his temple would overpower the truth tingling in his brain. Answering with a question of his own seemed to be the only way to quell the confessions. "What do you think we were doing?"

Rain put a hand on his bicep. "That's none of your business, Calista, and it doesn't have anything to do with the murders."

She arched an eyebrow. "He'll answer the question or this meeting will adjourn and you'll be handed over to the council."

"We were having sex." He put his hand over Rain's and cringed at the indecent way the words sounded on his lips. It had been so much more than that.

Calista grinned. "Who was on top?"

"What the hell, Calista?" What kind of sick individual got their kicks from forcing people to talk about their sex lives? The tingling in his head intensified. Sharing his private, intimate experiences with anyone but the woman he loved appalled him, but the spell forced him to answer. "She was."

The priestess looked at Rain. "You got a werewolf onto his back. Impressive. With his attitude, I expected him to be more…dominant."

She raked a heated gaze down his body. "I guess you're all bark and no bite."

Chase growled a warning, but what was the use? He'd have to endure her questioning if he planned to save his woman. "I respect her. What we do in the bedroom is a shared experience."

"I see." She flashed a wicked grin. "Tell me, Chase. If your alpha hadn't been here to stop you, would you have given me your blood to save her?"

Anger seared through his chest like a blade taken straight from the forge. "Goddammit, witch." She was setting him up.

Rain gasped. "She asked for your blood?"

"She did." He looked at Rain, and her eyes grew wide in disbelief. Then he cut his gaze to Luke, who kept his expression neutral, though he probably knew Chase's answer already. Speaking the truth out loud would be admitting he'd disobey the alpha and pack law. He might as well walk his ass back to the bar and lock himself in the pit right now.

"Answer the question." Calista's voice grew impatient. "Would you have disobeyed your pack law and given me your blood to save this woman?"

The air in the room pressed down on his shoulders, threatening to crumble him. He'd have to deal with whatever punishment Luke deemed appropriate. He gnashed his teeth and growled out his answer, "Yes."

As he uttered the word, Luke faked a giant sneeze, the sound so loud it echoed in the small room. "I didn't hear what you said, and I'm giving you a direct order never to repeat it."

Calista inclined her head. "Well played, alpha."

"No more games, Calista. Get the information you need and nothing more." He pinned Chase with a heavy stare. "I'm going to wait in the hall."

As Luke stepped through the door and closed it behind him, Chase tipped his head back and closed his eyes for a long blink. Even as he'd admitted his disobedience, his solid friendship with the alpha had saved him.

Calista crossed her arms, narrowing her gaze as she studied him.

"Interesting. What would the punishment have been if you'd given your blood to me?"

"Whatever the alpha deemed fit." Was she playing some kind of power game? Trying to exert her dominance over the werewolves?

"I see. Yet, you were willing to endure whatever he could dish out to save a magicless witch. Why?"

He looked at Rain, and he couldn't have stopped the words from spilling from his mouth if he tried. "I'd do anything for her. She's my fate-bound."

Rain's breath hitched, and tears collected on her lower lids. "I am?"

He tucked a strand of hair behind her ear. "This wasn't how I planned to tell you, but yes."

Her bottom lip trembled. "How long…? Why didn't you tell me?"

"I was afraid I'd scare you away. I wanted to give you time to fall in love with me." The longer he spoke, the faster the truth tumbled from his lips. "I hope that you'll be my mate, but since you're not a werewolf, I was afraid this bond would overwhelm you."

She threw herself into his arms, burying her face in his chest. "It's not scary, Chase. I feel it too."

She couldn't possibly, but he'd let her believe it if she wanted to.

Calista let out a dry laugh. "If I'd known this juicy detail, I would've gotten *her* to ask for your blood."

He stiffened. "She would *never* ask for such a thing." He kissed her forehead as she slid from his arms. "She knows me too well."

"Can we get on with this?" Rain's brow furrowed as she sank into a chair. "Let us tell you what happened so we can stop anyone else from dying."

The priestess narrowed her eyes. "Fine. Tell me who's killing witches."

Chase explained the story of Rain's ex showing up in her shop and everything that led up to the event. Calista's pen flew furiously across a sheet of paper as she took notes. She asked for precise locations where they'd seen the tulpa each time, and he showed her on a map where Isaac had gotten hold of him in the swamp.

"I don't recommend sending any of your witches out hunting for him. He's proven he can kill. Let the werewolves handle it."

Calista stared at the map and tapped her pen on the spot in the swamp. "You have twenty-four hours to *handle* it before I send my own team after him."

He grumbled. If the witches went hunting, they'd expose the whole damn magical community. They didn't care about secrecy. Didn't require it like the other supernatural beings living in New Orleans. "We'll take care of it."

Calista held his gaze, hesitating to let them go. "You'd better. For her sake. She is the reason this lunatic is here after all." She rose to her feet and motioned toward the door.

Chase didn't give her time to change her mind. He grabbed Rain's hand and tugged her to the exit.

Luke met them in the hallway. "And?"

"We're free to go. Let's get Snow and get the hell out of this place."

CHAPTER TWENTY

RAIN LEANED AGAINST THE COUNTER IN HER BAKERY, STARING AT Chase's magnificent backside as he conferred with Luke. Calista had activated the coven's emergency call tree, and every witch in New Orleans had been accounted for...all alive and well and on high alert for any suspicious activity. Isaac would be weak after the encounter last night. He didn't pose an immediate threat, which gave her mind time to ponder Chase's admission.

She was his fate-bound.

Her heart did a little flip in her chest. She needed to get him alone so they could talk about what this meant. He'd said he hoped she would be his mate, and she wanted to reassure him that she wanted the same. Of course, if she could get him alone, there wouldn't be much talking going on for a while.

Warmth bloomed below her navel, spreading through her body to chase away her fatigue. She'd slept maybe an hour last night, but she'd stay up all day if it meant sharing her bed with the sexy werewolf standing in her doorway.

She ran her tongue across her teeth, wrinkling her nose at the gritty sensation. She hadn't showered or used a toothbrush in more than twenty-four hours. A quick glance in the mirror revealed disheveled hair and mascara rings beneath her eyes.

She grabbed a napkin and wiped at the day-old makeup as Snow approached from the kitchen. "I double-checked all the totems. As soon as the guys get out of the doorway and lock it, the charm will be good to go."

Rain nodded, trying to wipe the grin from her face. She shouldn't have felt this happy when her life was in danger, but she couldn't help it. "I'm his fate-bound."

Snow smiled. "So I heard."

Chase looked over his shoulder and caught her gaze as he motioned for her. She pushed off the counter and stepped toward him, and he took her hand. "Tell him what you told me about the tulpa. How to defeat it."

"The only person who can stop it is Isaac, but he's not going to do it voluntarily."

Chase squeezed her hand. "But it's not real…"

She nodded. "It's a figment of Isaac's imagination that he's managed to make other people see, but in reality, it doesn't exist. As long as you can convince your mind it's not real…"

"Then it can't hurt you," Chase finished for her.

"Unless it gets ahold of a weapon. It can manipulate objects." She shivered. "It held a knife to my throat."

Luke cringed. "The blue moon tonight is good timing. Our wolves will be at their most powerful, so if we can find him, we can take him out."

Chase stiffened. "My wolf is bound." He looked into his alpha's eyes. "The bastard tricked me into taking a binding spell. I can't shift."

"Shit." Luke narrowed his gaze. "Why didn't you tell me this?"

"I was embarrassed. I…Crap." He looked away. "Goddamn truth spell. I didn't want you to think any less of me. You and your old man…y'all saved my life. I wouldn't be here today if not for the pack, and I don't want to let you down. How can I be your second if I can't even shift?" He chuckled and wrapped his arm around Rain. "That's a truth I didn't even know myself."

Guilt snaked its way into Rain's chest, squeezing it tight. "I'm so sorry."

He pressed his lips to her hair. "It's not your fault."

Luke shook his head. "I don't have to tell you all the things that could've gone wrong when we went into that coven house…and I'd have been fighting alone."

"Not alone. I can fight." He leaned into her side. "I'm sorry, man. I let you down."

Luke inhaled deeply. "On the plus side, you won't have to fight the blue moon to take care of your woman tonight. You'll stay here with Rain. Macey will be your backup."

"Doesn't she have to work?" Poor Chase. She could tell he didn't like his friend thinking him unable to guard her on his own.

"Macey hasn't taken a vacation since she joined the police department. She's got plenty of days saved up." He clapped Chase on the shoulder. "We're hunting in turns. Call the bar if you need help. Someone will be around."

Chase nodded and tightened his grip on Rain as Luke strode out the door.

Rain locked it, activating Snow's protection charm, and turned to Chase. "What does he mean 'hunting in turns?'"

Chase shuffled to the counter and sat on a stool. "The younger, weaker wolves have a harder time fighting the shift on a blue moon. They'll hunt first. The strongest go last, since they can hold the beast longer. We can't have a hundred wolves hunting in the swamp at the same time, especially since the pull of the moon is so strong that we usually kill the first living thing we see."

She moved toward him, situating her hips between his legs and wrapping her arms around him, pushing the image of his last statement from her mind. "Luke doesn't think you're weak. You didn't let him down."

He sighed. "I did. I let you all down. I should've known that tulpa wasn't you. Anytime you're near me, I feel the bond in my heart, and now that I look back, I didn't feel it then. It didn't act like you. Hell, it wouldn't even speak. I let my guard down and got distracted, and I wasn't there for you when you needed me."

"Chase." She cupped his face in her hands, running her thumbs through his beard. "This is a ghost from *my* past. He's going after you to hurt me. I accept all the blame, and *I* am sorry for letting you down."

He smiled weakly. "You're pretty with your hair all messy like this." He ran his fingers into her mane and tousled her curls, but his attempt at flirting didn't mask the sadness in his eyes.

"Is something else bothering you?"

He pressed his lips together and lowered his gaze, obviously wanting to say no, but the truth spell wouldn't allow him to lie.

"You can trust me. With your secrets. With your heart. I will never hurt you."

"I know." He looked into her eyes. "Doesn't make it any easier to admit weakness. I'm second in command of the sixth largest wolf pack in the country. I'm not supposed to show my pain."

She kissed his forehead. "Let me be your safe place."

"I've never missed the blue moon hunt. My wolf is bound, but there's a humming in my blood. An ache. And I'm under orders to stay here, but I really want to hunt the bastard down. I want to break this spell, remove your curse, and dammit…I want to live happily ever after with you. Beauty and the Beast did it. Why can't we?"

She smiled. The more he spoke, the more compelled he'd be to keep going. To spill all his emotions. It was how truth spells were designed to work. "I have to admit, I like all this raw honesty."

He blew out a hard breath. "You know I'd never lie to you. Truth spell or not."

"I also know you wouldn't willingly wish…out loud anyway…that our lives were like a Disney movie."

He chuckled. "You know me well."

"I have an idea." Snow strolled in from the kitchen with her hands clasped behind her back. An excited look danced in her eyes. "I think you can both have your happily ever after. Rain, you could create an unbinding spell to free Chase. Your magic is strong enough."

Rain rested her hands on Chase's thighs and shook her head. "No, Snow." A trickle of dread inched down her spine. *Please shut up. Not this. Not now.*

"I'm not sure if we can take his blood now, or if we need to wait until the sun sets." She glanced out the window. "We might as well wait. There's an hour of daylight left. What do you think?"

Oh, goddess, no. She said it.

Chase stiffened. "Who's blood?"

"Yours. Duh." Snow pranced toward them and held the unbinding spell in front of her. "And look. We haven't even collected the blood, and the incantation has already appeared with him simply being here."

"You...want my blood." He blinked at her, the incredulous look in his eyes piercing her heart. Sliding off the stool, he stepped away from her and took the spell from Snow's hand.

Rain's heart pounded against her ribs. "No, Chase. It's not like that."

Snow continued, apparently oblivious to the tension. "With Chase's blood, I can complete the spell and unbind your powers. Then, with your magic back, you can write a spell to unbind Chase's magic, and boom. Happily ever after for both of you. Isaac won't stand a chance against both of you with your magic intact."

Chase scanned the paper and read the words aloud. "Two drops of blood from a first-born werewolf, given willingly, beneath a blue moon." He dropped it on the counter. "All this time, you've been after my blood?" His eyes tightened, his brow pinching as his expression wavered between unbelieving and appalled.

Her hands trembled with the need to touch him, to comfort him, but as she reached for him, he stepped away. "No. I mean...yes, the unbinding spell requires werewolf blood, but I wasn't going to ask you for it after..."

"But you *were* going to ask me for it before, weren't you?" The confusion in his eyes tore her heart to shreds. "Is that why you agreed to date me? So you could get my blood for your spell?"

She could have denied it. Sworn she'd never intended to ask, but she couldn't lie to him. "Originally, that was the plan."

"Well, shit. And there just happened to be a blue moon around the corner, so you thought you'd..." He raked a hand through his hair and turned away from her. "What the hell, Rain?"

"This isn't coming out right." She curled her arms over her head, clutching at her hair as she looked to her sister, widening her eyes in a *help me out* look.

Snow chewed her bottom lip and drummed her fingers on the counter. "She's been hot for you since you met. The fact that you're a werewolf and can break her curse is a bonus."

He growled.

"I'm not helping, am I?"

Rain glared at her. "No." She stepped toward Chase and put a hand on his arm.

He jerked away. "Don't."

Her breath lodged in her throat at his rejection. "Please let me explain." She reached for him again but let her hand drop to her side. She had to make him understand. "I've been living with this curse for seven years. When the council sent me the spell to break it, I was over the moon. The ingredients have been revealed one by one as I gather them, and the final one appeared the day after I met you."

The muscles in his jaw flexed as he ground his teeth, but he let her continue.

"Seeing werewolf blood as the final ingredient, I thought I was doomed. I'd never find a werewolf willing to give me his blood. But you know how fate works. Was it really a coincidence that a werewolf couple wanted me to make the cake for their wedding right before a blue moon? Then you came back to apologize, and I thought maybe…"

He let out a hard exhale and narrowed his eyes.

She hurried to finish before he stopped listening. "But then I got to know you, and I fell in love with you. And when you told me your story…with what happened to you when you were a kid…I knew I could never ask you for the same thing that hurt you back then."

He looked at the door. "Maybe I wasn't wrong to distrust witches."

"Chase, please." She took his hand, and he didn't pull away. "I wasn't going to ask you. I should have told Snow I didn't plan to ask." She looked over her shoulder at her sister.

Snow lowered her head. "I'm sorry."

"I love you, Chase."

His phone rang from his pocket, and he slipped from her grasp to answer it. "Hello?"

He paused as the other person spoke.

"What happened?"

Another pause. "All right. I'll leave as soon as Macey gets here."

He shoved his phone into his pocket and looked at her, his eyes finally softening. "There's been an emergency; Luke needs me at the bar."

"What happened?"

"I don't know. He sounded weird. Called from a number I don't recognize, so it must be important." He jerked his head toward the door at the sound of Macey knocking. Disengaging the lock, he swung the door open, stepping past Macey as she entered.

"I thought I was your backup, not your relief," Macey said.

"I have to go." He stopped outside the door and turned to Rain. "Macey will take care of you." Shoving his hands in his pockets, he turned and strode away.

"Everything okay?" Macey shut the door and turned the lock.

Rain opened her mouth to answer, but no words came. Nothing was okay. The man she loved thought she was using him, and she hadn't tried to stop him from walking away. Her deranged ex-boyfriend was killing innocent people to make her suffer. What if the emergency Chase had to attend to was dangerous? Would he do something stupid trying to prove himself and wind up getting hurt? "I have to go after him."

"Hold on." Macey put her hands on her shoulders. "You're supposed to stay put until the threat is neutralized."

"Yeah, Rain." Snow shuffled around the counter. "I'm sorry for blabbing about the spell. I thought you guys had talked about it already."

"Well, we hadn't." Her voice came out as a trembling whisper.

Macey let her go but didn't move from the doorway. "Whatever it is, I'm sure you'll work it out when he gets back."

"I'm not." Pressure mounted in the back of her eyes. "I'm going to take a shower and lie down for a while." She turned on her heel and trotted through the kitchen to her bedroom. Grabbing her robe, she headed to the bathroom and turned on the shower.

She had to get through to Chase somehow. To make him believe he could trust her. That she wasn't just another witch out for his blood. She stood beneath the stream, setting the water as hot as she could stand it and breathing in the steam. The warm moisture filled her nose, opening her airways and clearing her mind. She'd make this right somehow.

With her skin pink and softened from the heat, she shut off the water and slipped on her robe. She padded to her bedroom, pulled on a pair of sweatpants and a T-shirt, and gazed at her disheveled sheets. Her heart ached at the memory of sharing her bed with Chase. Picking up a pillow, she pressed her nose against it and inhaled deeply. His musky, masculine scent lingered on the soft fabric, and a sob caught in the back of her throat.

A tapping sound drew her gaze to the window, and she glanced out the glass in time to see a shadow dart from right to left.

She started for the window, but her phone chimed from the bedside table. She picked it up, and a message from an unknown number lit up the screen: *I have your boyfriend. If you want to see him alive, come to the swamp. Alone. My tulpa will guide you.*

Isaac. Her hand trembled, and the phone slipped from her grasp, landing on the bed. The screen dimmed, extinguishing the message as terror twisted in her gut. She couldn't let him hurt Chase. She would never forgive herself if anything else happened to the man she loved. To anyone.

Tiptoeing to the kitchen, she peeked into the storefront. Snow and Macey sat at the table, drinking coffee, so she grabbed a chopping knife from the block, padded back into her bedroom, and slipped it into her shoulder bag before shoving her phone in her pocket.

Before she could talk herself out of it, she snatched the bride and groom cake topper from beneath the dishtowel on her table and broke the couple apart, shattering the protection charm Snow had placed on the building. Opening the window, she crawled outside and ran to her car. Her hands trembled as she shifted into drive and headed to the swamp.

Tonight would probably end with one of them dead, and she had to make certain it wouldn't be Chase.

CHAPTER TWENTY-ONE

Chase pushed open O'Malley's front door and shuffled into the pub. Amber stood behind the bar, and his sister sat on a stool near the corner.

Bekah spun in her seat to look at him, her face contorting into a mask of concern as she met his gaze. "What happened?"

"Noth—" The word got stuck in his throat. Damn it, he couldn't even lie and say "nothing."

"None of your business." That was the truth. "Luke in the back?"

Amber furrowed her brow. "He's not here."

"Shit." He plopped onto a stool and checked the clock on his phone. Whatever this emergency was, Luke had better get there fast. Chase had bigger problems on his plate.

Honestly, when the call had come through, he'd been relieved to get away from the bakery. Away from Rain. A million thoughts spun through his head, but he couldn't seem to catch onto any of them. And with the truth spell active in his system, he might've said something he'd regret if he'd stayed.

Then again, truth spell or not, the thought that he should be there protecting her anyway clawed at the edges of his mind.

Bekah sat on the stool next to him. "You look like death warmed over." She put her hand on his. "You feel like it too. What happened?"

He pulled from her grasp. The last thing he wanted to do was talk about his feelings with his sister. "Where's Emma?"

"Mom took her to Shreveport to see the Imagination Movers show. They're spending the night in a hotel."

He nodded and checked the time again. Where the hell was Luke? As mixed up as his thoughts were about Rain, he didn't like leaving her when a madman was after her.

Bekah narrowed her eyes. "Did you break up with Rain?"

"Not yet. I…"

"Not *yet?*" Amber stepped toward him and rested her hands on the bar. "You can't break up with her. That's not how I felt your future."

Damn these women and their empathic abilities. He let out a dry chuckle. "How do you *feel* the future, anyway?"

Amber crossed her arms. "Tell us what happened, Chase."

His head tingled, the truth rolling through his brain and out his mouth before he realized what was happening. "She needs my blood for a spell. She's wanted it all along."

Bekah's eyes widened. "Does she know about…?"

"Yeah, she knows. She knows everything." He fisted his hands on the bar. "I trusted her, and she betrayed me. All this time I thought she was falling in love with me, but in reality, she wanted my blood. Turns out my disdain for witches was well-founded after all."

Bekah pursed her lips, tilting her head. "She does love you. I felt it in her the last time she was at the house."

A flutter of hope shot through his heart, but he squelched it. "She loves what I can do for her."

"What can you do? Why does she need your blood?" Amber asked.

He clamped his mouth shut as the truth spell tried to force the words from his lips. What the hell? If he stayed with her, the pack would find out about her curse eventually…and if he left her, what did it matter? "She's cursed. Her powers are bound, and two drops of my blood can break the spell. Apparently, werewolf blood is a highly coveted ingredient for potions."

Bekah gave him a confused look. "So you're upset with how she asked you? I don't understand the problem."

"She didn't ask."

"Then how do you know she needs your blood?"

"Her sister showed me the spell. Two drops of blood from a first-born werewolf, given freely beneath a blue moon." A sour sensation formed in his stomach. "Rain said after she learned about my past, she didn't plan to ask me, but..." He balled his hands into fists, unable to stop the truth from flowing. "Why would fate bind me to someone who wanted to use me?"

"Exactly," Amber said.

"Fate wouldn't." Bekah put her hand on his shoulder. "You're bound to her because you're supposed to be together. Because you need each other. I think you should give it to her."

How could she even suggest that, knowing what the punishment would be? He shook his head. "It's against our laws. Calista asked for some in exchange for Rain's freedom earlier today, and Luke forbade it."

"He wouldn't let you give it to *Calista*," Amber said. "Rain is your fate-bound, he won't stop you from giving it to her." She looked him hard in the eyes. "I know my brother...and you know him too. Stop using the alpha as an excuse."

He let out a slow breath and mumbled, "I'm scared." *Damn this truth spell.*

Bekah laughed. "I doubt two drops will hurt her."

"It's not that." He stared at the bar and traced the wood pattern with his finger.

"What are you scared of then?" His sister leaned an elbow on the bar. "You found your fate-bound. That's pretty damn special."

His shoulders drooped. "But she's not a were, so it only works one way." Shaking his head, he huffed and lifted his gaze. "My heart is bound to hers for the rest of my life, but she could walk away at any time. That would crush me. What would I do then?" Hell, where had that come from? What else had he been lying to himself about?

Bekah laughed. "Wow. This is the most emotion you've ever shared out loud."

He glared at her. "Don't get used to it."

"She's not going to walk away." Amber put her hands on her hips. "Fate wouldn't bind you to someone who would. Besides, my premonitions about your future have been strong. Your heart is bound to hers forever. I think she's worthy of receiving your blood."

Who was he kidding? He couldn't walk away from Rain if he wanted to. And deep down, he didn't want to. He loved his witch with every fiber of his being, and if his blood would break her curse, why wouldn't he give it to her? He'd give her the moon if he could pluck it from the sky.

"Do you believe her?" Bekah asked. "That she wasn't going to ask you for it?"

"I do." He pressed his fingers to his temples. "She was willing to sacrifice her unbinding spell to keep from hurting me."

Amber gave him a pointed look. "That says a lot about her character."

"You're right. There won't be another blue moon for two years. I can't let her live with her powers bound another day. Not when I can do something about it."

As soon as he finished whatever Luke needed him to do, he'd go to the bakery and break her curse. He checked the time again. "Where the hell is Luke? He told me to meet him here."

Amber furrowed her brow. "Luke took a group of teens out for the first hunt. I'm surprised he didn't ask you to chaperone too."

"He called me half an hour ago. Said there was an emergency."

"He was already in the swamp by then. He wanted to have the kids away from civilization before the sun set, so they didn't do anything stupid."

His stomach tumbled into his boots. The odd quality of Luke's voice. The unfamiliar number the call had come from. "Shit." He shot to his feet.

"What?" Bekah asked.

"If Luke comes back, tell him to call me ASAP." He darted out the door and climbed onto his bike.

Peeling off the curb, he sped down St. Philip toward Royal, weaving his way around taxis, narrowly missing a pedestrian who stumbled into the street. When he reached the intersection of Bourbon, a crowd of partiers stood in the street, oblivious to the line of cars trying to get by.

The driver of a Mercedes laid on the horn, and a couple of people shuffled out of the way. A belligerent drunk man yelled a string of profanities at the driver and gave him a one-fingered salute.

"Hell, I don't have time for this." Chase revved his engine and wound around the string of vehicles. His shoulder bumped the drunk, knocking him out of the way of the Mercedes as he sped past.

Hanging a right on Royal, he plowed onto the sidewalk in front of the bakery and parked against the wall. Snow and Macey sat at a table inside the store, and Snow padded toward the door as he pounded on it.

"Where's Rain?" He pushed through the entrance and marched through the storefront, into the kitchen.

Snow followed. "She's sleeping."

"Are you sure?" He flung open her bedroom door and found it empty. His stomach churned as he stepped into the room.

"Maybe she's in the bathroom." Snow ducked out and returned a few seconds later. "You don't think she…"

"She went after Isaac." He picked up the broken wedding cake topper he found lying in her bed. Half the groom's arm hung from the bride's hand where the two pieces had been connected.

Snow's eyes widened. "She broke my totem. The circle of protection." She took the bride half of the figurine from his hand. "Why would she go after him alone?"

His throat thickened. "She did it for me. To prove that I can trust her." He dropped the totem on the bed. "Damn it. The bastard lured me away so he could get to her." He brushed past Snow and stormed into the storefront.

Macey stood by the door. "What's the plan?"

"I have to go after her." He dialed her number, and it rang five times before going to voicemail.

"I can track her phone." Snow pressed a few buttons on her screen. "She's here." Pointing at the map, she angled the phone for him to see. "There's nothing out there but swamp."

"That's where he's hiding. I saw his tulpa there the night he tried to drain me. Shit." He clenched his jaw. He couldn't shift. He could handle the witch himself, but that damn tulpa was another story. Real or not, it could do some major damage. "If Rain had her magic, could she beat him?"

"Goddess, yes. She was the most powerful witch I've ever met. Are you willing to give us your blood?"

He glanced at Macey. She'd be obliged to tell Luke, but dammit, he didn't care. "I told you I'd do whatever it took to break her curse. Give me a knife."

"Hold on." Snow took a wooden box from a shelf and pulled out a copper bowl. "She has to pay me for mixing each ingredient or the curse will get me. If you give me your blood now, I might not make it out the door." She poured a thick liquid from the bowl into a small glass jar. "We'll do it when we find her. If she drinks the potion as soon as it's mixed, the curse should lift before it has time to affect me." She capped the jar and stuffed it in her pocket as she strode to the door. "I'm coming with you. I've got the incantation memorized."

He nodded and looked at Macey. "Will you stay here in case she comes back?"

"Of course."

"If you hear from Luke…"

She nodded. "He'll understand."

"Wait." Snow darted behind the counter and took a cookie from the display case. "Eat this. For clarity."

He looked at the blue-frosted question mark and shook his head. "I know exactly what I need to do."

She held it toward him. "Rain said that if you can convince yourself the tulpa isn't real, it won't be able to hurt you. This will help. Trust me."

Last time he ate a magic cookie, he lost his wolf. He cut his gaze between the cookie and Snow and clenched his teeth. Without the ability to shift, he'd need all the help he could get. He shoved it into his mouth and chewed. A tingling sensation spread across his tongue and down his throat as he swallowed.

Snow grabbed one for herself and followed him to his bike. He tossed her a helmet. She put it on and climbed on behind him, wrapping her arms around his waist. "We'll find her."

God, he hoped so.

Rain exited the highway and parked behind a cypress tree. With the cover of night and the dense forest, no one would notice her car in the trees until morning, and hopefully she'd be out of here before sunrise.

She climbed out of her car and clicked the door shut before peering into the trees. The blue moon hung high in the sky, casting the swampy forest in a silvery glow. Spanish moss wept from the branches of towering cypress trees, and a bullfrog croaked in the distance. The dank scent of rotting foliage hung in the thick, wet air, and as her eyes adjusted to the darkness, she caught sight of a shadow bounding through the trees.

Hopefully it was the tulpa and not a werewolf. She shook her head. Did she really hope the monster lurking in the trees was the slave of the man who lured her out here to kill her? According to Chase, Isaac and his tulpa weren't the only predators in the swamp she needed to worry about tonight.

She crept deeper into the trees, carefully placing each step to avoid slipping and breaking an ankle. Her shoes squished in the mud as if she walked on a wet sponge, the ground becoming soggier the deeper she ventured into the woods.

Her heart thrummed. Was Chase already dead? Had Isaac called her into the swamp to watch him bury the man she loved before he killed her too? She couldn't think that way. Not if she wanted to stand a chance against Isaac.

A rustling in the brush sounded off to her right, and she jerked her head toward the noise. The shadow rushed her, knocking her into a tree before darting off to the left. Her arm scraped against the bark with stinging pain, but she caught a glimpse of the dull-gray aura before the tulpa disappeared into the darkness.

She leaned her back against the tree and tried to calm her breathing. What was she thinking coming out here alone? Without her magic, she'd have to rely on strength and wit to outsmart the man who'd spent seven years planning his revenge. She'd rushed out here with no plan. No idea how to stop him.

Slipping her hand into her shoulder bag, she gripped the knife handle and tiptoed in the direction the shadow had run. Maybe she could reason with Isaac. Maybe she could convince him to…what? Let Chase go? Forgive her for sending him to a fate worse than death?

She stepped around a thick tree trunk, and her breath caught in her throat. Isaac stood in the clearing, his spine straight, the skin that clung to his bones filled out as if there were muscle beneath, the life-less body lying at his feet evidence he'd fed.

Her heart stopped for a moment, but the form was too small to be male. He'd drained a woman, using her life energy to rebuild his own body, gaining temporary access to whatever magic she possessed.

"Rain, you're just in time." Isaac smiled as the tulpa scooped the woman from the ground and tossed her body into the murky water.

"Where is Chase?" She tightened her grip on the knife in her bag.

Isaac laughed. "I've changed my mind about your boyfriend. I'm going to kill you first, so you can leave this world knowing that even your death couldn't save the ones you love from suffering."

Her lungs tightened until she could hardly breathe. "Why hurt them? It's me you want."

He tilted his head. "Because hurting them hurts you, my love."

Her jaw clenched, and the nails of her empty hand dug into her palm. "Don't call me that. You never loved me. You loved my magic."

"That's where you're wrong. I was infatuated with you from the moment I saw you, but you weren't the slightest bit interested in me. You were too focused on your goals. Opening your bakery. Gaining your place on the national council. I wasn't skilled enough to cast a love spell; you know how hard those are to create. An obsession spell, though…" He stepped toward her, clutching his back as if the move-ment caused him pain. "It wasn't an easy task, but it worked." He laughed again. "Boy, did it work."

The tulpa hovered next to her, inching closer, making her palms sweat. *It's not real. It can't hurt me.*

The shadow swiped a fist toward her face, and its hand turned to mist, disintegrating around her head and reforming behind her. She swallowed the bile creeping up the back of her throat.

Isaac narrowed his eyes, and the tulpa grabbed her bag, twisting it around her shoulder and pinning her arm behind her back. She held in a groan as sharp pain shot through her arm. She wouldn't give him the satisfaction of seeing her cry.

"He can still manipulate objects, whether you believe in him or not." The tulpa used her bag to throw her to the ground.

She landed on the same shoulder, and another wave of pain shot through her body. Using her hands, she pushed into a sitting position. "Let's talk about this, Isaac. You don't need to hurt anyone else."

"We could have talked about it when you caught me draining you…before you tried to kill me. Now, it's too late."

"I wasn't trying to kill you. I was trying to make the one you loved most hate you. How was I supposed to know you loved your power more than anything? I never would have done it if I hadn't been under your spell."

"We aren't so different, you know?" He took another step toward her and grimaced as he clutched his hip. "You loved your power more than anything too. You didn't have time for love until I made you make time."

"That wasn't love." She crab-walked backward until her shoulder smacked a tree.

"Obviously not."

Using the trunk for support, she pushed to her feet. "We've both suffered."

"You call your little curse suffering?" He spat out a dry laugh.

"I can fix this. The council…they sent me a spell to break the curse. If I get my powers back, I can undo the spell I put on you. We can both be free."

He paused, rubbing the raw skin on his jaw. Confliction clouded his eyes, his brow furrowing as he contemplated her offer. The tulpa reached into her bag, yanking out the butcher knife, and Isaac's gaze hardened. "We can both be free? Is that why you brought a knife?" The tulpa pressed the tip against the base of her throat.

She swallowed, and the sharp point pierced a shallow layer of skin. "It was a precaution," she dared to whisper.

"The council may think you've served your punishment, but I'll watch you burn in hell for what you've done."

With the blade pressed against her neck, she couldn't convince her mind the shadow wasn't real. It grabbed her arm, wrenching it behind her back, and forced her to her knees.

CHAPTER TWENTY-TWO

THE SIGHT OF RAIN ON HER KNEES WITH A KNIFE TO HER throat sent Chase's heart into overdrive, and he charged toward Isaac, barreling into him and knocking his boney body to the ground.

His concentration broken, Isaac's control of the tulpa slipped, and Snow dragged Rain away from the shadow. Chase drew his arm back to slug the bastard in the face, but the tulpa hurled the knife, jabbing it into his back.

Searing pain spread through his muscles, and he staggered to his feet, reaching behind, barely grasping the handle and yanking it from his back. His head spun. Blood gushed from the wound, and the muffled sound of Rain's scream reached his ears before his knees gave out.

Isaac scrambled into a sitting position, clutching his arm and grinding his teeth so hard that blood dripped from the corners of his mouth.

Gripping the knife, Chase advanced on the sadistic witch. The tulpa charged, knocking him to the ground again. The impact knocked the breath from his lungs, and electric pain shot from his wound through his chest. The edges of his vision darkened, and nausea churned in his stomach.

"It's not real, Chase," Rain called.

He squinted through his tears to find Snow clutching her arm, holding her back.

"It can't hurt you without a weapon," she said. "Use the magic from the cookie."

The shadow sat on his chest, a two-hundred-pound weight crushing his ribcage. "I don't believe in you." Chase closed his eyes and focused his mind. The magic from Snow's spell tingled behind his forehead, bringing his thoughts into crisp focus. "You're a figment of this sick bastard's imagination." The weight of the shadow lifted, and Chase stood, passing through it like a mist.

Using the trunk of a tree for support, Isaac clambered to his feet. He stumbled forward, narrowing his eyes in concentration, and the tulpa lunged for Chase again.

It's not really there. Chase stopped, closing his eyes briefly as the shadow passed through him yet again. He chuckled. "It's you and me now, Isaac."

Chase advanced on the witch, trying to ignore the searing pain ripping through his back. If his magic hadn't been bound, he'd have healed by now. Instead, he could barely get enough air into his lungs, and stars danced before his eyes as he closed in on the man trying to hurt his fate-bound.

The *snap* of a tree limb breaking barely distracted him from his target. He raised the knife, and something hard smacked into his back, knocking the air from his already starving lungs. He went down, the knife slipping from his grip and landing somewhere in the mud. The tulpa lifted the branch to strike him again.

Rain screamed and charged toward them. She grabbed onto the branch, engaging in a tug-of-war with the imaginary being, giving Chase a chance to stumble to his feet. His head spun. The world tipped on its side and his stomach roiled, but he grabbed a branch to hold himself upright. It was time to end this.

Isaac leaned against a tree, his body too damaged to move, but his mind agile enough to control the tulpa as if it were an extension of him.

Where the hell was the knife?

"Chase." Snow lifted her hand from the murky water and tossed him a two-foot-long icicle with a razor-sharp point. The intense cold stung his hand like dry ice, and a thin mist rose from the makeshift weapon like a magical aura.

Rain grunted as the tulpa spun around, pinning her between the branch and a tree. "Chase." His name came out as a squeak as the shadow pressed the air from her lungs.

He paused, momentarily paralyzed as the primal need to save his fate-bound fought to control his movements. Instinct to hurl himself at the shadow propelled him forward, but the only way to stop this monster stood behind him.

He turned to Isaac and hurled the frozen spear at him, piercing his chest. The witch gasped, his eyes widening in disbelief before he crumpled to the ground.

A strangled gurgling sound emanated from Isaac's throat as the tulpa dropped the branch, and it splattered in the mud. The entity reached for something on the ground and lunged for Chase.

The knife sank into his chest, an explosion of searing pain sending him to his knees.

"No!" Rain screamed and ran to him.

His vision tunneled, and he fell to his side and rolled onto his back. The tulpa rose behind Rain, lifting a branch above its head.

Chase gasped for breath to warn her, but he couldn't suck in any air. The sound of Isaac's hacking cough echoed in the night. Then it ceased. The tulpa dissolved, and the branch thudded to the ground.

Rain knelt by Chase's side, her head throbbing as if her heart had leapt all the way up to her skull. This couldn't be happening. Her mind reeled, a million thoughts ricocheting around in her brain, scrambling for coherence.

She put her hands on his chest. It barely rose and fell with his shallow breaths. "Oh, goddess, no. Chase? Talk to me, please. You're going to be okay."

"We need to get the knife out so he can heal." Snow grasped the handle and ripped the blade from his chest, and the wet, sucking sound of metal leaving flesh made Rain's stomach turn.

He groaned, his head rolling from side to side, his eyelids fluttering as blood gushed from the wound. Rain pressed her hands to the gash, trying to slow the flow, but blood pooled between her fingers, the deep-orange glow pulsing as his magic tried to break its bond.

"Why isn't he healing?" Snow's voice tipped with panic. "He's a werewolf. He should be healing."

Tears streamed down Rain's face, her heart wrenching in her chest. "His magic is bound. He's not going to heal. We need to get him to the hospital."

"No." His voice was barely audible as he put his hand on hers. "Take my blood. Break your curse."

"My curse is the last thing I'm worried about. I'm calling an ambulance." She fumbled for her phone and found it dead, the screen cracked, her distorted, tear-streaked reflection staring back at her from the blank surface. "Dammit!"

She looked at Snow, who held a small bottle in her hand. "What are you doing?"

"He offered his blood, so I'm taking it. There won't be another blue moon for two years."

Why were they both so concerned with her curse? Her soulmate lay dying. Saving him was all that mattered.

Chase coughed, sending more blood oozing from his wound. Rain pressed harder on the gash. "I don't care about my curse." She couldn't live without this man. He meant the world to her and spending a single second without him by her side would be unbearable.

"Take it, Rain." His voice was raspy and strained. "Fate bound us together for a reason, and it wasn't so I could die without helping you. I'm meant to break your curse."

"No." Hot tears stung her eyes. "Our hearts are bound because we're meant to spend forever together."

He gripped her hand. "Some forevers aren't that long."

A sob bubbled up from somewhere deep in her soul. This wasn't how it was supposed to end. She should've been the one lying on the ground, bleeding out. *She* was the one who deserved to die.

Snow lifted his shirt and pressed the bottle to his side beneath a stream of blood. The first drop fell into the nearly-completed potion, and nothing happened. Then the second drop splashed into the liquid, and a burst of light filled the bottle with shimmering orange sparkles.

Chase's eyes fluttered shut as Snow whispered the incantation.

Panic surged through Rain's veins. "Chase?" She took his face in her hands. "Don't die, Chase. I need you."

His lids opened into slits. "I love you, Rain."

"I love you too. Please don't leave me."

His eyes closed, and it felt as if the knife were driven into her own chest, filleting her heart into a million microscopic pieces.

Snow grasped her hand and closed her fingers around the bottle. "Take it, Rain. Don't let this all be for nothing."

She looked at the shimmering liquid in the glass. The cure for her curse. If she had the ability to heal, she'd down the potion in a heartbeat and use her powers to heal her werewolf. But she didn't. Her magic was useless against the wound draining the life from the man she loved.

She sucked in a breath. She couldn't heal Chase...but his wolf could.

Her heart was bound to his like a tether, their souls intertwined as if they were two parts of the same whole. Maybe...

She tugged on his chin, parting his lips and holding the bottle to his mouth.

"What are you doing?" Panic laced Snow's voice. "The spell was written for you. It won't work on anyone else."

"It will work on him. Fate didn't bind us together to rip us apart." She poured the potion into his mouth. "Swallow it, baby." She rubbed his throat, encouraging him to let the magic flow into his body. "Please. For me."

Nothing happened. His chest stopped moving. The potion glowed deep-orange inside his mouth, but he didn't swallow it.

Ice flooded her veins. "Chase?" She patted his cheek as a sickening nausea churned in her stomach, reaching up to tangle with the pieces of her shattered heart. "Swallow the potion, Chase." She moved his jaw to close his mouth and tapped on his throat. "Swallow it, dammit."

Snow grasped her shoulders. "He's gone, sweetie. I'm so sorry."

"No! He's not gone." She wrenched from her sister's hold and threw herself on top of him. "He can't be gone. He can't!"

With tears flooding down her cheeks, she sat up and positioned her hands over his chest. Locking her elbows, she pushed down forcefully, sending blood spewing from his wound. She pushed again, willing his heart to beat.

"Rain, please." Snow rested a hand on her shoulder. "You're making it worse."

"You're. Not. Leaving. Me," she said between chest compressions. Her entire body trembled. She couldn't get enough air into her lungs. Collapsing on top of him, she sobbed into his shirt, fisting the material in her hands. He couldn't be gone. Not after everything they'd been through. She squeezed her eyes shut as a gaping hole tore in her chest, hollowing her heart, ripping her world apart.

She gasped for breath and choked on a strangled sob. "No, Chase. Don't leave me."

CHAPTER TWENTY-THREE

RAIN PRESSED HER FACE INTO CHASE'S CHEST AND SLID HER hands to his cheeks. He couldn't be gone. She refused to accept it.

His arm jerked, and she sat up. The muscles in his throat contracted, and he gasped, choking on the potion. His lids slammed open, his eyes wide with confusion as a coughing fit wracked his body.

"Chase!" Rain's heart lurched into her throat, beating a frantic rhythm as she stroked the hair from his face and leaned over him. "It's me. You're okay." She ran her hands across his forehead and down his cheeks before pressing a kiss to his head.

"Rain? What?"

She lifted his shirt, her eyes widening in astonishment as the knife wound began to heal. The fibers of his skin stitched themselves back together, closing the gash and stopping the bleeding instantly.

He rose onto one elbow and felt his chest with his other hand. "How?"

Fresh tears streamed down her cheeks, but this time, they were tears of sheer joy. "I gave you my unbinding spell."

Snow knelt next to her. "Unbinding spells release your magic in a gush of power. That's why you healed so quickly."

He sat up, and she reached for him, wanting more than anything to hold him in her arms forever.

But he put his hand on her shoulder, gripping her tightly. "My wolf."

Her shoulder ached. Apparently, his strength had returned in that same rush of power. "You're hurting me."

His face pinched, and he yanked his hand off her arm. "Get away from me."

His words stung, but she refused to move. "What's wrong?"

"I can't control my wolf."

"Oh, shit." Snow shot to her feet and yanked Rain up by the arm. "He's going to shift. We need to run."

"No, we don't. I've seen him shift before." She planted her feet and pulled her arm from her sister's grasp.

"It's a blue moon. Werewolves attack the first living thing they see. He said so himself." She tried to drag her away, but Rain held her ground.

Chase's body shimmered, engulfing him in magical light as he transformed into a massive wolf with dark-chocolate fur rolling over his body. He bared his teeth and let out an ear-splitting howl.

"Crap, those teeth are big." Snow's voice trembled.

"Stay behind me." Rain took a step toward him. "He won't hurt me."

He growled as she approached, and her heart sprinted in her chest. She reached a shaky hand toward him and stroked the soft fur on the side of his face. "You need to hunt?"

He exhaled a huff through his nostrils.

"I love you, Chase. Go."

Lowering his head, he turned and bounded into the trees.

Rain let out her breath, and a strange mix of relief, exhilaration, and shock tumbled through her system, making her limbs tremble.

Snow moved to stand next to her. "Holy crap. I can't believe that worked."

Rain laughed and threw her arms around her sister. "He's alive."

"And Isaac is dead. It's over." She took Rain by the shoulders and held her back to look into her eyes. "Are you okay? You may never get rid of your curse now."

"I don't care. Chase is alive, and that's all that matters. I'll gladly spend the rest of my life cursed, as long as I get to live it with him."

Snow smiled. "I suppose his life is worth whatever the curse decides to throw at me for completing the spell without getting paid."

Rain cringed. Her sister would pay dearly for what she had done. "I'll write you a check as soon as we get back to the bakery. Maybe that will be good enough to spare you."

She nodded. "I'll call Macey and see what she wants to do about these bodies."

"Good idea. I—" Her stomach quivered like a swarm of moths had been turned loose inside her. Her head spun, and she pressed a hand to her temple.

"Are you okay?"

"I…don't know." The fluttering spread to her chest and down her limbs, buzzing and humming with a familiar power, though the intensity felt like her veins would explode. She gripped Snow's arm for support as her magic unfurled in her core, filling her with energy that rolled over her body in waves.

The hum spread, connecting her soul to her element, every molecule of water in the air buzzing with her magic, preparing to do her bidding.

She laughed, straightening and throwing her arms to the sky, sending her energy into the clouds. The water obeyed her command. Drop by drop, she collected the elemental liquid, drawing it toward her as if she were magnetized. Thunder clapped, and the sky darkened as she gathered the storm.

Snow backed away. "Did you get your magic back?"

"It sure feels like it." She unleashed an explosion of energy, and rain poured down on them. It washed away the blood and the muck, cleansing her body and soul as the energy welled inside her. Another burst of electricity flew from her fingertips, and thunder boomed from above.

"Can you rein it in?" Snow asked. "I don't want to get struck by lightning."

The overwhelming sensation rolled through her body, awakening her cells, filling her heart with exuberance. "I can't, but I'll try to take it with me."

Snow smiled. "I'll take care of the mess here, and I'll meet you at the car when you're done."

Rain nodded and strode deeper into the trees, running her hands along the rough trunks, breathing in the fragrance of the storm, *feeling* things as if she were feeling them for the first time.

An act of selflessness would end her curse. She'd saved Chase at the cost of never breaking the spell, putting his life above everything else.

She wandered through the woods to a clearing and stood in the center, looking up at the sky. As her burst of magical energy waned, the sky began to clear, the pouring rain relenting to a light shower, with the blue moon peeking from behind the clouds.

Chase bounded through the forest, the elation of having his wolf back driving him to run harder than he'd ever run before. He'd hunted, his instinct guiding him to his alpha to assure Luke everything was okay. Now that the beast had been satiated, the man needed to be with his woman.

She wasn't hard to find. He simply followed the downpour to its center, where his fate-bound stood beneath the falling droplets, lifting her face toward the sky. Soft moonlight glinted off her dark curls, giving her a magical glow.

He shifted into human form and stepped into the clearing as the rain lightened into a fine mist that hung in the air like a fog. She met his gaze and smiled, and he stood there for a moment, absorbing her beauty. Water dripped from the ends of her hair as it cascaded over her shoulders. Her wet shirt clung to her curves, the fabric darkened from the downpour.

A peacefulness settled around her, and she put her hands on her hips, looking more comfortable and complete than he'd ever seen her. "How was your hunt?"

"Good." He moved toward her, taking her in his arms. "I figured with your name you had some kind of water power, but…you can really control the weather?" He gazed into her dark-gray eyes, reveling in the magic energy dancing across her skin.

"I can only make it rain."

"Impressive." He leaned down, touching his lips to hers, and electricity shot through his body, the combination of their magic and their emotional chemistry mixing into a whirlwind of desire. "Thank you for saving my life."

"Thank you for breaking my curse." She held him close, resting her cheek against his shoulder and running her fingers through the hair on the back of his head.

He kissed her temple and sighed as he memorized the perfect way she fit in his arms. The vapors in the air settled on the ground, and he inhaled the sweet scent of clean air mixed with the feminine fragrance of the woman he loved.

She pulled from his embrace and cupped his cheek in her hand. Her touch was warm. Soft. Her eyes brightened with her smile as she placed a tender kiss on his lips. "Snow is waiting for me at the car. Will you come home with me?"

He laced his fingers through hers and kissed her palm. "I'd go anywhere with you."

He led her through the swampy forest toward his bike, making a wide berth around the place they'd defeated Isaac. The tulpa had disintegrated, so Isaac had to be dead, but Chase wasn't taking any chances.

He was still high on adrenaline and magic, and he knew the perfect way to expend his energy.

With the way Rain looked at him, she seemed to have the same idea. "There are so many things I need to say to you, but I can't seem to form a coherent thought."

"We'll have plenty of time for talking. Right now, let's just ride."

They reached the road and found Snow leaning against the hood of Rain's car, an amused grin lighting on her lips. "Hey, you two."

Rain squeezed his hand before releasing him and running to her sister. She hugged her tightly, and Snow laughed. "Since you seem to have another way home, I'm going to wait here for Macey. Give me your keys, and I'll drop off your car at the shop later today."

Rain handed her the keys, and Chase pulled Snow into a hug. "Thank you. For everything."

She patted his back and whispered, "Anything for my future brother-in-law."

He chuckled. "I like the sound of that."

"Me too."

Rain gave him a curious look. "The sound of what?"

He took her hand and led her to his bike. "I'll tell you later. Let me update Luke, and we can head home."

He grabbed his cell phone from a pocket on his bike and dialed his number. "Hey, man. Checking in."

"Everything's under control on this end. You okay?" The smile behind Luke's voice was evident.

"Never better."

"Take the night off. I'll handle the rest."

"Thanks." He shoved his phone in his pocket and tossed Rain a helmet. She put it on, sat behind him, and wrapped her arms around his waist.

They flew down the freeway toward the French Quarter, the crisp air biting into his skin, his wet clothes intensifying the chill. With Rain hugging him from behind, his body blocked most of the wind from her, but she shivered as he exited I-10 onto the frontage road.

As he stopped at a red light, she loosened her grip, resting her hands on his thighs. He squeezed her fingers. "We're almost home, *cher*."

Without saying a word, she slipped her hands beneath his shirt, tucking the tips of her fingers into the waistband of his jeans. The magic on her skin tingled against his stomach, tightening his muscles and hardening his dick. Holy hell, he couldn't wait to get her home.

The light turned green, and he sped into the French Quarter, parking in the alley next to the bakery. Rain slid off the bike, and when Chase dismounted, chunks of mud fell from his pants legs onto the cobblestone walkway.

"We can't walk through your kitchen like this. We'll make a mess." He kicked off his boots and set them next to the door.

Rain stepped out of her shoes and peered at her legs. With a wicked grin, she slipped her pants off, dropping them in a heap next to her shoes. "Better?"

His pulse quickened. "Getting there."

She unlocked the door as he shoved his pants to the ground and stumbled out of them, wrestling to yank the wet denim from his legs. She'd disappeared into the building by the time he got the damn things off.

He stepped into the dark kitchen, and the door slammed shut behind him. He spun around in time to catch Rain as she flung herself into his arms. She kissed him hard, slipping her tongue between his lips and moaning into his mouth.

Her taste. Her scent. The vibration of sound moving across her lips. It was enough to drive him mad. Between the unbinding spell unleashing his magic in a rush and the power of the blue moon, his instincts had sharpened to a fine point. He needed her to be his and his alone. To belong to him, like he belonged to her.

He broke the kiss, trailing his lips to her ear. "Rain?"

She stepped back and grinned. "I feel dirty."

His heart thudded. "What kind of dirty are you talking about?"

She took his hand and tugged him through the kitchen. "Shower with me."

The thought of his hands on her naked body, slick with soap, hardened him even more...if that were possible. He followed her into the bathroom. "I still don't know what kind of dirty you mean."

She laughed as she took off the rest of her clothes and stepped into the shower. Tipping her head back, she let the water flow down her body, drenching her from her hair to her toes. It ran in rivulets over her soft curves, caressing her skin as it washed away the grime from the swamp.

Damn, she looked good wet.

"Are you going to stand there or are you going to come help me get clean?" She lathered the soap between her hands and ran them down her stomach and up to her breasts.

Holy hell. He stripped and joined her in the shower. His fingers twitched with the urge to touch her, but watching her washing herself...touching herself...sent his heart racing. Warm water beat down on his shoulders as Rain slid her hands to her throat, leaving a trail of suds along her skin. She closed her eyes as she massaged her neck and glided her hands to her breasts again, cupping them and circling her nipples with her thumbs.

She opened her eyes. "Want to help?"

His stomach tightened. "I want to watch."

She lathered more soap in her hands and continued washing herself, putting on the sexiest show he'd ever seen. As she bent to slide her palms along her legs, her hair brushed his dick, sending a jolt of electricity to his core. He didn't want the sensation to stop.

Straightening, she looked at his hand gripping his cock and grinned. "Like what you see?"

He chuckled. "How'd you guess?"

She wrapped her fingers around his hand, moving it up and down his shaft. "It's kinda obvious."

He shuddered. Her hand on his, guiding it on his dick, helping him pleasure himself…he wouldn't last long like this. He'd never had a woman show him how to jerk off before, but damn it if she wasn't better at it than he was. She knew exactly how to move, how much pressure to squeeze with, the perfect spot to twist her grip. He ground his teeth, staving off the orgasm coiling in his core.

As if she felt his climax building, she released her hold and ran her hands up his chest. "Not yet."

He let out a shaky breath and put his hands on her hips. "You're good at that."

"I'm good at a lot of things." She poured more soap into her hands and spread it over his torso. Her soft touch raised goose bumps on his skin, and he closed his eyes, memorizing the way her hands felt on his body.

Her magic tingled on his skin as her fingertips caressed every inch of him, setting his soul on fire.

"All clean." She pushed him under the stream, and bubbles spiraled down the drain.

He glided his hands along her slickened curves, holding her close as the scents of soap and Rain filled his senses. Everything about this moment felt so right. The woman he loved in his arms.

Their magic intertwining, dancing across his skin, seeping into his being.

Though they stood skin to skin, he couldn't get close enough. He needed her. To be inside her. To become one with her.

With her back against the wall, he pressed his body to hers, his cock sandwiched between their stomachs, aching to fill her. He nipped at her collarbone, gliding his tongue along the delicate skin of her throat to find her mouth.

She tangled her tongue with his and moved her hand between their bodies to grip his dick. Heat flushed through his veins, igniting his nerves with electricity.

"I love you, Chase." Her words pierced his soul, filling him with emotion, weakening his knees with their sincerity.

"I love you too." His voice was thick, and she must have sensed his need because she hooked one leg around his hip and guided him to her entrance.

He pushed inside her, delicious wet warmth squeezing him as he filled her, and she let out her breath in a slow, satisfied hiss. Holding still for a moment, he gazed into her stormy eyes and ran his hand over the creamy flesh of her thigh. He pulled out slightly, and her breath hitched, her lids fluttering before her focus returned.

Her foot slipped, and he caught her leg, lifting her from the floor to settle his cock deep inside her. She moaned and leaned her head against the wall, arching her back toward him to take him in even farther.

Holding her ass, he rocked his hips, sliding in and out and creating a delicious friction that awakened every instinct inside him. She moved with him, using the wall as leverage to match his thrusts beat for beat.

Gripping his shoulders, she cried out his name as she came, her body writhing against him and her sounds of ecstasy dancing in his ears. She was a goddess. An angel…no, an elemental witch.

His witch.

He buried his face in her neck, pinning her against the wall as she clutched his back, thrusting his hips harder and faster until his orgasm coiled tight like a spring and exploded through his body.

Her breath came in pants as she clung to him, resting her head on his shoulder, trembling from her own release. He leaned into her, stroking the hair from her face and trailing kisses along her neck.

Unwilling to break their intimate union just yet, he pushed deeper inside her. "You're mine, Rain Connolly."

She lifted her head from his shoulder, and a tiny smile played on her lips. "I know."

Slowly lowering her legs to the floor, he slipped out of her but held her close. She shivered as the once warm water of the shower turned cold, and she stepped out of the stream. "I suppose we've wasted enough water."

As he reached for the faucet, Rain lifted her hands, palms up. The water stopped, droplets suspended in midair as if she'd pressed a pause button on the flow.

"This is incredible." He ran his hand through the water as if the drops were glass beads, holding steady to their spots in the air. Taking one between his thumb and forefinger, he plucked it from the stream and rolled it in his hand. Squeezing it, the droplet crushed, returning to its liquid state and dripping from his fingers.

He looked at the amazing woman before him and smiled. He'd known she was powerful the moment he'd met her, but to control an element? "Amazing."

"Can you hit the faucet?"

He turned the knob to shut off the flow, and Rain released the droplets from their semisolid state. They splattered on the floor of the shower and cascaded down the drain.

"I'd forgotten how amazing my powers were…are." She grabbed two towels from a rack and handed him one before patting herself dry. "When I was young, it was all I really cared about. Elemental witches are rare, but for some reason, my power never seemed like it was enough."

She hung the towels over the shower curtain rod and guided him to the bedroom. "I always wanted more. I thought getting a seat on the national council would be my greatest achievement, but I doubt I would have even been satisfied with that."

Chase climbed into the bed with her and pulled her into his arms.

"There's nothing wrong with wanting more. Ambition is a good thing."

"Maybe, but spending seven years cursed and powerless helped me get my priorities straight. Power and position won't make me happy. I know that now, thanks to you."

He kissed her forehead. "Me? What did I do?"

"You have power...and position, but that's not what makes you tick. Your pack...your friends and family...they're what matter most to you. From now on, they're what matter most to me."

His heart pounded. "Speaking of my pack...and family." He rolled to his side to face her, taking both her hands in his and entwining their legs together. "You are my fate-bound."

She smiled. "I know. That's why the unbinding spell worked on you, even though it was created for me." Holding his hand, she touched his palm to his own chest and then to hers. "The bond works both ways. You're stuck with me."

He held her gaze, losing himself in the deep-gray of her eyes. The raging storm had settled, and now all he could see when he looked at her was the rest of his life. "Will you be my mate? My wife?"

Her eyes sparkled as she smiled and rested her hand on his cheek. "All I can promise you is forever."

He laced his fingers through hers and kissed her palm. "Forever is all I need."

EPILOGUE

Rain took a deep breath to calm her sprinting heart as Chase stood beside Luke near the alter. She sat in the audience, on the second row next to Bekah, with little Emma situated between them.

Chase caught her gaze and winked as he adjusted the lapels of his jacket. Though her husband looked damn fine in a suit and tie, he'd be ripping at his collar by the end of the night. She bit her bottom lip as thoughts of helping him out of the confining garments danced through her mind.

They'd been married and mated for a month, living in the apartment above the bakery for three weeks. Though Chase was second in command of the pack, since he didn't belong to the first family, his wedding hadn't required the pomp and circumstance of the alpha line. He and Rain had taken their mating vows beneath the last full moon, and Luke's father officiated the marriage ceremony immediately after.

She grinned. That was the first time she'd helped Chase out of an uncomfortable suit.

With her curse broken, she'd finally reunited with her parents. Though she missed them, New Orleans was her home now, and Chase's pack had welcomed her as if she were one of them. Like family.

The organist began the wedding march, and Rain stood, along with the other four hundred or so wedding guests, to watch Macey walk down the aisle.

Emma giggled and tugged on Rain's hand. "She looks so pretty."

Rain smiled and put a finger to her lips, reminding the little girl to stay quiet.

Luke held his eyes wide as Macey approached. From her view in the audience, it appeared as if he fought back tears.

Rain understood the feeling. She hadn't been able to stop her own tears from flowing when she married Chase. She'd barely been able to keep the rain from falling from the clouds that had gathered like they tended to do when she was in a state of heightened emotion. The love of a werewolf was intense, loyal, and unwavering, and she thanked fate every day for leading her to Chase. She was the luckiest witch alive.

Rain ducked out as soon as Luke and Macey said their vows, and she headed to the ballroom for the reception. Snow was putting the finishing touches on the cake display when she arrived, and Rain stood back to admire the massive wedding cake she'd created with her sister.

Frosted in buttercream, with an intricate basket-weave design, the five-layer cake was topped with an array of yellow roses that cascaded down the sides in a waterfall pattern. She'd accented her classic vanilla-almond cake with a raspberry cream filling that Chase swore was the most decadent thing he'd ever tasted.

Snow adjusted a flower and stood next to her. "It's our best one yet."

"We should take some pictures for the portfolio before the guests get here."

"Good idea." Snow ducked behind the table and pulled her phone from her purse.

As she snapped pictures of the cake, Rain turned to survey the ballroom. Dozens of tables drenched in white linen filled the space, and a band had set up on a raised platform at the end of the room. A set of wooden steps led up to a series of French doors that opened onto a balcony overlooking the French Quarter.

As the first guests entered the ballroom, the band started in with some smooth jazz. The people mingled, mostly werewolves, but mixed with the leaders and other important people from the entire magical community.

Calista caught her gaze and gave her a warm smile as she approached. "The cake is beautiful."

"Thank you." Rain braced herself for the questions. With her curse lifted, and her true powers revealed, the high priestess had tried to become her best friend.

"Are you sure you won't join the coven? We could use an elemental witch in our group."

"I told you I haven't made up my mind yet. Until I get settled into my new life, I'll keep paying the fee to operate a witch business." Her acceptance into Chase's pack increased her number of customers tenfold. She made more than enough money to pay the rent on the shop and her new apartment, along with the fine for not joining the coven.

Calista inclined her head. "My offer stands. A seat on the board is yours if you want it."

"Thank you. I'll keep that in mind." A few months ago, she'd have jumped at the chance to be on the board. It wasn't the national council, but it was prestigious in its own right. Now though, the position wasn't the slightest bit appealing, especially since the person offering it had previously wanted her dead. Rain had her bakery, her husband, the support of a werewolf pack, and her sister. She didn't need anything else.

The wedding party arrived, and she sat next to Chase at the head table. The werewolves dined on filet mignon, and Rain had a goat cheese ravioli with pesto sauce.

When they finished dinner, Rain stood next to Chase on the dance floor as Luke and Macey swayed to the music—their first dance as husband and wife.

As the song ended, Chase tugged her into his arms for their own dance. He held her close, his hard body pressed to hers, his masculine, woodsy scent filling her senses, making her head spin. Would she ever get used to the way this man affected her? She hoped not.

He took her right hand in his left and ran his thumb across the small tattoo adorning the inside of her wrist—a wolf head centered on a fleur-de-lis, like the one on Chase's shoulder. The tattoo wasn't a requirement of joining the pack, but getting it seemed…right.

Since she'd broken ties with the Miami coven and her powers had been unbound, her magical crest had dissolved from her skin. This tattoo was made of mundane ink and would be a part of her forever. She would be a part of this pack…be Chase's mate…forever too.

She ran her hand over his shoulder and down his jacket lapel. "This suit looks good on you."

He chuckled. "It'll look even better on the floor when we get home."

"Hmm…" She leaned back to take in his form. "I think you're right."

They danced to a few more songs before Luke called Chase to the stage to give a toast.

Alexis stood next to Rain and bumped her with her elbow. "That cake was amazing."

"Thanks." Rain glanced at Alexis, but the werewolf focused her attention on something across the dance floor. She followed her gaze to what had intrigued her friend. "Macey's partner is cute, isn't he?"

Alexis's cheeks flushed pink. "Bryce?" She looked at the floor. "He's okay. He's human."

"There are a lot of humans here."

Alexis nodded. "Macey grew up in the human world." Her gaze drifted back across the dance floor.

"Bryce seems like a nice guy."

Alexis drew her shoulders up. "I'm leaving town tomorrow. Don't know when I'll be back."

Rain smiled. She could take a hint. "Take care of yourself."

"I'll see you around." The toasts ended, and Alexis strode toward her sister, pulling her into a hug.

Chase hopped off the stage and met Rain on the dance floor. Taking her by the hand, he led her up the steps and out onto the balcony, where soft moonlight painted the city in a silvery glow. She leaned on the railing and looked at him, and so much love filled her heart she couldn't help but smile. "Luke and Macey leave for their honeymoon tomorrow. Are you ready for two weeks as pack leader?"

His hazel eyes sparkled as he returned her smile and shook his head. "Five years ago, if someone had told me I'd be married to a witch and running a pack, I'd have laughed in his face."

"And now?"

He wrapped his arms around her waist. "I'm ready for whatever fate has planned. It hasn't steered me wrong yet."

"Fate does have a way of leading us to the things we need most, doesn't it?"

"That it does."

The balcony door opened, and Bryce shuffled through. "Sorry, guys. Didn't mean to interrupt. I needed some fresh air."

Chase slipped his hand into Rain's. "No worries. You going to make it without your partner for two weeks?"

"I'll be fine." Bryce gazed through the window into the ballroom. "I can call you if we come across anything weird?"

"You've got my number."

Rain tugged Chase toward the window and followed Bryce's gaze. Alexis stood on the edge of the dancefloor, laughing at something James said. A lopsided grin spread across Bryce's face, and a look of longing sparkled in his eyes.

Rain nodded toward Alexis. "Macey's sister is pretty."

Bryce's grin widened. "She is cute, isn't she?"

BOUND BY BLOOD

✤THREE✤

CHAPTER ONE

ALEXIS GENTRY TUGGED AT THE TOP OF HER STRAPLESS bridesmaid gown as she paced across the dance floor toward her sister. She could count on one hand the number of times she'd needed a formal dress in her life, and Macey's wedding made number three. After barely scrounging up enough money to pay for the two-hundred-dollar dress, the thought of only getting to wear it once had made her cringe.

Macey had chosen a beautiful burgundy satin number, though, and if Alexis found herself needing to attend another formal pack gathering in the future, thankfully, this dress would do the trick. Not that she *ever* planned to attend another pack meeting. With her sister mated to the alpha, she was already closer to this pack than she'd intended to get.

A pair of crystal chandeliers illuminated the hotel ballroom, and hundreds of people milled about the massive space, dancing and drinking to celebrate the alpha's wedding. Had she ever been in the presence of this many werewolves at once? She shook her head. Macey's human friends didn't have a clue.

Plush carpet squished beneath her shoes as she stepped off the wooden floor and approached her sister. Delicate beadwork accented the top and bottom edges of Macey's simple, white gown, and a pair of satin stilettos added four inches to her petite height.

"You're the most beautiful bride I've ever seen." Alexis hugged her, and a strange pressure formed in the back of her eyes as her throat thickened. She released her hold and straightened the top of her dress again.

Macey smiled as she brushed a strand of hair from her forehead. She'd piled her long, blonde locks on top of her head in elegant curls, and a few shiny spirals cascaded around her face, accenting her eyes. "Thank you. That gown looks gorgeous on you."

Gorgeous, but completely impractical. If she wasn't careful, the damn thing might end up around her waist before the night ended.

"I've got you to thank for that." She returned the smile and scanned the room, hoping to catch another glimpse of Macey's sexy detective partner, Bryce Samuels. She'd met him several months ago, when she and Macey had first reunited after a twenty-year separation, and her wolf had insisted she at least say hello to him every time she'd swung through town since.

Her duties as maid of honor had kept her too busy to speak to him so far, but now that the formalities had ended, she could placate her wolf with a short conversation with the man. When she couldn't find him, an odd mix of disappointment and relief spiraled through her chest and came out as a sigh.

Macey touched her elbow. "Are you going to be in town when I get back from my honeymoon?"

"Oh." She bit her bottom lip. "No, I found a job a few towns over that will take me a while to complete. Room and board are included." That last part was a lie. She wouldn't room with the person offering if he tripled the payment. She'd learned her lesson with Eric two years ago, and she would never go back to that abusive bastard again. But she couldn't resist the money he'd offered, and small-town motels were cheap enough. Or she'd sleep in her car; she was accustomed to both. Either way, she'd do the job, get the money, and get the hell out.

Her sister's brow pinched. "You could stay at my place while I'm gone, and then work for Luke when we get back. If you need money, I can—"

"I don't need a handout." The last thing she wanted was for her little sister to think she couldn't take care of herself. "Anyway, I've already agreed to do this job. It's not that far away; I'll stop by and see you when I can."

"You know you're always welcome—"

"So…" She couldn't bear another second of their current conversation. Macey only *thought* she wanted her to stick around. "What's it like working with Bryce? He seems a little cocky." And too hot for his own good. Why did she always find herself attracted to men like that? "Does he get on your nerves?"

Macey sighed. "He is a little sure of himself, but he's got a big heart. I love him like a brother."

"He doesn't wear a wedding ring. Does he have a girlfriend?" She clamped her mouth shut. Her voice had sounded way more hopeful than she'd intended.

Her sister cut her a sideways glance. "Bryce hasn't had a relationship that's lasted past the third date as far as I know. We don't share a lot about our personal lives."

"I remember." Bryce didn't even know Macey had a sister until a few months ago. Alexis gritted her teeth to quell her irritation, reminding herself *she* had been the one to run away. She couldn't expect Macey to tell her partner about a sister she hadn't seen since she was ten. "You spend all day with the guy. What *do* you talk about?"

"Work. Shallow stuff. We joke around a lot." She shrugged. "Bryce has lost most of his family. He's not the most emotionally open person, but I can't imagine working with anyone else."

A man with baggage, emotional scars, who didn't like to share himself. He sounded exactly like her type, but she was done with men. Especially men who needed saving. She'd spent her entire adult life trying to heal people's wounded souls, thinking that maybe if she fixed someone else, she could fix herself in the process.

Her enhanced healing powers only worked on physical wounds, though, not emotional ones, and she should have learned that lesson by now. She was attracted to damaged men because she was damaged beyond repair herself.

But she couldn't ignore the flutter in her stomach as she caught

Bryce's eye through the balcony window. Her lips curved into an involuntary smile, so she pressed them together and lowered her gaze to the floor. "Good thing he's your partner, then. You don't have to work with anyone else."

"He won't be for long."

She glanced at Macey. "Is he moving?"

"He's up for a promotion to sergeant, and he's applied for a position as a negotiator. He's been studying for it, so I know he'll get it." Her shoulders drooped. "I'm going to miss him. Everything in my life seems to be changing."

"Change is the only constant in my life." The one thing she could depend on.

"It doesn't have to be that way."

"Hell of a party, ladies." James sidled next to them and tossed back the contents of his glass. "Can I buy you a drink?" He winked before raising his dark brows.

Alexis laughed. "At the *open* bar? Sure. Why not?" She smiled at Macey. "I'll talk to you later."

Taking a deep breath of relief, she followed James toward the bar. "Thanks for that."

He paused and turned to her. "You looked like you needed a little help. Family squabble?"

She cast her gaze to her sister as Luke swept her into a spin on the dance floor. The band belted out a slow version of Frank Sinatra's "My Way," and she chuckled at the appropriateness of the song. "Not a squabble. She expects me to drop everything in my life and settle down in New Orleans to be with her. I can't do that."

James shuffled toward the line at the bar. "I hear ya. You've got a life to live too."

"Exactly. I'm a rogue. Always have been. She can't expect that to change. People don't change."

He rubbed at the scruff on his chin. "That's where you're wrong. People *can* change if they want to."

"Situations change. People don't." She'd learned that the hard way. Several times.

He arched an eyebrow as he stepped toward the bar. "If you say so. What are you drinking?"

"Whiskey, neat."

James turned to the bartender, and Alexis gazed toward the window where she'd seen Bryce, but he was gone.

"Excuse me, ma'am, would you care to dance?" Bryce's deep, rumbly voice came from right behind her, and she jumped.

Her heart fluttered, and she pressed a hand to her chest as she spun to face him, discreetly running a finger over the top of her dress to be sure nothing had popped out when she'd startled. A quick glance down assured everything was in place. "Do you always sneak up on women like that? Trying to shock me into saying yes?"

Shrugging one shoulder, he grinned and held out a hand. "Whatever works."

His dark suit accentuated his broad shoulders, and he wore a gray shirt with a charcoal tie. Alexis pressed her lips together and glanced at his outstretched arm before looking into his eyes. That was her first mistake. The little brown flecks in his hazel irises seemed to sparkle with his smile, drawing her in and holding her. Mistake number two happened when she placed her hand in his and let him lead her to the dance floor.

She hadn't thought about it. Her arm acted of its own free will, extending toward his until their palms touched and his fingers closed around hers. By the time she realized what she'd done, Bryce's right hand rested on her hip, and his left hand held a firm grip on hers.

James caught her gaze as he sauntered toward the dance floor with two glasses of whiskey in his hands. He grinned and tossed back one of the shots before taking a sip of the other and winking. What had she gotten herself into?

"It was a nice wedding."

Bryce's voice drew her attention, and she glanced at his lips before looking into his eyes. Mistake number three. No lips should look that inviting. She swallowed the dryness from her mouth. "Yeah. It was."

He chuckled. "I never thought I'd see the day Macey got married."

"Why do you say that?"

"She never was one to share much about her emotions. I'm glad to see she finally let someone in." He tugged her closer as he eased into a spin.

With her face this close to his neck, she couldn't help but take a sniff. He had a masculine, woodsy scent with a hint of citrus that made her mouth water. Damn it, why did he have to smell so good? She cleared her throat. "Funny. She said the same thing about you."

"She knows me better than anyone." As the spin slowed, he loosened his grip, putting some much-needed space between them. "It's been a while since I've seen you."

"You've seen me every time I've been in town."

"You should be in town more often then." He looked into her eyes, and a familiar sensation stirred in her soul.

A sense of longing tightened her chest—a feeling that seemed to grow stronger every time she was near this man. The same words coming from her sister would have irritated her, but for some reason, when Bryce suggested she should be around more often, something deep inside her wanted to agree.

Snap out of it. She needed to put an end to these stirrings right now. She was done with emotionally unavailable men. Why did she keep having to remind herself of that? "I'm a busy woman. I stop by when I have time."

He nodded. "I respect that."

Sure, he did.

"Do you want to have dinner with me tomorrow night?" So much for respecting her busy life.

No, she definitely did not need to have dinner with him. "I'm leaving town tomorrow. I don't know when I'll be back."

"How about tonight then?"

"We already ate."

He pursed his lips as if he were thinking. "How about this? After this shindig is over, we'll go to Café du Monde for a *café au lait* and maybe split an order of beignets. Will that work?"

The man was persistent; she'd give him that. "I prefer my coffee black."

He grinned. "Got it. *Café* without the *lait*. No problem; we can do that too."

Why was she having such a hard time telling him no? Half of her wanted to say to hell with the job she had lined up and stay in New Orleans so she could have that dinner date with Bryce. The other half —the logical half—wanted to turn tail and run out the door right now. She didn't need yet another man's emotional baggage weighing her down, trying to drown her. She'd been there, done that too many times already.

Maybe spending some alone time with Bryce would wake her up to the fact that he was no different than any other man she'd tried to save. He was damaged goods, like all the guys she'd fallen for, and that would never change, no matter how hard she tried to fix him. Then she could squelch that nagging message her wolf had been trying to wriggle into her brain since the moment she met him.

"I do love beignets, but it will be awfully late."

He shrugged. "I don't mind if you don't. I work nights, so I'm used to it."

"Not for long, I hear. Macey said you might be getting a promotion."

He eased her into another spin, and his masculine scent danced in her senses again. Having coffee with him would also satisfy the half of her that wanted to get to know him better. Well, that half wouldn't be completely satisfied until she'd gotten to know what was beneath his tailored suit, but that would never happen. Not if she could help it.

Sliding his arm around her waist, he tugged her closer so their hips touched, and against her better judgment, she didn't pull away.

He grinned triumphantly, as if he thought he'd broken down one of her walls, but he had no idea who he was dealing with. Her walls were fortified with titanium.

"Did Macey use the word *might?* Surely she thinks more highly of me than that."

She fought her eye roll. If he kept up the cocky attitude, she'd have no problem telling him goodbye after coffee tonight. "I didn't mean to bruise your ego. What were her exact words?" She gazed at the ceiling, feigning deep thought.

He let out an irritated *hmph.* "It takes a lot more than that to hurt my pride."

She narrowed her eyes at him. Something told her he wasn't as tough as he pretended to be. "She said you were up for a promotion and wouldn't be her partner much longer."

His grin returned. "That's more like it. I knew she had faith in me. I'm going to be promoted to sergeant." He straightened his spine, inclining his chin like he had no doubt the job was his. "A spot as negotiator opened up, so I applied for that too. I want to get into community policing—be present at the area schools, get to know the kids. Hopefully I can save a few lives so no one will have to investigate their deaths later."

"That's noble of you." And a little bit hot.

He shrugged. "Being a homicide detective is noble too, but this is what I've always wanted to do. My life's purpose."

The song ended, and as she stepped away, Bryce tightened his grip on her hand. The band played a cover of Billy Joel's "Just the Way You Are," and he tugged her to his body.

"One more dance? I love this song."

"Sure." And there she was telling him yes again, when she should have said no. His muscles were firm beneath his suit, and as he slid his arm tighter around her waist, she leaned into him, allowing herself… at least for the moment…to enjoy the feel of his strong arms wrapped around her.

She'd never dated a human before. Maybe Bryce would be different since he wasn't a werewolf. Maybe without an animal side, he… *No, no, no.* She'd made a promise to herself, and she intended to keep it. No more relationships.

The song ended, and she stepped away before he could pull her into another inviting embrace. "I need to use the restroom."

He walked with her to the edge of the dance floor. "No problem. I'll find you again before the party ends."

She flashed a weak smile, turned on her heel, and strode out of the ballroom. And hopefully out of Bryce's life forever.

Bryce shoved his hands in his pockets and watched as Alexis strutted away. Her maroon dress hugged her curves in all the right places, and her hips swayed in time with the music as she drifted through the door. *What a woman.*

He couldn't fight his smile. He'd jokingly asked her out a few times...well, every time he'd seen her since they first met, but she'd never taken him seriously, especially since Macey was always around when he did it. After a pep talk from Chase's wife, Rain, on the balcony, Bryce had gathered up the courage to ask her out for real this time, and his pulse was sprinting from her answer.

Wait...she hadn't exactly said yes, had she?

She hadn't said no either, though.

Alexis was mysterious, and he liked that about her. Most of the women he'd dated wanted to spill all their secrets and load him down with their problems before they'd gotten to second base. Not Alexis. She was a woman who knew how to handle herself.

He'd had to fight the urge to slide his fingers into her silky, blonde hair while they were dancing. She smelled like cinnamon and vanilla, and she'd fit in his arms perfectly. He could get used to holding a woman like that.

"You're smiling." Rain grinned as she and Chase moved closer to him from the dance floor. Her long, dark curls swished across her back as her husband spun her under his arm before pausing in front of Bryce. "I guess it went well?"

He tried to flatten his mouth into a neutral expression. "We're having coffee tonight."

"Good for you." Rain waved as Chase led her into another turn.

His own smile returned as soon as she looked away, so he sauntered to the bar and ordered a Jameson. Sipping his whiskey, he kept an eye on the door, watching for Alexis to return.

He couldn't explain the way he felt about the woman. There was something about her that made him want to dive into her mystery and swim through her soul. Independent and strong, she didn't give a damn what anyone else thought of her. She was who she was, and she made no apologies. He could learn a lot from a woman like Alexis.

The band played three more songs, and Bryce ordered another

drink. After another three numbers, she still hadn't returned, and a sinking feeling formed in his stomach.

Grabbing his third drink from the bar, he found Macey sitting at a table near the wall. He strolled toward her and settled into a chair. "Congratulations, again."

She smiled. "Thanks. Thirty more minutes, and we can get the hell out of here. I've dealt with enough people for one day."

He chuckled. "I bet."

"I saw you dancing with Alexis." Her brow puckered, her eyes holding way too much concern.

His stomach sank a little further. "I'm supposed to take her out for coffee after this is over, but I haven't seen her in a while." He set his drink down and drummed his fingers on the cloth.

Macey reached across the table and stilled his hand. "She left."

He blinked. "She went to the restroom. She's coming back."

"She left fifteen minutes ago. Said she wanted to make the drive to her new job tonight so she'd be fresh in the morning."

"She…" He let out a heavy sigh. "She didn't tell me that."

Macey squeezed his hand before leaning back in her chair and crossing her arms. "Her excuse was a load of bull if that makes you feel any better. Between me trying to get her to stay at my house while I'm gone and you asking her out, we probably scared her away. What else did you talk about?"

"Nothing really. I was my usual charming self. Don't think I've ever scared a woman away before." He tossed back the whiskey and focused on the burn it caused on its way down to his stomach. At least that was a welcome burn.

"She's skittish. It may not feel like it now, but it's better this way."

He arched an eyebrow.

"She ran away when she was thirteen. I didn't see her for twenty years, and now she's been in and out of my life so many times in the past year that I've lost count. I love her, but…Alexis always leaves. It's the only dependable thing about her."

There had to be more to it than that, but if the woman didn't want to go out with him, he wouldn't push it anymore. Despite what he led people to believe, he was no stranger to rejection. It had been a while since it had happened, but he'd get over it. He always did.

Plastering on his most confident grin, he straightened his spine. "She's still pretty, though."

Macey rolled her eyes. "You're impossible."

CHAPTER TWO

(THREE MONTHS LATER)

A feeling of dread twisted in Alexis's core as she stopped outside a one-story brick house in Pearl River, Louisiana. Three massive pine trees towered over the squat structure, creating an intricate pattern of needle-sharp shadows jutting across the front lawn, and a tricked-out black Ford Mustang took up most of the short driveway. She let out her breath in a hiss. Eric's ego was probably parked right alongside it.

Sinking in her seat, she gripped the steering wheel in her sweaty hands and stared at the front door. Bile crept up the back of her throat. This was a bad idea. She hadn't spoken to Eric in two months. Not since she'd finished the job. He'd declined to pay her for the work when she'd refused to stay and be his mate. What made her think he'd pay her now?

Prying her hands from the steering wheel, she rested her fingers on the door latch, but she couldn't make herself open it.

She squeezed her eyes shut and rubbed her forehead. Coming here hadn't been an option two years ago; it had been survival. When a Biloxi pack member's drug deal with the area rogues went awry and three of them wound up dead, Alexis—the only other rogue in town —had been blamed for the murders. Mississippi wasn't known for having the most civilized packs in the nation, so when the second-in-command had offered her a way out, she'd jumped at the chance to move to Pearl River and keep an eye on his son in exchange for her life.

Though she'd been paid to watch Eric and report his actions to the pack, she'd also tried to save him. To heal the wounds that made him into an abusive, cocksure, wannabe alpha male. She couldn't help it; healing—fixing people—was in her nature. But she couldn't fix someone's personality, and he'd given her plenty of bruises to prove it.

Eric wasn't mate material. Hell, there was only one person her wolf would allow her to take as a mate, and she'd been steering clear of him since her sister's wedding.

A rogue couldn't be tied down, and no matter how much she wanted to belong somewhere, she never would.

"What am I doing?" She eased her foot onto the gas pedal and continued down the street. She'd traded in her Honda Civic for a small stack of cash and this beat-up Ford when she'd finished the job. Eric wouldn't recognize it, and something in her gut told her she should keep it that way.

She drove to a strip center a half mile from the neighborhood and parked in front of a doughnut shop. A pair of police officers sat inside the small store, chatting up the waitress behind the counter. *How cliché.* A diner anchored one end of the center, while a small grocery store occupied the other. People wandered in and out of the shops and restaurants all day. Leaving her car here wouldn't raise suspicion.

With her phone and wallet locked in the glove box, she slipped the car key into her pocket and trekked up the street to Eric's house. Winter wind bit at her cheeks, whistling through the trees and whipping her hair into a mess. She crossed her arms over her chest to ward off the cold and marched up the driveway.

Alexis hovered her finger over the doorbell. *Go in, convince him to give me the money, and leave. That's all I have to do.* Then she'd never have to see the abusive bastard again. He owed it to her anyway. Soundproofing a room wasn't easy. Or cheap. Twenty-seven years old, and he wanted to start a metal band. *Meathead.*

When he'd called her three months ago, asking her to do the job, instinct had told her to say *hell no*. But even werewolves couldn't survive on hunting alone. Her human side needed to eat too, and the last twenty dollars she had to her name sat locked in the glove box of her car.

She rang the doorbell and waited. Silence answered. Her knuckles wrapped on the wood as she knocked. Nothing. "Eric, I know you're home. Answer the door."

He was probably in his music room, fumbling with the new guitar his daddy bought him. She twisted the knob. Cold metal bit into her palm as the latch disengaged, and she pushed open the door. Small town folk trusted their neighbors way more than they should have.

Alexis peeked her head inside. "Eric?" She stepped into the foyer.

Stifling heat blasted through a vent in the ceiling, and she slipped out of her jacket and dropped it on a ratty, overstuffed sofa in the living room. A football game played on an eighty-inch television. Surround-sound speakers hung from each corner of the room, but thankfully they were muted. A pizza box lay open on the kitchen counter, grease congealing on the surface of the leftover slices, and dirty dishes filled the sink.

She covered her nose. With a sense of smell ten times better than a human's, how could any werewolf live like this?

Eerie silence filled the home, and a sinking feeling twisted her gut tighter. Something was off. Her instinct to run battled with her curiosity to figure out what was going on. Curiosity won.

"This is a bad idea," she whispered as she crept down the hall, the beige carpet masking her footsteps—not that anyone inside a sound-proof room would have heard her approaching. Her arm hairs stood on end as she rested her hand on the knob and twisted it. Figured. Eric felt the need to lock this door, but not the front one. Detaching the bobby pin from her keyring, she jiggled it in the lock to disengage it and flung open the door.

Her breath caught in her throat.

Eric crouched, in wolf form, his gray fur standing in a ridge down the center of his back. Saliva dripped from his bared teeth as he snarled over a trembling woman. Blood soaked through the thigh of her khaki pants. Eric's head snapped toward Alexis, his gaze locking with hers for a split second before she reacted.

"Eric, no!" She called on her wolf, her body tingling with magic as her form shifted. Plowing into his side, she knocked Eric off his feet, and the woman scrambled into a corner. Eric lunged at Alexis, clamping his jaws on her front leg. His teeth tore into her flesh, cracking her bone, and she yelped and jerked from his grasp. She threw herself toward him, and they tumbled over each other, fighting for dominance. Alexis didn't stand a chance against a wolf as powerful as Eric, but she couldn't let him tear a defenseless human to shreds.

The woman screamed. Alexis glanced her way to find the victim sitting beside a mangled, bloody body. Eric barreled into Alexis's side, knocking the breath from her lungs as she crashed to the floor. The woman stumbled to her feet before falling onto her side.

Why wasn't she running? The door was wide open.

The woman clutched her leg and peered at the torn flesh, gritting her teeth as her complexion paled. Alexis glanced at Eric. What was this sick bastard doing?

She bared her teeth, growling a warning for Eric to stay away as she backed toward her. The woman's chest heaved as she tried to scramble away. Eric crouched low, preparing to lunge. She had seconds at most.

Alexis placed her front paw on the victim's leg. A high-pitched squeal escaped the woman's throat, a mixture of garbled fear and pain. Magic pulsed from Alexis's core, and she focused it into her paw. She felt the woman's torn muscles stitch back together as the wound closed.

She clutched her leg. "How?"

Alexis's head spun, but she nudged her with her nose. She wanted to scream, "*Get out*," but her wolf mouth couldn't form words. Another nudge, and the woman shot to her feet and raced to the door.

Eric lunged for his victim. Alexis caught his back leg between her teeth and yanked him to the floor. The sharp tang of were blood oozed into her mouth as she tightened her grip on his leg. The woman took one last look at the body before sprinting away.

With his victim gone, Eric relaxed beneath her grasp. He shifted to human form, the sensation of matted fur turning to skin and denim on her tongue. She growled a warning, refusing to release her hold.

"C'mon, Alex. Let me go."

Her nostrils flared as she blew out a hard breath and tightened her jaw. Nausea churned in her stomach, her power waning from the energy she'd expended to heal the human. She'd need rest to regain her strength, but she couldn't let Eric see her weakness.

He winced. "I wasn't trying to kill her."

Yeah, right. She flicked her gaze toward the crumpled corpse in the corner.

"That was an accident." He shrugged. "Let me go, and I'll explain." His eyes didn't hold a single hint of remorse, but that shouldn't have surprised her. He'd tried to convince her she deserved the beating he'd given her, right before she'd run away.

She released her grip on his leg and backed up. Ribbons of blood flowed down his skin, splattering on the tile floor. She hesitated to shift. Eric was stronger than her no matter what form he took. As a man, he stood six-four with two hundred pounds of pure muscle. In her weakened state, at least as a wolf, she'd have a fighting chance if he tried to pull something.

He rubbed at the gash in his leg, wiping the thickening blood from the wound. The flow was already subsiding. "I haven't seen you in two months, sweetheart. Show me your pretty face."

Asshole. Alexis blew out a hard breath and shifted to human form. The gash on her arm had already healed, and the bone had mended where it cracked.

Eric rose to his feet and dusted off his shirt, flexing his pecs so the garment strained across his chest and grinning like they'd had a friendly wrestling match rather than a full-blown fight. His charming smile added an innocent look to his sharp, handsome features. But a coldness hovered behind his eyes, turning the light blue irises to ice. "That's better. Now we can talk like civilized people."

"Civilized?" She looked at the heap of flesh in the corner and shuddered. "Nothing about this setup is civilized."

"No? I soundproofed the room so it wouldn't disturb the neighbors. Well, *you* soundproofed it actually. Great job, by the way. You've always been good with your hands." His gaze raked up and down her body as he took a step toward her.

Her heart rate kicked up, but she held her ground and stared him hard in the eyes. "What's going on here?"

He walked his fingers up her arm, and chills crept down her spine. "Why don't you come to the bedroom, and I'll tell you all about it?"

"Not a chance." She slapped his hand away, but he caught her by the wrist.

"I knew you'd come back to me."

"I came back for the money you owe me." She jerked from his grasp. "If you weren't trying to kill her, what were you doing to that woman?"

Sighing, he stepped toward the man in the corner. "I was really hoping he'd pull through." He nudged the body with his boot. "Of course, if I'd have known about your little gift of healing, I would have waited until you got here. How long have you known you could do that? I'm hurt that you kept it from me after everything else we've shared."

She clenched her jaw. "We never *shared* anything. I gave. You took. Now, you've got thirty seconds to tell me what the hell is going on or—"

"Or what? What will you do? Run to your sister's pack in New Orleans? They won't help you. This isn't their territory." A wicked grin turned up the corner of his mouth. "And you're just a rogue."

That sinking feeling she'd felt earlier slammed her stomach into her knees. *Just a rogue.* That was all she'd ever be. Even with her blood-ties to the pack, the law forbade them from interfering outside their territory.

She was on her own.

He rolled the corpse onto its back and rotated the head from side to side. "Damn. Definitely dead. I'll have to find another one."

"Another one?" She gaped.

"Well, you turned my next patient loose, didn't you? I'm not a murderer. I'm trying to help these people." He crossed his thick arms over his chest, purposely flexing his biceps.

She mirrored his posture, though she left the flexing to the meat-head. "By tearing them to pieces?"

"I want a pack of my own. I deserve to be alpha, no matter what my old man thinks. I need at least twenty members before the national congress will even consider giving me pack status, but there aren't enough weres out here that are willing to follow. Right now, I have three: Trevor, Justin, and you."

She scoffed. "You don't have me. And what does that have to do with killing humans?"

"Like I said, I'm not trying to kill them. I'm trying to turn them. Make them into werewolves."

Her eyes widened. "That's illegal." And impossible. Even a rogue knew that.

He lifted one shoulder in a dismissive shrug. "Since when do you care about laws?"

Was he completely insane? "You can't turn someone into a were-wolf by attacking him."

He gave the body another kick. "No? You've never been part of a pack, but the first and most important law weres learn is never to attack a human while in wolf form...unless it's a fight to the death."

She clenched her fists. "I'm aware of the laws." Alexis had been on her own since she started shifting at thirteen years old, and the first rogue werewolf she'd met had taught her the rules. She shuddered at the memory of the *other* things he'd taught her.

"So? Why do you think that law was created?"

"Because attacking humans is wrong." Werewolves were supposed to be peacekeepers, not monsters.

He chuckled and shook his head, giving her that condescending look he always used when he wanted to make her feel stupid. "Because if you leave them alive, they'll turn into werewolves themselves. My dad is second of the Biloxi pack; he has access to ancient records. I've read about humans being turned. That's why the congress outlawed attacking humans without killing them. To keep people from trying this." He opened his arms, gesturing to the dead man in the corner.

She swallowed the sour taste from the back of her throat. "This is barbaric."

"I won't argue with that. But once I master the process, it'll be much more efficient. Finding the right balance of blood loss and venom is proving impossible, but you can help. If I attack them, you can heal them right before they die. Then if the change doesn't take, we can try again and again. We'll be a team. What do you say?" His charming smile returned as if he'd asked her to go to an amusement park rather than become an accessory to murder.

"You're sick." *And deranged.* Werewolf venom? There was no way in hell she'd take part in this. She backed toward the door.

He wiped his hands on his pants and stepped toward her. "We could be more than a team, babe. If I'm going to be alpha, I'll need a mate. We already know we're compatible in the sack." He reached for her hand.

Her wolf revolted, the thought of going to bed with him making her skin crawl. She crossed her arms and took another step toward the door. "No way. I want the money you owe me, and I'm leaving."

He winked. "I'll give you the money if you stay."

"Keep dreaming." She stumbled through the threshold into the hallway. Sure, she was broke, but no amount of cash made any of this okay. She'd find another job somewhere. Sell what few belongings she had left. Hell, she'd cut out her own kidney and sell it on the black market before she'd take part in Eric's macabre plan. "Does your dad know you're doing this?"

"That dick wad doesn't know shit. I'm not the fuck-up he thinks I am." He prowled toward her. "C'mon, Alex. Don't make this difficult. You know I care about you, and you care about me too."

Her lip curled. "No, I don't."

"You used to."

She clutched the doorframe, every muscle in her body tensing to bolt. "That was before I got to know you." When she'd had her blinders on. Before she'd figured out she couldn't fix a broken soul. Eric *wasn't* the fuck-up his father thought he was…he was worse.

He sighed. "You know I can't let you leave. I've told you too much. Stay with me. Be my mate, and I'll take care of you. You'll never have to worry about money again. My old man's cash flow will cover everything."

She backed down the hall toward the front door, never tearing her gaze away from the deranged man who pursued her. He didn't know it, but his dad's money had been the reason she went to Pearl River in the first place. He was the one who'd financed her undercover mission, and now it seemed she'd have to do some pro bono work for her old boss. "You can't make your own pack out of innocent humans. I won't let you do this."

"How are you going to stop me?" He lunged, wrapping his arms around her waist and dragging her to the floor. Her head hit the fireplace hearth with a crack, and splitting pain shot through her temple. Darkness tunneled her vision. She blinked away the stars that swam in her eyes as she struggled beneath him, but she may as well have been wedged beneath a concrete block. He had the strength of an alpha, but no pack would ever accept Eric as leader.

He pinned her shoulders to the ground. "Please don't make me kill you. I'd much rather make love to you."

As her vision cleared, she spotted a canister of fireplace tools to her left. If she could get her hands on the poker... Her breathing slowed in spite of her racing heart. She tried to relax. To play the part of the lesser wolf giving in to the alpha's advances. She curved her lips into a seductive smile and sighed. "You're right, Eric."

"I am?" He loosened his grip on her shoulders.

"Of course. It's a genius plan. Making your own pack from scratch, they'll do whatever you tell them to. You can train them." She licked her lips. "Think of the power."

He released her and rose to his feet. "Exactly, baby. And with your healing powers, no one else has to die. Think of all the lives you'll be saving." He didn't offer her a hand up. Typical.

The room spun as she stood, but she held her seductive expression, running her fingers along the mantel and stepping toward him. "I'd be a fool not to stay with you, wouldn't I?"

"I knew you'd come around." He grinned and adjusted his crotch. "Let's go back to the bedroom and make things official."

She rested her hand on the handle of the poker. "There's one problem with that." She tightened her grip.

He crossed his arms and raised his eyebrows. "Oh, there is?"

"I wouldn't touch you with a ten-foot pole." Gripping the poker, she swung it at his head. The pointed end sliced through his cheek, the shock of impact knocking him to the ground.

"Three foot, maybe. But not ten." Her weapon clattered on the floor as she turned and sprinted out the door.

"Damn it, Alex! I didn't want to kill you." Eric barreled after her, gripping his bloody cheek in his hand.

Alexis tore through the front yard and darted across the country road into a field. She didn't dare look back. She could feel him getting closer as she ventured farther and farther into the grassy pasture. As she hurdled a barbed wire fence, her pant leg caught on a spike. The fabric ripped, and she crashed to the ground, taking in a mouthful of bitter grass and dirt. Spitting out the mess, she scrambled to her feet as Eric leapt the fence and caught her by the arm. He hauled her to his body, gripping her from behind.

His breath was hot against her ear. "Maybe I'll kill your sister too. That's a fair trade, huh? Stay with me and Macey lives."

He lifted her from the ground, and she planted her boot square in his knee. His scream muffled the loud pop of the joint dislocating. She wiggled free and sprinted through the field. The gash on his face had already healed; his knee wouldn't take long. She'd bought herself seconds at most.

She could shift and fight him as a wolf. At least the fight would lean toward fair. But to shift in public, in daylight, and expose herself to humans, would earn her one of the harshest punishments the werewolf congress handed out. Rogue or not, some rules simply could not be broken. She could never beat him anyway. The guy was a machine. Her best option was to run, but to where?

She poured on the speed, but not enough. Even with the injured leg, he gained on her. He caught the hem of her shirt and yanked. She stumbled. His arms wrapped around her waist, and he tackled her to the ground. She scrambled away, kicking him in the face, and jumped to her feet again. An electrical transmission tower stood ten feet away, and she darted toward it.

Gripping the cold steel beams, she hauled herself up. Hand over hand she climbed the structure towering one hundred feet into the air.

She didn't have a clue what she'd do once she reached the top, but it didn't matter. Eric wouldn't follow her ascent.

She climbed until her palms bled and her arms shook with exhaustion. Eric grabbed the tower and pulled himself onto the first crossbar. Alexis froze. Was he actually going to climb it? Cursing, he jumped to the ground and spat at the steel.

"Damn it, bitch, you know I'm afraid of heights." His body shook with rage. "You can't stay up there forever. As soon as you come down, you're dead." He fought the urge to shift; his eyes strained with the pain and concentration it took to hold back his wolf. The intensity of the situation called on her own beast as well, but even Eric knew better than to shift in public.

The wind picked up, whipping through her hair and cutting through her clothes like knives. She gripped the cold steel tighter, wrapping an arm around the bar and hooking it with her elbow, using all her energy to hang on. Her muscles trembled, fatigue threatening to make her fall.

What the hell was she supposed to do now? Like most times in her life, she'd acted rashly, climbing the tower without considering the consequences. Now she was screwed—like a kitten stuck in a tree, but no fireman would come along and rescue her. Unless...

Eric stood on the ground below, smiling as she struggled. "You might as well come down. What else are you gonna do?"

"What's going on out here?" A heavy-set woman wearing a bathrobe and rubber boots stomped toward Eric. "What's all this racket about?"

This was her chance. She couldn't out run him. She couldn't beat him in a fight. But she could always outsmart him. "I'm going to jump," she called to the surly neighbor below. "It's all his fault."

The woman's head snapped up, her eyes widening as she realized Alexis hung at the top of the tower. "What did you do to her?" She smacked Eric on the shoulder, and he flinched, ducking his head. A wannabe alpha...scared of an old woman. Alexis chuckled.

"Me? I...I didn't do anything. I don't even know her. I saw her out here climbing the tower, and I came to see what she was up to." He glared at Alexis, and a vein throbbed on the side of his forehead.

For her plan to work, she needed a bigger crowd. More witnesses. "I'll do it." She pretended to slip on a beam and let out an emphatic scream.

"You stay put, young lady. I'm calling for help right now." The old woman pulled a phone out of her bathrobe pocket and pressed it to her ear.

"Help me! I can't hold on!" She smirked at Eric, and his vein throbbed harder.

More neighbors appeared from their houses and rushed into the field. Eric held up his hands, swearing he had no idea who she was. The police were on their way. If she came down now, with all these witnesses, she'd be able to get away.

But she knew Eric too well. He wouldn't stop until she was by his side or dead, and she wouldn't give him the pleasure of achieving either.

He'd threatened her sister's life, though. There was only one thing she could do to keep Macey safe. He had to *think* she was dead.

She swallowed hard and leaned away from the tower. A square of concrete surrounded the structure—not a soft landing pad. If she jumped out far enough, she might be able to make it to the grass. Either way, the fall would be fatal for a human. Even a normal were-wolf wouldn't survive, but she was banking on being *not* normal, hoping her enhanced healing powers would keep her alive.

If she didn't survive, at least Macey would be safe. Eric would have no reason to go after her if Alexis were dead. Her sister's life was worth more than a miserable rogue's.

Closing her eyes, she said a prayer to whatever gods might be listening and let go. The collective gasp from the crowd rang in her ears as she plummeted to the ground. The impact shattered her bones. Searing pain rolled through her body like a wildfire, consuming her in its torrid hell. She wanted to scream, but she couldn't move. She couldn't breathe. She lay there an eternity before blissful darkness swallowed her whole.

"No! Oh, God no." Eric Anderson watched in horror as Alexis fell from the tower. She hit the ground with a jarring *thud*, and silence engulfed him. He rushed to her side and pressed his fingers to her neck. No pulse. A pool of blood spread on the concrete beneath her head, and her legs jutted out at unnatural angles.

Broken. Everything was broken.

Old Mrs. Livingston waddled over to him. "Ambulance is on its way, but it looks like we're too late for that."

His mind reeled. She couldn't really be dead. Any second now, she'd start breathing again. She was a werewolf; she had to survive. She was supposed to be his mate. She was the answer to all his problems. *Shit!* What had he done?

A siren sounded in the distance. He dropped to his knees to compress her chest. Maybe he could get her heart beating again. As soon as he pressed on her breastbone, a rib snapped. He jerked his hands away. "She can't be dead."

The paramedics arrived and ushered everyone away. Eric peered over their shoulders as they examined her. An EMT checked her pulse in her neck. Another one tried her wrist. He covered her mouth and nose with a mask and squeezed a plastic bubble, forcing air into her lungs, and a sickening, gurgling sound resonated from her throat. They started chest compressions, but they didn't try hard enough. Within a few minutes, they gave up.

"What are you doing? Get your ass back over there and use a defibrillator or something. She's not breathing!" He needed her powers, damn it. They couldn't let her die.

A dark haired EMT shook her head. "I'm afraid there's nothing else we can do. She's gone."

The words slammed into his head like a baseball bat shattering his skull. "No." She couldn't be.

A police officer tapped him on the shoulder. "I need to ask you a few questions, Mr.—?"

"Anderson." The police? What the hell was he supposed to do now? His father would shit a brick if he got into trouble with the fuzz again. He might even cut him off. Technically, Eric belonged to the Biloxi pack. He had to obey their laws.

"How did you know the victim?"

"Victim?" His hands trembled. Alexis wasn't a victim. He hadn't done anything wrong. "She killed herself."

"Right." The pig pushed his glasses up his greasy nose. "And how did you know her? Girlfriend? Relative?"

He shook his head. "I didn't know her at all. I looked out my window and saw her climbing, so I came out here."

"Why didn't you call for help?"

"I…Mrs. Livingston called. I was trying to talk her down." If he acted innocent, like he had nothing to do with it, they'd have to let him go. He'd lost his potential mate, but at least she wouldn't be able to screw up his plans.

The pig asked him a few more questions and seemed satisfied with his answers. As soon as he left him alone, he stepped away from the crowd and pulled out his phone.

"Trevor, it's Eric. We've got a problem. That Jane Doe you picked up for me this morning?"

"She met your requirements." Panic raised Trevor's voice an octave. He was about as useless as a werewolf could be, but at least he followed orders. "I did exactly what you asked."

"I know, but she got away. I need you to go find her. Now."

He paused. "Umm…I would, boss. But I'm at work, and if I miss any more shifts, they'll fire me. Can I go find her this evening?"

"I don't give a damn if you're in the middle of open heart surgery, you'll go find that woman now or I will make your life a living hell. Do you understand me?" He had to get that Jane back before she went around spreading stories about werewolves. The last thing he needed was to have the congress on his back about exposing their kind. And if they ever found out he was trying to turn humans, he'd be a dead man.

Trevor cleared his voice. "Yes, sir. I'll get right on that."

"Good."

He shoved his phone into his pocket and strolled toward the scene. The paramedics loaded Alexis's body onto a stretcher and covered her head with a sheet. If she hadn't started breathing by now, there was no way she'd recover.

A pang of regret flashed through his chest, and he winced. He'd miss the blonde bombshell, that was for sure, but he'd miss her healing powers more. That shit would have come in handy. He'd master the art of making a werewolf soon enough, though.

He ran his hand along the small dent in the back of his skull where his dad had hit him with a baseball bat when he was a teen. He'd spent his entire life trying to make that man happy and avoiding the beatings that ensued when he failed. Then the dick wad had banished him to this God-forsaken town to "keep him out of trouble." He'd show the old man trouble. Once he ran a pack of his own, his dad would have to respect him.

CHAPTER THREE

BRYCE PARKED ON THE CURB IN THE CENTRAL BUSINESS District and popped a stick of gum into his mouth as he stepped out of his car. A brisk December breeze tumbled through the streets, stinging his cheeks like the cold slap of an ex-lover. He zipped up his jacket and squinted toward the top of the twelve-story brick building. The structure seemed squat compared to the towers of steel and glass soaring around it, but it was tall enough to be deadly. Shielding his eyes from the sinking sun, he could barely make out the jumper's silhouette. A heavy-set man balanced on the ledge, his back pressed against the brick.

Bryce strode toward the police tape cordoning off the area and nodded at the officer in charge of crowd control.

The officer returned the nod. "Sergeant."

"What have we got?"

"Seventeen-year-old male snuck into an empty office," the uniform replied. "Johnson's been up there thirty minutes. No luck talking him down."

Christ, he's just a kid. "Got a name?"

The officer mumbled into his radio and nodded as the reply came through. "Michael Benson."

Bryce choked on his gum, the mint burning its way down his throat to sour in his stomach. "Shit."

"One of yours?"

"My neighbor." He shoved his way through the crowd that had gathered and jogged into the building. Jabbing the button for the eleventh floor, he twisted his brother's college ring on his finger and prayed he'd make it up there before the kid did anything stupid.

The elevator doors opened, sending a blast of frigid air into the compartment. Cold sweat beaded on his forehead. The drab beige hall stood empty, save for a lone guard standing outside the office doorway. Bryce nodded to the man and stepped inside. Papers lay strewn across the floor, the winter wind having scattered them in its wake. Most modern buildings in the Central Business District didn't have windows that could open, but this structure was from a time before central AC rendered them obsolete.

"Why don't you come inside, and we can talk about it?" Lieutenant Able Johnson, lead negotiator, reached a hand toward the kid on the ledge, but Michael scooted farther away.

"I got this, boss." Bryce waited for Johnson to crawl down from the window before sliding into his place.

Johnson nodded. "Remember. Start gentle. The kid's scared shitless."

"Have a little faith." Bryce had only been in the unit two months, but this was Michael. If anyone could talk the kid down, it was him. He latched on a harness and eased his way out onto the ledge, careful to keep his legs inside the window.

His heart raced. Even with the safety cord snugly secured, he kept one foot hooked under the edge of a desk. Instinct forced him to look down, and his stomach rolled. He took a deep breath and closed his eyes for a long blink. Rule number one—don't look down. Why did he forget that?

"Hey, Michael."

The kid swallowed hard. "Sergeant Samuels? What are—" His foot slipped off the ledge, but he caught himself on the edge of the window. A strangled squeal emanated from his throat as he dug his fingernails into the brick.

"You're okay." Bryce scooted closer. The kid was a mess. Bright-red capillaries zigzagged across the whites of his eyes, and his dark umber skin held an ashen tinge. It couldn't have been more than forty degrees outside, but sweat poured down his face, soaking the neckline of his sweatshirt.

"No." He shook his head and bit his bottom lip. "I'm not. I'm a lard-ass who doesn't deserve to live."

Bryce inched closer. "Now, where on Earth would you get an idea like that?"

Shutting his eyes, he tipped his head back against the brick. "Social media."

Of course. "What happened?"

Michael sucked in a shaky breath. "April Cunningham."

Bryce bit back a curse. The Queen Bee of Central High School had been on his radar for months. After his first anti-bullying speech in the school auditorium, three different girls approached him about her behavior in the hallway. Now it seemed she'd taken up cyber-bullying too. "Girls like that aren't worth your time. They're definitely not worth your life."

"All I did was tell her I liked her haircut." Tears streamed down Michael's face. "She posted a picture of me eating at lunch with the caption, 'This fat bastard thought he was good enough to talk to me. He should go jump off a building and spare us all from looking at his lard ass.'"

His jaw clenched. "She's a bully, Michael. She's not worth it." He unhooked his foot from the desk and eased out onto the ledge. A few inches more and he'd be able to reach the kid, if he didn't pass out from the adrenaline first. *Note to self: next time, skip the coffee.*

"Everyone saw it. You should see the other kids' comments. They're just as bad. Everyone hates me." He shuffled farther down the ledge.

"Not everyone." Icy wind whipped through Bryce's hair, stinging his eyes. He gritted his teeth and inched closer to his neighbor. *Please let this cable hold.* "I don't hate you. I think you're a pretty cool guy. So does Sam."

"Sam." He looked at Bryce, making eye contact for the first time. "I'm supposed to walk him this afternoon."

"I know he's looking forward to it. He always tells me about your walks when I get home."

Michael shook his head. "He's a dog."

Bryce shrugged. "Maybe not in words, but I know he loves you. So does your mom."

He gasped. "My mom."

"Think about how she'd feel if you did this."

His bottom lip trembled. "I can't leave her all alone."

"No, you can't." He reached for the boy. *Almost there.*

Michael leaned toward him. He was nearly in his grasp. "But what else can I do?" He jerked away, and Bryce let out a hard breath.

"You can come with me. I can help you through this."

The kid peered over the ledge and squeezed his eyes shut. "What do you know about being bullied, besides what they taught you at police school?"

His heart ached at the pain Michael must have been going through. "I know a lot more than you think. I was bullied too."

Michael let out a dry laugh. "Yeah, right. Look at you. You're a big, buff white guy. No one would ever mess with you."

His throat thickened. He'd known when he'd taken this job that his embarrassing past would come to light eventually, and he'd gladly share a little bit about himself if it meant saving a family from experiencing what he'd gone through. "I wasn't always this good-looking, kid. When I was your age, I weighed about a hundred and twenty pounds. I was a scrawny little nerd. In order to keep the bullies off my back, I had to do their homework for them."

Michael furrowed his brow. "I don't believe you."

Bryce sighed. "All right. You're the only person I've ever told this to, and I've *never* shown this to anyone." He reached for his wallet and pulled out a small photograph. "This was me at seventeen." He turned the picture toward Michael.

"I can't see it."

"Come closer then. If I get any farther away from this window, I'm going to vomit."

Michael inched closer, shuffling his feet along the ledge. Reaching out, he snatched the picture from Bryce's hand. Bryce glanced inside at Johnson and nodded as he slid back toward the window. He almost had him.

"You wore glasses," Michael said.

"Thick ones. I was nearly blind."

"And now?"

"Surgery."

"Well, that's not so bad. So you had to do some people's homework. At least they didn't publicly humiliate you."

"Well, now." He took a deep breath and cringed inwardly. He was going to have to say it. This kid's life was worth more than his shameful secret. "That's not entirely true. Once, I didn't do Aubrey Taylor's homework. He was beyond pissed."

"What did he do?"

"Our water wasn't running at home for a while, so I got to school early every day to shower in the locker room. When Aubrey figured that out, he followed me in and took all my clothes. When I came out of the shower, I didn't have so much as a towel to cover myself with. So, there I was, buck-naked and dripping wet in the boys' locker room when the first period bell rang."

Michael's eyes widened. "What did you do?"

"The other kids chased me into a stall. I barricaded myself in until Coach finally found me and gave me some sweats to wear home." His face heated, the shame of the memory adding to the nausea churning in his stomach.

"Ouch."

He laughed dryly. "Tell me about it. Can I have that picture back?"

"Why do you carry it around anyway?" Michael slid toward the window to hand the picture to Bryce. As soon as the kid got within arm's reach, Bryce grabbed him and yanked him inside.

All two-hundred-fifty pounds of Michael landed on top of him, knocking the wind from his lungs—a small price to pay for the opportunity to save a life. He regained his breath and pulled Michael to his feet.

His neighbor threw his arms around his neck and sobbed into his shirt. "I'm so sorry, Sergeant Samuels. I don't...I don't know what I was thinking. I don't want to die."

"Hey, you're fine now. The paramedics are going to take you to the hospital. We'll get your mom to meet us there, okay?"

"I'm scared." He clutched his stomach, his lips paling to a light grayish-pink.

Bryce grabbed his shoulders. "Did you do something else?"

"Vicodin." He doubled over, vomiting down the front of Bryce's shirt. Two paramedics took his arms and eased him onto a stretcher. "I'm sorry."

"It's okay." Bryce peeled the sticky, wet fabric away from his skin, the sour reek of stomach acid making him want to vomit himself. Johnson tossed him a box of tissues, and he wiped the muck from his shirt. "How many did you take?

"Twelve."

Bryce let out a slow breath through his nose. "You want me to ride in the ambulance with you?"

He looked at him with frightened eyes. "Please?"

Alexis's eyes fluttered open and adjusted to the fluorescent lighting. A small TV hung from the ceiling in the corner of the white room. Thin sheets and a scratchy blanket covered her achy body up to her chin. A metronomic beeping sound drew her attention toward a humming machine and a set of monitors, and as she turned her head, she focused on an IV drip and a tube that led down under the blankets, into her arm.

Oh, no.

Werewolves healed a hundred times faster than humans. Alexis even more so. After a fall like that, she should've been dead. Would've been if she didn't have extra healing abilities. How would she explain her recovery?

She'd rather have died from the fall than face the wrath of the congress if she exposed their secrets. Closing her eyes, she inhaled a deep breath, and sharp pain stabbed at her lungs. Why hadn't she thought this through?

She shoved the covers down and yanked the oxygen tube from her nose. Bruises mottled her arms in varying shades of red and purple. She moved her legs. Yesterday, the bones were broken. Or had it been two days? How long had she been out? She reached for the IV, ready to yank it from her arm, when a cheerful nurse with fiery red hair and pale green scrubs entered the room.

"Oh, good. You're awake." She shuffled to the bed and adjusted the blankets on Alexis's lap before placing the oxygen module back into her nose and lacing the tubes over her ears. "You're in New Orleans General Hospital." Her fingers flew across a keyboard, and she squinted at the screen. "Well, that can't be right."

Alexis stared at the woman. Thoughts scrambled through her brain as she tried to devise an escape plan. Eric must have thought she was dead, or she wouldn't be breathing. At least that part of her plan had worked.

The nurse tapped a manicured nail on the table. "According to this, your face was swollen beyond recognition a few hours ago. But I don't detect any edema now." She pressed her icy fingers against Alexis's cheek bones. "Does this hurt?"

She held back a wince. "No."

"Well, you're lucky to be alive. That was quite an accident you had." She returned to the computer. "What's your name?"

"Alexis." She clamped her mouth shut. She'd said too much.

The nurse typed on the keyboard. "Last name? You weren't carrying ID."

She scratched the back of her neck. "It's...um...Sinclair." If Eric thought she was dead, she was safe for the moment. Macey was safe. She could lay low for a while and figure out what to do about stopping Eric's cockamamie plan—if she could get out of the hospital.

"Is there someone I can call for you? A relative? Friend?"

It felt like her brain slammed against her skull as she shook her head. It was best if no one knew where she was.

The nurse gave her a warm smile and patted her hand before hanging a new bag of fluids on a hook and connecting it to the IV tube. "I'm going to give you a little something for the pain. It might make you sleepy." She picked up a syringe and reached for Alexis's hand.

She jerked it away. "No. I'm not in pain. I don't want the medicine."

"Oh, nonsense. I can't even see your real skin color through all those bruises."

Alexis covered the IV with her hand and glared at the nurse. "No medicine." No way in hell was she spending another second in this place. "I want my clothes. I want to leave."

"I can't let you leave until a doctor dismisses you. The police need to talk to you too." She squinted at the computer screen. "Something's not right about the details of your accident. It says you fell a hundred feet. Do you remember what happened to you?"

She cringed inwardly. Talking to the police was the last thing she needed. "Where's my stuff?" She could put on a show to convince them she was well enough to leave, but it was a matter of time before they figured out she'd given them a fake name. She had to get out before they started asking questions.

"Your things are somewhere safe, and you'll get them back as soon as you're released. Until then..." She reached for her hand. "Please... this will help you feel better."

"I feel fine."

The woman sighed and laid the syringe on a tray. "I'll go get the doctor."

As soon as the nurse shuffled out the door, Alexis sat up. Sharp pain ricocheted through her abdomen as if she were being stabbed by three knives at once. Clutching her side, she gingerly lay back on the mattress. Her enhanced healing abilities weren't healing her fast enough. She closed her eyes and breathed through the pain. As soon as she was capable of standing, she'd be out of there.

Bryce changed into a set of hospital scrubs and shoved his soiled clothes into a plastic bag. Michael would survive. They'd pumped his stomach, and the doctor seemed to think his liver would recover. Hopefully his mom would get him some counseling. Something. Anything to intervene in the downward spiral that had tempted him to the ledge. Bryce wouldn't give up until the kid got the assistance he needed. This was one cry for help that would not go unanswered.

He knocked on the door to Michael's hospital room. "How's it going in here?"

Karen, Michael's mom, sat on the edge of the bed, holding her son's hand. Her dark-brown hair was mussed, as if she'd raked her hands through it too many times, and tear stains streaked her cheeks. "He's going to be okay." She wiped beneath her eyes, smearing makeup across her face. "Thank you for saving him."

Bryce used his thumb to turn the ring on his right hand...the symbol of the life he couldn't save. "Any time. And you know I'm right upstairs if you ever need anything. Both of you." He squared his gaze on Michael. "I mean it."

Tears pooled in the corners of the kid's eyes. "I'm sorry I can't walk Sam today."

"Don't you worry about that old fur bag. He'll have to settle for walks with me for a while, but he'll survive." He looked at Karen. "You've got my number. Don't be afraid to use it."

She nodded. "Thank you."

"I'll see you soon, kid." He gave Michael a soft punch on the shoulder and then swallowed the lump from his throat as he stepped into the hallway and headed for the elevator. Michael was a good kid. No one deserved that kind of treatment, especially a kind-hearted soul like him. So far, Bryce hadn't been able to bring any charges against the bully, but this time...he was going to get through to that girl one way or another.

The fact that she could get under his skin the way she did presented another set of issues, though. To consider suicide as a viable option to solve his problems meant the kid needed professional help. Bryce knew how to recognize the signs...now that it was too late for his own family...but he'd be damned if he'd let it happen to another one.

As he made his way down the hall, he spotted Lauren, a red-headed nurse with brown eyes and freckles, and he ducked his head, hoping to pass by unnoticed.

"Sergeant Samuels." Excitement raised her voice an octave. She trotted over to him and batted her eyelashes. "Nice scrubs." Her gaze raked up and down his body.

He held up his bag of soiled clothes. "Occupational hazard. Have a good evening, ma'am." He tried to step around the nurse, but she caught him by the arm.

"I think we're beyond '*ma'am*.'" She grinned. "Congratulations on the promotion, Sergeant."

He flashed her a tight-lipped smile. "Thanks. It was a long time coming."

"You know..." She stepped closer, resting her hand on his shoulder. "My shift ends in a few hours. If you want to come over, I could give you a *proper* congratulations."

"Lauren..." He tried to make his voice firm and compassionate at the same time.

She pouted her lower lip. "My bed's been awful cold without you."

"That was one time, six months ago, and I told you I wasn't looking for a relationship." He removed her hand from his shoulder and gave it a squeeze before dropping it. "I thought I made that clear." This was exactly why he did his best to steer clear of women. He wasn't the settling-down type of guy, but they never seemed to understand that...always wanting to *get to know him*. They may have liked the package, but there was nothing on the inside they'd really want to know.

She sighed. "You did. I just thought..." She shrugged. "Anyway. Before you go, there's an alleged suicide attempt in room two-eleven. Jumped from a transmission tower. They pronounced her dead at the scene, but she woke up in the ambulance on the way to the morgue. The details of the accident seem...off. Not a single broken bone."

He looked at his watch and blew out a breath. His shift had ended two hours ago.

"There's a detective coming to talk to her about it, but I thought…since you're into rescuing people now and all…that you might want to see her."

Another suicide attempt? His shoulders sagged as the weight of her words pressed down on him. "Show me the way." He followed Lauren into the room and found a woman lying on her side, her back to the door.

Her short blonde hair stuck out in every direction, and she grumbled as they approached the bed. "I don't want the medicine."

"That's okay." Lauren rested a hand on the woman's shoulder. "This is Sergeant Samuels. He needs to ask you a few questions."

The woman rolled over gingerly, grimacing in pain from whatever had happened to her. Her arms were mottled with bruises, and a ring of dark purple encircled her left eye.

Bryce's pulse thrummed. She was battered, and her hair was shorter, but he would have recognized that face anywhere.

His breath caught in his throat. "Alexis?" He stepped closer to the bed and took her hand in his. "What happened to you?"

Her eyes widened, and she squeezed his fingers. She gave a tiny shake of her head and furrowed her brow. His heart wrenched at the sight of her, but the imploring look in her eyes stopped him from saying more.

"Oh, you know her?" Lauren typed something on the computer. "She didn't want me to call anyone for her."

He glanced at the nurse. "I do. I can take it from here."

Alexis released his hand and let out a long breath.

"Okay. I've got other patients to check on, so go ahead and do your thing, Sergeant." She swung her hips as she sauntered past him, stopping to rub her hand up his arm. "If you change your mind about this evening."

He stiffened. "I won't." And with Alexis back in town, he never would. She was the one woman he wouldn't mind getting to know.

"Well, if you do, you know where to find me." Lauren winked and slipped into the hallway.

As soon as the door clicked shut, he squared his gaze on Alexis. She closed her eyes and rubbed her forehead like she had a headache.

From the looks of her, everything probably ached. His chest tightened. Even battered and bruised, she was the most beautiful woman he'd ever laid eyes on. The moment he'd met her, some long-dormant part of his heart had opened up, and he hadn't been able to get her off his mind since.

Meeting his gaze, she flashed a half-hearted smile. "Hi, Bryce."

She'd seemed fine at the wedding a few months ago. What could have caused her to spiral down so quickly? "What happened to you?"

"I…got in an accident."

He narrowed his gaze. "The report says you jumped from an electrical tower, trying to kill yourself. They pronounced you dead." Simply saying the words aloud caused the weight on his shoulders to press down harder, threatening to crumble him. First his neighbor, and now Alexis. He couldn't handle losing anyone else he cared about.

"No, the report is wrong. I didn't fall from that far up, and I was conscious the entire time. I…" She ran a hand down her face. "It was stupid, and I never should have tried to climb it, but I swear I wasn't trying to kill myself."

The urge to take her in his arms and hug away the hurt overwhelmed him, so he shoved his hands in his pockets. "You're gonna have to give me more than that."

She gazed at the IV in her hand and shook her head. "I got into a little bit of trouble and had an accident."

He could think of one kind of trouble that would leave a woman this beaten and scared, and his hands curled into fists as he pulled them from his pockets. "What's going on? I can help you."

"No, you can't. I'm about to be released; it's no big deal." She gripped his hand, and his fist relaxed. "Please, Bryce. Promise me you won't tell Macey." Determination offset the fear in her eyes.

He sank onto the edge of the bed. "Alexis, if this wasn't a suicide attempt. If someone did this to you, I can help. You need to get the police involved."

"No one did this." She folded her hands on her stomach. "It was an accident, and I'm going to be fine. I feel better already. Macey's got enough on her plate now; I don't want to worry her."

"She's your sister. She would want to know." He knew his ex-partner well, and if there was anything she could do to help her sister, Macey would do it. As strained as their relationship was, she loved her.

"Everything will be fine." She blinked up at him, her emerald eyes pleading. "Please don't tell her."

He chewed the inside of his cheek. Her bond with Macey was rocky at best, so who was he to insist she confide in her? His brother had been his best friend, and look at what had happened. He took a deep breath and let it out in a huff. This was going to come back to bite him in the ass somehow.

"All right. I won't say anything." *Yet.* For some reason, he believed her story that the report was wrong. Eye-witness accounts were often inaccurate and conflicting, and his gut told him to trust her that it wasn't a suicide attempt. He'd bet his left nut the bruises hadn't been put there by accident though. "Can I do anything for you? Tell me what you need."

"I need my stuff." She picked at the lint on the blanket. "They took my clothes and put me in this stupid gown, and the nurse keeps saying she'll give them to me, but she hasn't. Can you get them for me? I want to be ready when they release me." She laid her arms by her sides. "I hate hospitals."

"I can get your stuff." He put his hand on hers, and her gaze flicked to where they touched. "Where will you go when you're released? Where do you live? I can give you a ride." Anything to make sure she didn't go back to the man who'd done this to her.

"I...nowhere right now. I'll figure something out."

"Nowhere? You're homeless?"

She smiled, but it didn't reach her eyes. "I'm resourceful. I'll find somewhere to stay until I can go back to work."

He didn't doubt her resourcefulness; she'd been taking care of herself since she was a kid. But there was no reason for her to be homeless when she had people who cared about her. "If you don't have anywhere to go, stay with me."

She pulled from his grasp. "What? No."

"I've got plenty of room at my place. You can stay with me until the trouble blows over. I won't say a word to anyone."

She pursed her lips and gave him a quizzical look. "That's very sweet, but you don't need to be involved in this."

"I already am." And, damn it, he *wanted* to be. She may not have needed a knight in shining armor, but she did need a friend, whether she wanted to admit it or not. He could be that for her. He could be anything she needed him to be.

"Thank you. But getting my clothes will be enough. I can take care of myself."

"You sound just like your sister." Macey had been his partner for seven years. She was independent and stubborn as a mule. It appeared to run in the family.

He slipped out the door and made his way behind the nurse's station. Alexis's personal effects sat in a plastic bag on a shelf. He tucked the parcel under his arm, grabbed a pen and a sheet of paper, and strode toward her room.

Ducking into a bathroom across the hall, he examined the items in the bag. A pair of jeans, a dirty, black T-shirt, a car key, and a matching set of blue satin unmentionables. His cheeks flushed with warmth as he shoved them back into the bag.

He scribbled his address and phone number on the paper and slipped it, along with his house key, into the pocket of her jeans. The temperature would be near freezing tonight, and she'd have to go somewhere. He'd sleep better knowing she was safe and warm. Shoving everything into the bag, he took it to her room.

She sat up when he walked in, a smile lighting on her lips as she eyed the bag. The bruise around her eye was already fading. Or maybe her smile made it less noticeable.

He tossed the package onto the bed. "My offer stands." Plastering on a fake grin, he winked. "Most women would jump at the chance."

She rolled her eyes. "Keep telling yourself that."

He paused as the ache in his chest grew stronger. "I can stay with you until you're released."

Clutching the bag, she shook her head. "That's okay."

"Are you sure? I don't—"

"Go home, Bryce."

Inhaling deeply, he held her gaze. The logical part of his brain barely overruled his intense desire to scoop her into his arms and carry her home with him so she'd be safe. But he recognized the stubborn set of her jaw. Like her sister, when she set her mind to something, there was no use arguing. If the woman didn't want his help, all the charm and wit he could muster wouldn't be enough to change her mind. "You just...be careful." He turned and left the room.

CHAPTER FOUR

BRYCE PARKED HIS CAR ON THE CURB AND CLIMBED THE STEPS to his half of the two-story duplex on the outskirts of the Garden District. Growing up, his family had barely scraped by in their three-bedroom rental on the wrong side of the tracks. He'd always dreamed of owning one of the big mansions in the area. While sharing a split-level with another family didn't exactly count as owning a mansion, at least he was in the right neighborhood.

A single massive oak tree filled the small front yard and shielded most of the yellow and white house from the street. Karen and Michael had wrapped the thick trunk with twinkling white lights for the holidays. That was as festive as Bryce was willing to get.

He lifted a fake fern out of a clay pot on the landing and grabbed his spare key from the bottom. Sliding it into the lock, he pushed the door open.

"Sam, I'm home." He stepped into the living room and braced himself for impact. His eighty-pound Siberian husky leapt from the couch and barreled toward him. He bent his knees to receive the goof-ball of a dog with open arms, and Sam showered his face in kisses, whining and wagging like he hadn't seen his owner in days.

"All right, boy. Calm down. You missed your walk today, didn't you?"

Sam woofed.

"You go do your business in the back yard, and I'll walk you after dinner. Deal?"

The dog licked his hand and darted to the back door.

"Out you go." Bryce flung open the door, and Sam raced onto the terrace and scrambled down the steps into the small back yard. He left the door open a crack and watched through the window as Sam chased a squirrel into a tree. "Crazy dog."

He grabbed a beer from the fridge and leaned against the counter, appreciating the peaceful silence of his home as he took a long drink. The effervescent liquid cooled his dry throat, and the quiet calm soothed his frazzled nerves.

The events of today had hit way too close to home, and while most of the guys on the team liked to let off steam at a crowded sports bar or night club, Bryce sought refuge in the solace of stillness. Michael would be okay, and Alexis...

He was done being the badass cop for today.

As soon as Sam came back inside, Bryce popped his last frozen dinner into the microwave and sighed. A trip to the dreaded grocery store was in order.

As he finished his last bite of Salisbury steak, he rinsed the plastic container and tossed it in the recycle bin. His favorite book sat on the end table, begging him to read it, but he'd promised Sam a walk after dinner. It was the eighth time he'd read *The War of the Worlds,* anyway. The Martians probably wouldn't change their plan of attack while he was out.

He picked up the leash, and Sam wagged his tail so hard his hind end could have fallen off. "Let's go, boy."

Sam darted out the door, dragging Bryce down the steps. The husky's tongue lolled from his mouth as he pranced down the street, sniffing and hiking his leg on every tree and bush he could find.

Normally, a cold, crisp night like this would clear Bryce's mind, but Alexis clouded his thoughts tonight. The official report said attempted suicide. A sickening feeling formed in his stomach. He couldn't live with himself if he'd left her there alone to enable another attempt. He twisted his brother's ring.

Stop second-guessing yourself. She'd sworn she wasn't trying to kill herself, and he believed her. In all his years as a detective, he'd gotten good at spotting a lie. This wasn't one. She had gotten into trouble though, and damn it, he promised he wouldn't tell her sister. Macey would want to know if someone had hurt Alexis. Now he was stuck between a boulder and a brick wall.

Macey trusted him explicitly. If he didn't tell her, she'd never forgive him if something happened to Alexis. But if he did tell her, who knew what kind of mess he'd stir up between the sisters? Alexis would probably never speak to him again. He hardly knew the woman, but based on the way his heart raced when she was around, he wanted to know more of her. A lot more.

Alexis double-checked the address Bryce left in her pocket and climbed the stairs to the second floor. Sharp pain shot through her knees with each step as she clutched the wooden railing and dragged her aching body up. She hesitated on the landing, toying with the key in her hand. This was a bad idea.

But what else could she do? Her sister would've been happy to help, but she couldn't get Macey involved. Eric was right. The Crescent City pack couldn't help her stop his sadistic plans. Their territory ended where Eric's began. All they could do was report it to the congress, and nobody listened to a rogue.

She had to handle this herself. Her life depended on it, and going to Macey would put her in danger too. Worse than that, Alexis would have to admit she'd gotten herself in over her head.

No, she'd figure something out. She needed a safe place to lay low for a while, at least until she recovered enough to shift. Then she could get her car from the parking lot in Pearl River and at least have her clothes and her phone back. After that… Eric's father might listen to her. If anyone could put an end to his scheme, it was David.

She put on a mask of resolve and knocked. No answer. She

chewed her bottom lip. Bryce wouldn't have given her a key if he didn't want her to use it, so she slipped it into the lock and opened the door.

Warm air enveloped her as she stepped inside, relaxing the tension she carried in her shoulders. She expected the place to be a pigsty, typical of the cocky smartass type Bryce appeared to be, but this was no standard bachelor pad. The countertops gleamed like they'd been freshly polished, and the furniture looked brand new. The living room smelled of lavender with a slight undercurrent of dog fur so faint she could barely detect it. The place had such a homey feel that she found herself standing in the entry, brow scrunched, unable to move for a moment.

"Bryce, are you home?" Soft carpet squished beneath her boots as she tiptoed through the living room and down the hall toward the bathroom. A bedroom door hung open, and she resisted the urge to peek inside to see where he slept. Her mouth went dry. She'd imagined him in the sack plenty of times since she'd met him, and seeing his actual bedroom would add fuel to the fire she was trying to extinguish.

A second door stood shut, and curiosity got the better of her. She gave the knob a twist and found it locked. What secret was he hiding in there? As long as it wasn't another soundproof room, it didn't matter. As soon as she recovered, she'd thank him for his help and be out of his life. Let the man have his secrets.

Avoiding the bathroom mirror, she stripped out of her blood-crusted clothes and stepped into the shower. Warm water cascaded from the showerhead, the droplets stinging as they pelted her bruised skin. The purple marks were already fading to a greenish-yellow, but they hurt like hell. Everything hurt.

She turned off the water, stepped out of the shower, and stared at her reflection in the mirror. What the hell was she doing here? Bruised and broken, she'd barely escaped from one arrogant male, and she'd run straight into the home of another one.

Sure, Bryce was handsome. Smoking hot. She'd felt something stirring deep inside her soul the moment she'd met him, but she'd squashed the sensation like dead bug as soon as she'd caught it wriggling its way into her mind. A rogue couldn't be tied down to a human. Especially to a cop. She had a hard enough time following supernatural laws; being near Bryce would force her to consider human ones too. It would also force her to face her feelings for him.

If he really had lost most of his family like Macey said, he'd have deep emotional scars. Wounds like that hardened men, and every time she scratched away the sexy, self-assured surface, she found an asshole underneath. Maybe Bryce would be different, but…

She sighed. It didn't matter. Getting close to him would end in heartache. Either she'd leave like she always did when she started getting comfortable somewhere, hurting him, or he'd turn out to be an asshole like all the other men she'd fallen for. It would never work.

Still, she couldn't deny the spark she'd felt when she shook his hand over Macey's hospital bed last year. It wasn't the spark of magic that she always felt when she touched someone with supernatural abilities—Bryce was all man—but looking into his bright, hazel eyes had made her heart stutter and her wolf howl.

And when Macey was hurt, he'd stayed by her side like she was family. He seemed to genuinely care. Macey trusted him, and that was the reason she'd come to his house for refuge. But he was a man, and Alexis was done with men…no matter what her wolf—or fate—had in mind.

She chewed her bottom lip. Speaking of fate…a vague memory of waking up in the ambulance rattled through her mind. She remembered clutching the EMT's hand and feeling a buzzing, supernatural energy seeping from her skin. The rhyming rhythm of a healing spell knocked around in her brain, but she couldn't remember the words. It was no coincidence she'd ended up in a witch's ambulance.

She grabbed a towel and wrapped it around her chest. She didn't need to justify her decision to come here—to herself or anyone else. Once she could shift, she could run back to Pearl River and get her car. This arrangement was temporary—like the rest of her life.

Bryce paused on the terrace with his hand on the doorknob. He remembered locking it when he left. His pulse quickened as he gazed in through the window. Light illuminated the hallway, but he always turned them off. Keeping Sam close by his side, he slipped inside and took his pistol from a drawer in the kitchen. It could've been Alexis, taking him up on his offer of refuge. It also could've been an intruder, and he wasn't taking any chances.

He padded into the hallway to find the bathroom door ajar, the scents of soap and shampoo wafting out with the dissipating steam. Widening his stance, he held the gun by his side. "Come out where I can see you."

The door opened fully, and he couldn't help but focus on the pair of shapely legs stepping through. He dragged his gaze up, over the midnight blue towel that covered her torso, and regarded the most disarming set of green eyes he'd ever seen. "Alexis." His posture relaxed, and a strange mix of relief and hope fluttered in his core.

A sly smile curved her lips as she raised her hands. "Don't shoot."

Sam lunged, yanking the leash from his hand. The dog whined and barked, shaking his whole body in excitement as he danced around her feet.

She grinned and reached down to pet him. "Some guard dog you got here."

"Sorry. He's not used to visitors." He picked up the leash and pulled Sam away, ducking into his bedroom to set the gun down.

"It's okay. He's sweet."

He returned to the hall. "Anyway, a badass cop like me doesn't need a guard dog." He winked and unhooked the leash. "Go to the living room, boy. Go."

Sam whimpered and looked at Alexis.

Bryce raised his voice. "Sam…Go."

The dog reluctantly sulked away, and Bryce focused on Alexis.

Damn. His chest tightened. Even the mottled bruises covering her body couldn't take away from her beauty. She stood about five foot ten, and her legs had to be a mile long. The towel barely covered the important parts. Heat flushed through his body, probably turning him ten shades of red. He was staring, but his brain couldn't seem to form a coherent thought to break the trance.

Resting her hands on her hips, she shifted her weight to one side. "You act like you've never had a naked woman in your house before."

He forced the words over the lump in his throat. "You're the first."

"Yeah, right." She stepped into the bathroom and came out with a wad of clothes. "Do you have a washing machine?"

"Yes." His mouth worked, but the rest of his body hadn't processed the shock.

She arched an eyebrow. "Can I borrow it?"

"Oh. Yeah. Here, let me take that." He took the laundry from her hands and padded to the washing closet. "Mind if I throw some of mine in with it? I had a rough day at the office."

"Fine with me." Her voice came from right over his shoulder.

He tensed. Her close proximity had his arms aching to hold her, and the scent of his soap on her body turned him on way more than it should have. He'd given her his key so she'd have a safe place to sleep, but he hadn't thought about what having her here would do to him.

He groaned inwardly. He had to get her out of that towel and into something more modest before he exploded. "Do you want to borrow some clothes while you're waiting on these?" Flipping on the washing machine, he turned to face her.

"Would it make you more comfortable if I did?" Amusement lilted her voice.

"It would, unless you..." He clamped his mouth shut before the automatic smartass comment could slip out. After what she'd been through, asking her if she wanted him to get naked too would be a dick move.

"Unless I, what?"

"Nothing." He sidestepped around her.

"Okay then." A muffled chuckle slipped from her lips as she followed him to his bedroom.

Pausing at the door, he considered saying it anyway. She seemed amused by the effect she had on him, but he wasn't lying when he'd said Alexis was the first naked woman he'd had in his house. Now she'd be the first one in his bedroom too. His home was his sanctuary. His quiet place to relax and recharge his batteries. He'd never been big on guests, especially overnight ones. He'd make an exception for

Alexis, though. She needed him, and something about being able to provide for her had him aching with his own need.

He dropped the leash on the dresser and moved his service weapon to the drawer next to his personal firearm before pulling out a pair of sweatpants. "Here." He handed them to her. "They have a drawstring, so you should be able to keep them up."

In his closet, he reached for a white T-shirt, but the thin fabric would've been more revealing than the towel. He handed her a dark green one instead. She took the clothes and looked around at his bedroom.

"What?" he said.

"Nothing." She shrugged. "It's not what I expected."

"My room?" He turned off the closet light and crossed his arms. How many times had he imagined having Alexis in his bed? And now here she was, nearly naked and standing three feet away from him.

"Your whole house."

"What did you expect?" And why did her answer matter so much to him?

"A pigsty. Tough guy. Lives alone. No time for cleaning since he's always out fighting bad guys and seducing women."

He flinched. "You don't know me."

"I know your type." She turned and headed for the bathroom.

Her statement stung, though it didn't surprise him. He'd worked hard to build up his no-bullshit reputation. To make sure no one saw the scrawny little nerd who'd had to do other people's homework to avoid getting his head shoved in the toilet. He'd created his confident, tough guy persona with a purpose. But for some odd reason, he didn't want Alexis to view him that way.

He shuffled into the living room and dropped his keys into a bowl near the door. Turning around, he found Alexis there in his baggy sweatpants and T-shirt. Thankfully, the garments hung shapeless on her body, hiding her curves. Then again, seeing her wearing his clothes was another kind of sexy entirely.

"Why are you wearing scrubs?" She gestured to his shirt.

He glanced at his clothes. "That rough day at the office I told you about? I got puked on."

"Ew." She wrinkled her nose. "That's what I smelled."

"Yeah. I'm going to shower real quick." He started down the hall, but he paused. "Are you going to be here when I get out?"

She winced as she lowered herself onto the couch. "I'm not going anywhere."

Sam jumped onto the sofa and licked her face. Bryce was about to scold his dog, but she laughed and scratched the fleabag behind the ears.

Warmth spread through his core. "If he's bothering you, I can put him in the back yard."

"He's fine. Mind if I turn on the TV?"

"Go for it." He hurried down the hall and showered and changed as fast as he could, tossing the scrubs into the wash with the other clothes. He even brushed his teeth just in case. Not that he was planning on kissing her—or even getting that close to her—but better safe than sorry, right? Holding his breath, he padded back to the living room. Fear that she'd be gone when he entered the room had his stomach in knots.

But there she sat, in the same place on the couch, Sam curled up next to her with his head in her lap. *Lucky dog.* "Can I get you anything? Water? Tea?"

She grimaced as she shifted her position. "Got any whiskey?"

"I've got a bottle of Jameson, but should you really be drinking in your condition?"

She stiffened. "In my condition, I could use a little pain relief."

"Do you want some ibuprofen?"

"Just the whiskey."

What a woman. "Yes, ma'am." He opened the bottle and poured two glasses. Offering her the drink, he settled onto a chair next to the sofa.

She sipped the whiskey and closed her eyes. "*Mmm.* That's better." As her lids fluttered open, her gaze locked with his. "What?"

Damn it, he was staring at her again. "Nothing. Are you hungry?"

"Starving."

Setting his glass on the coffee table, he shuffled to the kitchen and rummaged through the cabinets and the fridge. He'd eaten his last frozen dinner that evening. He had nothing with sustenance to offer her. "All I've got is a tube of Pringles and some Snickers bars. I can run out and pick something up for you."

"Chips and candy are my favorite." She grabbed the book from the end table. "*The War of the Worlds*? I didn't take you for a sci-fi nerd."

"I'm not." And he planned to make damn sure she never found out he was. Yanking the book from her hand, he set the food on the coffee table. Sam raised his head. "None for you, boy. You know what it does to your stomach."

She raised an eyebrow. "Junk food doesn't agree with him?"

"You thought *I* smelled bad. We'd need gas masks if he ate any."

She smiled and shoved a chip into her mouth. "This beats hospital food any day."

He slipped the book between the cushion and the arm of the chair, thankful he'd been able to change the subject. He'd prefer to talk about his farting dog any day over his love of science fiction. Alexis didn't seem like the type of woman who went for geeks.

She polished off half the tube of Pringles before moving on to the Snickers. Any woman who was happy with chips and candy for dinner was a keeper in his book. He sipped his whiskey and smiled. He could get used to this kind of company.

Aside from Macey's occasional visits, the only other woman who'd been in his house was Karen, and he usually tensed up when his neighbor overstayed her welcome. But something about Alexis being here added to the calm of his sanctuary rather than detracting from it.

She brought the chocolate to her lips and paused. "You're staring at me."

"Sorry." He set his glass on the table and yanked his head down from the clouds. "When are you going to tell me what really happened to you?" Nobody climbed a hundred-foot electrical tower unless they had a death wish or they were being chased.

Alexis sipped her whiskey and eyed him warily. "I'm not."

It figured. He'd have to be delicate with his interrogation if he wanted to get anywhere with her. "Whatever it is, I can help you."

She let out a cynical laugh and took a bite of the Snickers bar. "No, you can't. Believe me. You don't want to get involved."

"I already am, and I think I already told you that." He held her gaze, and for a moment, her eyes softened. Her lips parted slightly, and she inhaled as if she were going to speak.

She shook her head.

"Look, I'm going out on a limb here by keeping this a secret. Macey may not be my partner anymore, but she trusts me. And she's my friend." He sighed. "She'd expect me to tell her if I knew you were in trouble. You've gotta give me something. Let me help."

She stroked Sam's fur, and he nuzzled into her lap. What Bryce would have given to be in that dog's place. "You are helping. Letting me stay here tonight is all I need. Tomorrow, I can go get my car back, and everything will be fine."

"Where's your car?"

"Pearl River."

He furrowed his brow. "That's forty miles away. How'd you end up in a New Orleans hospital?"

Drawing her shoulders toward her ears, she looked into his eyes. "Fate?"

He chuckled. "There's no such thing. Try again."

She paused and pressed her lips together, as if considering her words, and cut her gaze to the left. "Then, I have no idea."

"Okay." He'd let her hold on to this lie. It didn't matter how she ended up there; he was involved now, whether she wanted him to be or not. "Let me drive you to your car."

"Oh, I don't think so." She bit her bottom lip and focused on the dog.

"What are you going to do? Walk there?"

She shrugged. "Maybe."

Stubborn. Independent. Like her sister, she didn't know how to accept help. "Let me take you. I've got nothing better to do."

She arched an eyebrow. "I highly doubt that, but, okay. I'll let you take me to Pearl River and drop me off at my car. That's it, though. No more questions and you stay out of my business."

"Deal." He crossed his arms and leaned back in the chair. There was no way in hell he was staying out of it. But at least if he drove her there, he might be able to pick up a few clues as to what was going on. Then he'd decide if he needed to get Macey or the police involved.

She stretched her arms over her head and cringed. "Ow. I should probably get some sleep. Can I borrow a blanket?"

"You can sleep in my bed."

She raised her eyebrows, and he could practically see the thought forming in her mind.

"Not with me in it. I'll take the couch. You're too sore to sleep out here."

"I'll be fine."

Man, she was beyond stubborn. "No, you won't. You need a good night's rest. You're sleeping in my bed."

She paused and regarded him, a tiny, heart-melting smile curving the corners of her lips. "Well, if you insist."

"I do. And if you need anything at all…ibuprofen, water, more whiskey…whatever…let me know. I'll be right here if you need me."

Her brow furrowed, a look of confusion clouding her eyes. "Thanks, Bryce. I appreciate that."

CHAPTER FIVE

Sunlight filtered through the blinds, casting a golden glow in the bedroom. The softness and warmth of Bryce's bed enveloped Alexis as if she were sleeping in a cloud. The last time she'd been this comfortable, she'd spent the night in a hotel room before Macey's wedding. After scrounging together enough money to buy her bridesmaid dress and pay for one night in the lush hotel, she'd been broke ever since. She needed to find a job fast.

Rising onto her elbows, she spotted her clean clothes sitting on the nightstand, folded into a neat stack. The house key she'd left in the living room last night lay on top.

She rolled onto her side and pressed her face into the pillow. As she inhaled deeply, a masculine, woodsy scent with a hint of citrus danced in her senses. She pulled the pillow on top of her head, allowing herself to get lost in the magnificent scent of Bryce. He'd been nothing but kind to her all evening. She'd fully expected him to try to climb into bed with her. No man was that nice without expecting something in return.

But Bryce had told her goodnight and left her alone all night. Maybe he really was different. Maybe not. She hugged the pillow tighter.

A knock on the door roused her from her thoughts, and she flung the pillow away from her face. Bryce stood in the doorway wearing nothing but a pair of gray sweatpants. His light brown hair was mussed on one side, making a sort of wave on top of his head. Just enough scruff peppered his jaw to give him a rugged look, and glorious muscles rippled down his stomach to disappear into the waistband of his sweats. Her own stomach fluttered, and she had to tear her gaze away.

He grinned and stepped into the room. "Were you smelling my pillow?"

Her ears burned. "No. Why would I do that?"

Grabbing a shirt from the closet, he slipped it over his head. "Yes, you were. You were sniffing it. What's it smell like?"

She ground her teeth as the heat from her ears spread across her cheeks. "It smells like you, dumbass." She chunked the pillow at his head, but he caught it in his hands.

His smile faded. "Dumbass? Is that what you think of me?"

She opened her mouth for another sarcastic answer, but the hurt in his eyes made the words stick in her throat. "I don't know what to think."

He set the pillow down and looked at her quizzically. Sinking onto the edge of the bed, he took her hand in his and ran a finger up her forearm. His gentle touch lit a fire in her core and sent shivers running down her spine. She wasn't used to gentle.

"The bruises are gone." His fingers grazed her forehead as he brushed the hair away from her face, and her breath hitched. "Even your eye. How is that possible?"

She pulled from his grasp and slipped her arm under the blanket. "I'm a fast healer. Always have been."

He held her gaze. "You fell a hundred feet."

"No, I wasn't up that high. I told you, the report was wrong."

"Why were you up there?" So much concern emanated from his voice that she almost believed he cared about her.

She inhaled deeply. Something about Bryce made her want to open up and tell him everything. Maybe it was his kind eyes or his open posture. Possibly the smolder in his gaze. Her wolf insisted on another, much stickier reason, but she intended to ignore that instinct like she'd been doing since she met him.

It was probably a trick he learned in police school to get people to confess their crimes. If she told him about Eric, she'd have to leave out the supernatural part. Then the testosterone would kick in, and Bryce would insist on going after him. Cop or not, he was no match for a werewolf.

She faked a smile. "I'm starving. Got any more Snickers?"

He sighed and pressed his lips into a line. "There's a café a few blocks away. I'll go grab some breakfast while you get dressed. Then we can get your car." Rising to his feet, he pulled a pair of pants from a drawer. "Will you be here when I get back?"

"I will."

Nodding, he hesitated in the doorway before turning on his heel and striding out of the room.

Alexis lay in bed until the front door opened and closed and the key turned in the lock. Taking one more deep inhale of Bryce's masculine scent on the sheets, she sat up and stretched her arms over her head. A mild ache replaced the excruciating pain from yesterday.

Would it be wrong to stay in bed and invite Bryce to join her when he returned? The stirring she'd felt in her soul when she first met him was back in full force, and if she wasn't careful, her wolf would try to claim him. A low growl rumbled in her chest. Who was she kidding? Her wolf was already trying.

Would that be such a bad thing?

Yes, it would. She was a rogue, and he was a human. Her wolf was wrong about this. She wouldn't be bound to any man.

Slipping out of bed, she got dressed and padded into the kitchen to open the fridge. A six-pack of beer, a half-empty carton of two-percent milk, and what was left of a loaf of bread. His fridge screamed typical bachelor, but nothing else about him fit the stereotype. A whine from the living room pulled her attention to the goofy dog on the couch. He rested his chin on a cushion, and his bright blue eyes stared at her with intensity.

"I'm sorry, Sam. I forgot to tell you good morning."

The dog jumped off the sofa and bounded toward her. She

scratched him behind the ears, and he licked her face before wagging his entire body and prancing around her feet.

"Maybe we can play later, okay?" She scanned the kitchen countertops for a coffee maker. Her head hurt from the fall, and a little caffeine might fix it. She found a bag of coffee and some filters in the cabinet—at least he had all the essentials—but when she filled the machine and flipped the switch to run it, nothing happened.

"Damn it. I need my caffeine." She unplugged the machine and rummaged through the drawers to find a screwdriver. The back of the contraption popped off, and she turned it around to examine it. A wire had come loose from a terminal. A simple fix. With a few turns of a screw, she reattached the wire and tightened the connections of the others. She replaced the cover, plugged the machine in, and flipped the switch again. The little red light blinked on as the coffee started brewing. "Thank God."

"We've got a problem," Bryce said as he stepped through the door. "Their coffee machine is down, and mine broke—" He inhaled deeply. "Wait. Do I smell coffee?"

She took two mugs from a cabinet and set them on the counter. "It had a loose wire. I fixed it."

"Fantastic." He grinned and dropped a white paper bag on the table. "I got sausage kolaches. I thought you could use some protein to build up your strength."

"Thanks." She poured the coffee and carried it to the table.

"I got some beignets too." His gaze locked with hers, and her breath caught.

Why did he have to bring this up now? "I'm sorry about that. I lost track of time, and I had to be somewhere." She sank into a chair and lowered her gaze to her mug.

Dropping into a seat, he pulled a French doughnut from the bag. "No big deal. I found someone else to go with me."

Something in his tone said that her leaving the wedding without saying goodbye had hurt him more than he wanted her to know. "Who'd you go with?"

He narrowed his eyes briefly before focusing on the beignet. "Best to eat them while they're warm." He shoved it into his mouth. "So good."

A thin layer of powered sugar dusted his lips, and she could almost taste the sweetness on her tongue. Her mouth watered. Why did he have to be so damn hot?

She always found herself attracted to the same type of men: muscular, good-looking assholes with tragic pasts. She'd convince herself that their cocky, abrasive attitudes were simply masks covering their wounded, softer sides. The softer sides didn't exist, though. Not in her experience.

Bryce seemed different. Sure, he was full of himself—most good-looking men were—but an undercurrent of kindness laced his actions. And she couldn't help but notice the fire that coursed through her veins when his tongue slipped out to lick the sugar from his lips. Oh, the places she'd like to feel his tongue. She shook her head to chase away the thoughts. "Thanks for taking me to get my car."

"My pleasure." He sipped his coffee. "What are you going to do once you have it back?"

"What do you mean?" She took a bite of the beignet and savored the sugary flavors dancing on her tongue.

"Are you staying in Pearl River? Do you live there now?"

She stopped chewing, clamping the mushed-up dough between her teeth. The thought of what to do next, where to go, hadn't crossed her mind. What *would* she do? She swallowed the beignet and took a sip of coffee. "I told you. I don't really live anywhere. I'm a wanderer." She forced a smile.

"You like living out of your car?" No judgment laced his words, simply curiosity.

She shrugged. "It suits me." Hell no, she didn't like it. But she'd spent her entire life on the run, first moving from foster home to foster home, then living on the streets. She didn't know how to stay in one place. Didn't know if she *could*. Every time she got comfortable somewhere, anxiety would get the best of her, and she'd run away. A rogue could never have an easy life, and that was all she'd ever be.

He shook his head. "It's too cold to sleep in your car. You can stay with me as long as you like."

Her stomach tightened around the butterflies attempting to take flight. Why was his offer so damn appealing? After she'd left Eric more than a year ago, she'd sworn off men all together. Then she'd met Bryce, and her wolf had been protesting her decision ever since.

Going back to Eric when he'd called her to do the sound-proofing job should have solidified her decision that men were bad news. Then again, if she hadn't done the job and gotten into trouble with him, she wouldn't have been sitting across from the sweetest, sexiest man she'd ever met. Fate had led her to this moment, but...

She shook her head. "Thank you, but I'm not going to steal your bed another night."

"If it means you're safe and have a warm place to sleep, I will gladly take the couch. Plus, you fixed my coffee maker. Saved me from buying a new one, so I owe you." He winked. "Think about it."

There he went with that kindness again. "I'm sure your red-headed nurse would be jealous if I stayed."

He stopped mid-swallow, choking on his coffee. Setting the cup down, he gave his head an adamant shake. "Lauren? She's just a friend."

The words "back off" had nearly slipped from Alexis's lips when the nurse had come on to Bryce in the hospital, but that would have been her wolf talking. As a woman, Alexis knew better than to get involved with him. *Yeah, right.* "Seemed like more than that to me. I may be injured, but I'm not blind. I saw the way she looked at you."

He straightened his spine, a cocky grin lifting the corners of his mouth. "I am easy on the eyes."

See, she wanted to tell her wolf. *He's no different from all the others.* She leaned back in the chair and crossed her arms. "And you're proud of it."

"So? I've worked hard to look this way. Don't tell me you don't know you're beautiful. You've probably got men tripping all over themselves to be with you."

"It's different for a woman."

"How so?"

Being with the man wasn't the issue. What happened afterward always proved to be the problem. Men didn't want to love her; they wanted to conquer her. It was either wham, bam, thank you ma'am, now get the hell out of my house, or they wanted to dominate every part of her life and treat her like an object rather than a person. She shrugged. "It just is."

His gaze locked with hers. "Lauren was a one-and-done deal. Don't worry about her."

"I'm not worried, but maybe you should have informed her of that. Women don't like to be used."

His posture deflated as worry knit his brow. "I did. We both agreed before it happened. I don't know why she keeps it up."

Because he was smoking hot. No woman would be satisfied having him once. Alexis sure wouldn't. "It's not her fault if she's fallen for a womanizer."

"Womanizer?" His gaze hardened, and he straightened his spine. "Let's get one thing straight. I *never* use people. Never." He snatched the empty doughnut bag from the table and chunked it in the trash. Then he yanked a wet wipe from a plastic dispenser and cleaned the table. Every muscle in his body tensed as he furiously wiped the wooden top.

Maybe the name-calling was a little harsh. "Hey, I'm sorry." She stood and placed a hand on his arm to still him. "I was out of line. Your love life is none of my business."

He inhaled deeply and straightened to face her, his body mere inches from her own. Heat radiated from his skin, and his woodsy citrus scent made her head spin. She looked into his unreadable hazel eyes and fought the urge to press her lips to his. They looked soft, the scruff on his skin around them rough, masculine. Her comment had sparked a passion in him she'd never seen before. Would it be wrong to kiss him now?

He leaned in, his face drifting toward hers. No sugar remained on his lips, but she could imagine the taste on her tongue. Sweet, with a hint of coffee. She parted her lips, and her pulse thrummed in her throat.

He bypassed her mouth and hovered near her ear. "Damn right it's none of your business. Let's go get your car." He stepped past her, grabbed a jacket from the coat rack, and tossed it to her.

She caught it and stood there watching as he turned and bounded down the stairs. Slipping her arms into the sleeves, she pulled the jacket tightly around her. She'd barely scratched the surface with Bryce, and a hint of that mythical softer side had already been revealed. How could she convince herself he was like all the other men she'd dated, when his actions repeatedly proved otherwise?

Bryce gripped the steering wheel and focused on the road. Neither of them had spoken since they'd left his house, but it was just as well. His mind couldn't have formed a coherent sentence if his life depended on it. The woman had him so riled up he didn't know if he wanted to kiss her or take his key back and never speak to her again.

Alexis stared out the window and toyed with the buttons on his jacket. His chest tightened. Something about seeing her wearing his clothes turned his insides to mush and his outsides rock hard.

But she thought he was a womanizer. A dumbass. He could see why she would think those things. In his quest to rid himself of the nerd he used to be, he tended to come off as aloof at times. Stoic. He'd rather people saw him as detached than a geek.

But not a womanizer.

"I really don't use women." He glanced at her and focused on the road. "I told Lauren I wasn't interested in dating anyone. She said she felt the same, so I didn't think any harm would come of it."

She looked at him, her expression hard, distant. "You don't have to explain yourself to me. It's none of my business."

"I don't want you to think poorly of me." More than that, damn it, he wanted her to like him. To feel the same heat he felt every time he touched her.

"It doesn't matter what I think." She lifted a shoulder and returned her gaze to the window.

He gripped the steering wheel tighter. "It matters to me."

Letting out a sigh, she shifted in her seat to face him. "I don't think poorly of you. But I do have a terrible habit of being attracted to the wrong kind of men, so you'll have to excuse me if I keep my distance."

His pulse quickened. "You're attracted to me?"

She grinned and mussed his hair. "Who wouldn't be? Take a left here. My car's in the lot on the right."

He turned left and rolled into the parking lot. Her gaze darted around like she was looking for something. Possibly for the reason she climbed that damn electrical tower in the first place. Seemingly satisfied, she looked at him and smiled.

He let go of the steering wheel and fisted his hands in his lap. "What makes you think I'm the wrong kind of man?"

"You all are." She offered him the house key.

"Keep it. My offer stands. If you get too cold, or...if you need a shot of whiskey, my door is open."

She slipped the key into her pocket. "Thanks, Bryce. For your help and for not asking too many questions." She leaned across the console and pressed her lips to his cheek.

Electricity shot through his core as her mouth hovered near his face. He turned toward her, their noses brushing, her breath warming his skin. Her gaze landed on his lips, and she swallowed. His pulse thrummed. He hesitated, giving her plenty of time to move away, but she didn't.

Leaning in, he tentatively brushed his lips against hers, fully expecting her back away or slap him. Instead, she returned the kiss, parting her lips as her breath hitched in her throat. She tasted like sugar and coffee, and as he slipped out his tongue, a slight moan resonated from her chest.

He moved closer, reaching across the console to slid his fingers into her hair, deepening the kiss. Her lips were soft, her skin warm, and as her fingers grazed his neck, he closed his eyes and lost himself to the moment.

With a shuddering breath, she pulled away and cupped his cheek in her hand. Though her eyes held passion, her brow knit with worry. "Thanks again." She slipped out the door before he could respond.

His oversized jacket nearly swallowed her, the slight horizontal motion of the fabric the only indication of her hips swaying as she walked to her car. His mouth tugged into an involuntary grin as he imagined what her curves looked like beneath the coat. He sucked his bottom lip into his mouth and ran his tongue over the surface, savoring the last hint of Alexis on his skin.

As she reached her car and stuck the key in the door, a burly, dark-haired man carrying a doughnut box called her name. Alexis spun around, and fear flashed in her eyes. The man's brows lifted briefly in surprise before he hardened his gaze and marched toward her, stepping so close that her back pressed into the car as he set the box on the top.

Bryce flung open his door and stomped toward them.

"I thought you were dead, baby." The man reached a hand toward her face.

She slapped it away. "You thought wrong."

"Is this guy bothering you?" Bryce stepped next to her, trying to create some space between Alexis and the man, but the guy wouldn't back off.

Alexis glanced between them and focused on the dark-haired man. "Everything's fine. Isn't it, Eric? *Sergeant* Samuels was nice enough to bring me to my car once I got out of the hospital."

He didn't miss the emphasis she placed on his title, like she was warning Eric not to make a move. This guy must have been the reason Alexis fell from that tower. Was he her boyfriend? The "wrong kind of man" she'd said she was attracted to? He had to wonder if some of the bruises mottling her skin yesterday were there before she fell.

"Oh, yes, Sergeant." Eric's voice oozed with false charm. "I'm so happy to see my *girlfriend* alive after that tumble she took." He reached for her hand, but she yanked it away.

"I'm not your girlfriend."

"Hey, man." Bryce put a heavy hand on Eric's shoulder. "Back off."

Eric took a swing. Bryce jerked away, the man's fist narrowly missing his jaw. Bryce moved forward to return the favor, but he stopped short as Alexis stepped between them.

"Boys." She held up her hands. "There's no need for this."

"You're right," Bryce said. "There's not. Get in the car, Alexis. Let's go home."

"She's not going anywhere with you." Eric shoved Alexis out of the way and lunged at Bryce. His fist connected with the side of his head, sending him careening to the ground, and an explosion of pain ricocheted through his skull.

He blinked away the kaleidoscope dancing in his vision and got to his feet. Alexis clung to Eric's arm, but he jerked it away and charged Bryce again. He took another swing, but Bryce ducked and rammed a shoulder into his stomach, knocking him off his feet. He tried to pin him to the ground, but the guy had super-human strength. He flipped Bryce onto his back and landed another punch square in his jaw. Eric grabbed him by the shirt, and Bryce could've sworn the guy started to shimmer and vibrate. He squeezed his eyes shut to chase away the wavering vision, and the pain in his head made his stomach turn. How hard had he been hit?

"Stop it, Eric," Alexis said. "There's people. Cameras."

Bryce turned his pounding head toward the strip center, where a crowd of patrons had gathered to witness the fight. Several people held their cell phones out, recording the incident. *Shit.* Just what he needed.

Eric glanced at the crowd and growled before rising to his feet and dragging Bryce up with him. "Sorry about that, officer." He smoothed the front of Bryce's shirt.

Bryce grabbed his arm, wrenching it behind his back before snatching his cuffs from his belt and slapping them on his wrist. "You're under arrest for assaulting a police officer." He cuffed the other hand and shoved Eric to his knees.

Eric laughed. "Looks more like battery to me, dude. I beat your ass."

Ignoring the jibe, he phoned the local police to make the official arrest. Within five minutes, an officer arrived and put Eric in the back seat of the squad car. Bryce gave his statement, and the officer turned to Alexis. She told him everything that happened in the parking lot, but she didn't elaborate further.

"Tell him what he did to you, Alexis," Bryce said. "If you want this guy to stay locked up, you need to tell him how he hurt you."

Her eyes widened as she shook her head. "He didn't hurt me. I'm fine."

He would never understand why so many women defended the bastards who beat them. Stepping closer to her, he lowered his voice. "It's for the best. Please tell him."

She chewed her bottom lip and stared hard into his eyes, as if she were pleading with him to understand. "That's it, officer." She looked at the uniform. "That's all I have to say. Am I free to go?"

The officer cut his gaze from Alexis to Bryce and nodded. "We'll be in touch."

As soon as the patrol car left the parking lot and the crowd dispersed, Alexis turned to him with panic in her eyes. "You have no idea what you've done."

"I put an abuser in jail where he belongs."

"Eric's more than an abuser. He's…Oh, forget it. I have to go." She reached for the door handle, but he grasped her hand. Her fingers felt like ice, and the color had drained from her cheeks.

"He's what, Alexis? What aren't you telling me?" He winced as a new flush of pain throbbed through his head. His eye pounded, his vision narrowing into a slit. No one had beaten him this badly since high school.

"Nothing." She took a deep breath and searched his eyes…or eye. He could only see out of one. "Oh, Bryce." She swept her fingers across his cheek and placed a soft kiss on his brow.

The throbbing in his head subsided, replaced by a dull ache. How could a simple touch from this woman ease his pain? "Let me help you. Unless someone posts bail, he'll be locked up for a few days. After that…" He shoved his hands in his pockets. After that, the usual would happen. If she wouldn't press charges, Eric would find her. Abusers always did. "I can protect you."

She smiled and brushed her thumb across his lower lip. "I don't need protection. But thank you."

He let her open the door this time and watched as she climbed inside. "You have my key. I hope you'll use it."

CHAPTER SIX

AFTER MAKING A FEW STOPS ON HIS WAY HOME FROM WORK, Bryce pulled into his driveway and stared at the file folder on the passenger seat. He'd run the scumbag's information, and Eric had a Mississippi driver's license, with a home address in Biloxi.

A quick search of the database had revealed another address in Pearl River and a criminal record. Mostly assaults, bar fights, evading arrest. The guy obviously had a temper. Unfortunately, he didn't have any outstanding warrants. Nothing to guarantee a lengthy stay behind bars, so he could get out on bail.

He might get six months for assaulting a police officer, but if Bryce could get Alexis to admit Eric hurt her—if she would testify—then he could lock the son of a bitch away for a nice long time. But she was protecting him, and something in his gut told him the reason ran deeper than thinking she deserved whatever he gave her.

A glance in the rearview mirror revealed a small, yellow bruise beneath his eye. No swelling. No blood. He looked again. Maybe Eric hadn't hit him that hard after all.

He climbed out of his car and shuffled up the walkway to the first-floor apartment. Karen opened the door as he approached. Her smile didn't mask the worry in her eyes.

"How is he?" Bryce asked. "I stopped by the hospital, but they said he'd been released."

"He's in the living room. Come on in."

He wiped his feet and stepped through the door. The floorplan matched his own upstairs: kitchen and dining area straight ahead, living room and hallway to the right. A bathroom and two bedrooms lay down the hall, though Bryce used his second bedroom as an office.

Michael sat on the pale-blue sofa, his gaze glued to the television. His skin still held an ashen tinge, but the puffiness encircling his eyes had eased.

"How ya feeling, buddy?" Bryce sat on the couch and put a hand on his shoulder as Karen turned off the TV.

Michael stared into his lap. "Better."

"Hey, look at me." He waited for the kid to return his gaze. "There's nothing to be ashamed of. We all go through rough patches."

Michael nodded, tears brimming in his eyes.

"The important thing is that you're alive. You're home with your mom. She loves you. Sam loves you. Hell, even I love you, kid. We're all glad to have you back." He wrapped his arms around him as Michael sobbed on his shoulder, and his heart wrenched. This was why Bryce did what he did. Everything he'd worked for from the day he graduated high school led him to this moment. Saving lives was all he'd ever wanted to do.

"Thank you, Sergeant Samuels." Michael wiped the tears from his cheeks. "I don't know if I said that before."

"I'm sure you did. So, what's the plan now?"

"He'll be seeing a therapist twice a week," Karen said. "And he's supposed to get back to his 'normal' routine as soon as possible." She made air quotes with her fingers. "Though I don't think going back to school right away is a good idea."

Michael fiddled with his hands in his lap. "It's almost winter break anyway. I can go back in January."

"When does therapy start? Not in January...?"

Karen sank into a chair. "His first appointment is tomorrow."

"That's good." He closed his eyes for a long, relieved blink and nodded. "And when you do go back to school, you won't have to worry about April Cunningham. She'll be spending the rest of the year at an alternative campus."

Michael's eyes widened. "Because of me?"

"You aren't the only one she's bullied. More kids are stepping forward with their own stories of harassment, and lucky for us, your school has a zero-tolerance policy when it comes to bullies."

His posture relaxed. "If it's okay with you, I'll start walking Sam again tomorrow."

Bryce smiled. "He'll be happy to hear it." He rose to his feet. "If there's anything you two need, I'll be right upstairs. Just give me a holler."

Karen walked him to the door. "How's your mother doing?"

He shoved his hands in his pockets. Karen and Michael had been his neighbors for five years. They knew his mom when she was functioning. His dad when he was alive. "Oh, you know. Same ol' same ol'. Sometimes she knows who I am. Sometimes she doesn't. She's progressively getting worse."

"I'm so sorry. I know she's all the family you have left, and I…" She shook her head.

And when she was gone, he'd have no one. But choosing to take on this tough cop persona and not letting anyone know the real him had been his decision. He may have been living a lie, but at least he could help people this way. A familiar ache tightened his chest. "She's seventy-five, and it runs in the family. It was bound to happen sooner or later."

She pulled him into a tight hug. "Thank you. I can't say that enough. Michael is my life. How can I ever repay you?"

"You being here for him is payment enough. I'm pretty fond of that kid." He patted her back, and she released her hold. "That's a pretty Christmas tree." He nodded to the sparkling fir standing in the corner.

"Thank you. Michael helped me decorate it last week. I can't…" Her voice cracked, and she cleared her throat. "I can't imagine what Christmas would have been like if he…"

"You don't have to imagine it. He's sitting right there. Go be with your son. I'll be upstairs if you need anything."

"Thank you, Bryce."

"You're welcome, ma'am." He stepped through the door and trudged around the building to the stairs. Christmas was a joyous time for people who had a family to share it with. He'd visit his mom on Christmas day, like he visited her every week. If he was lucky, she'd remember his name. Other than that, he'd be spending his holidays alone with his dog, like he had the past three years.

Sam greeted him at the door, doing his famous full-body wag. The tension melted from Bryce's shoulders, and he stooped to pet his dog. The house already felt too quiet. Like a piece of it was missing. Sam looked expectantly at the front door and whined when no one else stepped through.

"She's not here, buddy. I'm sorry."

The dog sat and tilted his head.

Bryce scratched him behind the ears. "You like her, don't you?"

Sam let out a soft *woof* and continued looking at the door.

Bryce sighed. "I do too."

He plopped onto the couch and ran a hand over his face. Where could she have gone? Temptation to call Macey had him reaching for his phone, but he thought better of it. Alexis had been adamant that she not know she was in any kind of trouble. She wouldn't run to her sister now.

Hopefully she found somewhere warm to spend the night. He shuddered at the thought of her huddled in her car somewhere in the cold. The temperature wouldn't drop below freezing tonight, but it wouldn't be pleasant either. Would she go back to that scumbag's house? Bile lurched into his throat. Surely, she wouldn't. Even with the bastard spending the night in jail, the image of her taking refuge under his roof had Bryce reaching for his car keys.

He had Eric's address, but what would he do if he found her there? She was a grown woman, and if she didn't want his help, he wouldn't force it on her.

Instead, he closed his eyes, and the image of her leaning toward him filled his mind. He could still taste her lips on his, the soft, velvety feel of her skin lingering in his memory like a warm summer day. She wore his jacket. She'd smelled like his shampoo. He had no claim on her, but the idea she had something of his with her—wher-ever she was—made him smile. Hopefully it would make her smile too.

Alexis pulled into the parking lot at the Barataria Nature Preserve and dialed David Anderson's number. She hadn't spoken to Eric's father in months, and her stomach turned as it rang once, twice…three times. Would her call be a welcome one?

"To what do I owe the pleasure, Alexis?" His powerful voice held a hint of wariness. It always did when she'd made her weekly reports.

"It's about Eric."

"Your relationship with my son was your choice. I paid you to get keep an eye on him for me. No bonuses for sleeping with him."

She gripped the phone tighter. "I'm not sleeping with him."

"Not anymore. But you're off my payroll, so why are you calling?"

Chewing the inside of her cheek, she took a few slow breaths before speaking. "Eric's in jail. He assaulted a police officer." She told him how he attacked Bryce in the parking lot.

"Goddammit. That little shit got in trouble with the law again." He sounded more tired than angry. "I sent him to that Podunk town to stay out of trouble. His ass can sit in jail. I'm not sending bail."

She closed her eyes and leaned her head against the seat. She'd be safe for a few days at least. "That's not all. That sound-proof room he begged you for wasn't so he could start a metal band. He wanted it built so the neighbors wouldn't hear the screams of his victims."

He paused. "His victims?"

"I know it sounds crazy, but I witnessed it first-hand. He's trying to start his own pack by attacking humans. He thinks they'll turn into werewolves if he tears them up enough and they survive." She crossed her fingers that he'd believe her story. Pack members trusted the word of a rogue about as much as they'd trust a life boat made from papier-mâché.

David let out a long sigh. "Has he been successful?"

"Not yet. He says he's trying to find the right balance of blood loss and werewolf venom."

"Werewolves aren't venomous. The idiot has no idea what he's doing."

Silence hung on the line as she waited for him to continue. "Looks like I'll be making a trip to Pearl River," David finally said. "Thank you for the information, Alexis. We'll be in touch."

The last visitors exited the parking lot, leaving Alexis alone. She moved her car behind a dumpster and shut off the engine before turning off her phone and locking it in the glove box. Eric had been happy to move to the tiny Louisiana town to get away from his controlling father. Hopefully David would enforce some of that control and whisk him back to Biloxi. Then she'd never have to deal with the jackass again.

A twenty-pound weight lifted from her shoulders as she climbed out of her car and strolled into the woods. She'd done all she could do.

She climbed over a game fence and slipped into the trees. Though mostly made up of wetland, the twenty-three-thousand-acre Barataria preserve held plenty of dense forest. A wolf could easily spend the night in the brush unnoticed.

Curtains of Spanish moss cascaded from the leafless branches of bald cypress trees, creating a canopy around the thicket, and dry grass crunched beneath her boots as she made her way deeper into the forest. A wooden boardwalk led off the right, winding through the trees before jutting out over the marsh. Alexis turned left, away from the trail.

Wrapping Bryce's jacket tighter around her shoulders, she inhaled his scent. Memories of his warm bed flooded her mind. The feel of the soft cotton sheets sliding across her skin. The way his pillow cradled her head. The way his scent lingered in the blankets like it did in his jacket. She'd much prefer Bryce's bed over the forest floor, especially if he were in it.

But she couldn't go back to him. She definitely shouldn't have kissed him. Her lips still tingled every time she thought about it. A peck on the cheek was all she'd meant to give him, but once she'd gotten close, she couldn't pull away. Everything about that man drew her in. Made her want to stay.

Part of her craved companionship. She wanted to have a real relationship with Macey—and with Bryce—but so far all she'd managed was a brief visit once a month. If she was going to settle down somewhere, New Orleans would be the place. The city was alive with culture, music, food, magic. Her sister was there. Bryce was there.

She shook her head. What was she thinking? She hardly knew the man. He couldn't possibly be as kind and gentle as he seemed.

Then again, he'd shown her more kindness in twelve hours than she'd seen her entire life. The more she thought about him, the more she needed him. She slipped her hand into her pocket and toyed with his house key. Cold and hard against her skin, it contrasted the warmth and tenderness she felt from him.

Every fiber of her being screamed at her to go to him. To take comfort in the safety of his arms. But what could she offer him in return? She had nothing. No job. No money. She was a flake. A drifter. A rogue. He deserved so much more than she could ever dream of giving him.

She released the key and ran her hand along the coarse bark of a cypress tree. Rough, like her. Bryce deserved a woman more refined, educated, feminine.

Alexis needed to clear her head. Thinking about Bryce did her no good.

It had been ages since she'd hunted. Maybe a quick chase would do the trick. Hunt. Sleep. Get on with her life tomorrow. It sounded like a good plan. As she shifted into wolf form, everything she wore and carried in her pockets was absorbed by the magic. When she shifted back, everything would be in its place. She'd never given it a second thought until now, but she felt comforted to know that a part of Bryce—even if it was just his jacket—would be with her through the night.

CHAPTER SEVEN

Bryce put the finishing touches on his anti-bullying PowerPoint and shut down his computer. Macey's shift would be starting soon, and he had to know if she'd heard from her sister. The temperature had dropped to forty-two last night, and the thought of Alexis shivering in her car, parked somewhere all alone, had him grinding his teeth in frustration. If he could get her phone number. If he could hear her voice to know she was okay, maybe he could relax.

He strolled by Macey's desk, but it sat empty. His promotion had earned him a coveted spot on the day shift; Macey worked nights. It didn't matter what time of day he went to bed, as long as he got to sleep, but working without his former partner had left an emptiness inside him he hadn't expected.

It had taken years of hard work and studying to earn his position as a negotiator, and saving lives and his work in community policing provided a satisfaction like nothing else. Though he'd never felt any kind of romantic stirrings for Macey, losing her as a work partner felt a little like losing a life partner. She was the closest anyone had ever gotten to actually knowing him. If Alexis would let him in, he wouldn't mind letting her get to know him too.

"Hey, Samuels." Lieutenant Johnson hovered in his office doorway. He kept his curly, dark hair sheared short, and the sprinkling of gray at his temples gave him that distinguished, senior officer look. A look he wore well. A series of fine lines etched into his forehead revealed the stress of the job.

Bryce made eye contact, and Johnson stepped back into the room and settled into his chair—his way of saying, "Come see me in my office." He was a man of few words. Bryce could appreciate that.

"What's up, LT?" He leaned against the door jamb.

"Sit down." His brow knit as he opened a file folder.

Bryce lowered himself into a chair and waited for the man to speak.

"I'm impressed with your work at the high schools. The kids are connecting with you. The principals are singing your praises."

A grin tugged at his lips. "Thank you, sir. Just doing my job."

"You're doing it well. But…" He pulled a photograph from the folder and slid it across the desk. Michael's red-rimmed eyes stared back at him. "You didn't tell me you knew him."

His throat thickened. "Oh. Yeah, he's my neighbor."

Johnson slipped the picture into the folder and let out a slow breath. "There's a reason we don't let friends and family talk to the jumpers when they ask for them. Do you remember why that is?"

He twisted his brother's ring on his finger. "More often than not, the loved ones will be a trigger. When emotions run too high, the jumper's more likely to go over the edge." *Shit.* He'd broken a rule. He was Michael's friend, and it hadn't even crossed his mind that he might be a trigger. He'd only been concerned with getting the kid off the ledge.

"Exactly."

"But, technically, he didn't ask for me. I happened to be there by coincidence."

Johnson pushed the folder aside and folded his hands on the desk. "It doesn't matter. You put that boy's life at risk by being there."

Bryce gripped the arms of the chair. "I saved that boy's life. You want to tell his mother I shouldn't have been there?"

"I know you did. That's why I'm giving you a verbal warning. Your record is nearly spotless. Not a single reprimand since you joined the force—aside from the cigarette incident."

When he'd first made detective, he'd dropped a lit cigarette onto a body, singing the skin a bit. It happened six years ago, but no one would let him live it down. "That was an accident." He hadn't had a smoke since.

"I know. I'll see you tomorrow." Johnson turned to his computer, ending the conversation.

Bryce grumbled as he left the office and turned down the hall toward Macey's desk. Thank God he'd gotten a verbal warning. He was proud of his nearly-untarnished record. He didn't need it blemished for saving a life. Rules and laws were made to be followed. His job was to enforce them. He couldn't go around breaking them; that would make him a hypocrite.

He stopped by the vending machine on the way to Macey's office —out of Snickers bars again—and he bought a Milky Way. Macey sat at her desk, examining a case report.

"How's it going, boss?" He stood in the doorway and took a bite of the candy bar.

"I think I should be calling you boss now, shouldn't I, Sergeant?" Macey smiled, her green eyes sparkling in the fluorescent lighting. He'd never noticed how similar they were to Alexis's eyes. They had the same hair color too, though Macey's golden locks flowed past her shoulders when she wore it down. Alexis had chopped hers into a short style that showed off her slender neck and heart-shaped face.

He sauntered into the room and plopped into a chair. "If I've learned one thing in all my years, it's that the woman is *always* the boss."

Macey rolled her eyes. "As long as she's cooking for you and keeping the house clean?"

He grinned. "You said it, not me." She knew damn well he'd never expect a woman to wait on him hand and foot, but it was fun watching her bristle when he joked about it.

She shook her head. "How's Michael?"

"Better. He's home now."

"That's good. I heard you pulled him in. Going out on the ledge like that? I don't know how you do it. It's amazing."

He shrugged. "Johnson doesn't think so. Seems I broke a rule."

She laughed. "You? That's a first."

"What can I say? I'm becoming a rebel in my old age."

"And mixing things up, I see." She nodded to his candy bar.

"Machine was out of Snickers." He shoved the last of the chocolate in his mouth and dropped the wrapper in the trash can. "You working on anything important?"

She arched an eyebrow. "Nothing pressing."

He drummed his fingers on the arm of the chair. "I ran into your sister the other day. Have you talked to her lately?"

She picked up a bunch of papers and tapped them on the desk, evening the stack. "Not in about a week. Where'd you see her?"

Crap. He should've figured out a story before he brought it up. "Convenience store. Stopped to get gas. Where's she staying now?"

Macey sighed. "I have no idea. She comes and goes. I'm trying to give her space…you know, time to warm up to the whole family thing again. She's been on her own so long, I don't think she knows how to stay in one place."

"That's hard, having family you can't be close to." He knew that better than anyone.

"It is. But it's been twenty years. It's going to take time for us to have a real sisterly relationship again."

He wiped his sweaty palms on his pants and flashed her a grin. "You wouldn't happen to have her phone number, would you?"

She crossed her arms. "Seriously? How many women live in New Orleans? And you have to crush on my sister?"

"She's pretty." He shrugged and cringed inwardly. Alexis was so much more than a pretty face.

"So are ten thousand other women in this city."

"Please?" He couldn't explain it to her. The possessiveness he felt in his heart. The overwhelming need to keep Alexis safe. It didn't make sense for him to feel this strongly about a woman he hardly knew, but he couldn't deny it.

She let out her breath in a huff. "Bryce."

"C'mon, Mace. It's just a phone number. I'm not asking for a blood sample. Let me ask her out. If she says 'no,' then no harm done."

She licked her lips and narrowed her gaze. "I don't want to see either of you get hurt."

He raised his hands in a show of innocence. "I'm not going to hurt her." He wouldn't dream of it.

"I'm more worried about you."

Really? He scoffed. "Have I ever let a woman hurt me?"

"Have you ever dated one long enough to give her the chance?"

He leaned forward, resting his forearm on her desk. "If my memory serves right, a year ago you were scared to get that close to a man." He winked.

She sat up straight. "People can change."

"I know that's right."

Tugging on her bottom lip, she furrowed her brow as she considered his request. "Alexis can be…flaky. I don't know what her life was like for the past twenty years, but from what's she told me, it's been rough." She punched some numbers on her phone. "Be careful."

His phone chimed with the incoming message. Alexis's number lit up his screen, and the fist gripping his heart released its hold. "Thanks, Mace. I will."

Macey's phone beeped. "Lovely. Just fished a body out of the Mississippi." She grinned at him. "I haven't been assigned a new partner yet. Want to ride along for old time's sake?"

"I'd love to."

Bryce rode shotgun as Macey maneuvered the black SUV up Chartres Street in the French Quarter. This part of the city was built in the 1800s, and the narrow streets weren't made for cars this size…or any size for that matter. Two and three-story buildings in varying shades of red, beige, yellow, and blue lined the street. Wrought-iron railings wrapped around the balconies, and wooden shutters covered the windows, blocking the winter chill from creeping inside. Elaborate wreaths and twinkling lights decorated the terraces, giving the city a festive aura.

Everyone would be celebrating the holidays with their families soon, while he sat at home with his dog. He looked at Macey. She knew him better than anyone, and he trusted her with his life. Most of what she knew was the mask, but her comment about Alexis hurting him made him wonder if she didn't see a little more deeply into him than he'd thought.

She glanced at him. "What?"

"What makes you think Alexis is going to hurt me? Aside from what you said before?"

The corner of her mouth tugged into an almost-grin. "What is it that you see in her? And don't just say she's pretty."

"She's independent, capable, smart." He shrugged. "I know she doesn't stick around, but she seems to be there for you when you need her most. Like that time you were in the hospital."

Macey took a deep breath and let it out slowly. "And she left as soon as I recovered."

"She came back though. She was here for your wedding. She loves you." He smiled. "I admire her tenacity. I don't see why you think she's going to hurt me."

She narrowed her eyes. "You're a lot more sensitive than you lead people to believe, but you can't fool me. I'm psychic, remember?"

They hung a right on St. Philip and another on Decatur to pass Café Du Monde. Macey pulled onto the curb, got out of the car, and started up the steps toward the riverbank.

Bryce followed, mulling over what she'd said. "I thought you could only talk to dead people?"

She laughed and continued her climb.

He stopped on the sidewalk. "Go ahead without me. I'll be there in a second."

Macey turned around when she reached the top of the stairs and put her hands on her hips. "Tell my sister I said, 'hi.'" She shook her head and continued to the river.

He clicked Alexis's number and held his breath as it rang. Voicemail. Of course.

"Hey, Alexis. It's Bryce. I wanted to make sure you're okay…after what happened yesterday. And to remind you that you have my house key. I hope you'll use it." His stomach soured as he pressed end and jogged up the stairs to the scene.

The moon reflected off the river, causing the muddy water to sparkle like the stars, and lights from the Crescent City Connection bridge illuminated the water with a reddish glow. A massive white steamboat docked down to the right, and a crowd of uniforms stood in a semicircle around the body. Bryce caught up to Macey as she began to ask questions.

"What have we got?" she asked a man in blue.

"Male. Mid-forties. A couple found him floating face down a few feet out. Hasn't been in the water long, but it looks like something tried to eat him."

Bryce followed the man's gaze to the mangled body lying in the grass. Jagged tears covered the dead man's flesh from head to legs, and obvious teeth marks punctured his arms. Bryce's skin crawled. After seven years of working cases like this, he was happy to be saving lives rather than investigating deaths.

"What do you think, boss?" he said to Macey.

She slipped on a pair of blue latex gloves, snapping them at the wrists, and bent to examine the body. "Looks like an animal attack to me. Maybe a wolf or rabid dog." She gestured to his arms. "See the teeth marks here?"

"I don't know. The neck's clean. Seems like a wolf would go for the throat on instinct to kill its prey before eating it."

She yanked off her gloves and tossed them in a trash bag. "Then it was a dog."

"A dog dumped the body in the river?" Was she serious?

"Maybe he fell in while trying to run away. Anyway, I don't think a person did this, but we'll see what the autopsy says."

He followed her while she investigated the scene, though he hesitated to call what she did an investigation. A half-ass glance, maybe. She shined a flashlight on the ground in a few spots and walked along the bank where they'd dragged the body from the water for a total of two minutes and thirty-seven seconds. Then she nodded to a uniform. "I've seen enough. Pack it up."

"What about your spirit sensors?" Bryce asked as she made her way toward the street.

She shrugged. "No objects to touch. Let's go."

"Yes, ma'am." Bryce may not have had psychic abilities, but his cop sensors screamed murder. Macey had never been one to overlook evidence, but the way she dismissed this as nothing more than an animal attack seemed downright strange. It was her case, though, so he'd let it go. For now. "Hey, can I buy you a cup of coffee or a beignet? It's been a while." He slid into the passenger seat and clicked his seatbelt.

"I would love that, but I've got a lot of work to catch up on." She turned onto Decatur and headed back to the station. "Besides, your shift ended an hour ago. Don't you want to go home and get some rest? Leave the night shift to us lowly detectives?" She playfully punched him on the arm.

"Yeah. That's fine."

"Rain check. I promise. Hey, maybe you can come to dinner with me and Luke sometime. I cook a mean pot of gumbo."

"Sure. That sounds great." He stared out the window.

She stopped in a parking space and shut off the engine. "I guess Alexis didn't answer?"

"Voicemail."

"That's not surprising."

He got out of the car and walked around to Macey's side. "Need any help with your paperwork? I remember how to investigate a murder."

She cast him a sideways glance and shook her head. "This wasn't a murder, but no thanks. I've got it."

He shoved his hands in his pockets. Her answers didn't sit right with him. She was hiding something, but he knew her well enough to know she wouldn't share it until she was ready.

"Go home, Bryce. Tell Sam I said, 'hi.'"

"Will do, Mace. Take care." He got in his car and headed out of the French Quarter, through the Central Business District, and into the grandness of the Garden District. The "American" part of New Orleans. Massive Victorian, Greek Revival, and Italianate homes built on generous lots populated the neighborhood along St. Charles. A streetcar chugged along the track as he made a left into the neighborhood and pulled into his driveway.

Karen sat on her front porch, sipping a mug of coffee. Light from the television flickered in the window behind her, and she waved as Bryce trekked up the sidewalk.

"Evening, ma'am." He stopped and rested a hand on the railing. "How's he doing?"

Her smile didn't reach her eyes. "Shaky, but better. Sam's a good stress reliever."

"That he is." He nodded to her mug. "Careful. That stuff'll keep you up all night."

"It's decaf."

"Good deal." He tipped an imaginary hat and started toward the stairs.

"I made you dinner," she called after him.

He stopped and turned around. "You didn't need to do that. A man can be sustained on candy bars and potato chips."

"It's just to say thank you. Again. I can't say it enough."

"You don't have to say it at all." Rules be damned. Seeing Michael safe at home with his mom trumped any kind of reprimand Bryce could have received, verbal or not.

She folded her right leg beneath her left and gripped the mug with both hands. "You worked late, so I left it in your fridge. I hope you don't mind."

He smiled. "I would never be opposed to finding a home-cooked meal in my fridge. Thank you."

Once inside, he gave Sam a good scratch behind the ears and headed straight for the refrigerator. A large plastic container occupied an empty shelf. A handwritten note on pink stationary sat atop the blue lid.

Thank you for saving Michael's life. You're a hero. —Karen.

He set the note on the counter and scooped out a generous helping of jambalaya. Covering the rice and sausage dish with a paper towel, he popped it in the microwave while he poured himself a glass of whiskey. The smooth liquid warmed his insides as he settled onto the sofa and flipped on the TV.

When the microwave beeped, he retrieved his dinner and found *Star Trek: The Next Generation*—the best TV series ever created—on Netflix. The herbs and spices of Karen's jambalaya danced on his tongue as he savored the tangy sausage. Sam sat on the floor, his snout resting on the edge of the sofa, his sorrowful puppy-dog eyes pleading.

"Sorry, buddy. You know the rules."

Sam let out a pitiful whine. Bryce took another bite as his front door swung open.

CHAPTER EIGHT

Alexis hesitated in the doorway as Bryce's eyes widened. He fumbled with the remote, dropping it in his lap twice before he mashed the power button and turned off the TV.

She rested her hand on the knob. "I'm sorry. I should've knocked."

"No, no." He stood and wiped his palms on his pants. "I gave you a key. I wanted you to use it."

As she stepped into the living room, she slipped out of his jacket and hung it on the coat rack. She immediately missed its warmth and woodsy scent. It had been like a permanent hug from Bryce over the last couple of days. "I got your message."

His Adam's apple rose and dipped as he swallowed. "Good."

Sam bounded toward her, his tail wagging like a tornado, and she bent down to pet him. "What were you watching?"

He ran a hand through his hair and cast his gaze to the TV. "Oh, uh…football."

She suppressed a grin and ran both hands over the dog's shoulders, giving him a good scratch as his left leg thumped the floor. "Who's playing?"

Bryce chuckled. "The Saints, of course."

"The Saints?" She straightened and put her hands on her hips. "Didn't they play last night?"

He scratched his head and looked at his dog. "I DVR'd it."

"Right." What was he up to, and why didn't he want her to know what he was watching?

He picked up a plate from the coffee table and rushed into the kitchen. "Are you hungry? Karen made some amazing jambalaya. Want some?"

Her heart dipped into her stomach to swim through the jealousy boiling there. He had a woman cooking for him? "Sure. Who's Karen?" She shuffled into the kitchen and picked up the pink stationary lying on his counter. It would be her luck if he had a girlfriend he'd neglected to tell her about. "She have the hots for you?"

He stopped and looked at her, and the corner of his mouth tugged into a crooked, kissable grin. "She lives downstairs. Read it." He gestured to the paper.

She scanned the note. "Who's Michael?"

"Her son. I talked him down from an eleventh-story window ledge. That's why I was in the hospital that day. When I found you." He locked eyes with hers, and her stomach fluttered. When he'd *found* her…like she'd been lost.

Maybe she had.

"You…Wow." Her chest warmed as if her wolf were saying *I told you so*.

He shrugged. "It's my job."

"You act like it's no big deal." Of all the things for him to be proud of himself for, saving lives should have topped the list. She set the stationery on the counter.

He took a deep breath and twisted the ring on his finger. "I know it is a big deal, but I have to play it down. Ultimately, it was his decision to let me grab him and pull him to safety, like it would have been his decision if he jumped. If I go around saying *I* saved his life, then what will I have to say if I lose someone?" His hazel eyes held a deep sadness, as if the safety of the world rested on his shoulders.

Having that kind of responsibility was unimaginable. She sank into a dining chair as he put a plate of food in front of her. What a stressful job that must have been. "I never thought of it that way. Have you ever lost anyone?"

He hesitated, his gaze growing distant before he blinked and shook his head. "No, but I've only been doing this for a few months. I know people who have." He settled into the chair next to her.

"Still, it's amazing what you do."

"Thanks." He held her gaze, the look in his eyes somewhere between a smolder and curiosity. He was either going to drill her with questions or pull her into his arms and kiss her, and she couldn't handle either at the moment.

Focusing on the food, she took a bite of jambalaya. The overwhelming heat of the spices burned her tongue, but she couldn't seem to stop eating. She shoveled it in and had cleaned her plate before she realized it.

The corners of his eyes crinkled when he smiled. "Hungry?"

She took a sip of whiskey. "I can't remember the last time I had a home-cooked meal. Tell Karen I said it was delicious."

Bryce cleared the dishes from the table and washed them in the sink. Alexis watched his backside as he dried the plates and returned them to the cabinet. He was meticulous in his ways, putting each dish in its proper place before wiping down the counters and the table and pouring two more glasses of Jameson.

He was a walking, talking contradiction. Cool and cocky on the surface, but inside he was so much more. He saved lives for a living, dedicated his life to helping others. Her initial perception of Bryce had been all wrong, and her wolf was gloating in her soul.

"Shall we?" He gestured to the living room.

She followed him to the sofa and sat next to him, shifting her knees toward his so she faced him. The intensity in his gaze held her as he pressed the glass to his lips and took a sip. A tiny drop of alcohol dripped onto his lower lip, and his tongue slipped out to retrieve it, sending a warm shiver cascading down her spine.

He set the glass on the table, never taking his gaze off hers. "What made you decide to come back?"

She rubbed the goose bumps on her arms. "It's pretty cold out tonight. Didn't want to sleep in my car again."

"I see." His eyes searched hers, penetrating her soul, making her want to open up to someone for the first time in her life. Could he really be the one? Was she ready to listen to her wolf?

"That's a lie." Her body involuntarily drifted toward him.

"I know." He didn't move away.

"I came to see you. I couldn't stop thinking about you." She reached behind his head and pulled his face to hers. Their lips met, and warmth spread through her body like a wildfire consuming a forest. She closed her eyes as her tongue brushed his, and he slid a hand to her hip. She wanted him. To feel his hands on her body, his bare skin pressed to hers. Taking his face in her hands, she kissed him harder, trailing her lips across his jaw and down his neck.

"Alexis." He gripped her shoulders gently and pushed her away.

His eyes swam with emotion, the greenish-gold irises almost molten, the brown flecks seeming to shimmer as he blinked. He looked at her with desire, but his mouth pressed into a hard line. "As much as I enjoyed that. I need answers before it happens again."

She slumped her shoulders. Of course he needed answers. He deserved them. He deserved so much more than she could give him.

He released his hold and leaned back on the couch. "This Eric guy. He your boyfriend?"

She stared at her hands folded in her lap. "I used to date him a long time ago, before I met you. I guess he still thinks there's something between us, but there isn't. I swear." She raised her eyes to meet his gaze. "It's kinda like you and that red-headed nurse."

"Not even close." His jaw clenched, the tendons in his neck tightening like wires. "Is he the reason you climbed that tower? Was he trying to hurt you?"

She swallowed. "Yes."

"Why did you lie to the police?" He stared at her, his silence willing her to continue.

She held her breath as a hundred different lies flitted through her mind. There were a thousand ways she could spin this story, but in her heart, she didn't want to lie to Bryce. "I did a job for him."

He arched an eyebrow.

"Not like that. I do construction work. I fix things. It's how I make a living. I soundproofed a room for him, so he could start a heavy metal band and not disturb the neighbors." That wasn't a lie. She never would've done the job if she'd known the real reason he needed the room.

He let out a dry laugh. "That sounds about right for a guy like that."

"When things didn't work out between us the first time, I left him. Then he called me a few months ago to do the job, and I needed the money so I agreed, but he never paid me. He gets an allowance from his dad, and he said he was late on the deposit, so I waited. When I went back to collect, he still didn't want to pay, but he *did* want me to stay."

Bryce's hands balled into fists. "And he hurt you."

Her gazed drifted to the floor, and she forced the word over the lump in her throat. "Yes."

His eyes softened. "Why won't you press charges?"

This was the hard part. She couldn't tell him the real reason, but he could obviously spot a lie. She'd talked to Eric's dad and done all she could to stop his idiotic plan.

"I want it to be over. I don't want to deal with all that, and I never want to see him again. Please." She reached for his hand, and his fist relaxed under her touch. "Can we let it go?"

The sound of his teeth grinding told her the answer. "He's the 'wrong kind of guy' you always go for?"

She clutched her hands in her lap. "I guess so."

He leaned away from her. "And that's what you think I'm like?"

"No. I...I don't know."

He rose and shuffled behind the couch. "Well, you're not doing a very good job of keeping your distance if I'm the wrong kind of guy."

She twisted around to face him. "I'm trying to figure out what kind of guy you are. You're cocky one minute, and then you're the kindest person I've ever met the next. You care about people, but you act like nothing bothers you. I can't stop thinking about you, though I honestly don't know who you are."

"Who do you want me to be?"

"I want you to pick one. Either be the sweetheart or be the jerk, but don't keep me guessing which one is real."

He crossed his arms and studied her. His gaze narrowed as he chewed his bottom lip and drummed his fingers against his forearm. "You want to know who I really am?"

"Yes."

"I'll show you the real me, but you're not going to like him." He hesitated then slowly moved around the sofa and took the remote from the coffee table. "You wanted to know what I was watching? Here you go."

He pressed a button, and the TV flickered on. A bald man in a futuristic red and black shirt filled the screen. "*Star Trek*. I was watching *Star Trek*." He picked up the book from the end table. "I've read *The War of the Worlds* eight times. You accused me of being a sci-fi nerd, remember?" He lowered his gaze to the book and sighed. "Well, you were right."

Why didn't he want her to know he'd been watching *Star Trek*? "Just because you like science fiction, it doesn't make you a nerd." She grinned, trying to lighten the mood. "Eric likes *Star Wars*. You can still be a jerk."

He sucked in a breath like he planned to say more, but then he clenched his jaw shut. He tossed the book onto the table and dropped into the chair. "Yeah, I guess you're right. I'm a jerk."

"That's what I thought." *Not even close.* She stood and paced around the couch.

Bryce stared at the TV screen. "Get me a beer while you're up." Though he'd tried to make it sound like an order, the inflection on the final word lifted, turning his attempted command into a request.

She stifled a laugh and continued to the front door. "Nice try." He was too sweet to bark orders. Turning the knob, she pulled it open.

Bryce shot to his feet, a hint of panic tightening his eyes. "Hold on, now. You don't have to leave."

She straightened. "Maybe I want to."

He let out a defeated sigh. "It's too cold to sleep in your car. Stay here. Please?"

"That's not a very jerk thing to say." She suppressed a grin.

"Even an asshole wouldn't want you to freeze to death."

He had no idea. "All right. I'll stay. I'm going to get some clothes from my car." She stepped through the threshold before he could respond and slammed the door to keep in character.

Crossing her arms over her chest to ward off the cold biting at her skin, she trotted to her Ford she'd parked on the curb. Opening the back door, she glanced at Bryce's apartment and found him peering through a slit in the curtains.

That man couldn't pull off asshole if he tried. The more time she spent with Bryce, the more she saw through his smartass exterior, and that conversation proved it. There was a lot more to Bryce than met the eye, and now she was determined to know the man beneath the mask.

She shoved some clothes and toiletries into a backpack and shut the door. As she turned toward the window, the curtains fell shut, and when she returned to the living room, she found Bryce sitting in the chair, beer in hand, staring at the television.

If he wanted to pretend he was a jerk, she'd let him. If he'd admitted to being the sweetheart she knew he was, she might not have been able to resist him tonight. She had no clue what she was going to do about her blossoming emotions for the man, but sleeping with him wouldn't be the best place to start. First, she needed to get to know him. The mask would have to come off sometime.

"Mind if I use your shower?"

He didn't look at her. "Whatever you want to do."

"Okay then." She shuffled to the hall and glanced at him.

He flicked his gaze toward her, and his eyes held so much confliction, she almost apologized for calling him a jerk. Instead, she turned and headed for the shower.

Fifteen minutes later, she emerged from the bathroom to find Bryce sprawled out in his bed, his arm draped over his eyes. Lamplight seeped into the hall from the living room, but all the other lights were off.

She stood in his doorway. "I'm not climbing into bed with you." No matter how tempted she was.

"I didn't invite you." He folded his hands on his chest and met her gaze. "There's a pillow and blanket on the couch."

"What happened to you gladly giving up your bed if it meant I was safe and warm?"

"You can be safe and warm in the living room. I'm a jerk, remember?"

She rested a hand on the door jamb. "You're not a jerk, and your couch is actually pretty comfortable. I've been treated a lot worse."

He rolled onto his side and propped his head on his hand, and her chest tightened. Her wolf wanted her to climb into bed with him and end this ridiculous charade, but pride kept her feet glued to the floor.

"If you want to talk about it, I'm happy to listen." He paused, pinning her with a heavy gaze as he waited for her to respond. When she didn't, he rolled onto his back.

Would it be so wrong to talk to the man? In her heart, she trusted him. In her soul, she wanted to share everything with him. And that was the problem, wasn't it? If she allowed herself to fall for Bryce, she'd want to stay. Rogues never stayed, and people never changed. "Goodnight, Bryce."

CHAPTER NINE

ERIC SQUINTED AGAINST THE BRIGHT HEADLIGHTS STREAMING through the windshield. His asshole of a father had made him spend two nights in that damn cell before bailing him out. He'd remember that when he became alpha of his own pack.

Neither man spoke on the drive from the jail to Eric's house. He stomped inside and tried to slam the door behind him, but his old man caught it with his meaty hand.

"I drove an hour to bail your sorry ass out of jail. The least you can do is thank me." David stepped through the threshold and let the door shut behind him.

"Thanks." Eric plopped onto the couch and rested his feet on the coffee table. "Now leave."

"You assaulted a police officer. What the hell were you thinking, son?"

"I caught him making out with my girl. What was I supposed to do?" His insides burned as the image of his woman pressing her lips to the pig's face flashed in his mind. They were both going to pay for that little display of affection. Alexis would learn not to cheat, and Sergeant Samuels would learn to stay away from his property.

David shook his head like he was disappointed. The man was

always disappointed. "Alexis hasn't been your girl since you beat the shit out of her for denting your car." He crossed his arms over his chest and stood over him. Trying to intimidate him.

It wouldn't work this time. Eric put his feet on the floor and sat up straight. "How'd you know I was talking about Alexis?"

"She called me. If she's *your girl*, why'd you try to kill her?"

"I didn't mean...Wait. Why'd she call *you?*"

David narrowed his eyes as a reptilian smile curved his thin lips. "How do you think she ended up in this God-forsaken town? I paid her to keep tabs on you."

Eric tried to take a breath, but it got caught in his throat. "You... paid her?"

His old man shrugged it off. "She got into some trouble with the pack in Biloxi. I got her out of it and sent her here to watch you."

Eric fumed with anger. No wonder she'd turned down his offer to be mates. She was nothing more than a prostitute, and his own father was her pimp. "I didn't try to kill her. It's not my fault she fell off the electrical tower. She tried to kill herself."

"But she survived, even though you left her for dead."

"I thought she *was* dead." He should've known she'd survive. He'd seen her healing powers first-hand, and they obviously worked on herself too.

"Come on, son. You wanted her dead. She told me about your cockamamie plan to build your own pack out of humans. Are you trying to get yourself killed?"

He crossed his arms, tucking his fists beneath them to stop himself from punching the bastard. He hated the old man with a passion, but he needed his money. He had to play it cool. "Build my own pack?" He forced a laugh. "Alexis told you that? She was probably trying to squeeze more money out of you. She seemed destitute when she came here. She practically got on her knees begging me for some cash." He rose to his feet. "She's good on her knees, if you know what I mean, but I didn't give her the money."

His dad cocked an eyebrow. "Who knows what you've been up to? She hasn't worked for me since she left you."

"Exactly, Dad." He put a hand on the old man's shoulder. "She's broke. She'll do anything for a few bucks."

His dad eyed him warily. "Let me see your music room."

"Yeah, sure. No problem." He led his father down the hall and pushed open the door. A drum set sat on a raised platform in the corner, and several guitars hung from a rack on the wall. The tile floor had been hosed down and cleaned with bleach after his last unsuccessful attempt at turning a human, and thankfully the bodies were in a freezer at Trevor's place. David wouldn't find a lick of evidence in this house. After Alexis had shown up unannounced, Eric had made sure he wouldn't be caught off-guard again.

His father may have thought him a stupid loser, but he took plenty of precautions. He'd even taken care of the Jane that Alexis had set free. Now, he had to take care of Alexis.

David scanned the room, running his hand along the wall and fingering the strings of the bass guitar. Eric held his breath, hoping the old man wouldn't ask him to play it. He hadn't touched the instrument since he hung it up. His dad opened the closet door and peeked inside. It was empty. He stepped in front of Eric and stared him hard in the eyes. "Where are the bodies?"

Eric let out an exasperated breath. "There are no bodies. I told you she was lying. She's desperate, Dad, and she's just a rogue. Believe me."

"Why do I smell bleach?"

Shit. Would he ever let up? "I got a little crazy on a guitar solo and knocked a six-pack off the table. It shattered on the tile. You smell floor cleaner. That's all."

David sighed and walked to the front door. "I don't understand why she'd make this up, but your story checks out, son. If there is something unethical going on here, I will find out."

"There's not. Everything's legit. I swear. And I'm sorry about getting in a fight with that cop. When I saw him with Alexis...you know how I feel about her. Jealousy got the better of me. It won't happen again."

"You're damn right it won't. You've embarrassed the family name enough. I'd like you to come back to Biloxi one day, but not until you've gotten your act together. The pack won't tolerate miscreants."

"I understand, Pops. I'm trying." No way in hell would he step foot in Biloxi again. He'd go completely rogue before he'd be under his old man's thumb.

His dad stepped through the door, and the new motion-sensor camera he'd installed on the doorbell made his phone chime. "All right. I'll see what I can do about getting you out of this assault mess if you promise me you'll stay out of trouble."

"You have my word." He closed the door and marched into the living room.

That bitch. He rammed his fist through the sheet rock. White powder rained onto the floor as he jerked his hand from the wall. Alexis could fix the hole. She could fix everything. He hadn't been successful in turning a human into a werewolf a single time. The bodies were piling up, he was no closer to having his own pack, and now he had his dad on his back.

At least she'd run to a human for help and not her sister's pack. Cops he could handle. His old man he could handle. Starting a war between Biloxi and New Orleans he could not. Luckily, Alexis didn't catch on to the hollowness of his threat to harm her sister. If he could hang that over her head, he had leverage.

Her sister was a cop. He had enough bodies in the freezer to easily pull her in without getting the pack involved. Trevor had already dumped the first one in the river, and there were plenty more to keep her busy. Samuels would be easy to find too. Alexis was bound to turn up on one of their doorsteps sooner or later, and then she'd be his for the taking. She'd come back to him on her own once he was done.

CHAPTER TEN

BRYCE ROLLED OUT OF BED AND STOOD STILL FOR A MOMENT, listening for a sound that Alexis might have actually stayed the whole night. Sam's soft snoring filled the otherwise silent house. He fought the urge to tiptoe into the living room to see if she was there and shuffled to the shower instead.

After the way he'd treated her last night, he'd be surprised if she stayed. *Asshole.* What had he been thinking?

She'd convinced herself he was just like her dipshit ex-boyfriend, and instead of proving her wrong, he'd given her exactly what she wanted—a dickhead.

He groaned as he shut off the water and toweled off. Jabbing the toothbrush into his mouth, he scrubbed his teeth, and then he stomped to the bedroom to get dressed. He shoved his legs into his pants and struggled with the buttons on his shirt.

Taking a deep breath, he let it out slowly, hoping to calm the anger making his heart pound like a hammer. If her opinion of him mattered so much, why the hell had he acted like an asshole?

After fumbling with his belt for half a minute, he finally got the damn thing buckled and pulled on his shoes. He'd make it up to her —if she ever spoke to him again.

He shuffled to the living room and found Alexis curled up on the couch next to Sam, stroking his fur as he snored away happily. Her boots sat next to her backpack by the front door, and she'd folded the blanket and stacked it with the pillow on the chair.

Shoving his hands in his pockets, he nodded. "Hey."

She looked at him, and her green eyes sparkled in the early-morning sunlight streaming through window. "Hey."

"I...didn't think you'd be here."

She glanced at her stuff by the door. "Do you want me to leave?"

"No." He sauntered into the room and sat on the arm of the couch. "I'm glad you're here. I want to apologize for the way I acted last night."

She narrowed her eyes and studied him, the seconds stretching into an eternity. "Why *did* you act like that last night?"

He let out his breath in a huff. "I was childish. There's no excuse for my behavior, but..."

Sam raised his head and peered at Bryce sleepily before sliding off the couch and walking to the back door.

"Hold on." He shuffled to the door and opened it, and Sam scrambled outside and down the steps. Bryce left the door cracked and turned to find Alexis on her feet, leaning against the back of the couch.

She crossed her arms, and the corners of her mouth twitched. "You were saying..."

"Here's the deal. I like you, and when you compared me to that jackass you dated..." He sighed. Why couldn't he spit it out? "Like I said before, I don't want you to think poorly of me, but you're not giving me a chance. I got frustrated and acted like an ass, and I'm sorry."

She smiled. "Apology accepted. And I'm sorry for assuming the worst of you. You're nothing like Eric or any other man I know."

"Thank you." The tension in his shoulders loosened. Stepping toward her, he took her hand. "Let me make it up to you. If you'll stay here today, I'll make dinner for you tonight."

"You can cook?"

"I can learn."

She gazed at their entwined fingers before blinking up at him. "I don't know, Bryce. I..."

"Where else are you going to go?"

She drew her shoulders toward her ears. "I was thinking about seeing Macey."

"One more night. Please? Have dinner with me, and then if you don't want to see me anymore you can leave. I won't bug you to stay." He held his breath, waiting for her answer.

"I guess dinner won't hurt." She smiled. "I'll go see Macey this afternoon, and I'll be back in time for dinner. Does that work for you?"

The knot in his chest unfurled in a flush of warmth. He still had a chance. "Be home by seven?"

"Sure."

He could have lost himself staring into her emerald eyes. Her irises sparkled like actual jewels, and they held so much depth he felt as if he could swim through her soul, if she would let him in. As she held his gaze, a strange energy passed between them, and he could have sworn he felt a piece of her wall crumble. He leaned toward her. "Is this the part where we kiss and make up?"

She laughed and pulled her hand from his. "Don't push it, mister."

He held up his hands. "Okay. Okay. I have to go to work. I've got a school visit this morning."

"Michael's school? Is he going back already?"

He grabbed his keys from the bowl and dropped them in his pocket. "The bully's been removed, but Michael's not going back until January. I need to check on the other kids. Make sure things are running smoothly."

She caught his gaze, and her smile held so much warmth the entire world seemed to pause for a moment. "Those kids are lucky to have you looking out for them."

He cleared his throat. "You're welcome to stay here as long as you want. Sam enjoys your company."

A knock sounded on the door, and Bryce tore his gaze from hers to answer it. Michael stood on the landing, holding a metal pan.

Alexis moved behind Bryce and rested her hands on his shoulders.

His stomach tightened at the casual way she touched him. It felt way more intimate than it should have.

"Do you always have your meals delivered?" She moved a hand to his bicep and peered into the dish. White icing melted on top of four giant, fluffy cinnamon rolls.

The kid's gaze cut back and forth between Alexis and Bryce. "I... uh...Sorry. I didn't know you were busy. My mom wanted me to bring you these."

Bryce smiled and patted her hand. "No problem, man. I'm never too busy for your mom's cooking. This is my friend, Alexis Gentry."

She offered him her hand to shake.

"Hi. I'm Michael."

Alexis glanced at Bryce, and he gave a small nod of confirmation as he took the cinnamon rolls.

"Well, I'm going to go. Have a nice day, Sergeant Samuels." He raised his hand in a timid wave. "Nice to meet you, Ms. Gentry."

Bryce closed the door and carried the cinnamon rolls to the table. "I'll have to take mine to go." He snatched a plastic container from the cabinet and pulled a roll from the tray. Gooey icing dripped down the sides onto his fingers as he dropped it into the container.

He stuck his finger in his mouth to lick off the frosting, and Alexis bit her bottom lip. Her gaze slid from his eyes to his mouth and back again, and his knees nearly buckled beneath him.

She sank into a chair. "Sweet kid."

Bryce blinked away the memory of the way her lips had felt pressed to his. "Yeah, he is." He grabbed a plate and a paper towel and set them in front of her. "Help yourself. They're best when they're warm."

"Thanks."

He poked his head out the back door. "Sam." The dog stopped and looked at him for a second before lowering his nose to the ground and ignoring him. "C'mon, Sam, I've got to go to work."

"You can go. I'll watch him." She took a bite of her breakfast, and icing dripped onto her lip.

He couldn't help but stare as she flicked out her tongue to lick it off. Blood rushed to his groin, and a shudder ran down his spine.

Watching a woman eat shouldn't have affected him this way, but he'd never met a woman like Alexis. Everything she did had sex appeal. "I appreciate that." He sauntered to the door, fighting the urge to adjust his crotch. "I'll see you at seven?"

She stood and padded toward him. "I'll be here." Leaning in, she placed a soft kiss on his cheek. "Thank you. For everything."

He nodded and opened the door. "My pleasure, ma'am."

Warmth filled Alexis's core as she watched Bryce through the window. He had a slight spring in his confident gait, and she hoped she'd put it there. She let the curtain fall shut and sank onto the sofa. Maybe nice guys did exist after all.

She checked her phone. Nothing from Eric or David, so hopefully that debacle had been taken care of. As second in command of the Biloxi pack, David should have been able to keep control of his son. He just needed to tighten the leash.

A high-pitched whining noise sounded from the kitchen, and she turned around to find Sam sitting by the back door, licking his front paw. She shuffled toward him, and he whined again.

"What's the matter, buddy?" She reached for his leg, and he shied away, flattening his ears against his head. "I can't help you if you won't let me look."

She gently took his paw and examined the underside. A huge bur wedged between the first and second pads, so she pinched it between her thumb and forefinger and pulled it out. Sam licked his paw one more time and jumped to his feet, doing his adorable full-body wag.

Alexis laughed and tossed the bur in the trash. "You're welcome."

She closed the back door, and the sound of a key turning in the front lock sent her heart racing. The door swung open, and a woman in her mid-forties stepped into the living room. She had medium-length, dark hair styled into a classic mom-cut. High-waisted jeans and a button-up blouse completed the look.

The woman closed the front door and fisted her hands on her hips as she turned to face Alexis. "Who are you, and what do you want from Bryce?"

Whoa. She got right to the point. "You must be Karen, right? My name is Alexis. It's nice to meet you."

Her eyes widened, and her aggressive posture relaxed slightly. "Yes, I'm Karen. I live downstairs." She crossed her arms. "How do you know Bryce?"

Alexis mirrored her posture and tried to ignore the territorial instinct that had her wolf wanting to growl. How many women had a key to Bryce's home? "We're friends. Macey, his ex-partner, is my sister."

Karen dropped her arms to her sides and let out a slow breath. "Is that your car on the curb?"

"Yes. I can park somewhere else if it bothers you."

She nodded. "I know your type."

"Excuse me?"

"Everything you own is in the back of that car, isn't it? You drift from man to man, sleeping with whomever will take you in, using him until you get tired of him or he stops spending money on you."

"You don't know a thing about me." How dare this woman force her way in here to corner her? She had no right to make accusations like this. Alexis didn't use men. If anything, her life had been the exact opposite, and Bryce…she wouldn't dream of hurting him.

What kind of person waltzed into a man's house and started spouting insults at the woman he *had* invited over? She ground her teeth to fight the rumble trying to roll up from her chest.

Karen raked her gaze over Alexis's cargo pants and sweatshirt. "I know enough. Bryce is a great guy. He deserves someone who's going to treat him with respect, not someone who's using him for a free ride."

Alexis straightened her spine. "I'm not using him. I care about him." *He's mine.*

Whoa. Where did that thought come from? She'd dealt with plenty of territorial women in the werewolf community, and her wolf was standing her ground. That's all it was. She hadn't *actually* claimed him.

She took a deep breath and let it out slowly. "Karen, I appreciate that you want to protect Bryce. He is an amazing man, but you have to understand that he's an adult, and who he invites into his home is his business. Unless you have some kind of claim on him?"

The muscles in Karen's jaw tightened as she turned for the door. She paused with her hand on the knob. "Please don't hurt him. He deserves better."

Alexis sank onto the couch as Karen shut the door and trotted down the stairs. Sam jumped onto the cushion next to her and made a whining sound in his throat.

She scratched his head. "I really do care about him." Way more than she should have. Karen was right, though. He did deserve better.

CHAPTER ELEVEN

BRYCE'S LEG BOUNCED BENEATH HIS DESK AS HE SCOURED THE internet for recipes. Alexis had been impressed with Karen's jambalaya, and he wanted to give her another home-cooked meal to prove he wasn't the jackass she'd thought. That he could be a provider. The kind of man she wanted.

He'd known Alexis for more than a year now, seeing her with Macey every now and then when she'd popped into town for a few days. She never seemed to stay in one place for very long, and from the way she talked, it sounded like she'd never met a man worth staying for.

Bryce wanted to be that man. He *would* be the reason she stayed this time. And if he had to learn how to cook to convince her he was the right man for her, so be it. He'd do anything.

His computer pinged with an incoming e-mail, and he clicked the tab to open it. His pulse quickened. The autopsy report on the body they'd pulled out of the river had finally come through.

He scanned the contents, and a sickening feeling pooled in his gut. Macey had tried to write it off as an animal attack, but the body temperature had been seven degrees below the ambient temperature of the Mississippi in that area.

If the body had been colder than the atmosphere they'd found it in, it must have been refrigerated—or possibly frozen—before the killer dumped it in the river. He didn't know any wolves that had access to freezers, let alone opposable thumbs and the brains enough to put a body in one. Let Macey try to dismiss this as an animal attack now.

Johnson knocked on his office door, his expression grim. "Jumper on the CCC. Let's go."

A brick settled in Bryce's stomach. The Crescent City Connection, the bridge between the Mississippi's East and West banks, hosted a couple of suicide attempts annually. This would make number three for this year.

He followed Johnson out of the station and climbed into his SUV. Flipping on the siren, he high-tailed it for the bridge and said a silent prayer they'd make it in time.

When he approached the bridge, the uniforms already had the westbound lanes closed, and a line of cars blocked his access. He cut the wheel right and took the shoulder the rest of the way before killing the engine and sliding out of his seat.

Adrenaline made his nerves hum as he paced up the street toward the bridge entrance. Frigid wind whipped into his face, biting at his skin, and a thick blanket of clouds covered the sky, masking the sun. A harbor police boat chugged through the murky water below, and a chill wound up Bryce's spine. He zipped his jacket.

A uniform approached, shaking his head, and a heaviness pressed on Bryce's shoulders as if he were Atlas, trying to hold the weight of the world. A fist of dread yanked his heart into his stomach, and he quickened his pace.

The uniform put up his hands. His name tag read Blanchard. "Dude already jumped. Harbor police are searching the water to see if he's alive, but you know how this goes."

"Goddammit!" Bryce clenched his jaw so tight a sharp pain shot through his temple. If he'd been five minutes earlier, he might've been able to save that man. He *would* have saved him.

"Hey." Blanchard slapped him on the shoulder. "At least he's out of his misery now, right?"

Bryce's nostrils flared as he inhaled the stifling odors of car exhaust and muddy river water, and the corner of his mouth twitched. Misery? He had no idea the kind of misery this man had left behind for his loved ones. Pain. Guilt of not doing enough to help. Remorse for not paying attention to the signs. The suffocating agony of never having an answer to why. Drowning in a sea of a thousand regrets, unable to break the surface to simply breathe...

Blanchard shook his head. "I don't know why we try to stop them, honestly. If they want to die—"

"Walk away, Blanchard." His anger morphed his words into a growl. That man probably had a family. Parents. Friends. *A brother*. People who cared about him. His suffering may have ended, but theirs was just beginning...and for what? Because of the screwed-up way society viewed depression? Because people thought it was something to be ashamed of rather than an illness that could be treated? People were all too willing to talk about their physical problems...cancer, heart disease, diabetes...they'd tell you all about the treatments and medications they took. But as soon as the problem had to do with the mind, people acted like it was a personal weakness. He curled his hands into fists.

"All I'm saying is, who are we to decide who lives and who dies?"

"You've got five seconds to get your ass off this bridge before I plant my fist in your face."

Blanchard raised his hands in surrender. "All right, I'm going. Man, all you negotiator guys got a chip on your shoulders." He shook his head and strode away.

"Chip on my shoulder, my ass," Bryce grumbled. Most of the guys on the team had witnessed firsthand the aftermath of a suicide. It wasn't a chip. It was a deep desire to stop it from happening to anyone else.

Another slap on his shoulder pulled him from his thoughts.

Johnson scowled. "Body's already on the bank." He nodded to the left, where a team dragged a corpse from the water. "Once we get ID, I'll handle notifying the next of kin. You can head back."

"Yeah." Bryce stared out over the water as a familiar numbness spread through his core and down his limbs. Too late to save him. If he'd only known sooner.

He closed his eyes and let out a slow breath. Internalizing would do him no good, so he wiped the emotion from his face and made his way down the riverbank. He'd save the next one. And the one after that.

Seeing the body wouldn't help, but he always had to look. Maybe one day he'd find a clue to the reason a person could slip into such a state of distress. Could feel so alone, even when he had people who loved him.

He peered at the body lying in the grass, and his heart stuttered. "I thought the jumper was a male."

"He was," an officer answered.

Bryce took a step closer. A series of jagged tears covered the woman's arms and legs. Her torn shirt revealed teeth marks in her shoulder, and the gash in her neck probably severed her carotid artery. He backed up as Detective Sharon Dupuis crouched to examine the body.

She shook her head. "Looks like another animal attack." She addressed a uniform. "Weren't there reports of wolves in the surrounding area last year?"

"Yes, ma'am. I believe so," the officer replied.

She stood. "We'll need to contact the park rangers and see if there have been any recent reports." She typed something into her phone and turned to walk away.

"Now, hold on a minute, Detective." Bryce strode toward her. "Have you seen the autopsy report on the other one?"

She crossed her arms. "Sergeant, what are you doing here?"

"I was on the bridge for the jumper. Have you seen the report?"

Her brow furrowed as she fought off a cringe. "Not yet."

"The first *animal attack* victim measured seven degrees colder than the river. Unless you know a wolf that keeps a deep-freezer in its den, I'd say it was more than an animal attack."

She tilted her head. "You're a negotiator. Why were you looking at the autopsy report?"

Damn it, why did it matter? "I was helping Detective Mason."

"I see. Well, I'll be sure to let her know if the case is the same with this one." She flashed an insincere smile, turned on her heel, and strutted away.

Bryce ground his teeth on his way back to his SUV. Something fishy was going on with these bodies, and though murder investigations were no longer in his job description, he'd be damned if he'd let any criminal roam free. He'd give Macey a chance to get up to speed with the inconsistencies in the autopsy report, and if she didn't start treating this case like the crime it was, he'd do it for her.

Alexis tugged Bryce's jacket tighter around her shoulders and pressed her nose against the collar. His warm, masculine scent filled her senses, stirring the strange feelings deep in her soul. What was it about this human that commanded her wolf's attention?

She strolled up Royal Street toward the Gumbo Place, absorbing the scenery and relishing the warmth Bryce provided against the cold. Two and three-story wooden structures rose on both sides of the street, their colorful facades reflecting a time long ago. Festive holiday colors decorated the wrought-iron railings that trimmed the balconies and galleries, and a three-piece band played an upbeat version of "Have Yourself a Merry Little Christmas" on the corner of St. Louis Street.

She passed Spellbound Sweets, and her witch friend Rain leaned her head out the door. "Hey, Alexis. I didn't know you were back in town." A gust of wind kicked up, whipping her dark curls into her face. "Do you want to come in for a minute?"

"Thanks, but I'm on my way to meet Macey for lunch."

Rain smiled and raised her eyebrows. "Have you seen Bryce lately?"

She paused, unaccustomed to talking about her feelings, and warmth unfurled in her chest. "I'm seeing him tonight." Was that giddiness bubbling from her stomach? No, it had to be heartburn.

"Good. Stop by if you have a chance before you leave town."

"I will." She grinned and hung a left on St. Peter. It might not hurt to stick around for a while this time. She hadn't heard a peep from Eric or his dad, so that mess had probably blown over. Knowing David, he tore Eric a new one the second he stepped out of jail and then hauled his ass back to Biloxi to keep a closer eye on him.

She had friends here now. Macey was here…and Bryce. Her stomach fluttered. It might be nice to see where things went with him. To explore these strange emotions stirring in her soul.

She opened the door to the Gumbo Place and found Macey and her sister-in-law, Amber, sitting at a table by the window. Macey smiled, and Amber waved her over. Zydeco music played through the speakers in the ceiling, and Alexis sashayed past a row of booths covered in red-checkered cloths.

Macey had pulled her blonde hair back into a ponytail, and it swished over her shoulder as she hugged Alexis. "I was wondering if you were ever going to call me."

Alexis hugged Amber and settled into a chair. "No visit to New Orleans is complete without seeing my little sister." She ignored the pang of guilt squeezing her heart. She was here now, and that was what mattered.

Macey opened her mouth to speak, but the waiter arrived to take their orders. Amber asked for a roast beef po-boy, and Macey ordered a muffuletta.

"I'll have a glass of water." Alexis pressed her lips into a tight smile.

As the waiter nodded and turned to walk away, Macey held up a finger to stop him. She lowered her voice. "I can buy your lunch. Go ahead and order something."

Alexis straightened her spine. "I don't need you to pay for me." She shrugged. "I'm not very hungry."

Macey put her hand on hers. "I don't want you to have to sit there and watch us eat."

Alexis let out a slow breath. Because she was a homeless rogue, everyone immediately assumed she didn't have a dime and couldn't be depended on. Macey may have been right about the money, but Alexis could take care of herself and anyone else that came along.

"All right. I'll get a little something, but I'm paying for it myself."

She scanned the menu. "I'll have the half ham sandwich. Separate checks, please." At $5.99, after tax and tip, the half sandwich would eat up half her life savings, but it was better than admitting she was broke.

The waiter shuffled away, and Alexis picked at her unpainted nails, unable to look Macey in the eyes.

Amber broke the awkward silence. "What brings you into town, Alexis?"

"Oh, umm…" Heat climbed her neck and settled in her cheeks.

"I'm the one who gave him your number, remember?" Macey smiled, but it didn't mask the wariness in her eyes. "I'm pretty sure that's his jacket too."

Wrapping her arms around herself, Alexis stroked the soft fabric. The central heating in the restaurant provided enough warmth that she didn't need to wear the jacket inside, but it had become a sort of security blanket.

She deserved every bit of doubt her sister had about her, but earning it didn't make it any less painful. If she'd have stayed last year, when they'd first reunited, things would be different. The alpha had given her a job. She'd had a place to live. Family. But as soon as she'd gotten comfortable, she'd gotten scared, and she'd left like she always did. Being a rogue, Alexis had learned the hard way that letting her guard down—getting comfortable—set her up for people to take advantage of her. To hurt her. She knew in her heart that Macey and her friends here weren't like that, but a lifetime of being on the defensive wasn't easy to change.

She popped in and out of town, but it didn't provide the kind of relationship her sister wanted. Hell, it wasn't the kind of relationship she wanted either.

This time would be different. "I'm seeing Bryce."

Amber looked at Macey. "Your old partner?"

Macey nodded.

"That's sweet." Amber tucked her light-brown hair behind her ear and folded her hands on the table. "I knew you'd get to keep him in your life somehow."

Alexis's breath hitched. As a second-born werewolf, Amber's psychic power was empathic premonitions. She felt things about the future that usually came true. "Have you seen anything about him? Or…me?"

"No, I meant that Macey and Bryce were too close to let a little promotion end their friendship. I only have premonitions about people I see on a regular basis."

"Oh." She slumped her shoulders.

"Maybe if you stick around a while this time." Amber grinned and raised her eyebrows.

"How long are you planning to stay?" Macey asked.

The waiter delivered their food—and an ounce of relief—and Alexis used the distraction to avoid answering the question. She took a bite of her sandwich. The earthy aromas of the whole-grain bread offset the sweetness of the ham, and the Cajun seasonings in the mayonnaise added a zip to the medley of flavors on her tongue. She mushed the food around in her mouth longer than necessary before swallowing and taking another bite.

The heaviness of things unsaid hung over them as they ate in silence. Macey flicked her gaze toward her, inhaling as if to speak several times, but she didn't. She didn't need to. The words were apparent in her expression.

Amber must have sensed the tension, because she focused on her po-boy, lifting her gaze from her food occasionally.

Alexis finished her sandwich and folded her hands in her lap. "I like Bryce. A lot."

Macey wiped her mouth with a napkin and dropped it on her plate. "He likes you too. More than I've seen him like anyone in the seven years I've known him."

Her lips tugged into a smile. Hearing those words from someone who knew Bryce well had her pulse racing.

Macey gave her a curious look. "Please be careful with him. He pretends he's a tough guy, but he's more sensitive than he'd like anyone to believe."

His sensitive side was the reason she was still in town, planning to have dinner with him in a few hours. The reason she was falling head over tail for a human. "I know you're worried about him, but I promise I don't plan to hurt him. I care about him."

Macey shook her head. "You care about me too, don't you?"

"Of course I do." How could she even ask such a thing? "After I ran away from foster care, I spent the next twenty years looking for you."

She swallowed hard, her gaze lingering on her crumpled napkin before locking with Alexis's eyes. "You hurt me every time you leave."

Her breath hitched. "Macey, I…"

"I don't know where you go. I don't know what you're doing. Half the time you don't answer your phone when I call. I…" She clamped her mouth shut and took a deep breath. "I guess what I'm trying to say is that you tend to hurt people without realizing it."

Did Alexis not realize it? Or had she been ignoring the pain she'd seen in her sister's eyes every time she'd said goodbye? Convincing herself she wasn't the cause because nobody cared about her enough to be hurt by her absence? "Why haven't you told me this?"

She shrugged. "Would it have made a difference?"

Fisting her hands on the table, Alexis inhaled deeply. "I started shifting on the first full moon after my thirteenth birthday. I had no idea what was happening to me, so I ran. Do you know *why* I ran?"

Macey held her gaze. "You were scared."

"That, yes, but I also ran because that's what Mom and Dad did. You were too young to remember, but we moved eight times before I turned six. It seemed like every time I got close to making a friend, we packed up and moved."

Amber's brow puckered. "That must have been hard."

"That's just how it was. I didn't know any better." She returned her gaze to Macey. "Then we went through four different foster homes after they died, and none of our foster families gave a damn about us. You had nightmares. You'd wake up screaming, and when an adult would come in to spank you for waking them up, I'd take the blame. I took the beatings, but I couldn't stop the nightmares. I couldn't fix you."

Macey's eyes shimmered. "I remember that. I remember when you were there for me."

"I failed you. No matter how much I tried to help, I couldn't fix the pain in your heart."

Her shoulders drooped as she slowly shook her head. "You didn't need to fix me. I just needed you to be there."

Alexis folded her hands on the table. "Me being there didn't seem to do anything for you. It never did. Our parents weren't the best role models for reliability. They never had any friends. I had zero social skills, and then I turned into a freaking wolf. I ran, and instinct led me to a rogue that I found hunting one night. He took me in. Promised to keep me safe. To take care of me." She swallowed the sour taste from her mouth. "He made sure I took care of him too."

Macey sucked in a sharp breath. "He didn't..."

"He did. And I didn't know any better, so I let it happen. I thought it was how werewolves behaved." She sipped her water, washing the dryness from her throat. "Now I know that's just how assholes behave, but...you're lucky you got adopted when you did because when I came back looking for you..." She didn't need to finish the sentence. The horror in her sister's eyes said she understood.

Amber shifted uncomfortably in her seat, casting her gaze to her lap.

"Eventually, I got away and started living on my own, but I was already broken. He made me think I was worthless, and I still struggle with that today. I've never had a healthy relationship. Nobody trusts a rogue. My life has never had a positive impact on anyone, so I'm not used to anyone caring what I do...or whether I live or die for that matter." Pressure built in the back of her eyes, so she blinked it away. She would not cry. Crying meant weakness, and she was anything but weak. "I'm sorry."

Macey reached across the table and took her hand. "People do care. I care, and so does Bryce."

Heaviness settled in her chest, squeezing her insides from her heart to her throat, making it hard to breathe. "I love you, Macey."

"I love you too. I'm so sorry you went through that."

She shook her head. "It's over now. Bryce is a good man, and I don't want to hurt him."

Macey leaned back in her chair. "You need to understand that when people love you, your actions have consequences. If you get close to him…if you bring him into our world and tell him what we are, his life will turn upside down. Don't do that to him unless you plan on sticking around."

Alexis focused on her hands folded on the table. Things were different now. She had the beginnings of a romantic relationship with an amazing man, but the biggest difference resonated in her soul. Her wolf wanted to stay this time, and that was something she'd never felt before. It was time to stop fighting these emotions and go with her gut.

Lifting her gaze to Macey's, she smiled. "Is Luke hiring?"

"You know you have a job here if you want it. We've got an extra bedroom too." The hopeful look in Macey's eyes tugged at her heart.

Could she stay this time? She opened her mouth to say she would, but fear clamped her throat, blocking the words from flowing. Her pulse sprinted, and nausea churned in her stomach. She wanted to stay. God, she *needed* to. Her wolf craved the companionship and comfort of the people she cared for, and Bryce… He wasn't like any man she'd ever met. She'd gotten a tiny peek behind his mask, and a hardened asshole didn't reside beneath it. He was kind and gentle.

She squared her shoulders toward her sister and straightened her spine. "I'm going to stay." She had to. She was done running.

Macey raised her eyebrows. "For how long?"

"For as long as you can stand having me around. It's time I put down some roots, don't you think?"

"I agree." Her smile finally reached her eyes.

Amber had remained silent during their exchange, but as she paid her tab, she took both their hands in hers. "I've got an extra room too, if you'd rather stay with another single lady." She winked and rose to her feet. "I have to get back to work."

"Yeah, I have things to do too." Alexis handed her last twenty to the waiter.

Macey paid her tab and stood. "I'll talk to Luke for you. And please…be careful with Bryce. He's a skeptic at best. Bringing him into our world won't be easy."

Alexis stayed at the table when Macey and Amber left the restaurant, her stomach tying itself into a massive knot as Karen's words echoed in her mind: *he deserves better*. Rising to her feet, she fisted her hands at her sides. She could do this. Bryce wanted to be with her, and she wanted to—she *would*—be the woman he deserved.

CHAPTER TWELVE

BRYCE FILLED A POT WITH WATER AND SET IT ON THE STOVE before washing a saucepan in the sink. His mom had bought him the cooking set when he'd graduated college and gotten his first grown-up apartment, but they'd sat unused in every place he'd lived since the day he'd moved in. How a layer of dust had managed to settle on the dishes in a cabinet he never opened, he wasn't sure, but he'd be giving his kitchen a thorough cleaning on his next day off.

He'd been a nervous wreck all damn day. First losing the jumper before he could get to the scene, and then witnessing yet another suspiciously mutilated body retrieved from the river. He'd left Macey a message about the autopsy, but she hadn't returned his call. She'd been acting so strange lately she probably wouldn't. He added getting to the bottom of her out-of-character behavior to his mental to-do list.

Rolling his neck, he stretched the soreness from his muscles and popped open a jar of tomato sauce. Pouring it into the saucepan, he set it on the counter and peeked inside the oven. A gelatinous mixture of flour, soda, and salt coagulated in another pan he'd never used until today. It didn't look much like bread, but it had another ten minutes to cook.

The saucepan clanked as he set it on the stove, and then he turned on the burner. Orange flames whipped out from the contraption, licking upward and nearly engulfing the small pan in fire. "Shit." He twisted the dial, making the flames fit beneath the pan, and pulled his buzzing phone from his pocket.

Alexis's name lit up the screen, and his heart raced as he pressed the device to his ear. "Hey there, beautiful."

She missed a beat in her response. "Hi, Bryce."

"Dinner's almost ready. Are you on your way?"

She took a deep breath. "If I told you I was leaving town tomorrow, would you want to see me tonight?"

His stomach tightened. Leaving tomorrow? Had she already made up her mind before she'd given him a chance? "Yeah. Of course I would. I mean…any time with you is time well-spent."

"Okay."

The crunching sound of a key sliding into a lock reverberated through the phone and in his living room. The front door swung open, and Alexis strutted in wearing skinny jeans, black lace-up boots, and an olive-green sweater that dipped below her collarbone, accentuating the delicate curve of her neck. She dropped her backpack and locked the door as Bryce slipped his phone into his pocket.

She turned to face him, and her brow furrowed, a look of determination falling across her features. She raked her gaze from his head to his toes, and when her eyes met his, their intensity stilled his heart in his chest.

The corner of her mouth twitched as she closed the distance between them in three purposeful strides. Without saying a word, she slipped one hand behind his neck and the other around his waist and planted her soft lips on his.

Fire shot through his veins. This wasn't the hello he'd been expecting from a woman who intended to leave town tomorrow, but he wasn't about to complain. Instead, he wrapped his arms around her, tugging her close, and deepened the kiss.

She tasted like warm honey, and as he coaxed her lips apart with his tongue, a tiny growl rolled up from her chest. She pressed her body harder against his and opened for him, lapping at his tongue, brushing it with hers before catching his bottom lip between her teeth. With a gentle tug, she released him and glided her lips across his cheek to nip at his earlobe.

A moan rumbled in his chest, and he slid his hands down to cup her ass. "If I'd known this was the reward for making a woman dinner, I'd have learned to cook a long time ago."

Biting her bottom lip, she leaned back and ran her hands down his chest, stopping above his jeans. She gripped the hem of his shirt and tugged it up toward his head. He could've stopped her. Told her to slow down, take her time. But, damn it, he wanted this woman as much as she seemed to want him.

He helped her tug it over his head, and as his arm came down to hold her, he hit the saucepan handle, knocking the pot to the floor. Tomato sauce splattered across the tile, and Alexis had the common sense to jump out of the way. Bryce stood there in a daze as red goo plastered his pants and shoes.

"I'm so sorry." She grabbed the pot and dumped it in the sink before tugging the roll of paper towels from the rack. When he didn't move, she stopped and put a hand on his chest. "Are you okay?"

The warmth of her skin touching his sent blood rushing to his groin. Was he okay? He was half-naked with the woman of his dreams standing in his kitchen. He was a hell of a lot better than okay. "Yeah." He took the paper towels from her. "I'll clean this up; I knocked it down."

She pulled a string of towels from the roll and knelt on the floor. "You knocked it down because *I* tried to get you naked while you were cooking. I'll help."

"Wait…you were trying to get me naked?" He knelt beside her and wiped up some of the mess.

She grinned. "I didn't plan on stopping with your shirt."

Heat crept up his neck. "Oh."

She laughed. "You really haven't had many women over, have you?"

"I told you. You're the first." And if he got his way, she'd be the last. He didn't plan to leave a trace of doubt in her mind after tonight. She couldn't leave town tomorrow. She couldn't leave *him*. He gathered the mess of paper towels and tossed them in the trash. "We've got a problem."

"What's that?" Her gaze lingered on his chest, and she licked her lips.

Dear Lord, if she didn't stop looking at him like that he'd never be able to speak a coherent sentence again. "Umm…" He cleared his throat. "That was my only jar of tomato sauce. I've got nothing to put on the spaghetti now."

She sucked in a sharp breath and blinked before looking him in the eyes. "You've got ketchup, right? Isn't that tomato sauce?" Peering into the fridge, she pulled out a bottle of Heinz. "It's in a bottle rather than a jar, but the first ingredient is tomato sauce. This should work if we heat it up."

"I never thought of that, but I think you're right. Let's do it." He washed the pot in the sink and set it by the ketchup before grabbing the dried pasta from a shelf.

Alexis wrinkled her nose. "What's that smell?"

He paused and inhaled, and a faint, sweetly pungent odor with the sharp reek of something burnt greeted his senses.

She nodded to her left. "I think it's coming from the oven."

"Oh, crap. The bread." He yanked the oven door open, and cloud of black smoke billowed into the kitchen. It rose quickly, wafting toward the ceiling, and he fanned it out of his face as he chased it toward the smoke alarm.

Too late.

A high-pitched squealing sound filled his apartment and probably half the block. Grabbing a paperback, he fanned the book in front of the device to dissipate the smoke, but the damn thing wouldn't turn off. He mashed the reset button with his thumb and blew into the plastic cover. Nothing would silence the incessant screeching, so he tore it from the wall and yanked out the battery. Glorious silence filled his throbbing ears.

He took a deep breath and set his jaw. This was no big deal. He could save face. He'd go back in there, they'd laugh it off, let a restaurant cook them dinner, and maybe they'd finish the other thing they'd started this evening.

He sauntered to the kitchen and found Alexis with her backside pressed against the counter, her hands gripping the Formica so tightly her knuckles turned white. Sam sat at her feet, a ridge of hair down the center of his back standing on end.

Karen stood at the sink, fanning the smoke out the window. "If you're going to try to cook for him, at least figure out what you're doing before you burn our house down." Her voice held a venom he'd never heard from her before, and from the look on Alexis's face, Karen had done more than insult her lack of cooking skills.

He moved to stand next to Alexis and draped an arm across her shoulders. "Thanks for your concern, Karen, but we've got this under control."

"You obviously don't. Spaghetti with ketchup?" She picked up the bottle and curled her lip before setting it down. "You shouldn't be in the kitchen with your shirt off, especially with an inexperienced cook like her. You could have been burned."

He grabbed his shirt from the counter and yanked it over his head. "I had tomato sauce, but it spilled on the floor. And *I* am the inexperienced cook. I was making dinner for Alexis."

She flashed an unbelieving look. "And what is this supposed to be?" She gestured to the burnt mess she'd retrieved from the oven.

"I was trying to make bread."

Alexis slid her arm behind his back. "And it was a sweet gesture, Bryce. I appreciate the effort." She kissed him on the cheek and rested her other hand on his chest.

If he didn't know any better, he'd say it felt a little bit like she was claiming him. He suppressed a grin. Something about the idea of Alexis feeling the need to fight for him warmed him from the inside out.

Karen ignored her comment. "What did you put in it?"

Bryce shrugged. "Just what the recipe called for. Flour, salt, soda… I used Dr. Pepper. Should I have gone with something clear?"

Karen laughed. "Soda means *baking* soda. Not the kind you drink." She shook her head. "You know what? I made a pot roast, and there is plenty for everyone. Why don't you come down and have dinner with Michael and me?"

Alexis tightened her grip on his waist, and he could've sworn he heard a growl rumble from her chest. "We'll pass."

He gave her shoulder a squeeze and stepped away to usher Karen to the door. "I do appreciate the invitation, ma'am, but this was supposed to be a date. I'll take her out somewhere for dinner."

He stepped onto the landing and closed the front door before lowering his voice. "What are you doing, Karen? You can't let yourself into my house when I've got company over and start insulting my girlfriend."

Karen crossed her arms. "She's your girlfriend?"

"With any luck, she might be some day. I'm working on it." He crossed his arms to chase away the chill in the air.

She glanced at the Ford on the curb and huffed. "She lives out of her car."

"She's going through a rough patch right now. It can happen to the best of us."

Her jaw clenched. "She's using you."

While he appreciated Karen's concern, her judgment of the woman he cared for grated on his nerves. He needed to nip this cat fight in the bud before it turned ugly. "She's not using me." He chuckled. "I practically had to beg her to come over."

"I know you like to save people, but believe me, this won't end well. You can't save someone like her. I tried once, and I ended up alone and pregnant."

He sighed. "She's not Bobby...and I don't have the parts to end up pregnant, so the worst she can do is break my heart. Cut her some slack, huh? She's Macey sister."

Karen swallowed and nodded. "You're right. I'm sorry I turned into a mother hen on you. I just...I need to protect my boys." She flashed an apologetic smile. "I'll give her a chance."

"That's all I'm asking. Tell Michael 'hi' for me."

"I will."

He stayed outside as she shuffled down the stairs toward her own apartment. Hopefully he'd seen the end of the turbulence with Karen. Convincing Alexis to stay was already hard enough; the last thing he needed was another woman driving her away. When he opened the door, Alexis stood in the living room with her arms crossed over her chest.

A fire burned in her emerald eyes, and as she arched a brow and drummed her fingers against her bicep, he fought off a smile. "Does she do that often?" she asked.

He shoved his hands into his pockets. "Do what?"

"Let herself in whenever she wants."

"She didn't mean any harm. I'm sorry about that." Damn, she was cute when she was jealous. "She heard the smoke alarm, and if my place burns down, hers does too."

She inclined her chin. "Is there something going on between you?"

"What? No." He moved toward her. "Karen is like...she looks out for me...like a second mom."

"A mom who would've been ten years old when she had you."

"Okay...how about an older sister? I swear, Alexis, there is nothing going on between me and Karen." The only woman he wanted to have anything going on with was standing right in front of him. If she didn't understand that by now, he'd have to do a better job showing her.

She narrowed her eyes, studying him. "Her pupils dilated when she looked at your chest. She finds you attractive."

He laughed. "Who wouldn't?"

Alexis rolled her eyes. "I believe there's nothing going on between you because I don't think you'd lie to me...and...you've got no game." She grinned.

His mouth dropped open. "I've got game."

"Do you?" She slinked toward him and ran her fingers up his chest before placing a soft kiss on his lips. Then she nodded toward the kitchen. "You call that game?"

His teeth clicked as he clenched his jaw. He wanted to argue...to defend his manhood, but what could he say? "I see your point. Let me get rid of that godawful science experiment and get cleaned up." Then he'd show her game. He strutted into the kitchen. "Would you have known baking soda wasn't the stuff you drink?"

She laughed. "Everyone knows that."

Not everyone. He grabbed the bread pan with both hands, and searing pain exploded across his skin. "Godammit! Shit!" Dropping the pan on the counter, he peered at his palms. "Damn thing's still hot."

Bright-red marks covered his palms and fingers where he'd made contact with the heated glass. His skin warped, as if the top layer no longer connected to the skin beneath. His hands throbbed, and he bit the inside of his cheek to hold in a groan. "That's gonna blister."

"Let me see." Concern danced in her eyes as she gingerly took his right hand in hers. She tilted her head. "That's not so bad."

"If you say so." His voice sounded strained, and he took a deep breath to rein in the wuss and act like a man. The skin on his fingertips was already puckering, moisture building beneath the loose layer of flesh. He held in a whimper. Men didn't whimper.

Alexis gently ran her fingers over the burned areas of his hand, and he'd be damned if the woman didn't have a magic touch. The throbbing subsided, and as she brought his fingertips to her lips and kissed them, the pain ceased entirely. She did the same thing to his left hand, and just like that, the agony was gone.

"You bring kiss-it-and-make-it-better to a whole new level." He looked at his hands, and his eyes widened. "The burns are gone. How'd you do that?" He turned his hands over a few times and rubbed his palms together. No trace of the injury remained. His mind reeled. All she did was touch him. His skin should've been a blistered mess by now.

The woman had a way of making him feel better whenever she was near, but there was no way in hell she'd healed his wounds with a touch. It wasn't possible. "Alexis?"

He looked at her, and she closed her eyes, her body swaying as if she were on the verge of passing out.

"Are you okay?" He clutched her shoulders, steadying her.

With a deep inhale, she opened her eyes and nodded. "I'm fine. Those burns were pretty deep." She cupped his face in her hands, running her thumbs across his cheeks. "I'm okay. Why don't you put some clean clothes on, and I'll take the pan to the trash outside? That smell is horrible." She grabbed a dish towel from a hook and folded it over, using it as padding to pick up the mess. "I don't think the pan is salvageable."

"Yeah. Okay." He stood motionless as she walked to the door, his mind running in circles. *What just happened?*

She paused in the threshold. "Go change, goofball." She grinned and shut the door.

Goofball? Well, it was better than dumbass.

He dumped his dirty clothes in the washing machine and pulled on a pair of clean jeans and a black T-shirt. Sinking onto the edge of the bed, he stared at his hands. No matter how hard he wracked his brain, he couldn't come up with a logical explanation for what she'd done to him. How had the pain stopped instantly like that? And where were the blisters?

He took a deep breath and blew it out hard. Macey had her psychic ability to read spirit energy. Her friend Rain claimed to be a witch, and they both insisted she could cast spells. It was possible Alexis had the ability to heal, wasn't it? Hell, why not? Plenty of faith healers claimed to have powers like this. Maybe they weren't all scam artists after all.

He put on his shoes and padded to the living room, where he found Alexis on the couch, petting Sam. She looked so comfortable in his apartment, lounging with his dog like she belonged there. His heart couldn't decide if it wanted to race or skip a beat as he paused to look at her. Having her here felt almost too good to be true. Almost…magical.

He shuffled to the couch. "Are you ready to tell me what you did to my hands? Do you have some kind of weird power like your sister and her spirit sensors?" He sank onto the cushion next to her.

She bit her bottom lip in that oh so sexy way of hers, and her eyes tightened with uncertainty. "What I did…drains me. Can we get some food, and then I'll try to explain?"

He held her gaze, searching for a sign that she planned to avoid the issue, that she was concocting a lie to appease him. He only found fatigue. "Fair enough. There's an Irish pub a few blocks away. Good food. Great whiskey."

She smiled. "Sounds fantastic."

"Are you too tired to walk? I can carry you on my back if you are."
He winked.

"Really?" Her musical laugh danced in his ears, adding warmth to
the hominess she already brought to his apartment. What would it
take to convince her she belonged here?

"Or we can drive."

Giving Sam one last pat on the head, she rose to her feet. "A walk
would do me good, but...can I borrow your jacket again? I lost mine."

He sauntered to the door, took the one she'd worn a few times
from the rack, and held it out to her. "How'd you lose your jacket?"

She slipped her arms through the sleeves and kissed him on the
cheek. "I left it at Eric's."

The mention of her abusive ex stopped Bryce in his tracks. The
fact that sorry excuse for a man had hurt Alexis fanned a fire of hatred
in his heart so hot that he might not be able to stop himself from
tearing into the asshole if he ever saw him again. A sour sensation
burned in his stomach, and he caught her hand. "Have you heard
from him lately?"

"Not a peep." She laced her fingers through his. "Let's go eat."

CHAPTER THIRTEEN

ALEXIS HELD BRYCE'S HAND AS THEY STROLLED THROUGH THE neighborhood toward the tavern. Massive oak trees wrapped in twinkling white lights created a canopy over the sidewalk, and wreaths and tinsel adorned the homes along the path. Quaint, modest houses sat next to huge nineteenth century buildings with white columns and gas lamps for porch lights. The area had a cozy, welcoming ambience that she'd like to get used to.

Bryce remained quiet on the walk, giving her time to figure out how much to tell him. She wanted to spill it all. To tell him everything about herself, about her abilities. But to expose the werewolves to him would be a bigger step than she was ready to take.

Werewolves shared their secrets when they planned to make a serious commitment. While she knew, without a doubt, that she wanted to be with Bryce, the idea of settling down…of trusting someone…had her insides tied in knots.

If she could get out of her head and let her wolf take the lead, she'd be able to admit he was her fate-bound. Hell, her wolf had been trying to convince her to make the man hers since the day she met him. It was time she started listening.

She clutched his bicep with her free hand and leaned into his side.

He was warm, strong, kind. He deserved to know everything, but could he handle the truth? Would he believe her?

He patted her hand on his arm. "We're almost there. You doing okay?"

"I'm good." She caught his gaze, and the words *I'm a werewolf* danced on her tongue. She bit them back. "Why don't you have a Christmas tree?"

He laughed dryly. "I don't do much for the holidays anymore."

"Why not?"

"There's not much to celebrate when you're alone." A sadness she'd never heard before laced his voice. An ancient pain she didn't dare drag up for him to relive. Bryce was charismatic, friendly...everyone seemed to like him. A man like him wouldn't be alone unless he chose to be.

"Surely there are plenty of single guys at the station throwing parties, going to bars. Why don't you celebrate with them?"

"I do occasionally, but..." He stopped and faced her. "It may not seem that way, but I'm an introvert at heart. I enjoy hanging with the guys, but it drains me. I need my alone time to recharge my batteries." He opened the pub door and motioned for her to enter. "And speaking of doing things that drain you, I believe you owe me an explanation."

The wooden floor creaked as she stepped through the doorway, and she slipped out of Bryce's jacket, folding it over her arm. Dim, green-shaded lights hung from chains above the twenty or so tables scattered about the restaurant, and an impressive assortment of whiskey bottles lined the shelves behind the dark wood bar. A hostess seated them at a small table in the corner, and Alexis ordered the shepherd's pie, while Bryce went for an English breakfast. As the server scurried away to enter their orders, Alexis excused herself to the restroom. She hoped the extra time would give her a chance to come up with an easy way to explain to a skeptic that magic was real, but she returned to the table with nothing.

As she slid into her seat, Bryce leveled a heavy gaze on her.

Her stomach tensed. There was no easy way to say it. Bryce liked to deal with facts, so that was what she'd give him. "I healed you. I have…healing abilities."

He blinked at her, saying nothing.

"Like how Macey can read spirit energy, I can access my own healing energy and share it with others. It takes a toll on me, though, so I don't do it very often."

He shook his head. "That's impossible. You can't heal someone with a touch."

"I…" She paused as the waiter delivered their food. "I can, Bryce, and I did it to you. Twice."

The muscles in his jaw worked as he ground his teeth. "Twice? You mean both hands?"

"Also when Eric hit you."

He exhaled in a huff and scooped a forkful of beans into his mouth. She could practically hear the gears turning in his mind as he rolled over what she'd said. She'd had a hard time believing in magic herself in the beginning, even after she'd transformed into a werewolf the first time.

She gave him time to process and picked up her fork to break open the layer of mashed potatoes on top of her meal. Steam wafted out of the pie, and she swirled the utensil through the ground beef, picking up a scoop of meat, potatoes, and veggies and placing it on her tongue. The savory medley melted in her mouth, and she took another bite as she waited for Bryce to respond.

He finished half his plate before he spoke. "I'm a skeptic. Always have been. But what I saw you do today, and what you apparently did before…I can't explain it." He looked into her eyes with a gaze so intense it pulled the breath from her lungs. "I also can't explain the way I feel about you. The way *you make me* feel. But just because I can't explain it, that doesn't make it any less real."

He smiled and reached for her hand across the table. "You've got magical powers. I can live with that."

If he only knew the half of it. She smiled tentatively and gave his hand a squeeze.

"Since Macey has her own abilities, I take it this runs in the family?" He went back to eating like they were having the most normal conversation in the world.

"Something like that. You know Chase's wife, Rain?"

He nodded. "The witch."

"Her sister thinks we might be related, so that could be where it comes from."

He shrugged. "Makes sense."

"Does it?"

"Not really, but if I keep pretending it does, then maybe one day it will."

He'd taken it so much better than she'd thought he would. The way Macey had made it sound, she'd expected him to put his hands over his ears and refuse to listen the moment the idea of magic got tossed into the conversation. Maybe learning about the werewolves wouldn't turn his life *completely* upside down.

They finished dinner and walked hand-in-hand to Bryce's apartment, making a wide berth around Karen's front porch. She was nowhere to be seen. *Thank God.* That was another issue she'd have to address with him, but she'd save it for another day.

Once inside, they settled on the sofa, and she snuggled into his side as he draped his arm across her shoulders. She could get used to this feeling of belonging. Of finally being home.

He kissed the top of her head and held her tighter. "Are you really planning on leaving town tomorrow?"

She sat up to look at him, and the worry in his eyes tore at her heart. "Actually, I was planning on sticking around for a while, if that's okay with you."

The tension in his shoulders eased. "I'd like that very much."

"I will be out of your hair soon, though. Luke offered me a job on his construction team, and his sister has a spare room she's going to rent me."

"You're welcome to stay with me as long as you need to." He brought her hand to his mouth and kissed her fingers. "As long as you *want* to. What made you decide to stay?"

A warm shiver raced up her spine at the tenderness in his eyes, in his touch. "I'm staying for you, Bryce. I…" She looked at their entwined fingers as her heart beat at a hummingbird's pace. "Now that I've gotten to know you, I think I kinda like you."

A look of confliction furrowed his brow, and he let out a slow breath. "You don't really know me. Not the real me."

"I think I do. You're not the asshole I first thought you were." She sighed. "Actually, I never really thought you were an asshole. Most assholes have game, and you've got none." She winked and poked a finger at his stomach.

He shook his head. "There's a lot you don't know."

Not the reaction she was expecting. She leaned away, narrowing her gaze. "Then tell me. Tell me everything I need to know…to know the real you." She grinned slyly. "Because I'd like to know every inch of you."

"Come with me." His tone serious, he took her hand and pulled her off the sofa.

She followed him down the hall, past his bedroom, to a closed door. His hand rested on the knob. "You haven't looked in this room, have you?"

She shook her head. "You keep it locked."

"So you have tried?" He reached above the door and took a key from the trim.

Her pulse thrummed. Was it a sex dungeon? Or maybe a storage closet for his homemade taxidermy? She shivered. "I might have given the knob a twist the first time I was here alone. I figured it was an office or a home gym or something."

"It is my office, but no one has been in this room but me. No one knows about this side of me but my mom, and she rarely remembers who I am anymore." He squeezed her hand and pushed open the door.

Alexis held her breath as she stepped into the room. A large oak desk sat against the far wall beneath a window overlooking the back yard. Stacks of Sudoku puzzle books lay on either side of the laptop computer.

No torture devices. No dead animals. She released her breath.

Bookcases overflowing with paperbacks lined the walls to the right and left. He must've had more than a thousand books crammed into the small space. She fought the grin that tugged at her lips. Who would've guessed this sexy cop was really a nerd? "I was expecting whips and chains. Why do you keep it locked?"

He shrugged. "Karen and Michael come in to bring me food and take care of Sam. Even they don't know this side of me."

She ran her hand along the spines and stopped on a copy of George R. R. Martin's *A Game of Thrones*. "I've seen this show. It's good."

"The book is better." He stepped behind her, so close his breath warmed the back of her neck.

She closed her eyes for a moment, the close proximity of his body making her nerves tingle. If he thought she wouldn't like him anymore after showing her his intellectual side, he was dead wrong. "Have you read all these?"

"Every one."

The wall opposite the desk held two large shelving units. Every type of *Star Trek* toy imaginable occupied the space. She stepped toward the toys, his heated gaze following her every move, and she pulled one from the shelf. "Why are the dolls still in boxes?"

He took the package from her hands and gently set it in its place. "They're action figures, and they're collectibles. They're worth more in the box."

"Why are you showing this to me?"

"If you're going to stay in New Orleans for me, you need to know what you're getting." He gestured to the room. "*This* is me. No matter how cool and tough I try to be, this is who I really am inside. I'm a fake." He dropped into the chair and rubbed his forehead.

"So you like to read. Big deal. I don't understand why you think you have to hide it. And lots of people like *Star Trek*, obviously, or they wouldn't make the toys to begin with. Why are you ashamed?"

***

Why wouldn't he be ashamed? Why was he even telling her this? "It's not just the books and the toys. I'm a certifiable nerd. Always have been. I'd rather stay home and work math puzzles than watch a football game at a sports bar. Everyone thought I'd end up being a computer programmer or a rocket scientist or something. Hell, I probably should've been."

Her eyes held an emotion he couldn't read. Pity maybe? "Then why did you decide to become a cop?"

He'd told her this much. He might as well go all in. "Believe it or not, I was bullied in school. A lot."

"You? I don't believe it. Look at you. You're hot, and I know you know it."

He fished his wallet out of his pocket and pulled out the photograph. "I didn't always look this good." He passed her the picture.

Her brow furrowed as she looked at it. "This isn't you, is it?"

"I'm afraid it is."

She examined the photograph more closely, a tiny smile tugging at the corners of her mouth. "Huh. Once you see past the braces, glasses, and acne, you've got the same sweet eyes. You were kinda cute."

Yeah, right. He took the picture and slipped it into his wallet. "You wouldn't have thought so in high school."

"I never went to high school. You don't know what I would've thought. Why do you carry it around?"

"To remind me of who I was and why I do what I do. This was my junior year. The lowest point in my life. I had to do the football team's homework every week to avoid getting my ass kicked."

She grimaced. "That's awful."

"Tell me about it. I can't stand football. I made it through high school and decided I had two options: I could be a victim or I could do something about it."

"So you became a cop."

"I started working out. I went away to college and got a criminal justice degree. I decided to dedicate my life to fighting bullies. I changed the way I look. I changed the way I act. But no matter what I do or how hard I try, I can't seem to change the person I am on the inside. This." He gestured to his body. "This isn't really me. I will always be the kid in that photo."

She knelt by the chair and laced her fingers through his. The warmth of her touch tempered the chill running through his heart.

Aside from his confession to Michael on the ledge, he'd never told anyone about his past. He did his job, followed the rules, enforced the law, and that was all anyone needed to know about him. But not Alexis. For some reason, he wanted her to *know* him. Everything about him.

Blonde lashes shielded her emerald eyes from his view as she stared at their entwined hands. How could she even want to touch him now that she knew his whole persona was nothing more than a mask?

She lifted her gaze to meet his. "You did change. I think this really is you. You're the kid in that picture, and you're the tough, sexy cop."

He shook his head.

"Why can't you be both?" She moved to the front of the chair, keeping a firm grip on his hand and situating herself between his knees.

"When I'm Bryce the cop, I feel like I've got Bryce the nerd locked away somewhere inside me, and he's screaming to get out. It's almost like this persona is invading my body and taking over, but it's fake. You can't be two people. It doesn't work that way."

Her eyes tightened. "Sure it does. The bullied kid in that picture is the reason you're the person you are today. And this person you are on the inside…" She rested her other hand on his chest. "That you so desperately try to hide from the world. This is exactly who you should be. This is the part of you I've been getting to know. The part of you I'm falling for."

His heart slammed into his sternum. "So, you're okay with all this?"

"Well…" She leaned into his lap and traced the outline of his pecs with her finger. "It's a little intimidating, seeing as how I never finished eighth grade. But brains *and* brawn? You're the complete package. Incredibly sexy."

He took her hand and pulled her into his lap. "Why did you run away when you were so young?"

"That's a conversation for another day, but I will say this: I've been running my entire life because I've been scared. Now, I can't remember exactly what it was that I was afraid of."

He could live with that answer. She'd already opened up to him about her impossible ability, and she hadn't run away when he'd confessed to being a fake. But how could she find him attractive? "For some reason, it's easier to believe that you have magic powers than that you're falling for me after seeing all this."

"I've shown you my powers. Apparently, I'm not doing a good job of showing you how I feel about you. Let's change that." She leaned in and pressed her velvet lips to his mouth. His heart seemed to stop for a moment, then stuttered to restart. Gliding her hands up his chest, she hooked them behind his neck and slipped her tongue into his mouth. A moan rumbled from his chest to his throat, and he took her face in his hands as he kissed her. Her skin smelled like his soap, and she fit in his arms like she was made for him to hold.

Shifting from his lap, she turned to straddle him, pressing her soft curves into his chest. His core tightened, his dick hardening beneath her, and he wrapped his arms around her, crushing her body to his. Kissing her here, in the room where he kept his true self locked away, in the midst of everything he hid from the world, was enough to send him over the edge.

This part of him...the real him...had never been with anyone before. He'd always donned his mask of machismo before he'd hopped in the sack. No one ever bothered to look beneath it.

But Alexis did.

Her hips rocked, sending a jolt of electricity from his dick to his heart.

He groaned.

She found the hem of his shirt and yanked it over his head. Her tongue slipped out to lick her lips as she trailed her fingers down his chest, over his stomach, to grip his cock through his jeans. *Holy shit.* She fumbled with his belt, and he reached out to still her hands.

She looked at him with uncertainty in her eyes. "You want me to stop?"

He laced his fingers through hers. "Oh, no. I want to keep going, but are *you* sure you want to do this?"

She rose to her feet, pulling him with her. "This is exactly what I want."

"Well, then." He cupped her face in his hand, rubbing his thumb across her smooth skin. "Let's slow down and do this right." Lifting her in his arms, he carried her to the bedroom.

Alexis lay on the bed, and Bryce climbed to his knees on the mattress. Soft moonlight filtered through the blinds, washing the room in a silvery glow. Mischief danced in his hazel eyes as a slow smile turned up the corners of his mouth, and anticipation tightened her stomach.

He shifted to the end of the bed and unlaced her boots. "It's kinda unfair, you know?" He slipped off her shoes and socks and dropped them on the floor.

"What is?"

He took her foot in his hands, massaging the sole. "That you know so much about me now."

"And I like everything I know." She started to sit up, so she could talk to him face to face, but his firm hold on her foot kept her in place. He rubbed his thumbs in circles on her arch, sending tingling warmth shooting up her legs.

"But I know so little about you." He stood on his hands and knees above her, his gaze traveling from her eyes to her lips. He kissed her mouth then trailed his lips along her jaw to nip at her earlobe. "And I want to know *all* of you."

He sat back on his heels and slipped her shirt over her head. She tried to sit up again to undo his pants, but he caught her hands in his. He kissed each palm and gently laid her back.

"You first," he said. "It's only fair." His gaze roamed over her body. "Where to start?"

He bent down and pressed his lips to her stomach. Her breath hitched as warmth spread below her navel, and he roamed his hands up her body to cup her breasts. He continued to kiss, working his way up her stomach, stopping at the clasp on the front of her bra. Tracing his fingers along the edge of the material, he grinned.

"This needs to go." He unclasped the garment and laid it open. "Much better." He took his time, tasting every inch of her body, his tongue slipping out to tease her nipples into tight pearls. Then he pressed his body to hers, trailing kisses up her neck to find her mouth once more.

His warmth enveloped her, his tender touch sending shivers from the base of her neck down to her toes. Never in her life had she been touched this gently. This unselfishly. Pressure built in the back of her eyes as she finally gave in to her wolf's demands. Bryce was the one. Her soulmate. Her fate-bound.

She squeezed her eyes shut and willed the tears away. She would not ruin this moment by crying.

"Now for the fun part." He shifted to the end of the bed and unbuttoned her jeans, slipping them over her hips. When he pulled her panties off, she sucked in a shuddering breath.

He paused. "Are we okay? Do you want to keep going?"

She nodded, swallowing the dryness in her throat. "Yes. God, yes."

He grinned and slipped out of his clothes. His body was lean and firm, his defined muscles sculpted to perfection. He stood beside the bed, and his dick, thick and rock-hard, had her mouth watering to taste it, her fingers twitching to touch it. She reached for him, but he caught her hand and brought it to his lips.

"Not yet. I'm getting to know *you* right now."

Good God. Who knew selflessness could be this hot?

Crawling onto the mattress, he trailed more kisses below her navel as he settled between her legs. Massaging her inner thighs, he explored her body with his tongue, kissing up one hip and down the other. His mouth hovered above her center, his warm breath teasing her skin. Anticipation knotted in her core as she gripped the bedsheets, and she arched her back, raising herself closer to his lips.

He slipped out his tongue and tasted her. Warm wetness enveloped her clit, and she gasped as he slid a finger inside her. Fiery electricity shot through her veins, setting every nerve on edge.

She knotted her fingers in his hair. Dear lord, the sensation was maddening. Her hips rocked involuntarily, and he dared to slip a second finger inside. Her core tightened, the orgasm coiling inside her as he continued the tortuous pleasure. She cried out as the climax ripped through her body, wave after wave of uncontrollable ecstasy rocketing through her core.

Panting, she tried desperately to catch her breath as the elation subsided into a tranquil hum. As her breathing finally slowed, Bryce looked up at her and grinned.

She sucked in a shaky breath. "I take back what I said about you not having game."

He chuckled and lay beside her, the length of his body warming more than her skin. This man lit her soul ablaze.

She gazed into his eyes, mesmerized as the tiny flecks of green and brown seemed to dance in his irises. He looked at her with an intensity that made her heart flutter, and a deep feeling of possessiveness stirred in her core. Her wolf had claimed him, and now it was the woman's turn.

Rolling toward him, she took his length in her hand and stroked him. He inhaled deeply, and his lids fluttered shut as he let out an aroused *mmm*. She pressed her lips to his, and he opened his eyes.

"Make love to me, Bryce."

He cocked an eyebrow. "My pleasure."

As he started to move, he let his head fall onto the pillow and rolled onto his back. "Okay, you win. I've got no game."

She trailed her fingers up and down his stomach, reveling in the way his muscles tightened and goose bumps rose on his skin. "You've got plenty. No one has ever made me feel the way you do."

He let out a heavy sigh. "I don't have a condom."

She cupped his cheek in her hand, turning his head to face her. "Go grab my backpack. I've got some."

With a grin, he hopped off the bed and returned with her bag. "At least one of us is prepared."

Unzipping the front pocket, she took out a condom and whisked off the wrapper. "I was hopeful."

"Nothing wrong with that." He took the rubber and rolled it on.

Positioning himself on top of her, he settled his hips between her legs and pressed his tip against her. She bit her lip as she gazed into his soulful eyes, and he filled her. An electric tingling sensation shot from her center to her chest, and she pulled his face to hers to take his mouth in an urgent kiss as they became one.

Rocking his hips, he slid in and out, sensuous friction making every cell in her body hum. She clutched his shoulders and hooked her heels behind his thighs, driving him deeper inside her with every thrust. She couldn't get enough of him. He trailed his mouth from her lips to her neck, searing her with kisses before nipping at her skin.

His woodsy scent. The salty taste of his skin. The warmth of his body on hers... She was on sensory overload and relishing every goddamn second of it. This man was made to be hers. It didn't matter that he was human. He belonged to her, and she belonged to him.

She found his lips with hers and drank in his essence, giving herself to him fully. As he moaned into her mouth, the vibration sent warm shivers running across her entire body. She held him tighter, the orgasm building in her core like a river behind a dam.

His rhythm increased, his thrusts growing harder and more determined. She gasped as the dam broke and a tidal wave of ecstasy crashed through her body, shattering her senses.

Tossing her head back, she cried out his name. He groaned in response, a shudder running through his muscles as he slowed his motion and relaxed on top of her.

He nuzzled into her neck and slipped his fingers into her hair. "I like your haircut. I don't think I've told you that."

"Thank you. I like...everything about you."

"That's good to know." He rose onto his elbows before sliding to his side. "I happen to like everything about you too." Rolling out of bed, he tossed the condom in the trash and settled next to her again.

She turned to face him, and he took her hands and entwined his legs with hers—a tangle of limbs and pounding hearts. Sleeping with Bryce was nothing like she'd expected. He was unlike any man she'd ever known, and he'd forced her to reconsider everything she believed about human nature. People *could* change. Bryce was living proof. He'd taken the hand he was dealt and turned himself into the most amazing man she'd ever met. If he could go from zero to hero by sheer force of will, a rogue could learn to settle down and stay in one place.

So many emotions coiled and twisted through her soul. Sensations she'd never felt before. For the first time in her life, she hadn't had sex —she'd made love.

"I'm glad you decided to stay." He kissed the back of her hand and gazed into her eyes like he was looking into her being.

"Me too." She had so many secrets, and at that moment, she wanted to share them all. To tell him everything about her—her past, her abilities, the werewolves. But she couldn't. Not yet. If he couldn't accept that his nerd side combined with his cop side to create his whole being, how could she expect him to accept that she was both a woman and a wolf?

"How was lunch with Macey? Did you talk about anything interesting?"

She grinned. "We talked about you. She warned me not to hurt you. All your friends seem to think I'm going to."

His brow furrowed. "I don't think you're going to hurt me."

"I don't want to hurt you."

"Well." He glided his fingers down her side to rest on her hip, leaving a trail of goose bumps on her skin. "I believe ours are the only opinions that matter in this case. Don't you agree?"

"I do."

His expression turned somber. "Did you tell her about your trouble with Eric?"

She drew her shoulders toward her ears. "It didn't come up in the conversation."

He arched an eyebrow. "You should tell Macey. She'd want to know."

"Tell her what? That I stupidly attempted to climb an electrical tower while trying to get away from an abusive ex-boyfriend? I'm her big sister. I should be taking care of her. She doesn't need to know I can hardly take care of myself. Anyway, that mess is over now." If he would stop bringing it up, maybe she could put her past behind her and focus on making a future with him.

He propped himself on his left elbow and used his thumb to fiddle with the ring on his right hand. "She's your family. You're lucky to have to that."

Alexis was damn lucky; she knew that. But she *didn't* know how to handle people who actually cared about her. This new life she was trying to make...staying in one place for good...would require baby steps. She was finally willing to accept that she could change, but he couldn't expect her to dive right in and act like she'd been here all along. "What about your family? Where are they?"

He let out a sigh, untwined their legs, and rolled onto his back. She immediately missed his warmth and scooted closer to rest her hand on his chest.

"My mom is at Autumn Winds Nursing Home. She has Alzheimer's." A mask of sadness covered his features, and his eyes grew distant.

She sidled next to him, pressing the length of her body to his side and propping her head on her hand to catch his gaze and keep him grounded in the present. "Do you ever see her?"

"I visit her every week." He stared at the ceiling. "Most of the time, she doesn't even know I'm there. She..." He inhaled a shaky breath. "She doesn't remember she has a son."

Her own mother had died when she was six, and she would give anything to see her one more time. To ask her the questions that had burned in her mind since she discovered she wasn't human. But for Bryce's mom to be alive and not recognize her own child... She could imagine the hole that must have left in his heart. "I'm so sorry. That must be hard."

"Yeah." He inhaled a quick breath. "How do your healing abilities work? Could you...?"

She smiled sadly. "No. I can only heal physical wounds. Diseases..." She shook her head. "I can't. I've tried." Her wolf made her immune to disease, so she had no need for the ability to heal them. "Is she all you have left?"

He looked at her and rested hand on top of hers. "My dad died of a heart attack three years ago. He was seventy-six. My mom started going downhill after that. She couldn't live without him. They had such a strong bond. So much love." A small smile curved his lips. "No matter what life threw at them, they always made it through because they had each other. And believe me, life threw some pretty wicked curve balls." He laced his fingers through hers. "Family is important. Don't shut your sister out."

Family. It was hard to believe she actually had one now. "I know you're right, but I don't want to be a burden on her. Luke's already giving me a job, and…"

"Family is never a burden." He swallowed. "I had a brother. He was six years older than me." He sandwiched her hand between his palms and raised their hands to his lips. "He killed himself when I was seventeen. Overdosed."

"Oh, Bryce. I had no idea." Her throat thickened. "And then you saw me in the hospital, and you thought that I…I'm so sorry."

His eyes began to glisten, so he blinked and shook his head.

"And then Michael… How do you do your job when it's so personal? How do you handle it?"

He laid her hand on his chest and rubbed his ring. "It's *why* I do it. The bullying is part of why I became a cop, but I became a negotiator so I could help people. So I could keep it from happening to anyone else."

"Because no one helped your brother?"

"I didn't know anything was wrong with him. He…" He paused and blew out a hard breath. "He had severe chronic depression, and he suffered in silence for years. Nobody knew. At least…*I* didn't know. I hadn't exactly mastered my people skills back then, so I wouldn't have recognized the signs if he'd broadcasted them. He put on a mask around his friends and family. Pretended to be happy. To be someone he wasn't." He laced his fingers through hers. "His smile never reached his eyes, though. I should've…" He pressed his mouth into a hard line. "Not a day goes by that I don't regret not knowing. Not helping."

Turning his head toward her, he pinned her with a heavy gaze. "If he had opened up and let me know what was going on, I might have been able to help him."

"But you didn't know."

"Doesn't make it hurt any less. Suicide doesn't stop the pain. It passes it on to someone else. Don't shut Macey out of your life because it isn't as perfect as you'd like it to be. She loves you no matter what."

She snuggled into his side and draped her arm across him. If only her healing powers worked on broken hearts. "That ring isn't yours, is it?"

"It was my brother's college ring. He'd just graduated when..." He let out a hard breath. "I wear it to remind myself why I do what I do."

"And because it keeps him close to you."

He wrapped his arms around her, pulling her even closer to his side. "That too."

A familiar ache expanded in her chest, and she closed her eyes. "I used to have my mom's wedding ring. It was a simple, gold band, but it meant a lot to me."

"What happened to it?" His chest vibrated against her cheek.

"I pawned it." She buried her face in his neck, the shame of losing her connection to her mother twisting a knife in her heart. "I was broke. Hadn't eaten in days. I used to steal people's junk that they'd thrown to the curb and pawn it, but the broker wasn't interested in the busted bicycle I tried to sell him. He offered me fifty bucks for the ring and gave me a month to buy it back."

"You didn't make it in time?"

"No, I did. I came back three weeks later, but he'd already sold it. I lost the one thing I had of my mom's for fifty bucks."

"I'm sorry. I guess he wasn't willing to track down the buyer and try to get it back for you?"

She laughed dryly. "No, he wasn't, but I hear you about family. I'm going to do my best to repair my relationship with Macey. She's all I have left."

CHAPTER FOURTEEN

Bryce woke and reached for Alexis, but the bed was empty. Panic fluttered in his chest. He'd dumped so much on her last night…his fake persona, his family, his brother's death. Had she changed her mind about staying? Decided he carried too much baggage? He rose onto his elbows, and light shining from beneath the bathroom door eased his fear. When he put his hand on the bed where she had lain, her warmth remained in the sheets.

Her sweet scent lingered on the pillow, and he pressed his face into the fabric, inhaling deeply. The bathroom door swung open, and Alexis stepped into the room, wearing nothing but a towel. His mind flashed back to the first time he'd seen her in a towel, and he smiled. Not a single bruise marred her skin now, and she was finally opening up to him. Letting him into her world.

"Now you're doing it." She strode across the room and sat on the edge of the bed. The towel slid up until it barely covered the important parts, and heat pooled in his groin.

"Doing what?"

"You're sniffing the pillows. And smiling about it."

He swung the pillow behind her back, clutching it with both hands and pulling her to his chest. "You smell good." He nuzzled into her neck and took a deep breath. The scent of his soap mixed with a sweetness that was all Alexis, making his mouth water to taste her.

She laughed. "I smell like you. What's with the citrusy shower gel?"

"I like it. Especially when it's on you." He trailed kisses up the curve of her neck to take her earlobe between his teeth.

She shivered. "Don't you have to go to work?"

He tossed the pillow onto the bed and lay back, lacing his fingers behind his head. "Not for a few hours. It's six a.m."

Her gaze traveled the length of his body before settling on the tent he'd made of the sheets. She grinned. "I don't start my new job until Wednesday. Mind if I do a little exploring?" Her fingers brushed his stomach as she slid the sheet down. "Or do you have something you need to be doing?"

His core contracted, and his dick twitched beneath the sheet. "The only thing I need to be doing right now is you, darlin'."

"Darlin'?" She unknotted the towel from her chest and tossed it on the floor. "I've never let anyone call me that before."

Damn, she was gorgeous. All fair, flawless skin and delicate curves. He'd call her anything she wanted him to if she'd crawl into bed and press her supple body against his. "Would you like me to stop?"

"I like it coming from you." She tugged the sheet from his legs and climbed on top him.

Every nerve in his body hummed as she lay against him, coaxing his lips apart with her tongue. She tasted like mint toothpaste, and as he wrapped his arms around her, he couldn't seem to hold her close enough. He needed to be in her. To be one with her.

His home had always been his sanctuary. His place to be alone when the world became too much to bear. He'd never realized how lonely he'd been, isolating himself like he had. Now, with Alexis in his bed, her scent lingering on the sheets, her essence filling his space with promises of companionship, he couldn't imagine a life without her in it.

She glided her tongue down his neck toward his chest, and antici-pation knotted in his muscles.

"You know," he said. "You don't have to move in with Luke's sister."

"I don't?" She trailed kisses across his right pec and flicked out her tongue to lick his nipple.

His stomach clenched, and he sucked in a sharp breath. "Not if you don't want to."

"Where would I live then?" She grazed his sensitive flesh with her teeth and sucked his nipple into her mouth.

Electricity shot straight to dick, his hips involuntarily bucking with the sensation. "You could stay with me."

"I could?" She kissed her way down his stomach, his muscles coiling tighter as her lips neared his groin.

He rose onto his elbows to look at her. "I like having you here, and I plan on spending every free second I have with you."

"Do you, now?" She grinned as she took his length in her hand and stroked him.

His lids fluttered, but he forced his eyes open. She knew exactly what to do. Where to touch. To lick. She was made for him, and he needed her to know exactly how he felt about her. "I don't know how to describe it, but there is something about you. I felt it the first time I met you, and it's gotten stronger the more I spend time with you."

She stroked him again, and a bead of moisture gathered on his tip. A moan rumbled up from his chest, and she stroked him again.

"Maybe I do know how to describe it. Alexis, I…"

She flicked out her tongue to lick him, and the thoughts evaporated from his mind like a fog burned away by the morning sun. He dropped his head onto the pillow and closed his eyes as she took him into her mouth. Warm and wet, her tongue massaged the underside of his dick as she sucked him deeper. Then she slid her head up until only his tip remained between her lips before taking his entire length into her mouth again. A shudder ran through his body as she repeated the motion again and again, pushing him closer to the edge.

He could barely suck in enough air to speak. "I need you. I…"

She rose to her knees and grabbed a condom from the nightstand, rolling it on before she straddled him. Gripping his cock, she guided him to her center and sheathed him before he could finish the thought. Her gaze locked with his, and she rocked her hips, sending searing electricity pummeling through his veins.

With her hands on his chest, she rode him, her gorgeous breasts swaying with her movements. She was sheer perfection, and the connection he felt with this woman ran deeper than he'd imagined possible. He belonged to her. Every part of him.

He licked his thumb and pressed it to her clit, and she gasped, straightening her spine and increasing her rhythm. His climax coiled like spring in his core, and has she tossed her head back and cried out his name, an explosion of ecstasy ricocheted through his system and sparks danced before his eyes.

Breathless and trembling, Alexis collapsed on top of him. She clutched his shoulders and showered him in kisses, and he glided his fingers across her sweat-slickened skin. Her hair was still damp from the shower, and he ran his fingers through it, brushing it away from her face.

"One of the perks of moving in with me?" He kissed her cheek. "Mornings like this."

She lifted her head and smiled. "I'll think about it."

His chest tightened, and three little words danced on his tongue. He bit them back. She said she'd think about it, and he didn't need to press his luck by saying more. He would give her all the time she needed to warm up to the idea of being his. Right now, he'd find satisfaction in the fact that she was staying in town.

He held her for another half hour before showering and getting ready for work. Alexis dressed and followed him into the living room, where she gave Sam a scratch on the head and let him out the back door.

"Mind if I make some coffee?" She kissed him on the cheek and padded barefoot into the kitchen.

A fluttering sensation formed in his stomach as she made herself at home, opening cabinets, taking out cups, and filling the machine to brew. He stepped behind her and slid his arms around her waist. "Will you be here when I get home?"

She turned her face toward him and kissed his cheek. "Do you want me to be here when you get home?"

"You know I do." Today and every day for the rest of his life.

"Then I will. Once my job starts, I'll have to figure out this whole staying in one place thing. It's scary."

He released his hold and moved to face her. "The last thing I want to do is scare you away. If I'm coming on too strong, please let me know."

She put her hand on his face. "I'm not scared of you, Bryce."

"That's good to know, darlin'." He kissed her palm. "Do you like frozen waffles?"

"I prefer them heated."

He laughed and popped some Eggos into the toaster—a feat of cooking he could actually handle. They ate and cleaned up the mess together, the routine as effortless as if they'd already lived together for months.

She walked him to the door and kissed him on the cheek, and he paused to take in her beauty.

"You are an amazing woman, Alexis Gentry. I'll see you tonight."

She smiled. "Bye, Bryce."

He tugged the door open and stumbled over a heap of fabric blocking the exit. A brown envelope slipped from the pile and landed at Alexis's feet. The color drained from her face as she bent and scooped the fabric and the envelope into her arms.

"This is my jacket." Her voice came out as a raspy whisper.

Bryce's heart slammed against his ribcage. "The one you left at Eric's?"

She nodded, and he wrapped his arm around her, pushing her back inside before locking the door. He should have expected this. Abusers never let go that easily.

Standing utterly still, she stared at the envelope in her grip. "He found me."

Bryce took the envelope and carried it to the kitchen. "I guess someone bailed him out of jail." He tore it open and dumped the contents onto the counter. A stack of glossy photographs slid across the Formica, and anger burned in his chest. "Bastard's been watching us."

Alexis peeked over his shoulder as he spread the photos out on the surface. Pictures of his car parked at the station, Alexis's Ford on the curb in front of his house. The two of them walking hand-in-hand beneath the oaks on their way to dinner last night. A shot of them embracing in the living room, taken through the open blinds.

She picked up an image of her and Macey having lunch in a restaurant. Dropping it on the countertop, she covered her face with her hands. "I'm so sorry. I really thought this was over."

"Guys like that don't take rejection well. I'm not surprised at all." But he *had* let his guard down. He'd been so caught up in his feelings for Alexis that he'd been careless. Sloppy. The bastard had been following him, and he hadn't even noticed. He was a detective, for Christ's sake; he should have caught on.

Her hands trembled as she stacked the pictures. "I'll go talk to him."

"No, you won't. This." He gestured to the photographs. "This is stalking. He's already hurt you once."

She dropped her gaze to the floor, and ice flushed his veins.

"At least once." He didn't need to know exactly what the asshole had done to her. The look on her face said enough. He ground his teeth. "You need to get the police involved. Get a restraining order, so if he does something like this again, I can arrest him."

She opened her mouth as if to argue, but she let out a defeated sigh instead. "Okay. You're right. I'll get a restraining order." She fumbled with the pictures, nervously stacking them face-down on the counter. When she reached the image of the two of them embracing in the living room, she swallowed hard and shoved it into the middle of the pile.

He called Sam inside and locked the back door. "Put your shoes on, and you can come to the station with me. I'll take the day off and stay with you until we can get this sorted out."

She inhaled a shaky breath. "If you don't mind, I think I'd like to get Macey's help with this." She glanced into his eyes before lowering her gaze again. "After our talk last night, I feel like she would want to help."

Hooking a finger under her chin, he raised her eyes to meet his.

"You won't regret that." He tugged her into a firm hug. "I'll follow you to her house to be safe."

"You don't have to do that." Her face was pressed against his chest, muffling her voice.

"I want to." If he didn't trust Macey with his life, he'd insist she go to the station with him. Macey would keep her safe, though, and this might be exactly what they needed to mend their rocky relationship.

She sighed and pulled from his embrace. "Okay. Let me get my things from your room. I'll just be a minute."

Alexis gazed at Bryce through her rearview mirror on the way to Macey's house. Even at a distance, his clenched jaw and furrowed brow were unmistakable. His concern for her safety warmed her soul, and part of her actually considered his suggestion of letting the police handle Eric. Maybe another run-in with the law would convince his bully of a father to take him back to Biloxi. Then again, if he hadn't bothered this time, he'd probably washed his hands of his delinquent son.

She pulled to a stop on the curb in front of Macey's house and said a silent prayer thanking whatever god was responsible for ensuring that cars lined the rest of the road so Bryce had nowhere to park. He stopped in the middle of the street and rolled down his passenger side window.

Alexis slipped out of her car, lightly shutting the door to avoid bringing any attention to her presence. Resting her hands on the door, she stuck her head through his SUV window. "Thanks for the escort, officer."

He pressed his lips together, his brow knitting as he held her gaze. "I know Macey can protect you, but…if you need anything, please call me. I—"

"I will." She couldn't let him finish the thought. Not if it was the same thing he'd tried to tell her this morning. He might change his mind after what she was about to do.

A car stopped behind him and honked.

"You better get out of the road. I'll see you later." She straightened and wiggled her fingers. "Bye, Bryce."

He nodded. "Be careful."

"I will."

He hit the button to roll up the window and slowly drove away.

Alexis spun around and made her way toward Macey's front door, but as soon as Bryce turned the corner, she got in her car and sped off in the opposite direction.

Eric wouldn't stop until Alexis was by his side or dead, and being anywhere near Bryce put him in danger. A restraining order would do nothing to stop a werewolf. She had to handle this herself.

She turned onto Interstate 10 and headed to Pearl River. Maybe she couldn't beat Eric in a fair fight, but she could outsmart him again. She'd take care of this problem for good, and then she'd come back to New Orleans and settle down with Bryce like her wolf had been begging her to do.

And once her sadistic ex was no longer a threat, she'd tell Bryce what she was…tell him everything. She'd bring him into her supernatural world once it was a safe place for him to be.

Her stomach soured as she pulled into the driveway and parked behind Eric's Mustang. She shoved some clean clothes into her backpack and slung it over her shoulder as she paced up the walk. A new video doorbell hung beside the frame, and she pressed the button before smoothing her hair into place. A red light blinked beside the camera, and a few seconds later, the lock disengaged.

Eric crossed his arms and leaned against the jamb, a smug smile contorting his features. "I knew you'd come back to me."

"You didn't give me much of a choice."

"You always have a choice, baby. You finally made the right one."

She clenched her jaw, trying to keep her expression neutral. "If I help you, you *will* leave Bryce alone. Macey too."

His grin widened as he drew a cross over his chest. "You have my word."

"Like that means a lot." She pressed her hand against the small of her back—where Bryce's gun fit snugly into the waistband of her jeans—and pushed past Eric to enter his home.

CHAPTER FIFTEEN

Bryce set his phone on the desk and stared at the blank screen. Two hours had passed with no word from Alexis. She hadn't shown up at the station to report the bastard yet, and anxiety had him wound up so tight his muscles ached. His knee bounced incessantly beneath his desk, and he popped a piece of peppermint gum into his mouth, clenching it between his teeth.

He'd called her half an hour ago and gotten her voicemail. She was doing exactly what he'd suggested: getting Macey involved, building the bond with her sister. And he trusted Macey with his life. She could handle whatever that bastard threw at them, but damn it, not knowing where Alexis was made him crazy.

He'd almost told her he loved her several times that morning, and now he was cursing himself for not forcing the words from his lips. She'd had a hard life. Wasn't used to people caring about her. She didn't understand how profoundly her actions could affect the people who loved her. If she changed her mind and went after Eric on her own...

Shit. Why hadn't he told her?

His computer chimed with an e-mail, and he clicked it open—the autopsy report on the female they'd retrieved from the river. He scanned the document and squinted at the body temperature. That couldn't be right. Bryce rubbed his eyes and looked again. Thirty-eight degrees.

He scrolled down to the examiner's comments. *Evidence of freezing after death.*

What the hell? He pulled up the other case. Nothing new since Macey suggested an animal attack. Had she even seen the autopsy? Or was something else going on that she was trying to cover up?

A sour sensation crept from his stomach up the back of his throat. Had Macey gotten involved in something sinister? No way she'd voluntarily participate in something like this, but if she were being forced…and he'd sent Alexis to her for help.

He mashed the button on his phone to dial Macey's number.

"Bryce? Is everything okay?" Her voice was raspy, and the sound of rustling sheets filled the silence.

His heart sank. "Were you asleep?"

"It's not even ten a.m. What's wrong?"

He swallowed the thickness from his throat as icy tendrils of dread wound their way up his spine to grip his neck. "So you haven't seen Alexis today?"

"No. What happened?"

"Nothing. I'm sorry I woke you." He pressed end and slammed his phone onto the desk. How could he have been so stupid? Alexis never had any intention of asking her sister for help. She was stubborn and overly confident, and he'd let love blind him to her faults. He should have known.

Assholes like Eric couldn't be reasoned with. Bryce had been on his fair share of domestic abuse calls, and these guys never quit.

He dialed Alexis's number. Straight to voicemail. A quick search of the database gave him Eric's address, and he grabbed his jacket and stormed out of the station.

His mind reeled on the drive to Pearl River. What exactly was he going to do when he got there? He had no warrant. No legal reason for busting in and beating the shit of the dude. Alexis went there of her own free will, so as a cop, his hands were tied.

But as a man…

He yanked his badge from his belt and tossed it on the passenger seat. If he'd have been thinking straight, he'd have stopped by his house to grab his personal firearm, but he didn't plan on needing to use it. He was simply there to talk. *Right.*

Pulling into the grass on the side of the road in front of Eric's house, he tightened his grip on the steering wheel. Alexis's car sat behind a Mustang in the driveway, and Bryce closed his eyes, gritting his teeth until pain shot through his jaw.

He wasn't breaking any laws. Yet. He'd knock on the door and ask for Alexis. If the bastard wouldn't let him talk to her, then…he'd cross that bridge when he got to it. Prying his fingers from their death-grip on the wheel, he opened the door and slid out of the car.

Sunlight glinted off his badge lying on the seat, and he slammed the door. If he did cross any bridges today, the emblem wouldn't shine so brightly as his boss confiscated it. His career would end. He squared his shoulders toward the house and marched to the door. He'd choose Alexis over his job any day.

Ignoring the doorbell, he pounded his fist against the wood. A muffled shout sounded from somewhere inside, and a tiny red light blinked beside the camera on the bell. The sound of something hitting the floor resonated from the other side of the door, and Bryce's heart rate kicked up.

He clenched his hands into fists, ready to defend himself if the asshole tried to catch him off guard, and he took a step back as the lock disengaged. Alexis's face appeared by the jamb, and his breath caught in his throat.

She glanced over her shoulder before stepping through the doorway and shutting it. "You shouldn't be here."

"Like hell I shouldn't. I told you not to try to talk to him." He took her hand. "C'mon. We're going home."

She pulled from his grasp. "This is my home, Bryce, and you don't get to tell me what to do."

"No, Alexis, this isn't…you don't have to stay here. We'll get the restraining order, and if he tries anything else, I'll throw his ass in jail. I will take care of you."

"I don't need you to take care of me." She crossed her arms and lowered her gaze to the ground. "I don't want you to."

"What?" He blew out a breath. "What are trying to say?"

The muscles in her throat worked as she swallowed and lifted her gaze to his. "I'm saying I *want* to stay here. With Eric." Her lip curled as she said his name. "This is where I belong, and I'm sorry for leading you on. I..." She cut her gaze to the side before making eye contact again. "I was using you until the heat blew over. He forgives me now, so you should go."

As she held his gaze a moment longer, a tiny shard of doubt wriggled into his mind before he slammed the door on it. After everything they'd shared last night and this morning, there was no way. "C'mon, darlin'. You don't mean that."

"I do."

She didn't. The rapid blinking, cutting her gaze to the left, holding eye contact longer than was natural when she did look at him...they were all classic signs of lying. And the way her brow knit as she glanced over her shoulder at the window, she couldn't hide the fear in her eyes if she tried.

The red light on the doorbell camera blinked, indicating Eric was watching every move she made. Bryce stepped toward her, lowering his voice and resting his hand on her elbow. "Did he threaten you? Is he making you say this?"

"No, Bryce." Her gaze hardened, and she whispered, "Look, we had sex, okay? It doesn't mean I want to move in with you. Just...go home and forget about me."

"That's enough, babe. Time to come inside." Eric's massive frame darkened the doorway.

Alexis's shoulders tensed.

Bryce clenched his fists. "Please, Alexis. Come home with me. I love you."

She locked eyes with him, and a thousand emotions played across her features. As she opened her mouth to respond, her lower lip trembled. "I could never love a man like you. Go home, Bryce."

Eric grabbed her arm, but she yanked from his grasp and stomped inside. He turned to Bryce. "Whatever you thought you had with my girl is over. I don't want to see your pig face again."

He didn't move as Eric slammed the door. Not a word of truth had spilled from Alexis's lips, but what else could he do? Bust the door down and drag her away? If she wouldn't listen to him, he'd call in backup.

Turning on his heel, he ground his teeth and strode to his SUV. This was far from over.

Alexis leaned against the kitchen counter, careful to keep her back toward the wall. Eric hadn't let her out of his sight since she'd knocked on the door, and she needed to stash Bryce's gun somewhere she could get to it later.

A fissure tore through her chest as pressure built in the back of her eyes. Bryce had said the words, and they'd nearly crumbled her. Fate had bound her heart to his, and hearing him confirm it had her wolf howling with joy.

And then she hurt him.

Lying to Bryce had been the hardest thing she'd ever done, but she'd had to do it to keep him safe. If he thought he didn't have a chance with her, surely he'd give up long enough for her take care of Eric. Then, with the threat extinguished, she could crawl back to Bryce on her hands and knees and beg for forgiveness.

What else could she do? The man held her heart in his hands, and Eric would tear Bryce's throat out if he knew.

"Don't look so sad, babe." Eric adjusted his crotch and sauntered toward her. "He's a human."

She blinked back her tears and nodded. "You're right. I don't know what I was thinking running to him. I was stupid."

"Damn right you were." He slid a hand up her shoulder, and she recoiled.

Clutching her chin between his thumb and forefinger, he forced her gaze to his. "I think I need to fuck you 'til you forget him." He grabbed the back of her neck with his other hand. "What do you say?"

She shrugged out of his hold and paced toward the couch. "I'm on my period."

Following, he leaned toward her and sniffed the air. "I don't smell blood on you."

"I wear tampons, dumbass. Of course you don't."

His lip curled in disgust. "Nasty bitch."

"Wow, Eric." She hung her backpack over her shoulder. "If you're trying woo me, you might want to watch your language."

He shuffled around to block the front door. "Where do you think you're going?"

"To the bathroom to change my tampon."

"Hold on." He jerked the bag from her shoulder and opened it. "What you got in here?" He stuck his hand in the bag and rummaged around.

She rolled her eyes and unzipped a side pocket before yanking out a handful of feminine hygiene products.

He wrinkled his nose and shoved the bag toward her. "Make it fast."

She shook her head. What kind of alpha male was afraid of a little period blood?

Padding down the hall, she slowed her stride as she passed *the room*. The stench of bleach assaulted her senses as she peered inside the pristine area. All the musical instruments hung seemingly untouched on the wall, and the tile floor shone like it had been freshly polished.

Her stomach turned. How many people had he killed in that room?

Ducking into the bathroom, she turned the lock on the knob and pulled the gun from her waistband. She shoved it into her backpack and covered it with clothes before opening a tampon and tossing the wrapper in the trash. She flushed the rest of it to hide the evidence— she wasn't due to start her period for another two weeks—and looked at her reflection in the mirror.

The bruise Eric had given her had thankfully faded right before Bryce arrived. She'd taken the beating like the "dutiful girlfriend" Eric expected her to be, but she was biding her time. All she needed was a little evidence to show the council, and she'd be justified in what she planned to do.

With the gun hidden in the bottom of her backpack, she crept into the living room to find Eric lounging on the couch with a beer in his hand.

He grinned and unzipped his pants. "Come on over here, darlin'."

Her skin crawled hearing Bryce's name for her spilling from that meathead's lips. "Don't call me that."

"Since I can't fuck you for a while, why don't you come suck me off to show me your appreciation for taking you back."

The Eggos she'd had for breakfast threatened to make a reappearance as she set her bag against the wall and crossed her arms. "I'm not in the mood."

He narrowed his eyes. "You will be. You'll learn to love me again."

Looking at him now, with a beer in one hand, the other hand in his pants, she couldn't recall an ounce of positive emotion that she'd ever felt for the man. He had a muscular body, strong jaw, and symmetrical features. All the things a woman was supposed to find attractive in a man. But the hatred and idiocy that spilled from his mouth overshadowed any amount of physical appeal he possessed. "I never loved you, dickhead."

He laughed. "I like it when you're feisty."

A chime sounded from a speaker in the hall half a second before his phone buzzed. The back door opened and slammed shut, and a male called, "I got one, boss. Better make it quick, though. The chloroform is wearing off."

"All right." Eric stood and zipped his pants. "Let's get to work then."

Bryce parked on the curb in front of Macey's house and chewed the inside of his cheek. His stomach had tied into a knot on the drive over, and his heart flipflopped between aching for Alexis and burning in rage for the man who was holding her captive. She may not have wanted her sister involved, but she'd left him no choice.

He strode to the front door and pressed the bell. Laughter resonated from inside, and light footsteps sounded on the floor. He let out a breath. At least he hadn't woken her.

The door opened a crack, and Macey peeked through the slit. "Hey, Bryce. This isn't the best time." She wore her police uniform, though the shirt was untucked and the top four buttons hadn't been fastened.

"It's important. It's about Alexis."

Macey sighed and opened the door. "What did she do this time?"

He tilted his head as he stepped through the threshold. "Why are you wearing your uniform? Did you pick up an extra shift?"

Her husband, Luke, padded in from the hallway, wearing unbuttoned jeans and no shirt, and examining a pair of handcuffs. His light-brown hair hung loose, nearly brushing his shoulders. "You're sure you've got the key for these, babe? I'd hate to have to break them when we're done."

Heat crept up Bryce's neck as he cut his gaze between Macey and Luke. This was a sight he could not unsee.

Macey plastered on a fake smile. "We've got company, dear."

Luke lifted his gaze. "Oh, hey, Bryce." He glanced at the cuffs in his hand. "This…" He looked at Macey apologetically. "Isn't what it looks like?"

She laughed. "It's exactly what it looks like. Come sit and tell me what my sister has gotten herself into." She buttoned her shirt and led the way to the living room.

"I'll leave you two to it. Good to see you, Bryce." Luke nodded and shuffled down the hall.

Bryce followed her and sank onto the sofa, trying to ignore the images of the scene he'd interrupted that his brain kept projecting behind his eyes. She wasn't kidding when she'd said this wasn't the best time, but what he had to say was too important to wait. "Alexis went to her abusive ex-boyfriend's house, and he's holding her there against her will."

Macey lifted an eyebrow. "Abusive? How do you know?"

He hesitated. Breaking the trust of the woman he loved wasn't the best way to start out a relationship, but damn it, she needed help.

"Hear me out." He told her about finding Alexis in the hospital and how she had been staying with him on and off for the past week. "He's been stalking us. He left a stack of photos on the doorstep this morning. Alexis told me she was coming to you for help, but she went to him instead. She lied to me."

She folded her hands in her lap, and her eye twitched as if she fought to keep her expression neutral. "Wow. You must really like her. It's not like you to miss a lie."

He scrubbed a hand down his face. Did she even care that her sister was with an abuser? "Mace, I'm in love with her."

"Oh, Bryce." She shook her head, sympathy softening her eyes. "I warned you not to do this. She's not the settling down type."

His chest tightened. "She is. She was. We talked about it last night. She said she was starting work with Luke on Wednesday and that his sister offered her a room in her apartment. She was making plans to stick around until her jackass ex left that package on my doorstep." He shifted toward her. "Her first instinct was to go talk to the dude. Try to get him to stop. But I convinced her not to."

He stared at his hands in his lap. He *thought* he'd convinced her not to.

Macey put her hand on his. "What do you want me to do?"

"Talk to her. See if you can get the truth out of her. Get her to let you file a report." He raked a hand through his hair. "He's hurt her, Mace, and when I tried to get her to leave with me, she refused. If she won't press charges, I don't…" He could go back, beat the shit out of the guy, and drag Alexis away. But then he wouldn't be any better than Eric. He huffed. "I don't know what else to do."

"Do you know his name?"

"Eric Anderson. Dude's got a record but no outstanding warrants."

"Anderson?" Luke's brow puckered as he sauntered into the room. "Is he from Biloxi?"

Bryce's heart rate kicked up. If he couldn't convince Macey to do something, maybe he could appeal to Luke's protective nature. "Yeah. You know him?"

"I know his old man." Luke exchanged an unreadable look with Macey and strolled into the kitchen.

Macey sighed. "Let it go, Bryce. If she wants to be with Eric, there's nothing you can do about it."

He clenched his fists. "He's an abuser."

"But she won't press charges, and she refused to leave."

"No, I couldn't get her to, but I—"

"She can take care of herself." Her voice turned firm. "You need to let her go." She stood and shuffled to the front door, casting a glance toward the kitchen as he followed her. She whispered, "Seriously, Bryce, don't get involved."

"I already am." He'd been involved since the second he stepped into her hospital room, and he wouldn't give up now when she needed him the most.

Opening the door, she stepped onto the porch and motioned for him to follow. "You're not. Her business doesn't concern you, so please stay out of it."

"The hell it doesn't. Mace, what's going on? You've changed."

She flinched as if he'd slapped her. "What do you mean? Nothing's changed."

"You have. You're missing evidence, blowing off cases, looking for the easy answers rather than digging for the facts."

She crossed her arms. "We're not partners anymore. You don't know how I handle cases."

He stiffened. "That body they pulled out of the river had an internal temperature seven degrees lower than the water they found it in, yet you're calling it animal attack."

She cut her gaze into the house. "Bryce…"

"It's not since I got promoted. Ever since you met Luke, you've been different. You're hanging out with all these people with magical powers. Psychics and witches that I wouldn't have even believed existed if I hadn't seen them work their tricks with my own eyes. Are you in some kind of cult? Is that why Alexis doesn't stick around? Because of what you're involved in?"

She dropped her arms to her sides and tilted her head. "You know me better than that."

"Do I?" He wasn't sure about anything anymore.

"I'm not in a cult." She narrowed her eyes. "I'm married to the man of my dreams who happens to have some friends with abilities similar to mine. I finally belong somewhere, and you're accusing me of nefarious acts?"

He opened his mouth, but the words got stuck in his throat. What the hell was he doing? Arguing with Macey wouldn't help Alexis, and priority number one was getting her out of that abuser's house. "I'm sorry, Mace…"

"Go home, Bryce, and leave Alexis alone. She's not worth it." She marched inside and slammed the door, leaving him alone on the porch.

He'd always held Macey in high regard, but if she didn't give a damn about her own flesh and blood…maybe he didn't know her as well as he'd thought he did.

CHAPTER SIXTEEN

ERIC LEANED AGAINST THE SOUNDPROOF WALL AND CROSSED HIS arms. If he could turn this guy into a werewolf, he'd promote him to second as soon as he shifted. Hell, the dude's muscle mass alone was comparable to any alpha he'd ever seen, and man, had he put up a good fight. Tearing him to pieces had been fun.

Sweat beaded on Alexis's forehead as she repaired the damage Eric's teeth had done. She'd screamed at him to stop during the entire attack, her voice cracking with anger or fear...he didn't care which. Seeing her all worked up like that had gotten him all worked up, and now he was so goddamn horny his dick felt like a blocked water pipe about to explode.

He could force her to give him a blowjob, but he didn't trust that bitch's teeth anywhere near his family jewels at the moment. "How much longer you gonna be on your period, babe?"

She wiped her brow with her forearm and glared at him. "A week."

Damn, she was sexy when she was mad. If she'd been clean, he'd have bent her over the table right then and reminded her why she really came back. She wanted him, whether she was ready to admit it or not.

"How's the patient?" He pushed from the wall and strolled toward his mate-to-be. Peering over her shoulder, he marveled at the final flesh wound stitching itself back together with the help of Alexis's magic.

She turned her face toward him, and her skin had taken on a grayish color. She'd never admit weakness, but healing drained the life right out of her. He gave her shoulder a shove, and she fell onto her side before rolling onto her back and squeezing her eyes shut. *Frail little bitch.*

The man's eyes rolled beneath his closed lids, and Eric knelt, gripping his forearm and waiting for the tingle of werewolf energy to seep into his skin. He felt nothing. "Damn it, Alex, you healed him too fast."

She grimaced as she pushed to a sitting position. "Any slower and he wouldn't have made it. You almost tore his throat out."

He shot to his feet and clenched his fists. "We'll try again then. I'll stay away from his neck this time."

Alexis rubbed her forehead. "No, Eric. He's been attacked and healed three times now. Doing it again isn't going to change anything. Maybe it takes time for the magic to bond with his blood."

"No. It's almost a full moon; it should be immediate." He narrowed his gaze at Alexis. "You're distracted. That's what it is."

She leaned her back against the wall. "Of course I'm distracted. You're insane."

"No. It's that damn cop. You're still thinking about him." He'd seen it in her eyes, even as she'd told the dude to leave her alone. She had feelings for a human. His nostrils flared as a jealous rage boiled in his gut.

"I'm not thinking about him. All I can think about right now is how I wish you'd clean up all this blood. It's making me nauseated."

What could a human cop give her that he couldn't? At the moment, the one thing Samuels had that he didn't was power. That would change soon enough. He had a new strategy in the works. His men were already out finding him someone weaker to practice on. Once he perfected the method, then he'd move on to creating strength in his pack. He'd need weaker wolves to do his grunt work anyway.

"You can clean it up when we're done. We've got a new patient on the way."

"You need to give this one time. Let him at least wake up before you hurt anyone else. The magic might hold."

"No. He's too strong. It's not going to work." A chime sounded in the hall. His minions had arrived with his next experiment. "Stay here with the dead guy."

"He's not dead."

"Not yet." He slipped out the door to meet them at the back.

Alexis took a deep breath and leaned her head against the wall. Her stomach churned at the coppery scent of fresh blood, but she pushed to her feet. She couldn't let Eric see how weak healing made her.

She shook the man's shoulder. "Wake up, dude."

His eyes rolled from side to side, but they didn't open. The third time Eric had attacked him, he'd nearly killed him. It had taken every ounce of energy Alexis had to keep the guy alive, and he was still unconscious.

She put her hands on either side of his head and tried to push more healing energy into him. If she could get him to wake up before the dickhead and his flunkies came back, he might be able to escape out the front door.

"Goddammit, Trevor, I told you no more women." Eric's voice grew louder as they approached the room. "Alexis is going to be my mate."

Her skin crawled at the thought of getting her body anywhere near that meathead. She pressed her back against the wall as Eric slammed the door open and stomped into the room, followed by his two prospective pack members.

"You said you wanted someone weaker," Trevor said as he lowered the unconscious woman to the floor.

"Not that weak. A new pack needs a solid foundation of strong werewolves. I can make males strong, but females aren't going to cut it."

"Sorry." Trevor lowered his gaze, while Justin hovered near the door.

Eric scratched the scruff on his jaw as his gaze danced between the victims, his men, and Alexis. "Here's the plan. Trevor, go get me the kid we talked about."

Trevor rubbed the back of his neck. "The kid? Are you sure you wanna go there, boss?"

Eric puffed out his chest like an overstuffed peacock. "Are you questioning your alpha?"

He lowered his head. "No sir. I'm on my way." He scurried out the door.

"Justin, after I take care of these two, dump them in the river, and then get your ass back here to help Alexis clean up the mess." Eric cracked his knuckles. "I don't want any contamination when the kid gets here."

"Yes, sir." Justin gave him a mock salute.

She stepped toward the woman. "Take care of them? What are you going to do?"

Eric smiled wickedly and shifted into his wolf form.

Alexis screamed.

He lunged for the unconscious man, going straight for the neck, and ripped his throat out before Alexis could move. Then he turned to the woman.

"Eric, no!" She threw herself on top of her. "Don't kill her. Let her go."

He paused, a low growl rumbling in his throat. His gaze flicked to Justin and back to Alexis.

Justin grabbed her arm, trying to haul her up, but she clutched the woman's shoulders, hanging on tight. She couldn't let him kill her or anyone else. This had to end.

"Come on, woman," Justin said. "You heard the alpha. We have to get rid of her."

"No. She hasn't even woken up. Let her go."

Justin pulled his arm back, fisting his hand to deliver a blow, but Eric barreled into him, knocking him into the wall. Alexis clung to the woman, her head spinning from exhaustion, nausea churning in her stomach. Eric would have to go through her if he wanted to kill another innocent human, and in her current condition, she'd be dead before she had the chance to shift.

Eric returned to human form and yanked Justin up by the collar of his shirt. "No one lays a hand on the alpha's mate," he growled.

"I'm sorry." The lackey ducked his head, averting his gaze. "You want me to haul her off and take care of her myself?"

"You'll have to kill me first." Alexis tightened her grip on the victim's shoulders.

Eric arched an eyebrow at her before turning to his minion. "Did she see your wolf form?"

"I knocked her out with the chloroform from behind. She never even saw my face." He smiled smugly.

Eric grabbed Alexis's elbow and dragged her to her feet before wrapping an arm around her. "You heard my future mate. This one lives. Dump her in the woods before she wakes up and leave her." He pressed his putrid lips to Alexis's head, and her stomach turned. "See, babe? I told you this would be a partnership. You saved a life today."

She shook from his embrace. "And you took one, asshole."

He shrugged. "As soon as we figure out the formula, no one else will die."

She clenched her teeth. Someone else would die tonight, and it wouldn't be another human.

CHAPTER SEVENTEEN

EVERY MUSCLE IN BRYCE'S BODY TENSED AS HE DROVE OVER THE Crescent City Connection bridge onto the East Bank. He'd been driving aimlessly for the past two hours, rolling over his conversations with Alexis and Macey in his head, gripping the steering wheel until his knuckles whitened and his joints ached.

Had he been wrong about Alexis? He'd missed every single sign when she'd lied to him about going to the bastard's house. He could hardly see through the thick cloud of love covering his eyes, and his judgment suffered for it. Was he only seeing what he wanted to see?

No, she hadn't used him like she'd said. It was a lie—all of it—but *something* was going on. She may have gone to Eric's willingly, but she wouldn't stay with him unless she had a reason. She was smarter than that.

Whatever it was, she did not need to be anywhere near that abuser. He had to figure out a way to get through to her. Maybe she really couldn't ever love a man like Bryce, but she deserved so much better than an asshole like Eric.

He groaned and exited the highway onto Tchoupitoulas Street and made his way into the Garden District. A few shots of caffeine and a rush of sugar ought to wake his mind up. Help him think straight.

He hadn't slept much last night with Alexis in his bed. The corner of his mouth twitched as images of her sexy body wrapped around him danced behind his eyes. She had feelings for him; of that he was sure.

But he'd come on too strong. What the hell had he been thinking asking her to live with him? He should've been satisfied when she said she'd stay in town, but he'd pushed her too hard and sent her straight into that asshole's house. That's what Macey would have him believe, but the wriggling sensation in the back of his mind told him something else was going on. And in his heart...damn it, in his *soul*, he knew Alexis was the one for him. If he believed in fate and soul mates and all that crap, he'd say she was his. He couldn't deny the strong connection he felt with her. She felt it too. She had to.

He pulled into a parking lot and zipped his jacket as he trekked into the coffee shop. Half a dozen tables sat scattered about the room, four of them occupied, and a row of stools lined the counter in front of the kitchen. The rich aromas of espresso and cinnamon tickled his senses, and a woman laughed, disturbing the quiet hum of conversation filling the air. Grabbing a seat at the counter, he ordered black coffee and an apple fritter, and he played his conversation with Alexis in his mind for the fifteenth time. There had to be something he'd missed. Some clue.

"Hey, Bryce. How's it going?" A tall man with dark hair and blue eyes slid onto the seat next to him.

Bryce sat up straight. "James, right?" He offered his hand to shake. "Good to see you." Macey had so many new friends since she'd married Luke, it was hard to keep up with them all.

James shook his hand and ordered a roast beef po-boy. As the waitress delivered Bryce's food, James chuckled. "Late breakfast?"

"I didn't realize it was already lunch time." He broke off a piece of the fritter and shoved it into his mouth. The combination of apple and cinnamon normally made his taste buds zing, but he could hardly taste it now.

"You okay?" James's eyes held brotherly concern. "You look like you lost your best friend."

He let out a dry laugh. "Close. I might have lost the woman I love."

James palmed his shoulder. "I'm sorry man. That's tough."

"Tell me about it." He scrubbed a hand down his face. He normally kept his mouth shut about his personal life, but at least this guy had some sympathy for his situation. Macey had had none. "She went back to her abusive ex."

He sucked in a breath through his teeth. "There's nothing I hate more than a man who hits a woman. You need any help kicking his ass, you let me know."

"I might take you up on that." He took a gulp of coffee. Lukewarm, like his love life.

James's food arrived and they ate in silence. The waitress refilled Bryce's coffee, and it was a little warmer this time. Still, nothing compared to the fire Alexis had lit inside his soul. He shoved his plate away. If he could clear his head—get his mind off his emotions—then he could look at the facts and figure out how to get her back.

He turned to James. "What's your super power?"

James choked on his iced tea. "Pardon?"

"Seems like all Macey's new friends have some sort of psychic ability. What's yours?"

He bit into his sandwich and took his time chewing before he answered. "I don't have any psychic abilities." He cut his gaze to the side and ran his hand over his mouth.

"Good to know I'm not the only one." Bryce sipped his coffee and eyed the man. "How long have you known Luke?"

"Since we were kids. We grew up together, close as cousins." He rubbed the back of his neck. "Listen, man, I'm serious. If you need help getting your girl out of a bad situation, hit me up."

"Thanks."

"What's her name?"

Bryce straightened his spine and held his gaze. "It's Alexis. Macey's sister."

James's eyes widened briefly, and he pressed his lips into a hard line. He slapped a twenty on the counter before giving Bryce's shoulder a squeeze. "Take care, man." He hustled out the door.

The waitress grinned as she picked up the money James had left. "Is he paying for yours too?"

"No, ma'am. I've got mine."

Her smiled widened as Bryce paid his tab, and he shuffled out of the restaurant. James was hiding something, like Macey and Luke and everyone else she'd gotten herself involved with. From the look on James's face, Alexis was mixed up in it too, and it seemed this Eric guy was at the center of the mess.

He got into his car and started the engine. It looked like he'd be putting his detective skills to the test on this one.

His frazzled nerves should have smoothed as he made his way toward his home. Being alone inside his apartment always brought him a sense of calm, but the tension wound tighter as he pulled into the driveway and cut the engine. He kept adding pieces to the puzzle, but he couldn't get any of them to fit together.

He climbed out of the car and cut around the side of the house to the staircase, and his heart dropped into his shoes. A mass of white fur lay at the bottom of the steps, and icy dread clawed through his veins as he approached. *Please don't be Sam.*

His throat thickened. It was Sam.

Bryce dropped to his knees and put a hand on his dog's side. Sam's ribcage rose and fell with his shallow breaths, and he whimpered, lifting his head to look at his master.

"Aw, buddy. What happened to you?" Bryce ran his hands along the dog's fur, and Sam yelped as he touched his back leg. "Can you get up? Come here, boy." He scooted a few feet away and patted his legs to call his dog.

Sam wiggled and tried to push to his feet, but he let out an ear-piercing howl and crumpled to the ground.

"All right, goofball, let's get you to the doctor." He scooped the eighty-pound canine into his arms and carried him to the car. Shifting the dog's weight to one arm, he fumbled with the handle, cursing at the damn thing until he got it open.

Sam whined as Bryce positioned him on the back seat and unhooked the leash from his collar. "I'll be right back."

He shut the door and marched to the house. Michael was probably inside, crying on the couch. No telling how Sam had hurt his leg, but the kid would blame himself since it happened on his watch.

He banged on the door. "Hey, Michael? What happened to Sam?"

Silence answered.

He knocked again. Nothing.

Fishing his keys from his pocket, he unlocked the door and poked his head inside. "Michael?"

A lamp burned in the corner of the living room, but all the overhead lights were off. Pausing, he listened for sounds of movement, for any indication someone was home, but the apartment sat silent. Empty. He wiped his feet on the rug and crept inside the eerily quiet living room. His heart sprinted as thoughts of Michael's delicate mental state flashed through his mind. If the kid had done something to himself because Sam was hurt...

He shook the idea from his head and searched the place, finding every room empty. No sign of Michael anywhere. "What the hell?"

He locked the front door and dialed Michael's number as he paced to his car. Sam whimpered as he climbed into the driver's seat and started the engine. Michael didn't answer.

"Hey, Mike, it's Bryce. I found Sam hurt at the bottom of the steps and wanted to check in with you. Call me as soon as you can."

He shifted into drive and headed to the emergency vet as he dialed Karen. The call went straight to voicemail, so he left her a message too. Hopefully they were together, but Karen would have called if she'd known Sam was hurt.

Maybe Michael left the door open, and Sam escaped that way, tumbling down the stairs on his way to freedom. But why would the leash have been attached?

If Michael had left in a hurry, he might have forgotten to unhook the leash and left the door ajar. It was the only logical explanation... but Bryce had glanced up at his apartment from the bottom of the stairs. The door was closed.

He tried both their numbers again, hanging up before the voicemail greeting ended, and then carried Sam into the clinic. The technicians took the dog to the back to sedate him and run tests and X-rays, and Bryce dropped into a chair in the waiting room.

He called Alexis first, but the call went straight to voicemail, so he tried Michael and Karen's cells again. Nothing. He sent all three of them a text before calling the landline at Karen's house. The machine picked up, so he left another message there before shoving his phone in his pocket and wringing his hands.

He took a deep breath, and the scents of lavender and antiseptic greeted his senses. A fake plant stood in the corner of the room next to a short table littered with magazines. A woman and her young daughter occupied two chairs on the opposite wall, the mother reading quietly from a thick-paged book.

He could call Macey, but what good would that do? He'd already pissed her off with his cult comment, and James's strange responses during their conversation had him all the more suspicious.

Bryce had never felt more alone in his life.

Alexis showered and shoved her bloodied clothes into the washer before ducking back into the bathroom and tossing another tampon wrapper into the trash to keep up the charade. With Bryce's gun hidden at the bottom of her backpack, she shoved the bag under Eric's bed and cringed. She'd have to crawl under these blankets with the dickhead tonight if her plan was going to work. She might even have to make out with him. Her stomach lurched, and she covered her mouth with her hand as she shuffled toward the sound-proof room.

She and Justin had cleaned up the bloody mess while Eric jerked off in the bathroom. *Sick bastard.* And now Trevor was probably back with whatever kid Eric planned to turn. Alexis gritted her teeth. She would *not* let him hurt a child.

Glancing toward the bed, she eyed the edge of the backpack beneath it. She could grab the gun and end this now, but she'd only get one shot. If she fired and missed, she'd be dead. Since she'd never shot a gun before, it was better to wait until he slept tonight. She swallowed the sour taste from her mouth and turned away from the bedroom.

Twisting the knob, she pushed open the door, and her heart shot into her throat. Michael sat alone on the floor, gagged, his back against the wall, his hands tied to his ankles.

"Oh, no." Alexis ran to him, dropping to her knees at his side and pulling the gag from his mouth. "Are you okay?" She put up a finger to keep him from answering and rushed to slam the door, blocking the sound from escaping. "Did he hurt you?"

Tears collected on his lower lids. "I'm okay. He knocked me out with something on a rag, but Sam…" His lip trembled and the tears spilled down his cheeks. "He hurt Sergeant Samuels' dog." He sucked in a shaky breath. "Sam was trying to protect me, and he kicked him. I heard something snap, and he yelped, and I tried to help him but…" He bit his lip.

She clenched her teeth. "He won't get away with this." The urge to grab the gun and end this now grew palpable in her core. Her legs tensed, her body willing her to follow through, but she fought the impulse. She had to wait for the right moment.

Squaring her gaze on Michael, she put a hand on his shoulder. "I'm going to help you, but I need you to play along, okay? And when I tell you to run, you need to *run*. No questions asked. Got it?"

He nodded.

The knob turned, and Eric sauntered into the room. "Damn. He's awake." He closed the door. "I wanted to make this fast, so you don't get all teary and soft on me."

Alexis shot to her feet, clenching her hands at her sides. "Leave him out of this, Eric."

"Oh, he's in this, babe. He was in it the moment you ran to that cop for help. Now everyone he knows is in this."

She swallowed her bitter anger and softened her gaze. Eric liked it when she seemed weak. "Please don't hurt him. I'm here. You got what you wanted, and I promise I won't leave you again." She unclenched her fists and clasped them together over her heart, batting her lashes to add to the effect.

He hesitated, his mouth opening a few times as he attempted to speak, and her pulse thrummed.

"I'm sorry, Eric. I'm here." She held out her hands to him. *Please let this act work.*

His brows slammed together in a scowl. "Your body may be here, but your mind ain't." He cracked his neck, and shimmering vibration engulfed him as he shifted into wolf form.

Michael screamed.

"Damn it, Eric." Alexis widened her stance, blocking the kid from his attack.

Eric rocked back, ready to spring, and Alexis had two choices: she could shift and fight him, or she could get torn apart on his way to his target.

"I promise I won't hurt you," she said over her shoulder to Michael before calling on her own wolf and shifting form. Crouching low, she growled a warning but didn't advance. Even with all her strength intact, she didn't stand a chance against a powerful wolf like Eric.

He lunged, feigning right then left. Alexis snapped her jaws, purposely missing on each advance. He was toying with her, and she refused to give him a reason to attack.

Ears back, Eric lowered his head and let out a menacing growl. Michael whimpered behind her, but she didn't dare turn her back on the wolf to check on him. She growled in return, and Eric blew out a hard breath through his nostrils before backing up and sitting on his haunches. He tilted his head, and his body shimmered as he shifted back to human form and laughed. "Come on, babe. Let's not fight."

This was her chance. If she leapt for him now and went straight for the throat, she could take him out before he knew what hit him. But the uncontrollable sobs from the terrified teenager behind her glued her to the spot.

She'd wait. Bide her time like she originally planned. Another warning rumbled from her chest before she shifted to human form. "Let him go." With her wolf hovering near the surface, her voice sounded more like a growl.

"He's seen our wolf forms now. You'll be in deep shit too, if we do that."

She knelt beside Michael, and he recoiled from her touch. "It's okay. I promise no one will hurt you."

He stared at her with wide eyes. "Are you a…are you a werewolf?"

She pressed her lips together and gave a tight nod.

"You'll be one too, by the time I'm done with you." Eric rose to his feet as a speaker in the corner of the room buzzed. He grumbled and pulled his phone from his pocket. "Goddammit. It's my old man."

He slammed his phone onto a table and grabbed two guitars from the wall, shoving them at Alexis. "Hold these."

He yanked the ties from Michael's wrists and ankles and dragged him to his feet. "Give him the bass. Sit there and pretend like you're practicing." He raked his hands through his hair and mumbled as he stomped out the door. "Piece of shit's got the worst timing."

As soon as the door shut, Alexis swiped Eric's phone from the table. It took her less than a minute to download a rideshare app, connect it to his credit card stored in his virtual wallet, and request a car.

She crept toward the door and peeked down the hall. No sign of the men. Eric must have wrangled his dad into the living room.

Motioning for Michael, she whispered, "Hang a right and go out the back door. Keep running straight through the neighbor's yard and you'll come to a road. Go left and head for the convenience store on the corner. A rideshare car will be there to pick you up, and it's taking you to O'Malley's Pub."

He furrowed his brow as his frightened gaze danced about the room. "A bar? I don't understand."

"Ask for Macey Mason when you get there. You know who she is, right?"

"Sergeant Samuels' old partner."

"Right. Now, listen to me, Michael, this is important. You need to tell her *everything* you saw here."

His eyes widened. "Even about how you…?"

"She's my sister. She knows what I am."

He nodded.

"Don't tell Sergeant Samuels anything, okay? He doesn't know, and it's important no one else ever finds out. For my safety and yours. Don't talk about this to *anyone* but Macey. Do you understand?"

"Yes, ma'am. I'll tell Detective Mason everything, and I won't say a word to Sergeant Samuels."

She leaned into the hallway. "Run, Michael. Don't stop until you get in the car. Go!"

Stepping away from the door, she shoved Michael through. He stumbled in the hall, catching himself on the wall before regaining his footing and barreling toward the exit. Alexis held her breath as he fumbled with the knob, and when he finally threw the door open, a chime sounded from the hall speaker.

Alexis's heart pounded against her ribs as she closed the door and settled onto a chair with the guitar in her lap.

Eric stormed into the room with a look of fury in his eyes so hot he could have shot flames. "Where's the kid?"

David stepped in behind him and narrowed his eyes at Alexis.

She plastered a huge smile on her face. "His mom called, and he had to go home." She turned to Eric's dad. "It's good to see you again, David. What brings you out to our neck of the woods?"

"I'm checking up on my son."

Eric's hands clenched into fists, and a vein in his forehead throbbed. "And everything is fine, so you can go now."

Alexis stood and hung the guitar on the wall. "Don't be rude, Eric. He drove all this way." Eric couldn't do a damn thing while his dad was around, so the longer she could keep David in the house, the more time Michael would have to get away. "Why don't you stay and visit a while? Can I get you a beer or some coffee?" She padded toward the door.

David cut a suspicious gaze between Eric and her. "I'll take a beer."

"How about you, babe?" She slapped Eric's ass on her way to the hall. "Want a cold one?"

"Sure." The word was barely audible over the sound of his grinding teeth.

The men shuffled into the living room as she popped the tops on two cans of Bud Light and handed them the beers. David settled into a recliner, and Eric glared at her as he dropped onto the sofa. She flashed him a smirk and perched on the arm of the couch.

David's gaze bore into her as he set his beer on the coffee table and crossed his arms. "After that story you told me about my son, I wonder why you're here."

She swallowed, lowering her gaze and trying to look ashamed. "I'm sorry about that. We had a little tiff, and I was mad at him. I thought getting him into trouble would make up for him hitting my friend, but..." She glanced at Eric. "It was a stupid thing for me to do. I apologized, and he forgave me. Didn't you, babe?"

Eric grunted in response.

David eyed her skeptically. "So you two are together now?"

Forcing a smile, she rested a hand on Eric's shoulder. "'Til death do us part."

She managed to keep Eric's dad in the house for another half hour, and by the time he left, two more veins had popped out on Eric's forehead. He watched from the window as David drove away, and as he turned to face her, his face flushed red.

Her blood turned to ice in her veins, but she held her ground, planting her feet firmly on the floor and lifting her chin defiantly. Eric backhanded her, and searing pain exploded in her cheek, the momentum of his swing knocking her to carpet.

"You'll pay for this." He patted his pockets. "Where the hell is my phone?" He stomped down the hall and returned with the device. "You ordered a car with my phone?"

"You hid mine."

His eyes narrowed. "You sent him to O'Malley's? Isn't that the pack's headquarters?"

"He's being protected now."

"Like hell he is." Growling, he punched some buttons on the screen. "The kid got away. Go find him." He paused as the other person spoke. "I don't give a damn what you're doing; go get that kid."

CHAPTER EIGHTEEN

Bryce lifted his head from his hands as a vet tech shuffled into the waiting room. She had a warm smile, and she looked him in the eyes, putting his fears at ease. "Mr. Samuels?"

"How's my boy?"

"His leg is broken and a few ribs are bruised, but he's otherwise healthy. He's sedated, and we'd like to keep him overnight for observation." She offered him a tablet to sign.

He scribbled his name on the screen. "Can you tell how it broke? Did he fall down the stairs?"

Her eyes tightened. "From the X-ray, it looks like some sort of blunt force trauma caused the break. A boot or something else hard."

He sucked in a sharp breath. Whoever hurt his dog would pay.

"We'll call you when he wakes up and let you know when you can get him."

"Thank you, ma'am." Bryce nodded and turned for the door. As he exited the building, his phone buzzed, and he fished it from his pocket. Karen's name lit up the screen.

He pressed the device to his ear. "Where are you? Where's Michael?"

She paused. "I'm at work. I was in a meeting when you called, and Michael's at home. Is everything okay?"

Dread sank in his stomach like a brick. "He's not there, and I found Sam at the foot of the stairs with his leg broken and the leash attached to his collar."

She didn't respond.

"Karen? Have you heard from him today?"

"No." Her voice was a whisper.

He scrubbed a hand down his face and climbed into his car. "Meet me at the station. We'll file a missing person's report."

Silence.

He slammed the door and buckled his seatbelt. "Karen? Did you hear me?"

"Yeah. I'll meet you there."

He tossed his phone in the cupholder and sped to the station. When he arrived, Karen was already talking with an officer. Tears dripped from her eyes, and she threw her arms around Bryce when he approached.

"He hasn't been missing for twenty-four hours." She sobbed into his shirt.

Bryce narrowed his gaze at the officer. "He's a suicide risk. File the report."

Karen sobbed harder.

The officer nodded. "Yes, sir. Ma'am, can you give me a description."

Releasing her hold on Bryce's shirt, she wiped her eyes. "He's tall. A little chunky."

"He's one of mine," Bryce said. "Michael Benson. The report should have everything you need. And put in a call to the area hospitals; he might be injured."

Karen stared blankly at the wall as she sank into a chair. Lacing her fingers together, she clenched them tightly until the tips turned purple. "We're moving."

Bryce sat next to her. "Where are you going?"

She inhaled a shaky breath. "To stay with my mom in Texas. I thought it would be good for Michael to get a clean start. I put in my two-week notice today." She covered her mouth and sobbed.

"Hey." Bryce rubbed a hand across her back. "We're going to find him."

Her phone rang, and she yanked it from her purse. "It's our landline." She held it to her ear. "Michael?"

She let out an enormous sigh and leaned back into the seat, her shoulders slumping in relief. "Are you there alone?"

Her brow furrowed as she listened. "Okay. Stay put. I'm on my way." She shoved the phone into her purse and shot to her feet. "He's okay. He's at home. There's an officer with him."

Bryce glanced at the dispatcher, who lifted his hands and shook his head. "Which officer?"

"I don't know." She strode to the front door.

Bryce followed her home and stood in the doorway as she hugged her son. She showered him in questions and affections, and Bryce cut his gaze to James, who stood in the living room. *Officer, my ass.*

"Good to see you, Sergeant Samuels." James held out his hand to shake. Bryce accepted. "Detective Mason wants to speak with you ASAP. She's at home, waiting."

Bryce lowered his voice. "What the hell is going on?"

James glanced at Karen and gave him a pointed look. "I'm not at liberty to discuss the case, but Detective Mason will fill you in on the details."

"I'm so sorry, Sergeant Samuels." Michael hung his head and shuffled toward him. "Sam fell down the stairs, and when I couldn't get him to stand up, I freaked out and ran away. Detective Mason found me by the riverbank, and she brought me home." He rubbed at his nose as he spoke, looking anywhere *but* at Bryce. "Is Sam..." He glanced into Bryce's eyes and looked away. "Is he okay?"

"He will be." Bryce glared at James, who clamped his mouth shut. The kid was lying. James was lying. The whole story smelled like a wharf in the summertime.

Karen wrapped her arm around Michael's shoulders. "We'll pay Sam's vet bill."

"I'm sorry." Michael stared at the floor.

"That won't be necessary. I'm glad you're okay." He reached for the doorknob. "If you've got this under control…"

"We're fine. Thank you for your help, Bryce. Officer." Karen nodded at James.

"A word, *officer?*" He jerked his head, silently telling James to follow him outside. Stepping off the porch, he shuffled around to the stairs.

"We've got a man watching each side of the house. They're safe." James handed him a slip of paper. "My number. I meant what I said about getting your girl back, but Luke can't know."

He squinted at the paper. "Luke?"

"Say the word, and I'll be there." James climbed into a pickup truck and slammed the door, revving the engine before Bryce's mind caught up with the conversation. Why did it matter if Luke knew? And what *men* were watching the house?

He got into his car and dialed Macey's number. "What the hell's going on, Mace? Since when is James an officer of the law?"

She paused. "Not over the phone. Come to my house."

He let out a slow breath. "Is Michael safe?"

"We've got…people…watching him. Get over here. Now." She hung up.

Bryce reversed out of the driveway and hightailed it to the French Quarter. His emotions flipflopped between satisfaction that his suspicions about Macey and her new friends were well-founded and sickening dread for the same reason.

He parked two blocks from her house and hoofed it up the sidewalk to her front porch. As he lifted his hand to pound on the door, it swung open and Macey ushered him inside. Luke lounged on the sofa in the living room, and Macey sank down next to him, gesturing to the chair for Bryce to sit.

He paced in front of the coffee table instead. "I want answers, Mace. You've got a man impersonating an officer. Michael's lying about where he's been. James is lying. You. Alexis. Shit, everyone's lying." He threw his arms in the air. "What the hell is going on?"

Macey tugged on her bottom lip and glanced at Luke. "You're going to want to sit down for this."

"I don't want to sit down." He didn't mean to yell, but goddammit, he needed the truth.

Luke leaned forward, resting a protective hand on Macey's knee.

Bryce took a slow, deep breath, trying to calm his sprinting heart. Unclenching his fists, he lowered himself onto the chair and rested his palms on the arms. He pried his teeth apart and tried to keep his voice calm. "I'm sorry. Will you please tell me what's going on?"

Macey sat up straight. "You were right about everything."

"I..." Her confession took the breath from his chest. "What do you mean everything?"

Luke grasped her hand and nodded. "Tell him. It's time he found out."

"You accused me of being different since I met Luke, and you're right. I am. Or...I haven't changed, but I finally understand *what* I am."

"*What* you are? Mace..." He squeezed his eyes shut and pinched the bridge of his nose. "Will you please try to make some sense? I need facts. What happened to Michael? Why is James posing as a police officer? Why are you ignoring the autopsy reports for the bodies we pulled out of the river?" He scrubbed a hand down his face. "And what's going on with Alexis?"

She locked eyes with him. "Werewolves."

"What?"

"We're werewolves."

He held her gaze, waiting for her to crack a smile or roll her eyes and tell him he'd been overreacting. But she returned his stare, her eyes tightening as if she were willing him to accept the absurd remark.

Blowing out a hard breath, he leaned back into the chair and crossed his arms. "C'mon. Be serious." Did she take him for some kind of idiot? "Whatever you're involved in, it's affecting the people I care about. You can either tell me the truth, or I'll figure it out for myself." *Werewolves, my ass.*

She scooted to the edge of the couch and gave him a sympathetic look. "This is going to require some open-mindedness, so please hear me out."

"My mind is open to facts. Tell me the truth."

"We're werewolves." Her face held the most serious expression he'd ever seen, but there was no way.

He threw his arms into the air. "This was a waste of time. I'm going to get a *real* officer to look out for Michael, and I'm going to get Alexis back." He shoved to his feet.

"Sit down, Bryce." Luke's voice boomed with so much authority Bryce planted his ass in the seat without thinking twice. "My mate is trying to give you the facts, and you're going to listen to her."

His *mate?* What the...? And who the hell did this guy think he was giving an order like that? Bryce opened his mouth for a comeback, but Macey beat him to it.

"It's okay, hon. I've got this." She patted Luke's knee and scooted closer to Bryce, turning to him again. "Are you ready to listen?"

"Yeah, sure. Why not?" She'd probably spin some crazy story about magical creatures lurking in the shadows all around that no one had ever seen, but maybe he'd be able to glean a few bits of actual information from the tale.

"You believe in my ability to read spirit energy, right?"

"I've seen you do it. Of course I do."

"And you remember Chase's wife, Rain? She's a witch; she can cast spells."

He nodded. "She told me spells are like prayers, but they're something else, aren't they?"

"They're a way of manipulating energy. Magic is, at its core, energy manipulation."

Crossing his arms, he arched an eyebrow. "What are you trying to say?"

"Magic is real."

Had she told him that a week ago, he'd never have believed it. Hell, he didn't believe in ghosts until he'd seen how she could read spirit energy. But after the way Alexis healed his burns with a simple touch, he couldn't deny it anymore. "I know. Alexis said you were related to witches."

"We are, way back in the family tree." She furrowed her brow. "What else did she tell you about us?"

He shrugged. "Nothing I didn't already know about your parents dying when you were young. And she showed me her healing powers."

Her eyes widened. "Healing powers? When she was hurt?"

"Yeah. Then she healed me when I was hurt."

Macey gave Luke a quizzical look, and he shrugged. "It's not unheard of," he said. "The witch genes could be active in her system."

She shook her head. "Anyway, you *do* believe in magic, whether you want to admit it or not."

He had no problem admitting to things that could be proven. "Go on."

"Do you remember last year, when those women claimed some kind of animal saved them from the attackers?"

He closed his eyes for a long blink. "I remember."

"And then I saw a wolf in the woods behind the crime scene?"

A lump formed in his throat. This story was starting to make too much sense. She couldn't be serious.

"That wolf was Luke. I didn't know that he…that *we*…were werewolves at the time. Once I figured it out, everything fell into place."

"Hold on, now. You had me going for a minute there, Mace, but how could you be a werewolf and not know it? Do you black out every time you sprout fur and forget?"

"Only the first-born child of a werewolf couple can shift," Luke explained. "Macey was raised by humans, and Alexis went rogue as soon the change came, so she never knew until they reunited."

"Wha—?" He clamped his mouth shut. Questions ricocheted around in his head, but he couldn't grab on to one long enough to speak it coherently. Luckily, Macey knew him well enough to give him the answers he couldn't ask for.

"A rogue is a werewolf who doesn't belong to a pack. Alexis didn't know what she was until the first time she shifted when she was thirteen. She freaked and ran away and has been living on her own ever since."

His mind didn't want to believe it, but somewhere deep in his soul it made sense. Why the hell would something so ridiculous make sense? He'd been working too hard. Too many distractions had his thoughts wound up in a jumbled mess. He needed sleep. Or an appointment with a psychiatrist. "You're telling me that Alexis…is a werewolf?"

"She is."

He shook his head. Nonsense. It was all nonsense. "Werewolves aren't real."

"We are."

He crossed his arms. It wasn't possible. "I'll believe it when I see it."

Macey looked at Luke. "That's your cue."

"I'm on it." Luke stood and strode down the hall.

Leaning toward him, Macey took Bryce's hand as he uncrossed his arms. He hadn't realized how cold his own had turned until the warmth from her palm seeped into his skin. "It took a lot of convincing for me too," she said, "but I think this will do it."

A shuffling noise sounded from the hallway, and in padded the biggest wolf he'd ever seen. Light-brown fur covered its massive body, and as it opened its mouth to pant, fangs the size of daggers filled its enormous maw.

Bryce's heart rate kicked up, and his muscles tensed, ready for fight or flight…he wasn't sure which. "What the hell?"

The wolf approached Macey and sat at her feet as she rested a hand on its neck. "This is Luke."

"No, it's not. It's a pet. A mutated Siberian huskey or something." There was no way. That beast couldn't be… Luke wasn't a…

The animal licked Macey's cheek from jaw to ear. She laughed and pushed it away. "What have I told you about that? Show him."

The wolf paced to the center of the room. A shimmering mist gathered around its fur, almost as if it were glowing, but not quite. Bryce rubbed his eyes and looked again. As the mist grew denser and the image wavered, the wolf rose onto its back legs and transformed into…

"Luke?" Bryce's mouth fell open. How could he—? "But you—"

Luke laughed. "Convinced?"

It wasn't possible. Supernatural creatures didn't exist in this world, yet he'd watched a wolf turn into a man right before his eyes. He stood and paced toward Luke. Reaching out his arms, he hesitated before clapping his hands onto his shoulders.

All the blood in his body seemed to settle at his feet, making his head spin. "It's really you." He dropped his arms to his sides.

"Yep." Luke patted him on the back and plopped onto the couch next to Macey.

"Do you believe it now?" she asked.

He sank into the chair. "I suppose I have no choice." He'd always been a *seeing is believing* guy, but what he just saw he couldn't explain. Focusing on *how* a giant wolf had waltzed into Macey's living room and transformed into her husband made his head spin. The important thing was that it *had* happened. He'd deal with the how later. "Can Alexis…?"

Macey nodded. "She's first-born, so she can shift."

How could his sweet, soft woman turn into a massive beast? "I never would've guessed it." He shook his head, trying to get the spinning thoughts to form into some sort of coherence. The woman he loved was a werewolf. His partner of the last seven years was a supernatural being. Her husband too. "James?"

"He's a werewolf," Macey said. "So is Chase. Michael is safe with them watching him, but Alexis is in trouble." Her expression softened. The mask of supernatural secrets she'd been keeping dissolved, allowing her true concern for her sister to finally show through, and his doubts about Macey dissolved right along with it.

Her words focused his thoughts into pinpoint precision. His world may have been turned upside down, but having the woman he loved safe and back in his arms was all that mattered. "I assume you're telling me all this because Eric is a werewolf too?"

Macey's expression turned grim. "I haven't been ignoring the autopsy reports on those bodies. I've been trying to cover them up. Those people were killed by werewolves."

"One werewolf in particular," Luke said.

"Eric." He fisted his hands on the arms of the chair. "Why would Alexis go back to him?"

Macey straightened. "We think she wants to stop him. He's trying to turn humans into werewolves, and those bodies we found in the river were his failed experiments."

Bryce rubbed his forehead in an attempt to slow the merry-go-round of thoughts whirling though his mind. "How do you know all this?"

"Michael didn't run away." She cringed. "One of Eric's men kidnapped him."

He slammed his fist on the arm of the chair. "The bastard hurt my dog too."

"Alexis helped Michael escape, and she sent him to me. I think she's safe for now, but we don't know how long he'll keep using her."

His stomach soured. "What's he using her for?"

"If she can heal other people like you say." She took a deep breath and looked at Luke. "He must be attacking the humans and having Alexis heal them in hopes that they'll turn into werewolves."

"Is that possible?" He cut his gaze between Luke and Macey. "Can someone be turned into a werewolf?"

"It's possible," Luke said. "But extremely unlikely to happen. The human would have to lose a considerable amount of blood and put up enough of a fight to cause some damage to the wolf attacking him. Get enough werewolf blood into your system, and it's going to wreak havoc on your DNA."

Bryce scrubbed a hand down his face. "Why attack people then? If he's kidnapping people and knocking them out, why not give them a blood transfusion and avoid the hassle?"

"He probably doesn't realize it's blood his victims need." Thor, Macey's brown tabby cat, jumped into Luke's lap, and he stroked its back. "Werewolves are taught two basic laws from the time we're old enough to understand them. One: never attack a human while in wolf form, unless it's a fight to the death. Two: our blood is sacred and can never be shared." He passed the cat to Macey. "Breaking those laws is punishable by death."

Macey set the cat on the floor. "He probably thinks the first law exists because people will turn into werewolves if they're attacked. Most people think that."

"The chance of survival after losing the amount of blood required for the change is slim," Luke said. "I know of four cases in our history of it actually happening, and they were hundreds of years ago, before the laws were in place."

Bryce's mind spun. It was all too much to process. More than his brain was ready or willing to comprehend. He focused on the one thing he did understand...his own heart. "I have to get Alexis out of there."

Macey swallowed. "Yes, you do."

"That guy is inhumanly strong. Tell me he's not bulletproof."

"You have to hit him in the head or the heart," Luke said. "Anywhere else, and he'll heal easily."

He rubbed the back of his neck. Murder wasn't on his radar, but it sounded like having a civilized conversation with this guy was off the table. He might have to shoot him in self-defense, but the ramifications of what he was about to do could end his career and land his ass in jail.

"Don't worry about the police." Macey seemed to have read his mind. "Werewolves have been covering up our less-than-humanly-legal activity for hundreds of years. Get Alexis out. We'll take care of you."

He looked from Macey to Luke, and they both met his gaze with sincerity in their eyes. Bryce trusted them to his core, and it didn't matter what happened to him. Eric was a murderer who needed to be stopped, and Alexis needed saving.

"Got it." Bryce shot to his feet. "We'll stop by my place first to get my personal firearm. You've got your own, right, Mace?"

Macey glanced at Luke. "We...can't help you."

He cocked his head. "Why not? She's your sister."

"I know, but..." She sighed. "Eric belongs to the Biloxi pack. If New Orleans werewolves attack, it will start a war between the packs. He's not on our territory."

"War? We're talking about stopping a murderer, not assassinating a political figure."

"It is political. His father is second in command of Biloxi." Luke rose to his feet and paced in front of the couch. "We've contacted the Biloxi alpha and put a call in to the national congress. Our hands are tied until one of them acts."

"But he's killing people."

Macey stood next to Luke. "We don't have any proof."

"We have bodies."

Luke ran a hand through his hair. "And the connection to Eric is based on the word of a human who shouldn't know we exist."

"What about Alexis? She knows what's happening."

"She's…a rogue." Macey lowered her gaze to the floor.

Luke put his arm around her. "The word of a rogue is as useful as wet toilet paper, no matter who she's related to."

"I don't believe this." Because Alexis wasn't a card-carrying member of their group, they refused to help her? Were they insane? Didn't they even care? He crossed his arms. "You called the Biloxi alpha. I want to talk to the man in charge of New Orleans."

"You are talking to him," Macey said. "Luke is the alpha."

"Damn it, Mace. Why didn't you tell me any of this before?"

"You were on a need-to-know basis."

"And I didn't need to know until now. I get it." It sucked that she'd kept so many secrets from him…but he got it. He reached for the doorknob. "James gave me his number."

Macey drew in a breath. "That's great. You should call him and go have a beer sometime."

"He said—"

She opened the door and pushed him through it. "I'm sure *whatever* reason he had for giving it to you is between you and him." Widening her eyes, she gave Bryce a pointed look before glancing at Luke and closing the door.

"Right." Luke couldn't know because he was the alpha and sending in pack members would start a war. James was offering his help outside the pack.

"I know it seems like I don't care about her, but this is a complicated situation. When a werewolf decides to go rogue, they understand that they're giving up all support from the pack. Alexis has had an open invitation to join us since the moment she came back into my life, but she's chosen to remain rogue."

He shook his head. "Doesn't matter. She's your blood."

"I know. That's why you *have* to help her. For seven years, I've trusted you with my own life. Now, I'm trusting you with my sister's."

"I'll get her out of there." Or he'd die trying.

Macey pulled him into a tight hug. "Be careful. You're living outside the law now."

"She's worth it." He patted her shoulder and stepped away. "I won't let her down."

CHAPTER NINETEEN

BRYCE CLIMBED INTO THE PASSENGER SEAT OF JAMES'S TRUCK and slammed the door. He'd torn his bedroom apart looking for his Smith and Wesson when it wasn't in its drawer. His personal firearm was gone, and he hadn't misplaced it. He chewed the inside of his cheek. "If Alexis can turn into a wolf, why would she need a gun?"

James arched an eyebrow. "Good question. A werewolf using a gun is like cheating. Our teeth and claws are our weapons. My guess is that she knows she can't beat him in a fair fight."

His mind flashed back to the scuffle in the parking lot, and he cringed. One punch had landed Bryce on his ass. "How does werewolf justice work? Since this guy's part of another pack, if they don't want to stop him, he can keep on killing people?"

James started the engine and backed out of the driveway. "Unless another pack can prove he's breaking our laws, attacking him would be equivalent to attacking his pack. That's why I'm going rogue tonight." He shifted into drive and headed for Pearl River.

"What will happen to you if Luke finds out you're helping me?"

Resting his left elbow on the window frame, James rubbed at the scruff on his face. "Depending on how far south this all goes, I could serve time in the pit."

"The pit?"

"Werewolf prison. A human cell won't hold a supernatural being." He cast a sideways glance toward him before focusing on the road.

Bryce stared out the window as they exited the residential area of the city and entered the highway. "You're risking jail time to help me. Why?"

His brow furrowed as if the question confused him. "It's what friends do."

Friends. "Thanks, man." He'd have to buy him a beer when this was through.

The corner of James's mouth twitched. "Jail time is better than execution. That's a possibility too."

He balked. Firm laws and harsh punishments served their purpose, but execution for trying to save someone from a murderer? What kind of man was Macey married to? "Luke would kill you for this?"

"Our laws are strict to keep our existence a secret. They've worked for hundreds of years." He chuckled. "Our alpha is bound by the national congress to enforce them, but he knows when to look the other way. Sometimes laws have to be broken."

"Yeah, I guess they do." He'd spent his entire life playing by the rules, doing what everyone expected of him. Human laws had served him well, but the world as he knew it ceased to exist a few hours ago. Where did he fit in now?

He was in love with a werewolf. How could he compete with a supernatural being? What could he offer a woman who came from a magical world he'd had no idea existed? A sinking sensation formed in the pit of his stomach. "What if she doesn't want to be saved?" He looked at James. "What if she went back to Eric because she really does want to be with him?"

"She doesn't want to be with that asshole. Believe me."

He wanted to believe him. To believe he hadn't imagined the connection he'd felt with Alexis. But the rug of life had been yanked out from under him, and he didn't have a clue what was real and what wasn't anymore. "How do you know?"

"I know Alexis. She's got a good thing with you."

He rested his arm on the edge of the window and watched the

trees zooming by in a blur. "Is it even allowed? If she were in a pack and followed the rules, would she be allowed to date me?"

"We can date anyone we want. We can't reveal our true selves unless we plan to take the person as a mate, but since you're already in on the secret, you're good to go."

A weight lifted from his shoulders, but his stomach tensed as they exited the highway and turned onto Eric's street. James tightened his grip on the steering wheel, and Bryce glanced at his four-fingered hand. "Mind if I ask what happened to you?"

James loosened his grip and flexed his fingers. "Construction accident."

"I thought werewolves were fast healers."

"We are, but we can't regrow limbs." He cut the wheel to the right and stopped in a grocery store parking lot. "We'll walk from here."

Bryce tucked his service weapon into the waistband of his jeans, and they trekked into the field behind the store. He'd left his badge and holster at home. His cuffs too. He'd lose his job if he got caught in an act of vigilante justice. Hell, he might even lose his life.

The nearly-full moon hung high in the night sky, casting a silver glow on the damp grass. Shadows danced around his peripheral vision, and his pulse thrummed in his ears. If werewolves existed, what other kinds of monsters lurked in the darkness? A shudder ran down his spine. He didn't want to know.

A rustle sounded in the grass, and he jerked his head toward the noise, his hand instinctively reaching for his firearm. Adrenaline coursed through his veins, setting him on edge.

"It's a fox." James stopped walking and pointed. "Look closely and you'll see the light reflect in its eyes."

Bryce repositioned his gun in his pants and squinted into the darkness. A little flash of something glinted in the moonlight, and a shadow darted through the grass. "I suppose you have some kind of enhanced werewolf vision?"

"It's better in wolf form, but yeah. You'll never see a shifter needing glasses."

He huffed and continued his trek toward the house. The eye surgery he'd had a few years back had turned his own night vision to shit. Add that to the list of reasons he couldn't compete with a were-wolf, and he began to wonder exactly what Alexis saw in him.

As the house came into view, James let out a whistle. "Looks like our friend has company."

Alexis's car sat behind the Mustang, and an F-150 had parked in the grass by the road. They crept into the yard and scanned the outside of the house. The massive pine trees appeared black against the moonlit sky, and light burned in the living room window. No security cameras hung from the eaves, and no motion-sensor lights turned on as they approached.

"Do you know if he has a security system?" James asked.

"He's got a video doorbell, the kind you can easily install yourself, but I haven't noticed anything else."

James nodded. "Can you pick a lock?"

"If I had the tools."

He pulled a black bag from his pocket and handed it to Bryce. "I'll knock on the door and keep them occupied. You go in through the back and get Alexis out. Got your phone on you?"

Bryce patted his pocket.

"Get pictures. Any kind of evidence you can find. Paperwork, blood, bodies, whatever. If we can prove what he's doing, the pack can move in and end it."

Bryce took a deep breath, centering himself, and the nervous jitters he'd experienced on the way over dissolved, leaving behind nothing but the calm before the storm. "And if there's a confrontation..."

"We end him."

"I'm glad we're on the same page."

James darted around to the front door, and Bryce slipped into the backyard. He pulled the tools out of the bag and jimmied them into the lock. The faint sound of voices emanated from the front, and the tool slipped from his sweaty fingers. He cursed under his breath and wiped his palms on his jeans before retrieving the instrument and shoving it back into the lock.

After a few minutes of fumbling, the bolt disengaged and he

pushed the door open. An alert chimed in the darkened hallway, and he held his breath as the voices stopped.

"What the hell's going on?" Eric's voice boomed.

"Stop!" Alexis screamed, and the sound of scuffling ensued. Then a growl. Then a snarl, and the scuffle turned into a full-blown brawl.

Holy shit, he was about to witness a werewolf fight.

Instinct to break it up drew him toward the fray, but he stopped as the sound of footsteps thudded toward him. They needed evidence. He leaned into a door on the left and twisted the knob. Locked.

"Bryce!" Alexis whispered as she ran toward him. "What are you doing here? You have to leave. It's not safe." She tried to push him down the hall, but he caught her in his arms and held her to his chest.

Relief unfurled in his gut, and he pressed his lips against her hair. "I'm here to bring you home." The sounds of snarling and jaws snapping echoed from the living room, and he tightened his arms around her.

"I can't go home. Not until I stop Eric." She pushed him toward the back door. "Please go."

He gripped her shoulders. "I know what you are. I know you're a werewolf."

She glanced behind her toward the living room. Someone yelped as glass crashed on the floor. "Then you should know how dangerous it is for you to be here. I promise I'll come home, okay? Let me finish this."

"What do you need to finish, babe?" Eric stood at the end of the hall and crossed his arms over his barrel of a chest.

Bryce shoved her behind his back and leveled his gun at the bastard's heart.

Eric smirked and raised his hands. "Aren't you going to read me my rights first, officer? Your case will never stand in a court of law if you don't."

His finger hovered over the trigger. "What you're doing is so far beyond the law that I've appointed myself judge and jury."

He laughed. "If that's how you want to play..." Eric's body shimmered, and in an instant, he transformed into a wolf. Dark-gray fur rolled over his massive body, standing in a ridge along his back. Baring his razor-sharp fangs, he prowled toward them.

Bryce's heart slammed into his throat, and he squeezed the trigger, firing a shot into the wolf's shoulder.

Eric paused and shook his coat as if the bullet had merely stung his skin. Then he rocked back on his haunches and sprang.

"No!" Alexis screamed as she shoved Bryce against the wall and turned into a wolf in mid-air. She lunged at Eric, and Bryce stood motionless as they tumbled over each other snapping and biting at their necks. Alexis yelped, and blood matted in her sandy-colored fur above her shoulder.

Gripping his gun in both hands, Bryce pointed it at the bigger wolf, but he couldn't get a clear shot. A gray wolf appeared behind them, but a black one latched onto its neck and dragged it into the living room. Bryce couldn't tell which one was James, so he'd have to let them fight it out. But Alexis, he would save…if she'd get out of his way.

"Alexis, move," he shouted.

She faltered, whipping her head around to look at him, and Eric latched on to her neck. Lifting her from the ground, he hurled her massive body toward Bryce, and she slammed into him, the momentum busting open the door.

He landed on his back, with Alexis the wolf on top of him, and the air left his lungs in a gush as the gun skidded across the floor. Alexis scrambled to her feet, and Bryce blinked until his vision focused on his surroundings. Musical instruments hung from the padded walls, and the sounds of the other werewolf fight ceased. This must have been the sound-proof room she'd told him about.

Eric's massive body filled the doorway, blood matting his dark fur on his neck and shoulder. Alexis barreled toward him, but he tossed her aside as if she weighed nothing, slamming her into the wall.

"Alexis!" *That's it. This guy is dead.* He scrambled for his gun, but Eric leapt at him, clamping his jaws onto his shoulder. Bryce let out a garbled yelp as dagger-like teeth sliced through skin and muscle, shooting searing pain through his core. With a jerk of his head, Eric dragged him away from the gun and swiped his claws across his stomach.

The flesh on Bryce's abdomen ripped open, the wolf's claws penetrating to the organs beneath. Pain exploded through his gut, first as the pressure of a Mack truck rolling over him, and then the burning, stinging sensation and fear that his guts would spill onto the floor. He groaned as the massive wolf loomed over him, his body growing cold beneath the animal's heated breath. Paralyzed in agony, Bryce gasped for air and turned his head toward where Alexis had lain, his only thought that she should be the last thing he saw before he left the world.

She was gone.

His vision tunneled, and he straightened his head to look into his killer's eyes. Eric reared back, opening his maw for another strike, and time slowed to a crawl. Numbness spread through Bryce's body as he stared into the werewolf's open mouth. Hot saliva dripped from Eric's canines and splashed onto Bryce's cheek. His heart should have been pounding as the teeth neared his throat, but the sluggish muscle barely beat in his chest. He couldn't move. Couldn't fight back, so he prayed for a quick ending.

The explosion of a gunshot pierced the room, and the wolf's head jerked to the side. Another shot, and it went limp, collapsing on top of him, the pressure shooting another burst of agonizing pain through Bryce's body. Stars danced in his wavering vision as the weight of the wolf was lifted, and Alexis's emerald eyes came into view.

Worry knit her brow as she knelt beside him, and he tried to focus on the beauty of her human face. Her flawless skin. Her cropped, blonde hair sticking out in every direction. Darkness closed in around him as he opened his mouth, and no words would pass from his lips. Alexis was alive—uninjured—and he'd go to his grave with the satisfaction of knowing that she'd survived.

She rested her hands on his stomach. "He got you pretty good." Her lip trembled, and a tear slid down her cheek. "You've lost a lot of blood, but I'm going to fix you, and then we'll get you to the hospital. Hold on for me, okay, Bryce?"

He wanted to nod. To tell her yes, he would hold on. That he'd never leave her. But his head spun and his lids fluttered shut, betraying his intentions. His abdomen tingled where she touched him. He forced his eyes open to meet her gaze, and streams of tears ran in rivulets down her face.

"James!" she screamed, her voice hoarse and trembling. "If you're done with Trevor, I could use some help." Her skin paled, and she swayed as she moved toward his shoulder. She closed her eyes and tipped to the side, catching herself with her hand before her head smacked the tile floor.

"Alexis." Bryce's voice came out as a croak.

"I'm here." She sat up and clutched her head. "I healed your stomach. Your shoulder's in pretty bad shape too."

"Stop." He forced the words through his thickening throat. "You're draining yourself."

"I'll be fine." Though her voice sounded calm, it didn't mask the anguish in her eyes. "Let me heal you so we can go home."

He touched his stomach. Cooling blood congealed on his torn shirt, but he couldn't find a trace of injury. Lifting a hand to her face, he brushed the hair from her forehead, leaving a swipe of red across her skin, and she closed her eyes, nuzzling her cheek into his palm. "Where is home?" he asked.

She smiled weakly. "It's anywhere you are, dummy."

A werewolf snarled behind her, and as she turned toward it, the wolf lunged, clamping onto her throat. It shook her violently, dropping her on top of Bryce, and her body fell limp. Lifeless.

The growl of a second wolf and sounds of another fight retreating through the open door barely registered in his mind, and the pain shooting through his shoulder paled in comparison to the agony of his heart wrenching in his chest.

"Alexis?" His throat thickened, and tears stung his eyes as he tried to move her with his good arm. Her head lolled like her neck had been snapped, and his breath hitched. *No.*

She couldn't be dead. She was his soul mate. The woman he was meant to spend the rest of his life with. "Darlin', you have to heal yourself." He stroked her matted hair and then rested his hand on her back, searching for the gentle rise and fall to prove she was breathing. That she was healing.

She lay utterly still.

This couldn't be happening. She had to live. This amazing woman who could heal with a touch had accepted him for who he was, and she'd taught him to accept himself. She meant the world to him; she couldn't be gone. "Come on, sweetheart. Don't leave me now." Damn it, he needed her. Tears rolled down his cheeks, choking his words. "I love you."

When she didn't respond, a sob bubbled up from somewhere deep in his soul—the sound of his heart breaking beyond repair.

He nudged her, and blood gushed from her wound, flowing into the gash on his shoulder.

It seared the exposed muscle, and the fiery sensation shot down his arm and into his chest, spreading through his body as if he were being burned from the inside out. He tried to scream, but he couldn't get any air into his scorched lungs. An inferno raged inside his body, and agony consumed him as a burst of blinding white light flashed in his vision.

Then the world went dark.

CHAPTER TWENTY

ALEXIS GASPED AND SHOT TO A SITTING POSITION. "BRYCE!" HER heart sprinted as she clutched a soft fabric in her hands and blinked her eyes into focus. "Where?"

"He's here." Macey sat next to the bed and gestured to the spot beside Alexis.

A knot formed in her throat as she shifted her gaze to Bryce. He lay on his back, his arms by his sides, a peaceful expression softening his handsome features. Too peaceful. "Is he…?"

"He's alive."

"Oh, thank God." She reached for him, running her fingers down the side of his face, and a tingling sensation seeped into her skin. She cupped his cheek in her hand, and the faint prickling shimmied up her arm. "Why do I feel magic in him?"

"We were hoping you could answer that." Luke stood beside Macey and rested a hand on her shoulder. "James found you both unconscious on the floor. He thought you were dead."

She looked from Luke to Macey and finally took in her surroundings. Sheer drapes covered a bay window, and morning sunlight filtered through the glass, softly illuminating the bedroom. She sat in their bed, the alabaster duvet covering her legs. The white cotton T-shirt and flannel pajamas pants she wore didn't belong to her, and as she ran her fingers through her hair, flakes of dried blood drifted onto her lap.

Blood. Her breath caught. *Bryce's shoulder.*

She put her hand on his chest and gazed at his unmarred skin. No trace of the bite marks remained. Tugging on the neck of his shirt, she moved it aside to see what should have been a massive gash. He was uninjured. She hadn't healed him, had she?

"Can you tell us what happened?" Macey put her hand on Alexis's leg.

Alexis blinked, her mind reeling to understand. "I was healing him. Eric had torn him up, and I healed his stomach. I shouted for James, and I was about to heal his shoulder when…" She cupped her neck in her hands. "Trevor tried to rip my throat out. He broke my neck." Her body trembled as the memory ran through her mind. "What happened to James?"

"I'm fine." He stood in the doorway, leaning against the jamb. "Sorry, Trevor got away from me. I took care of him, but I really thought you were dead. There was blood all over you. All over him. I thought it was Bryce's blood, but when I rolled you off him, he didn't have a scratch. Your neck healed pretty quick after that, but neither of you would wake up."

"How did we get here? What's going to happen?" She took Bryce's hand, lacing her fingers through his. The same faint tingle of magic seeped from his warm palm. "Is Bryce…did Eric turn him?"

"Rain is on her way over to read his aura." Macey squeezed her leg and stood.

Luke put his arm around her. "I don't think Eric turned him. The shot to the head killed him, but he didn't lose much blood before that. Only werewolf blood—a lot of it—has the power to turn a human into a shifter."

Blood. That was why Eric's plan didn't work. It never would have worked, no matter how violently he attacked his victims, but… "Then why does Bryce have a magical signature?" She rubbed her temple, trying to put the pieces together, but it didn't make sense. Bryce had lost too much blood. Even with her healing powers, she couldn't have saved him without a transfusion. He'd needed a hospital.

"We think you turned him." Macey gave her a sympathetic look.

She gazed at Bryce. "But it's not possible."

"It's possible," Luke said. "If he lost enough blood, and then yours mixed with his...with your healing ability...he could have magic in his veins now."

Magic in his veins? *Her* magic. What had she done?

Bryce drew in a deep breath and mumbled, "Alexis."

"I'm here." She put her hand on his cheek and hovered her face above his.

His lids fluttered open, and his brow pinched in confusion. "How? I watched you die."

"I'm not that easy to kill." She smiled and stroked the hair away from his face. She may have forced him into a supernatural life, but he was alive. That mattered most. "How do you feel?"

He rubbed his shoulder where the bite had been and glanced down at his body. "Not hurt." He pushed to a sitting position and leaned his back against the headboard. "But not quite...right."

He looked at Luke and Macey, and his eyes widened as if he'd just realized they were there. "Where?" His gaze danced around the room, and he clutched his shirt.

"You're in our house," Macey said.

"Whose clothes are these?"

"They're mine." Luke shuffled closer to him and bent down to look into his eyes. "You're not in any pain?"

"Surprisingly, no." He tossed back the blanket and swung his legs over the side of the bed. "I feel weird though. What happened?"

James pushed from the wall and sauntered toward him. "We got your girl."

Bryce looked over his shoulder at Alexis and took her hand, pulling her toward him. "We sure did."

She moved to sit next to him, holding his hand in both of hers. "Eric is dead." Her chest tightened, and she looked at Luke. "I don't want to cause any trouble with the pack. Should I...leave?"

Bryce's grip on her hand tightened. She didn't want to go

anywhere without this man, but if killing Eric would bring war to the pack, she'd have no choice.

Luke shook his head. "You stopped a madman who was breaking the law. You don't have to go anywhere."

She let out a slow breath and leaned into Bryce's side.

"We found a body in Trevor's fridge," James said. "Found his roommate casing Michael's house, and he was in on it too. Confessed to the whole plan."

"I've contacted the national congress and Biloxi." Luke crossed his arms. "We're in agreement that Eric was to blame and he was killed in self-defense."

Alexis nodded. The ordeal had been messier than she'd planned, but it was over. Eric couldn't hurt anyone else.

The doorbell rang, and she glanced at Bryce. "That'll be Rain."

"I'll let her in." James strode out of the bedroom.

"More company?" Bryce gestured to the sweatpants he wore. "I'm not dressed for guests."

"We need her to read your aura," Macey said. "If you're both feeling okay, let's move to the living room."

Bryce stood. "My aura? That's really a thing?" He shook his head. "Of course it's a thing. I keep having to remind myself this is all real."

Alexis held tight to his hand as Luke and Macey shuffled into the living room. The guilt of not revealing her secret to Bryce herself gnawed in her gut. She was done keeping things from this man. Moving to face him, she rested her hands on his shoulders. "I need you to know something."

He grasped her hips and gazed into her eyes. "Tell me you didn't mean what you said before about wanting to be with Eric."

The lies ended now too. From this moment on, she planned to tell him everything. She swallowed the thickness from her throat. "I didn't mean a word of it. I was trying to stop him."

His lips tugged into a smile. "That's all I need to know." He flicked his gaze to the door and leaned in, taking her mouth with his. Vibrating energy danced across her lips, shooting straight to her heart.

She'd been an idiot to think she could handle Eric on her own, defaulting to her old ways when her future stood right in front of her.

When she'd held her fate-bound in her arms. She didn't have to be alone anymore. She had her sister, a pack who would accept her, and a man who loved her.

She brushed his lips once more and pulled away to look into his eyes. "There's something else you need to know, and it's something I should have told you a long time ago." Brushing his hair from his forehead, she cupped his face in her hand. "I love you."

He smiled. "I love you too."

She threw her arms around his shoulders and hugged him tight, the wolf and the woman rejoicing in her acceptance of what she'd known deep down all along. She belonged with him, and now, she could spend forever with him. "There's one more thing I need to tell you before we go out there. It might come as a shock."

"In the past twenty-four hours, I found out that werewolves are real and I'm in love with one. I don't think anything you can say will shock me."

She pulled from his embrace and furrowed her brow. "You might *be* a werewolf now."

He blinked.

Macey popped her head in the doorway. "Rain's ready."

"How?" Bryce cocked his head and narrowed his gaze at Alexis before following Macey into the living room.

Alexis held her breath as she sank onto the couch by Bryce. Rain sat on a chair next to the sofa, and Chase stood behind her. Macey perched on the arm of the couch, and Luke stood in front of them.

"What do you see, *cher?*" Chase asked.

Rain's eyebrows pinched as she studied Bryce, and she opened her mouth a few times as if to speak, but then she clamped her lips together.

Alexis's stomach sank. Why did she get the feeling the witch didn't have good news?

"He's…" Rain tilted her head. "He has two auras. I see a pale-blue hovering around an orange one like a halo. It's…I've never seen anything like it."

Bryce swallowed. "What does that mean?"

Alexis took his hand. "It means you have werewolf magic in your blood now."

He looked at Luke. "You said it wasn't possible. You said no one would survive the kind of attack it would take..."

"You shouldn't have survived." She drew in a shaky breath. "Your stomach was..." A shudder ran up her spine at the memory. "You'd lost so much blood." She bit her lip to hold back the tears threatening to spill down her cheeks.

His eyes widened. "It was your blood...from where the wolf bit you. It burned."

"Burned?" James gave Luke a wary look. "That doesn't sound good."

"Can you describe the burn?" Luke asked.

"It felt like my whole body was on fire. I thought I was dying." He rubbed his forehead. "What does this mean? Am I going to be like you?"

"You might." Alexis put her hand on his leg and gave him a squeeze. "Or the magic might not hold, and the moon will draw it out of you. Either way, we'll find out soon. The next full moon is tonight."

"I wouldn't mind having super strength like you guys. That's not so bad." He laughed, but it sounded forced. "And the night vision would come in handy at work."

Luke's expression turned grim. "The magic could also be too much for your body to handle. You might not make it."

Macey gasped and covered her mouth. Rain lowered her gaze to her lap as Alexis tightened her grip on Bryce's hand. He had to make it. Her blood coursed through his veins. Her power. Her healing ability. The magic—the wolf—in her blood was bound to Bryce as much as her heart was. Her wolf would never hurt the man she loved.

"Super strength," he said through clenched teeth.

"Sorry." She relaxed her grip and swallowed the bile from the back of her throat. "You're going to make it. If the magic is too much, I'll heal you. Whatever it does to your body, I'll fix it."

Bryce nodded absently and looked at Luke. "So, I might not make it through the night?"

Luke pursed his lips, his brow raising apologetically. "It's a possibility."

He pulled from her grasp and cracked his knuckles. "Hey, Mace? Can you take me home?"

"Bryce." Alexis reached for his hand, but he shot to his feet.

"I need to go home."

"I can, but, Alexis, we brought your car back," Macey said. "It's parked down the street."

Alexis stood. "I'll take you home." She couldn't begin to imagine what he must've been feeling, but she planned to be there for him through the full moon and every second that led up to it. All of this was her fault. She'd run to Eric to ensure Bryce's safety, and now he might die because of her.

Clenching her fists, she strode toward the door. She wouldn't let it happen. She couldn't live without him.

Macey padded into the hallway and returned with Alexis's backpack. "The guys found it in the bedroom." She handed it to her. "I washed your clothes, and Bryce, your keys and wallet and both your guns are in there too."

He looked at the backpack and nodded before shuffling toward Alexis. "Thank you, everyone, for your help. Really, I can't thank you enough, but I need some time alone to…" He inhaled deeply. "This is a lot to take in."

"We'll need to take you to the swamp tonight for the full moon." Luke shook his hand. "Whatever happens, you won't be alone."

"Thanks." He glanced at Alexis and walked out the door.

Bryce's mind reeled as he stepped onto Macey's front porch and jogged down the steps. He'd learned werewolves existed less than twenty-four hours ago, and now he might be one?

Or he might be dead before dawn.

The brisk morning air raised goose bumps on his skin, and he rubbed his arms to chase away the chill. Alexis followed behind, but he didn't dare turn around. With the amount of pressure building in the back of his eyes, looking at her would probably make the tears fall, and he refused to look weak in front of her.

Spotting her car on the curb, he slid into the passenger seat, closing the door before she caught up. He managed two deep breaths before she got in the driver's side. She shoved the key into the ignition and started the car, but she didn't drive.

Dropping her hands into her lap, she looked at him with sadness in her eyes. "Please talk to me. Tell me what you're thinking."

What *was* he thinking? Between the strange electrical sensation tingling through his body and the news that he might have less than twelve hours to live, not a single coherent thought had formed in his mind in the last twenty minutes. "Take me home. Please."

Her breath caught, and she nodded before pulling away from the curb. They meandered through the French Quarter, and Bryce stared out the window at the architecture. The festive displays in the windows of the historic buildings reminded him of the upcoming holidays.

He glanced at Alexis, who clutched the steering wheel in a death grip and stared straight ahead. He might not see Christmas this year— or tomorrow for that matter—but if he did survive, and she stuck around, he wouldn't have to spend another holiday alone.

He needed to say something. To let her know he planned to spend the rest of his life with her, whether that meant the rest of today or the next fifty years. But he couldn't make his mouth form the words. Instead, he shifted his gaze to the scenery.

They reached Canal Street and stopped at a light, waiting for a streetcar to pass before heading onto St. Charles and leaving the French Quarter behind. Highrise hotels and more modern architecture replaced the nineteenth-century buildings, and the roads widened as the traffic increased.

They entered the Central Business District, and he glanced up at the twelve-story building where Michael's life had almost come to an end. A heaviness settled on his shoulders. Would the kid and his mom be safe living below him now that he was part of this supernatural world? At least they were moving in two weeks, but what would happen with the new neighbors?

As they left the CBD and approached the Garden District, he admired the Colonial and Greek Revival houses. How many times had he driven by these homes, not even noticing the grand columns and pristine gardens surrounding the structures? Today, he took it all in. The ornate fences, the detailed trim, the elaborate wreaths hanging from the doors, and the Christmas trees illuminating the windows. He'd overlooked the beauty of this city for far too long.

The beauty of life.

Alexis turned onto his street and stopped on the curb in front of his house. "Here we are."

"Home sweet home." He reached for the handle.

She put her hand on his thigh. "Can I come inside?"

He glanced at her, and the pressure in his eyes built again so he looked away. "I expected you to."

As he climbed out of the car, Karen's front door opened, and she struggled to drag a giant suitcase down the porch steps. He jogged toward her and lifted it from the ground. "Where you headed?"

She hit a button on her key fob, and her car chirped, unlocking the doors. "To my mom's."

"I thought you were staying another two weeks." He followed her to the driveway, lugging the suitcase.

"After what happened yesterday, I…" She opened the trunk, and Bryce put the bag inside. "I want to get Michael away. It's time."

"I understand." They'd be safer there, and if he didn't make it tonight, at least they'd be far away. "Take care of yourself." He gave her a hug.

"Oh, I have something for you." She rummaged in her purse and pulled out a white envelope. Handing it to him, she glanced toward Alexis's car and gave him a half-smile. "It's a gift certificate for couple's cooking classes. I thought it might be something you'd have fun doing together."

She turned to Alexis as she approached. "I'm sorry we got off on the wrong foot. I judged you when I should have gotten to know you."

Alexis smiled. "Thank you."

"Take care of him. He likes to pretend he can handle himself, but he needs a good woman around."

"I will."

Michael brought out another suitcase and paused, his gaze cutting from Bryce to Alexis. The corners of his mouth twitched like he wasn't sure if he should smile or not. "Is…everything okay?"

Bryce forced a smile. "Never better. I'll see you around, kid."

"Bye, Sergeant Samuels."

Alexis slung her backpack over her shoulder and followed him up the stairs. As they reached the landing, she handed him his keys, and he unlocked the door. Silence greeted him as he stepped into the living room, and a sense of calm settled in his core.

"Where's Sam?" Alexis asked.

"He's at the emergency vet. Someone beat him up when they kidnapped Michael. Do you have my phone?"

She dug in her backpack and handed it to him. He had several missed calls and a voicemail from the vet. As he listened to the message, he let out a slow breath. "He's okay. I'm going to take a shower and go pick him up."

"I can get him. He'll be good as new by the time I get him home." She smiled weakly. "It's my fault he got hurt to begin with."

"It's not your fault." None of this was her fault. He'd gotten involved of his own free will, and he'd tell her so if he could compose himself enough to speak. If she'd give him five minutes to breathe, he might be able to pull all the broken pieces of his thoughts together and talk to the woman. He took a credit card from his wallet. "But if you could get him, I'd appreciate it. I'm not sure I should be driving with the way I feel."

She put a hand on his arm. "How do you feel?"

"Like I've got electricity running through my veins, battling with my blood."

"What do you feel when I touch you?"

He put his hand over hers. "Soft skin. Warmth. Concern, though I think that's because I see it in your eyes."

"Nothing else?"

"No. Should I feel something else?"

She dropped her arm to her side and lowered her gaze as her voice softened. "I guess not. I'll go get Sam."

CHAPTER TWENTY-ONE

A WEIGHT THE SIZE OF A BOWLING BALL SETTLED IN ALEXIS'S stomach as she drove to the emergency vet clinic. Getting more than two words out of Bryce had felt like wringing grape juice from a raisin. The moment he learned about the magic in his blood, he'd become distant, acting as if she were nothing more than an acquaintance.

He had every reason to hate her. She'd endangered his job...his life and Michael's...all because she was a rogue. She never should have tried to collect the money from Eric in the first place, much less gone back to him a second time to try and stop him on her own.

What the hell was her problem? She parked in the back of the clinic parking lot and smoothed the wrinkles out of her sister's shirt as she strode to the door.

The receptionist stopped talking mid-sentence and stared as Alexis made her way to the desk. "Can I help you?" Her gaze lingered on Alexis's hair.

She ran a hand through her locks, cringing as little flakes of dried blood rained down on her shoulders. She should have showered and changed clothes before she came, but Bryce had needed some alone time. "I'm here to pick up Sam, the Siberian husky."

"Right, his owner called and said to expect you." She rose to her feet, but hesitated. "Are you okay?"

Alexis smiled. "I was painting an accent wall. Forgot I got it in my hair."

The receptionist let out a nervous giggle. "A technician will be bringing him out. He'll need to lie on his side. Do you have room in your back seat?"

"Sure do." She gave the woman Bryce's credit card and cringed when she saw the eight-hundred-dollar charge. She'd pay him back, even if it took her five years to save up the money.

A door swung open, and a burly man cradling the dog in his arms stepped through. Sam whimpered, and she sucked in a sharp breath as guilt stabbed her in the heart. *Poor boy.* She stroked his head, and his tail swished.

"Thank you." She held out her arms to take the dog.

"He's heavy. I'll carry him to your car."

"I can handle it." She took Sam into her arms and shuffled toward the door. Taking a deep breath, she began healing his bruised ribs on the way to the car. As she situated him in the back seat, she focused her energy on his leg.

Her head spun as the bone mended, and she stumbled around to the driver's seat when she finished. Sam sat up and licked her cheek, leaving a trail of warm saliva on her skin.

She laughed. "Thanks, boy. We'll get the bandages off of you after we get home, okay?"

Sam let out a quiet woof and sat in the back seat. The dog had forgiven her. Now, she'd have to work on the man.

Thankfully, Karen and Michael were gone by the time she brought Sam home. She killed the engine and let out a sigh. At least she wouldn't have to explain how the dog had magically recovered. She opened the back door, and Sam jumped out and hobbled on his cast to the staircase. It took him a while to climb all the steps, which gave her time to figure out what she would say to Bryce.

A profuse apology would be step one. She'd follow that with another confession of her love…and hope he could find forgiveness somewhere in his heart.

She opened the door, and Bryce's face lit up as Sam limped inside. He dropped to his knees and took the dog in his arms. "Hey, buddy. How you feeling?" He lifted his gaze to hers but quickly looked down. "Can we take the cast off?"

Her throat tightened. Was he so angry he couldn't even look at her? "Yeah. He's all healed."

He rummaged under the sink and took out a small saw. "Can you hold him?"

"Sure." She wrapped her arms around the dog's chest as Bryce cut into the cast. Sam wiggled, desperate to be free, and Bryce grunted, making tiny back and forth motions with the saw.

Sam twisted in her arms again, and Bryce rubbed the dog's head. "Be still, buddy. I don't want to saw your leg off."

"I can probably get it from here."

The corner of his mouth twitched as he set the saw on the counter and took the dog in his arms. "Super strength?"

"Something like that." Grasping the cast in both hands, she pulled it apart at the cut he'd made. Sam shimmied free from Bryce's grasp and danced around the room, wagging his entire body.

She handed Bryce the receipt and his credit card. "I'll pay you back for this."

His eyes widened at the amount before he dropped the paper on the table. "There's no need. You saved him from a week or two of pain."

With her hand on the back of a chair, she traced her finger along the smooth wood, unable to meet his gaze. "He wouldn't have been in pain at all if it weren't for me."

Bryce rested his hands on her shoulders and finally looked her in the eyes. "None of this was your fault, so stop blaming yourself. I don't blame you."

Her breath hitched. "You don't?"

"No." He dropped his arms to his sides, and the sadness in his eyes caused his brow to pinch. "But considering what could happen tonight...I'm going to see my mom."

Sam nudged his leg, so he leaned down to pet him.

Alexis swallowed the lump from her throat. "I understand." Of course he would want to see his mom and anyone else he cared about. Spending the day with the person who doomed him to possible death wouldn't rank high on his last-day-of-life to-do list. "I'll wait here for you."

He straightened. "I was hoping you'd come with me."

She missed a beat. "Really?"

"It could be the last time I see her, and I'd like her to meet the woman I love."

A swarm of butterflies unfurled in her stomach, flitting its way up to her chest. "I thought you were mad at me."

He sighed and took her face in his hand. "I'm sorry if it seemed that way. I needed a moment to gather my thoughts, but I'm okay now. If anything, I love you more after everything that's happened." He chuckled. "I didn't think that was possible, and maybe it's because I've got your blood…your magic…running through my veins, but I feel connected to you."

He had no idea the connection she had to him. Now that he had werewolf magic inside him, could he possibly feel the bond between their hearts like she did? She rested a hand on his chest. "We're bound by fate."

"More like by blood, but you can call it fate if you want to." He shrugged. "Whatever it is…blood, magic, something supernatural…I could never be mad at you."

He didn't believe in fate, but after tonight, he would. Once the magic took hold, he'd understand. They were meant to be together. To be mates.

"I'm either going to end the night as a werewolf, a human, or dead, so I'm going to make the most of the day. Will you come meet my mom?"

She smiled and pressed a kiss to his lips. "I would love to meet your mom. Let's go."

He stepped back and gazed at her, the corner of his mouth tugging into an adorable grin. "I think you look beautiful like you are, but the nurses might not appreciate the blood in your hair."

She cringed. "Maybe I should shower?"

"Probably a good idea." He dropped onto the couch and held out his arms to Sam. The dog bounded toward him and licked his face.

Alexis shuffled toward the bathroom and paused in the doorway, turning to look at him. Her fate-bound. "I love you, Bryce. I mean that."

He smiled. "I love you too."

"Don't expect much." Bryce pressed the elevator button and took Alexis's hand. His heart felt like it was beating in his throat as the doors slid open and they stepped inside. "She might not recognize me. Sometimes she thinks I'm my brother."

"That's got to be hard." She squeezed his hand. "Don't worry about me. I'll follow your lead."

He kissed her on the cheek, and they exited the elevator, heading to his mom's room. Pausing outside the door, he took a deep breath to calm the hummingbird trying to escape his chest. He lowered his head, saying a silent prayer to whatever gods—supernatural or not— that might be listening for his mom to be coherent. If this turned out to be the last time he saw her, he'd like to go out knowing she remembered him.

Alexis rested her hand on his back, calming him. "Are you okay?"

He forced a smile. "I'm good."

Cold metal greeted his clammy palm as he twisted the knob and opened the door a crack. He leaned his face in the space between the door and the jamb. "Hey, Mom? You decent?"

"Bryce? Is that you?"

He closed his eyes and tipped his head back as he whispered, "Thank you," to whomever answered his prayer. He opened the door wider and smiled at his mom. She sat propped against a mound of pillows in her bed, her legs covered with the blue afghan she'd knitted a few years back, before the arthritis in her hands forced her to give up the hobby. Someone had curled her hair and applied bright-pink rouge to her cheeks.

Grasping Alexis's hand, he tugged her through the door. "You look like you're having a good day."

She beamed a smile, and her eyes were bright and coherent. "I am. And who is this lovely young lady?"

"I'd like you to meet my girlfriend, Alexis." His smile widened as Alexis gave his hand a squeeze.

She waved. "Hi, Mrs. Samuels. It's nice to meet you."

"Come here, hon." His mom held out her arms. "I'm a hugger. You too, Bryce, honey, I haven't seen you in ages."

He'd visited his mom last week, but she hadn't recognized him at the time. Alexis shuffled forward and leaned over the bed to give his mom a hug, and he sucked in a shaky breath. He'd never believed in fate or getting signs from above or any of that nonsense. But after everything he'd learned about the supernatural, he couldn't shake the feeling that his mom being coherent was a sign he wouldn't make it through the night. Maybe fate was granting him one last visit with his loved ones before his life ended.

"That's a beautiful ring." Alexis gestured to his mom's wedding ring.

She held it up and admired the stone. "It's been in the family for ages. It belonged to Bryce's grandma, and I think his great-great-grandma before that. Keeps getting passed down."

"What a lovely tradition." Alexis moved aside for him to hug his mom, and pressure built in the back of his eyes.

She held him tight and whispered in his ear, "She's a keeper. I like her."

"So do I." He swallowed the thickness from his throat and blinked back the moisture threatening to drip from his eyes as he settled into a chair next to Alexis.

They chatted for another twenty minutes, Bryce filling her in on how he'd come to date his ex-partner's sister after all these years working with Macey. When her lids started to flutter shut, he gave her a kiss on the cheek and led Alexis to the door.

His mom sucked in a sharp breath as she woke. "Wait, Bryce. I need to talk to you."

Alexis patted his shoulder. "I'll be in the hall."

He shuffled to his mom's bed and sat on the edge. "You should get some rest."

"I will. I will." She tugged the ring off her finger and put it in his hand. "You love this girl?"

"With all my heart."

"Then you better put that ring on her before she gets away."

He gazed at the stone, a one-carat diamond nestled in a scalloped circle of tiny diamond flecks. "Are you sure you're ready to give it up?"

She closed his fingers around the ring. "I'm ready for you to make good use of it."

He kissed her forehead. "Thanks, Mom. I will."

Bryce dropped the ring into his pocket and shuffled toward the door. Pausing with his hand on the knob, he glanced back at his mom, sleeping peacefully, and a sense of calmness settled over him. Had he come to terms with the fact that this might be his last night on Earth? Not really. But if he did go, at least the people he loved knew he cared about them.

His throat thickened as he toyed with the ring in his pocket. He'd like to drop to one knee and put it on Alexis's finger as soon as he stepped through the door, but he'd wait. If he asked her to marry him now, she might say yes out of guilt or pity, and that was no way to spend the rest of his life with the woman of his dreams.

If he survived whatever the full moon had in store for him, then he'd propose. She could say yes...or no...with a clear conscience.

A tiny smile tugged at the corners of Bryce's mouth as he stepped through the door, and Alexis couldn't help but smile in return. His nervousness had rolled off him in waves on the way to visit his mom, but now he seemed calm. Maybe even at peace with everything that had and would happen.

She took his hand. "Everything okay?"

"I never thought my fate would lie with a lunar cycle, but yeah. Let's go home." He guided her to the elevator, and they stepped inside.

She waited until the doors closed before turning to him. "I thought you didn't believe in fate?"

The elevator stopped and opened into the parking garage. "That's the first time my mom has been coherent when I've visited her in a month. It could be a coincidence, or it could be God or the *gods* or fate or…whatever…granting me one last moment with her before I die."

Pain gripped her heart, and she stopped walking. "Don't talk like that."

He took a few more steps before turning to her. "Whatever's gonna happen is gonna happen. Nothing I can do about it, right?"

"I'm not going to let you die." She marched past him and got in her car, slamming the door. This nonsense had to stop. There was no way in hell she'd let anything happen to him, and he needed to stop talking like this was the end. She started the engine and checked the clock on the radio. They had four hours until they had to meet the pack in the forest, and she intended to use those hours to show Bryce she was worth living for.

He sidled into the seat next to her and buckled his seatbelt. "I'm sorry."

"Don't." She ground her teeth as she pulled out of the parking lot and headed to his home…*their* home.

He didn't say anything else on the drive, but he reached across the console to hold her hand, and tears almost spilled from her eyes.

They greeted Sam as they entered the house, but even his signature full-body wag couldn't lift the weight pressing down on her shoulders. When he was satisfied with their affection, the husky returned to his favorite spot on the couch and curled into a fluffy ball.

Alexis looked at Bryce. "You are not going to die, so don't even mention it again today, okay?"

He knit his brow and cupped her cheek in his hand. "It's a possibility, darlin', so we have to consider it. And by the look on Luke's face, it seems highly likely."

She slapped his hand away. "No. Luke doesn't know what I can do. He's never seen me heal." She'd survived a hundred-foot fall from an electrical tower that broke every bone in her body. The same magic that saved her now ran through Bryce's veins. Fate didn't lead her to this man—give her the ability to heal him—to take him away from her when she needed him most. He *would* survive this. He had to.

"You said yourself you can only heal physical injuries. This one might be in my blood."

Her entire core tightened, twisting her insides until she couldn't breathe. She grabbed his shoulders and shook him. "I can't lose you. Do you understand? For the first time in my life, I've found something worth staying for. That something is you, Bryce. You've made this place my home. *You* are my home."

A thousand emotions danced with the brown and green flecks in his eyes as she held his gaze, and the corner of his mouth tugged into a grin. "That's the nicest thing anyone's ever said to me. I still might die, though."

"Stop talking." She took his mouth with hers, and the tingle of werewolf magic on his skin mingled with the electricity shooting through her body. He responded with a masculine growl emanating from somewhere deep in his core as he slid his arms around her waist and pulled her close.

A spark of hope ignited in her chest. She'd never heard such a wolf-like growl from Bryce before. Taking his face in her hands, she pressed her forehead to his. "What do you feel when I touch you?"

He kissed her jaw, trailing his lips down the curve of her neck before whispering in her ear, "Passion. Adoration. Love."

Sweet, but not the answer she wanted to hear. "Do you feel my magic?"

"Everything about you is magical." He gripped the hem of her shirt and tugged it over her head before stepping back to admire her. "Wondrous." Grabbing the back of his shirt, he yanked it over his head.

She ran her hands up his chest, resting them on his shoulders. "You don't feel a tingling sensation when I touch you?"

"Should I?"

She lowered her gaze. "If you were a werewolf, you would."

"Hey." He hooked his finger under her chin, lifting her head toward his. "That's not to say I won't be after the moon comes out. We have no idea what's going to happen tonight, so let's enjoy right now while we can."

She inhaled deeply and gazed at him. Whatever fate had planned, she couldn't do anything about it now. All they could control was this moment. "That's the best idea I've heard all day."

With his hand on the small of her back, he pulled her to his body, taking her mouth in a kiss. She parted her lips, and as her tongue brushed his, fire shot through her veins. This was *her* man. Whether he became a werewolf or stayed human, she didn't give a damn. At this moment, he had magic in his veins, and that magic called to her, awakening a primal instinct in her soul. The overwhelming need to possess him had her burning with desire. Throwing her arms around his neck, she pushed him against the wall and crushed her body to his.

He grunted and broke the kiss. "Watch out with that super strength. I know you can heal me, but I'd rather not get broken."

She nipped at his collarbone, gliding her tongue up his neck to take his earlobe between her teeth. "I'm sorry. You have no idea what it's like to finally be able to be my true self with someone. For you to know everything about me and want me anyway."

"I know *exactly* how you feel." The heat of his breathy whisper warmed her ear, sending shivers down to her toes.

She fumbled with his belt, trailing kisses across his chest, as she finally unbuckled it and yanked it from his jeans. She couldn't undress him fast enough. Jerking at the buttons on his fly, she shoved the rest of his clothes to floor and took his dick in her hand. She needed to be closer. To be part of him. To make him understand how much he meant to her and that dying was not an option for him tonight or any night in the next fifty years.

Gripping her hips, he leaned his head against the wall, his lids fluttering shut as she stroked him. He was thick and hard, and as a bead of moisture collected on his tip, she had to taste him. Lowering her head, she circled her tongue around him before taking him into her mouth and reveling in the salty-sweet taste of him.

Sliding his fingers into her hair, he rested his hand on her head—not to move her or force her into a rhythm—but to gently caress her scalp as she sucked him.

Another growl rumbled from his chest, and he stilled her head, moving his hand to her shoulder to guide her back up to his mouth. He undid her pants as he kissed her, working them over her hips and pushing her clothes to the floor.

He toed off his shoes and stumbled out of his jeans before grabbing her by the ass and lifting her onto the table. Pushing her onto her back, he dragged a hand down her body and stroked her clit with his thumb.

Electricity shot through her core, and she bit her bottom lip as he pulled her pants from her ankles and spread her legs with his broad shoulders. He caressed her inner thighs, and she rose onto her elbows to find him gazing at her with so much passion in his eyes that it took her breath away.

"You're so beautiful, Alexis."

"I need you inside me. Please."

He pressed his lips to one thigh, and then the other. "If this is my last night on Earth, I want to savor you first."

"Stop saying—"

The warmth of his tongue bathed her sensitive nub, taking the words from her lips. She lay back and closed her eyes as he lifted her legs onto his shoulders and stroked her folds before slipping a finger inside her. She sucked in a breath between her teeth when his tongue circled her clit again. An *mmm* vibrated across his lips, the sensation intensifying the climax coiling in her core.

He continued pleasuring her, adding a second finger inside, working her in circles until she lost control. Her orgasm slammed into her center, ricocheting through her soul and shattering her senses. She tangled her fingers in his hair, panting his name until he brought her down. But she was far from satisfied.

She needed this man inside her like she'd never needed anything in her life. Sitting up, she pushed him into a chair and straddled him. He inhaled deeply, gazing at her with passion-drunk eyes as she guided his cock to her center.

He moaned as she sheathed him, and she stilled, pressing her naked body to his, memorizing the way he filled her, relishing the magic emanating from his skin. Taking his face in her hands, she pressed her forehead to his. "I love you, Bryce."

"I love you more than you can imagine."

"I can imagine." She rocked her hips, and he gripped her thighs as he sucked in a sharp breath.

Clutching his shoulders, she held him close as she moved up and down his thick shaft, delicious friction making every nerve in her body hum. He held her hips, moving his own in unison, creating a choreography that felt as if it were ingrained in her soul. She belonged to this man. Every part of her.

His rhythm increased, each thrust of his hips sending a thrilling jolt through her core. Her climax built slowly, steadily, and when her name crossed his lips in his growl of release, she lost control. Her orgasm consumed her, burning her in its flames, and Bryce raised her from the ashes.

A sleepy, satisfied smile curved his lips as he ran his fingers through her hair. "Talk about going out with a bang."

This would not be the last time she made love to him. They had many, many years ahead of them, and tonight was only the beginning.

So, why did her throat thicken at the thought? Tears she'd refused to shed collected on her lower lids, and she wrapped her arms around his shoulders, burying her face in his neck to hide them.

He held her and stroked the back of her head. "Are you crying?"

"No."

"Then your eyes are leaking on my neck. Hey." He gently pushed her back to look at her. "I'm sorry. I shouldn't have said that."

"No, you shouldn't have. You're not going to die."

"You're right." He touched his own chest and then hers. "This connection I feel with you is going to hold me here. I haven't spent nearly enough time with you, and if fate decides it's my time to go, well...fate can kiss my ass."

CHAPTER TWENTY-TWO

BRYCE HELD ALEXIS'S HAND AS THEY CREPT TOWARD A CLEARING in the trees. The sinking sun cast long, jagged shadows across the forest floor, and the sound of dry leaves crunching beneath his boots filled the silence. The sense of calm he'd achieved with Alexis earlier was slowly draining away, and a ball of nervousness twisted in his gut.

A week ago, no amount of money would have been enough to convince him to venture into the swamp at night unarmed. Snakes, gators, and who-knew-what other kinds of creatures lurked in the shadows, waiting to make an unsuspecting human their next meal.

Well, now he did know what other kind of creatures hunted these woods, and all he could do was hope they didn't have the taste for human flesh.

Alexis squeezed his hand. "Almost there. Luke and some other weres will be there to help you if you shift, and I won't leave your side no matter what happens. You won't be alone through any of this."

If he shifted. But if he didn't? "What do werewolves eat?"

"Boar, gator, whatever. You can start with a prey animal—a deer or even a nutria for your first hunt."

"Swamp rat?" He curled his lip. The idea of killing any animal with his mouth and then eating it raw made his stomach churn.

She shrugged. "It's what I went for my first time. Of course, I was hunting alone and had no clue if I'd even turn human again."

"That must have been scary."

"It was terrifying." She stopped walking and looked at him. "But it won't be like that for you. You've got a pack and a woman who loves you to guide you through it."

Her words loosened the knot in his chest. For once in his life, being alone didn't sound the slightest bit appealing. "Do werewolves ever eat humans?"

Now it was her turn to curl her lip in disgust. "We aren't cannibals."

"You aren't exactly human."

"We are half-human, and that's the side that's in control. Even in wolf form, our human minds are fully functioning." She cupped his cheek in her hand. "Don't be scared. No one is going to hurt you tonight."

He stiffened. "I'm not scared."

She kissed him on the cheek. "I would be."

Who was he kidding? He was scared shitless. Not that he thought his friends would actually eat him, but the list of things that could go wrong tonight was too long to count.

They reached the clearing and found Luke standing with his thick arms crossed over his chest. Was the alpha always the biggest man in the pack? Once the shock of this situation wore off, he'd have to wrangle the mess of questions running through his mind into a manageable list.

Chase leaned casually against a tree trunk, and James stood with his hands in his pockets as if a bunch of French Quarter men hanging out in the swamp was the most natural thing in the world. For these men, he supposed it was.

Alexis nodded at the alpha, and he stepped forward to shake Bryce's hand. "Welcome to our hunting grounds. This goes without saying, but no one can know about us or where we hunt."

"Your secret's safe with me." He stared into the trees. "I'm still having a hard time believing it myself."

Alexis held his bicep. "Even after everything you've seen?"

"When you've been a skeptic your entire life, and you're suddenly thrust into a world you never knew—refused to believe—existed, it takes a while for your brain to catch up."

Chase pushed from the tree and strode toward them. "We're running out of daylight. You ready?"

His pulse thrummed. Could he ever be prepared for what could possibly happen to him in the next few minutes? "As I'll ever be. Hey, can you really talk to ghosts?"

Chase laughed. "Nah. I'm just a werewolf."

"So those weird cases you helped on…"

"I was determining if they were supernatural or not and what evidence we'd need to hide. We're like the paranormal police force of New Orleans."

The pieces of the puzzle finally clicked into place. All the evidence that went missing over the years wasn't from poor management of the lab and the morgue. The werewolves had been stealing it. And if Bryce became a werewolf, he'd have to find a balance between enforcing the law like he'd been doing his entire adult life and breaking it to keep supernatural secrets.

Could he do that? If the safety of humanity was at stake, he damn well could. Super strength. The task of protecting humans from real-life monsters. This werewolf gig didn't sound half-bad.

James grinned. "Breaking laws has its advantages." Luke cut him a sideways glance, and he stiffened. "Only human laws. I never break pack laws." He clapped Luke on the shoulder and winked. "I swear."

The last rays of sun disappeared behind the horizon, and everyone looked at Bryce.

Alexis wrapped her arms around his waist. "How do you feel?"

He took a deep breath and focused on his body. The hormones he'd released by making love to Alexis continued to course through his veins, giving him a natural high. But adrenaline and—if he were honest with himself—a trickle of dread created a nauseating, hyper sensation that made him feel like he needed to jump out of his own skin.

Otherwise…nothing unusual. "Honestly, I feel completely human. I don't even feel that battle in my blood anymore."

She furrowed her brow and took his face in her hands. "I feel the magic on your skin." Every time she mentioned the magic she felt in him, she got a hopeful look in her eyes. While he'd be thrilled if he simply survived the night, he couldn't shake the feeling Alexis wanted him to be a werewolf. With all the things he *couldn't* do as a human, he didn't blame her.

He took her hands and held them against his chest. "You want there to be magic in me, don't you?"

"I couldn't care less. I want you to be you, whether the magic binds with your soul or leaves you completely. As long as you're my sexy, sci-fi loving, introverted, tough guy, I'll be the happiest woman in the world." She held his gaze with conviction in her eyes. She meant every word.

Maybe he wasn't a fake after all. If she could be both a wolf and a woman, why couldn't he be the scrawny, bullied kid from his past and the cop of today? Hell, he could even be a wolf too. They were all parts that made up the whole, and he was done hiding behind a mask.

"Feeling anything yet?" James asked.

He shook his head. "If I shift, is it going to hurt?"

"It shouldn't." Alexis kissed his cheek.

"Well…" Luke rubbed at the scruff on his face. "It might. Werewolves are born with the magic already ingrained in their souls. Yours needs to bond with your blood, so it might be painful at first." His eyes tightened. "It probably will be."

"Fantastic." He tipped his head back and looked at the moon. A light mist of clouds stretched across the silver sphere, and stars glistened around it. How could a hunk of rock orbiting the Earth have so much control over his future? He sighed and shook his head. If it could control the tides, why not his fate?

"Still nothing?" Alexis asked.

"Do I need to say some kind of magic chant or pray to the moon god or something?"

They all chuckled, but he'd been serious.

He let out his breath in a huff. "Maybe nothing's going to happen. Maybe—" He clutched his stomach as a burning sensation expanded in his gut.

Alexis grabbed his shoulders. "Are you okay?"

"Unless this is really bad heartburn, no." He doubled over, supporting himself with his hands on his knees. "God, it feels like it did when you bled on me." His jaw involuntarily clenched, his teeth cutting into his tongue. The coppery taste of blood filled his mouth, and he dry-heaved as the burning intensified.

Alexis held on to him, pressing her lips to his ear. "I'm here. Whatever happens, I'm here."

He spit blood onto the ground, and she gasped. "Oh, God. What's hurt? Let me heal you. Is it your stomach?" She tried to make him stand upright, but he pushed her away.

"I bit my tongue. I'm fine." He dropped to his knees. His blood burned like acid, each beat of his heart forcing another pulse of caustic sludge through his veins. He wanted to scream, but he couldn't get enough air into his lungs.

Alexis knelt beside him and wrapped her arms around him. "Why is it hurting him so bad?" she screamed at Luke. "Why is it taking so long?"

"I don't know. Nothing like this has happened in hundreds of years. This is new territory for all of us."

Bryce squeezed his eyes shut and prayed for a quick ending. He would either spontaneously combust or he'd black out from the pain. At this point, he'd take either.

"I don't know what to heal." Alexis rubbed his back. "I can't find anything broken."

"It's okay." He forced the words out in a breathy whisper as he turned his gaze to meet hers. "If this ends the way it feels like it's going to end, please know that I loved you with every fiber of my being."

Tears streamed down her cheeks. "You're not going to die. Do something, Luke!"

Luke straightened his spine and nodded. "Everyone shift. Maybe seeing our wolves will bring his out."

Bryce squinted through his wavering vision as Luke, Chase, and James became wolves. They circled him, their intelligent eyes boring into him as if they were willing him to shift too. "That's not helping."

Alexis stroked his hair. "I'm going to shift too. It's my magic doing this to you, so maybe *my* wolf needs to bring yours out."

He nodded and dropped his hands to the ground to stop himself from collapsing.

"I won't be able to talk once I shift, but I'll still be me, okay? Just...whatever is happening inside you...don't fight it. Give in and let the magic take over." She rose to her feet. "I love you, Bryce."

Her body shimmered, and in seconds, she transformed into a beautiful, sandy-colored wolf. She lay on her stomach, resting her head between her paws, and gazed at him with emerald-green eyes.

His chest squeezed, and a swarm of wasps seemed to come to life in his stomach. The stinging, fluttering sensation spread through his body, electrifying his veins and making his head spin. He closed his eyes to stave off the dizzying effect and tensed his muscles against the pain.

Don't fight it. Alexis's words rang in his ears. *Let the magic take over.*

He inhaled the deepest breath his starving lungs would allow, and then he let go. Collapsing onto his side, he let the world slip away and focused on Alexis's eyes. Her gaze grounded him, her wolf silently calling to something deep in his core, and a cooling sensation spread from his chest out to his fingers and toes.

His body vibrated, and Alexis rose to her feet. She whimpered as she took a tentative step toward him and nudged his shoulder with her nose. Something inside him responded, and the vibration intensified until it consumed every cell in his body.

Then, it stopped. The pain ceased. He inhaled a deep breath and was met with an array of scents from the swampy forest. Dirt, cypress, decaying foliage, and the distinct aroma of dog fur danced in his senses.

He lifted his head and gazed at the wolves surrounding him. The forest seemed almost as bright as day. Raising his gaze to the full moon above, a shudder ran through his body, and he shot to his feet.

No...to his paws. And did he have a...? He swished his tail, and Alexis trotted toward him, bathing his face with her tongue. He was an honest-to-God werewolf.

He tried to laugh, but the sound came out as a grunt. Alexis nudged him toward the bayou, and he gazed at his reflection in the water. Dappled, reddish-brown fur covered his entire body, but his hazel eyes somehow looked like his own.

His stomach growled, and the urge to hunt overwhelmed him. He looked at Alexis, and she met his gaze, seeming to understand what he needed. Somehow, the thought *follow my lead* entered his mind, and he knew it came from her. Could he read her mind?

He stared at her intently, trying to figure out her thoughts, but what he received was more of a feeling. She was urging him to hunt with the pack, though no words were exchanged telepathically.

He turned around to find the other wolves watching him, and Luke's command to follow him registered in his mind. Bryce hesitated. Hunting had never appealed to him before, and he expected to be repulsed at the idea. But his wolf's needs outweighed his own.

He ran with the pack, reveling in the exhilaration of the hunt and the sensation of using his senses for what felt like the first time. Every sound, from leaves crunching underfoot to rodents scurrying to hide, registered in ears, and the scents of the forest delighted his senses.

Alexis stayed by his side, silently guiding him, being a calming force like she had been since he awakened with magic in his blood. Magic that it seemed would be with him forever now.

As the expedition concluded, the rest of the wolves shifted back into human form, laughing and congratulating each other on their successful hunt. Bryce's heart thrummed as Alexis sashayed toward him, her hips swaying and a smile lighting on her lips. He had no clue how to turn human again and no way to tell her his problem.

She took his face in her hands and stroked his fur. "You are the sexiest wolf I've ever seen, but you're even sexier as a man. Come back to me, Bryce."

He whimpered.

"Focus your intent and imagine yourself human again. Let the magic running through your veins change you."

He blew out a hard breath through his nostrils and did as she said. As the image of himself as a human formed in his mind, his body vibrated, the sensation running up and down his form in a wave as he transformed into himself.

As soon as he was upright, Alexis hugged him and showered his face in kisses. His skin tingled each time her lips brushed his cheeks, and as she took his mouth with hers, magical energy shot straight to his heart. "Is this what you were wanting me to feel before? This electricity dancing on your skin?"

Her smile brightened her eyes. "Yes, it is."

He felt it, and his love for her had grown exponentially in a matter of minutes. The wolf inside him loved her as much as he did, and it was time to make her his. He sucked in a sharp breath and pressed his hands to his pockets. "Oh, shit." Where was the ring?

Alexis laughed. "Everything you had on you is there. It gets absorbed by the magic and returns to its proper place when you shift back."

He ran his finger around the circle of metal in his pocket and let out a breath.

The men approached, and Luke clapped him on the shoulder. "Glad to have you back, my friend. Macey insists y'all come by the bar to celebrate."

Alexis took his hand. "Is that okay with you? We can stop by tomorrow if you're too overwhelmed."

A few days ago, his first instinct would have been to say no. To retreat to the quiet and comfort of his home. But he was a pack animal now, and he couldn't ignore the new duality of his nature. His wolf craved the company of his friends. "I'm the first human-turned-werewolf in hundreds of years. I'd say that's something to celebrate."

"I'd also like you to join the pack," Luke said. "You can be rogue if you want." He glanced at Alexis. "But there are benefits to joining the pack…if you don't mind following a few more rules."

Bryce laughed. "More rules? Where do I sign up?"

Luke smiled. "Let's not waste the full moon then. We can perform the induction ceremony when we get back."

"I want to join too." Alexis wrapped an arm around Bryce's bicep. "I'm ready to stay in one place, if you'll have me."

"How can I say no to my mate's sister? Macey will be thrilled." Luke shook both their hands. "I'll see you two at the bar."

Alexis started to follow Luke and the others, but Bryce didn't move. Slipping his hand into his pocket, he moved his lips as if silently practicing lines for a play. He must have been overwhelmed, his mind reeling.

The first time Alexis had shifted, she'd felt the call of the moon and run deep into the woods. But what happened once she'd gotten there had turned her entire world upside down. She could imagine what Bryce must have been feeling, but he'd have the pack and her for the rest of his life. He'd be fine if she could get him out of the woods and back to humanity.

She laced her fingers through his and gave his arm a gentle tug. "We don't want to keep the alpha waiting."

He blinked, focusing on her. "No, I guess we don't."

She led him to her car, and they rode in silence to the bar, Bryce letting everything sink in, and Alexis basking in the joy that her fate-bound had survived. They parked a block away, and as soon as they reached the sidewalk in front of the bar, Macey ran out and threw her arms around Bryce's waist.

"I'm so glad you're okay." She hugged him tightly and grinned at Alexis. "I bet you're glad too." She let Bryce go and hugged her sister.

Alexis wrapped her arms around her, and those pesky tears collected on her lower lids again. "I'm going to take care of him."

Macey pulled back and wiped a tear from her cheek. "I know. Luke said you're joining the pack."

"I am." She reached for Bryce's hand. "*We* are."

"Come here." Macey wrapped her arms around both of them and kissed their cheeks. "I am *so* happy."

Rain and Chase stepped onto the sidewalk, and the witch smiled. "His aura is all werewolf now." She moved closer and squinted at him. "The orange has completely taken over."

Macey let them go and stepped into Luke's arms as he and his sister, Amber, joined them on the sidewalk.

A giddy sensation bubbled up from Alexis's chest as her wolf rejoiced in the company of the pack. She'd be with her sister and the man she loved for the rest of her life. As she slid her arms around Bryce's waist, the woman in her celebrated too.

James leaned out the door. "Would all you happy couples care to come inside and have a drink?" He scanned their faces and sighed. "I'm going to have to find some more friends. All you lovebirds are cramping my style."

Amber laughed. "Enjoy your style while you can, my friend. I'm sensing change in your future."

He narrowed his eyes. "I'll pass."

Alexis laughed. "You won't have a choice."

"You can't fight fate." Bryce kissed her on the cheek. "What's meant to be will always be."

She squeezed his hand. "Oh, you believe in it now?"

"How could I not?"

Luke motioned toward the door. "Let's go in and get this induction ceremony started, so we can celebrate."

They all filed in, but Bryce held her back. "Hold on. I need to talk you about something." He reached into his pocket and pulled out a ring. Holding it in both hands, he gazed at the stone.

Her breath caught in her throat, and a shiver ran through her body. "Is that your mom's ring?"

He let out a nervous chuckle. "It is. She gave it to me when you left the room this afternoon." He held it up to the light, and the diamond glinted. "It can never replace your own mom's ring, but I would be honored if you'd wear this one. Alexis, will—"

"Wait." She held up a hand. "Before you say anything else, you need to know something about werewolves. In order to get married, we would have to become mates."

His brow furrowed. "Mates?"

"It's kind of like marriage, but it's an oath you take under a full moon to be together forever. Werewolves mate for life, so once you're in there's no way out. There's no such thing as werewolf divorce."

"I like the sound of that." He closed the distance between them. "I've never been a quitter. Anyway, you said yourself we're bound by fate. I didn't understand what you meant at first, but after what happened tonight in the woods, I finally do. We're connected somehow, and I couldn't imagine myself with anyone but you. I'm in this for the long-haul. Forever."

Forever was exactly what she wanted. For him to be a permanent fixture in her life. She was done with temporary. "You are my fate-bound."

"We're each other's fate-bounds." He took her left hand in his. "So...can I put this ring on you now?"

"I would be honored to wear it."

He slipped the ring on her finger and pressed his lips to her hand. "It looks good on you. Now, call me old-fashioned if you want...I did spend most of my life as a human...but, werewolf or not, I want to marry you. How do we become mates so I can make you my wife?"

She slid her arms up his shoulders to hold the back of his neck. "The alpha performs the mating ceremony on the night of a full moon."

He arched an eyebrow. "Really?"

"Mm-hmm." She licked her lips in anticipation of what she hoped he'd suggest.

"There happens to be a full moon tonight, ma'am, and the alpha is already performing one ceremony. Do you think he'd mind adding one more to the agenda?"

"I doubt he'd mind."

He smiled and ran his fingers through her hair. "Well, what do you think about becoming mates tonight?"

She gazed up at the full moon glowing brightly in the midnight sky and offered a silent thank you to fate for finally forcing her to get her life together and for bringing this amazing man to her. Looking into Bryce's eyes, she ran a finger down his chest and hooked it into the waistband of his jeans. "I think we should stop burning moon-light. Let's get hitched."

ALSO BY CARRIE PULKINEN

New Orleans Nocturnes Series

License to Bite

Shift Happens

Life's a Witch

Santa Got Run Over by a Vampire

Finders Reapers

Swipe Right to Bite

Batshift Crazy

Collection One: Books 1-3

Crescent City Wolf Pack Series

Werewolves Only

Beneath a Blue Moon

Bound by Blood

A Deal with Death

A Song to Remember

Shifting Fate

Collection One: Books 1-3

Collection Two: Books 4-6

Haunted Ever After Series

Love at First Haunt

Second Chance Spirit

Third Time's a Ghost

Love and Ghosts

Love and Omens

Love and Curses

Stand Alone Books

Flipping the Bird

Sign Steal Deliver

Azrael

Lilith

The Rest of Forever

Soul Catchers

Bewitching the Vampire

ABOUT THE AUTHOR

Carrie Pulkinen is a paranormal romance author who has always been fascinated with things that go bump in the night. Of course, when you grow up next door to a cemetery, the dead (and the undead) are hard to ignore. Pair that with her passion for writing and her love of a good happily-ever-after, and becoming a paranormal romance author seems like the only logical career choice.

Before she decided to turn her love of the written word into a career, Carrie spent the first part of her professional life as a high school journalism and yearbook teacher. She loves good chocolate and bad puns, and in her free time, she likes to read, drink wine, and travel with her family.

Connect with Carrie online:
www.CarriePulkinen.com

Milton Keynes UK
Ingram Content Group UK Ltd.
UKHW011930140823
426877UK00013B/325/J